MW00980197

DAY OF JUDGMENT

A NOVEL

HEATH DANIELS

Copyright © 2019 Heath Daniels

All rights reserved.
No part of this book may be reproduced, stored in a retrieval system,
or transmitted by any means, electronic, mechanical, photocopying,
recording, or otherwise, without written permission from the author.

This is a work of fiction. Any resemblance to persons living or
dead is entirely coincidental. Actual persons mentioned in the
dialog are based entirely on wide-spread media accounts.

Photograph on page 468 was taken by Maximilian Opheim. Photograph
on page 626, of burro in Carizozo, was taken by Claudiu Crivat. All other
photographs were taken by the author or taken from public domain sources.

Published by ITO Press

Cover Design by Monkey C Media
MonkeyCMedia.com

Printed in the United States of America
Second Printing

ISBN: 978-0-9974413-3-8

Library of Congress Control Number: 2017909492

BOOKS BY HEATH DANIELS

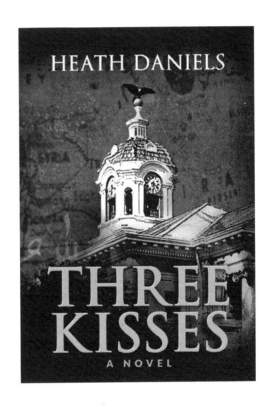

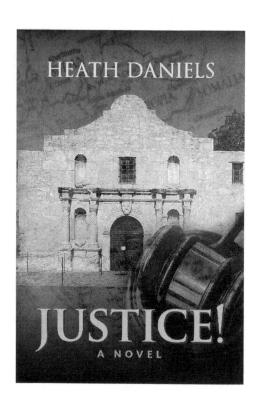

Visit HeathDanielsBooks.com for news of upcoming books.

List of Characters Day of Judgment
In alphabetic order by first name or nickname (except when last name is mostly used)

Abou Nidal [Jamal] al Khatib – Palestinian refugee, resettled in Southwest Virginia. Cousin of Nassar.

Abou Tarek [Ousama] al Shaeer – Cousin of Nassar who lives in Arlington, Virginia.

Ahmed Hammoud – young Palestinian American, born and grew up in mountain and valley area of Southwest Virginia. Son of Nassar and Roula; brother of Marwan and Fatima.

Ali Salman – Syrian medical doctor who agreed to be made into a duplicate to infiltrate the US. He was caught and moved to Iraq by the CIA.

Ashley Sue Hunter – U. S. Public Defender attorney for the Western District of Virginia, Roanoke, Virginia.

Bart [Bartholomew Lee Jackson] Reynolds – Retired U.S. Marine Corps General, father of Frank.

Beasley, Walter – First Sergeant, U.S. Marine Corps, Deputy Commander, U.S. Marine guards, National Security Agency.

Bishop, Martha – Judge, U.S. District Court, Western District of Virginia, Roanoke, Virginia.

Brad [Bradley] Spencer – Arabic language specialist working in the National Security Agency listening to Arabic language conversations.

Cranford Brooks – FBI agent in the Washington, DC, office.

Dieter Müller – Executive with German automobile manufacturer in Tuscaloosa, Alabama, Married to Greg.

Elsie [Elsbieta] Ferris – Flight attendant, wife of Patrick.

Fatima Hammoud – young Palestinian-American, born and grew up in mountain and valley area of Southwest Virginia. Daughter of Nassar and Roula. Sister of Ahmed and Marwan.

Felicia Ramos, nee Cavanaugh – Filipina married to Pete, widow of US Air Force pilot, mother of Denise and Timmy.

Frank Reynolds – U.S. Marine Corps major, commander of U.S. Marine Guards at National Security Agency, former coworker of Felicia and Patrick.

Gordon Hicks – Assistant principal of Shawsville Middle School, Marwan's coach, father of Jordan.

Granger, Otis – Colonel, U.S. Army, U.S. Defense Department Inspector General office.

Greg Hanson – Human resource specialist for German automobile parts supplier in Tuscaloosa, Alabama. Friend of Patrick. Married to Dieter.

Imran Ashfaq – Professor at Virginia Tech, leader of Muslim community in Blacksburg, Virginia.

James Edward Goodwin – young staff attorney for the U.S. Attorney General, Western District of Virginia in Roanoke, Virginia.

Jason Henderson – artist, friend of Brad, Frank, Joe, Omar, and Paco.

Joe [Yusef] Shaito – Young staff attorney for the U.S. Attorney General in Washington. Arab-American Muslim from Dearborn, Michigan.

Jolene Robbins – Pastor White Memorial Methodist Church in Shawsville, Virginia.

Jordan Hicks – computer salesman, friend of Marwan, son of Gordon.

Keith Barnes – unemployed from rural Montgomery County, Virginia. Friends with Kody Bates and Kyle Bates.

Kody Bates – unemployed from rural Montgomery County, Virginia. Friends with Kyle Bates and Keith Barnes.

Kyle Bates – unemployed from rural Montgomery County, Virginia. Friends with Kody Bates and Keith Barnes.

Larry [Lawrence] Briscoe – CIA specialist on Middle East.

Marcus Porter – Young judicial reporter for the *Roanoke Times*, Roanoke, Virginia.

Marian Spencer – Elementary school teacher in Minneapolis, Minnesota. Mother of Brad.

Marwan Hammoud – Young Palestinian-American born and grew up in mountain and valley area of Southwest, Virginia. Brother of Ahmed and Fatima.

Nassar Hammoud – Palestinian Refugee resettled in Southwest Virginia. Husband of Roula and father of Ahmed, Marwan, and Fatima.

Omar Abu Deeb – Visiting Fellow at Georgetown University and part-time imam at the Islamic center in Washington, DC. Originally from Yemen.

Paco [Francisco] Mendoza – practical nurse with the U.S. Veterans Administration hospital, friend of Frank

Patrick Ferris – U.S. Army captain. Weapons system engineer, NATO, Brussels. Former work colleague of Frank and Felicia.

Pete [Peter] Ramos – Chief of protocol, U.S. Naval Academy. Husband of Felicia.

Ralf McWhorter – Owner McWhorter Funeral Home, Blacksburg, Virginia.

Randy [Randolph] Walker – U. S. Attorney General, Western District of Virginia, Roanoke, Virginia.

Rhonda Philips – Political and foreign policy liaison and specialist, Headquarters, Defense Intelligence Agency.

Rich [Richard] Harris – Young attorney in Roanoke, Virginia, public defender.

Robert Vandam – airline pilot, coworker and friend of Sean, coworker with Elsie.

Roger Chen – Attorney with the U.S. Attorney General Office in Washington.

Rosie [Roosevelt] Jordan – Chief of Operations, FBI Operations Technology Center, Quantico, Virginia.

Ross, Edward – Colonel U.S. Air Force, Deputy Associate Director of the National Security Agency.

Roula Hammoud. Palestinian refugee resettled in Southwest Virginia. Wife of Nassar; mother of Ahmed, Marwan, and Fatima.

Sean Johnson – Flight attendant, friend and coworker of Elsie and Robert.

Shane Roberts – construction worker, Lafayette, Virginia, neighbor to the Hammoud family. Husband of Velma.

Timo [Haitham] Haider – Young Lebanese refugee, acquainted with Joe and Omar.

Velma Roberts – Bank employee, Shawsville, Virginia, neighbor to the Hammoud family. Wife of Shane.

Wissam Salameh – Young Palestinian-American, born in Washington, DC, area; grew up in Arlington, Virginia.

Yuhanna Khalil – Iraqi refugee, attorney, resettled in West Virginia, works part time as a public defender.

PROLOGUE

PROLOGUE 1

The ringing sounds of Skype were replaced by the image of Muhammad Faisal Abdulla al-Qhatini, imam at the al-Aqsa Masjid mosque in Arlington, Virginia, to whom Abdulmalik Abu Salim said, "Good afternoon dear friend Abou Khaled," in Arabic. He used the name 'Abou Khaled' in the Arab tradition of *abou* or 'father of' plus the name of his oldest son for intimacy and respect.

"Nice to see you my friend Abdulmalik," Abou Khaled replied in Arabic. "Good you're using Skype. So far no indication it's monitored, but good to be cautious."

"Yes," Abdulmalik replied in Arabic. "I'm in Cyprus; they wouldn't monitor calls from here. Can't wait until we eliminate that place that monitors our phone calls."

"We're eager to help," Abou Khaled stated in Arabic.

"Thanks for applying for my work visa," Abdulmalik said in Arabic; "I tried to process it here, but they said I have to do it in Beirut."

"With the shortage of imams," Abou Khaled said in Arabic, "we got our embassy to apply pressure. Still they drag their feet approving imams."

"It'll be interesting to be an imam," Abdulmalik said in Arabic. "I've been lots of things, but not an imam."

"As you know, there're no formal requirements to be a Sunni imam," Abou Khaled replied in Arabic. "We had to stretch things a little bit to convince them you're qualified."

"I should go now," Abdulmalik said in Arabic. "Just wanted to check in and say things are in motion here."

PROLOGUE 2

Monday, May 23, 2004
Elliston, Virginia, USA

In the dull noise and subtle food smells in the lunchroom at Eastern Montgomery High School, Ahmed Hammoud was eating with other students. At eighteen, he was five feet nine inches, had medium-short slightly wavy dark brown hair, sparkling deep brown eyes, and a slightly dark complexion. He dressed stylishly with medium quality clothes, always clean and pressed, making a favorable impression, especially with girls.

The modern school building served the mostly rural area of eastern Montgomery County with its two small bedroom communities of Lafayette and Elliston, the slightly larger community of Shawsville, and a small cluster of houses called Ironto. It had an Elliston postal address, but was between Elliston and Shawsville on old highway US 460 and 11.

A girl about his age asked, "Your sandwich has flat bread with a pocket. Where'd you get that?"

"My mom gets it in Blacksburg at a shop next to the mosque," he answered.

"What's that?" another girl asked. "Like a church?"

"Yes," he answered. "Where Muslims go to pray."

"Up with the high and mighty Tech people," she said.

"Yeah," he agreed. "We just go pray and don't have much to do with them."

Another attractive girl smiling flirtatiously asked, "What'd you do over the weekend, Ahmed?"

He answered, "Went to prayers on Friday and worked for my dad in the garage."

A boy asked, "Your dad has a garage?"

"Yeah, at the Ironto exit; gas station too," he answered.

"I know that place," the boy replied. "An old man who doesn't speak English well works there. He your dad?"

Ahmed answered, "My uncle. Not really my uncle, but we call him that. A cousin who came from Lebanon with my parents. My dad's usually in the garage working on cars."

"Your folks Lebanese?" a girl asked.

"Palestinian," Ahmed replied. "Came from a refugee camp in Lebanon."

When the group of girls had taken their trays, one of the boys leaned closer, "Ahmed, you got a prom date yet?"

Ahmed, surprised, said, "No."

"Brittney said she hopes you ask her," his friend said.

Ahmed blushed, saying, "Hadn't thought about the prom." To himself, *Never thought about going to the prom. Might be fun. Wonder if folks'd let me. Do pretty much as I please now I'm eighteen, but have to get a car from Dad. Never thought about dating a local girl, but Brittney's cute and nice. Dad always talks about finding me a Palestinian girl.*

Meanwhile, Marwan Hammoud, Ahmed's younger brother, was sitting with friends at another table. He was seventeen, slightly taller at five feet ten inches, thinner than his brother with similar hair, complexion, and eyes, and an athletic build reflecting several years' playing soccer. Black wire-rimmed glasses made him look geekish, obscuring intense dark brown eyes. He, too, wore clean, stylish school clothes.

"What'd you do this weekend?" asked a buddy who was dressed similarly and slightly geekish as well.

"Went to prayers," he answered. "Yard work, planted flowers, worked in my dad's station some, and worked on that computer project we have due."

"The friend asked, "Say, could I look at your project? Just look; I'm hung up on one thing. You know my father'd kill me if I copied."

"Yeah," Marwan chuckled. "Vice principal of the middle school who handles discipline cases, his own son caught. Probably kill me too for letting you copy. He's known me since I was six on the soccer team."

"What're you two computer geeks going to do when you graduate next year?" another friend asked.

"Haven't really thought about it," Marwan asked.

"Maybe go to New River Community College and study computers," the geekish friend answered. "Maybe you could go too, Marwan."

"Ahmed's going next year to study auto mechanics; he graduates this year," he answered. "Don't know if dad can afford both of us going at the same time. For sure he wants us to get education."

"You guys want to see if we can get a soccer game on Friday?" yet another friend asked.

"Friday's when we go to pray," Marwan replied. "Otherwise I'd be down for it."

Meanwhile, two girls with unkempt hair and sloppy clothes sat next to Ahmed and his friend, overhearing his friend ask, "What are you going to do after you graduate?"

"Go to New River to study auto mechanics and go into business with my dad," Ahmed answered.

"Oh, you's one of the high f'lutin' types goin' to college," a girl said.

Ahmed replied, "Need to learn more about working on American and Japanese cars to expand the business."

"What're those funny bracelets y'got on your wrist?" the second girl asked.

"That's my rosary and miniature Q'ran," he answered. "Muslims use them to pray and show faith."

"I thought Catholics use rosaries," a boy commented.

"Muslims do too," Ahmed replied.

"You one of them A-rab terr'ists," the first girl said.

Ahmed, annoyed at the offensive mispronunciation of 'Arab', still trying to be pleasant, answered, "We're Arab, but I was born and grew up here; my sister and brother too. We definitely aren't terrorists."

"Ain't what we hears," the second girl sneered. "A-rabs bombed us, so you're terr'ists."

A bell signaled it was time to return to class.

PROLOGUE 3

Wednesday, May 26, 2004
Lafayette, Virginia, USA

On a warm, breezy late spring day, a Montgomery County school bus stopped where Ahmed, Marwan, and Fatima Hammoud lived with their parents in the small community of Lafayette. Fatima, aged 8, was about five feet three inches and slightly chubby. All wore nice school clothes as usual.

Hammoud family house in Lafayette, Virginia

Lafayette, a cluster of modest houses on narrow streets, was just inside the Montgomery County Line from Roanoke County between the old U.S. Highway 460 and 11 and the main line of the Norfolk Southern Railway; I-81 ran parallel on the other side of the railroad tracks. As in the neighboring community of Elliston—

all houses in Lafayette had an Elliston postal address—residents were hard-working, lower-middle-class people who respected law and order. Life centered around schools and churches, mostly in slightly larger Shawsville further along U.S. 460-11.

Ahmed grumbled to himself: *About to graduate and still have to ride the damned school bus with my little sister. Why the hell won't Dad let me have a car now? Says I have to wait until fall when I go to college.*

A dirty, faded gray old Saturn at least six years old came to a screeching halt almost in front of them.

"There you are, you fuckin' A-rab sissy boy," the driver said in a pronounced accent.

He was no more than 20, five feet ten, had long scraggly brown-blond hair, dull blue-grey eyes, a few days' growth of beard, and was sloppily dressed in tattered jeans and a t-shirt.

Two others got out of the car and started walking towards the three children, with eyes on Ahmed, and one said, "You're messin' with our girls, ain't ya?" Both were the same age as the driver, one over five feet eleven, husky, with scraggly brown hair and a couple days' growth of beard, dressed like the driver. The other, about five-nine, thinner, had sinewy muscles on his bare arms, closely cropped hair, dull brown eyes, and was clean shaven; he reeked of cigarette tobacco.

Ahmed tossed his backpack to Marwan and shouted, "Run home with Fatima, quick!" Defiantly to the bullies, "What 'n hell you talkin' about?"

While the two moved behind Ahmed, the driver scowled, saying, "No fuckin' A-rab's goin' t' mess with our girls."

"Just friendly at lunch," Ahmed stammered in a Virginia mountain and valley accent, not crude like the three others.

As he tried to run, the driver moved closer. The husky one grabbed Ahmed, saying, "Y'ain't goin' nowhere, y' A-rab asshole. You're a sissy boy, always dressed fancy. We know what to do with sissy boys, 'specially A-rabs."

The driver grabbed his shirt and said, "We're goin' to beat the livin' shit out of you and teach you a lesson, only w'ain't goin' t' do it here. Get 'n the car, you fuckin' A-rab."

The car reeked of tobacco and stale beer and had a shabby, torn interior. Ahmed tried futilely to open the back door as they sped away. He recognized they were driving past his father's gasoline station and garage, thinking, *I know all the roads, driveways, and hollows around here; been exploring them ever since old enough to go out on my bike.*

Nassar Hammoud's garage next to a gas station at the Ironto
Exit off Interstate Highway 81 near Elliston, Virginia

Soon they turned left into a badly rutted old driveway up a hollow and stopped at an abandoned shack evoking neglect; an ideal location for clandestine activity through the years. Ahmed thought: *We're so far from civilization no one'd hear us. Used to come here when I wanted to be alone.*

He was dragged from the car; before he could stand, the driver punched him in the abdomen. The husky guy grabbed him by the shoulders, pushed him down, and started punching him in the kidneys as Ahmed screamed in pain.

The skinny guy said, "Hey, I know what to do. He's a sissy boy and needs a good fuck, just like a girl."

"Don't know 'bout that," the husky guy said. "Ain't never thought about sticking my dick in another guy's ass. Kind of makes me feel creepy. Y'ever done it?"

"Naw," the skinny guy said. "May be fun; he deserves it. Pull his jeans down."

Ahmed broke out in a cold sweat despite the warm weather and felt a chill from the breeze. The other two complied, knocking Ahmed to his knees, holding him while the skinny guy stood in front of Ahmed's face saying, "Look. Not all of me's short and skinny."

Ahmed turned his face, knowing Muslims are not supposed to see private parts. The skinny guy used his free hand to grab him by the hair to force his eyes towards his midsection while the other two made him be still. The skinny guy forced himself inside; Ahmed screamed.

The driver became visibly aroused and pulled Ahmed's head by the hair, saying, "This's what's goin' inside you next."

"You're a good fuck, sissy boy, almost as good as a girl," the skinny guy said as he lit a cigarette. "Gotta have a smoke after a good fuck. Girls don't like it, but who gives a shit about this A-rab sissy."

The tall husky guy loosened his grip on Ahmed, grimaced with disgust, and said, "I ain't goin' inside of that! Too bloody and messy!"

The skinny guy finished and flipped the still-lit butt of his cigarette onto Ahmed's back as the driver said, "Now y' know what'll happen when you mess with our girls again. Don' cha think you c'n report us neither. There's three of us and we was just watchin' TV all afternoon."

Ahmed sobbed uncontrollably as the car sped away. He was in shock, unable to think. After several minutes, he started retching, continuing to tremble and shiver. He stumbled to a creek, washed himself as best he could, put on his jeans and shirt, tossing his briefs aside, and walked away, eyes watering, feeling the lingering pain.

What do I do now? Most kids have cell phones, but Dad says a waste of money; only uses his for work. I'll walk 'til I find a phone; nearest one's that Exxon station. Might as well go on to Dad's.

He forced his mind not to think about what just happened, using other thoughts to keep his composure while he trudged the two miles: *Abou Nidal'll notice. Treats me and Marwan like his own sons, but we still call him Abou Nidal for his own son. We think of him as our uncle, but he's only a distant cousin. Helped Mom and Dad escape slaughter in Lebanon; got 'em on a boat to Cyprus. Went back for his wife and son. She said she had to stay with her aging parents, and Nidal stayed with his mother, who had no means of support.*

Mom and Dad settled here; Dad opened the gas station and garage; Abou Nidal just came along. Couldn't leave him after he saved their lives. He ran a shop in the camp so now he runs the shop in the gas station, keeps the station open at night, and sleeps in the little one-room apartment at back.

Ahmed burst out sobbing again. *Those guys must be gay. Now I'm unclean. Can never get married. How'm I going to tell Dad I can't marry a Palestinian girl and bring her family here? He's convinced I'll stay and work in the garage with him; expand the business. Maybe just move in with Abou Nidal. Two broken men living together.*

Can't pray because I'm unclean. How can I tell Dad and Marwan? They'll wonder if I suddenly stop going to prayers. Maybe go and pretend. Will Allah punish me?

After several minutes, he could see the station and thought, *The car Dad usually drives is gone. Can't let Abou Nidal see me yet. Hope the restroom's unlocked.*

That night he lay in bed tossing and turning, thoughts running through his mind. *Can't let Marwan hear me cry. Be strong and get over it, Dad said, thinking all they did was beat me up. That's how they survived in the camp. You're stronger'n them. Mom's sympathetic; upset I wasn't eating. If they knew how they damaged me inside, inside my soul. Can't tell 'em. Can't tell anyone.*

Gay bastards ruined me. Americans hate gays; hear about it all the time. I want to kill every gay guy I find. Now I know why al Qaeda attacked to punish the U.S. because it has so many gays. Even Christian preachers, the ones right here in Virginia, Falwell and Robertson, said

13

nine-eleven attacks are God's punishment for not stamping out gays. Maybe al Qaeda's not so bad after all.

Finally, he crammed his head deep into his pillow with tears flowing silently while he felt the lingering, piercing pain.

BOOK 1

PRELIMINARIES

CHAPTER 1

On a bright fall day with a slight nip in the air, leaves turning gold, red, and orange, Felicia Ramos responded to melodic doorbell chimes, saying "Frank!" hugging him, and allowing him to kiss her cheek as he handed her a lavish fresh flower bouquet. "So good to see you. They're lovely! Please go on in. I'll put these in a vase."

She was hosting a reunion of persons who worked together recently at Wright-Patterson Air Force Base, Ohio, along with her husband, Navy Captain Peter Ramos, at senior officer quarters assigned to him at the U.S. Naval Academy.

She was wearing upscale blue jeans, a frilly red blouse, long red earrings, and casual red leather shoes with two-inch block heels to give more height to her five feet two inches and enhance her well-proportioned petite figure. Black wire-rimmed glasses complemented her bright brown almond-shaped eyes and straight black hair typical of her Filipino heritage. She was in her thirties.

A floor-length mirror on the wall called out to Marine Corps Major Frank Reynolds as he walked towards cheerful conversation sounds coming from the room at the end of the hallway. Instinctively he checked his "spit and polish" image of a Marine Corps officer, even in civilian clothes: polished cordovan loafers, perfectly pressed khaki pants, a green-striped long-sleeved Oxford cloth shirt with button down collar, and a navy blue blazer. He was in his mid-thirties, five feet eleven, with military-trimmed brown hair and intense green eyes.

He thought, *Interesting being in Felicia's home, senior officer quarters at that. Worked with her a few years, but didn't socialize; didn't socialize with much of anyone in their homes and didn't invite them to mine. Mom and Dad never entertained at home. Mom wasn't up to it; always had a buzz sipping vodka tonics. Entertaining was at the officer's club, and I usually wasn't included.*

Sure was a warm greeting; seems she really does want to see me even though she had something to do with Doc taking Patrick's place, knows I know, but probably afraid to say anything like I am. Here to see Patrick again, and he doesn't have a clue. Because of Paco, now I have feelings. Never allowed to have feelings, much less express them. Maybe that's why I feel weird here.

Upon entering the large family room-parlor, Pete Ramos jumped to greet him. "Frank, welcome! Haven't seen you since our wedding. Really wanted to have you over now that we're settled and the kids are in school."

Pete Ramos was five feet nine and in his early fifties. He had graying black straight hair trimmed military style, brown eyes, and Asian features, being second generation Filipino-American.

"This is our receiving parlor," he said. "These quarters were built back when Academy officers lived grandly and entertained more formally than we do. Some of my ancestors may even have been servants here; maybe smiling in their graves knowing I live here now. What can I get you? We're having wine. Growing up in the Corps, you might be used to something stronger. We have most things."

Reflecting on his parents' hard drinking, Frank replied, "Wine's fine."

Patrick rushed to Frank, put his hand on Frank's shoulder, and shook hands, saying in a Southern accent, "Hey, Bud, great to see you."

U.S. Army Captain Patrick Ferris, first generation Lebanese-American, was in his very late twenties, five feet nine, and had closely trimmed brown-red hair and sparkling brown-green eyes.

Although physically fit, he couldn't be described as slim and trim. He too dressed casually. Like Frank, he had been an engineer in weapons system acquisition at Wright-Patterson, now assigned to NATO headquarters in Brussels.

Frank smiled broadly and stammered, "You too." He thought, *Really seems glad to see me. That time at his house in Ohio, he gave me a hug and three Lebanese kisses; thought it was intensity of the moment when I'd just come out to him.*

"After dinner, I need to ask you something, sorta private," Patrick said in a low voice. He kept his hand on Frank's shoulder and said, "Come sit with Elsie and me; tell us about your new job, where you're living, and all."

Elsbieta Stankowski stood and smiled as she took Frank's hand, moved her face close for him to kiss her cheek, and said, "Frank, so nice to see you again."

At five feet eight she had a well-proportioned figure, shoulder-length styled blonde hair, pleasant blue eyes, and her flight attendant's composure. She wore designer blue jeans, a light blue sweater that complemented her eyes, simple gold earrings, and casual shoes. She too was in her late twenties, only slightly younger than Patrick.

Frank thought, *Gee, they're really touchy-feely, like they're really glad to see me.*

They talked about Frank's settling into Maryland, living in a rented townhouse in Laurel until his house in Ohio sells. His job as commander of the Marine security guards at the National Security Agency located nearby at Fort Meade didn't present challenges.

Better not tell them about my other supposed job to visit gay places to find about homosexuality for DIA and impact on military intelligence, he thought. *Could tell Patrick. He's told Elsie, I'm sure; made a point that she works with gay men and some're good friends. Doubt Pete and Felicia know; now's not the time to tell 'em. Pete's Chief of Protocol for*

19

the Academy, third generation U.S. Navy. Seems understanding, but I'm sure "don't ask; don't tell" applies to him.

Conversation drifted to Elsie's job working for a major airline. Frank barely paid attention as he mused, *Never knew anyone interested in me as a person; maybe never allowed anyone close enough because afraid of being found out. Whenever I was asked questions, I was suspected of doing something wrong; started with my parents. Then I met guys at the Serpent, but that's different. They have secret lives too; safe to talk to each other. Better get back in the conversation. They're asking Patrick about Lebanon. I just eat up this foreign affairs stuff.*

Shortly, Frank followed others into an expansive formal dining room with a large formal dining table. Dishes of cold food were on the table, and pleasant smells of warm dishes came from the kitchen. Casual tableware and paper napkins took away some of the formal stiffness.

"Another feature of these houses," Pete said smiling, "dining rooms so big, stiff, and formal it almost takes the appetite away. At least we can all sit down together."

Christina Ramos held out her hand to Frank, saying, "Hello, Major Reynolds, nice to see you again."

She had her mother's tallness, almost five nine, was slender and athletic looking, had closely cropped black hair, bright dark brown eyes, was in her mid-twenties, and had Asian features reflecting mixed-race parentage; her mother tragically passed away with cancer a few years back. She wore men's-type blue jeans, a plaid men's style shirt, casual white athletic shoes, and simple stud-type earrings.

"Christina lives in Northern Virginia," Pete said. "She's a software engineer. Sometimes returns to grace us with her presence, especially for big events like this. We think she likes to have us look after her and sleep in her old room."

Frank took her offered hand, thinking, *Should I kiss her cheek also? Damn, why'm I so awkward?*

She solved his dilemma by remaining a slight distance away, giggling at her father's comments, saying, "Here's our budding young cook for the evening."

Denise Cavanaugh, Felicia's daughter with her first husband who was killed in the first Iraq war, stood about five feet with slightly wavy brown hair and was dressed in white pants, a red blouse similar to her mother's, white athletic shoes, and simple studded earrings with faux diamonds, which she'd recently received for her ninth birthday. Lightly applied make-up made her look precocious.

She held out her hand and said, "Hello, Mr. Major."

How'm I supposed to greet children, Frank asked himself. *Hardly been around any.*

He awkwardly responded, "Hello," but with a smile.

Timmy bounded into the room with David close behind. Timothy Cavanaugh, Felicia's son with her first husband, reflected mixed-race parentage, was slightly smaller than a typical five-year-old, wore jeans, white athletic shoes, and a short-sleeved soccer shirt. David Ramos, an inch taller than his father, had brown hair, brownish green eyes, facial features of his mixed-race parentage, and boyish good looks reflecting his 20 years of age. He wore a sloppy Naval Academy sweat shirt, blue jeans, and well-worn Nikes.

"You remember my son, David," Pete said smiling, "He's in his last year at the Academy and lives in the Midshipmen's barracks. He gets to sign out for an occasional weekend home. For him, it's just a short walk."

Smiling, David shook Frank's hand and said, "I remember you from Dad and Felicia's wedding. You were dressed differently then; I was in my military tuxedo too."

Timmy squirmed, not remembering Frank, when Pete said, "You know Timmy from Ohio."

Frank thought, *I remember a little kid off in the distance at their wedding and Felicia sure talked about him in the office.* He impulsively bent at the knees to be at eye level and said, "Hi, Timmy. I've heard a lot about you. I'm Frank."

"Hi, Frank," Timmy said in his almost-six-year-old little boy's voice. "You like to play soccer?"

Frank stood, saying, "Some, when I was a kid. I mostly ran track." He thought, *Always moving around; didn't stay in one place long enough to fit into a team. Individual sports like track, yeah; I was a good sprinter.*

Felicia, Christina, and Denise brought big bowls of rice, hot spicy fish soup, chicken, and beef cooked Philippine style with aromas enhancing everyone's appetite.

Pete said, "Shall we pray." Each took the hands of persons on either side. After a short prayer, Pete said "Amen." All but Frank repeated "Amen" and made the sign of the cross.

He thought, *Paco should see me now. He's trying to get me to be religious, and he's a good Catholic too.*

CHAPTER 2

Saturday, October 21, 2006
Annapolis, Maryland, USA

After dessert, while drinking coffee, Elsie announced, "We're getting married the Saturday after Thanksgiving."

Patrick added, "We have to be legally married for quarters in Brussels; otherwise It'd be quarters for single and unaccompanied officers or we'd have to live on the economy, which is expensive. We decided to get married now."

"Where'll it be? Columbus?" Frank asked.

"No," Elsie began, hesitating. Patrick interrupted, "It didn't work out to have a church wedding in Columbus on short notice, and Elsie wants to get married later in a church in Munich, which is fine with me."

"I found an English-speaking priest in Munich who agreed we could be married there," Elsie continued, "but we'd need to discuss it more. He said church weddings aren't legally recognized in Germany; they're just religious ceremonies. People have to get legally married civilly."

"It's the same in Belgium," Patrick added. "We probably could've been married by a military chaplain and made it legal, but we didn't want that and decided to have a quick civil marriage now. Later we'll have our real wedding in Munich when we have time to arrange it properly. Maybe some distant relatives in Lebanon and Poland could come to Munich, but not to the U.S."

Elsie interjected. "Ever since I saw that church, I wanted to get married there. It's called the Lady's Church, *Frauenkirche* in German. It refers to Our Lady the Virgin Mary, but still a nice name."

"It suddenly hit me," Patrick continued, "we could get married in Alabama where my folks live. One of Dad's best friends in Kiwanis is a judge; he was my Little League coach. He agreed to marry us."

"It's fine with me," Elsie said. "It's a legal marriage; the real one'll be in Munich. If it makes Patrick's folks and some of their friends happy, so much the better."

"The whole town's invited," Patrick added, "everyone who shops at the store. Couldn't invite some and not others and piss off good customers. It's low key: wedding cake and punch; no formal reception with a dinner."

"I'll just wear a simple white dress," Elsie said. "I'll wear my *real* wedding gown in Munich. We want all of you to come to Alabama, but for sure we want you to go to the real wedding in Munich. You're even going to be my flower girl over there like you were for your mother's wedding, Denise. We'll make sure it's in summer when school's out so you and Timmy can travel to Germany."

"Don't misunderstand," Patrick said. "We really want you to come to Alabama too. I'd love my family to meet nice friends like you. If you think two weddings are too much, Munich's where we want people we care for most to come. No wedding gifts in Alabama either. Invitations ask people to make donations to a church or charity. We'll have shipped our household goods and don't want excess baggage."

"Well, I'm going to both weddings!" Felicia said. "And you're coming with me, Pete, aren't you?"

"Guess I don't have much choice," he replied, smiling.

"I always wanted to go back to Germany," David said. "Don't remember much when I was there as a kid. Let's see where I'm stationed then. Don't know about Thanksgiving. Things are busy with studies then."

Christina said, "I just started a new job. Don't know what it'll be like at Thanksgiving, but you'll have to tie me down to keep me from Germany."

"Let's go to the other room where it's more comfortable," Felicia said. "We ladies will clear the table."

Patrick said, "Say, Frank, there's a great view of the bay from the patio; let me show you." With a fresh breeze blowing, he continued, "Beautiful, isn't it? The Navy picked a great place to put its academy."

Looking at sparkling lights reflecting on the water of the bay, Frank replied, "Yeah. That's a big surprise, getting married in Alabama."

Patrick replied, "Big mess with Elsie's family over getting married there. I interrupted because it's painful for her. I'll tell you more, but now there's something special I want to ask you."

He moved closer and put his hand on Frank's shoulder; Frank felt his knees weaken, thinking: *Going to ask me not to go because I'm gay.*

"I want you to be my best man in Alabama," Patrick said. "I don't know how it'd be in Munich because you're not Catholic, but Alabama for sure. If you want to, that is."

Frank, stunned as though he had been struck by the proverbial bolt of lightning, was unable to speak.

"Hey, is something wrong, Bud?" Patrick asked. "You're the first person I wanted; been waiting to ask you in person. Is it something you don't want to do?"

"*No!* Just I don't know what to say. Yes, of course! I'd've never thought you'd ask me."

"Why not?" Patrick asked surprised. "Sorry, if I'm putting you in an uncomfortable position."

"*No!*" Frank said, putting both hands on Patrick's shoulders. "No one's ever asked me something like this."

"You're the best friend I've had here lately," Patrick said. "You told me that in the military great friends become great memories fast. I started dating Elsie right after I moved there and didn't develop many guy friends of my own, except you. She and I have friends together, mostly people she works with. Funny, her closest work friend, and he's a friend of mine, is gay. Even in this age of enlightenment, there's no way she could make him maid of honor. He's not a friend like you, someone I'd want to stand next to me at my wedding. You know I don't have a brother; my only cousins are in Lebanon and I barely know them. There're a couple of guys back in Russellville I halfway keep in touch with, but our lives are different so it'd feel funny having them stand up for me. Besides, Elsie doesn't know them."

Frank choked back tears, thinking, *That's the trouble with learning to feel at my age.* He said, "I'm overwhelmed, Patrick. Thrilled. Of course I will!"

Patrick replied, "Bud, I know you've had some hard knocks, and I'm thrilled you accepted. Of course Paco's invited. That best friend of Elsie's will be there with his partner. Guess what? Remember Greg, the gay guy I knew in the MBA program? I looked him up. He's back in Tuscaloosa; director of human resources for the local plant of a German company, supplier to the big Mercedes plant. He's coming too, bringing his partner."

"You've mentioned your home town in Alabama; Russellville or something like that?" Frank asked.

"Yes," Patrick answered. "Sort of close to Huntsville in the northwest part of the state; not all that far from Birmingham. Oh, you and I'll be in uniform; hope that'll be OK with you. Not the tuxedo type we suffered with at Felicia's wedding, just a full dress uniform. Not a military wedding, but uniforms go over big down there and most people remember me as the boy who went off to the Army."

"That's OK, but what about me being seen in uniform with Paco?" Frank asked. "Would people be upset seeing me with my boyfriend? Will other military people be there?"

"Pete'll be there, it seems," Patrick chuckled. "Right offhand, I can't think of any other military we'd invite. Not many'd want to come to Alabama, but, hey, you're not going to be making out in public or holding hands or anything like that with your uniform on, are you? You wouldn't do that if you brought a girlfriend, so why'd this be different?"

"Guess not," Frank said. "I'll bring him if he wants to come. Felicia and Pete will have to figure it out and deal with it if we're going to keep in contact and be friends."

"We should get back inside, I'm getting chilly," Patrick said. "But one more thing. I'd like to get together on Monday afternoon or night if you're free."

Frank replied, "I'd be pleased to show you around the NSA if you like. We were at your place for dinner last time; why don't you come to mine. There's someone I'd like you to meet if he's not busy. He's been to Lebanon and even teaching me to cook Middle Eastern food."

They made arrangements to meet, Frank offering to have Patrick stay overnight.

Inside Patrick was beaming as he said, "Hey, everyone, Frank says he'll be my best man."

Elsie said, "Oh, Frank, thank you so much. Patrick could hardly wait to ask you and I'm so glad. I wish Annalise could meet you; she's the matron of honor. Been working with her since my very first day."

"This calls for celebration," Pete said. "Cognac?"

Everyone but Frank said "Sure." Frank said, "Yes, but a small one. Need to drive back, and I've had plenty of wine."

Later he drove his three-year-old cream-colored Mercury Mountaineer home. His emotions told him to burst out in tears and joyous laughter now that he was alone.

CHAPTER 3

Monday, October 23, 2006
Laurel, Maryland, USA

L ate in the afternoon on an overcast fall day, wearing comfortable clothes in his family room, Frank handed a bottle to Patrick and asked, "Red OK? We're having lamb."

Frank's townhouse, Laurel, Maryland

Patrick, who had also changed to comfortable clothes, read aloud, "Chateau Ksara, Cabernet Sauvignon, Lebanon. Where'd you get this?" He thought, *Had lamb at home; folks ate it in Lebanon. Owning a supermarket, they could stock it. Only store around that did; got a few customers that way.*

"Store in DC," Frank answered.

Patrick said, "Wish I could get some for the folks, except I won't see them before I go to Brussels."

"How about I bring some for the wedding," Frank offered. "Might drive down if the weather's good."

"It's a dry wedding; lots of local folks don't approve of alcohol," Patrick said, "but, hey, folks'd like some."

"Sure," Frank said. "I talked to Paco; he might fly down and drive back with me."

"Good; things're going well with you two," Patrick said.

"So far," Frank replied. "If he drives back with me, it'll be an acid test. I told you about our big fight when we took a road trip together to Florida. He said it wasn't until he was with me alone for two continuous days that he could see what I'm really like, a robot with no feelings. That was my wake-up call; realized my whole life'd been robotic; how my parents raised me. I'm learning it's OK to have feelings and express them. Hasn't been easy, and I've got a way to go. He had to work on some things too."

"You were relaxed at Felicia and Pete's," Patrick said.

Frank replied, "One of the few times I've been in a warm family environment. Been with Paco's family a couple of times; they're Mexican. Nothing wrong with that, but have their own culture, people jabbering in Spanish."

"You really had me worried when you got stiff and quiet after I asked you to be my best man; thought you were going to turn me down," Patrick said.

"Sorry about that," Frank replied. "I was just shocked. Would never have thought anyone would ask me to do something like that, no straight guy anyway. You know I grew up a loner, Marine Corps brat and all of that."

Patrick added, "Greg was surprised too when I invited him to the wedding. When Elsie and I were down there, Greg and Dieter came up from Tuscaloosa for lunch. Just like back in the MBA program at Bama, he was grateful I'd gone out of my way to find him. Elsie liked him, and Dieter too. We even joked that she might throw her bouquet to one of them; said they're getting married in Germany soon. When we told them about our real wedding in Munich, we half-joked about having it the same time as their wedding in Stuttgart, that's where Dieter's from, so we could attend each other's weddings. Here I am rambling and not drinking."

Frank said, "I'm looking forward to meeting them."

"Any more on plans when you retire?" Patrick asked.

Frank replied, "The guy who's coming to cook's been giving me information; wants to study the same thing. He spent a semester abroad in Jordan with Arabic language studies. Works in the Arabic language section of the NSA. You probably heard about the shit over illegal monitoring of domestic phone calls."

"I remember," Patrick said. "You met him at work?"

"No, actually not," Frank said. "We met at a café in the gay district of Baltimore, Labor Day. He recognized me even out of uniform. Tried to avoid him, but he was persistent. I'm glad because he's become a good friend. Has a very steady boyfriend in Virginia."

"Sounds interesting," Patrick said, "especially if he's cooking lamb authentically."

"He's a great cook, especially Middle Eastern things," Frank said. "Even trying to teach me a few things. Let's start the charcoal. You said you'd tell me more about not having your wedding in Columbus, not that it's any of my business."

Patrick began, "Elsie went to the Catholic church in the neighborhood where she grew up and her parents still live. She talked to the priest there now, who was weird and wanted to know intimate details about her relationship with me. Turns out this priest has been accused of sex scandals with older girls and young women. No one really wants to talk about it, and the church is trying to keep it quiet. Rumor has it that he's been moved from parish to parish whenever he's involved in a scandal and was sent to this one that has mostly older parishioners like Elsie's parents."

Frank muttered, "Oh."

"Some of Elsie's relatives said they wouldn't come to the wedding if this priest were presiding," Patrick continued. "Now she understands why she felt creepy around him. She went to a couple of other parishes in Columbus, but they hemmed and hawed she'd be marrying outside her parish and they didn't know. By this time, she was pretty frustrated.

"She and I went together to see the priest in Fairborn, where we've been going to church for a couple of years, the one who married Felicia and Pete. He said it'd be OK, but we needed to have the required amount of prenuptial counseling. That didn't bother Elsie and me; all Catholics know counseling's required for a Catholic wedding. I mentioned I'd be in Brussels and maybe I could get some of the counseling there. The priest said no, counseling had to be together and with him. He dismissed us, saying we should go see the Catholic chaplain on the base."

"Gee."

"We were both pissed off and haven't been back to that church since," Patrick added, "or any church for that matter except with Felicia and Pete to the chapel at the Academy yesterday. You said you're not a church person, so maybe this is something you can't identify with."

"No," Frank answered. "My family never went to church except on rare occasion to an event at a base chapel when my father felt he needed to show up for political reasons. Paco's a good Catholic. He'd like me to be more interested in church. Brad and his boyfriend go to a gay-friendly church here in Laurel and have been trying to get me and Paco to go with them. Don't know if I'm ready."

Conversation had turned to the wedding when Frank's cell phone rang and he said, "Charcoal's going, come anytime."

Soon Brad arrived, wearing a jacket against the chilly night and carrying bags of food. Frank gave him a light kiss on the lips, took the bags, and gave him wine, which he swirled in the glass and smelled the bouquet.

Bradley Spencer was in his mid-twenties, five feet ten with a medium build, and had neatly trimmed, styled, longish slightly wavy blond-brown hair. He was wearing dark brown corduroy pants, well-worn dark brown penny loafers with brown socks, and a loose fitting Minnesota Gophers hoodie over a light blue oxford cloth shirt.

Frank made introductions and Brad said, "*Marhaba*; you're Lebanese," in Arabic.

Patrick responded in English. "My parents are Lebanese, but I don't speak Arabic. I did with my grandmother when I was a kid and some came back when I visited Lebanon, but it's all but forgotten now."

Brad asked, "When'd you go to Lebanon? I was there in fall 2004."

"Spring 2001," Patrick answered. "Discover my roots, so to speak."

"Where'd you go?" Brad asked.

"Pretty much all over," Patrick replied, "except the far south. My parents' families live around Beirut, but my father's family village is in the north, on the Syrian border."

"Cool," Brad said. "I'd love to hear about it over dinner. I should get busy cooking, or I should say *we* should get busy. I'm teaching Frank to cook Middle Eastern food."

In the kitchen, Brad said to Frank, "You can wash the parsley, mint, lettuce, and tomatoes, and then start chopping the parsley up really fine. Then the small tomato."

"Oh, tabbouleh," Patrick said. "Anything I can do?"

"Soon as I get the meat chopped, you can put the pieces on skewers," Brad said. "While you're doing that, I can start the rice and pine nuts."

"Yumm," Patrick said. "Haven't had that since last time I visited the folks and Mom made it."

When they sat to eat; Brad raised his now full wine glass and said, "*Sakhtein*."

Patrick smiled, hearing the word his parents used to begin the meals and said, "*Sakhtein*; to the chefs."

While eating, Patrick asked Brad, "Where in Lebanon did you go?"

Mostly around Beirut," Brad answered. "Didn't have much time. Stopped at some Roman ruins just at the foot of the mountain when we crossed from Syria."

"Anjar," Patrick said.

"Sounds like it, Brad responded. "The only major side trip was to the Roman ruins at Baalbek."

"Baalbek?" Frank asked. "Isn't that the Hizbollah stronghold that the Israelis bombed this summer?"

"That's it," Patrick replied, "except the ruins are outside the town and the Israelis were very careful to avoid damaging them. They knew the whole world would condemn them if they destroyed a UNESCO heritage site."

"Damn fuckin' Israelis," Brad exclaimed. "Americans still haven't figured out what bastards they are. At least they didn't destroy the whole country. Don't get me started on Israel; I can get pretty worked up."

"From what I heard from the folks," Patrick added, "the Israelis were very careful this time not to destroy Lebanon's economy and not completely wipe out infrastructure; just enough to keep weapons from coming in. I can get pretty worked up too, so maybe we shouldn't get started."

"On a brighter note," Brad said, "I loved those two big beautiful cathedrals on the mountain north of Beirut, Jounieh I think; we took the cable car to get there."

"Oh, Harissa," Patrick said his eyes lighting up. "That's my grandmother's village; the one who lived with us when I was a kid until she died. It's the village at the top; Jounieh's down below where you take the cable car."

They continued talking about travels in the Middle East and other topics. Brad brought out fresh fruit for dessert, saying, "This is what the Middle Easterners would eat."

"Yeah, that's what my parents do," Patrick said.

Brad made Arabic coffee, then they returned to the family room saying, "Too bad we don't have Lebanese sweets. You can get them in DC, but not around here."

"For sure I don't need them," Patrick said, chuckling. "I put on five pounds in Lebanon from eating so many."

Frank got out the brandy snifters and Cognac while they talked until fairly late. They exchanged three kisses all around upon Brad's departure.

CHAPTER 4

Monday, November 7, 2006
Elliston, Virginia, USA

On a crisp, cold, fall morning in the Appalachian region of Virginia, Ahmed drove a twenty-year-old Peugeot his father had repaired and refurbished as he and Marwan went to classes at New River Community College, thirty-five miles away in Dublin.

He said, "Didn't get to tell you last night: You know I begged Dad to stay over with our cousins in Arlington for the Eid, even if I did miss a couple of classes. We went to Eid parties. One guy took me to a mosque for Friday prayers and then to a meeting for young guys, mostly Palestinians. Talked about Arabs getting fucked over in this country and organizing to demand our rights. They hate this country just as much as you and me."

Marwan thought, *Why does he include me? I don't hate this country. He really turned bitter and full of hate after those rednecks beat him up. Sure, he's my brother and I don't like them beating him up, but not enough to hate everyone. He even went to Friday prayers up there; tries his damnedest to get out of going here.*

He mumbled "Yeah" while Ahmed continued, "People there hate gays, just like us. There were demonstrations in Washington that being gay's a sin and'll be punished by God. A church group came all the way from Kansas saying God punishes gays. Everyone knows it's the fuckin' gays in this country that caused al Qaeda to attack."

Marwan thought, *There he goes again, saying "just like us." What's he got against gays?* Again he mumbled, "Yeah."

Not paying attention to Marwan's minimal responses, Ahmed kept on, "Lots of Arabs up there. Met lots at the Eid parties and they're nice, not like at the mosque in Blacksburg, where there's no Arabs and others think they're so much better because they have more education and money than us. Even a high school for Arabs up there. We got stuck going to shitty Eastern Montgomery with all the rednecks and gay sons of bitches. Lots of Arabs up there have their own businesses and hire other Arabs. Even computer companies. You should check 'em out."

Marwan thought, *Maybe I could get a job up there when I finish. No jobs around here. Some guys I chat with are from up there; maybe meet them.* "You suppose Mom and Dad'd let us move up there when I finish New River?" he asked.

"Might let you," Ahmed replied. "You're the second son. Expect me to stay and work in Dad's business because I'm the oldest. Especially now that he bought the car carrier to get more business, got himself registered with the AAA, and got the state police to let him haul abandoned cars to his garage. Mostly American and Japanese cars. That's why he made me study auto tech. His specialty's European he learned in Lebanon. People who have French cars like this one drive miles around because he's the only one who knows how to fix 'em. Just enough work for one person now, he says, but when business picks up then he'll need me full time."

CHAPTER 5

Thursday, November 23, 2006
Lafayette, Virginia, USA

On a cold, blustery, overcast afternoon, the Hammoud family were eating Thanksgiving dinner in the cozy warmth of their house in mid-afternoon. Roula and Nassar had been in the U.S. some 25 years and adopted many local customs, including turkey dinner for Thanksgiving, although they had given up finding halal. They prayed for their fellow Palestinians in the Middle East that they be relieved from their suffering, and they conversed in Arabic, which the children barely understood, about being thankful for living in the U.S. where they could live safely and the children could go to school.

Yeah, right, Ahmed said to himself bitterly. *Great fuckin' country. Gays ruin me forever; can't get a job except working for Dad. Marwan can't get a job. All Fatima's classmates call her "Fatty" and make her cry. If I say anything, they tell me to shut up.*

While eating, Nassar answered his cell phone, saying, "OK, we'll get it. Mile 130, southbound lane, just inside the Montgomery County line."

(pause)

"Thanks, Happy Thanksgiving to you too," he said; in Arabic to Ahmed, "Abandoned car on the shoulder of I-81. You and I can go after we eat."

"Oh, let the two boys go," Roula said in Arabic. "You don't ever get to rest."

"Yes, guess I could," Nassar replied in Arabic.

"Get your old dirty clothes on too," Roula continued in Arabic. "One of you stay and watch the station after you get the car while the other brings Abou Nidal to have Thanksgiving dinner. I'm sure he hasn't been away from that place since the Eid."

Marwan and Ahmed both grumbled, "OK."

Bundled up against the winter cold, they arrived where a dull slate gray Saturn sat on the shoulder. It was difficult for Ahmed to get the auto carrier in position because of heavy Thanksgiving traffic on this, probably the busiest non-urban interstate in the U.S.

He turned even colder, stopped, and fright came over him, saying, "That car's familiar."

Marwan said, "It's the car of the guys who beat you up."

Ahmed said, "Get the fuck out of here, *now*."

"We gotta take the car; can't just leave it," Marwan said and dismantled the apparatus to connect it.

Ahmed retched, almost vomiting, and reluctantly helped load the car. They unloaded it behind the garage.

"Do you want to stay or should I?" Marwan asked.

"You!" Ahmed screamed. "I'll take Abou Nidal."

Later, Marwan was alone when a car with two young men came to a screeching stop, one saying, "Tryin' t' steal m' car, ain' cha."

"No," Marwan answered. "State police said pick it up because it was blocking traffic."

"We're takin' it now," the young man said.

"You have to give us a release from the state police and pay towing," Marwan replied.

"Like hell we do," the young man said.

"I'll call my dad," Marwan said.

The young man tried to start the car, the engine turning over slowly then with no further sound. Within five minutes, Nassar and Abou Nidal drove up in an old Peugeot.

Nassar asked, "What can we do for you?"

The young man said, "Want m' car back."

Nassar, knowing the driver had contacted the state police or else would not have known where to find it, replied, "You can have it back when you pay towing and storage and have a release from the state police."

"So how much I gotta pay you?" the young man asked.

"It's $35 for towing and $20 a day for storage," Nassar replied. "Storage's waived if we repair it."

"Ain't got that much on me now," the young man said.

"Come pay whoever's here," Nassar replied. "You'll get a receipt for the police. You'll have to bring something to move it or pay us to haul it somewhere."

"Storage don't cost if you fix it?" the young man asked.

"That's right. What happened? Why'd you leave it on the highway?" Nassar asked.

"Runnin' rough, sputtered 'n' died," he replied.

"Could be several things," Nassar said. "You didn't run out of gas, did you?"

"Shouldn't of," the young man said. "Put in some yesterday. Gauge's broken so can't say f'r sure."

"Maybe a clogged fuel filter or plugs fouled," Nassar said. "I can likely fix it tomorrow. If it needs parts, probably have to wait to Monday."

"OK," the young man grumbled and left.

Nassar asked Marwan to help him push the car into the garage, saying in Arabic, "Somehow I don't trust him. Better lock it up overnight in case he gets ideas about coming back to tow it away. Not sure I want to work on it, but at least I can keep it locked up until I get my money."

They drove home, leaving Abou Nidal at the station.

CHAPTER 6

Saturday, November 25, 2006
Russellville, Alabama, USA

Paco turned over onto his back after intense love making, saying to Frank, "We've got to get up if we're going to meet them for breakfast."

Francisco Mendoza, known by his nickname Paco, was six feet two and husky, but could never be called chubby. He was intimidating when need be as a practical nurse in the Veteran's Administration nursing home; soft green-brown eyes neutralized the impact. Short, dark brown hair was trimmed military style. Slightly dark complexion and facial features hinted at his Mexican heritage, but he could easily pass as Anglo-American.

Welcome to Russellville, Alabama

As they walked to the continental breakfast of the Winwood Best Western hotel, he said, "This town is more like South Texas than Alabama. Half the town is Mexican. *Taquerías, tortillerías, carnecerías,* and *iglesias* all over the place. Even the insurance agency says '*se habla español.*'"

Two men dressed in smart casual clothes for winter in the mid-South, one in his late twenties and the other in his mid-to-late thirties, greeted Frank and Paco, who joined them for breakfast. Sean Johnson was five feet nine, had dirty blond hair, blue eyes, and a smile one expects from a flight attendant. Robert Vandam, an inch taller, had medium brown hair with green eyes; he looked the distinguished airline pilot that he was.

Patrick arrived soon, removed his light winter jacket, and said with a more pronounced Southern accent than usual, "Hey, guys. I'll just get coffee; Mom wouldn't let me out of the house without breakfast."

Robert asked, "Ready for the big day?"

"Ready as I'll ever be," Patrick answered, grinning. "Couldn't ask for a better day: sunshiny and'll get warmer this afternoon." To Paco, "Elsie's folks really appreciated the angel wing Polish wedding cookies you brought from your cousin's bakery; they'll have them at the reception later." To Frank, "The folks really appreciated the Lebanese wine you brought; almost brought tears to their eyes. They want to do something in return; go to the store and get things to take back with you."

"Oh, I couldn't…" Frank began when he felt Paco's foot kicking him in the ankle, "but come to think of it, we could use some food to eat on along the way."

Small talk continued a few more minutes until Frank said, "We need to be going. My job as best man's to make sure the groom gets places on time."

Robert asked, "Anything Paco and I might do for you? Anything we can do to amuse ourselves?"

Patrick replied, "You could wander around downtown. Might be at the community center early to see if anything's come up. Mom's lady friends are taking care of the reception; might need something. Greg and Dieter said they'd show up about 11 for us all to go to lunch. Oh, here're invitations. They gave them out to everyone at the store."

Nadine and Raymond   *Maryja and Jacek*
Ferris   *Stankowski*

Request the honor of your presence
at the wedding of their children

Elsbieta Maryja Stankowski
and
Patrick Nabil Ferris

Saturday, November 25th, 2006
at
Three o'clock in the afternoon
A. W. Todd Centre
Russellville, Alabama

and the
Reception immediately following

The bride and groom request donations in their
honor to your church or favorite charity in lieu
of other remembrances of this blessed event

Robert and Paco arrived at the community center shortly before 11 a.m., Robert comfortable in a conservative navy blue suit, having worn a similar pilot's uniform for several years, and a trench coat. Paco, in contrast, seemed awkward and uncomfortable in a medium brown down-market suit with just an ordinary jacket over it.

Soon two matronly women asked in cultured Southern accents, "Would you two nice big young men come help us move something in the other room?"

When they returned, they saw two men dressed in trench coats, and Robert said, "You must be Greg and Dieter."

Greg Hanson was five feet ten and had professionally trimmed medium brown hair. Intense green eyes showed through the black wire-framed glasses that made him look older than his actual late twenties. Dieter Müller was about an inch taller and looked about ten years older, had dark brown hair and bright dark brown eyes. Both wore conservative business suits from the Hugo Boss outlet store near Stuttgart, purchased on their last business trip to Germany.

A. W. Todd Centre, Russellville, Alabama

After introductions, Greg asked, "You two together?"

"No," Paco said. "Boyfriends're in the wedding party."

Patrick came and gave Greg and Dieter warm handshakes and big smile, saying, "Hey, guys, great to see you. Let me get the others."

At a restaurant, the owner, a portly man in his fifties who was dressed in black slacks, a white long-sleeved shirt, and nondescript tie, said with a big smile, "Hey, Patrick, y'r big day. M' wife wouldn't miss y'r weddin' f'r the world. I'll be there too, least a little while, if we don't get too busy. Got a big booth set up f'r ya in the corner. Roast beef's 'specially good; made it for folks tired of eatin' turkey. Got cheese grits if y' don't want mashed p'tatoes. Shirleen'll be there in a minute."

A dowdy woman in her forties arrived with water; she was about five feet five, stooped, and had brown hair streaked with gray that hung limply to her shoulder. She was wearing a simple black skirt and white blouse.

She gave Patrick a warm smile and said in a very pronounced accent, "So y' done gone and gittin' y'rself married. Luvly gurrl. Saw her 'n' her fokes here yest'rday."

"Thanks, Shirleen," he replied, with an equally warm smile. "In a bit of a hurry; I'll have roast beef, cheese grits, some vegetables, and whatever salad you have."

All ordered the same to make it easier and save time. They conversed in small talk, which turned to Dieter and Greg's upcoming wedding, with comments about how great it is two men can get married in Germany.

Frank said, "I suppose it's a civil marriage because church weddings aren't legal in Germany."

"Yes," Dieter replied.

"Big event like Elsie and Patrick's there?" Sean asked.

"We'll have some kind of a party," Dieter began in fluent English with a detectable accent. "In Germany, civil weddings are usually low key with just the couple and a few others present; usually a party afterwards. If there's a church wedding at another time, the big party's usually after that."

"My folks'd like it to be a church wedding," Greg said. "They've always wanted that, but I turned out to be gay."

"My parents would like a church wedding too," Dieter said. "They're regular church goers, very strong Protestants, but no Protestant clergyman would marry two guys."

"I have a friend who goes to a gay church," Frank said. "Says they have gay ceremonies. Metropolitan Community Church; they're all over the world."

"I've heard of them," Greg said. "I checked if there's one in Tuscaloosa, but there isn't. Wonder if in Stuttgart."

While eating, Sean turned to Greg. "Do you have to find someone who speaks English? Elsie said she had to hunt to find an English-speaking priest in Munich."

"Not a problem," Greg answered. "I speak German. A language major undergrad, language geek like some guys're computer geeks. Helped avoid dealing with being gay. That's how I got the job I have; got an MBA and a German company snapped me up."

"I have a friend like that," Frank said; "his language is Arabic. Paco knows him and Patrick met him too."

"I bet you speak Arabic, Patrick," Robert said.

"No," Patrick replied and told about his grandmother.

Sean asked Greg, "Did you study other languages?"

"Spanish," Greg answered.

"*Hablas español, entonces,*" Paco said.

"*No mucho hoy día,*" Greg replied, "but I managed when we went to Spain."

"Oh, you've been to Spain," Paco said. "Maybe I can go there after I get my citizenship. I'd know the language."

"You're not a citizen?" Robert asked. "You speak without an accent."

"Parents came here when I was a baby," Paco replied. "I feel American, but still a Mexican citizen."

"Gee, am I the only one who speaks only one language?" Frank asked.

45

Robert answered, "I speak only English, sadly. I'd like to learn another language, but can't with my flying schedule."

"They teach us flight attendants a smattering of other languages when we start flying internationally," Sean said, "but I can't really speak any."

Noticing all had finished, Shirleen asked if they were ready for dessert. "Comes with th' meal. Just bread puddin'."

"I'll pass," Patrick said. "Elsie'll feed me cake later."

"Frank said, "You and I need to go soon. I'll pass too."

Sean said he should pass, but Paco said, "I'll have dessert and coffee. We have time while they get dressed."

Shirleen said, "I'll bring coffee f'r all ya. Know you likes it so much, Patrick. Surely y' got time f'r coffee."

"OK," Patrick said, "Please bring the check, also."

She returned with coffee and four small dishes of bread pudding with the owner close behind her who said, "This is on us. Not goin' to discuss it. You said no gifts, but that's 'cause you couldn't carry things with you, so your mom told m' wife. No problem carryin' this."

"Thanks, Jack," Patrick said, with a warm handshake.

Shirleen said, "Me too. Y' always tipped me good ever since you's a boy, not like others who didn't leave nothin' or just a nickel or dime. Not goin' to take a thing from you today. Can't get to your weddin' 'cause gotta work, but this here's my gift to you."

Patrick gave her a kiss on the cheek, saying, "Gee, thanks, Shirleen. That's my best wedding gift ever."

When she was out of earshot, Sean said, "That was really sweet. People in this town really love you."

"Well some of them," Patrick said blushing. "Shirleen had a handicapped child and was a single parent. She really struggled to get by working here and wouldn't take a dime from anyone except wages and tips. Now the kid's grown and in an institution, so she doesn't have to work so hard at home; works here even more because she's lonely; uses the extra money to buy things for the kid. We weren't very well off in those days, but had more than she did."

Frank thought, *Here I thought he was too nice for his own good. These people really do love him. No one ever felt that way about me. I was always nice to people and didn't mistreat 'em, but guess never did anything special; was probably so insensitive didn't even notice. Old men in Paco's nursing home love him too.*

He looked at his watch and then said to Patrick, "OK, time to go. I'm not going to be responsible for your being late to your own wedding."

CHAPTER 7

Saturday, November 25, 2006
Russellville, Alabama, USA

When it was time for the wedding, warm sunlight streaming through the tinted windows, Robert, Paco, Greg, and Dieter were sitting near the front of a big room in the A. W. Todd Centre, an empty chair next to Robert for Sean. He and a local friend of Patrick's were ushers scurrying to find more chairs and eventually directing people to stand.

The local friend escorted Nadine Ferris. She walked gracefully, beaming with pride. She was about five feet six, wearing a dressy navy blue dress with matching shoes; her medium brown hair with a few streaks of gray was perfectly styled for the occasion.

Raymond Ferris followed, standing about five feet eight inches with reddish brown hair like his son, gray around the edges. He had an average build and was wearing a grey suit made by an Armenian tailor in Beirut, along with a burgundy red tie. He too was beaming with pride.

Sean escorted Maryja Stankowski. She was slightly robust, about five seven, walking purposefully. She wore a medium blue lady's suit with a white blouse and had nicely styled, mostly gray hair reflecting her mid-fifties age. She looked very much the proud, happy mother of the bride.

A diminutive older lady, at least seventy, dressed elegantly in a pink lady's suit, sat at the piano. Judge Jasper Richardson, Patrick, and Frank entered, the latter two in full dress military uniforms. The judge wore a robe to cover his well-built figure.

The pianist struck the keys with a fervor unexpected of someone frail and delicate looking. She had been Patrick's and Anna Marie's piano teacher and for many children in Russellville, as well as pianist and organist for most weddings in town. Even though mostly retired, she would not have missed this occasion for anything in the world.

With the stirring chords of Wagner's wedding march, Elsie walked down the aisle wearing a simple solid white cocktail-type dress and elegant, solid white medium-heeled shoes. With a bouquet of white flowers surrounded with greenery, she beamed the beautiful bride, her hand on her father's arm. Jacek Stankowski stood about five ten with a husky build and graying dark hair. He would have looked more comfortable in construction clothing than in the down-market gray suit he was wearing with a navy blue tie. He was bursting with pride as he escorted his daughter and only child. The audience, those who were not standing already, stood to look at her smiling. Annalise followed wearing a pale turquoise dress with matching medium-heeled shoes. When the music stopped, Mr. Stankowski placed his daughter's hand in Patrick's and sat next to his wife.

Judge Richardson began, "My friends, we are gathered here to join this couple in matrimony...." He recited the short, somewhat perfunctory wedding vows with the exchange of rings and concluded, "... By the authority conferred on me by the State of Alabama, I pronounce you husband and wife. You may kiss the bride."

Patrick and Elsie, with broad smiles, exchanged a short, warm kiss and walked down the aisle hand in hand to the stirring chords of Mendelssohn's wedding march; Frank escorting Annalise followed.

All moved to an adjoining room. A long receiving line formed where Patrick, Elsie, the two sets of parents, and the rest of the wedding party stood. Two older ladies, both well into their sixties, stood to the side dressed in their best Sunday-go-to-church clothes, one in a lavender lady's suit, the other in a pink winter dress with a white shawl over her shoulders.

The one in pink looked to the other saying, "Violet, it looks like you're waiting before you get in the line also."

"Yes, Rose," her friend replied, "plenty of time; it'll take a while with this crowd."

Both spoke with the cultured and cultivated Southern accents typical of educated people in the area.

"Just look at little Patrick, big Patrick now," Rose said, "so handsome in his uniform. Seems just last year he was in my social studies class. Always wanting to know about different parts of the world, especially the Middle East where his folks are from. Seems he *really* did well in your classes."

"Oh, yes," Violet said. "Had a head for science and math. No wonder he went to Auburn to study engineering. Really nice scholarship, from what I recall."

"Army paid for an MBA in Tuscaloosa," Rose continued. "Always was a bright one, and hard working too."

"Now he's gone away," Violet added. "Good ones usually do. Not much in this town to keep them here."

"Well, he's in the Army, so he has to go," Rose said. "But, yes, you're right; probably won't be back now that he's married a Northern girl. She's lovely, though, isn't she? She's an airline stewardess, Nadine told Maude."

"Oh, yes," Violet agreed. "She is at that. I'm surprised they're getting married here, not at her home, and just a civil ceremony. Nothing against Jasper, and he's a good friend of Raymond, but most folks here have church weddings."

"Well, they're *Catholic,* don't you know," Rose said. "No Catholic churches here."

"Yes, I think I heard that," Violet said. "Now that I think of it, they didn't get involved in church things, but were involved in so many other things we just didn't notice."

"Maude said that Nadine told her that they had to get married in a hurry before moving to Europe, Brussels I think, and there was some problem getting married in a church so quickly up where she lives, so they just came down here," Rose continued.

"*Had* to get married," Violet said.

"Well, not that way," Rose replied. "Nadine didn't actually say she isn't pregnant, but she did go to great lengths to explain to Maude that they have to be legally married so she can go over there to live with him; and since they couldn't get married quickly up there, they came down here."

"Well, I guess we'll see in a few months," Violet giggled. "Nadine couldn't keep quiet about a grandchild even if it were over there and born a few weeks early."

"Nadine also said to Dora," Rose continued, "they're going to have a proper church wedding over there in some big fancy cathedral, in Munich, I think."

"Oh, Munich," Violet responded. "That's where those terrorists killed all the athletes during the Olympics way back in what year? 1972. But now aren't they getting uppity. Getting married in some big fancy cathedral in Europe."

"Well they'll live there," Rose offered, "and Nadine said it's easier for family to come from Lebanon and Poland."

"Oh, yes, that's right," Violet said. "They're foreign. Ferrises never seemed foreign, but they did come from Lebanon and bought that old grocery store. Sure made a good business out of it, so I guess no one notices any more that they speak with just a little bit of an accent. The bride has a funny name, parents too. Never knew of Polish people around here."

"Dora says that Nadine told her that she likes to be called Elsie, like 'Elsie the Contented Cow' in those milk commercials when we were young," Rose added.

"Well at least the Ferrises gave their kids good American names," Violet retorted, unaware that Patrick and Anna Marie

51

were Lebanese names. "Say, that matron of honor looks almost old enough to be her mother."

"Maude says Nadine told her that she's another stewardess she works with," Rose explained.

"That's a nice looking young man who's the usher," Violet said. "Suppose she works with him also. They call them flight attendants when they're men these days."

Rose said, "That's what Maude says Nadine told her."

"Seems like he's with that older good looking man over there," Violet said. "Wonder if they're homosexuals. I hear most men flight attendants are these days."

"Look at that distinguished handsome military officer who's Patrick's best man," Rose said. "Doesn't he look nice in that uniform, just like Patrick's, but a different color because he's in the Marines."

"I heard that tall husky guy over there was with him at the rehearsal dinner last night. Wonder what his connection is," Violet continued. "He looks a little bit like some of the Mexicans who've begun moving in here."

"Don't know," Rose replied. "Didn't hear anyone say. Must be some other military buddy, the way he has his hair trimmed like Patrick and his best man."

"But he's not in a uniform," Violet said.

"Well, maybe only Patrick and his best man were supposed to be in uniform," Rose offered. "Looks like the line's getting shorter."

"Oh, look, there's that colored woman, Fannie, about to greet them," Violet said.

"She was their maid and Patrick and Anna Marie's nanny when they were little and Nadine worked at the store," Rose said. "Kept her on until she wanted to retire. Look, Nadine's giving her a hug."

"In my day, colored'd keep their place," Violet stated.

"Isn't your day any more," Rose said. "Let's get in line."

They got behind a lady the same age wearing a white dress with a dark yellow jacket and white shoes.

Rose asked with a smile, "Are you last in line, Daisy?"

"Yes," she answered. "Aren't you two smart today."

"Oh, look," Violet said, "who're those Oriental people? The man looks distinguished and the woman is so pretty, diminutive, even if they are Oriental."

"Don't look like Chinese people who run restaurants up in Muscle Shoals," Rose commented.

"Well, Hilda told me they came into town yesterday. Saw them in the supermarket with Patrick and his girlfriend, now his wife."

"Those two children don't look completely Oriental like the two of them, like part American," Violet observed.

"Hilda said the two kids seemed really attached to Patrick," Daisy continued.

"You think they're his?" Violet suggested. "Come now, Violet," Rose said chidingly. "He's not old enough to have a child old as that girl. She looks a good nine or ten. Too much makeup too."

"Well, *biologically* he is," Violet retorted.

"Oh, come now," Daisy said. "He'd've been a student at Auburn. Came home at least once a month. Went off to the University and did the same. Couldn't have kids and do that. Besides, they don't look anything like him, American part, that is."

The three ladies continued gossiping. Elsie and Patrick cut the wedding cake together and fed each other. Elsie threw her bouquet so that Anna Marie with her fiancé Doug standing near caught it. They visited with the guests and then retired to change to their travelling clothes.

CHAPTER 8

Monday, November 27, 2006
Christiansburg, Virginia, USA

On another cold but sunshiny late fall day, Paco drove Frank's Mountaineer northbound on I-81 through the Appalachian Mountains of Southwest Virginia while Frank's thoughts drifted: *Wouldn't let us get away early; insisted we take all this food. Had to stay overnight in Tennessee; another nice night in bed with Paco.* "Say, how'm I doing?" he asked as he put his hand on Paco's thigh. "We've been together 36 straight hours."

Paco smiled and gave him a playful pinch on the cheek saying, "Just fine, doll. Hard to imagine the change since that trip to Florida. You were really open with everyone, especially me, except when you were about to say you didn't want to take food Patrick's folks offered you. Man, someone offers you something nice because they like you and want to show appreciation, you don't turn them down. Like Patrick accepted lunch and even the waitress's offer of no tip. Could really hurt their feelings if he didn't."

"Yeah, I realized that, pretty quickly," Frank said, "especially after you kicked me in the ankle."

"Hey, don't go get a big head, now," Paco teased. "You've got a way to go. Besides, you were under lots of stress that trip to Florida. I hadn't recovered from that long drive to Mexico and back, and was sensitive myself."

Frank said, "It woke me up to realize just what stress is and how it affects me. Never thought I was stressed, just cool, reserved, Marine Corps officer Frank Reynolds. It hit me: was *lack* of stress I didn't know; been under constant stress all my life; was the normal way I dealt with things."

Paco continued, "I actually read that book *The Great Santini*. Haven't gotten around to the other one, something about discipline."

"*Lords of Discipline*," Frank said.

Paco continued, "Helped me understand what you went through growing up. Have a few things to work on myself."

"Oh," Frank said.

"At first I was intimidated by that crowd all with college degrees, important positions. Realized I had a chip on my shoulder; looking for reasons to feel sorry for myself, a poor dumb Mexican who hasn't had advantages like other people."

"Really?" Frank asked. "You seemed to fit in just fine, especially when we went out Saturday after the wedding."

"It hit me having lunch and guys talking about languages they speak," Paco began. "I speak two languages, more than you do. Realized what I do as a practical nurse is every bit as specialized and important as what Sean does as a flight attendant. Patrick's parents aren't much different from mine, immigrants who came to this country for a new life, started basically from scratch. They've been successful with their supermarket, more than my folks who worked in factories, but we haven't done so bad. Dieter's father worked in a factory too, not that much different from my papi. I've got to get on with things. If I get a job in Baltimore, going to get a B.S. in nursing and see where I go from there."

Frank said, "Guess I won't be seeing much of you then."

"Don't worry, lover boy," Paco said as he squeezed Frank's thigh. "You'll see plenty of me."

After a few moments, Frank said, "Damn, I need to pee; looks like we've passed the last exit for this town. I'll look at the map to see if there's a rest area or another exit up ahead."

"Wouldn't hurt to get some gas," Paco said. "If we get some while you pee, it'll save time."

Frank said, "There's an exit ahead before a rest area. Maybe a gas station there."

CHAPTER 9

Monday, November 27, 2006
Elliston, Virginia, USA

Ahmed was working alone in the garage and Abou Nidal was working inside the gas station when a battered old car came to a screeching halt close to where an old slate gray Saturn was parked. A passenger was directed to the garage where he said, "Looks like mah car's ready."

Ahmed, whose head was under the hood of a car, said, "Go to the station; I'll be there in a minute to get your bill."

In front of the station, Ahmed became scared when he recognized the person dressed in a shabby well-worn winter coat and said, "That's $97.81; $35 for the towing and $62.81 for the repair."

"It's you, sissy ass, fuckin' A-rab," the other man said.

A cream colored Mercury Mountaineer drove up to a gasoline pump near them. Paco got out, shivering in the cold but not wanting to put on a heavy jacket just to pump gas. He heard, "Ain't paying no fuckin' bill. Told ya A-rabs don't b'long here."

Paco moved closer while Frank got his cell phone to call to 911 if needed and asked, "Where's the restroom?"

Ahmed stammered, "Outside door on the right."

Shivering in the cold, Frank thrust the cell phone into Paco's hand, put his credit card into the pump to pay, and rushed to the restroom.

Paco moved closer, asking, "What's the problem here?"

The car that had brought the man claiming the Saturn quickly drove away as the other ran towards his car, turned, and screamed, "We warned you fuckin' sissy ass A-rab. Next time we're bombing the shit out of that house where you live, just like you fuckin' A-rab terr'ists bombed us."

Paco pumped gasoline and kept his eye on Ahmed as the Saturn sped away with the driver screaming, "Get your fuckin' A-rab ass out of here or you'll get it reamed again."

"Looks like we got here at the right time," Paco said.

"Yeah," Ahmed stammered, shivering in the cold.

Paco said, "They did bad things to you, didn't they?"

Ahmed replied, "Damned fuckin' gays. Ruining the country. Treat Arabs like shit when we just work to survive."

Paco said, "Hey, man, not all gays're like that. Some'll fight to protect you."

Frank returned, took his receipt from the gasoline pump, and said, "He drove off without paying, didn't he?"

Ahmed replied, "Yes. My father'll be really pissed off."

"How much did he owe you?" Frank asked.

"A little under $100," Ahmed replied. "Why?"

Frank gave him five $20 bills, saying, "Now your father won't have to know."

Ahmed, stunned, not knowing what to say or do, barely muttered, "Thanks," as Frank and Paco drove away.

On the interstate heading north again, Paco said, "Nice of you to give the kid money, but sometimes best for people to work things out for themselves."

Frank replied, "All I could think of was my father pissed off at me, especially if I did nothing wrong."

"That's what I figured," Paco said. "Not criticizing, something to think about. The kid'd been raped by them."

"Oh, God," Frank said. "No one deserves that."

"Must've really made him bitter against gays," Paco continued and recounted what was said.

They continued in silence and small talk to Maryland.

CHAPTER 10

Monday, April 16, 2007
Lafayette, Virginia, USA

Relaxing before bedtime as they usually did, Nassar, Roula, Ahmed, and Marwan watched evening news. Tonight they watched scenes from the shooting of thirty-three people that morning on the nearby campus of Virginia Tech. Fatima had been sent to her bedroom to do homework.

"Those poor mothers," Roula said tearfully in Arabic. "Their precious children killed like that. The mother of that young Korean man too. How can she live knowing her son did such a horrible thing?"

"Thought we'd gotten away from violence when we settled here," Nassar said solemnly in Arabic. "Happens all the time in Palestine. This is right here, twenty miles away! Wonder if anyone at the mosque was hurt."

"One Israeli guy got killed," Marwan said in Arabic.

Ahmed said to himself: *Damn fucking Israeli; deserved it. So what if stupid arrogant assholes from the mosque were hurt. They don't show respect to us Arabs; fact we're Muslim like them don't mean shit. We're the only Arabs there. Don't know why dad goes and insists Marwan and me go along. Marwan and me've gotta get out of here; go to Northern Virginia where there's other Arabs who want to stand up and fight and demand people respect us.*

Marwan went to the bedroom he shared with Ahmed, saying in Arabic, "Have to study. Big project due."

Later in their bedroom, Ahmed said, "We got to get out of here. Foreigner's gunned down these people; they'll turn on us even though we were born in this fucking country."

Marwan thought, *There he goes, this "us" stuff. Don't treat me bad. Not always nice either. Mostly ignore me at the rest area. Maybe he's right; go where I can get a decent job.*

Ahmed continued, "Said he was upset and angry they'd treated him bad because he's foreign. Bet it was gays who hurt him. Damn fuckin' gays fuckin' up this country."

Marwan said, "Have to work on this program. If I get a good grade might help get a job up there, if Dad'd let us. Don't want to go up there alone."

"Mom'll never want either of us go," Ahmed replied. "If Dad says it's OK, she won't go against him. Maybe let us go again once your school's over."

Ahmed went to sleep. Marwan did the same about an hour later.

CHAPTER 11

Wednesday, May 23, 2007
Harrisonburg, Virginia, USA

In late morning on a clear warm day, leaving the DC metropolitan area after morning rush hour, Marwan was driving a 1980s vintage Mercedes-Benz on I-81 southbound when Ahmed said, "How'd you like the meeting with the guys and imam last night? Good thing Dad let us stay after he took off with the carrier and the other car I found. Now you see what Arabs there're like, ready to fight for our rights and make 'em respect us."

Marwan thought, *Full of hate, just like him. Something really bad happened to them too, or maybe the imam's stirring them up. Our mosque says Islam is peace and non-violence; this imam says the Prophet commanded Muslims to fight back, defend themselves, demand respect. Maybe I'm naïve.* He grunted, "Yeah."

Ahmed continued, "You heard me sayin' how gays're fucking up this country and defiling Islam too. The imam said so too, after he heard me. Gotta kill 'em all."

Marwan continued to think. *Really have to stop being gay. Imam says it's wrong. Trying to stay out of those chat sites and away from the rest area. Only went there once just before we left. Damn it felt good what that guy did to me.*

"You saw that Falwell guy's funeral on TV," Ahmed continued. "People from a church in Kansas came all the way to protest. Say being gay's a sin and all gays need to be killed. See, Christians think the same way. Arab Muslims kill gays, Christians'll see what we've done and respect us."

"You talk to Dad about moving there?" Marwan asked.

"Yeah," Ahmed answered, "when we went to get the car he bought. May have convinced him I can do more good up there finding old European cars and sell some of the ones he's fixed. Told him there really isn't enough work in the garage for two of us, and he reluctantly agreed."

"Really?" Marwan asked.

"Yes," Ahmed answered. "I suggested what he really needs is another person like Abou Nidal, who needs a place to live and work. Maybe fix up another little apartment."

"He agreed?" Marwan asked excitedly.

"Not really," Ahmed replied, "but didn't disagree. Told him I'd try to find someone."

"Did you?" Marwan asked.

"Asked a couple of people and some mentioned knowing about someone. What about you; any jobs?"

"Some," Marwan answered. "Heard about Arab-run computer companies. Some're expanding. Told me to get a résumé. Going to do that first thing when we get home."

They drove the rest of the way mostly in silence in their own thoughts, not paying attention to the beautiful mountain and valley scenery on such a clear day before the summer haze set in.

CHAPTER 12

Saturday, June 16, 2007
Stuttgart, Baden-Württemberg, Germany

Elsie, Patrick, Frank, and Paco shared a table amid the dull noise and mostly German conversation at Dieter and Greg's wedding reception in the Steigenberger Graf Zeppelin Hotel sipping German "champagne" called *sekt*. Small engraved folded cards were located on each table:

GREGORY WAYNE HANSON
UND
DIETER FREDRIK MÜLLER

16. Juni 2007

"Flew in yesterday and stayed in Frankfurt to look around," Frank replied to Patrick, who had asked. "Not much there; just another big city. Took the train this morning. Luckily this hotel's right across the street from the train station, so we didn't have to deal with taxis."

Elsie agreed. "When we fly to Frankfurt, it's kind of dull and boring; Munich's much more interesting."

"What about you?" Frank asked.

"Flew in this morning," Patrick answered. "Haven't seen much of the city. Seems nice; new and modern."

"My first time here, too," Elsie commented. "We don't fly here; Delta's the only U.S. airline that does. U.S. military activity here, I hear. They're required to use U.S. carriers if they can; Delta got here first."

"Headquarters Armed Forces Europe is here," Patrick added. "We coordinate with them; haven't been here yet."

Frank said, "I was here when I was a kid, early teens. Dad came for something, guess to that headquarters. Brought Mother and me because they didn't think I should be left alone," *although they would've liked to I'm sure*, he thought. "Tag along and be quiet; don't remember much." *She was drinking a lot, so I couldn't be left alone with her.*

"Old guys in the nursing home talk about being here," Paco said. "Not a very nice place back then, most of 'em say. Allies bombed the shit out it—oops; sorry, Elsie—and nothing but rubble. People pretty poor too."

"Yes," Frank concurred. "Daimler Benz factories all around; major place for German war industry. Studied about it in military history at the Citadel." To Elsie and Patrick, "You go to the civil ceremony?"

"Yes," Elsie answered.

"Place called Pleenygun, or something like that," Patrick added. "Last place Dieter lived before the company moved him to Alabama. We could see a building with the big Mercedes star on top not far away."

"It's Plieningen, dear," Elsie said. "You didn't miss much, a simple legal ceremony in German in an ugly concrete building; must have been built in the fifties when they rebuilt the city. Kind of a city hall."

"Called it the rat house," Patrick chuckled. "Expected rats to run out of the closets any minute."

Bezirksrathaus, Plieningen, Stuttgart, Germany

"We weren't invited," Frank said. "Only to the church wedding and reception. Now I see why."

"Greg was glad to have Americans there so he wouldn't be overwhelmed by Dieter's German family and friends," Patrick said.

"I was surprised so many showed up," Frank said.

"Some're work colleagues," Patrick added. "Company he works for's located here too, major supplier to Daimler. He comes here and they go to Tuscaloosa pretty often."

"Standing room only, in that small old church," Frank commented. "Just like your wedding in Russellville."

"There won't be that problem in Munich," Elsie added, smiling. "It's a huge old church. This one isn't all that old; built in the 1800s. Really interesting history. Always been an English-speaking church, but now shared by Anglicans and a German group, the Old Catholics. The city gave land to the Anglican Church in the 1800s because they were eager and pleased to have an English-speaking church here; made Stuttgart a cosmopolitan international city for its day. It's always been Saint Catherine's in English. Local people protected it and hid some of the members during the two wars. It was damaged a fair amount in World War II."

"Gee, you know a lot about churches," Paco said.

"I've always had a thing about old churches," Elsie replied. "Every time we overnight in Europe or in Mexico, I go looking for them. That's how I found the one in Munich where we're getting married. Here, I saw a leaflet in English that had the history. After World War II, there weren't enough English speakers to support it, so the building was given to a German-speaking church who're very similar in belief. Anglicans have the right to use it perpetually."

Saint Catherine's Church, Stuttgart, Germany

"Interesting ceremony," Paco commented. "Three priests, one a woman, and one native English speaking."

Patrick added, "Greg explained it to us. They followed through on your comment, Frank, and found one of those gay churches here; has a woman pastor. She was pleased to give them a church wedding; even suggested this church. When they talked to the two priests who use the building to get permission, the Anglican priest's from the United States. Greg said his family'd really like it if an American priest presided. The pastors agreed it'd be OK for the lady from the MCC to preside speaking German and the American priest speaking English, with the other priest taking a nominal role."

Frank asked, "How long're you staying?"

"We're taking the train to Munich in the morning," Elsie said. "Patrick hasn't been there to see what it's like."

"We're staying in this hotel, too," Patrick said. "All we have to do is walk across the street to get the train. I'll fly from Munich back to Brussels. Got work to do and not much to do while the women are seeing to the details. My folks don't arrive until later in the week, and they'll be busy with family coming from Lebanon. Anna Marie and Doug arrive later in the week."

"My mother'll be with me all week," Elsie said. "She really wants to get involved in this wedding, not like the last one where she felt kind of left out. Don't get upset dear; that's the way it had to be and she's not upset, but every mother wants to be personally involved in her daughter's wedding."

"What's this *Biergarten* place the invitation says you're having the reception?" Frank asked. "Sounds like an elegant wedding, not something that'd be at a beer garden."

"Oh, it'll be elegant," Elsie said smiling. "That's an outdoor courtyard used as a beer garden for the public. We reserved it for the evening so we can be outdoors. It's Midsummer's Day, longest day of the year. We thought it'd be nice outdoors to dance through the night. A string quartet'll play classical dance music. Hope it doesn't rain, but we have a tent reserved just in case."

Gee, string quartet and a tent reserved, Paco thought. *Must cost a fortune. Her father's a factory worker like mine.*

As if sensing Paco's thoughts, Patrick leaned closer and said, "We can tell you, but please don't tell others. We're making Elsie's parents think they're paying for most of it, but not telling them how much it costs. They don't understand how much a euro is in dollars. Make them think it's just a little bit more expensive than in Poland."

"We're putting in as much as we can," Elsie added. "We both earn OK salaries."

"Actually my folks are paying a good amount," Patrick added. "Lebanese have to show off to their families. Dad told me quietly the store's doing really well. Don't want local people to know just how well off they are. They're charging fair prices—have to with Super Walmart almost next door—not taking advantage of anyone, but good service and personal attention pay off. He also said he and Mom worked hard to get where they are and they're not going to deny me the opportunity. They're giving Anna Marie a big wedding too."

"What're you two doing this next week?" Elsie asked.

"Frank said we'd rent a car and look at places around here," Paco answered. "Maybe the Black Forrest, also Strasbourg where I hear they have a beautiful cathedral."

"Sounds nice," Elsie said, "especially the cathedral."

"We're going to the Hugo Boss outlet that Dieter and Greg told us about," Frank added. "It's close to here, almost a suburb. Then we'll take the train to Munich."

Food was served, and festivities continued well into the early morning hours. Frank and Paco gave their goodbyes and thank-yous early, claiming they were still jet lagged. Elsie and Patrick left early, saying they needed to take an early train.

CHAPTER 13

Saturday, June 23, 2007
Munich, Bavaria, Germany

On a warm sunshiny summer day, Paco and Frank walked down Müllerstrasse, the main street of Munich's gay district, feeling a bit rushed because Paco had been pressed into becoming an usher at the last minute because a cousin of Patrick from Lebanon couldn't get a visa in time and Paco was the only Catholic readily available. They saw the KraftAkt internet café they were looking for; Paco said, "That's Spexter across the street, the shop in the guide. Go ahead; I'll look quick and find you if anything's interesting."

Spexter sex shop, KraftAkt internet café, directly across the street from each other, Munich, Germany

Upon entering the café Frank exclaimed, "Patrick, what the hell're you doing here?"

The man turned pale and exclaimed, "Frank!"

Realizing Patrick wouldn't dress like this, Frank fumbled, "You, you're Doc!" recognizing the man who had been infiltrated into the U.S. as a duplicate of Patrick. "What the hell're you doing here?"

The man answered in flawless American English, "Yes, Frank, and I do have a name. I can ask you the same question."

Frank stammered, "Al, Ali? If you told me any other, I don't remember."

"Salman, Ali Salman, almost like the fish," he replied.

"I'm attending a wedding," Frank said, "and you?"

"Don't you think you should sit down so we can talk better, not standing up so everyone can see and hear you?" Ali said. "I'm in the middle of something, don't have much time left, and not much money to pay for more. If you want coffee, I'll join you when I finish."

Frank thought: *Can't let him out of my sight. Might run into someone who knows Patrick.* He said, "I'll wait here."

A few minutes later at a table, Frank buying coffee for both, he asked, "Your first time in Munich?"

"Yes," Ali answered.

"What do you think about it so far?" Frank said.

"It's interesting; different," Ali answered.

Frank asked, "Care to tell what you're doing here?"

Ali replied, "Here to meet people about opening a clinic; and you must be curious how I got here from Texas, where you left me with your two buddies."

As Frank was saying "yes," Paco walked in and said, "Hey, Patrick. Having coffee with us gay boys?"

Ali became pale; Paco noticed Ali's clothes and stammered, "You're not Patrick."

Ali said, "No. I don't know your name. Remember?"

"You're Doc," Paco stammered.

"Yes," he replied, standing to offer a handshake, "but I have a name, Ali Salman. Might as well sit. We're catching up since we last saw each other."

Paco shook his hand and said, "Paco Mendoza. What're you doing here?"

"Doc, er Ali, just started to tell me he's here to meet people about opening a clinic," Frank interjected.

"Oh," Paco said. "What kind of a clinic? Where?"

"Cosmetic surgery," Ali answered. "You should remember; you called me Doc. Clinic's in Iraq."

"Iraq!" Paco exclaimed. "How'n hell'd you get there? We left you in…"

"Mexico," Ali completed the sentence. "You might as well get coffee if you want before I start."

Paco ordered while Ali explained he and the three others had been captured by Mexican authorities suggesting Paco had set things up. He described how Mexicans had taken them to a secret location where they fell into the hands of U.S. authorities, and later transferred to a prison in Baghdad.

Paco exclaimed, "Baghdad! What about the others?"

"The tall skinny guy was killed. No idea about the other two," Ali replied while Paco asked himself, *Will they come back to haunt me too?*

Frank asked, "You went to Baghdad. Then what?"

Ali explained he had helped in the prison clinic. They employed him to work in another prison clinic, continuing, "I worked there for a while, then someone had an idea the U.S. should fund a cosmetic surgery clinic for people who survive bomb attacks and war injuries, also Iraqi soldiers and police; build goodwill with the community. Funded by the U.S. Agency for International Development and private charities." To himself: *Don't think I should say it's mostly a CIA project.*

"You're running it?" Frank asked.

Ali replied. "A local doctor is nominally in charge; I'm associate medical director in charge of plastic surgery."

"What's it like in Baghdad, opening a clinic in all the chaos?" Frank asked.

"It's in Sulaymaniyah in the Kurdish area that's stable," Ali replied. "Part of a burn, plastic surgery, and emergency hospital. It's the cultural capital of Kurdistan, big city of over a million, but quiet and low key. Name's spelled lots of ways in western characters; you can find it with an online search."

"What're you doing here, then, if this is an American operation?" Frank continued to ask.

Can't say the CIA operates from here, Ali thought, then said, "German and Austrian charities with support from their governments want to help. Want our business for equipment and supplies. They're quietly investing in the Kurdish area because it's stable. I've got to pee bad. Let me find the restroom."

Frank said to Paco, "Keep your eyes on him and that restroom door. Don't want him bolting out of here and ending up somewhere he can be seen by the others. We could invite him to lunch and to Salzburg tomorrow."

"Huh?" Paco said surprised.

"You said put myself in another person's position," Frank replied; "understand what they're feeling."

Paco agreed, "Yeah. He must be shocked as we are; afraid the past'll come out."

"Yes," Frank said. "Lonely too, a strange country, not knowing the language, overwhelmed."

"I'd be too," Paco concurred, "if it weren't for you."

"If we show empathy, be friendly and nice, invite him to be with us," Frank continued, "get his confidence so he'll cooperate and not allow himself to be seen."

"Hey, love, you're really catching on fast," Paco said with a big smile as he stood and kissed him.

Ali saw the kiss and said, "You two are together?"

Paco said, "Er, yes."

Ali said, "In Mexico, you were with someone else."

"Oh, that's my cousin," Paco replied. "We've been 'doin' it' for years; Frank's my main squeeze now. What're you doing in a gay place? Don't go saying you just happened to find this internet café while walking along some street not knowing where you are."

Ali blushed as he answered, "I've been curious and was sort of forced to start thinking. Difficult, but like your buddy said, better accept it because it's much easier to deal with. In Kurdistan, I don't have an opportunity to even be curious and explore, so here I thought since I don't have anything else to do this weekend, I'd see what I can find. Took some effort to find where gay places are, but I managed. And yes, I did just happen to find this internet café walking along the street."

Frank said, "Say, Ali we're having lunch around here; come with us. We have to go to a wedding in the afternoon, but tomorrow we're taking a short trip to Salzburg; you can come with us. Mozart's home and all that."

"It's Patrick who's getting married here, isn't it?" Ali asked. "You want to keep me out of the way so I don't run into someone who'd be shocked. Don't worry. I'm eager as you are not to have a confrontation. I'll stay close to my hotel. Don't have money to go out anyway."

"That's part of it," Frank said. "We really do want you to go with us. Circumstances weren't good last time, so we want to make it better this time. Besides, doesn't cost any extra with a family ticket. Ali, you really do have to change your appearance. Let your hair grow; grow a moustache."

"Yes, I know," Ali said. "I'm not ready. I was happy being a regular American. Until recently, I've been around U.S. military people and wanted to fit in."

"I'll buy your lunch," Paco said. "Make up for that crappy food we fed you."

Ali, "Gee, thanks, but I don't know."

"Come on, quit being polite," Paco said as he put his hand on Ali's shoulder. "I'm taking Frank to the shop across the street to look at some leather and other things. You want to explore gay things, so might as well come along. Then we'll find something to eat."

After lunch, Paco said, "Gotta go get into my tux."

"Go ahead," Frank suggested. "I'll stay with Ali and find out where he's staying."

"I can meet you at your hotel," Ali offered.

"Not a bother," Frank said. "Besides, we're staying at the same hotel as the wedding party."

"Oh," Ali gulped. "hadn't thought about that."

Paco gave Frank a kiss, put his hand on Ali's shoulder, and said, "See you tomorrow."

CHAPTER 14

Saturday, June 23, 2007
Munich, Bavaria, Germany

From bright summer sunshine, Frank entered the dark Frauenkirche, stopping to allow his eyes to adjust. He was wearing a new Hugo Boss charcoal gray suit with a white Hugo Boss shirt, and conservative navy blue Hugo Boss tie. Paco ushered him to a seat alongside Greg, Dieter, Robert, and Sean. Pete, Felicia, David, and Christina sat nearby. The altar had lavish arrangements of red, white, yellow, and blue early summer flowers and ample greenery. Smaller identical flower arrangements indicated seats for the mothers.

Frauenkirche, Munich, Germany

Frank thought, *A fair number showed up, but feels like just a few in this big church.*

Nadine Ferris, escorted by Doug, was dressed elegantly in a summer satiny blue dress befitting a proud mother of the groom.

Paco escorted Maryja Stankowski dressed slightly less elegantly in a complementary blue dress. The priest and male members of the wedding party stood in front of the altar facing the people; all but the priest were wearing elegant tuxedos.

The traditional Wagner wedding march sounded on the pipe organ. All stood to see Denise Cavanaugh, wearing a blue satiny dress, throwing white rose petals. Elsie, wearing an elegant white wedding gown with a long train and carrying a bouquet of the flowers adorning the church, was escorted by her father in a tuxedo. Annalise, the matron of honor, and two maids of honor, all in identical elegant blue dresses and carrying similar smaller bouquets, followed. Timmy Cavanaugh, wearing a miniature tuxedo, carried a pillow with rings.

Mr. Stankowski placed Elsie's hand in Patrick's, bowed toward the altar and crossed himself, and sat next to his wife.

Frank observed, *Can you believe all of those tourists walking around? Don't they stop tours when private things are going on?*

Frank did not follow the prayers and liturgy, his mind drifting to the shock of meeting Ali. The formal mass ended and a Maronite priest, a distant relative of the Ferrises from Lebanon, delivered a marriage blessing in Arabic. The organist stuck the chords of Mendelssohn's recessional.

Later in the *Biergarten,* converted into a gala reception site, a lavish dinner was served with German Franconian white wine and Lebanese Cabernet Sauvignon. Dancing continued late into the night with Dieter and Greg and then Robert and Sean joining other couples on the dance floor. Frank dragged Paco onto the dance floor for a Viennese waltz to which they danced badly; Paco would have been much more comfortable with the *Cumbia* like at the Mexican block parties back in Ohio.

At the first sight of dawn, which came early in Germany on Midsummer's night, the party broke up and all retired wearily to their hotels, Patrick and Elsie to the bridal suite.

CHAPTER 15

Wednesday, July 4, 2007
Lafayette, Virginia, USA

On a very warm but not hot summer day typical of the mountain and valley region of Virginia, Ahmed drove his mother home to prepare a cookout, asking himself, *Where's Marwan? Can't wait to tell him.*

Soon Marwan rode up on his bicycle, thinking, *Ahmed and Mom are home. Good thing I left the rest area; too busy for anything to happen. Why'd I have to go there? Got chatting online and couldn't control myself.*

Ahmed said excitedly, not noticing Marwan's mood, "Hey, where've you been? I've been waiting for you."

He answered, "I just went out riding; boring around here. Fatima's off at a friend's."

"Guess what?" Ahmed said. "Dad says we can move to Northern Virginia. All we have to do is find someone to help in the station and with the car carrier."

Marwan's mood changed. "Really? I think I have some good job prospects up there." *Now I can quit being gay*, he said to himself. *Maybe someone up there'll find a girl for me. That'll stop me being gay.*

"Hey, why don't you come back to the station with me," Ahmed said. "Dad can tell you himself. Things are pretty busy with the Fourth of July traffic and Mom here."

As they drove the short distance to the station, they saw American flags being displayed and heard firecrackers.

"Stick those firecrackers up your gay asses," Ahmed said, as Marwan cringed.

CHAPTER 16

The beep of his cell phone jolted Frank out of idleness in mid-morning; a text message read, "Late lunch?" He knew Brad would be on morning break and had lunch at 1 p.m.

Must be important, Frank thought, *or he'd call at home tonight.* He replied: 'BE' indicating Bob Evans restaurant.

Frank was looking at a menu when Brad arrived and handed him a sheet of paper. "Look at this while I decide."

Frank said, "might be good. Weeknights are free unless Paco works weekends and comes over. You enrolling?"

"Thinking seriously about it," Brad replied. "Just saw this at HR this morning. Not much else to do except sometimes things at church. Jason lives so far away, weekdays're open for me too."

Frank looked over and said, "Not sure I'd want to go alone, first class in over fifteen years, but definitely interested."

"I'd want graduate credit," Brad said. "Probably have to get accepted by George Washington, show transcripts, and the like. Wonder who's this teaching? Definitely Arabic name. Probably an old fart from some half-assed university in an Arab country; U.S. government paid him to come for a semester as a goodwill gesture. Says he's a post-doctoral fellow, whatever that means. Still might be interesting.

The Role of Islam:
Religious Issues in Contemporary International Politics and Conflicts

Fall Semester 2007
Wednesdays 6 to 9 p.m.
First class: September 5

HOWARD COMMUNITY COLLEGE

Graduate and undergraduate credit through
George Washington University
or non-credit

Lecturer: Dr. Omar Abu Deeb, Post-Doctoral
Fellow, George Washington University

Enrollment on college website or in person;
deadline Friday, August 25, 2007

"Can't tell much from his name. Omar's one of the most common names in Arabic. Abu Deeb could be from anywhere. 'Abu' means 'father of.' Used mostly as a nickname given to a man when his first son is born, but a nickname that shows esteem and respect, especially when trying to butter someone up. Sometimes a family name."

Frank said, "Making sense. At Patrick's wedding, Lebanese relatives were calling his father 'something Patrick'; must have been Abou Patrick. They're Christian."

"Probably," Brad said. "Not a Muslim thing, cultural Arab. In Jordan I saw an occasional Abou George or similar among Christians, and in Lebanon there were a fair number of French names like Abou Pierre and Abou Antoine."

"Abou Patrick doesn't sound French," Frank said.

"Patrick is a French name," Brad continued. "Not the most common. Lebanese Christians, especially Maronites, give their children names of saints. Even though St. Patrick's Irish, he's still revered."

"His sister's Anna Marie, mother Nadine, and father Raymond," Frank said. "All fits."

Brad said, "Pronunciation different in English but very French. French was my second language, undergraduate."

"Does this guy have a son named Deeb?" Frank asked.

"Probably not," Brad answered. "When it's a family name it's usually written 'Abu,' but when it's a nickname usually 'Abou'; pronounced the same. Almost certain the Abu Deeb became a family name. If by chance he does have a son named Deeb, not likely he'd be called that on a formal document."

They continued with small talk, eating quickly so Brad could return to work on time.

CHAPTER 17

Wednesday, September 5, 2007
Columbia, Maryland, USA

With summer leisure and vacations past and a hint of fall in the air, Brad and Frank were sitting at the front of the classroom at Howard Community College when the teacher, in his middle twenties, arrived. He was five feet eight with medium build, had nicely trimmed, slightly wavy black hair, intense dark brown eyes showing through frameless glasses, and a medium dark complexion reflecting Arab heritage. He wore a stylish short-sleeved plaid shirt, a solid dark burgundy red tie that complemented the shirt, khaki-colored Dockers pants, and dark brown loafers with brown socks.

So much for some old fart, Brad thought.

The teacher wrote his name on the board and then said in fluent, slightly accented English, "Good evening. My name is Omar Abu Deeb." He asked students to write their names on large folded sheets of paper and gave a brief background, saying that he was from Yemen, had just completed a PhD in Islamic theology at the University of Minnesota, was a post-doctoral fellow at George Washington University, and was a part-time assistant imam at the Islamic Center in Washington. He them asked them to introduce each other in pairs.

Brad said to Frank, "Don't say anything about speaking Arabic; want to tell him myself later. How much you want me to tell about your military background?"

Frank answered, "Just say I'm commander of the Marine security guards at the NSA. You could say I've been stationed a few places, but don't say in Okinawa."

"Education?" Brad asked.

"Engineering degree from the Citadel," he replied.

Brad said, "OK. Don't say that I have a degree in languages; just a bachelor's degree from the University of Minnesota and I'm considering a master's in political science. You can say that I work at the NSA; most assume everyone there's involved in cryptology."

After introductions, Omar Abu Deeb remarked, "You certainly have interesting and varied backgrounds. I'm looking forward to being with you.

"First, administrative matters...." He continued with details and concluded, "You might know Ramadan begins in a little over a week. Ramadan is the annual period of fasting when Muslims don't eat or drink during daylight hours for four weeks. That means I won't eat until sunset and I might be a little late, especially early in Ramadan when days are longer, but I will be here. I'm not going to sacrifice eating after fasting since breakfast before sunup. Maybe one day in Ramadan we can meet at a restaurant nearby and have *iftar*. *Iftar* is the name given to the meal where fast is broken. It's often celebrated with friends and co-workers and timed to begin exactly at the moment of sundown. This is not a class in Islamic culture or customs, but learning how our religion affects daily life might be interesting.

"Those wanting graduate credit will do a project and make an oral presentation the last couple of days of class. Please identify yourselves during break or after class."

During the break, some students rushed to him; Brad said to Frank, "Let's talk to him at the end of the class. This sounds interesting, maybe fun."

Frank said, "I feel intimidated. Haven't been in a university classroom in seventeen years, and the Citadel isn't the most stimulating intellectually. Maybe this's a test to see if I'm ready for more."

Omar Abu Deeb dismissed class early, saying eagerly he would see them next time.

After class Frank said, "Dr. Abu Deeb…"

He interrupted, smiling, and said, "You're Frank, Frank Reynolds. I hope you'll enjoy the class."

Frank replied, "It sounds interesting. I'm concerned because this's the first class I've taken in seventeen years."

"Don't worry," Omar Abu Deeb said. "Most of the others seem to take the class for fun. Relax and enjoy it."

"I want graduate credit," Frank said. "I might get a master's when I get out of the Marine Corps in four years."

Omar Abu Deeb replied, "I'm sure we can find an interesting topic for you. Your friend wants to talk to me too. Let's see what he has to say."

"*Marhaba*, Doctor Omar," Brad said in Arabic, "How are you tonight? Fine?"

Omar Abu Deeb was startled, not only that Brad was speaking excellent Arabic, but also called him "Doctor Omar," the title followed by the first name that is used as a sign of respect, esteem, and a small amount of intimacy in Arab countries. He also asked the traditional "How are you?" and then completed it with "Fine?" before the other person could answer, a Levantine way of greeting.

Omar Abu Deeb replied in Arabic, "You speak Arabic."

"Yes, I'm an Arabic language specialist, and I lived in Jordan a while," Brad replied in Arabic.

"Wonderful," Omar Abu Deeb said in English. "We should talk more about that. We should continue in English unless your friend speaks Arabic also."

"No, afraid not," Frank replied.

"We're here to talk about topics," Brad said.

"With your ability in Arabic, there're all sorts of possibilities,"

Omar Abu Deeb replied, "but we have to be careful we don't overwhelm the rest of the class. One thought I've been bouncing around in my mind has to do with Sunni-versus-Sunni conflicts within Islam. The media, politicians, and foreign policy makers are preoccupied with Sunni-versus-Shia conflicts, and understandably with tensions involving Hizbollah in Lebanon and Shia in Bahrain, Kuwait, and the eastern provinces of Saudi Arabia. There are other conflicts that are Sunni versus Sunni. There may be Shia versus Shia too.

"One of the big Sunni-versus-Sunni conflicts is Fatah and Hamas in Palestine, although Fatah claims to be secular. Also, Turks versus the Kurds in Turkey and Kurds versus Arabs in Iraq."

Frank thought: *Kurds versus Arabs in Iraq; that's where Ali is; he talked about that in Germany.*

"There are conflicts in other parts of the world that don't involve Arabs, but do involve Islam," Omar Abu Deeb added. "There are ethnic Malays and ethnic Thais in the southern part of Thailand, and Sunni insurgents in the Philippines."

Frank thought, *Felicia's Muslim, or was.*

"Can we work together?" Frank asked.

Omar Abu Deeb replied, "I don't forbid students working together and many do. In this case, I think you might be dominated by Brad because he speaks Arabic, no matter how determined you are and how hard you work to make sure it's a joint effort. Also, you might shortchange yourself, Frank, because you want to go to grad school later. Are you parked here? We can walk out together."

While walking, Omar Abu Deeb and Brad talked about being at the University of Minnesota and other small talk.

CHAPTER 18

Tuesday, September 18, 2007
Washington, DC, USA

"Good morning, Roger, you want to see me?" Yusef "Joe" Shaito said to his boss at the U.S. Attorney General's office.

Roger Chen replied, "We've hardly had time to talk since you got back from London."

Roger wore pants of a charcoal gray suit and a white shirt with a yellow tie that had small dark blue designs. He stood five feet ten inches, had straight, professionally trimmed black hair complementing his square-ish face, brown eyes, and features of his Chinese ancestry. Gold-color-rimmed glasses with rectangular lenses completed his lawyerly appearance.

Joe Shaito, about five feet nine inches, had slightly wavy, neatly trimmed black hair, an average build, and a slightly dark complexion reflecting Arab ancestry. Bright brown eyes showed through rectangular frameless glasses. A small goatee and moustache added age to his boyishly handsome face; he was twenty-five years old but could pass for a teenager in some places. A sharply pressed white shirt, red tie with nondescript designs on it, and the pants of a navy blue suit completed his lawyerly appearance.

Roger Chen reflected, *Really pushed to recruit him from Michigan Law School about a year and a half ago. Every law firm in the country and government agency did too. Not only one of the very best graduates that year, he's Muslim. Everyone, especially government agencies, needs at least one token Muslim; he certainly isn't token. We couldn't discriminate; maybe that's why he selected us. Hinted others seemed more interested in hiring a Muslim than in hiring him.*

Took him under my wing, having a sense what it's like as first Arab-American, having been one of few Chinese-Americans, myself. Really showed his stuff in Cuba. Kept his cool when the judge in Roanoke threw us out of the courtroom. Has lots of people skills and good intuition. Sent him to London for a joint British-American task force; was great there too.

"How're things at home, if I may ask?" Roger Chen said. "The war in Lebanon's settled down."

"Thanks for asking," Joe replied. "Better with respect to war tensions; pro-Hizbollah elements have retreated. Still tension about me getting married. The first girl got impatient, rather her family did; married someone else. She was getting too old by Lebanese standards, and they didn't want to take the risk she'd be too old for the right kind of man to marry. My father was pissed off; made him lose face."

"You were out of the country working," Roger Chen said. "Couldn't they understand? Of course we arranged it."

Joe replied, "When dealing with looking good and face, no rational explanation's ever good enough. Now there's someone else in mind for me to marry. I've been warned not to let them down this time. I'll have to face them when I go home at the Eid."

"The Eid?" Roger Chen asked.

"Big Islamic holiday at the end of Ramadan, Eid al Fitr," Joe explained. "Lasts three days. Families get together, exchange gifts; it's as important as Christmas."

"When's that?" Roger Chen asked.

"Starts October 12 this year," Joe answered. "I'll try to cut it short, but I couldn't fail to show up."

Roger Chen commented, "Every group in this country has some type of family baggage; Chinese for sure. Listen, the reason I asked to see you is we've had a potential contract resource referred to us; someone to consult and advise on Islamic issues; not undercover. We let intelligence services handle that."

"Who and what'll he or she consult on?" Joe asked.

"It's he," Roger Chen continued. "New person in Islamic studies at George Washington University. We'd be consulting on Sharia law; maybe related things. We have you for many Islamic issues, but we don't want to overburden you, and you're more valuable for other things. Nothing indicates you know Sharia law."

Joe said, "Any Muslim who's reasonably educated knows something about it, but I'm far from expert."

"We want to talk to you first and see what you think before approaching him," Roger Chen continued. "Then get your assessment of him before we formalize anything. He has a PhD in Islamic theology; we're told Sharia law is intertwined in theology."

"That's true," Joe confirmed. "If he's broadly educated, he'd know something about it. There are schools that teach nothing but Sharia law; it's highly specialized. There're no schools in this country and not many people, or at least not reliable ones, would've studied in one. Is he American?"

Roger Chen said, "Reliability's one of the issues. Not American, but he's been here a while. He worked for another Justice Department agency and was good; I can fill you in later if it's important. I was thinking you and I could invite him to lunch in one of our private dining rooms."

"But this is Ramadan," Joe stated.

"What does that mean?" Roger Chen asked.

"If he's a good Muslim, which he must be," Joe explained, "he'll be observing Ramadan, which means no eating or drinking between sunup and sundown. Lunch is out of the question unless you wait until Ramadan's over."

"When's that?" Roger Chen asked.

"October 12," Joe replied, "when the Eid begins. He likely wouldn't be keen during the Eid, and I won't be here. The earliest would be, let's see, October 15. You could meet for dinner now if you especially want to meet over a meal."

"We do have dinner meetings," Roger Chen said, "but that sounds too formal for something exploratory."

"Yes," Joe agreed. "Why not invite him here, preferably early in the morning so he won't be too hungry or thirsty. Don't serve coffee."

"Sounds like a good idea," Roger Chen said. "I'll set something up as soon as possible. When're you free?"

"I'll check my calendar when I get back to my desk," Joe answered. "I'm busy, but not many firm commitments since I returned."

"OK, good," Roger Chen said. "Glad we have you around. I'd probably have invited him to lunch and put him in an awkward position."

"Thanks," Joe said. "You're right; it would be awkward. You want him to consult on Islamic issues, but you don't know it's Ramadan and that he wouldn't eat. If he's like most educated Arabs, I'm sure he'd be gracious and kind, but still not enthusiastic about working for you."

Roger Chen said, "I was going to invite you to lunch just to be sociable; we haven't visited, just visited, since you got back from London. We could invite you for dinner again. Any problem with that?"

"No," Joe replied, "so long as it's after sundown, but I don't want to impose."

"Oh, no, no imposition," Roger Chen said. "We often have people over at 7:00 or 7:30. Last time we invited you on Sunday afternoon because the kids would be around and you could meet them. I don't set times without consulting with my wife; I'll get back to you."

CHAPTER 19

Thursday, September 20, 2007
Washington, DC, USA

Omar Abu Deeb was shown to Roger Chen's office where Joe, shaking hands, said, "Yusef Shaito, *marhaba*."

Omar replied, "Pleased to meet you," thinking: *He's obviously Arab or Arab-American. Maybe he clued them in about Ramadan even if he's Christian; no coffee, but Yusef's a Muslim name.*

Roger Chen greeted him and said, "You're new at George Washington, I believe."

"Yes," Omar answered. "I'm also an assistant imam at the Islamic Center."

Must be Sunni, Joe thought. *The Islamic Center's Sunni.*

"The people who referred you told us some of your background," Roger Chen continued. "You're from Yemen and studied in this country; Minnesota, I recall. They didn't tell us details. They just said they'd done a background check and had glowing praise for your good work."

Omar Abu Deeb replied, "That's good to hear. What would you want me to do?"

"Nothing secret or undercover," Roger Chen answered. "We might not tell the *Post*, but it can be as open or quiet as you like. We need someone to call on about Sharia law. We're increasingly involved in international law issues in which some parties are subject to Sharia law. Most are commercial, like when a Dubai company bought the company that operates ports in the U.S. Now the Dubai Stock Exchange wants to buy exchanges in the U.S.; Islamic banking is making inroads."

Omar Abu Deeb said, "I'm not a Sharia law expert. I don't have a background in business either. I'm a theologian. There are schools that specialize in Sharia law."

"From what we've heard," Roger Chen replied, "Sharia law is intertwined with theology, so we thought you might be a good general source. Joe gives us background on Islam in general, but he doesn't have a background in Sharia law, and we keep him busy with our common law. There's your proximity and, shall we say, your reliability."

Maybe Shaito is Muslim, Omar thought, *but he called him Joe; that's a Christian nickname.*

"All I know about Sharia law is what I learned in Islamic classes growing up," Joe added, thinking, *Shia have our own Sharia law. People here're more interested in Sunni Sharia law; that's where commercial interests are.*

Omar Abu Deeb thought, *So he is Muslim*, and replied, "You're right, it is intertwined with theology. There are five streams of Sharia law and I know something about all five, although not so much about the Shia school. I'm Sunni. You mentioned my availability. I have only a two-year temporary work visa. I'm sure you know how that works. George Washington said it'd support me getting a green card and indicated they'd be interested in having me in a tenure-track position if I perform adequately; I've already contacted an immigration lawyer."

"We can probably help," Roger Chen offered. "Nothing not above board. We have a good relationship with the immigration people. We can let them know our interest in your services; George Washington has a lot of clout."

Joe interjected, "You're an imam; that raises suspicions. I'm sure you're well aware of activities of the so-called imams in this country..."

Omar Abu Deeb interrupted. "That's one thing I'm trying to fight with every legal and ethical means I can. Islam is being desecrated by its own people."

Hope he's not including Shia, Joe thought, adding, "It shouldn't be a surprise that USCIS could drag its heels on a green card application for an imam. We could let them know you've been scrutinized by this other agency without revealing details."

Joe's brilliant and thinks fast, Roger Chen thought. *That wouldn't have occurred to me so quickly.* "Yes, we could do that," he concurred.

"Oh, good. Thank you," Omar Abu Deeb replied.

Roger Chen concluded, "As I told you on the phone, this is a preliminary meeting to explore mutual interest. We can meet again to discuss specifics if you're interested. I can say now we'd be interested in going to the next step."

"I'm interested," Omar Abu Deeb replied.

"Just so you know from the outset, you'd be engaged as a contractor, not an employee. There're no benefits; it's not part-time employment. No taxes are withheld; you deal with your own taxes. Just to make sure we all understand, you're expected to report this on your taxes; we do not contract with persons who do not comply with tax law."

"I understand," Omar said. "My work with the other agency was that way. The immigration lawyer told me I'd need a certificate from the IRS that I'm clean on everything."

Roger Chen explained the likely financial terms, emphasizing it was not a commitment.

Gee, Omar Abu Deeb thought, *with that kind of money if they have work for me, I can pay the immigration lawyer and maybe get a better car.*

Roger Chen concluded, "Joe can show you our facilities. We're not a high point on the tourist circuit, not like FBI headquarters across the street, but you might find it interesting." He thought, *If Joe's as bright and quick as he has been, he'll know what we want. I've got a good hunch this guy's someone we can work with.*

Was the comment about FBI headquarters on purpose because I worked for them? Omar Abu Deeb asked himself. *Let's see where Yusef takes me. He seems nice and bright.*

Over the next several minutes, Joe guided Omar Abu Deeb through the facilities as they engaged in friendly, casual, small talk, their backgrounds at the University of Minnesota, University of Michigan, and Michigan Law School.

He's from Dearborn, Omar Abu Deeb observed. *That's where lots of Shia settled and some Druze. He talked about mosques, so not Druze; must be Shia. Makes no difference. He's nice to talk to and nice looking; nice Arab features.*

Joe said, "Let's sit down and visit. There's not much of interest here; just a bunch of lawyers' offices." He thought, *Roger obviously wants me to find out more informally. He seems interesting and nice.*

They visited in a conference room, Joe asking about his studies, research, and work as an assistant imam.

Omar Abu Deeb thought: *Of course they want him to get to know me casually. It'd be nice to have friends my age, just friends, not people I work with or students. Should wait for him to initiate any social contact.*

As if sensing Omar Abu Deeb's thoughts, Joe asked, "Do you have plans for *iftar* this evening? I'm tired of eating alone and it's an awkward time; I've mostly lost touch with people here because I was in London most of this past year."

He seems lonely too, Omar Abu Deeb said to himself. *Why not go to* iftar *with him; someone different.*

"I'll gladly join you," Omar Abu Deeb replied. "The formal round of *iftars* is over at George Washington. You know, being Muslim yourself, the first week or so of Ramadan everyone has an *iftar* party, then it fizzles into everyone going to eat at home or alone. I could find someone around the university to eat with, but I see them all the time. What do you have in mind?"

"There're some places close to DuPont Circle on 18ᵗʰ Street in the Adams-Morgan district, not far from where I live," Joe answered. "Some're halal, too."

"I've walked up in that area, but never ate there," Omar Abu Deeb said. "Be good to see what it's like."

"Great," Joe continued. "There's Jury's Hotel right on DuPont circle, corner of New Hampshire Avenue. We can meet in front. What time is *iftar* today?"

Omar Abu Deeb replied, "Close to 5:45. Say, if it works for you, why don't we meet at 5:30."

"Sounds good to me," Joe said smiling.

Omar Abu Deeb stood and said, "I should get back to the university if there's nothing else here. I'm sure students want to see me, and you must need to get to work."

"Yes, I always have plenty to do," Joe answered. "Say, what do you teach?"

"A couple of basic courses in introduction to Islam," Omar Abu Deeb replied. "They arranged an extra course for additional pay, out at a community college in Maryland."

"Sounds really interesting," Joe commented. "You can tell me more tonight."

CHAPTER 20

Thursday, September 20, 2007
Washington, DC, USA

On a pleasant early fall night, Joe arrived for their *iftar* date wearing neat, clean blue jeans, a nice casual long-sleeved sport shirt, white athletic shoes, and a nice, casual lightweight jacket over his shoulder in case it got chilly, as it often did in late September in Washington. Omar soon arrived, wearing the same clothes he'd worn earlier, but no tie. After warm greetings, Joe led the way up 18th Street through Adams-Morgan until they found a place that suited. Food and soft drinks were served at *iftar* time, and they ate and drank eagerly after a day's fast.

Omar asked, "You say you live close, Yusef?"

"Call me Joe if you like; everyone does," he said. "In school, other kids teased me and couldn't pronounce my name right. I said it was like Joseph. They started calling me Joe and it stuck. And, yes, but need to move soon. When I went to London, I needed a place to keep belongings and sleep when I came back from time to time. I found a room to rent in a couple's apartment. They're nice enough and it's clean and decent, but claustrophobic. I'd like more privacy, especially, during Ramadan. I get up before sunup to make breakfast and have to be careful not to wake anyone. No urgency to move; I can tolerate it until I can find the right place. Rent in DC's so damned high."

"I know what you mean," Omar said. "I'm staying in student accommodation until I find something. It's OK. I lived in enough student accommodation in Minneapolis, but now I've outgrown it. As a faculty member, it doesn't feel right living among students. Rent's high here; I'd like to save on rent to buy a new car."

"Oh, you have a car," Joe said. "I didn't dare bring my old clunker from Michigan. Got by walking and on public transport until I went to London. Saved a fair amount over there being on per diem. Probably have enough for a down payment on a car, but I have student loans to pay. To make car payments and pay rent at the same time would stretch things. If I bought a nice car, I'd have to live in a better neighborhood, rent a garage, or both, and that costs money."

Wonder if he'd like to share an apartment, Omar thought. *Two of us get a place that's half decent. Too soon to bring up the idea now; we're just getting to know each other.*

Wonder if he'd like to share an apartment, Joe thought. *He'd likely have good living habits. Too soon to bring it up; we've just met.*

"What'd you do in London?" Omar asked.

"I was our Arab, Islamic advisor on a joint U.S.-British task force coordinating legal policy issues," Joe began. "You can imagine terrorism issues are big in both countries. We agree in principle on almost everything, but have differences in implementation. Extradition of alleged terrorists is one. Immigration is another big issue. U.S. is suspicious of imams immigrating and discourages it in various ways; thinks British are too lenient because imams there can travel here easily if they have British passports. British in turn realize they need to tighten up and look to us for guidance."

"I can see that," Omar said. "Maybe that's why the Islamic Center here was eager to have me; easier to get someone already here legally than someone from outside the country, even if I still need a green card."

Joe added, "Another big issue is arranged marriages to allow whole families to come to the U.S. or the U.K. I'm sure you know about arranged marriages."

Omar nodded. "Yes, but not first hand."

"Started when I told Roger my family's putting lot of pressure on me to marry a girl in Lebanon so she could move here and bring her family," Joe continued.

"Oh, are you married? Waiting for a wife to get a visa and join you?" Omar asked thinking: *Guess he isn't a candidate for sharing an apartment.*

"Oh, no," Joe said emphatically. "Thankfully, that one fell through. I don't want to get married any time soon! Putting pressure on me again right now. I'm determined to hold my ground, but I'm not getting any younger. What about you? You said your parents are dead. Any other family pressure in Yemen?"

"No," Omar said, and explained other family in Yemen are distant. "You're Shia, aren't you? You have problems in Dearborn during the war in Lebanon against Hizbollah? There was Hizbollah support there."

Joe merely answered, "Yes," thinking, *He's not a candidate for a roommate; trying to find out if I'm Shia.*

Omar quickly added, "It's OK. I'm an Islamic theologian, not a Sunni theologian, even if I am Sunni. I don't get hung up on things that happened a thousand years ago, except from a historical perspective. One of the senior professors I work with is Shia from Iran. Karen Armstrong commented in her book *Islam* that the only difference between Sunni and Shia is political, not theological. One of my best friends in Duluth is Shia; refugee from Iraq. Owned two Middle Eastern restaurants. Very popular. Used to hang out there a lot; food halal too. Great guy."

Maybe he could be a roommate after all, Joe thought, then said, "People back home thought since I'm called Joe, I'm trying to pretend I'm Christian and deny I'm Muslim. People here started avoiding me, thinking I'm Hizbollah just because I'm Shia."

"Oh," Omar said. "You doing anything rest of the night? It's early and the weather's nice. Wouldn't mind walking around playing tourist. I'm still new here; plenty to see."

"Sure," Joe said smiling. "Let's pay and go."

Waiting for a check, Omar asked, "What's with guys walking around the circle holding hands? I know they do that in places like Pakistan, and this is an international city, but these look like ordinary Americans."

Joe replied, "DuPont Circle's the gay area."

"Is that why you want to move away?" Omar asked.

"Having gays around doesn't bother me," Joe replied reflecting on wandering around Soho in London near where he stayed. "Not looking to move out of the neighborhood, just get out of the place where I'm living. Very convenient here."

Omar said, "There wasn't a gay area in Minneapolis I knew of, but gays there like everywhere. To each his own."

They walked through Georgetown, stopping for coffee at one of Georgetown's trendy coffee shops, talked about courses Omar taught, exchanged other small talk, and generally enjoyed each other's company. Finally, they ended up where they had started.

"Say, would you want to do this again tomorrow night?" Joe asked tentatively.

Omar replied. "Sure. If you like, we could go to the center for Friday prayers, it's close to here, and then eat, if you don't mind a Sunni mosque."

"I've been to Sunni mosques," Joe said. "The Shia Islamic Center is in Alexandria and a hassle to get to. Usually I pray at the Islamic Center where you work."

They exchanged phone numbers and agreed to meet again.

CHAPTER 21

Saturday, October 13, 2007
Harrisonburg, Virginia, USA

In late morning on a beautiful clear day typical of fall in the Shenandoah Valley, Ahmed and Marwan were travelling to spend the Eid al Fitr holiday with their parents when Ahmed, driving an old Mercedes Benz, said, "Aren't you glad we waited until this morning to drive down? We could meet with the imam and the guys to begin making plans."

"Yeah," Marwan muttered.

Ahmed continued, "You gave the key when you mentioned the place that monitors phone conversations."

"Yeah," Marwan mumbled, "the NSA."

"You heard me say I'm going to go check it out," Ahmed continued. "There's bound to be some way we can get inside, like maybe cleaners or food service."

"Yeah," Marwan mumbled again.

"Damn fuckin' country," Ahmed kept on. "Only place they let Arabs have jobs is doing women's work, but works for us this time. At least you and I have proper work."

"Yeah," Marwan muttered and said, "The guy I work for is an asshole even if he is Palestinian. Didn't want me to take off yesterday even if it is the Eid."

"Don't you see that's the way it was supposed to be?" Ahmed said. "Allah wanted us to go to the meeting."

"I guess," Marwan said.

"Anyway," Ahmed said, "Gotta find out how someone gets a job there and get one of the guys to apply. Must have a big turnover with those shitty jobs. Good thing I spend most of my time finding cars for dad and selling some; easy to go to Maryland. When you find gay places, it'll all work out."

Marwan became alert and thought, *That's what he said last night, I find the gay places. Didn't ask me first. Does he know what I did back home? He must've, or why else would he say it had to be me? I've quit being gay since I've been in Northern Virginia; even found that girl at work who's sort of interested in me.* "Why me?" he blurted out. "Get one of the other guys to do it."

"You just turned 21," Ahmed answered. "You can check out the bars. You don't have to drink alcohol."

"Wouldn't know where to start looking for gay bars," Marwan protested. *For sure I can't let him have a clue the guys I used to chat with told me about places. Some around DuPont Circle, wherever that is,* he said to himself.

"Check it out on the internet," Ahmed said. "You're on that damned thing all the time anyway. You showed me how to find persons who wanted to buy and sell old foreign cars. Surely you can find gay bars."

Marwan thought: *Can't deal with this now. Gotta change the subject.* He said, "It'll be weird sharing a bedroom with Abou Nidal. I know he's like our uncle. Always there, played with us when we were kids, but he always slept at the station. With the new guy in his old place, he's in our room."

"I don't give a shit," Ahmed replied. "I'm not ever going to live there again. Didn't even want to go back now for the Eid, but no good way to get out of it. We've got to find some way to keep from going back for Eid al Adha. We'll be getting things ready then. We need passports. You can look that up on the internet too."

Whatever, Marwan thought, wanting to scream.

101

CHAPTER 22

Wednesday, December 19, 2007
Columbia, Maryland, USA

At the end of the semester with holiday distractions increasing, Omar greeted Brad and Frank with a smile, the night he returned exams and projects, saying, "You two got the highest grades by far."

"I wanted to see what you thought of my paper, and maybe talk more," Brad replied.

"Same here," Frank echoed. "This course gave me confidence to go for a master's. I'm hoping you have information about George Washington's programs."

"Me too," Brad said. "My job's dead end, but I want to keep using my Arabic skills."

Omar said, "First your papers. Yours was great, Frank. You wrote very insightful things about Sunni Kurds and Sunni Arab Iraqis; you even brought in Shia and the minority group Alawites. Where'd you get access to that material? I'll let you look at the paper and see notes I wrote on it."

To Brad he grinned and said, "I know where you got your sources about Bedouin versus Palestinian conflicts in Jordan; most of that material is available only in Arabic. That's why the western world doesn't know much about it. I'm really eager to know more what you do and how you came to speak Arabic, but look at the paper first."

Frank thought as he looked at the paper, *Felicia turned me down when I asked about Muslims in the Philippines. She was kind and gracious, even apologetic. Said it's a part of her past that's painful and the pain is fresh. Too fresh? She left the Philippines ten years ago. Oh! That's how she was involved in Doc's coming to the U.S.; al Qaeda in the Philippines must've forced her.* He said, "I know someone in Kurdistan and did a lot of emailing."

Omar commented, "I noticed the clinic in your paper brings people together, including Shia. I'd like to know more about it; could be a good research topic. When I get my green card, I might go there. Have to publish or perish."

Oh, God, Frank thought. *Omar goes to meet Ali? Don't even want to think about it.*

Brad was thinking, *Do I tell him what I do? How'll he react about spying on Arabs?* Hesitating slightly, he said, "I'm in the Arabic language section of the NSA."

"Oh, I read about that," Omar replied. "Scandal over monitoring domestic calls." *He seems hesitant to tell me,* he thought. *Maybe he thinks I'd be upset about U.S. spying on Arabs. In a way I am, but I did undercover work for the FBI; anything to stop al Qaeda.*

"For sure we don't monitor domestic conversations!" Brad replied.

"How'd you come to learn Arabic in the first place?" Omar asked. "Minnesota has a good Arabic language program. I had students take classes there, but were just learning a little bit, not planning a career."

Brad thought. *How can I tell him I was a language geek to cope with being gay?* "I got into it and liked it," he answered. "Thought it'd be fun to go to the Middle East in the study abroad program. After a semester in Jordan, I realized I wanted a career, at least for now. This was the first job that came my way, so I jumped. I guess you know native Arabic speakers get the good interpreting jobs. *I'll let him figure out native Arabic speakers aren't welcome in this job, so*

I had an advantage, he said to himself. He said, "We thought, now that there's no student-teacher relationship, you might have dinner with us tonight."

"Yes, please do," Frank said enthusiastically.

"I'd really like to," Omar answered, "but I already have plans. Maybe you know Eid al Adha begins tonight. There're always big dinners, especially the first night. People I work with are having the dinner tonight but, hey, it doesn't start for a while and doesn't matter if I'm late. I'd be pleased to join you for coffee. It'd be good to visit with you two some more."

Brad said, "I remember Eid al Adha when I was in Jordan. That's the holiday when Muslims commemorate Ibrahim's taking his son Ishmael up the mountain to sacrifice him; Allah appeared to him to say 'no', and told him to sacrifice a ram instead. You eat lamb for dinner."

"Oh, you know the Islamic version of the story," Omar said. "I assumed you're Christian."

"Yes, I'm Christian," Brad said, "very much so, but that doesn't mean that I'm not open-minded or that I accept everything in the Bible as literal truth."

In a snack bar they talked about their backgrounds and experiences. After a while, Omar said, "What're you two doing Friday night? Come to our place. My roommate and I are having an Eid al Adha party. You probably know, Brad, Eid al Adha parties are where lots of people are invited, not just close friends. You two'd fit in well. You can meet people from my department at George Washington, who can tell you more about studying there. Many of them are Muslims, like my roommate and me, but some aren't. There's one Jewish guy we think'll come; lots of Jewish students at George Washington, maybe you know. My roommate's inviting a man he works with and his wife; they're not Muslim. Neither of us is much of a cook, but we can manage lamb, we hope. The rest we'll just pick up somewhere."

Brad said eagerly, "If I'm free I'd really like to. I might have plans. Can I get back to you?"

"Same here, Frank said. "I need to check one thing."

"Why don't we exchange cell phone numbers," Brad said. "Maybe you can tell us where it is and how to get there now, so we don't have to do it on the phone."

After exchanging information, Brad said, "Maybe see you Friday. I'd really like to go."

Frank also shook Omar's hand saying, "Me too."

While riding home, Brad said, "Not sure if Jason and I'll get together Friday night or not. He's leaving Saturday morning to drive to his parents' for Christmas. We talked about me going with him so I can meet them. Kind of scary thinking about going down there, their being such fundamentalist homophobes. Yeah, I know I'm rambling. If I do go there, it'll be the next week for New Year. I have to work between Christmas and New Year. Also depends on what the weather's like; can get icy this time of year. Anyway, if I do go, we won't get together on Friday."

"Yeah, like with Paco and me, especially now that he's taking classes," Frank said. "I'm pretty sure he's working Friday night. He's trying to work it out so he'd be off between Christmas and New Year. What should we take with us? Obviously no wine, and I can't imagine flowers."

"Arabs wouldn't give flowers for a dinner party unless they know each other very well and are pretty intimate," Brad explained. "The thing to take is Arabic sweets. Baklava. Especially on Eid al Adha."

"I thought baklava is Greek," Frank said.

"It is, I guess," Brad replied. "Must be an Eastern Mediterranean thing, but for sure it's Arab and there're lots of different kinds of baklava. I'm sure they'll have some, but it's hard to have too many. That's definitely what guests take when invited to dinner, at least in Jordan, and the sweets are included in the dessert."

"Where do we get that?" Frank asked.

"There're places in DC," Brad answered. "We can stop on the way. We'd better order ahead of time; with the Eid, the shops might be sold out if we wait. I'll call on a break tomorrow. The people who run these shops are mostly Arabs and I can order in Arabic. Of course they speak English too, but we'll get better treatment if I order in Arabic."

They continued mostly small talk on the way home.

CHAPTER 23

Friday, December 21, 2007
Washington, DC, USA

Bundled up for the first cold spell of winter, in early evening, Brad and Frank were greeted by Omar and Joe at their plain, simply furnished apartment on 20th Street near DuPont Circle. The furnishings were basic secondhand. Walls were bare except for framed diplomas in a corner of the living room, visible but not "in your face."

Joe and Omar's apartment building,
DuPont Circle area, Washington, DC

"*Marhaba*, Brad Spencer," he said, shaking Joe's hand.

"You speak Arabic," Joe said in Arabic. They mentioned their backgrounds briefly, and then he shook hands with Frank, saying, "You're Frank. Omar told me about you too. Welcome. We'll speak English tonight."

Frank handed a box to Joe, who said, "Oh, is this for us? Baklava. *Shouqran*. How'd you know it's traditional to bring Arabic sweets on this occasion?"

"Oh, Arab sweets," Omar said. "How'd you know? Yes, of course. You were in Jordan."

Omar introduced them to Roger and Lisa Chen, who were dressed as they would for a dinner party. She was conversing with a well-dressed older lady wearing an obviously expensive headscarf completely covering her hair.

As they approached her, Brad hesitated, deftly positioned himself slightly to Frank's right, took Frank's right hand, pushed it behind his back, thinking, *Forgot to tell him Muslim women don't shake hands. Hopefully he'll get the hint.* He pointedly kept his right hand behind him so Frank could see as he was introduced to the lady and greeted her.

Frank thought: *He obviously wants me to do something with that hand, or maybe not do something. He's holding his right hand behind him, kind of awkward like. Is this a ritual when being introduced to Muslims?*

They quickly moved to an older man with Middle Eastern features who was dressed in a business suit. Frank thought, *He's almost certainly her husband. Better keep my hand in the same position.*

Frank was surprised when the man held his hand out to Brad for a firm professional handshake. Still confused, Frank took the older man's hand when offered.

Introductions continued to a couple in their thirties who were dressed "smart casual" and a younger man in blue jeans and nondescript sport shirt. Other than Roger and Lisa Chen, all were colleagues of Omar, some with significant others.

The table was crowded with stuffed vine leaves, hummus, moutabal, roasted nuts, dried fruits, a large pile of Middle Eastern bread, and Arab sweets with different kinds of baklava. Food was served on mismatched plates and bowls, mostly paper and plastic, and in deli containers; eating utensils were mostly plastic. There was fruit juice and mismatched plastic drinking glasses. Omar brought a bowl of rice of prepared Middle Eastern style with different kinds of nuts, and Joe brought a tray with lamb roast.

Omar said, "*Sakhtein*, everyone."

"Did you cook all of this yourself?" Lisa Chen asked.

"Oh, no," Joe answered, "Only the lamb. My mother told me how she cooks it; hard to mess up something basic like lamb." He thought, *First time I've been away from home for Eid al Adha. Mom was sweet and kind to tell me how to cook lamb, but I could tell from her voice she's sad with me not being there. Seemed to take away the pain to know I'm preparing food for our own Eid party. Deep down she knows I don't want to go back for another confrontation with Dad.*

"Here in Washington there're shops that sell good Middle Eastern food," Omar added. "It was a challenge in Minneapolis and not always halal. I'm sure you'd know, but just in case, this is halal."

"The rice has pistachios," the older Middle Eastern lady said, "just like in Iran. Did you cook that yourself?"

"No," Joe said. "We got it from the Persian restaurant on 18th Street."

"Oh, we go there, sometimes," she added.

Lisa asked after having put moutabal on a piece of bread, "What is this? It's very good."

"It's eggplant cooked over a flame so it gets a smoky flavor and then made into a paste," the Iranian lady said. "It's from Lebanon."

"We had it in Jordan, too," Brad commented.

When all had finished eating except for sweets, Joe prepared traditional Lebanese dark thick coffee in the traditional metal coffee makers he bought at a Lebanese shop in Dearborn; it was served in Styrofoam cups.

The remainder of the evening was spent with everyone enjoying conversation. Brad and Frank were the last there and began to say goodbye when Omar said, "Please stay a little longer. We really haven't had a chance to visit."

"Yes, please do," Joe said. "Omar told me about you, but it'd be good to visit more."

They talked about university experiences. Brad and Omar spoke Arabic while Joe told Frank his experiences in London and Frank shared his as a tourist. When it seemed all had a good rapport, Joe made tentative comments about struggling with his father's trying to arrange a marriage for him. Brad commented he was familiar with arranged marriages in Jordan and had seen the negative consequences.

Frank offered, "My parents make noises that it'd be good for my career if I were married, but I don't give a shit about any career anymore." He talked about how his attitudes had changed since he had non-military friends and would soon retire after twenty years' service. Brad talked about wanting to be more than merely a language specialist. Omar talked about wanting to stay in the U.S., the only place he felt at home because family in Yemen were either dead or distant; he hoped he could get a green card. Joe opened up about feeling pulled between two cultures; happy with his work, especially international issues he dealt with in London, but that he hadn't thought about long-run career plans. Well after 11 p.m., conversation dwindled, and Frank and Brad said they should go.

Omar said, "I'll get your coats."

Frank said, "I can get them. I need to use the facilities."

When Frank returned, Brad was saying goodbyes in Arabic and gave Joe three Arab kisses on the cheek, left, right, left, and repeated with Omar.

Frank also gave Joe three kisses, and he responded, "Oh, you know about Arab kisses too. Brad must've told you."

Frank said, "No, a Lebanese-American friend and Army officer, from Alabama of all places."

Omar gave three kisses to Frank. Frank and Brad then bundled up in their coats and scarves and left.

On the way to Laurel, Frank said, "Great party, and not a drop of alcohol. In the Marines, a non-alcoholic party is totally unheard of."

"Yeah, it was great, and I can imagine," Brad agreed. "In my student days in Minnesota, non-alcoholic parties were unheard of. Did you notice how much they seem like a couple? Always attentive to each other. Can't describe in words, but kind of like Jason and me when we were first settling into each other."

"Now that you mention it, I see what you mean," Frank said. "They don't sleep together, it seems. When I went to the bathroom and to get our coats, there were two separate bedrooms, both of which looked used. I didn't ask which one the coats were in and looked in the wrong one first."

"We should invite them over," Brad suggested.

"Maybe," Frank replied, "but would they find out about us? Maybe do it sometime like tonight when Paco and Jason are both busy, but they might think you and I are a couple."

"So what if they find out?" Brad said. "If a friendship develops, and I hope it does, they'll figure it out anyway. We don't have to flaunt anything in front of them, like me and Jason making out on the couch, but we wouldn't do that anyway. Invite them; and if our boyfriends are free to be there, so much the better."

BOOK 2

TRAGEDIES

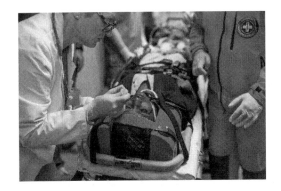

CHAPTER 1

Friday, February 15, 2008
Washington, DC, USA

Brad and his boyfriend Jason Henderson, bundled for winter cold, walked to Rory's, a gay bar near DuPont Circle, after dinner in Adams-Morgan and a visit to Kramerbooks and Lamba Rising Gay Lesbian bookstores. This was almost a monthly ritual; each would drive into the city, have dinner—tonight was Ethiopian—visit bookstores, and then stop at Rory's before going to Brad's for the weekend.

Kramerbooks and Lambda Rising bookstores, Washington, DC

Brad dressed in his usual preppie style, not changed after work. Jason, at five eleven, stood about an inch taller, had red-brown hair pulled into a ponytail that hung to the middle of his back, moustache and goatee, and steel-colored blue-gray eyes. He wore blue jeans with an ordinary long-sleeved shirt covered with a red wool sweater and boots.

In the bar, which was only moderately well lit, the bartender said, "Hey, guys, long time. The usual?"

He was in his mid-thirties, about five feet ten, had longish medium-brown hair pulled back into a small ponytail to comply with the health code, and wore somewhat faded blue jeans and a short-sleeved, nondescript shirt covered by a green apron. A large earring on his right earlobe and tattoos on his upper arm completed his appearance.

Both ordered their usual beers, Brad replying, "Hey, Chad. First time we've been into the city since before Christmas. Busy with holidays and all that."

"You guys do anything special?" Chad asked.

"We kind of broke the ice," Jason said in a Southside Virginia accent. "Brad came for New Year's."

Brad added, "We didn't come out to them or give them anything specific to go on. Good to meet everyone down there and see places Jason talks about."

"My folks're so wrapped up in their own narrow little world they probably didn't notice anything," Jason said. "Given enough time, they might. My brother and sisters might be getting the idea, but they've known I'm different for a long time. Some friends might figure it out too."

"Went to church with them on Sunday to that, shall we say, rather exuberant evangelical church," Brad commented. "That was an experience."

Jason smiled and said, "We went to a New Year's Eve party with some old friends, the few I have left there. That was another experience; he got to see how rednecks party."

When Chad tended to other customers, Brad said, "That guy over there's Arab; looks like guys I knew in Jordan, but doesn't look right. Nervous. Scared."

Jason saw a young man dressed in jeans, nondescript athletic shoes, and a loose fitting hoodie, and said, "He's probably just one of the Latin Americans who're flocking into here. This is DC. They come from all over."

"No, Arab," Brad persisted. "I saw enough of them." He got the attention of Chad and asked, "Who's that young guy over there, the one with the glasses?"

"Don't know," Chad answered. "He won't talk much. Started coming around Christmas, always alone."

"He looks really young," Brad said.

"I carded him once," Chad said, "but didn't need to; all he orders is juice. Still we don't want under twenty-one unless they're with someone. From what I recall, barely over twenty-one."

"He looks scared, nervous about something," Brad continued. "He looks Arab; it's tough to be gay for them."

"His driver's license's from around here somewhere," Chad said. "Virginia maybe. Didn't get my attention. Just stands and looks around; doesn't talk to anyone. Goes to the dark room. We keep an eye on guys like him at first, but he's done nothing to kick him out for. Excuse me."

They drank quietly, Brad deep in thought said, "I'm going to talk to him."

"Just let it be," Jason said. "Chad said he isn't causing problems. Besides, don't we want to go soon?"

"I just can't," Brad said. "Something's wrong; like with guys when I volunteered with the gay-lesbian organization at Minnesota, especially foreign students who got the courage to come to us. Really messed up, especially if they're Muslim. A few were glad to talk once they finally got over their fear; I was a safe person, and I could speak Arabic."

He took his half-finished beer, casually walked around the room, then walked up smiling, "Hi, how are you?"

The young man thought, *Damn, someone's hitting on me again.* "Fine," he answered.

"You new?" Brad asked. "Haven't seen you before."

"No," he answered.

"Can I get you something to drink?" Brad kept asking. "I see you don't have anything. What're you drinking?"

"Nothing," he answered, then added, "thanks."

"You seem tense and nervous, kind of frightened," Brad persisted. "You OK?"

"Yes, I'm OK," he replied.

Brad continued. "You look like someone I know. He was nervous and scared the first time. This your first time?"

When's he ever going to stop, the young man thought. "Er, no," he answered.

"He was from Jordan; thought you might be from there," Brad kept on. "You look Arab."

Damn! The young guy continued to say to himself. *Is someone spying, trying to find out what I'm here for?* He said, "I'm from here."

"You're gay aren't you, or else you wouldn't be here?" Brad said then thought, *He has an American accent, kind of a country one. Still, he's acting like the guys in Jordan who were reaching out for help.*

"No!" he screamed, and then said, "Not sure."

"I've been around gay Arabs," Brad said.

Is he police or something? The young man continued, asking himself. *Guys on chat said if someone's police, he must say so if asked. If he's police, maybe he'll just take me now and get this over with. Can't take this anymore.* "Are you with the police?" he blurted out.

Brad, stunned, thought, *Police? Why would he think I'm with the police? Some kind of trouble?* "No, not at all!" he replied. "Is something wrong? Do you need the police? It's OK. In this country, police're not out to get you, not like in the Middle East. I'll gladly listen; if I can't help you, I'll find someone who can."

No one can help me! he screamed to himself. "Please, just go; leave me alone," he begged.

"OK," Brad said. "I'm here if you need something."

"Thanks," the young man said softly.

Brad returned to the bar, moved his bar stool away from Jason and sat at an angle away from him, saying in a voice just loud enough for him to hear, "I'm pretending to ignore you, like I tried to pick you up and failed."

Jason said, "Huh? What happened?"

"Something bad's going on with him," Brad said. "Asked if I'm police. Scared shitless; looked like he was going to lose it. Chad needs to know this." To Chad, "I don't need another beer, but draw me one anyway so it looks good; put it on the tab. I'll pretend to drink it but pour it out, and I'm pretending to ignore Jason."

Chad said, "I've had strange requests, but this's the first for that. He blow you off like the others?"

"Yeah, but there's more," Brad replied. "Bring the beer and I'll tell you." He recounted the conversation concluding, "I thought you need to know if police are involved."

"For sure," Chad said. "Thanks for that."

"Pretty sure he's Arab," Brad continued. "When I mentioned Jordan, he got tense; said he's from here. Has kind of a country accent. I want to sit and think about it. Can't just get up and walk out. He needs help."

"Gotta go," Chad said, motioning towards a customer. "Look, he's going into the dark room like he usually does."

"I'm going in there," Brad said.

"No, I'll go," Jason said. "Might recognize you."

Brad suddenly said, "Joe. I'll call Joe. If anyone can help, it'll be him. Maybe he'll come over here."

Jason said, "Joe? A good Muslim come to a gay bar?"

"When we were at Frank's last weekend, he asked us straight out if we're gay," Brad continued. "Said he knew gay guys at Michigan and had stuck his head in gay places in London to see what they're like. Won't hurt to ask."

"Guess not," Jason said, as he went to the dark room.

Into his cell phone, "Joe? Brad. Hope it's not too late."

(pause)

"Good, you're at home. You might help us," he said. "I'm at a gay bar near you. Rory's, if you know it. There's a guy who's obviously Arab. He's in trouble. Nearly panicked when I talked to him and wanted to know if I'm police. Any chance you can come over?"

(pause)

"Give a second opinion; tell me I'm full of shit and to butt out, if nothing else," he added.

(pause)

"Good," he said. "Of course, no promises."

(pause)

He gave the location and concluded, "I'll be just inside the door in exactly ten minutes."

CHAPTER 2

Friday, February 15, 2008
Washington, DC, USA

While Joe was taking off his coat and scarf, Brad described his conversation with the young man and very briefly accounted for his experiences with young gay Jordanians. He concluded, "Jason and I are pretending we don't know each other, but we're talking with our backs to each other. I don't want the guy to think I'm with someone. Maybe you sit between us to make it look good."

Jason greeted Joe with a warm handshake and smile, "Hey, guy, rubbing elbows with the gay boys again."

Joe smiled and asked, "Who's the guy?"

Jason answered, "He's not out yet."

Joe, confused, said, "What d'you mean he isn't out yet? He's in a gay bar isn't he?"

Brad explained, "He went to the dark room and he hasn't come back out here yet."

Joe asked, "Huh? It's not all that dark in here."

Brad said, "We're using gay jargon. The dark room is off the corner and much darker. That's where some guys go to *do* things, if you get what I mean."

Joe blushed and said, "I wasn't aware of that."

Jason said to Chad, "This's our friend Joe. He came to have a drink with us. He's not likely to become a customer."

Chad winked at Jason, saying, "Got ya," and took Joe's order for cranberry juice.

Brad added, "Joe came to see what he thinks about the guy we talked about earlier; I asked him to help."

The young man came out of the dark room dazed by brighter light, thinking, *Damn, why'd that guy have to hit on me and make me gay again? I hate myself. I just want to die. Allah, please kill me now.*

"There in a maroon hoodie with glasses," Jason said as he and Brad moved to appear not to be together.

Joe said, "Looks Arab and doesn't look good. I'll talk to him. Lawyers get things out of people." He slowly walked to him and said, "You're the guy I'm supposed to meet."

Startled out of despair, the young man said to himself, *Is this a line to hit on me?* "Me?" he blurted out.

"Yes," Joe answered. "You fit the description."

The young guy thought, *I didn't give a description on chat, did I? Didn't tell anyone I'm here except Ahmed.* "I do?" he asked.

"Yes," Joe persisted. "You're obviously Arab."

The young man continued thinking, *Who'd know my description and that I'm Arab? Wait. Someone's supposed to contact me, and this guy looks Arab too.* He replied. "They said someone'd contact me, but didn't know it'd be here."

Oh, "they." Joe realized others were involved. "I've been looking for you since I came in," he continued.

The young man panicked, thinking, *Does he know I was in the dark room?* "I went to the restroom," he stammered, thinking, *I did go to the restroom.*

"Why not meet here?" Joe said. "We need someplace people wouldn't suspect us." He thought, *Maybe if I speak to him in Arabic he'd be more comfortable.* "We should speak Arabic if we're talking about something really secret," Joe said in simple Arabic.

The young man muttered "OK" in Arabic.

He seemed to understand that, Joe thought, and then said in Arabic, "You're not drinking anything. People'll get suspicious if you're not drinking. What can I get you?"

"Orange juice is fine," he replied in Arabic.

"I'll get it," Joe continued in Arabic. "Wait here. Don't move." *If I'm a little authoritarian he'll think I'm someone important*, he thought.

He ordered orange juice and said to Brad and Jason, "So far, so good. I won't come back to the bar. If I leave alone, wait a minute and act like you decided it is time to go, then follow me. We'll meet outside. If he and I leave together, follow immediately and try to keep us in sight."

"What? You're going to pick him up and get him to go with you?" Jason asked. "What makes you think he'll go with you when Brad couldn't?"

"Lawyer's intuition," Joe answered, and then said to Chad, "May I have a pen or pencil and some paper? Napkin's fine."

He pointedly paid for the juice, in case the young man was watching, and then took it to him, saying, "We can speak English now. Might be suspicious if someone heard us speaking Arabic too much. Did they tell you when it's going to happen? I haven't been told yet."

"Er, no," the young man answered. "Not yet."

"Why're they waiting?" Joe said. "Don't tell me much."

"Me, either," the young man replied. "They don't want me to know too much, but seems they're waiting until they can get someone inside the, er, other place, regular like."

Joe said, "Wonder what's keeping them. I'd have thought they'd have someone by now."

"I heard 'em say they think they know how someone can get a job in that place," the young man replied.

"What kind of job?" Joe asked. "I know people looking for jobs. What needs to be done? Any special skills?"

"Unless you consider cleaning to be a special skill, I don't think so," the young man answered.

"Where 'bouts is this?" Joe kept asking. "Some guys I know don't have cars and need to get there on a bus."

"In Maryland," he replied. "Don't know for sure."

"Where in Maryland?" Joe continued. "I think there's good bus service between here and Baltimore, but if it's out by Frederick, that could be a problem."

"Between here and Baltimore, I heard," the young man said. "A big military post near Laurel, I think. Don't know that area; only been here since September."

Maryland. Near Laurel, big military post, Joe thought. *That's where Frank and Brad work.* He said, "Who do they contact? Should I give your phone number?"

"No," he replied. "Wouldn't know what to tell them."

"OK," Joe said. "Not too many are supposed to know you and I are in contact. I should get your phone number so we can be in touch soon as something's worked out. Write it on here. My phone's in my coat pocket."

Joe thought, *So far so good; he's fallen for everything. He's young and naïve. Better not push him too far tonight.* He said, "I'll call you to confirm our next meeting. Who should they contact about a job out there?

"I guess the imam," the young man replied.

The imam, of course, "Joe said. "My car's died. I'll have to take the Metro. What station is nearest the Mosque?"

"Don't ask me," he replied. "We don't take the Metro."

So he goes with someone else, Joe thought. *Maybe one last stab and call it quits.*

"What street's it on or close to?" Joe asked. "I can find the Metro stop if I know that."

"We drive down Glebe Road to get there," he said. "I think I saw signs that said Ballston."

"OK, I can figure it out from that," Joe said. "We should meet soon and see if we've found out anything. What about Sunday night? Next day's a holiday. Might be a crowd here so we can just blend in and no one pay much attention to us. About the same time as tonight."

"OK," he grunted.

"I need to get out of here," Joe said. "Good Arab boys like us don't belong here except for what we're doing now."

"Er, OK," the young man mumbled. "I should go too."

"Good," Joe said. "We can leave together. We'll walk out with my arm around you. That way they'll think we're going somewhere together, like guys here.

CHAPTER 3

Friday, February 15, 2008
Washington, DC, USA

Omar, watching television, was startled when Joe entered. Omar said, "Oh, there you are, habibi. I wondered what happened to you."

"I had to go suddenly; you weren't here," Joe replied as he removed his coat and scarf.

"I was working late at the center," Omar said. "Oh, Brad and Jason are with you." After they removed their winter gear, he greeted them giving three Arab kisses and saying to each, *"Ahlan, habibi."*

Jason thought, *These Arabs, kisses, habibi here, habibi there. I'll never figure it out, but guess I have to if I hang out with them and my wannabe Arab boyfriend.*

Joe said, "We've got lots to tell you."

Omar turned off the television as Brad said, "Maybe we should start at the beginning," and told what happened before Joe arrived at the bar.

Joe told what had happened after he arrived, adding, "I haven't had a chance to tell you two. He's in big trouble. I'm no psychologist, but lawyers have to read people. I thought he was going to lose it. I was about to stop, but he mentioned an Army post in Maryland near Laurel."

"That's where I work!" Brad exclaimed.

"I know," Joe said. "Frank too. That's why I kept on. I made a date to meet him Sunday. If I walk out of the picture now, he might get suspicious and tell someone."

"What now?" Jason asked.

Joe said, "One thing is buy a cheap phone with another number and use that to call him to confirm Sunday night's meeting. Hope he gave me the right number."

"You want us with you on Sunday?" Brad asked.

"That's not necessary," Joe answered. "Your company's always good; if you'd go anyway, fine."

"Nah," Jason added. "We're at Brad's all weekend," thinking, *Maybe if I say something now, Brad'll get the idea.*

"Also follow up on the imam and mosque," Joe said.

Omar said, "I can ask at the center, but I have to be careful. You mentioned a street name."

"Glebe Road and Ballston," Joe repeated.

"Ballston's in Arlington," Jason said. "There's a Metro stop there, and I think Glebe Road's a major street."

Joe said, "We're forgetting Middle Eastern hospitality. Let's have coffee or tea; not sure what we have to eat."

Jason said, "Nothing to eat for me; had a big dinner."

Brad said, "If you have some of that yummy Arabic coffee you served at the Eid party, that'd be great."

"You mean that dark, thick, foul tasting stuff you try to force on me?" Jason asked with a laugh and a smile.

"Since when did I force anything on you, habibi?" Brad replied. "Joe knows how to make it and has the right kind of coffee maker."

"Oh, OK," Jason said. "I'll have some."

"We have tea also," Omar said.

"Coffee's fine," Jason said. "Had to give lover boy a hard time." *Hope they're not offended hearing me call him "lover boy,"* he thought. *Muslims have funny ideas about being gay, but they seem pretty cool about it. Both damned cute too.*

Joe asked Omar, "What about you, habibi?"

Gee, everyone's habibi, Jason thought. *When Brad called me that, he said it meant "dear"; thought it was something special for me. I'll get him for that this weekend.*

"Too late for coffee for me," Omar replied. "Just tea."

When Joe went into the kitchen, Omar asked, "What're you two up to? What brings you into the city?"

"It's kind of a ritual for us," Brad said and explained.

"Sounds nice," Omar said. "Which bookstore?"

"Lambda Rising, the gay-lesbian bookstore on Connecticut Avenue, next block up from DuPont Circle," Brad answered. "Sometimes Kramer's."

"I've seen that," Omar said. "I've been tempted to go inside to see what's there; didn't know it's gay-lesbian. Usually I'm with Joe, and he goes to Kramerbooks."

"Oh, that's a cool bookstore, too," Brad said.

"I didn't know either place until we started hanging out in this area," Jason added. "Now Brad has me involved in gay Christian books at both places."

"We're involved in discussions at church," Brad added. "Many guys like Jason come from homophobic church backgrounds. We help them realize they can be gay and Christian at the same time."

"How's that?" Omar asked. "You've said you're Christian and go to church. I've not asked you much because I like and respect you and didn't want to get too personal."

"Why shouldn't someone be both gay and Christian?" Brad asked.

"In my studies I learned some about Christianity," Omar replied. "The scriptures say homosexuality is bad."

"Where does it say that?" Brad asked.

"The story of Lot in Sodom," Omar replied, "in your book of Genesis. Lot condemned men of Sodom for wanting to have anal intercourse with other men."

"Oh, that," Brad said. "That's not about homosexuality; that's about hospitality."

"What?" Omar stated.

"Yes," Brad continued. "You're from the Middle East and know about hospitality codes in the culture. A moment ago, Joe said he'd forgotten Middle Eastern hospitality."

"Er, yes," Omar said.

Joe heard his name as he entered the room with the coffee. "What about me?"

Omar explained briefly. "The way it's told in our scriptures, and Jewish ones also, is this:" Brad began. "Three angels disguised as men came to Sodom needing food and lodging. Lot, following the *hospitality code* of the era and region, insisted they come to his home for the night."

"Yes," Omar said taking a sip of tea.

Brad continued, "The men of Sodom, who we're told are wicked and evil, demanded Lot turn over the strangers to them. Lot refused because it would violate the *hospitality code,* saying these men were guests in his house.'"

Omar again nodded.

Brad continued, "It's almost certain the men of Sodom wanted to rape them anally, but is this a sex act or an act of violence? From what I learned about culture in that era, the greatest humiliation one man could show to another was to treat him like a woman."

"Yes, that's right," Omar answered.

"Under the law, or at least the law today, there's a difference between rape and sexual activity," Brad said. "I'm no lawyer. Joe?"

"It's more complex than that," Joe said, "but that's the gist of it."

"When Lot condemned the men of Sodom and God punished them with fire and stones," Brad said, "it was not about male anal sex but about violence, and especially violation of the *hospitality code.* I'm no theologian, but that's what some respected theologians have said."

"Well, er, I've not heard anything like that," Omar said. "I need to think about this."

"On top of that," Brad continued, "Lot offered his two virgin daughters to the men if they'd leave the guests alone, because of the *hospitality code*. In Christianity, and Judaism too, forcing one's daughters into sex is certainly sinful, yet persons who use this scripture to condemn homosexuality don't say a word about that. What would Islam say?"

"Of course it'd be condemned," Omar replied.

"And," Brad added, "when Sodom had been destroyed, Lot's wife turned into a pillar of salt, and Lot was with his daughters drunk as a skunk; he had sex with them. Again, persons who use this scripture to bash gays say nothing about incest, not to mention maybe rape of one's own daughters. I'm sure Islam wouldn't condone that and drunkenness as well."

"No, of course not," Omar said. "You're right about hospitality and traditional Middle Eastern cultural norms' viewing women as lesser beings, although Islam doesn't take that view. I've not heard anything about this before, but Islamic theologians are mostly Middle Easterners and think culturally, not necessarily theologically."

"Sorry if I got carried away," Brad said. "I can get worked up about this. I'm certainly no theologian, but I can say these views have found their way into Christian theology only in the past thirty or so years, and there're still lots of Christians who don't accept this."

"Maybe if I had a chance to read more," Omar said.

"I've got tons of stuff I can give you to read," Brad offered, "and that gay-lesbian bookstore has lots more."

"Thanks," Omar said. "I might take you up on that, but I don't think I'll be going into that bookstore. I personally might find it OK to go there, but not sure it's a good idea for an assistant imam at the Islamic Center to be seen in there."

"I just thought of something else," Brad said. "This summer I attended a performance of a professional actor, playwright, one-man show that was fabulous. One of the sketches was exactly on this subject, the story of Sodom and Gomorrah. His name is Peterson Toscano. I have the DVD of his performance. I'll lend it to you too."

Peterson Toscano
http://PetersonToscano.com

"More coffee?" Joe asked.

"Oh, no, not for me," Jason said. "Thanks anyway."

"Not for me either," Brad said. "We should be going."

"Thanks for coming," Joe said.

"Thank *you*," Brad said. "You came over there."

"I can't say it was a pleasure," Joe added. "It's a pretty grim situation. I'm worried; but then I tend to go overboard."

"No, I think you're right, Joe," Omar said. "I don't think you're going overboard; all we can do now is pray."

Brad said as he stood, "Say, are you two guys doing something on Monday? It's a holiday. Come to my place; Jason'll be there of course. Maybe Frank and Paco can come too. Either of you alone if one is busy."

Joe said, "I'm not doing anything."

"I'm free," Omar said. "What time?"

They agreed on mid-afternoon while Brad and Jason bundled up for the cold weather.

CHAPTER 4

Sunday, February 17, 2008
Arlington, Virginia, USA

Marwan and Ahmed were eating pizza, washed down with Pepsi, at the kitchen countertop in their very shabby apartment with just chairs and two single beds.

Ahmed said, "You got your passport too."

Marwan mumbled, "Yeah."

"Now we have to book flights," Ahmed continued. "Have you figured out what we have to do?"

Marwan replied, "We can't book online unless we pay with a credit card, which we don't have. Need a date, too."

"We'll know the date soon," Ahmed said. "Wissam has a job there and figured out where the place is; just needs to make sure he's on the shift assigned to clean that place."

Whatever, Marwan thought, and muttered, "OK."

"So how're we going to do it?" Ahmed asked.

"Some guys at work said something about a travel agency Arabs use for flights to the Middle East," Marwan said. "We've never flown, so how do you expect me to know?"

"Well ask them," Ahmed said thinking: *He sure isn't showing much interest, and strange things are going on like that phone call he got yesterday. I'll just have to ride him; can't let things get fucked up now.*

"Yeah, right," Marwan said skeptically. "Tell guys at work, then the whole damned office knows."

"No! No!" Ahmed said impatiently. "Don't tell details; just ask about the travel agency. Maybe find two travel agencies, one for Canada and another one for England. Damn, if you could book online, then no one'd have to know."

"I said," Marwan replied, "you gotta have a credit card, and we don't have one."

"OK," Ahmed said. "I'll ask Abdulmalik what to do."

Marwan shoved his partly eaten pizza aside, took a couple of swigs of Pepsi, and sat listlessly, thinking, *Damn, a couple of weeks more. Don't know if I can take it that long. The boss already told me he's going to fire me if I don't shape up. I can't get fired the next couple of weeks, but then who gives a shit. Kahlil said we have to meet again tonight. Maybe I'll go early and really be gay.*

Ahmed asked, "Anyone contacted you yet about things you're supposed to get?"

"Yes," Marwan said indifferently.

"When're you going to get them?" Ahmed asked.

"Don't know," Marwan said. "Meeting him tonight."

"Oh," exclaimed Ahmed. "Where?"

"Said it had to be confidential," Marwan replied.

Ahmed thought, *Yeah, Abdulmalik said not to let too many people know who you're dealing with.*

"Do we have to keep talking about this?" Marwan said. "I'm sick of going over things again and again."

Gee, he's really spooked, Ahmed said to himself. *He doesn't look good; not eating.*

Both watched television until Marwan left.

CHAPTER 5

Monday, February 18, 2008
Laurel, Maryland, USA

Drinking beer in Brad's apartment on a sunshiny afternoon that took some of the chill away, Jason and Brad recounted events to Frank and Paco regarding the previous Friday. Jason's colorful paintings and drawings adorned the walls; Jason changed them frequently, always creating new conversation pieces.

Frank said, "Hopefully Joe'll tell us more when he gets here." To Paco, "We need to go to DC ourselves, like they do."

Brad's apartment, Laurel, Maryland

"Yeah," Paco agreed. "Friday nights're good for me if I'm not working. No classes, and I'm ready for a night off before hitting the books on the weekend."

"Why don't we all go together sometime," Brad said. "Washington has great ethnic restaurants."

They agreed on February 29 at a Himalayan restaurant. Jason laughed and said, "Himalayan; before I met this guy, the most exotic food I had was peanut soup."

"Peanut soup?" Paco asked.

"Virginia tradition," Jason said.

The doorbell rang and all greeted Omar and Joe, exchanging three Arab kisses. Brad took drink orders and brought cranberry juice.

Joe recounted details of his meeting with Marwan the previous night. Hearing the Arabic language section was targeted, Brad and Frank were alarmed.

"I need to tell everyone in the section tomorrow," Brad said agitated, "Look out for janitors who look Arab."

Frank replied, "Let me talk to my sergeant first; he's had thirty years' security experience. We need to stop someone before he gets into the building. If you put the word out now, it could create panic. Also, who'd believe you? You got this from someone in a gay bar? Plenty of people'd dismiss information from anyone in a bar, much less a gay bar."

"You have a point," Brad said, "but I can't just sit and let my co-workers be a target."

"Give me a day," Frank said. "Joe says it'll be a couple of weeks. Contact me tomorrow during a break."

After a few moments' silence, wanting to change topics, Omar asked no one in particular, "What about the election? Looks like McCain has it sewn up for the Republicans, now that Romney pulled out. I'm the only one here who can't vote, so maybe I can ask without being personally involved."

"Looks like it," Frank said. "I vote in Florida, and the primary there got things rolling for him. He's the only one who understands the wars in Afghanistan and Iraq."

"For sure, he's anti–al Qaeda and willing to go after bin Laden," Omar said. "That much is positive."

"You support wars there?" Jason asked.

"Can't say I support everything in Iraq," Omar replied, "but I certainly support elimination of al Qaeda."

Jason asked, "Why's that? Not that I disagree, but you seem pretty charged up."

"Al Qaeda killed my family, parents, brother, and sister," Omar replied, "and not for anything they'd done; just because they were in the way."

"Oh," Jason said. "Sorry if it's a bad topic."

Omar replied, "It's OK. I've worked through it, and I don't mind talking about it."

Brad said, "Don't be so sure that McCain's the only one who understands. Hillary Clinton surely understands after eight years in the White House and seven in the Senate. Looks like she has a fight ahead of her. I vote in Maryland, and Obama walked away with the delegates here."

"I voted for the first time since I just got citizenship," Paco said. "Was never interested in elections because most of our people don't vote. I may not've registered to vote if it weren't done automatically when I got a Maryland driver's license. Don't know much about what's going on in Maryland yet, but I managed to find the polling station."

"I'm one of the few non-blacks registered in the District of Columbia," Joe commented. "Makes me wonder if it's worth the effort. There're lively local contests I know nothing about, but otherwise DC's so overwhelmingly Democratic there's not much of a contest. I'm a government employee, so I can't get involved in politics anyway."

"Same for me in the military," Frank said. "That doesn't keep me from having opinions."

"I'm a U.S. government employee, too," Brad said.

"And I'm a government employee," Paco said. "Even if I'm not involved in politics and don't intend to be, one thing beginning to piss me off is the media talk about the Hispanic vote, the Hispanic vote, as though it were a foregone conclusion we're all going to vote the same. Hispanics have minds of their own and don't vote for someone because someone says we should. For sure I made up my own mind."

"Gee, I guess I'm out in left field," Jason said, "only one except Omar who's not a government employee and only one who votes in Virginia. Lot of the rednecks I grew up with don't bother to register and vote, but I got involved in political activism at VCU, especially in the gay-lesbian group against Jerry Falwell and Pat Robertson, both big Virginia Republicans. It's weird; in this election the most gay-friendly candidate was Rudy Giuliani, a Republican, until he dropped out. Who does that leave now? Lots say Hillary Clinton's lesbian, and that'd explain a lot; don't know if I'd vote for her just for that reason. Doesn't seem like McCain's anti-gay."

Brad said, "I need about fifteen minutes to cook the spaghetti. We're having spaghetti with a sauce I learned to cook from some Italian neighbors way back. Frank and Paco brought a salad."

When all had finished eating, Brad gathered dishes and asked, "Who'd like coffee? Maybe you two don't know it, but all gay households have to have an espresso machine, and we have Arab sweets that Joe and Omar brought."

After dessert and coffee, Omar said, "Thanks for the DVD. I'd like to take the book you mentioned and read it, if that's OK."

"Yeah, sure," Brad said.

"You've got me thinking," Omar said. "I need to do more research on why Islam comes down so hard on gays."

"Lots of Christians do too," Brad said.

"I have a question I hope you don't mind me asking," Omar said. "I've been wanting to ask, it's pretty personal."

"I don't mind," Brad said. "What's that?"

"Why would someone want to be gay?" Omar asked, "Especially since there's such a strong reaction against it and it's so unnatural."

Brad replied, "Who said anything about wanting to be gay. I doubt anyone in this room wants to be gay, or better said, *wanted* to be gay. I can't speak for others, but I can say I sure did not want to be gay. It took a while, but finally I realized this's the way I am. Being gay is a part of me, just like having blue eyes and wavy hair, so I might as well live with it. More than living with it, make the most of it, just like I always try to keep my hair trimmed to look my best."

Frank hesitated and said, "It wasn't until two years ago I could finally make my tongue and mouth say 'I am gay,' and for sure I didn't want to be this way. Now that I finally realize this's the way I'm made, I'm beginning to feel better about myself. It's a struggle, though."

"Why is it unnatural?" Brad asked. "Who said that?"

Omar said, "That's what I hear and read; against nature, contrary to God's order."

Brad tensed as he said, "Being gay's no more against nature than being left-handed. A minority, yes; but unnatural, I don't think so. I'm sure you know about left-handedness and problems these people face in the Middle East about touching someone with the left hand."

Omar replied, "Yes, I know, but there are other reasons for that too, and I am sure you know them."

"Yes," Brad said, feeling testy. "Without toilet paper, the left hand is used for certain things. At the risk of sounding overly pious, I can definitely say I know, I feel God made me gay for a reason. Part of surrendering to God's will is accepting that and discovering what that reason is."

Joe said with a smile and chuckle, "Hey, that's Omar's line, always at the risk of something."

"His line too," Jason said laughingly pointing at Brad.

"Yeah, that's my line," Omar said chuckling. "I see your point. As a man of God, so to speak, I know surrendering to Allah is the most fundamental part of Islam. The word *Islam* means 'surrender.'"

"I feel it to the depth of my soul and being," Brad said.

"I'm just now beginning to feel that way, too," Jason said, "thanks to going to the MCC with Brad. I accepted being gay a few years ago. Until now I struggled with the 'against nature' stuff; against God's natural order."

Paco spoke up, "I'm Roman Catholic and always go to mass; take communion with a clean heart and spirit, even if I am gay. The pope's anti-gay, but he's an asshole and not just for this reason. Doesn't mean that I can't be gay and a good Catholic at the same time."

"I'm not anything," Frank said. "Could say I'm agnostic. I don't worry about eternal condemnation because I'm gay."

"You've given me lots to think about," Omar said.

"Me too," Joe said. "I knew gay students at Michigan. I was around them in class and social settings, but not really close. They seemed like cool guys, and I didn't see any reason to avoid them because they're gay."

After several minutes of small talk, Joe said to Omar, "Shouldn't we go? I need to work tomorrow."

Omar replied, "Yes, I have some things to do too."

Joe said to Brad and Jason, "Thanks for having us. I really mean that. We've been letting down our guard, so I can say that it's been pretty lonely in Washington. A real letdown after Ann Arbor, where I was pretty sociable. Feels really good to be with people I can feel comfortable with."

"For sure," Omar said. "I'm so glad you two ended up in my class. Next time it'll be at our place."

CHAPTER 6

Tuesday, February 19, 2008
Fort Meade, Maryland, USA

While many people slowly began their work week after a long holiday weekend, Frank, with his steely reserve covering inner anxiety, asked First Sergeant Walter Beasley to come to his office very shortly after arriving for duty. Sergeant Beasley's sharp Marine Corps bearing was enhanced with a business-suit type uniform. Almost thirty years' experience in police and security work had earned him respect from all he worked with, superior and subordinate. He stood about five feet nine, had salt-and-pepper dark brown hair typical of late forties, and steel blue-gray eyes. He would soon retire and have a choice of many post-retirement jobs all over the country.

In response to Frank's asking about his weekend, he replied, "Good, Sir. The young kids were out of school, and the grandkids came over. My wife made cherry pies like people used to when the holiday was Washington's Birthday. What about your holiday?"

"Nothing special," he answered. "I was with a friend, a nurse from Baltimore. We met two other couples, one from Washington, which leads to why I called you in. One person works at a major government agency. Right now, it's probably wise not to tell which agency and his or her name, even to you. Let's just say this person has Arab-American connections and came across a rumor that an attack is aimed at the NSA and our Arabic language section."

"Oh?," Sergeant Beasley said.

"I've been around DC long enough to know rumors fly, and even if there's some truth, they can be exaggerated," Frank continued. "This person thought it best to tell me because we've been together socially. I don't want to react based on a rumor, but maybe it's best to err on the side of caution. What do you think?"

"For sure," Sergeant Beasley replied. "But shouldn't we run it through the DoDIG or FBI? If we act on our own, it might backfire; create a panic when it's not justified."

"This person's exploring what's best to do today," Frank said. "I wouldn't want to go to the IG or FBI until I've heard back, but I can't see not doing anything, either."

Sounds like this person might be with the State Department, Sergeant Beasley thought. *If so, there can be diplomatic stuff to be dealt with first. I can see why he's cautious. The Major's pretty sharp, even if he doesn't have a background in security.* He replied, "I understand. That's what makes working in the Washington area challenging and interesting. If this were in Utah, we'd report it to the FBI and be done with it."

"What should we do now, Sarge?" Frank asked. "I was thinking we should ratchet up security a little, maybe not suddenly so we don't call attention. If someone wants to know, we could hint but not lie that DoD thinks we're too lax, but that means you'd have to admit you're doing a bad job and we don't want to cause morale to go down."

He's sharp, Sergeant Beasley thought, *and understands morale for the troops. I'm sure he suspects we checked his background on the QT. I was concerned about Okinawa, but he knows how to protect his ass, but not screw his troops in the process.* "Let me handle that one, Sir," he replied. "I'll find some way to get them to ratchet up security, but sound like it's coming from somewhere else."

"If it helps, you can make me look at fault," Frank said. "It's no secret I'm putting in my twenty. I'm not going to neglect my duties; too much personal respect for that. If it takes that to keep this place secure, I can live with it."

"Gotcha, Sir," Sergeant Beasley said. "It's no secret I'm close to thirty myself. We think alike, so no need to spend time discussing. What's this about an Arab-American connection? We've got the Arab language section upstairs, but none of them are Arab-Americans. I'm pretty sure they wouldn't let Arab-Americans work there. Besides, those guys, and gals now, have gone through security checks."

"The person said the rumors were about contractor personnel, food service or cleaning," Frank added.

"We can't refuse to allow persons to work for contractors just because they're of Arab descent," Sergeant Beasley said.

"No," Frank agreed, "but we can unofficially try to identify Arab-Americans ourselves. Could you get me a list of new contractor personnel for the last couple of months?"

"I can do that," Sergeant Beasley said. "How soon?"

"Soon as it's convenient," Frank answered. "Maybe look like getting things in order for a surprise IG inspection, like we're overdue. Hasn't been one since I've been here."

Gee, this guy thinks of everything, Sergeant Beasley thought. "Anything else, Sir?"

"No, not right now," Frank replied. "Can you think of anything? You're the security expert."

"Not that I can think of, either," Sergeant Beasley said.

When Sergeant Beasley left, Frank called the Marine Corps personnel office at Wright-Patterson Air Force Base and said, "Good morning. This is Major Frank Reynolds. I'm hoping you remember me. I was there until a year and a half ago in a joint weapon's system office."

(pause)

"Oh, good," he said. "Maybe you remember in June of '06 there was a meeting with me and some colonels from Marine Corps personnel, NSA, and DoDIG," he continued. "If possible, I'd like to find the names of the persons there. I need to contact them."

(pause)

"No, I don't mind if you ask your director," he replied.

(pause)

"Yes, that's where I am now; and, yes, one of the persons was deputy associate director," Frank answered. "I'm not sure he's in. It's the day after a long holiday weekend. It's kind of a sensitive issue. I could try to get it from him in a day or two, if you don't have it."

(pause)

"Yes, thank you very much for understanding," Frank said, and gave a phone number and email address.

Sergeant Beasley returned, saying, "Here're the contractor applications for security badges the last three months."

"Thanks," Frank said, and started looking through them, saying, "Most of them are Hispanic."

"Yes, there's a high turnover in these types of jobs," Sergeant Beasley said, "and the most recent immigrants take them. Fortunately, most Hispanics aren't security risks."

"Here's one with the name Wissam Salameh," Frank said. "That doesn't sound Hispanic, but he looks Hispanic."

"His mother might be Hispanic," Sergeant Beasley suggested. "Lots of immigrants have names from their fathers, who come from who knows where."

Hispanics and Arabs look a lot alike, Frank thought. "Is Wissam Salameh an Arab name?" he asked.

"Hmm. Could be, I suppose," Sergeant Beasley said. "Not a name I'd recognize."

"Address in Arlington, Virginia," Frank said. "Isn't that a bit far to commute for a janitorial job?"

"Yes, if actually commuting," Sergeant Beasley replied. "Lots of them have extended families all over the place. They might put down one address on an application form, then move in with family somewhere else when they get a job."

"Citizen," Frank said; "born in Arlington, Virginia."

"I see what you're getting at," Sergeant Beasley said. "I don't screen these myself, and people who take them probably aren't as perceptive as you and I would be. After an initial screening, we give a temporary pass and give them to the IG for background checks. If we didn't give temporary permits, contractors would have problems getting people to work. No one working for these wages wants to sit without pay waiting for a clearance. Contractors would scream bloody hell, and Congressmen would get into the act."

"Yes, I imagine," Frank said. "What do we do now? We can't target this guy, especially with just this rumor to go on. Might scare him off."

"It could just cause them to send someone else and do a more careful job of who they pick to infiltrate," Sergeant Beasley said. "But we're getting involved in too many details for something that's based only on a rumor."

"What do we do, if anything?" Frank asked.

"A couple of ideas come to mind," Sergeant Beasley said. "We imply we're expecting a surprise inspection from the IG and have to get ready, general tightening of security. Another is seminars and briefing of all personnel about latest developments in security consciousness. We could say the greatest threat remains from young Middle Eastern men. We give an equally strong briefing about ethnic profiling; just look for anyone who acts strangely."

"That sounds like a plan," Frank said. "You always know what to do. How soon do we start?"

"Tomorrow," Sergeant Beasley said. "We have to get word to the troops that they have extra briefing sessions."

"OK," Frank said.

Sergeant Beasley added, "I also inquired when food service and cleaning staff are in the building. Food service is predictable and nowhere near the Arabic language section. Cleaning staff is mostly at night and on weekends. For places like the Arabic language section that operate twenty-four/seven, it's mostly weekends."

"Thanks for your good work," Frank said. "Please let me know what I can do. Something I can say to the troops?"

"Let me think about that," Sergeant Beasley said. "Maybe you should make a point of coming to one of the briefings, showing that *all* persons are required to attend."

When Sergeant Beasley left, Frank sent a text message: "Lunch. BE." Soon he had a reply that said: "Noon."

When Brad arrived at noon at Bob Evans restaurant in Laurel, Frank said, "Look at this name and see if it means anything to you."

Brad replied, "It's an Arab name for sure."

Frank added, "That's the name of a new person on the cleaning staff," Frank said. "It sounded Arab."

"Wissam is a common Arab name," Brad said. "It can be both Muslim and Christian. I'm pretty sure I've heard that last name in Jordan. We should ask Joe."

While eating, Frank briefly recounted the conversation with Sergeant Beasley, asking, "When is your section cleaned?"

"Never thought about it," Brad replied. "It's probably not on day shift I'm working now, or I'd have noticed. It's been so long since I've worked another shift, I don't remember. Not much to clean. They must sweep the floor and empty trash cans sometime. There's an ante-room where we hang our coats and make coffee. They could clean there and I wouldn't notice. I'll see if I can find out. I'm still nervous about leaving my co-workers at risk."

"So'm I," Frank said, further describing his interaction with Sergeant Beasley. "We should get in touch with Joe."

"He did say he'll be back in touch with us," Brad said, "but it's not his issue. He just did me a favor. He might just want to butt out, if it causes him problems at work."

"Somehow I doubt it," Frank said. "He seems the type that once he gets into something, he doesn't let go. He didn't have to go back to the bar alone Sunday night. When we get home tonight, if he hasn't called one of us, we can call him."

Brad said. "You want to come for leftover spaghetti?"

"Sure, why not?" Frank said. "I can bring wine. After a day like today, a couple of glasses of wine're just what I need, especially being close enough to walk home."

Later, back in his office in Fort Meade, Frank found an email message that merely had the names of two persons.

This lady really is good, he thought, and wrote an effusive message of thanks. He spent the rest of the afternoon trying to keep busy.

CHAPTER 7

Tuesday, February 19, 2008
Washington, DC, USA

After breakfast, Omar rummaged through his closet, asking himself, *Where'd I put that old phone?* He found and charged it, found a number, and called on another phone, "Hello, Gabe. Omar Abu Deeb. I worked for you summer of 2006."

(pause)

"Good, thanks," he said. "I'm in Washington now. How're things in Buffalo?"

(pause)

"I'm a part-time assistant imam at the Islamic Center," he replied, "and have a post-doc fellowship at George Washington University."

(pause)

"It's interesting, for sure, being right where the wheels of power turn," he replied.

(pause)

"I called because I need to contact your agency," he continued. "I'd rather it be you than a random person here in Washington. I got information indirectly about a possible plot against a sensitive place. An imam might be involved, like up there."

(pause)

"My roommate came across it," he continued. "He's Arab-American. He met another Arab-American who told him. My roommate got the information out of him. He's good at that because he's a lawyer working in a fairly sensitive job in a major agency here."

(pause)

"Yes, the Attorney General," Omar replied, surprised.

(pause)

"Yes, that's who he is." Omar was stunned.

(pause)

"Oh, you worked with him before," he said. "Yes, he's very capable. I'm lucky to have him as a roommate."

(pause)

Omar described briefly how he and Joe met and after a pause continued, "You know Roger Chen, too. Have you been keeping spies on me ever since I worked for you?"

(pause)

"I figured you'd turn this over to an agent here in Washington," he said, and gave his cell phone number. "Please have the agent text first; I might be in class or with students."

They disconnected after pleasantries.

In mid-morning at the university, Omar received a text message: "Gabe said call you. Please reply. C. Brooks."

In a private place, he called and made arrangements to meet for lunch at the Old Post Office food court.

At 11:30 a.m. Omar met Cranford Brooks, who stood six feet four inches, had short, black, tightly curled hair trimmed professionally, bright brown eyes, and black skin of his African-American ancestry. He was wearing a charcoal gray Brooks Brothers suit, a well-pressed white shirt, and a solid burgundy red tie, the "uniform" of the FBI.

Omar said, "I see what you mean; you do look like a basketball player."

"I played for the Georgetown Hoyas," he said, smiling, "a few more years ago than I like to think about. I wasn't good enough to get off the bench much, but it got me an education."

When both were seated, Omar said, "This's an interesting place. I've never been here, and it's not that far from the university."

"We come here a lot," Cranford Brooks said. "It's close to our office, and it's easy to get lost in the crowd and not draw attention to ourselves. Even so, we can't talk too much here. At least make contact and arrange another meeting. It seems you told your contact in Buffalo you have information about a possible incident at a sensitive facility."

"Yes," Omar replied, "and a so-called imam at a mosque in Virginia is apparently involved. I'm trying to find out more about the mosque, but I need to be careful. Did he tell you I'm a part-time assistant imam at the Islamic Center?"

"Yes, he mentioned that," Cranford brooks replied. "Apparently you didn't get this information directly."

"No, from my roommate," Omar replied. "He had direct contact with a person who revealed it."

Cranford Brooks said, "He told us who and also that he'd worked with your roommate before. Why isn't your roommate reporting this directly instead of you?"

Omar said, "I volunteered because I had the contact with the... your agency. Also, I have an interest myself. I don't know how much G..., the agent up there told you, but I have reasons to stop the organization that might be behind this."

"He told us a little," Cranford Brooks said, "but didn't go into details. It seems your roommate works for another government agency and some sensitive issues are involved."

"I presume you know which agency," Omar said. "There's more to it. The place he met the person is a rather sensitive place and he doesn't want to tell his agency quite yet and I didn't tell the agent up there either." He lowered his voice and said, "It's a gay bar in our neighborhood. My roommate isn't gay, or at least I don't think he is, but still he doesn't want to tell the people he works with right now. If it comes out later, I'm sure he will."

Cranford Brooks responded, "The fact he was in a gay bar doesn't affect anything one way or another, even if he is gay. It's now well known the founder of our agency was gay. But what was he doing in a gay bar if he's not gay?"

Omar briefly explained.

"This's getting complicated," Cranford Brooks said. "I'm not making notes on purpose, so it's difficult to follow."

"It's even more complicated," Omar said. "Yet another friend is in charge of security at that place."

"Oh," Cranford Books exclaimed. "Enough's enough. I was sure we'd need to meet again anyway. We, my agency that is, need to meet you and your roommate and probably both of those friends, not necessarily at the same time. How can we arrange it?"

"We'll be at home after work," Omar offered. "I'm not sure either of us wants to be seen walking into your office at that hour of the day; it's too late to pretend we're tourists."

"I can come see you, if there's no problem with an agent being seen at your place," Cranford Brooks suggested.

"No problem with that," Omar said. "That's what I expected. We'll be home about 5:30. I can send a text message and confirm with my roommate."

"OK," Cranford Brooks replied.

Omar sent a text to Joe: "FBI 5:30 our apt. OK?" then said, "If I don't get an answer before we go, assume it's OK unless I call you."

"OK," Cranford Brooks said. "Where do you live?"

Omar gave him the address. While they finished eating, Omar received a text message that merely said, "OK."

CHAPTER 8

Tuesday, February 19, 2008
Washington, DC, USA

After removing his professionally styled trench coat, part of the FBI "uniform," and neck scarf against the blustery winter weather, Cranford Brooks sat in Omar and Joe's living room, where they described Brad's and Frank's positions, how they became acquainted, and that they are gay with boyfriends. Joe added, "That leads us to Friday night," and described the events, including his return visit on Sunday night and their visit to Brad's on Monday, yesterday.

"I'll want to contact Brad Spencer and Frank Reynolds," Cranford Brooks said. "I could find their phone numbers, but it'd be a lot easier if you'd tell me."

Joe said. "I promised I'd call today. I'll call right now.

"Brad, it's Joe."

(pause)

Joe replied, "Good, we can talk to him too." To Cranford Brooks, "Frank's there too, and they have a name."

(pause)

"An FBI agent is here and wants to contact you," Joe said. "I'll put him on so you can make arrangements."

(pause)

Cranford Brooks introduced himself and said, "These gentlemen filled me in, but we'd like to see you in person. I don't know if it'll be me or someone else, maybe from the Baltimore Field Office."

(pause)

"Tomorrow, but maybe you don't want to be seen with us at your place of work," Cranford Brooks suggested.

(pause)

"Lunchtime's good," Cranford Brooks said. "We can meet Major Reynolds before or after in his office."

(pause)

They made plans to meet at Bob Evans in Laurel. Then Cranford Brooks asked, "Please give me a description that I can give whoever meets you?"

(pause)

He continued, "I believe Major Reynolds is there."

(pause)

"We'd like to visit you in your office," he said to Frank, "an official visit."

(pause)

"Immediately after we meet with Mr. Spencer, perhaps. Twelve noon, if that doesn't interfere with lunch," he said.

(pause)

"Yes, include the sergeant," he concurred. "We'll want to meet with you alone too."

(pause)

"Please give me that name now, and we can start checking," he said.

(pause)

When he disconnected, Cranford Brooks said, "Please bear with me while I enter this information. Can you tell me what Brad Spencer looks like? I want to make sure I have a good description if another agent makes the contact."

Omar gave the description; Cranford Brooks thought, *That matches the description he gave. Didn't suspect anything, but doesn't hurt to check.*

"Do you want Frank's description?" Omar asked.

"No, that won't be necessary," Cranford Brooks replied. "It'll be an official visit, so we'll go to his office and identify ourselves. He gave the name Wissam Salameh. Hope I'm pronouncing it right. Does that mean anything to you?"

"Wissam's a common Arabic name," Joe said, "There were a few guys with that name where I grew up in Dearborn. Last name doesn't mean anything special to me."

"It's a common Arabic name," Omar confirmed, "and Salameh is a fairly common family name, especially in the Levant region of Lebanon, Palestine, Jordan, and Syria. The name wouldn't mean anything, but it's definitely Arab."

Cranford Brooks said, "I'll give it to someone with background in Arab things. Is there anything you can add?"

"What about the telephone I bought and used to call the guy I met at the bar?" Joe asked. "He has that phone number, and I asked him to call if something comes up."

Cranford Brooks said, "Give the phone to me. If he calls, we probably won't answer, but make a note. We might have an agent who speaks Arabic return the call."

While Joe got the phone, Cranford Brooks asked, "Joe says he gave his name as Abed. Does that mean anything?"

Omar replied, "Abed's a very common nickname. It's usually someone whose name is Ahmed, but others use it too. It's also a generic nickname for someone who's a bit bumbling and stupid, especially Abou Abed. It's easy to see why this might be the first name that'd pop into his mind."

After Joe gave him the phone, Cranford Brooks said, "For now, I don't see a need to contact the agency you work for. If something significant develops, we'd notify you first. Also we'll be sensitive and cautious about disclosing information that came from a gay bar, but there're no guarantees. Likewise, we won't out your friends Brad and Frank. If there should be an arrest or some other public event, the media have ways of finding out."

"I understand," Joe said.

Cranford Brooks said to Omar, "We can probably keep you out of this. The FBI's good at protecting our resources. You may or may not hear back from us. Nonetheless, we really appreciate your reporting this."

After Cranford Brooks left, Joe said, "Say, what about dinner? Do we have any food here, or should we go out?"

"I want to go out and take my mind off things," Omar said. "I was naïve enough to think I'd put that behind me now that I'm in a regular job, actually two of them."

"Yeah, let's go out, even if it's just to KFC," Joe said. "You know I'm not much in the kitchen unless I'm on the phone with my mother, and I sure don't want to call her now. You haven't filled me in on what you did for the FBI. Is it something I need to know, now that this has come up?"

"Actually," Omar replied, "I was going to tell you anyway. The person I contacted knows you and Roger too."

"Oh, who?" Joe asked.

"Gabe Andreotti in Buffalo," Omar answered, "and I'm curious what you did with him. Just curious; I don't *need* to know, so don't tell me anything confidential."

"What? You worked with him?" Joe asked. *So he* was *involved in that situation*, he thought. *Omar must've been the undercover resource they mentioned.* "Yes, habibi, we have catching up to do, but let's go enjoy a meal, and then come back and figure out what to tell each other. I'll get out of this suit. Where do you want to go, so I know what to wear?"

"I had Chinese for lunch," Omar said, "so not that."

"What I'd like is some comfort food like my mother makes," Joe replied. "The best Lebanese restaurant I know is a couple of Metro stops away, up near the zoo."

"Let's go," Omar said. "I haven't been there yet."

Joe replied, "I won't wear my old skungie jeans. You know we Lebanese have to look good to each other."

CHAPTER 9

Tuesday, February 19, 2008
Washington, DC, USA

Inside Mama Ayesha's Lebanese Restaurant with its exaggerated Middle Eastern décor, conversation over dinner evolved to Joe's telling about being between cultures, growing up in the U.S., being a proud American, but not wanting to abandon Lebanese heritage, concluding, "Lebanese have always been westward looking, adopting western things, and embracing western culture. You'd know because of the classes you teach."

Mama Ayesha's Lebanese Restaurant, Washington, DC

Omar replied, "It's one thing to know and teach history in the abstract; it's another to actually live and experience it. Yemen's traditionally been closed. Well, not exactly; the southern port of Aden was a British colony, but the North where I'm from was isolated, even in the capital city, Sana'a. It was a big adjustment when I got here. Fortunately, the first place I went was Minnesota; people there are open and tolerant."

"Yeah, like Brad," Joe offered. "I'm not much into history, and what I did study was western civilization, roots of the English common law, and stuff like that. You know, Lebanese Shia stick to themselves. They settled in this country when things were tough in Lebanon but still stick to their community in Dearborn."

Omar replied, "You know other Lebanese immigrants have gone out of their way to blend in, especially Christians, but we don't deal much with Arab Christians in Islamic studies. Not many Yemenis in the U.S. One place there're some is Lackawanna, New York. Why they settled there is probably lost in history or no one ever told me. You probably figured out that's where I worked for that agency."

"Yes," Joe replied, "I was involved with a couple of guys from there, maybe Gabe told you."

"Gabe didn't tell me much," Omar replied. "Didn't say anything about you, just a comment on the phone this morning. What's it like growing up in an Arab community in Dearborn? It's pretty grim in Lackawanna. They stick to themselves, aren't well educated, and don't get involved outside their community. Young kids growing up there like those two guys have lots of stress of being pulled two ways."

"Wasn't that bad in Dearborn," Joe said. "Lebanese there're pretty well educated and work at different things: running small businesses, even medical doctors. My father works in an office, sort of an office manager."

"Lebanese are known for being adaptable and entrepreneurial," Omar commented, "and have the highest literacy rate in the Arab world along with Iraq, although Gulf states are catching up."

"I'd love you to go with me and see where I grew up and Ann Arbor where I went to school," Joe said, "but not now. Things are pretty tense at home."

"Oh, what's going on?" Omar asked. "Or would you rather not talk about it?"

"I'm glad to talk about it," Joe replied. "Really wanted to talk to you, but other things keep coming up, and now this." Joe explained tensions over his working for the U.S. government and his father wanting to arrange a marriage.

"I saw some pro al Qaeda feeling in Lackawanna," Omar replied, "so I can sort of imagine."

"Support for Hizbollah in Dearborn is mostly based on romanticized notions of what Hizbollah stands for," Joe added. "It's especially strong, now that their leader was assassinated in Damascus."

"I read the Israelis did it," Omar commented.

"In their minds. the U.S. did it even if someone else triggered the bomb," Joe added. "Even those who're not Hizbollah supporters view the U.S. as pro-Christian and now pro-Sunni; by implication anti-Shia."

"I teach some of that too," Omar said. "Just a couple years ago the U.S. cancelled a visa for an old Shia leader because of anti-American inflammatory statements."

"Nabih Berri," Joe answered. "An old has-been, but so are lots of older guys in Dearborn. Still fighting the civil war."

"How does this affect you right now?" Omar asked.

"You surely understand how important status is," Joe said. "Many view me as a traitor because I'm working for the U.S. government, and they don't stop letting my parents know that. Some of my father's friends have stopped calling him Abou Yusef now."

"Oh," Omar said. "That's pretty serious."

Joe continued, "You know Arab tradition that it's children's obligation to make parents look good, or at least not lose face. So far they haven't suggested I quit my job, but they've made it clear I need to redeem myself."

"Oh, habibi," Omar replied. "I know things're tense, but didn't know how much."

"That's one of the big cultural differences I feel torn over," Joe said. "American families support their children for the most part. Parents allow children to make their choices and accept and support those choices unless they're extreme. You know as well as I do Arabs are obligated to conform to the tribe and support parents' choices, but what're we supposed to do when our "tribe," so to speak, is a small minority in a much bigger society with conflicting notions?"

"That's the situation the Prophet faced when Allah anointed him to lead the faithful to new ways of thinking," Omar added. "Habibi, do what feels best inside. You don't need my advice, but you don't need some outdated tribal notion we Arabs have been burdened with."

"Thanks," Joe said.

"You mentioned redeeming yourself," Omar said.

Joe began, "They want me to marry someone in Lebanon who'll bring her family here. They have business connections to a family who want to get the whole family out of the conflict; no notion of children who'd be happy."

Omar said, "Again, be true to yourself."

Joe replied, "That's what I'm doing, but it brings up questions of what's marriage all about? What's it mean for two people to be joined together? Americans have a phenomenally high divorce rate. Even so, I get the idea their view of marriage is healthier than Arabs'."

Omar replied. "I don't know what to say. I've never thought much about getting married."

"It's good to have someone to talk to," Joe said.

"For sure," Omar said. "I really wanted someone to talk to, dealing with things two summers ago in Lackawanna. For a while, things were pretty tense between Gabe and me. Let's give it a rest for a while. I'm sure we have heavy stuff to talk about later. You want coffee or just go?"

"I can make Lebanese coffee as good as they can," Joe said while getting the waiter's attention. "This was good; lima bean stew with lamb, big fat lima beans like my mother makes. The big mezze plate too, with hummus, moutabal, vine leaves, and real Lebanese olives."

The bus boy, a young man in his early twenties, well-groomed with Arab features, came to clear the table and asked in accented English, "Did you enjoy your meal? Is that all?"

"Yes, very much," Omar answered in Arabic.

"You speak Arabic," the waiter replied in Arabic with a big smile. "Where're you from?

"I'm from Yemen," Omar answered in Arabic.

"I'm American," Joe said in Arabic. "My family's Lebanese."

"Oh, I'm from Lebanon," the bus boy continued in Arabic. "From Sur, or Tyr some call it. In the South."

"I have distant family there," Joe commented in Arabic. "I've not been there."

The bus boy replied in Arabic, "I left a few months ago. My family were killed, but I was able to get out."

Omar said in Arabic, "Sorry to hear that. My family were all killed too in Yemen. I know what it's like."

"You been here long?" the bus boy asked in Arabic.

"In the U.S. about six years," Omar replied in Arabic. "In Washington only five months."

"What do you do here?" the bus boy asked in Arabic.

"Assistant imam at the Islamic Center. Also work at George Washington University," Omar answered in Arabic.

"Oh, an imam," the waiter said in Arabic.

"Yes; come pray with us if there's not a mosque you usually go to," Omar said in Arabic.

"Yes, maybe," the bus boy replied in Arabic.

"I should tell you it's Sunni if that makes a difference to you," Omar said in Arabic.

Sensing dejection on the bus boy's face, Joe quickly said in Arabic, "I'm Shia too, and he's my best friend. We don't have religious differences here like in Lebanon." *OK, so I told a little lie,* Joe thought. *Allah will forgive me.*

"We're all followers of the Prophet," Omar said in Arabic. "All're welcome. I'm an Islamic imam, not a Sunni imam, but I did want you to know if you choose to pray and maybe do other things with us. I'm Omar, Omar Abu Deeb."

"Haitham Haidar, Timo," he said, then continued asking Joe in Arabic, "What do you do?"

"I'm a lawyer," he replied in Arabic. "Yusef Shaito."

Timo smiled and said in Arabic, "I was studying law at the Lebanese University."

Joe said in Arabic. "Maybe continue studying here. We need more lawyers with Middle Eastern backgrounds."

"That'd be a dream," Timo replied in Arabic, "but I need more money. I'd better not stay and talk any longer; I've got other tables. I'll send the waiter. Please come back."

Soon they paid and left, first giving a generous tip for Timo as well as for the waiter.

CHAPTER 10

Outside on a still winter night, wearing only jackets and scarves, Omar said, "Let's walk. It's not that cold."

"OK," Joe agreed. "We can go down Beach Street to Connecticut; take a shortcut."

"Timo's nice," Omar said as they walked, "attractive too. Bet the women customers like him. It's good to hear educated Lebanese speak Arabic, cultured and refined; easy to understand. Lebanese speak the best Arabic."

Joe said, "It's people like him the old farts in Dearborn don't know or don't care about. They're so hung up on the U.S. being anti-Hizbollah or anti-Shia they don't see situations where the U.S. is helping Shia also. Here's a decent guy. Family killed. Probably escaped to Cyprus and couldn't go back to Lebanon. Western countries parcel out refugees, so the U.S. took him."

"Couldn't go back to Lebanon? Why?" Omar asked.

"Likely persecuted by Hizbollah," Joe answered.

"What for? Was he helping the Israelis?" Omar asked.

"That's absolutely unthinkable," Joe replied. "He most likely helped the Lebanese Army. It remained neutral, but did try to maintain order. In the process they did things to piss off Hizbollah. If he was involved, he may have been targeted. If he was a law student, he probably wasn't a Hizbollah supporter. Doesn't mean he's anti-Hizbollah."

"Oh, I see," Omar commented.

"I hear things back home," Joe added. "When I see news or read the papers, I sometimes piece things together. I don't want to get started on what I think about the U.S. attitude towards Israel. Still doesn't mean it's anti-Islam or anti-Shia."

"For sure," Omar said. "I've been cautious saying things too. The U.S. has done a lot to support Muslims around the world. Look at Bosnia. Many politicians are too one-sided in support of Israel, but I don't want to start on that topic either."

They turned on Beach, a quiet residential street, and Joe said, "It's private here; maybe you can tell me about what you did for the FBI. When I worked with Gabe and others, it was a plea bargain for two young guys who they needed to get out of a secret location. I heard an FBI resource was driving to North Carolina for them. Must've been you."

"That was me," Omar admitted and explained his involvement with the FBI and Gabe Andreotti.

"Both seemed pretty decent guys who were exploited by the imam you mentioned," Joe said.

"Yes, they were," Omar confirmed. "Both from good families, poor, not well educated, but decent people who cared for them and they cared for their families. I never met the guys there, but I did meet them later."

"Later? How? They went to prison," Joe stated. "Wait. You were in Duluth and they went to prison in Duluth. The FBI had you watch them in Duluth?"

"No, no, no!" Omar replied. "I already had the job in Duluth before I knew they were sent there. When I found out there were Muslim prisoners, I got myself assigned as Islamic chaplain for the federal prison and met them there. I was really surprised it was the same two guys from Lackawanna."

"Federal prisons assign Islamic chaplains?" Joe asked.

"I had to apply," Omar explained, then described meeting them in prison and after their release their participating in the mosque where he was imam.

"Gee, what coincidences," Joe said. "I saw them a second time when I was at their trial in Roanoke. That's an interesting story, but not for now."

"Getting them out of that place wasn't the reason I was in Lackawanna," Omar said. He explained he was sent there to investigate a suspected al Qaeda cell run by a self-designated imam who also smuggled cigarettes and gasoline.

Joe replied, "Plenty of that going on in Dearborn, mostly to raise money to support Hizbollah. How'd you get involved with the FBI?"

"I did a couple of small jobs for them when I was in the Islamic studies program at Minnesota," Omar answered. "Nothing clandestine or under cover, although we kept it quiet. Mostly giving information about things in Yemen, reading documents, and giving my view on what they meant."

"How'd they contact you in the first place?" Joe asked.

"Still don't know," Omar replied. "Can only speculate. They must keep tabs on people in Islamic studies programs because they might be potential risks and potential benefits. I strongly suspect when I was admitted, there was a background check to find out my connections back home. After nine-eleven, I'm sure all students from sensitive countries are checked out. When they discovered al Qaeda killed my family and I have strong anti–al Qaeda views, they may have tested me to see how reliable I am. When this issue came up involving Yemenis, I was a natural."

"There must have been something in it for you, other than just hating al Qaeda," Joe commented.

"Yes, they paid me well," Omar admitted. "This assignment came when things were the most desperate financially and I thought I might not make it. At the risk of being overly pious, and I know that's my line, this's what Islam's about: Surrender and Allah provides. Mohammed also paid me. We're almost home now. There's that gay bookstore Brad and Jason talked about. What say we wait and I tell you more at home when we're relaxed over coffee."

Soon they were sitting in their living room sipping Lebanese coffee. Omar explained he'd been sent to Lackawanna because Mohammed, the would-be imam, needed someone to work in his side businesses. When he was induced to leave the country, Omar wound-up the businesses and paid himself generously with FBI guidance and blessing.

"I can see having someone to talk to would help," Joe said. "That's why I'm glad we found each other. I feel I can talk to you about anything and everything, except professional secrets at work. Maybe Allah brought us together."

"Maybe," Omar said with a big smile.

"Maybe your piety's rubbing off on me," Joe chuckled. Maybe it's time to let our minds rest. I wonder what's on television we can numb our minds with?"

CHAPTER 11

Thursday, February 28, 2008
Fort Meade, Maryland, USA

About an hour after arriving at work, Frank bounded up the stairs to the office of Air Force Colonel Edward Ross, Deputy Associate Director of the NSA, thinking, *What could he want me for?* He saluted and said, "You want to see me, Sir."

Colonel Ross returned the salute and remained seated, saying, "Yes, Major. Your security detail is harassing people. I want it to stop."

"Harassing, Sir?" Frank said.

"Yes, harassing," Colonel Ross repeated. "Thorough inspections; slowing people down. Big crowds backed up with people waiting outside in the cold."

"Sir, with all due respect," Frank stated. "Those security precautions are indicated by the circumstances."

"What the hell circumstances do you mean?" he demanded. "No circumstances require that kind of security."

"Sir," Frank continued, "we received word of a security threat to this installation and we're responding."

"Word from where?" Colonel Ross asked.

"From the FBI, Sir," Frank answered. *Thank goodness for the FBI visit so I don't have to lie. The bastard hasn't even asked me to sit.*

"When did the FBI tell you this?" Colonel Ross demanded. "I sure the hell haven't been notified."

"Last week, Sir," Frank replied. "On Wednesday an agent came to see me and Sergeant Beasley."

"That far back," Colonel Ross said forcefully. "Any threat would be gone by now. I want you to back off."

"We haven't been notified it's gone," Frank replied.

"Major, if you knew anything about your job," Colonel Ross almost screamed, "you'd know threats come and go. This one has gone if there was one in the first place."

"I've not heard that from the FBI or other authority," Frank said.

"Well, you're hearing it from me now, Major," Colonel Ross said, his anger increasing. "I'm telling you to reduce security back to what it was so people don't get upset."

"With all due respect, Sir," Frank began, "I'm the one who's in charge of security here, and it's me who'll be held responsible if anything serious happens."

Colonel Ross's face became red as he said, "That's an order, Major!"

Frank's steely resolve increased as he responded, "I will honor that order only if it is in writing and only after I have cleared it through the Marine Corps and the IG."

Colonel Ross's anger was so strong he could barely shout, "Major, you forget you are here on borrowed time, and not under the best circumstances. I didn't want you here in the first place, but you were forced on us."

"I'm not aware of any borrowed time, Sir," Frank said calmly. "I know my job and I'm doing it the way I know best. If someone wants to get rid of me, I'm prepared to fight publicly all the way. Now if there's nothing else, I'll go."

He saluted again and walked out, leaving Colonel Ross with anger so intense his face turned from red to white.

Frank walked to his office, palms sweating, knees weak, almost dizzy, thinking, *Here we go again. Okinawa all over. Only now I don't give a shit about my career, but I do care about my personal integrity.*

In his office, he quickly located the phone number for Colonel Otis Granger with the DoDIG, called, and said, "Good morning, Sir. This is Major Frank Reynolds; we met at a meeting at Wright-Patterson."

(pause)

"An issue has come up that I'd report to the IG under any circumstances," he began. "Because I know who you are, I thought it best to make initial contact with you."

(pause)

"Perhaps it's best not to discuss on the telephone unless we go to secure phones," he continued. "I'll come to your office to discuss it in person, and soon. It's urgent. I could come this afternoon if necessary. Anytime tomorrow also."

(pause)

"OK, ten tomorrow," he confirmed.

(pause)

He recounted to Sergeant Beasley the session with Colonel Ross and conversation with Colonel Granger, concluding, "I'll keep you out of this. I'll tell him I'm going against your advice by disregarding Colonel Ross's order. I'll give a written order to increase security so you and the troops will be protected."

Sergeant Beasley replied, "That's not necessary, Sir. I'm not advising you to follow Colonel Ross's order. It seems you're asking me in a backhanded way what my advice is. My advice is to keep doing what we've been doing, no matter what Colonel Ross says. He's not in our chain of command, and even if he were, his order is inappropriate. You did damned good to stand up to him like that."

"Thanks," Frank said. "I can still give a written order."

Sergeant Beasley replied, "If it makes you feel better, go ahead. I don't need a written order. If I may say so, Sir, you've really earned my respect over this one. You must've had some experience taking care of yourself and your troops."

"Let's just say that I've had to deal with some nasty business a couple of times before," Frank said.

Sergeant Beasley said, "On behalf of the troops, we appreciate it."

CHAPTER 12

Friday, February 29, 2008
Arlington, Virginia, USA

After a tedious drive on a drizzly winter morning through Washington area traffic, Frank finally found Colonel Granger's office in the labyrinths of the massive Pentagon, saluted, and said, "Good morning, Sir. Thank you for seeing me on short notice."

Colonel Granger was distinguished, in his late forties and wearing the business-suit-type uniform as would be expected of a senior military executive. At five feet ten, he reflected the confidence of a military officer at the pinnacle of power, his career still in ascendency.

Frank told details of the FBI visit and Colonel Ross's angry tirade, adding that Sergeant Beasley agreed they should maintain security at the current level.

"That is indeed serious," Colonel Granger agreed.

"There's more to it than that," Frank added. "I discovered this threat before the FBI came to visit me. Perhaps you remember you said the DIA wants to know more about homosexuality and how it affects the intelligence activities of the DoD."

Colonel Granger replied, "Major, you know as well as I do there was another reason behind that comment, and you're not expected to actively pursue this assignment."

Frank thought, *If I agree with him, that'd be "telling."*

"I took it seriously," Frank replied. "The information first came from gay bar conversations, but I wasn't in the gay bar. The persons who told me were. I didn't meet them in gay bars; I had class with one and from there met others. It doesn't take much imagination that one of the persons is gay and went to a gay bar for that reason. Some of the persons involved are in sensitive positions, so right now I'd prefer not to tell names and places. The FBI knows and has talked to them. The DIA may very well want to investigate; and I would, of course, tell details to your investigators. Perhaps you understand."

"Yes, I understand," Colonel Granger replied. "I don't have a need to know, and it wouldn't help for me to have the information and relay it to someone else. Is there something else you want to tell me right now?"

Frank replied, "No, but I'll answer any questions."

"I have enough for right now," Colonel Granger said. "I'm sure you understand I need to check with others and maybe the FBI. Certainly this is urgent; I'll get onto it right away. Thanks for bringing it to my attention."

"What about Colonel Ross's order to decrease the security level?" Frank asked.

"Let's wait and see if he does issue an order in writing; then you can bring it to me like you told him you would," Colonel Granger answered. "Right this moment, the less said the better. I agree it's best to err on the side of caution until we know more, and I agree with your sergeant. These experienced master sergeants are some of the best resources we have; you know that."

"Yes, Sir," Frank said standing. "Thanks for the time."

He started to salute, but Colonel Granger said, "At ease. I'm sure we'll be in contact again."

When Frank left, Colonel Granger called his administrative assistant, saying, "Please call Rosie Jordan, that's Roosevelt Jordan, Chief of Operations of the FBI Operations Technology Center at Quantico."

While he waited, Colonel Granger reflected on a task force in summer of 2006 involving the DIA, CIA, and FBI that Rosie Jordan headed: *Frank Reynolds again. That Marine colonel was probably right; he may be accident prone. He certainly seems drawn to situations not of his own making in which he has to defend the interests of the country and save his own ass at the same time. He went too far last time, but it sure saved a huge public embarrassment and panic over our security vulnerability. We need more like him. Too bad he's gay, or I presume he is. He was clever in deflecting my comment. If he'd agreed with me, that could be "telling."*

The phone rang; he said, "Hello, Rosie. How're things at your place? It's been a year and a half since we worked on that task force."

(pause)

"One of the characters has resurfaced, this time not for anything he's done," Colonel Granger said and gave a summary of his conversation with Frank.

(pause)

"I agree," Colonel Granger said. "I hope it doesn't come to a task force, but if it does, we're prepared."

(pause)

"I should give Rhonda a heads-up," Colonel Granger added. "Maybe we won't need her, but Rhonda's good. Doesn't hurt to inform her."

(pause)

"Likewise," Colonel Granger said, "I wish it were under better circumstances. Have a good day."

Colonel Granger hung up, reflecting on Dr. Rhonda Philips, political and international affairs expert and liaison for the DIA, who was the driving force in the last task force. *If this develops into something, it'll be good to have Rhonda involved from the beginning. She's one of the under-appreciated assets in this organization.*

CHAPTER 13

Friday, February 29, 2008
Lafayette, Virginia, USA

Just before bedtime, Shane Roberts donned a heavy jacket to walk the family's German-shepherd–Labrador-mix dog on a cold, clear mid-winter night. In his late thirties, he was five feet ten, had medium brown hair and green-blue eyes, typical of Scot-Irish who settled in the Appalachian mountain and valley region of Virginia over two centuries ago. A muscular build reflected several years of heavy construction work.

Roberts's house in Lafayette, Virginia, actually next
door to the Hammouds's house on page 9

Within moments, the dog began barking, straining at the leash, which Shane pulled firmly as he said, "Hush, Dodi."

When the dog continued to strain and bark, Shane, eyes now accustomed to the dark, saw in the moonlight a figure walking, almost running, around the corner of the neighboring house. He also saw taillights of a car driving to the dead end of the narrow street where a car could turn around.

His wife, Velma, came to the door dressed only in a long-sleeved shirt-blouse and pants and called, "Make her stop barkin' or you'll disturb the whole neighborhood."

She was tall, only about an inch shorter than Shane, slender, with longish medium brown hair almost to her shoulders, eyes more blue than green, also reflecting "mountain and valley" heritage. She was two years younger than Shane in her mid-thirties.

He shouted, "Bring my shotgun and call 911. There's a prowler at the Hammouds's house."

He loosened his grip on the leash, allowing the dog to lead. Velma returned quickly, handed Shane a shotgun, and rushed to the warmth of the house to telephone.

Taking care not to trip with the shotgun, he walked briskly approaching the neighboring house when a figure, visible as a husky young man about five-eleven with a shabby winter coat, came trotting quickly around the corner of the house.

Shane pointed the shotgun at him, released the dog, which jumped on the man and barked, and said, "Hold it right there. Get down on the ground, hands behind your head."

He sat and started to lie on his back.

"On your belly," Shane said.

He turned over and Shane put his foot on his back, saying, "Stay that way 'til the sheriff gets here."

The car that had driven by moments ago came back and stopped in front of the open area between the two houses. In the street light it could be seen as a dull, dark, older Saturn. At the same moment, a loud explosion was heard from the back of the house.

"Serves you right, you fuckin' A-rab assholes," the driver screamed. "You bomb us, we bomb you."

"Yeah, you mother-fuckin' A-rabs," a voice shouted from the passenger side. "There's more of this if you don't get outta here. Don't want no fuckin' A-rabs 'round here."

Velma Roberts, now wearing a winter jacket, was standing on the porch, shouting, "Shane? You OK?"

Another explosion was heard, and a red-orange-yellow glow came from the back of the neighboring house.

"Call 911 for the fire department," Shane screamed at Velma. "I'm goin' after 'em."

He took his foot off the man's back, let go of the leash while the dog snarled, saying, "One move and she attacks."

Shane ran as quickly as he dared to the car and heard the driver shout, "Kyle, c'm on. Gotta go *now!*" The young man on the ground screamed, "Get the hell away; don't wait for me."

Shane approached the car, holding the shotgun so it would be visible, and said, "Get out and hold your hands up."

At that moment, a law enforcement vehicle with blinking lights turned onto the street, distracting Shane momentarily. The Saturn quickly sped away, but not so fast he couldn't see the license plate. He rushed back to the husky man cowering on the ground with the dog snarling, and continued to repeat the plate number over and over.

Velma said loudly, "Fire truck's on the way."

Shane shouted, "Get a pencil and paper, quick!" and kept repeating the license plate number over and over.

Roula and Fatima Hammoud with Abou Nidal rushed out the front door of their house. Fatima was wearing pajamas and house slippers and was covered by a winter coat, frightened and crying, clinging to her mother. Roula wore a basic house dress covered with a winter coat. Her hair was uncovered because she had taken off her usual headscarf in preparation for bed. Her younger years growing up in the refugee camp taught her not to show outward expressions of emotion. Abou Nidal likewise was stoic, wearing work clothes and a winter coat.

Velma returned and heard Shane shout, "YPR 8468; write it down."

She wrote quickly and, seeing Roula and Fatima, rushed to them and said, "Come inside out of the cold," and quickly led the dog, Roula, and Fatima inside.

Shane, seeing Abou Nidal, called out, "Fire truck's on the way. Where's Nassar?"

"Turning on water," Abou Nidal answered and ran towards the back of the house.

The Montgomery County deputy sheriff swerved to miss the Saturn speeding away, parked, got out, and saw two men in the dim light, one with a shotgun, the other running towards the back of the house. Deputy Darrell Williams followed. He wore a tan uniform covered by a heavy leather jacket. He had a slightly husky build and stood about five feet ten, with closely cropped medium brown hair.

"What's goin' on?" he asked. "Got a call 'bout a disturbance."

"Saw this here guy prowlin' 'round the neighbors' house," Shane began. "He run back this way and I stopped him and made him get down on the ground. There was a loud explosion, two of 'em, and now somethin's on fire."

"Stand up and put your hands up," the deputy said. "Oh, you. What kind of trouble you got yourself into now?"

"Ain't sayin' nothin'," Kyle replied.

"Better see what's goin' on in back," Deputy Williams said. "You walk in front of me; if you think you're going to bolt and run, you know I got a pistol."

They saw Nassar holding a garden hose as if trying to coax water from the frozen tap.

"Fire truck's on its way," Deputy Williams said, then exclaimed, "Mr. Hammoud. This where you live? What's happenin'?"

"Heard a loud noise," Nassar said. "Then another and saw flames through the window. Looks like the gasoline can caught fire in the shed."

"Any others in the house?" Deputy Williams asked.

"No," Nassar answered.

"They're over at my place," Shane added.

Kyle was trying to get away in the confusion, but Deputy Williams clamped his hands on Kyle's shoulder roughly, grabbed his arms, attached handcuffs, and then locked him in the cruiser. The fire crew quickly extinguished the fire. In the dim light, remnants of dynamite sticks were seen next to a gaping hole.

"Prob'ly need to come investigate once it gets daylight," Deputy Williams said. "Can't do much in the dark. Don't think we need to keep someone here to secure the evidence; looks like we got the guy."

"He had guys helpin' him," Shane said. "Two in an old beat-up Saturn. Wife's got the license plate wrote down."

"Oh, them," the deputy said. "Sorry this happened to you, Mr. Hammoud. Any idea why someone'd do this?"

"No," Nassar replied. "Wait; old Saturn, beat up, you say? I towed one to my garage last fall when it broke down on the interstate. Made repairs and the guys who got it drove away without paying. Had to call your department to get them and make them pay. Can't see why they'd want to do something like this over it."

Shane handed a piece of paper to Deputy Williams who said, "Better go radio this plate right away. Maybe you'd like to go indoors where it's warm. I'll come find you."

"OK," Nassar replied and led them into the house.

Soon, Deputy Williams came in and said, "Can't stay long 'cause it's too cold to leave him sittin' in the cruiser. Anything else to add you haven't told me so far?"

"I heard 'em shoutin' things from the car," Shane said.

"What's that?" Deputy Williams asked.

"Don't rightly like to say in front of Mr. Hammoud here, but guess I ought to," Shane said.

"Yeah, good idea," Deputy Williams replied.

"One of 'em said, 'Serves you right, you blank A-rabs; we bomb you 'cause you bomb us," Shane said. "Th' other one said, 'Get out, you A-rab blank; don't want you here."

"I guess I know what you mean with them blanks," Deputy Williams said. "You might be called upon to say the exact words sometime. Anyone else hear 'em?"

"My wife might've," Shane answered. "She was standin' on the porch. Want me to go ask her?"

"Not right this moment," Deputy Williams answered. "Maybe ask her later and call me if she remembers."

"Anything else?" Deputy Williams asked. "Gotta get back to the car. Guys like him're too damned quick to claim mistreatment, 'specially if I leave'm too long in the cold. Don't want to cut you short, though."

"Can't think of nothin'," Shane said.

"You, Mr. Hammoud?" Deputy Williams asked. "Or you?" he looked to Abou Nidal.

Both answered, "No."

Deputy Williams stood and said, "Someone from the Sheriff's Department might be back to talk to you for more details. State Police and State Fire Marshall too, maybe."

Shane said, "Better be goin', too."

Nassar said, "I'll get my wife and daughter."

At the Roberts's house, Roula stood and said in halting English, "I get Fatima now."

"Let her stay here," Velma said. "She's in bed sound asleep with Amelia; pity to wake her. We can take her home in the morning."

Roula looked at Nassar.

Shane, realizing Roula expected her husband to decide, added, "We'd be pleased t' have her here rest of th' night. Kids can get pretty cranky if they're woke up."

Nassar said, "Thank you. It's been upsetting, and if she's asleep, we can leave her here."

177

Velma helped Roula with her coat, saying, "We're so sorry this had to happen to you. See you in the morning."

Shane shook Nassar's hand and said, "Again, sorry. We'll see you tomorrow."

When Roula and Nassar had gone, Shane said, "I'd better take Dodi out to do her business. She's pretty bad off if she's been holdin' it this long. Sheriff's deputy wants to know if you heard somethin' from the guys in the car when you was on the porch."

"Yes, heard ev'ry word," Velma replied, "but don't repeat those kinds of words, not even to you."

"I don't like repeatin' 'em to you, neither," Shane said, "but you'd better write 'em down. Somethin' tells me we might have to tell someone official like. I'm goin' to write down what I heard, when I get back from walking her."

CHAPTER 14

After nightly news on television, Joe and Omar headed for their bedrooms. Suddenly they heard a loud noise.

Joe said, "Sounds like an explosion."

Hearing sirens and seeing flashing lights of fire engines and ambulances out the window, Omar said, "It looks like over by 21st and R."

Joe shouted, "How could I have been so stupid!"

"Huh?" Omar asked.

Joe replied, "I focused on explosives to bomb the NSA. He wanted them to set off in the bar."

"Oh, shit!" Omar exclaimed.

"Remember Frank and Paco're going there tonight with Brad and Jason," Joe said putting on his winter coat.

Both rushed to the scene bundled for the clear cold night and were confronted by a policeman who said, "Sorry, you can't come any closer."

Friends of ours were in there," Joe said. "We want to get as close as we can to find out how they are."

"I'm clergy, in case I can help," Omar added hastily.

"Oh, yeah," the policeman said cynically. To Joe, "And who are you, the church secretary?"

"No," Joe answered indignantly. "I'm a lawyer."

"Oh, yeah," the policeman continued. "You got 'em covered both ways. One saves their souls while the other gets their money and turns it over to the church."

Joe retorted, "I work for a major U.S. government agency; I'm not in private practice. My friend here is an imam at the Islamic Center."

The policeman asked, "What're you doing here?"

"I'm an Islamic clergyman," Omar said assertively. "I suspect not many Muslims were inside, but I thought I'd inform you I'm clergy as a courtesy, in case I can help."

Joe said, "I hope you're not jumping to conclusions and engaging in ethnic profiling. We're law abiding citizens who respect law and order. We expect to *cooperate* with the police." *Omar's not a citizen, but oh well.*

The policeman said, "Step aside. We'll get you if we need you."

They moved as close as they could to the entrance, craning in the dim light to see who was being brought out. Joe noticed someone led by an EMT to a police car with serious cuts and gashes all over his face, scalp, and hands; his clothes were blood-soaked.

"That's Chad, the bartender," Joe half-shouted. He saw two male EMTs walking down the steps balancing a stretcher, trying to keep it level, with a large, tall, husky man walking behind and shouted, "That's Paco!"

Omar exclaimed, "That's Frank!"

They moved closer, watching EMTs load Frank's stretcher into the ambulance. Paco, limping and with cuts on his face and neck, attempted to climb in.

One of the EMTs said out of Omar's and Joe's earshot, "Sorry, we're using ambulances for those who can't walk."

"He's my friend; I've got to be with him. He needs me and wants me," Paco pleaded.

"Sorry," the EMT said. "We make exceptions sometimes for close relatives, but that's not you."

"But I'm a nurse; I can help," Paco pleaded.

The other EMT said, "Hey, man, I understand; I have a boyfriend too, but rules are rules. Besides we really need the space for those who're badly injured. If you're a nurse, maybe give first aid to some others; we're shorthanded."

Paco in a daze limped away; a female police officer said, "Come with me." Leading him to the car where Chad was waiting, she said to the driver, "Maybe take these two to the emergency room. They might treat them now before seriously injured get there."

Joe and Omar saw a tallish young man with a long ponytail holding his right arm and following a stretcher.

"That's Jason," Joe shouted.

"And that's Brad," Omar said, seeing Brad with a large gash running down the side of his head and face.

Jason, too, attempted to climb into the ambulance and the EMT whispered into his ear.

He dejectedly said, "OK," and walked away in a daze.

The female police officer saw him and directed him to the car with Chad and Paco.

Jason said to Paco, "You can't go with Frank either."

Paco muttered, "No."

The car and ambulance with sirens blaring drove away.

Joe suddenly broke through the police line rushing to ask, "Where're you taking them?"

"DC General," she replied, half shouting.

Joe quickly ran back to Omar and said, "Come on, we're going to chase ambulances."

As they walked away, he said, "Down at the corner on Massachusetts Avenue. Hopefully we can get a cab. Hospital's straight down Massachusetts by the river."

They continued half running, hearing the sirens.

CHAPTER 15

Saturday, March 1, 2008
Arlington, Virginia, USA

About 1 a.m., Ahmed woke from dozing, thinking, *Should've called by now. Wonder if it went off. I'll Check the radio.*

At the end of reports on upcoming primary elections in Texas and Ohio on a 24-hour news station, he heard, "Now breaking news: An explosion occurred in one of Washington's popular gay bars in the DuPont Circle area. We go to the scene."

Another voice said, "Reporting live on the scene at Rory's, one of Washington's popular gay bars: Emergency crews have taken injured to hospitals. The number of deaths and injuries are not known. Fire crews put out a small blaze, and no additional persons were found inside. Officials have not determined the cause of the explosion. Preliminary information points to a bomb blast. Back to you."

The original voice said, "Sources at DC General Hospital indicate numerous injured were taken to the emergency room. Hospital spokespersons will not speculate on the number of injured or dead nor the extent of injuries. Stay tuned for additional news updates as they occur...."

It went off, he said to himself. *So why didn't he return?*

"President Hugo Chavez of Venezuela issued another statement condemning the U.S. government for support of the Colombian government..." the radio continued.

That Chavez guy is really sticking it to the U.S. Good for him. Damn this fucking country, he thought.

He tried to call Marwan, and then thought, *Damn, no answer. It's ringing though. He didn't turn it off after he sent the signal to the bomb. Where the hell is he? We've gotta be at the airport before 6:00.*

He turned off the radio, set the telephone alarm, and drifted into fitful sleep.

At 4 a.m. he fumbled to turn off the alarm, thinking, *Damn, still not here. Be freshly shaved, dress nice, they said. Don't draw attention to yourself.*

He turned on the radio, hearing, "... President Hugo Chavez of Venezuela announced support in the form of oil, gas, and economic aid to Cuba. In a long speech to supporters, he rallied the support of fellow democratically elected socialists in Bolivia, Ecuador, and Nicaragua to form an alliance against imperialist aggression of the United States. He also announced he would supply gasoline, fuel oil, and other petroleum products to the Gaza strip to support Hamas, who he called valiant freedom fighters and champions of socialism seeking to liberate the Palestinian people from Israeli terror supported of imperialist allies...."

What? Support Hamas and Palestinians, he thought. *At least someone knows what the U.S. and all its gays are doing to us. Well we got rid of a few gays.*

"... So far there are no reported deaths from the explosion at Rory's gay bar in the DuPont circle area shortly before midnight last night," the radio voice continued. "Investigators report traces of explosive material were found at the site, confirming the blast was deliberately set. Police and hospital personnel decline further comment.... It is now only three days from primary elections in Texas and Ohio that are do or die for Hillary Clinton...."

What the hell could've happened to him? Ahmed asked himself as he went to shower. *Did it go off before it was supposed to? Instructions are if anything happens to one of us, the other has to leave the country. If both of us get caught, the whole group's in trouble.*

In the shower, he went over arrangements: *Drive to BWI Airport. Park in long-term parking; an abandoned car won't be noticed as soon there. Separate tickets Baltimore to Toronto and Toronto to Manchester on different airlines. Manchester, not London; not as much attention from immigration there. Address in Liverpool to put on British immigration form.*

Wait. Why do I have to go to fuckin' England? They're fucked up as much as this country. Blair and Bush are buddies, and Arabs there are treated like shit too. England fucked us over when they divided Palestine. They even taught us that in crappy East Montgomery High School.

I know where I'll go, and I'm not going to tell Abdulmalik. Hope I can remember how Marwan showed me to look up flight schedules. Hope they'll let me pay for the ticket by cash in Toronto. Got lots from Abdulmalik.

After shaving and dressing, he thought as he sat at the computer, *Yeah, there's a flight.*

He instinctively reached for his cell phone but tossed it aside, thinking, *Don't need this where I'm going.*

He put on his heavy coat and scarf, got his luggage, locked the door of the apartment out of habit, and drove to BWI Airport.

CHAPTER 16

Saturday, March 1, 2008
Washington, DC, USA

Joe and Omar sat wearily in the emergency room waiting area of DC General Hospital amid the dull roar from the commotion inside and traffic in and out. When not nodding off to sleep, Omar recited the sura of healing in Arabic.

Several minutes later, Paco walked out with a crutch, a cast on his foot, and bandages on his face and neck and blurted out, "What're you two doing here?"

"Waiting to find out about you guys," Joe replied. "We rushed to the bar when we heard the blast, saw you and Frank, and Brad and Jason, and came here. How are you?"

"Sprains, bruises, and superficial cuts," Paco answered.

"How's Frank?" Omar asked.

"Pretty bad," Paco replied glumly. "Nothing life threatening; broken ribs and thigh bone. Concussion. He'll be in intensive care at least through tomorrow."

"Do you know about Brad and Jason?" Joe asked.

Paco replied, "Brad's pretty bad. He'll be in the hospital a while. Jason's like me, cuts and bruises and a broken arm. He should be out soon."

A distant voice said, "The Muslim chaplain here yet?"

Another voice answered, "No, can't reach him."

Omar turned towards the reception desk and asked the others, "You hear that about a Muslim chaplain?"

Joe replied, "No. Wasn't paying attention."

Omar said. "I'm going to ask." To the receptionist, "Did I hear something about a Muslim chaplain?"

She replied, "The nurse asked for one. Why?"

"I'm an imam, Omar replied. "Maybe I could help."

"You're a what?" she asked skeptically.

"An imam." he answered. "A Muslim clergyman." Realizing his appearance and a full day's growth of a dark beard, he added, "I look scruffy. I came here when some friends were brought here; you can see one over there. I just thought I might help; not trying to push myself on you."

"Oh, OK," she said. Into the phone, "Aleeta, I think I have someone for you. This gentleman says he's an ee-mom, like a Muslim clergyman."

The nurse came and said to Omar, "We have a man who's badly injured and likely won't live. We think he's Muslim. We want someone to do what's supposed to be done before he dies."

Omar thought: *Never been around someone dying, but think I know what to do.* "Yes, there's a ritual for someone dying," he said. "What makes you think he's Muslim?"

"He had a tiny book on a bracelet that might be like a bible," she said; "also beads on a bracelet. We thought he's Catholic but staff who're Catholic said not a Catholic rosary."

"That's a moushaf, miniature Q'ran," Omar said. "Good Muslim men carry them and lots carry prayer beads."

Seems to be genuine if he can explain things, she thought, and said, "Can you come quick? We don't know how much longer he'll live; we're surprised he lived this long."

Omar gulped, thinking, *Maybe Joe'll go with me.* "I'll go with you now," he said, "but let me ask my friend to come with me. It should be done with two Muslim men if possible." *Allah will forgive me for wanting moral support. I've heard usually there's more than one family member. Doesn't have to be an imam.* He asked Joe, "Could you come with me? Someone's dying and they need someone to do the proper Islamic things. I've never done this before."

Joe thought, *I've never done anything like this either. Can I handle it? Omar's a special friend. I can't let him down.*

Omar said to Paco, "We need to go for a while. A Muslim man is dying and needs someone to recite the special verses. It's sort of like last rites for Catholics."

"Every religion has its last rites or whatever they call them," Paco replied. "I remember what it was like first time I was with someone who died. Glad someone was with me. Go ahead. I'm not going anywhere as long as Frank's in the ER."

In the treatment area, Omar and Joe put on sterile robes, gloves, and masks and were led to a screened-off area. The man was covered with sheets and blankets through which blood was soaking. He was unconscious, his breathing faint.

Joe turned even more pale and whispered to Omar, "That's him; the guy I talked to in the bar."

The nurse asked, "Do you want me to leave?"

"You can stay if you like," Omar replied. "He's supposed to be on his right side while I recite verses from the Q'ran into his left ear."

The nurse said, "That's the side that's badly injured."

Omar said, "My friend'll lift his shoulder just a little and we'll turn his head to whisper into his left ear." He whispered in English, "There is no God but Allah...." He continued in Arabic, reciting Sura 36, "... God gives life to the dead and records that which they have forwarded and that which they have left behind... And the trumpet will be blown and men will slide forth out of their tombs to their Lord."

Omar lifted his head, nodded to Joe to remove his hand, and said to the nurse, "Do you know anything about his family?"

"We turned personal things over to the office; they're in charge of notifying family," the nurse replied.

Omar said, "I could contact his family if you like. Might be better coming from an imam. If he's dying, maybe best to wait until the end."

"I'll tell the office you're willing to contact family," she said. "You around a while?"

"I'll be here as long as necessary," Omar answered.

"I'll have someone find you in the waiting room," she said. "Let me show you the way back out."

In the waiting area, they saw Jason next to Paco, his arm in a splint and sling, and bandages on his face.

He smiled faintly, greeting Joe and Omar. "Thanks for coming to check on us, but you don't look so good either."

"Omar just recited words from the Q'ran to a guy who's dying," Joe said. "It's the guy from the bar. I can't believe I was so stupid. It's my fault you're hurt like this."

"Lighten up," Omar said, his hand on Joe's shoulder.

"Yeah," Jason added. "No way you could've known."

"I should have," Joe continued. "I was so focused on the NSA, I missed signals about bombing the bar. A good lawyer picks up on those things."

"Hey, man, no one's perfect," Paco added. "Beating up on yourself isn't going to make anything better."

"Thanks," Joe replied. "I still feel like shit."

Omar asked, "What's the latest on Brad and Frank? What'll you two do now?"

"They won't tell me anything," Jason said dejectedly.

"I haven't gone back to see if I can get word on Frank either," Paco answered. "I'm going to stay here until I hear something. Probably rest of the night and morning."

"That's what I intend to do too," Jason said. "Need to move my car too. Not good to leave it there all night."

Paco added, "Frank has his car parked too. Better move it, but don't want to be too far away from the hospital."

"Why don't you go to our place," Omar said. "I need to stay; promised I'd stay until he passes. You go too, habibi."

"Don't you need me when you notify family?" Joe said.

"It's always good to have your support," Omar replied, "but I can handle it alone. Have to get used to things like this. Besides, it may be a good idea if one of us gets some sleep. Maybe best if it's you."

Joe replied. "OK. I should call that FBI guy from home when he'd be awake. Come to our place; we can take a cab. I can help with cars; neither of you's in a position to drive."

"You can sleep in my bed," Omar said.

"I don't have Frank's car keys," Paco said. "Need to lean on the nurses to get them and maybe they can give me an update." Eventually he returned with car keys saying, "Sorry it took so long. Really had to convince them and it took ages to find them. No real change in Frank or Brad. For sure they're not going to get out of intensive care for several hours, maybe a couple of days. We might as well get some sleep. Thanks for the offer of the bed."

While Joe put on his coat, Jason instinctively started looking for his and said, "Damn, where're our coats?"

Paco replied glumly, "Back hanging in what's left of that bar. I'll see if I can get blankets or something."

Omar gave Joe three Arab kisses saying, "Thanks for your support, habibi." He gave three kisses to Jason and Paco saying, "Take care of yourselves."

A few hours later, a nurse gently woke Omar, saying, "Please come this way. We found this number in his personal belongings. You can use that phone over there."

189

CHAPTER 17

Saturday, March 1, 2008
Fort Meade, Maryland, USA

On a cold overcast morning, U.S. Marine Corps Corporals Tyler Adams, Michael Kleinberg, and Daniel Morales worked the NSA security check point, Corporal Morales none too pleased to be recently assigned to early Saturday morning. Corporals Adams and Kleinberg were observing a slow but steady stream of persons who worked weekend shifts passing through metal detectors and watching an x-ray monitor; Corporal Morales watched for anything unusual and made detailed searches of bags.

He quietly said to Corporal Adams, "You see that guy with the dark wavy hair? He's walking funny."

"The one with baggy jeans?" Corporal Adams asked.

"Yeah," Corporal Morales said. "He walks funny, but not like he's handicapped; he's nervous. Find a reason to send him to me to examine. I'll tell Mike to look out too."

The young man put his coat and backpack on the belt for the x-ray machine, walked through without causing an alarm, and went to claim his belongings.

"Please step over here," Corporal Kleinberg said as he reached for the hand-held metal detecting wand.

"Uhhh, what?" the person asked nervously.

"Just an additional check," Corporal Kleinberg said. "Please spread your legs apart."

He ran the wand up and down the inside of his legs and thighs and thought, *Something doesn't feel like flesh or clothes*. He nodded to Corporal Morales.

Corporal Adams watching the x-ray machine whispered to Corporal Morales, "He has two cell phones."

Corporal Morales said, "Please come with me. Collect your belongings and hand them to me."

He led the young man to a sparsely furnished private examination room, saying, "Wait here. We'll examine you when another person is free. Your personal belongings will be locked in that cabinet so you can't have access to them." Outside, he said to the other two, "When one person can handle things alone, I need one of you with me."

Shortly, Corporal Kleinberg said, "I'll help Dan. I know where I felt something."

When the door was opened, the young man flung it aside, pushed past him, and ran towards the exit.

Corporal Morales shouted, "Mike, get him."

Corporals Morales and Kleinberg forcibly moved him back into the room, closed the door, and put on handcuffs saying, "We can put on leg restraints if you have any ideas of using your legs. Your jeans have to come down. You want to do it yourself, or do we have to do it for you? Don't go thinking we're going to violate your rights by looking at your private parts, so long as you have underwear on."

The man unbuckled his belt, unzipped the jeans, and pulled them down, exposing loose-fitting boxer shorts.

Corporal Morales commanded, "Turn and bend over."

The ends of wires and edges of plastic packages could be seen through leg openings of his boxers.

Corporal Morales commanded, "Stand up; stay that way. Police need to see this and take evidence properly."

"Why don't you call the police and Sarge," Corporal Kleinberg said. "Help Tye too. I can watch him."

After calling the military police for Fort Meade, he called again, saying, "Sarge, Dan Morales. Sorry to bother you. We caught someone entering with what looks like explosives," and explained briefly. "We're waiting for the MPs to collect the evidence properly."

(pause)

"See you soon," he concluded.

When two military policemen arrived, Corporal Morales said, "Thanks for coming so quickly. Could I please see your identification as MPs." After they complied, "You can hang up your jackets there. I'll call your unit." After he verified their identity, he led them into an office and said, "This looks like a terrorist plot to set off a bomb. Hopefully you understand why I need to be sure you're who you say you are. It's easy to get uniforms and ID cards."

He explained what they had done so far and led them to the examining room. With the door closed, Corporal Morales ordered the suspect to bend over. When he stood motionless, Corporal Kleinberg pushed the back of his head and shoulders. He bent over exposing wires and plastic.

One MP said, "We need to remove the evidence carefully; for that his shorts have to be down. Don't get ideas we're going to look at your private parts much less touch them. Four of us are watching and can testify we respected your privacy."

"We should make a video," the other MP said. "We can get the camera at the same time we get the evidence kit."

We should make a video too," Corporal Morales said. To his colleague, "If you want to get the camera, I'll stay." To the suspect, "You can stand up."

When they returned they started the cameras, put on rubber gloves, and said, "Pull up your pants and walk into that corner far enough that it'll be obvious on video we can't walk in front of you. I'm going to pull your shorts down far enough to get to the things you've stuck under them."

Two plastic packages about three inches square, one with wires coming out, were attached by adhesive tape immediately below the buttocks. The MP pulled them off, causing the suspect to jerk in pain.

"Let's see if there're any others," the MP continued, and moved his gloved hand between the suspect's thighs into the groin. Then he said, "Yep, just as I suspected; another one."

The suspect screamed as tape was yanked from his pubic hairs.

"Keep jerking, it'll get worse," the MP said, handing another package to Corporal Morales. "Let's see if there're more. ...That's all for now. If he has anything up his ass, we'll find it later when we can give him a proper body cavity search." To the suspect, "Get dressed. We're taking you to a police station where you'll be formally charged."

"The phones go in the evidence bag," the MP said. "Is there a anything else?"

That's all we've detected," Corporal Morales replied.

The MP stated, "He needs his jacket; it's cold."

Once the MPs and suspect were out of the building, the three Marine guard corporals looked at each other relieved; Corporal Morales said, "I need a strong cup of coffee. Actually I need something stronger. Sarge'll be here soon."

Sergeant Beasley exchanged greetings and said, "Looks like increased security paid off." To Corporal Morales, "Seems you're the most involved, Dan. You want to come in the office and tell me details?" When Corporal Morales finished, Sergeant Beasley said, "I get the idea. I'll save questions until later. I'd better hear what Mike has to say and look at the video."

After Corporal Kleinberg related details and they watched the video, Sergeant Beasley said, "Good professional job. Seems like the training paid off. You've all handled yourselves very well."

"Thanks," Corporal Kleinberg commented. "I suppose you want to talk to Tye now."

Corporal Adams told about discovering two cell phones, saying, "I probably wouldn't have noticed if Dan hadn't mentioned to me to look for something."

"Good for you that you did," Sergeant Beasley said. "All of you did good. Let's go back out."

When Corporals Morales and Kleinberg finished examining a cryptographer who had come to work on Saturday, Sergeant Beasley said, "Good job, you guys." To Corporal Morales, "You can get something to eat now, if you like. Sorry to have to say you need to stay close to your cell phone and not do anything you can't stop on short notice."

Corporal Morales gulped.

"You can go back to bed, shopping, out with your girlfriend, or whatever," Sergeant Beasley continued, "just don't go drinking or far off base until we can see how this's going to play out."

"What about tomorrow?" Corporal Morales asked.

"I doubt much'll happen on Sunday," Sergeant Beasley answered. "Go ahead with plans you have, but check with me first. If you want to do something tonight, it might be OK. Just check first. Before you go, Dan, for right now, let's keep this quiet. I'm sure this's going to come out and be big news soon enough, but we don't want word to get out prematurely. I have to notify the major, of course, and the NSA command post; maybe even the IG command post. Gotta see what the major says. I'll need to go to the MP station, too, and see what else they have. You guys should really be proud of yourselves. Now I'll get coffee."

In his office with coffee, he dialed Frank's home number and let it ring several times, thinking, *Just voice mail. Maybe with his girlfriend in Baltimore. I have his cell phone number too. ... No answer there, either. I'll keep trying him again and maybe call the IG myself.*

CHAPTER 18

Velma Roberts sleepily got out of bed, awakened by knocking, put a robe on over her nightgown, and walked to the door. Shane hastily pulled blue jeans over his underwear.

Recognizing Nassar, she opened the door, saying, "We didn't expect you so early. Fatima's still asleep."

"Sorry to get you up early," Nassar said, bundled for the cold weather. "Our youngest boy's been killed in an accident. We have to drive to Washington. Waited as long as we could."

Shane came into the room as Velma said, "Oh that's terrible. I'm so sorry. Come on in out of the cold a minute." To Shane, "Their youngest boy's been killed."

Shane gently put his hand on Nassar's shoulder, and said, "That's terr'ble. So sorry t' hear that."

"Thanks," Nassar replied with stoic composure. "The imam who called me said police have to keep him a while, but we have to identify him. Can't get our older boy."

"Ee-mom? Someone from the police?" Shane asked.

An imam is a Muslim prayer leader," Nassar explained. "About like your pastors. Can we get Fatima?"

Velma said; "Why not leave her here. Can't be a good place to take a young impressionable girl, even if it's her own brother. That way she won't miss school. I work at the bank in Shawsville and can take her to school and pick her up just like I do Amelia. I'll even tell the school office; know the school secretary and vice principal from church."

Shane said, "'Course you gotta do what you feel's best, but we're always pleased to help out neighbors, and it's no burden for us. Might be best for her, too, if she's not used to such bad things."

Nassar, replied, "I'll go ask Roula."

Velma said, "I'll be over in a few minutes to get her things soon as I get dressed proper."

Nassar merely said, "OK," and walked somberly away.

Velma said to Shane, "Oh, God. They don't deserve this. First them thugs set off a bomb and now their son's killed. I'll tell Jolene to say prayers for 'em at church tomorrow. They may not be Christian, but bible says we're supposed to pray for all. Oh, we've got to take Fatima to church with us tomorrow; can't leave her here alone. Not right to take her to Sunday school and church. They might not like exposin' her to a differ'nt religion. I'd sure not want them taking Amelia to where they goes, not without talkin' to me first."

"She could go to th' nursery, although she's old for that," Shane offered.

Velma replied, "Not too old t' help in the nursery. If not too cold tomorrow, might be lots of little kids. I'll tell Nassar and Roula when I pick up her things."

In the Hammouds' house, Velma saw Roula standing with no expression on her face, took Roula's hand in both of hers, and said, "So sorry to hear about your loss. He was a good boy."

Roula finally muttered something that sounded like, "shoo-kran. I get Fatima's bag."

Nassar commented, "Roula's not doing well. We appreciate your keeping Fatima. You're right, not good for her to go with us."

Velma said, "I'll have Fatima call you when she gets up. I's goin' to tell you we've gotta take Fatima to church with us tomorrow, can't leave her here alone, but want you to know we're not takin' her

196

to no religious stuff; not right, you being Muslim. Leave her in the nursery taking care of babies with some grown-ups in charge."

Nassar replied, "Thanks."

At home where Shane was drinking coffee, Velma said, "Somethin's wrong with Roula. She's not showin' any feelin' at all. I know she cares for her kids a lot, but she hasn't even been crying. I'll ask Jolene 'bout that too. She'd know, her bein' a pastor."

"Yeah, good idea," Shane said.

"Better fix some breakfast," Velma said. "Girls'll be up soon. Wonder what we should have. Don't seem right just having cold cereal on a day like this cold as it is. Wonder what she's supposed to eat or not eat. For sure no pork so can't have ham. Bet she might like some pancakes; Amelia does."

"Yeah," Shane commented. "Wouldn't mind some m'self. Some ham or sausage on the side sure'd be good."

"Nope," Velma said. "Don't know how she'd feel if others eatin' stuff she's not s'pposed to. How 'bout eggs?"

Later, Velma served breakfast to Amelia and Fatima and said, "I'm sorry to say your mom and dad had to go away. Your brother's hurt and they had to go to Washington quick. I said you'd stay here until they get back."

Fatima asked, "What's wrong?"

At twelve, now into puberty and losing her baby fat, she was an attractive, bright, capable, and precocious child.

"Said you'd call," Velma said. "I'll get the phone."

Fatima spoke in Arabic and handed the phone back.

"That was quick," Velma said. "You could've talked longer; I don't mind."

Fatima said, "My mom doesn't seem good. She wouldn't talk much; said my dad'd call me later. She wouldn't tell me about Marwan except he was hurt bad."

Velma put her arms around Fatima's shoulder as she was apparently trying to hold back tears, saying, "It's OK, honey; I'm sure they'll tell you more later. Why don't you girls go get dressed, take a bath if you want to. Then maybe you can help me in the kitchen. Say, why don't we make a special Saturday night supper. We can invite your uncle over, Fatima. What's his name?"

"We call him Abou Nidal," Fatima said, "only that's not his name. His real name's Jamal."

"Why don't you call him his real name?" Velma asked.

"That's what we call someone who has a son," Fatima said. "Nidal is his son who he hasn't seen in a long time. He doesn't like to talk about it much; makes him real sad."

"Oh, that's so sad," Velma said. "If we invite him for supper, what should we call him?"

"Abou Nidal, I guess," Fatima answered.

Velma said, "Let's see what we can have for supper. Would he eat chicken?"

"Oh, yes, he likes chicken," Fatima answered. "I do too. We have lots of that."

"Me, too," Amelia said with a smile.

"And mashed p'tatoes?" Velma continued asking.

"My mom usually makes them like French fries," Fatima answered, "but I like mashed potatoes and I think he's eaten them when we've been at KFC."

"That's what I like too," Amelia said.

"OK," Velma continued. "We can make some green beans, almost anyone'd eat that, and Jell-O salad."

"My mom says we're not supposed to eat Jell-O," Fatima said.

"Oh, why not?" Velma asked.

"Something about being made out of pigs," Fatima answered. "I eat it anyway, sometimes, when I'm somewhere else and they don't see me."

"Goody," Amelia said. "Jell-O Salad's my favorite."

"I'd of never thought that," Velma said. "No, honey, we got to respect other people and what they can't eat. No Jell-O salad if

Aboo Needle's here. Now you girls go on and get ready. Your mom packed a bag for you, Fatima. If you need any soap or towels or anything, we got plenty."

CHAPTER 19

Saturday, March 1, 2008
Washington, DC, USA

Omar fumbled with the key to the apartment, mentally, emotionally, and physically exhausted. Once inside, he thought, *Paco and Jason are in my bed; the couch for me.*

About two hours later, fully clothed, covered with his winter jacket, he woke up thinking he heard a cell phone alarm. Joe walked into the living room wearing briefs and a t-shirt. Still groggy, he saw Omar on the couch thinking, *Here I am with just my underwear.*

"Good morning," Omar said sleepily.

"How long you been home?" Joe asked.

Omar answered, "Got here about 7:30. What're you doing up?"

"Set the alarm to call the FBI guy," Joe replied. "Oh, I've got the number back in my phone."

Omar said, "I have it in my phone. I should call, being I made the initial contact and they confirmed the death to me."

"Oh, he did die," Joe said, "but was a matter of time."

"About 6:30," Omar said. "I called his father in Virginia. He's on his way; he'll call me when he gets here. I talked briefly to the police too; they need to keep his body for the medical examiner."

"They'd need to examine for forensic evidence to establish it's suicide or something else," Joe said.

"Police were understanding when I explained Muslim traditions with deceased persons."

Omar called, saying, "Damn, no answer. Wait, there's the voice mail. ... You may remember we met in the Old Post Office a couple of weeks ago. This line may not be secure, but if you know who I am, call back on a secure line. There's a very significant development."

Joe commented, "I moved the cars. It was late and cold, so I parked them in Jury's garage. Costs a fortune, but it's only money. Maybe you and I can find parking places later."

"OK, but now I need to sleep," Omar said with a big yawn. "The father will contact me in a little while, and I need to be halfway alert. Besides, the FBI might call soon."

"Say," Joe said, hesitating, "you can sleep in my bed; can't be comfortable here."

Omar, surprised, thought, *Never slept in the same bed with another person, except maybe when I was a kid, but yeah, lot more comfortable than here.* He said, "You sure, habibi? a lot better than this couch, but I've never slept in the same bed with someone."

"I haven't either," Joe said, "but if Paco and Jason can do it, no reason we can't. You need your sleep. I'm sure it won't keep me from sleeping, tired as I am."

A few hours later, Joe woke up thinking he heard noises in the apartment. He slowly moved himself away from the wall where he had been squeezed, crawled off the foot of the bed, and rummaged to find his jeans. He saw Jason and Paco in the kitchen, Paco on a crutch, Jason having only one free arm, both only in t-shirts and briefs.

Joe, startled seeing other men in underwear, thought, *I've seen guys in underwear in movies, but never in person. At school, there were enough Arab boys, we dressed privately.*

Jason said, "Hope we didn't wake you. We're trying to find some coffee and maybe something to eat."

"Hope you don't mind," Paco said. "We're really hungry, at least I am, and can't go out to eat."

201

"We have Lebanese coffee," Joe offered. "All we have for breakfast is cereal and juice; we were going shopping today. You're welcome to anything we have."

"I need coffee bad," Jason said. "Your Lebanese coffee is fine. How do I make it?"

"Oh, it's easy," Joe replied. "I'll do it."

He got a simple aluminum pot with a long handle that would hold about one and a half measuring cups, filled it with water, put in two heaping spoons of Café Najjar, stirred it, and sat it on a burner at the highest setting.

He said, "Keep your eyes on it and when it starts to bubble around the edges, let me know."

Jason asked, "Where's Omar? Did he come back from the hospital? Had to go out again?"

Joe replied, "Still asleep; has to go out this afternoon."

While Joe was getting food, Jason said, "Coffee!"

Joe quickly set things down, leaped to the stove to remove the coffee as a few drops sizzled on the burner, turned the burner down two notches, and stirred down the foam saying, "Let it come to a boil and stir it until it doesn't foam any more. I'll do it, but you asked how it's made."

Soon cereal, milk, and orange juice were on the table, coffee was poured, and all ate in silence, not in the mood for small talk. The phone rang. Joe leaped to answer.

(pause)

"He's asleep now."

(pause)

"I don't know; he was up until morning, but I can talk."

(pause)

"I made a big mistake when I said explosives were for …that place in Maryland. They were meant for here at the bar. There was an explosion there last night. The guy I talked to is dead; we saw him at the hospital. Say, it's safe to talk on this phone, isn't it?"

(pause)

"Oh, it's on all the news broadcasts," he said. "We just woke up and haven't turned on the radio or television."

(pause)

"Two guys hurt in the blast are here. You met Brad and Frank. They're in the hospital. Their boyfriends are here."

(pause)

"You can come over right away," he said. "We're finishing breakfast and'll be through when you get here."

Joe said, "That's the FBI agent; he's coming soon."

"We've got to get dressed," Jason said. "It was bad enough getting undressed to go to bed."

"It's easier to get undressed than dressed," Paco replied. "If I can stand without the crutch, I can help you. I've had plenty of experience with the old guys I tend to."

"I can stand with no problem," Jason said. "With only one hand, I can't be of much use to you, but we can try. Say, this might be funny. You got a video camera?"

"Well, er, I could help you," Joe said haltingly.

"OK," Paco said. "We'll call if we need you."

Jason said to Paco laughing, "Let's pretend we're Ernie and Bert and see if we can dress each other."

Ernie and Bert? Paco thought. *Oh, yeah, Sesame Street.*

They hobbled to the bedroom. Joe cleaned off the table, put the food up, and went to Omar's bedroom, where Paco was buttoning Jason's shirt, showing years of practice.

"We need some help putting on our pants," Paco said. "I can sit here on the side of the bed and hold out my legs while you pull them up as far as you can."

"I think that's what I need also," Jason said.

Joe very awkwardly pulled Paco's pants over his legs, being careful not to rip further the leg that had been cut in the emergency room. Paco moved his hips and wriggled, helping with his own hands to pull the pants over his thighs. He then stood up, using the crutch to balance himself, and tried to fasten the waistband and pull up the zipper.

"I think you're going to have to do this, too," he said.

Jason then handed his pants to Joe, sat on the bed, and stuck out his legs for Joe to pull on. When they were over his thighs, Jason stood holding his pants up with his one useable hand. He awkwardly attempted to pull the pants up, wriggling and moving his hips, but to no avail.

"You're going to have to help me too," he said. "Just grab one side and pull while I do the other."

Joe left; Paco got his crutch and said, "I'm not going to put my shoes on after that ordeal. Shit! Where's my other shoe? Must've left it in the ER. I won't need it right away, but don't want to lose it. I'll ask when I check on Frank."

"Can we see Brad and Frank today?" Jason asked.

"Don't know," Paco replied. "You better believe I'm going to try."

"I'm going with you," Jason said emphatically. "I'm not going to try putting on shoes either."

CHAPTER 20

After introductions to Paco and Jason, Joe asked Cranford Brooks, "Would you like Lebanese coffee? We want more."

"Like at the Lebanese restaurant by the zoo?" Cranford Brooks replied. "Don't mind if I do." Sipping coffee, he said, "Can you please repeat again what you said on the phone."

Joe repeated; then Cranford Brooks replied, "I don't think you made a mistake; I'll get to that in a minute. Only one person's dead, and it looks like suicide."

Joe replied, "I know who he is; Omar and I saw him in the hospital just before he died. That's why he called you."

"Please start from the beginning and tell me what you you know."

Joe explained. Cranford Brooks took notes, concluding, "Omar knows his name, if he notified the family."

Cranford Brooks asked, "How can you know he wasn't targeting Frank Reynolds and Brad Spencer at the bar?"

Joe replied, "I can't for sure, but he'd never seen Frank before. He met Brad once, but I can't imagine Brad would've said anything about where he works. Also, how would he know Brad and Frank were going there last night?"

"Maybe someone at the NSA was keeping tabs on them and fed him information," Cranford Brooks said.

"If I may add something," Jason interrupted, "We might possibly have told someone at church on Sunday we were going to Rory's the following Friday. I can't imagine anyone at church being a terrorist spy who'd target Brad."

"What church is that?" Cranford Brooks asked.

"The MCC, Metropolitan Community Church in Laurel," Jason answered. "New people show up, but none I can think of since we made plans to go to Rory's last night. Been trying to think who we might've told; can't imagine we'd've told more than one or two, if that many. We don't usually invite people to join us; this's our special time together, just the two of us. We did ask Frank and Paco last night because they'd never been."

"I can tell you for certain sure that Frank wouldn't've told anyone," Paco said. "Being a Marine Corps officer, he's not going to tell anyone he's going to a gay bar."

"That makes it unlikely they were targeted," Cranford Brooks said. "Makes it even more an issue for the Metropolitan Police, were it not for one thing. That's what I want to bring up next, but maybe we could do it in private."

Joe said, "We could go to a bedroom, but I can't think of anything Paco and Jason don't already know."

Cranford Brooks said, "Frank Reynolds is going to find out soon as we locate him, and likely Brad Spencer too. That means you two'd find out if you're close as you seem to be."

Paco said, "Frank's in the hospital unconscious, or was the last time I saw him. Even if he's conscious, he'll be in the ICU a while, and I doubt they'd let you talk to him."

"Brad too," Jason said, "but Paco's the last to see him."

Cranford Brooks brought up another file and said, "When I talked to you before, you said the person you spoke with at the bar said there were explosives and wondering if he were to share them with the other person in Maryland."

Joe thought a moment and replied, "Yes, that's right." *Wait a minute. He said I said 'share',* Joe said to himself.

"You said you spoke Arabic," Cranford Brooks said.

"Yes, both times," Joe confirmed.

"You said he said a person who'd be cleaning the Arabic language section could speak Arabic," he continued.

Joe replied, "Yes. He made a joke about it."

Cranford Brooks continued, "This morning Marine guards at the NSA caught a person on the cleaning crew with explosives. That's why we thought someone might've been observing Frank Reynolds and Brad Spencer there. He has an Arabic name, but we don't know yet if he speaks Arabic. We're investigating to see if he'd work in the Arabic language section. Your statement's the first evidence that links the cases together. Right now, bombing of the gay bar's a local matter to be handled by the Metropolitan Police; there's no federal issue. You'd know that, being with the AG. Entering a federal building on a military post with explosives is indeed a federal issue. With your statement, the FBI can take over the gay bar bombing case, but we might not want to, or might make it a joint case."

"Why's that?" Joe asked.

"We caught the guy in Maryland in time to keep it quiet," Cranford Brooks said, "not stir up panic in the public and especially in Congress; we often learn more without being under a microscope, so to speak."

"You have to charge him or let him go," Joe said."

"Yes, habeas corpus," Cranford Brooks agreed. "The longer we keep it quiet that the two cases are connected, the more freedom we have to get to the bottom of things. I suspect we'll let the Metropolitan Police be in charge of the gay bar bombing, at least nominally. We have a good working relationship with them; have to in this city. I'm getting ahead of myself. I'm just a field agent, even if it is a pretty important field office. Policy decisions are made at way higher levels."

"Joe said, "For sure I have to tell my office now; can't let them find out later when we're involved in prosecution.""

Cranford Brooks said to Jason and Paco, "You know you need to keep quiet in the interests of your boyfriends."

"I'm just a redneck from Southside Virginia," Jason said, his accent coming on strong, "but I ain't stupid. I know when t' keep mah mouth shut."

"I'm just a dumb Mexican," Paco said, "but I know when to keep quiet."

"I'll need contact details," Cranford Brooks said. "You seem to know each other well enough you don't mind others hearing them. I can take them in private if you prefer."

After both provided details, Jason added, "My cell phone's in my coat hanging up in Rory's. Any chance I'd get that back? I need my coat for sure."

Paco said, "I'd sure like my coat; only one I got."

Cranford Brooks finished typing then said, "I'll contact our liaison with the Metropolitan Police Force; need to do that anyway. I can ask them when they'd release evidence. My guess is it'd not be immediately, being a weekend."

Jason said, "There's a Burlington Coat outlet close to me if we get out there. Prices're pretty good."

Cranford Brooks asked, "Any idea when Mr. Abu Deeb'll be up? You gave lots of good information, but we'd like him to confirm the name of the person who died."

"I don't know," Joe replied. "I thought he might wake up by now with our voices, but he was really out of it. Do you want me to wake him up?"

"No, but could you please have him contact me when he gets up?" Cranford Brooks asked. "We won't press him for details today, but independent confirmation helps."

When Cranford Brooks left, Joe said, "I don't know about you two, but I sure need more coffee."

Sitting sipping coffee again, Joe said, "What do you two want to do now?"

"First contact the hospital," Paco said.

"Yeah," Jason agreed. "I need to get home, get a coat, and change clothes. I can probably drive with one hand. If they'll let us see them tonight, I'll be back for sure."

Paco said, "Go back to Baltimore and go get a coat too."

"I can drive you some places; maybe Omar too," Joe offered. "Wait, he said something about having to meet the guy's family when they get here. Maybe the first thing we need to do is get your cars out of the hotel garage before it costs a fortune. I can do that soon as I can get shoes on. Need to go to the grocery store too."

"I could help you with the cars and shopping if I had a coat," Jason offered. "You suppose Omar's might fit me?"

"Probably," Joe said, "but can you maneuver a steering wheel well enough with one hand to get out of a parking garage and into a parking place alongside the curb?"

With a dejected look Jason said, "Probably not."

"Let's not worry right now," Joe said. "I'm sure Omar and I can sort the cars out. Maybe simplest would be for you to stay overnight here again. Tomorrow might be calmer, and I could drive you to Baltimore and the place you live in Virginia. Maybe Omar too, if he's not tied up with that family. By then you'll know more about Brad and Frank."

"Yeah, maybe," Paco said, dejected.

"We can't keep on imposing on you," Jason said, "even if hospitality codes are part of your culture."

"Hey, habibi, don't worry about it," Joe said. "It'll work out. Who knows what you might do for us next time."

"If you're going to Baltimore with Paco tomorrow, maybe I can ride along and go to church," Jason added. "Having them pray for us would help a lot. In fact, if I can use your phone, I'd like to call the pastor this afternoon and tell her what's going on. I'm sure they're upset anyway, knowing a gay bar was bombed."

"Yes, sure, use the phone, Joe offered. "Right now, I'd just like a shower and get cleaned up. What about you two? You're welcome to use the bathroom, of course."

"For sure it'd feel good," Jason replied, "but I have this splint and they said keep it dry, and Paco has a cast on too."

"Not a problem," Paco said. "We deal with this in the nursing home. Put a large plastic bag over them and seal it with tape. You've got plastic trash bags, don't you, Joe?"

"Yes," Joe answered, "no tape though. But, hey, there's CVS on Connecticut Avenue just past DuPont Circle."

"If I could borrow Omar's coat, I can get it myself," Jason said. "Go take a shower if you like, and we'll figure it out. I can clean up the dishes with one hand. Might take a little longer, but I can do it."

CHAPTER 21

Saturday, March 1, 2008
Toronto, Ontario, Canada

Ahmed waited impatiently inside Lester Pearson International Airport, reflecting, *Didn't think they'd sell me a ticket. Damn, why didn't Marwan show up? Abdulmalik's going to have to find some way for him to escape. Don't suppose Abdulmalik has some secret plans for Marwan and that's why he's acting so strange? Go somewhere secret and not let me know? He acts kind of weird for an imam.*

Thought I'd blown it when security pulled me aside, asked all those questions. Good thing I thought up that story someone died there and my father needed me to represent the family because he couldn't travel on Palestinian identity papers, but I have a passport.

A television set suspended from the ceiling was showing a CBC report from the U.S. with the volume barely audible, "… In Washington, a bomb in a popular gay bar killed one person; several are injured, some seriously.…"

What, only one person killed? he thought. *He was supposed to take out a big group.*

"… A fire department spokesman confirmed no sign of a gas leak or other accidental causes but signs of a deliberately set explosion. A spokesman said Mayor Fenton will have a statement shortly because he was only notified within the last hour. The Westboro Baptist Church in Topeka, Kansas, issued a statement in the last hour, saying the church will offer praise tomorrow in worship services, thanking God for removing the scourge of homosexuality from the nation's capital."

Yeah! Ahmed said to himself almost out loud. *They're going to love us for trying to get rid of gays. Wonder how soon Abdulmalik's going to tell them that our group did it?*

"… Primary elections in Ohio and Texas…."

Nothing about the bomb Wissam's supposed to set off, he thought. *Why's it taking so long?*

CHAPTER 22

Saturday, March 1, 2008
Lafayette, Virginia, USA

Shane kissed Velma and asked, "What's f'r lunch?"

"Nothin'," she answered. You c'n make a sandwich. I'm not hungry and the girls had a big breakfast. We're makin' a special supper for that nice man who lives with the Hammouds. All this goin' on, he's probably not in a mood to cook for hisself."

"Nice," Shane said. "Just heard somethin' on the radio. Where's the girls? We need to watch the news on TV, but not let them see it. 'Bout their boy who's killed."

"Don't know," Velma answered. "Here'n th' house somewhere. If they're not in her bedroom, we can go in ours and look at the little TV."

While he prepared a sandwich, Velma looked and said, "They're down in the rec room watchin' TV."

In their bedroom, Shane put his arm around Velma's shoulders, cuddling. Their minds drifted during news of primary elections.

Suddenly Shane said, "There."

The line moving across the bottom of the screen read, "One person killed in gay bar in Washington DC. Several injured; some seriously."

Two news anchors appeared, one saying, "Returning to our main story: Police in Washington, DC, confirm one person has been killed in a bombing in one of the city's most popular gay bars in the DuPont Circle area, widely known as the gay district. An official spokesman reported only one person dead, several injured, some seriously. The spokesperson confirmed the fire department analysis that there were no gas leaks or causes of an accidental explosion. Evidence indicates the bomb was set deliberately. A source who spoke off the record because of not being authorized to confirm such matters indicated there are characteristics of a suicide bombing. The name of the person killed has not been released pending official notification of next of kin, who are en route to Washington at this time...."

"Oh, my God," Velma said. "You think that's him?"

"Guess we'll find out, but maybe," Shane answered.

"... The Mayor of the City of Washington, Adrian Fenton, condemned the bombing, especially targeting gays, saying all residents and visitors have the right to expect safety in private establishments catering to the public, regardless of their individual characteristics, including sexual orientation, so long as they are acting lawfully."

"The President's press secretary issued a statement on behalf of President George W. Bush, stating his concern for the victims of the horrible tragedy and his personal revulsion that such a thing could happen in this country almost in sight of the White House. Avoiding comment about sexual orientation, he offered the services of federal investigative agencies if desired by the Metropolitan Police.

"The three remaining major contenders for the presidential nomination each issued statements through spokespersons while on the campaign trail. Both Hillary Clinton and Barak Obama, expressing horror and sympathy for the victims, specifically stated they support the right of gays and lesbians to live without fear of injury or death. When asked if they would support federal hate crime legislation for attacks on gays and lesbians, both indicated support in principle and indeed both have long supported gay rights in the U.S., but would not comment further on specific legislation.

Senator John McCain, through a spokesperson from his home in Arizona while taking a weekend break from the campaign, said he condemned all violence directed towards law-abiding citizens. He declined further comment for the moment, having been informed only recently because of the time difference from Washington.

"In Topeka, Kansas, the Westboro Baptist Church issued a statement it will dispatch a delegation to Washington to demonstrate at the site of the bombing and at funerals of persons who were killed in the blast. ..."

"Oh, God," Velma said. "How c'n they call themselves a church? Didn't Jesus say we should pray for sinners, and I'm not so sure bein' gay's a sin, and be compassionate to them, not rejoice if they get killed."

Shane said, "Don't know if it's a sin neither; guys I work with make fun of gays, but wouldn't want to kill 'em."

Velma said, "They're going to demonstrate at funerals of the persons killed. Y'don't suppose if it's the Hammoud boy they'd come down here."

"Oh, m' God," Shane exclaimed. "Didn't think about that. Was bad enough with the big shootin' up in Blacksburg and people was all over the place, even 'round here."

Velma turned off the television set, saying, "I've seen enough. One of us better go out in case the girls come upstairs. If this's true, then Fatima's bound to hear it sometime. Just hope her folks calls to break the news to her first before she sees it on TV or somethin'. Say, I'd better call Jolene and tell her before we go to church tomorrow morning. She might want to say somethin' to Fatima."

"What about you sayin' to her folks about not exposin' her to religious things?" Shane asked.

"I'll just leave that one up to Jolene and God. Surely doin' something to comfort a little girl whose brother just got killed ain't against any religion."

CHAPTER 23

Saturday, March 1, 2008
Washington, DC, USA

Joe, freshly showered, shaved, and dressed, saw Jason with shoes on. Jason said, "If I can borrow a coat, I'll go to CVS."

Joe thought, *He's eager to get out. I would be too.* "You can use mine," he replied.

After Jason left, Joe asked Paco, "More coffee?"

"Nahhh," Paco replied. "Sorry, I'm bummed out; thanks for asking though."

Joe thought, *I can imagine. Stuck indoors. Hard to get around. Boyfriend in the hospital and doesn't know how he is.* "Just let me know," he said.

"Yeah, OK," Paco said indifferently. "I'm not very good company, sorry. I'm the one who takes care of others, the take-charge guy. Now I understand what it's *really* like for the old guys who can't take care of themselves any more. Got a shitload of studying to do, too, and don't have my books."

Joe asked, "How's school going?"

"Good," Paco replied. "If it keeps on as good as it is now, I'm going straight to get a master's."

"Great," Joe said. "Why'd you choose nursing?"

Paco replied, "My family're manual workers. Couldn't see beyond working in a factory getting a steady paycheck."

"People like that in Dearborn, too," Joe commented.

"Couldn't see myself doing that," Paco continued. "Day after day, same thing. Factories're automating, closing down, laying off, so I thought what else I could do. My family, well, most of the Mexican community, didn't believe in education. Waste of time and money, and no one got anywhere getting more education. Going to a university never occurred to me."

"Lots of local people in Dearborn like that, too," Joe concurred. "Not the Lebanese, but go ahead."

"There was a shortage of nurses and talk about good jobs," Paco continued. "Men were becoming nurses; some Mexican guys getting jobs as orderlies in nursing homes. Nursing homes liked them too, because some old people were more than women could handle."

"Back in Lebanon, so I hear," Joe added, "lots of men who are nurses; especially at the big American University Hospital, almost all nurses are men and have been for years. Good profession for guys."

Paco continued, "Against family opposition, I took practical nursing at the community college. Teased too; a big, husky guy like me becoming a sissy nurse."

"Yeah, people made fun of guys in nursing school at U of M too," Joe said, "but when some of them were getting the prettiest girls on campus, it changed people's minds."

"The VA recruited, almost begged guys to work for them," Paco continued. "Can't legally discriminate, but pretty clear they wanted guys, especially big ones like me. I could've gone lots of places, but Mexicans stay with their parents until they get married, so I took the closest job in Cincinnati and continued to live at home."

"Middle Easterners too," Joe said. "That's one reason I'm getting so much shit from home. How'd that work out?"

"Pretty good," Paco answered. "I was a good Mexican boy staying at home, serving the country too. Mexicans are patriotic, even if they're not all citizens, and most understood a nursing home for old soldiers needs male nurses."

"But you moved to Baltimore," Joe commented.

"Yeah," Paco said. "Frank's one reason, but not the only one. I'm thirty-five and it's time to get on with my life. I love my family, always will. Hurt like hell to be away at Christmas time, but we survived."

"I miss my family, too" Joe agreed. "It hurt to be away from them at the Eid. I know what you mean."

"The Eid?" Paco asked and then added, "Oh, that party you had and invited Frank and Brad. ... Go do what you need to do. Don't worry about me. I need time to sit and think, especially how I'm going to go see Frank tonight."

"Have you found out about him?" Joe asked.

"Called while you were in the shower," Paco replied. "They're in the ICU. Regained consciousness. We *might* be able to visit a little while during visiting hours."

"Great," Joe said. "We'll try to get you there. Take you to Baltimore, too, to get books and things," Joe continued, "most likely tomorrow."

"That'd work," Paco said. "Jason wants to go too. He called the pastor; the whole church's praying for them."

"What about your church?" Joe asked.

Paco answered. "Don't know who I'd tell. I go to mass when I can, but just know priests by sight. Doubt they'd remember me. For damned sure, not going to tell them I was at a gay bar, not even in confession."

Joe said, "Confession. That's legally protected speech. A priest can't be made to repeat what he's heard there."

"That's it," Paco said when Omar's cell phone rang.

Joe leaped to pick it up, spoke in Arabic, then went to gently shake Omar's shoulder, saying, "Habibi, sorry, but you need to wake up."

Still groggy, Omar said, "What's going on?"

Joe told him about the call, concluding, "I'll leave you to call Mr. Hammoud and make coffee."

Omar called, then came into the living room, saying, "Good morning, rather afternoon. How're things with you?"

"OK, considering," Paco replied, and then explained briefly his injuries and about maybe visiting Frank.

Joe asked, "You want coffee, habibi? I can get you tea. You want breakfast too?"

"Oh, whatever," Omar replied. "If you're making coffee, that's fine. I can get my own breakfast."

"No, sit down," Joe said. "You had a rough night, and looks like you might have a rough day. I'll bring it." While Omar ate, Joe asked, "You meeting Mr. Hammoud today?"

"Yes," Omar answered, "between 2:30 and 3:00 at the hospital morgue. Said I'd call the police and set up the meeting. He has family here, a cousin in Arlington, who can help him find the hospital."

"OK," Joe replied. "Maybe we can get the cars out before it costs a fortune. Jason and Paco need coats, too."

Omar said, "I can take one of the cars when I go to the hospital and park it around here when I come back."

Jason returned and Omar said, "Hello, habibi."

"You want some coffee?" Joe asked Jason.

"Yes, thanks," he replied. "It's cold; coffee'd be great." He pulled out bags of potato chips and cheese puffs, dip for the chips, disposable razors, a can of shaving cream, two toothbrushes, a tube of toothpaste, and two rolls of adhesive tape and said, "Hope this's the right kind of tape."

Paco replied, "That works; a shave would be good; glad you thought of toothbrushes too."

Joe brought coffee and said, "Omar has to meet the father of the guy who died. He can take one car."

"I can take my own car, of course," Omar interjected.

Jason said, "No take mine. If I can go to my place later, I've got a jacket there; with a sweater, it'd work unless we get a real cold spell. Paco could get something at Burlington Coat outlet. Maybe leave the car. I could come take a taxi and the Metro, go to the hospital to see Brad, and then take the Metro back." To Paco, "You could come with me; we could come back in the morning, and maybe go to Baltimore."

Omar said, "That's a lot of effort. Why don't you stay here at least another night. I could take you to the hospital, depending on what I might need to do with this family. An imam's first obligation is to his people, even if they're not a part of our mosque community. Hope you understand."

"Yeah, a good pastor too," Jason said.

"A priest too," Paco confirmed.

"That's what I told them," Joe said. "Stay another night, then we can sort things out tomorrow. But, hey, maybe we could all go to Jason's place tonight if Omar's free. Might be a decent supermarket there too."

"Thanks," Paco said. "What do you think? Don't mind staying here another night either, but can't keep imposing."

Omar replied. "Let's work that out later. I need to get cleaned up and call the police."

"Paco said to Jason, "Let's get taped up for the shower. Omar'll be out by the time we're ready to go in."

CHAPTER 24

Joe drove Jason's 2005 Toyota Celica along Massachusetts Avenue, grumbling, "All these circles. Washington sure wasn't laid out for automobiles." He suddenly remembered and said to Omar, "You're supposed to call Cranford Brooks."

After greetings, Omar said into the phone, "I'm on my way to meet the father and police for formal identification."

(pause)

"Yes, call any time, but if it's a weekday, text first in case I'm in class," he requested, and then said goodbye. To Joe, "He asked us to tell the police it's the same person you saw in the bar; that'd be enough for now."

Inside DC General Hospital, they saw two Arab-looking men whom Omar approached and said in Arabic, "*Marhaba*, is one of you Mr. Hammoud?"

Shaking hands, Nassar said in Arabic, "You're the imam? So young."

"I just finished university," Omar replied in Arabic. "I can see if I can locate someone older."

"No," Nassar replied in Arabic. "I talked to you, and we have an appointment. Let's go ahead."

Nassar introduced his cousin Ousama al Shaeer, Abou Tarek, who said in Arabic, "Thanks for coming to be with Abou Ahmed now."

Abou Ahmed, Omar thought. *The son who's dead is Marwan. He must have an older son.*

Omar notified the morgue while Nassar asked Joe in Arabic, "Did you know my son?"

"No," Joe lied, thinking in English, *Allah forgive me; I'm not going to tell him now how I met his son.*

"Are you an imam, also?" Abou Tarek asked in Arabic.

Joe answered in Arabic, "I'm a friend of Omar," and explained being in the hospital earlier and his background.

A young man in hospital whites led them to the morgue, where a police detective asked, "We'd like you to identify a person we believe is your son. Are you willing to do that?"

Nassar merely replied, "Yes."

"Will these gentlemen be with you?" he asked.

"I will," Omar answered before Nassar could. "I'm an imam, an Islamic clergyman."

"I'll go also if you like," Joe offered.

"Yes, of course," Nassar replied. "My cousin also."

"Please go with this gentleman," the detective nodded to the morgue supervisor. "You'll need your coats on."

Joe stayed behind with the detective, saying, "If I may have a brief word: I met his son earlier. It has a direct bearing on this case and I'm sure you'll want a statement from me; but, please, I don't want to describe the circumstances now in front of his father."

"OK," the detective said as both entered the morgue.

The supervisor pulled out a slab and Nassar stoically said, "That's my son Marwan."

Joe and Omar said almost simultaneously, "That's the person we saw here in the hospital earlier."

The detective said gently, "Mr. Hammoud, if you would please follow me to sign the forms."

Nassar signed, asking, "When can we have him?"

The detective replied, "We need a medical examiner to look for evidence. Because it's the weekend, medical examiners won't be here until Monday. It depends on how much work there is and what priority. You'd better count on Tuesday at the earliest. That'll give you time to arrange a funeral director to pick him up."

"Why a funeral director?" Nassar asked, confused. "We just want to prepare him properly and bury him."

The supervisor said, "We release remains only to licensed funeral directors. That way they can be embalmed and the family can have whatever service they like."

Nassar said, "He can't be embalmed. His body must be whole to be lifted up when Allah claims him."

Omar gently put his hand on Nassar's shoulder and said, "Allah understands. If a Muslim has to be embalmed to comply with the law, it's OK. Allah can find a way."

The morgue supervisor said, "I saw you folks're from Virginia. I heard Virginia doesn't require embalming, but we do have to release the remains to a licensed funeral director. Where do you plan on burying him?"

Nassar said, "Montgomery County's the only home we know; only home he knew. It'd have to be there."

"If I may suggest," the supervisor continued, "we get plenty of out-of-town people in this city. Simplest thing is to arrange a funeral director where you live to come here."

Omar, sensing Nassar was overwhelmed said, "Thanks for that. He'll work out details later. It seems we have until Monday at least. Is there anything else?"

"No," the detective replied. "The orderly can show you out. We're sorry for your loss, Mr. Hammoud."

In the elevator, Nassar asked in Arabic, "Can you tell me how he died? Why do police need to examine him?"

Oh, Allah, give me the words, Omar thought. "Let's find a place to talk quietly," he said in Arabic.

Joe said in Arabic, "Hospitals usually have a place where family can have private conversations. Lawyers often talk to people there. I'll find out."

He led them to a multi-faith chapel where Omar said in Arabic, "I'm sorry to say the police think Marwan set off a suicide bomb in a gay bar and want evidence to confirm."

Nassar, shocked, fumbled words in Arabic. "What, my son a suicide bomber? That can't be; Islam does not allow suicide except for a jihad. There's no jihad here."

Abou Tarek interrupted in Arabic. "Maybe it's that imam in Ballston, trying to incite a jihad."

"What imam in Ballston?" Nassar asked in Arabic.

"I haven't told you yet," Abou Tarek answered in Arabic. "An imam in Ballston meets with a group of young men, supposedly for prayer and support. My boys are too old, but know about it."

Nassar asked in Arabic, "What's a gay bar?"

Omar explained in Arabic. Then Nassar, anguished, said in Arabic, "My boy's a good Muslim. He wouldn't go to a bar. He can't be homosexual. If this is true, he can't go to heaven on the day of judgment."

Omar said in Arabic, "Allah is merciful. There's a period of purification in the grave when persons who have much good in them, but have committed sins, will be allowed to enter heaven on the day of judgment. All good Muslims who truly believe in the one true God will be allowed the joy of entering heaven."

Nassar replied in Arabic, "He was a good boy; a good Muslim."

"Maybe he thought he was doing the right thing if that imam convinced him it was holy jihad," Abou Tarek suggested in Arabic.

Omar recited the Fatiha in Arabic, "In the name of God, the Compassionate and the Caring...."

Recognizing the words, the others joined.

Omar asked in Arabic, "Do you have an imam in Arlington who you and Abou Ahmed can talk to?"

Abou Tarek replied in Arabic, "The imam at the mosque where we pray is Hamas. He collects money to send to them. We were Fattah back there; they don't like to associate with us because we don't give money."

"I can have an older imam at the Islamic Center contact you," Omar said in Arabic.

"Thank you," Abou Tarek replied in Arabic. "You're a good man, a true follower of the Prophet. Abou Ahmed's lucky to find you; maybe Allah sent you to him. There's no need for another imam."

Omar asked in Arabic, "Do you have an imam where you live? You know an imam's not needed for a burial."

Nassar replied in Arabic, "No, the Islamic community is mostly big important professors and doctors in Blacksburg, not simple people like us. Sometimes they give sermons and lead prayer, but they have other jobs. We don't talk to them much; just go pray."

Like when I was in Duluth, Omar thought, *but I took time for everyone, not just professors and doctors.*

Nassar said in Arabic, "Could you come recite the holy scriptures and maybe help get his body ready? I can't contact my older boy. I have two men who work with me, but they're just simple guys like me. The big guys from Blacksburg wouldn't want to do something like help wash his body."

Omar, surprised, thought, *What? Go down there? I don't know where this place is. I've heard of Blacksburg after the big shooting there, but didn't pay attention to where it is. He shouldn't be so sure men there wouldn't help. At least men at UMD would help a fellow Muslim in need. That's what Islam is all about!*

After Omar hesitated, Nassar said in Arabic, "Sorry, you must be busy. We'll take care of things."

"Oh, no," Omar said in Arabic, "I was just thinking how I could arrange things to go do it."

"Oh, wonderful," Nassar responded in Arabic.

Joe asked in Arabic, "The man in the morgue said it's best to find a funeral director close to where he'll be buried. Where exactly do you live?"

Nassar replied in Arabic, "In Montgomery County, just across the line from Roanoke County. We're in a little community called Lafayette, but the mail address is Elliston."

Roanoke, I've been there, Joe thought, "What's the nearest town with a funeral director?" he asked in Arabic.

"Christiansburg's the county seat; it's bigger," Nassar answered in Arabic. "Blacksburg's even bigger, but further away. Salem and Roanoke are pretty big, but they're in the next county in the opposite direction. Never paid attention what's there except to get auto parts and things like that."

"If you want, I can check," Joe continued in Arabic.

"Oh, thanks," Nassar replied in Arabic, relieved.

Thank you for that, Joe, Omar thought. Then he said in Arabic, "We'll call you."

Nassar stood and took both Omar's hands, saying in Arabic, "You're a kind man. I am so glad you will be with us for our son's burial."

CHAPTER 25

Saturday, March 1, 2008
Washington, DC, USA

Alone in the chapel, Omar took both Joe's hands and said in English, "Thank you, habibi. It's so good to have you with me. I'll need to do this on my own in time, but this's my first time; I can't say how much it means to me."

Joe, said, "It's OK, habibi. As you keep saying, an important part of Islam is one person supporting another. I'm surprised you agreed to go down there."

"The words just came out of my mouth," Omar said. "I wasn't planning to say that. Must've been Allah's doing."

Joe said, "You want me to go with you?"

Omar replied, "I wouldn't ask you to do that, habibi. You've been a great support, but that's too much."

Joe asserted, "You're not asking me; I'm volunteering. Like you just said, the words just came out of my mouth. Maybe that's Allah's doing too."

Omar said, "I'd love to have you with me. Are you sure you want to touch a dead body?"

"Someone has to do it," Joe said. "I've never done this either. I have to talk to Roger anyway on Monday; I can ask for days off. I have plenty of vacation time built up. I've been to Roanoke before. You remember the trial of the guys who're now in Duluth? It was in Roanoke."

"Oh, good," Omar said. "Maybe you can tell me more about it and how to get there."

"We flew," Joe said, "so I don't know much, but can find out. Let's try to see Brad and Frank."

At the reception window, Omar said, "We'd like to see Brad Spencer and Frank Reynolds."

She looked at a computer then said, "Bradley Spencer and Frank Reynolds? They're in intensive care. No one but immediate family and clergy. You got ID proof?"

"No, not related," Omar said, "but I'm a clergyman."

"Yeah, right," she said. "Look honey, we've had guys all afternoon claiming to be family, clergy, and just about everything else to see patients. Sorry, we have rules."

Omar forcibly contained himself while Joe pushed in front and spoke, "We're in this hospital in a legitimate capacity. My colleague is a clergyman, an Islamic one."

"Now I've heard everything," she replied with a smirk. "People try to get around our rules but this is the first time I've heard something like this."

Joe said forcefully, "If you don't believe us, you can call your morgue. We were there moments ago in his capacity as an Islamic clergyman. Early this morning in the emergency room, too. You can check. May I also remind you it's a violation of both federal law and that of the District of Columbia to defame a person's religion and discriminate against Islam or any religion."

The receptionist said, "Please calm down. I'll call." Into the phone, "Two gentlemen who *claim* to be clergymen are here to see patients Reynolds and Spencer. Is it OK if I send them up?"

(pause)

Then to Joe and Omar, "You can go up but a maximum of five minutes. Directory's on the wall next to the elevator."

I didn't claim *to be a clergyman,* Joe thought, *but for damned sure I'm not going to correct her.*

In the ICU, a young man in a white nurse's uniform with a name plate reading "Malcolm Carter, RN" said, "You're here to see Brad and Frank. You must be their boyfriends. They've been asking about you."

"We're not their boyfriends," Joe answered.

"I'm a clergyman," Omar said. "Didn't she tell you?"

With a sheepish look, the nurse said, "Sorry. Some guys really want to see their boyfriends or partners. It'd help them a lot to recover, and I want to cooperate to the extent I can without breaking rules; maybe bend them a bit."

Joe said, "Their boyfriends are at our place. We're here on his business as a clergyman. We want to see them for just a few moments; we can tell their boyfriends how they are."

The nurse smiled, saying, "That's good of you. You can't stay more than five minutes with each. They've been conscious a while and not in critical condition, but not well enough to have visitors. I'll take you to Brad; he's closest. …Brad, someone to see you."

Brad's left leg was in a cast strung by a wire to an overhead rack so his leg was above his body at an angle; the left side of his face and head were covered with bandages. An intravenous drip was connected to his right arm. Seeing Omar, he tried to smile and speak.

The nurse said, "It's painful for him to talk, so best not say anything that causes him to speak."

Omar said softly, "Joe's here too. We saw you and Jason being brought to the hospital last night. We had to come here today, so we came to see you."

"You saw Jason?" Brad pleaded, clearly in pain.

"He's at our apartment," Omar answered. "His arm's in a sling, and he has some bandages, but otherwise he's OK."

"Oh, thank God," Brad murmured.

"He's worried about you," Joe added. "He's going to your church tomorrow; says they are all praying for you."

Brad tried to open his mouth, but Omar said: No, don't say anything. I'll recite the Fatiha for you and then we'll go."

He began reciting in Arabic, "In the name of God, the compassionate the Caring…. We'll be back when we can."

"We'll tell Jason we saw you," Joe said. Yalla, bye."

The nurse asked, "What kind of a clergyman are you? You were praying in a foreign language."

"I'm an assistant imam, an Islamic clergyman. It wasn't a prayer; I recited a verse from the Q'ran. We use it like a prayer; it's called the sura of healing. He's an Arabic language specialist and understands."

"You're a gay Muslim couple?" the nurse said, "and you're a clergyman? I didn't think Muslims allowed gays."

"We're not a gay couple," Joe answered firmly, "but we're human beings and have different kinds of friends."

"You're right," Omar said more softly. "Muslims don't accept homosexuality for themselves, but that doesn't mean we condemn them, either."

"Oh, sorry, here I go jumping to conclusions," the nurse said. "You said his boyfriend was going to church tomorrow."

"Yes, they're devout Christians," Omar said. "Christians are children of God; we call them 'people of the book.' We can recite the sura for healing for Christians."

"Amazing," the nurse said. "I'll tell my boyfriend about this. Here we are. Someone to see you, Frank."

Frank lay flat on his back with a cast on his right thigh over his hip and bandages around his body covering his ribs. An intravenous drip was connected to his left arm.

Frank smiled as he exclaimed, "Omar and Joe!"

"We were in the hospital anyway and they let us see you," Omar said.

"Paco's really worried and has been calling the hospital, playing his 'I am a nurse' card to get information," Joe said.

"Oh, Paco's not hurt?" Frank asked.

"His ankle's sprained and in a cast," Joe said, "and he has bandages in a few places. He's at our place; Jason too."

"Oh, Jason." Frank said. "How is he?"

"Arm in a splint, and bandages, but OK," Omar said.

"Brad's right here in ICU," Frank said.

"Yes, we've just seen him," Omar replied.

"I have to contact people where I work," Frank said.

"We've been in touch with authorities," Joe said.

"But..." Frank said when the nurse interrupted, "That's enough for now. Don't worry. Things'll be taken care of."

Omar said, "We'll be back to see you when we can."

Joe added, "We'll be sure to tell Paco we saw you; I'm sure he'll be here as soon as he can manage a way."

Omar and Joe followed the nurse out who said, "It's good you told them their boyfriends are OK and with you."

Joe replied, "They're both anxious to see them as soon as you let them. Maybe you heard me say that Frank's boyfriend is a nurse. Someone told him maybe tonight. What time could they come?"

"It's not a good idea tonight," the nurse replied. "We want them calmed down and to sleep as early as we can. If you can get them here right away, I can get them in."

"Oh, great," Joe said."

"Do you live close?" the nurse asked.

"Just by DuPont Circle," Omar answered.

"I know DuPont Circle," the nurse said, chuckling.

"Don't let your mind go places," Joe added. "Living near there doesn't mean anything. Both of us work close."

The nurse said, "You didn't recite anything to Frank."

"Frank's atheist or maybe agnostic," Omar replied. "His boyfriend's working on that; doesn't mean I can't recite the sura of healing for him, just not out loud."

The nurse warmly shook hands saying, "If you can get their boyfriends while I'm still on duty, I'll take them in."

"How do we get them past the receptionist?" Omar asked. "She is… let's say she wasn't very nice."

"Best thing is just to walk right past her like you know where you're going and what you're doing," the nurse answered. "If they're in splints and casts, people'll think they're here for themselves, not to visit someone. If she gives you any shit, tell her to call me. Malcolm X knows how to get things done in this hospital."

Waiting for the elevator, Joe said, "Makes it easier to go to Jason's place tonight if they come now."

Omar said, "Maybe they can use the blankets they used last night and take a taxi down here; takes less time."

Joe thought then said, "Wouldn't work. Can't have 'em stand out in the cold on DuPont Circle wrapped up in blankets trying to get a cab. Bad enough getting a cab under normal circumstances. Call them to be ready waiting for us."

CHAPTER 26

Saturday, March 1, 2008
Maiquetía, Venezuela

Carrying his heavy winter coat and backpack, Ahmed rushed from the Air Canada jet to passport inspection at Simón Bolívar International Airport serving greater Caracas, saying nervously, "I want political asylum."

"Excuse me, what did you say?" the official asked in accented English. "Do you have your passport?"

"I want political asylum," Ahmed said more forcefully.

The surprised official thought in Spanish, *What stupidity is he talking about? Asylum!*

"No jokes," the official said. "Your passport, please."

"It's no joke," Ahmed said. "I want political asylum."

¡Ay, caramba!, the official thought in Spanish. *He arrived from Canada and he wants asylum here?*

"Why do you want asylum here?" the official asked.

Ahmed replied, "Your president supports Palestinians."

Palestinians, the official thought in Spanish. *They're Arabs. He does look Arab.* "Do you have a passport?"

Ahmed handed it to the official, who thought in Spanish: *He's gringo, not Canadian, but seems like an Arab name.* "This is a U.S. passport," he said.

Ahmed spat out the words, "I'm Palestinian! I was born in that fuckin' country and that's the only passport I can get. I renounce my U.S. citizenship."

"I have to call my supervisor," the official said.

After some minutes, an older uniformed official arrived and asked in Spanish, "What's going on?"

"This guy asked for asylum," the first official said in Spanish, handing him Ahmed's passport. "He says he's Palestinian and renounces his U.S. citizenship."

The older official looked at Ahmed, opened the passport to the picture page, looked back at Ahmed, and said in English, "Come with me; bring your things." In his office he asked, "You want political asylum?"

Ahmed, replied, "Yes, sir."

"Why do you want political asylum here?" he asked.

"Your president Hugo Chavez helps Palestinians struggling against the imperialist American oppressors who allow gays and Jews to do indecent things to get their own way. I helped get rid of gays in the U.S., and want to help your great president do it in other places."

The official, startled, thought in Spanish, *Gays,* maricones, *and our marvelous president. He's crazy for sure. This'd be hilarious if it weren't so serious.* After a few moments, with Ahmed increasingly nervous, the official suddenly thought in Spanish, *I know what I can do.* With an ingratiating smile, he said, "Please excuse me a moment. I'll make arrangements for a special guest like you. We weren't expecting asylum seekers on a weekend." He told his lieutenant in a low voice in Spanish, "Watch the door. I don't think he'll escape, but we have to make sure."

Upon returning, the official said to Ahmed, "We've made temporary arrangements for you. I'll take you to the Defense Forces base on the other side of the airport. It's secure if imperialist Americans want to come after you. Give me your baggage claim check. We'll claim your luggage. Give me your coat and backpack too; we'll take them also."

The official summoned the lieutenant, gave him the backpack and claim check, and said in Spanish, "Get his bag and examine these *thoroughly*, if you know what I mean. To Ahmed, he said in English, "Please come with me. I'm taking you there personally to make sure you are taken care of properly. We'll keep your passport so we can make arrangements. My assistant will bring your belongings later."

Ahmed, nervousness subsiding, followed.

CHAPTER 27

Sunday, March 2, 2008
Lafayette, Virginia, USA

"Fatima sure is a brave girl; she cried when her father told her that her brother was dead, but held up really well," Velma said, dressing for church in what she sometimes also wore to work, a red winter dress with tasteful white patterns.

"Yes," Shane replied as he put on a dark brown polyester-wool suit, yellow shirt, brown tie with small patterns, and brown socks and shoes. "Maybe they has differ'nt ways of dealin' with things when someone dies."

"I's a bit concerned 'bout Amelia," Velma said. "This's the first time she's been around death of anyone sorta close. Glad in a way Fatima didn't break down and cry much; might've been too much for Amelia right now. 'Course we don't want to keep her from bein' exposed. We all got to face death sometime and not good to wait until she's grown."

"Yeah," Shane replied. "Kinda glad I knew 'bout fun'rals before my cousin got killed in a car wreck when I was a teenager."

"Good thing I got Jolene," Velma said. "She might say somethin' to Fatima and include her family in prayers."

"She's a nice lady and a good preacher," Shane said. "Didn't know how I was goin' to react to a woman preacher, but she's who the bishop sent. She's good as any man."

"Better," Velma said. "I'm ready."

In the car on the way to nearby Shawsville, Virgina, dressed for a typical winter day in the mountain and valley area, Velma asked, "Does your family go worship together somewhere like we do, Fatima?"

"Sometimes," Fatima answered. "There's a mosque in Blacksburg. Women pray in a separate part. My mom and I go sometimes, but she's not all that interested. There's an Arab food store there she likes to shop. It's mostly my dad, Ahmed, Marwan, and Abou Nidal who go from the station; Mama stays at the station, and I stay with her."

At the White Memorial United Methodist Church, Velma led Fatima to the Reverend Jolene Robbins, a tall woman about five feet ten inches with average build. She looked in her mid-forties with medium brown hair turning gray that she wore stylishly short, and she had soft blue-green eyes. Today she wore a plain navy blue skirt that matched the jacket of her conservatively styled woman's winter suit. A simple pale pink blouse complemented the suit, as did the plain navy blue shoes with block heels.

"You're Fatima," she said with a soft, Eastern Virginia accent. "Let's sit over there; Ms. Roberts can stay with us, then we'll take you to the nursery. We always appreciate help from big girls like you. You ever taken care of little children?"

"No," Fatima answered.

"We're sorry about your brother," Jolene Robbins said.

Fatima's eyes turned moist as she said, "He's my favorite brother. Ahmed was good to me too, but Marwan liked to take care of me when I was little."

"Allah has a special place for boys like him; he'll be lifted up to heaven on the day of judgment," Jolene Robbins said. "We'll say prayers for him and your family today."

She seems so nice, Fatima thought. *She's saying what Baba said on the phone last night.*

237

Jolene Robbins said, "Let's go meet Lucy. She's been taking care of little children here for a long time."

She led the way, resisting her natural instinct to put her arm around Fatima's shoulder, knowing many Muslim women do not like to be touched and unsure when a Muslim makes the transition from girl to woman. Entering the nursery, she introduced Fatima to Lucy Simpson, a spritely, well-built woman in her early sixties who was unaware of any taboo and immediately put her arm around Fatima's shoulder.

"We got just this one little boy, now," she said in a pronounced local accent. "There'll be more later."

Outside the door, Velma took Jolene Robbins's hands and said, "Thank you so much. Fatima's such a nice girl."

Jolene Robbins said, "She'll be OK. God is gracious and merciful." *And works in marvelous and mysterious ways. I was sure that book on Islam was here in my office, but there it was on my bookshelf at home.*

A little over an hour later, Jolene Robbins stood before the congregation wearing her pastoral robe, leading the usual items in the order of worship. Then she began her sermon, "It's with sadness and concern that I say there's a family in our community who needs our prayers. The Hammoud family, next door neighbors to the Robertses, suffered the tragic loss of their son, only twenty-one years old, in an accident in Washington, DC. This occurred only hours after persons from our area set off a bomb at their house. The saddest thing is that the persons setting off the bomb said they were targeting the Hammouds because they're Arab. The Hammoud family are Palestinian Arabs and Muslim. They're fine, upstanding, members of the community and have been for over twenty years. You may know Mr. Hammoud's garage and gas station at the Ironto exit.

"Some of you've heard about Muslims and bad things they're trying to do to this country and around the world. Let me remind you, the first religious terrorism in the world was by persons who considered themselves to be good Christians during the Crusades. We're not going to dwell on that today, but maybe in the future we might look at it in one of our special studies.

"For now, let's say there's no reason for Muslims and Christians to be in conflict. Jesus tells us several times we must reach out and pray for all people, especially those in need. The story of the Samaritan woman at the well in Jericho is just one of many. In the words of Muslims, we are all 'people of the book,' along with the Jews, believers in the God of Abraham which in the Arabic language is Ibrahim and Allah is merely the Arabic word that means God.

"Now I want to read for you one of the most commonly recited passages in the Koran, a message of healing and comfort Muslims recite for many important life events such as death. Listen, and I'm sure you will find it, as they do, relevant for us as Christians and believers in the same God.

> In the name of God, the Compassionate the Caring
> Praise is to God, the sustaining Lord of all words
> The Compassionate the Caring
> Master of the Day of Judgment
> You do we worship
> And you we ask for help
> Guide us on the straight road
> The road of those whom you have given on them
> Not those with anger on them
> Nor those who have gone astray

"Now, in this season of Lent, three weeks before Easter Sunday, let us think about the text for the day...."

CHAPTER 28

Joe, sprawled on the couch, dozing after a day of driving Frank's SUV to places in Baltimore and Laurel, was startled when Omar came home and asked, "How was your trip?"

"Hectic," Joe began. "First to Paco's to get his things."

"What's it like?" Omar asked.

"My Lebanese mother wouldn't approve," Joe said, "but not bad; not cluttered like Jason's we saw last night. An old garden apartment complex in a reasonable neighborhood.

Paco's apartment in Baltimore

"Then we went to the nursing home. The old men were all over him, feeling sorry for him. Rest of the staff really like him too. The Catholic chaplain and some old guys begged him to go to mass; he always helps when he's on duty on Sunday. He tried to beg off, but Jason and I said go ahead. While we had coffee, some old guys doted on Jason being injured, and on me too."

"Then we went to Laurel, where Jason and Paco got things for Brad and Frank. After a late lunch, we went to the church Brad and Jason go to. I hoped Jason didn't want to stay for a service, but he returned soon.

"We came back to Washington and stopped at the hospital to leave off things they'd brought. They found out Frank and Brad'd be put in a regular room; Paco had leaned on them to put them in the same room and let him and Jason stay overnight. Brought them here to get overnight things, then took them back to the hospital. Oh, we had two sets of keys to the apartment made for them. Hope that's OK."

"No problem," Omar said. "I'm surprised the hospital let them stay overnight."

Joe replied, "Paco says these days hospitals like to have family and close friends stay. Helps patients recover, knowing someone close's there. Hospitals are short staffed; having someone to do little things helps. Say, what'd you do today?"

"Talked to an older staff member about Islamic burial in this country," Omar began. "He confirmed Islam accepts local requirements or compromises with them."

Joe commented, "As in so many things, laws in this country were based on assumptions everyone's Christian."

Omar continued, "He confirmed Muslims reluctantly accept embalming if required. Laws and regulations are for public health, sanitation, and safety, and it's in the interests of Muslims to follow them. He told me a place that sells traditional scents for the body during preparation. Turning the body to face Mecca usually's not possible; preparation tables are fixed in place. In cemeteries, the way the graves are faced is usually fixed."

"Maybe I need to go see what cemeteries are like in Dearborn," Joe commented. "Do they wrap them in white cloths, or are they required to use a casket?"

241

"Yes, they use cloths," Omar replied. "Some funeral homes don't like it because they make money selling caskets. Here in the city, there're enough poor people that funeral homes are used to providing cardboard boxes or cheap wooden caskets."

"There's more to this than I imagined," Joe said.

Omar continued, "I went to Abou Tarek's place. Nassar's wife isn't well at all; like she's shut down. He apologized for her and said this started when hoodlums set off a bomb at their house and caught it on fire. They got the fire out, but she was really scared. Then next morning they got my phone call. She's barely spoken since then."

Abou Tarek's home, Arlington, Virginia

"Oh, God, sounds awful," Joe said."

"Yes," Omar agreed. "Also, can't locate their older boy, Ahmed. He and Marwan shared an apartment here. They can't contact the landlord on Sunday. The car he was supposed to take to Nassar is gone too.

"I asked Nassar about the Islamic community where he lives," Omar continued. "He gave me the name of a professor at Virginia Tech, a Pakistani. They're not close, but he knows his name. I asked about Islamic activities there; a big university like Virginia Tech's bound to have Muslims. There's a mosque, but no regular imam, although the professor's sort of a leader. The group's mostly non-Arabs, one reason why Abou Ahmed and his family aren't involved other than Friday prayers. Mostly I think it's socio-economic class difference. I agreed to contact the Pakistani professor. I hope to find out about funeral homes in Blacksburg or other places, so you may not need to."

"Good," Joe said. "Any more contact from the FBI?"

"No," Omar said. "They'll probably wait until at least tomorrow to contact Frank. I'm sure someone's going to ask me about that imam in Arlington; don't know how much I should tell. Information about the older son and the name of the imam is told to me in my role as an imam."

Joe said, "You can't be required to tell things told to you in confidence in your capacity as an imam. That doesn't keep them from asking, and you can tell voluntarily."

"But morally and ethically..." Omar began.

"I'm getting there," Joe said. "This protects persons from self-incrimination. Just like persons can't be required to testify against themselves, something they tell to a clergyman, doctor, lawyer can't be used either. These people have to have personal information to do their jobs properly and have a bond of trust that allows persons to give information without fear it'll be passed on to their detriment.

"It's not clear whether things Nassar and Abou Tarek told you about the imam and the older son are in this category. The information isn't direct and not directly implicating. I'd need to research privileged communication and see what the courts have decided.

"As you said, what's allowed under law and what's moral and ethical are two different issues. You have your own ethics to do what you feel's in the best interests of persons you're dealing with. If you follow your conscience and decide not to disclose this information, I doubt seriously anyone'd try to hold you responsible unless you're protecting terrorists under the guise of religion."

"The imam may be involved in terrorism," Omar said.

"But you're not protecting him," Joe replied. "If anyone, you're protecting Abou Tarek and his sons."

"OK," Omar replied. "I don't know yet what my conscience is telling me. You know how much I hate al Qaeda, but I don't want that to cloud my judgment."

"Sit on it for a while," Joe suggested. "No one's after you for information now. Look at it this way: The FBI's going to find out eventually if Nassar reports his son missing and notifies police about the missing car. You might benefit everyone by getting the information to the FBI sooner. Maybe lean on Nassar to notify Arlington police and then you notify the FBI. They won't know you notified the FBI."

"Maybe you're right," Omar said.

"It's not a matter of being right," Joe said. "I'm sure not going to tell you what you should feel and do as an imam. If I give you information that helps you draw your own conclusions, fine."

"Thanks, habibi," Omar said.

Joe said, "What about something to eat. Lunch's wearing off."

Omar said, "They had lots of food at Abou Tarek's place, and of course I couldn't turn them down."

Joe said: I'll find something in the kitchen. Good thing we stocked up on food last night at a proper supermarket when we left Jason's. You want something?"

"No thanks," Omar replied. "I'll see what's on TV."

Both became alert when they heard, "Today in Washington, members of local area churches demonstrated near Rory's, a gay bar near DuPont Circle that was bombed Friday night, claiming the bombing was God's punishment of homosexuals...." Images of placards read, "God punishes gays for their sins" in large block letters.

"Members of local congregations of the Metropolitan Community Church staged a counter demonstration." Images of placards showed, "God loves me and I am gay." "Police separated the two sets of demonstrators to prevent violence. Demonstrators from the Metropolitan Community Church emphasized Christianity does not condone violence, and they will turn the other cheek if attacked.

"The Westboro Baptist Church in Topeka, Kansas, issued a statement today that members would arrive in Washington tomorrow for further demonstrations at the bar and at funerals of those who were killed. Police confirmed only one person is dead; hospital officials say others are in serious but not critical condition...."

"Shit!" Omar exclaimed. "Are they going to his burial to demonstrate? That's the last thing the family needs."

Joe said, "They'd have to know when and where it is."

"What's the likelihood of that?" Omar asked.

"Pretty low, unless police release details," Joe said. "DC has to issue a death certificate quickly; it'd have to before the body's released. How soon they'd file it in public records is the question. Best we can do is appeal to the police to sit on it when they ask us to confirm the identity, likely be tomorrow. It's in the hands of Allah."

"Yes I know," Omar said. "What else's on television? I need to get up early and deal with a lot tomorrow."

CHAPTER 29

Monday, March 3, 2008
Washington, DC, USA

"I'll close the door if it's OK," Joe said entering Roger Chen's office. Surprised, Roger agreed and replied, "How was your weekend?"

"Not good," Joe replied. "That's why I need to talk."

"Roger Chen asked, "More trouble at home?"

"Not home as in Michigan," Joe replied, "although things there haven't changed. Do you remember two guys from Omar's class who came to our Eid dinner?"

Roger Chen answered, "Yes, the Marine Corps officer and the Arabic language specialist at the NSA."

Joe described, with his usual preciseness, events since then up to his visit to the gay bar, emphasizing he discovered they were gay later, saw no reason to terminate the friendship, and that he went to the gay bar only because Brad asked him.

He sure is going to some length to distance himself from their being gay, Roger Chen thought. *He's dragging this out too.* He said, "This obviously has you concerned. There've been gays in the military before, some in positions of importance. It's mildly embarrassing at times when it comes out, but not a big deal. Homosexuality is a fact of life we accept and deal with and wouldn't affect anything here in the AG office. Why'd you wait two weeks to tell me? There must be more to it."

When Joe said he wanted to keep it quiet that an Attorney General employee was in a gay bar, emphasizing he wouldn't go there otherwise, Roger Chen interjected, "Even if you did, it wouldn't make a difference. What you do in your personal life's no concern so long as it's not illegal, unethical, or compromises your work. There must be more, if you're bringing it to my attention now."

Joe then described events of the weekend, including FBI and police contacts, emphasizing he had identified himself as being with the Attorney General's office only to the FBI and Metropolitan Police. "...You see, I'm further implicated and one of the few who can connect the bombing at the gay bar with the guy caught at the NSA."

Roger Chen said, "I haven't heard about a bomb at the NSA; I might not until he's charged, if then. I appreciate your telling me. Is that everything?"

Joe answered, "One more thing about taking time off, but that's all concerning this situation."

Roger Chen said, "You handled things the way you're supposed to: always professional, showing good judgment. It's hard to imagine you'd be involved in prosecution of the guy caught at the NSA, so there wouldn't be a conflict of interest. It's remotely possible you could be called to testify, but unlikely. That wouldn't be a conflict of interest, but it could be tricky. Let's worry about that if the time comes."

"That's what I thought," Joe said. Then he told details of burial arrangements, concluding, "... They live on the other side of Roanoke. I'd like time off to go with Omar. I don't have to, but he needs support because this's the first time he's done it. To be honest, I want to go. I've got plenty of vacation time. It's short notice, but I can arrange my work."

Roger Chen replied, "Yes, I understand. I have no objection in principle. Why don't you come back and let's review what you're working on and how it'll be handled. How long will you be gone?"

"Can't say for sure," Joe answered. "Tomorrow's the earliest we could go if they release the body today. They might have a burial tomorrow, which is the Muslim tradition, but they might have to wait until Wednesday. We could possibly come back on Wednesday, but I don't think Omar'd leave the family so quickly. We might come back on Thursday, so I could come in Thursday afternoon, but for sure on Friday. That could change, of course, depending on when police release the body."

"There you are, being super conscientious," Roger Chen said. "Don't worry about coming back on Friday; take the rest of the week off, assuming your work's covered."

"Thanks," Joe said.

"Thanks for telling me," Roger Chen said. "Take it easy. This is stressful. Don't push yourself too hard."

CHAPTER 30

Monday, March 3, 2008
Christiansburg, Virginia, USA

Montgomery County Sheriff Jack Bellows sat in the office of James W. Pierce, Commonwealth's Attorney, in the courthouse in the center of town. Christiansburg had been a sleepy county seat and commercial town until recently, when Virginia Tech in nearby Blacksburg grew to over 25,000 students. That had changed the character of the county, much to the dismay of long-time local residents, including public officials like these two.

The sheriff ran the county jail and was the first interface between persons arrested and prosecutors. Jack Bellows, from a local family, was portly, in his late forties, and wore a winter uniform like those of his deputies. James Pierce, slightly younger, was dressed like a small town lawyer. He too came from an established local family. The sheriff always informed him about arrests that he would prosecute on behalf of the state, a regular Monday morning activity over coffee.

"Just one case," the sheriff stated, sipping coffee and handing him papers. "Local rednecks bombed a house in Lafayette; one arrested on the spot; other two soon after."

James Pierce glanced at the documents and asked, "Two Bateses related?"

"Prob'ly cousins," Jack Bellows answered. "So much intermarriage, if they bother to get married, everone's related t' everbody else.

They're from out east of Blacksburg, real rednecks, don't work too hard; dig up wild plants to sell for landscaping; and a few other enterprises, shall we say."

"Know who you mean," James Pierce replied. "Seems you know a fair amount about them."

"Lots of little run-ins," the Sheriff began. "Disturbin' the peace, truancy, and harassin' people 'round th' high school. Couple of run-ins lately for possession of small amounts of mar'wana. Lots switched to growin' it when moonshine wasn't profitable anymore. Most of th' mar'wana stuff is state police responsibility; we only get involved if we stop 'em f'r somethin' else and find it."

James Pierce continued, "Says they're charged with arson, trespassing, destroying property, and other things. Sounds lot more serious than disturbing the peace and possessing marijuana."

The sheriff concurred, "That's why it's surprisin'. I'm not sure an arson charge'd stick. Read the fire department's report; says the fire was caused 'cause explosives were too close to a gas can. Seems he didn't set out to burn down the house. I ain't no lawyer, but don't seem like arson to me. 'Course there's other things to charge 'em with."

"Yes, that's right," James Pierce concurred.

"Besides, only one of 'em allegedly set off th' explosive," the sheriff continued. "Guys in the car just shouted things."

"Well, there's conspiracy," James Pierce said. "Don't see people whose house was bombed preferring charges."

"No one there," the sheriff replied. "Couldn't locate anyone at the house over the weekend, and when we went to the station today, guy who works there said Mr. Hammoud's off to Northern Virginia."

"Station?" the Commonwealth's Attorney asked.

"Guy whose house was hit runs a gas station down at the Ironto exit on 81," the sheriff explained. Then he described the other businesses, including specializing in European cars, concluding,

"Sometimes buys old cars in DC area and sells them up there when he fixes 'em. Must've took off for one."

"You know lots about his business," James Pierce said.

"Me 'n' the deputies sometimes deal with him over cars he hauls in, plus stop by for bathroom breaks and gets coffee," the sheriff continued. "Don't deal with th' owner hisself much, 'cept if some problem haulin' in a car; he's usually back in th' garage. Seems OK. Talks kind of funny, bein' a for'ner; all of 'em who work there do, 'cept his kids."

"Where they from?" James Pierce asked.

"Don't know for sure," the sheriff answered. "Must be some A-rab place. Read down through the deputy's report where neighbors said guys in the car shoutin' they don't want no A-rabs here."

James Pierce skimmed through the pages then said, "That sure doesn't sound very nice, but using the 'f' word isn't a crime. Anyone talk to the neighbors?"

"Not since Saturday when they called to give statements. Sent a patrol car out this mornin' when I read the report; we got patrols out in that part of the county most of the time. No one home. Pro'bly at work."

"Yes, probably," James Pierce agreed. "What evidence you got? I can read later, but can you tell me now?"

"Statements of neighbors and catching Kyle Bates on the spot; there's dynamite sticks," the sheriff said. "No fingerprints 'cause he wore gloves, cold as it was."

"Did you seal the place off and do a forensic search?" The Commonwealth's Attorney asked.

"No," the sheriff answered. "Waitin' 'til today to see if I wanted to bring in State Police and Fire Marshall."

James Pierce said, "I need to look this over in more detail, but based on what you've told me so far, we'd have a hell of a time getting a conviction on anything serious enough to be a felony. Maybe best thing is see if we can get a plea bargain out of 'em. Like charge 'em with malicious mischief and sentence 'em to six months' community service. For sure they couldn't pay a fine."

"And havin' 'em sit in a jail cell wouldn't 'complish nothin' 'cept cost the taxpayers money," the sheriff said.

"I'm pretty sure that Grafton at the General District Court would go along with it," James Pierce said.

The sheriff said, "Don't they have to have an attorney? We read 'em their rights."

"Yes, of course, but guys like them aren't going to pay for an attorney even if by some miracle they do have money," James Pierce said. "They'd just want a public defender, but you've got a point there. Might be best to see who we'd get for a public defender. Might get someone who'd be a stickler for making sure they had a full and fair trial on everything. Let me get Judy to find out. There's a duty roster where lawyers in the county have to take turns being public defenders." Into the phone, "Judy, would you please call Judge Grafton's office and find out who's next on the duty roster to be public defender?" To the sheriff, "If we do it this way, we see to it they get some punishment. If we go to trial and the jury acquits, they get off scot free."

"Yeah," the sheriff agreed. "My department decides th'community service. Always picking up the trash on roads."

"Serve them right to have to clean out the bedpans at the nursing home," the Commonwealth's Attorney offered, "but wouldn't want those guys too close to any patients."

"Yeah," the sheriff agreed. "Wait; we can assign 'em to clean out the animal shelter."

The Commonwealth's Attorney chuckled as his secretary handed him a slip of paper and then said, "I know him. I'll probably be having lunch with him and some others today, anyway. I'll put the deal to him. He'll go along."

CHAPTER 31

Monday, March 3, 2008
Washington, DC, USA

At 2 p.m., Sergeant Beasley entered Frank and Brad's hospital room, saluted to Frank, and said, "Good afternoon, Sir."

"Sarge!" Frank exclaimed. "Sorry I can't return the salute. You didn't have to come to the hospital just because I had someone call that I couldn't come in. Pull up a chair."

Sergeant Beasley said in a low voice, "Sir, as much as I'd like it to be, this isn't a social visit. I've been trying to get you the last two days because of something serious you need to be informed about, even if you're in the hospital. I came at the earliest possible moment visitors are allowed. We really need to talk privately if possible."

Frank asked, "What's happened? One of the guards get in trouble, something to be kept quiet?"

"No, Sir," Sergeant Beasley replied. "It's when we made a decision and that person from another agency came to see us; you had an incident on Thursday."

Frank said, "Oh, the FBI. Then, gesturing to his roommate, he continued, "The guy over there is Brad Spencer. He works in the Arabic language section. He knows all about this. The FBI talked to him too. He doesn't know what happened Thursday and my trip to the Pentagon on Friday, but it's not going to hurt for him to know."

Sergeant Beasley said, "Saturday morning our guys caught someone entering the facility with hidden explosives, the same person who you suspected with the Arabic name."

Frank said, "Oh, shit! Now these two cases are connected for sure."

Sergeant Beasley replied. "I'm confused. Two cases?"

Frank began, "Brad and I were injured Friday at the same place when a bomb was set off. It was he who was suspicious and discovered the plot at the NSA. Now I realize both are connected. I could tell more, but now I need to contact Colonel Granger at the DoDIG urgently."

Sergeant Beasley thought, *Only place a bomb's gone off was at the gay bar.* He asked, "Er, you were at that place where the bomb went off on Friday night?"

"Yes," Frank answered. "As strange and bizarre as it might sound, it was in the line of duty."

"Line of duty?" Sergeant Beasley asked, perplexed.

"Becoming commander of the Marine Guards at our place wasn't the only reason I was reassigned here," Frank explained. "It was a good cover. Surely you've figured out."

Sergeant Beasley replied, "Well, yes, but not what for."

"Maybe Colonel Granger can fill you in more." Frank explained his dual assignment, concluding, "Is it possible you could see Colonel Granger at the Pentagon today? It's urgent for our unit. My personal stuff can wait."

Sergeant Beasley replied, "I have my car. How can I contact him? You have his number?"

Frank answered, "It's written down at my desk and can be looked up on the computer easily, but no computer here."

Sergeant Beasley said, "I'll call the guys on my cell phone. (pause)

"Tye? Sarge. I'm in the major's hospital room. He's OK. Bunged up, but OK, considering. Tye, I'm glad it's you. It's about that incident on Saturday morning. Look up a phone number on the computer." He gave details, waited, and concluded, "Got it. I'll go to the Pentagon this afternoon. You can call me on this phone."

(pause)

"Yes, I'll tell him," Sergeant Beasley said. "Bye now.

"They said tell you to get well soon. Good thing it was Tye. We're keeping things quiet."

Frank said, "Tyler Adams. He's a good Marine."

"One of the best," Sergeant Beasley agreed. "Other two were Dan Morales and Mike Kleinberg. Damned good too."

"Yes," Frank agreed.

Sergeant Beasley called Colonel Granger and agreed to go the Pentagon as soon as possible.

(pause)

"Probably half an hour," Sergeant Beasley continued.

After saying goodbye, he said to Frank, "There's something else. This was in the morning distribution."

"Oh, shit, so he did write it!"

"His secretary came rushing, trying to retrieve it. I pretended I hadn't seen it."

"Great thinking!" Frank exclaimed.

"I've had to cover my ass a few times, too, Sir," Sergeant Beasley said. "I made a few copies and have one here for you. Maybe the original needs to be locked up. I'm sure you want me to show it to Colonel Granger."

"Yes," Frank answered. "Colonel Granger might want the original, which's OK."

At that moment, Paco and Jason came in, Jason stopping at Brad's bed, Paco hobbling to Frank's side.

Paco hesitated when he saw Sergeant Beasley and said, "Oh, sorry, you have company." Paco turned to leave, but Frank said, "No, stay. This is Sergeant Beasley; you called him this morning. Sarge, this is Francisco Mendoza."

29 February 2008

Major Frank Reynolds, Commander
U.S. Marine Corps Security Detail
National Security Agency
Fort Meade, MD

It has come to my attention that you are exceeding your authority in applying a level of security that is not justified by the circumstances. You are hereby directed to return to the previous level of security until further notice.

Edward L. Ross, Colonel U.S. Air Force
Deputy Associate Director

They shook hands and Frank said, "Paco was hurt the same time I was. He's staying here to help me; he can't work. He's a nurse at the VA nursing facility in Baltimore."

Sergeant Beasley thought, *Nurse from Baltimore. Of course.* He smiled and said, "Nice to see you're in good hands. I'd better be going."

"Thanks a lot for coming," Frank said.

Sergeant Beasley said, "You take care now."

CHAPTER 32

Monday, March 3, 2008
Maiquetía, Venezuela

"Good afternoon," the senior immigration official said when he knocked on Ahmed's door in a VIP detention facility for persons for whom a conventional jail cell could cause difficulties. "I'm sorry to keep you so long without contact. I hope you were comfortable and the food was tasty. We made some of our very special dishes."

"Er, yes," Ahmed answered. *It's about time*, he thought. *It feels like I'm in jail, only jails aren't this nice, from what I see on television.*

"We weren't able to do anything yesterday because it was Sunday," the official explained, "but I've been working all day to make special arrangements for you. I arranged for you to have asylum for only $4,000 instead of the usual $5,000 because you're a young man and you'll work hard for us." He thought in Spanish, *He has a little more than $3,000 in his luggage, the lieutenant said. Probably took a tip for himself.*

Ahmed said "Er, I don't have that much."

"That's unfortunate," the official replied. He paused as though deep in thought and then said, "I might be able to convince him to take a little less. Maybe promise you'll do extra work for us. What did you do where you came from?"

"I worked on automobiles," Ahmed answered. "Do you really think he'd take less?"

"I can take him what you offer and see," the official said. "How much could you pay?"

Ahmed thought, *I should have about $3,000. I thought I had more in the backpack. Must've counted wrong.* "Er, I can pay $3,000," he said.

"Give me $3,000 and we'll see," the official said.

"Er, OK," Ahmed said as he counted $3,000.

We can take the rest when we make a medical exam, the official thought in Spanish. He then said, "Tomorrow afternoon, we'll take you on a special airplane to a place you can be very useful to us. Our President, His Excellency Mr. Chávez, is doing humanitarian work to free captives on the Colombian border," He thought in Spanish, *I didn't say he'll go to the Colombian border.* "If I don't tell you otherwise, please assume it'll be OK. Tomorrow morning you'll have a complete medical examination. We need to make sure persons where you came from have not infected you with diseases like they did in Africa."

"They wouldn't know I'd be here," Ahmed replied.

"We need to be sure," the official said. "Just in case there's something, we have the best medical care to make you well. Have a good evening, and enjoy your evening meal. We're making it special, just for you."

"Er, thanks," Ahmed said, amazed at the nice treatment he thought he was receiving.

CHAPTER 33

Monday, March 3, 2008
Washington, DC, USA

At home after work, Joe took off his trench coat, scarf, suit, and tie, dressed casually, and collapsed on a chair, thinking about going the next day.

Omar came home, disturbing his dozing, saying, "Oh, hello, habibi."

You look even more frazzled than me," Joe said. "Let me get you a cup of tea; I'll have more myself."

Omar smiled faintly. "Must be a bad day if you're having tea. I'd love some."

Soon after, Joe brought tea, asking, "What about tomorrow?"

Omar replied, "Hearse'll be here about noon; we'll go directly to the funeral home and see what we do next. We'll have to squeeze in the hearse with the driver, or else one of us rides with the Hammouds. I'd rather squeeze in the hearse; but if you want, I can ride with them."

"For sure, squeeze in the hearse," Joe replied. "It'd be pretty tedious for you to ride with them."

"Not sure how long we'll be there; can't rush back immediately," Omar continued. "I made arrangements at the university to be gone the rest of the week; I'll need to be at the center on Friday."

Joe said, "I'm off the rest of the week. I suppose you gave a statement to the police."

Omar replied; "Did it out rushing around."

"I went to their office about three," Joe added. "Asked them not to release information too soon so this church group wouldn't go demonstrate."

"I was there later," Omar said. "I asked them to delay releasing information too; made a point of not telling police where the burial'll be. What say we go eat?"

Soon they sat in a quiet corner of a trendy sandwich and salad shop where Omar began, "I called the Pakistani professor. Nice guy; a biochemistry professor. He confirmed the Hammouds stick to themselves. He was sad to hear about Marwan's death. Said it was an accident and didn't go into details. He seemed pleased the Hammouds found an imam, me, relieved more wouldn't be expected of him. He'll meet us at the funeral home tomorrow afternoon. If the burial doesn't conflict with classes, he'll be there too. He gave me the name of a funeral home that's well thought of, especially the way they handled the Virginia Tech killings. It's more likely to be sensitive to Muslims than a funeral home in other towns."

"I can imagine a funeral home in Ann Arbor would be more sensitive than one in Ypsilanti," Joe added.

"I called the funeral director," Omar continued. "He was very nice and open to serving Muslims, but they haven't had a full Muslim burial; just an occasional death for which they prepared the body to ship somewhere else. They recognize they need to be prepared now that a small stable Muslim population is there. Regulations and insurance might not allow anyone but a licensed funeral director in the preparation room. He'll check."

"Makes sense," Joe said. "Suits against funeral homes could be lawyers' tickets to fame and fortune."

"He said maybe the family could apply perfume in a private location," Omar said. "Good thing I talked to him before I talked to Nassar. I suspect he'd actually try to do it in his basement. With the bad wound and his wife not well, it'd be a disaster. The funeral director said he'd call funeral directors who've had Muslim burials to find out. He said he'd see about orienting the body towards Mecca, but most things are fixed in place.

"I called again later about the burial plot; I'll get to that in a minute. He asked about caskets, and I explained Muslims aren't buried in caskets, only wrapped in three white cloths. He seemed unhappy about that. I told him it's up to Nassar, but unless there's some strong reason, it just wouldn't be in the Muslim tradition so I doubt that Nassar'd want to buy one. He emphasized there has to be something to transport the body from DC to Blacksburg; they can't have a body wrapped in cloth all that distance. He mentioned inexpensive plywood caskets or in extreme cases cardboard boxes."

"Makes sense too," Joe said. "People driving by could freak out if they saw a dead body wrapped in cloths; another invitation to a lawsuit."

"He said they arrange the burial, contacting the cemetery, opening the grave, and those things," Omar continued. "He recommended a new cemetery in Blacksburg. He said they own a part interest and he wants us to know that, but that's not why he's recommending it. The old town cemetery's full, and other cemeteries in the area have a strong Christian atmosphere. The new cemetery's almost empty and has plenty of available plots. The cost would be about the same as other cemeteries. He can't guarantee any'd face Mecca, but it's hilly and not oriented in true directions, so it's possible. He has to talk to Nassar himself and get a commitment from him. He also said he requires payment before he sends a hearse."

"Yes, of course," Joe said. "They're in business too."

Omar concluded, "After that I went to Arlington to talk to Nassar. Maybe we should be more private."

Walking to their apartment, Omar continued, "It was interesting to see Nassar's composure even if it's his son's burial. He knows how to drive a hard bargain. Must be hardened, growing up in a refugee camp, but Palestinians have been shrewd operators for centuries; they're not well liked in the Middle East."

"That's the impression I get from old-timers in Dearborn," Joe said. "Palestinians bring lots of their problems on themselves and brought some with them when they were forced to Lebanon."

"There's a lot of truth in that," Omar said, "but we're getting into one of my lectures. Nassar tried to talk the funeral director out of buying a casket. He challenged him on each item the funeral director said he had to charge for. I thought he was going to offer to dig the grave himself. He even wanted the funeral director to provide three sheets to wrap the body. The funeral director offered to buy them and charge Nassar. In the end, Nassar said he'd get the sheets himself. I think his grief affects him and he isn't thinking clearly; he automatically reverts back to behavior he learned from the camps: always wary of anyone; automatically assume they're out to take advantage of him.

"Nassar and Abou Tarek got a key to Marwan and Ahmed's apartment and went this morning. Marwan's bags were packed to go somewhere, probably with Ahmed. Ahmed's suitcase and backpack weren't there, and some clothes were missing. His cell phone was on a chair like it'd been tossed aside."

Joe said, "Maybe he went somewhere U.S. cell phones won't work; mine didn't in London."

Back home sprawled on the couch, Omar continued, "I encouraged Nassar to go to the Arlington police to report Ahmed as a missing person and report the missing car; offered to go with him. Abou Tarek thought he should tell police the imam's behind this, but I said 'no.' Words just came to me to say it wasn't the right place."

"Good thinking," Joe said.

"Then words just came to me again to say I'd tell the authorities and give authorities Ahmed's telephone," Omar said. "I said I'd be in touch with them anyway; I didn't say which authorities.

"I met Cranford Brooks at the Metropolitan Police Station, gave him the name of the imam, the address of the apartment and what they found there, the car information, and Ahmed's cell phone. After that, I went to the university to deal with things before taking off."

"I had to work late, too," Joe said. "I hate to ask, tired as we are, are we going to see Brad and Frank tonight?"

"Guess we should," Omar answered, "especially since we'll be gone a few days. They need to know what's going on with the FBI in case they contact them."

CHAPTER 34

Monday, March 3, 2008
Washington, DC, USA

Brad had the back of his bed raised and was wearing glasses with one ear piece removed when Omar and Joe arrived, commenting it was good to see him up and alert.

"That was Paco's doing," Jason said.

"Just a bit of Mexican ingenuity," Paco said, smiling. "Taught 'em that trick in the nursing home."

"Omar said to Brad, "You look better. You can't talk, but maybe someone'll tell how you're doing."

"He's perking up a bit," Paco said.

"What've you two been up to?" Frank asked. "You look frazzled."

Omar replied, "Mostly helping the father make burial arrangements. We're going there tomorrow; hope it doesn't bother you we're participating in the burial of the guy who caused your injuries and might've killed you."

"Didn't you see the news tonight?" Jason interjected. "Police say he tried to get as far away from others as he could, screaming 'stay away'; he won't be gay any more, and something about virgins in heaven."

Omar's exclaimed, "Oh, my God!"

"They conclude he's a Muslim distraught over being gay, acted alone intending to kill only himself," Jason said.

"That's not true," Joe said, also horrified. "He wasn't acting alone. They're keeping it quiet."

Frank concurred and said, "That's a strong reaction from both of you. Is being gay so terrible for Muslims?"

Omar stated, "It's the reference to virgins on the way to heaven. The Q'ran says the path to heaven is guided by attractive young women. Many jihadists interpret this as meaning they're literally virgin and will give sexual favors along the way. It's easy to dismiss that as manipulation to convince suicide bombers. When a young gay Muslim uses it to justify suicide, which is forbidden, to stop being gay, that's a whole new dimension Islam has to deal with."

Paco stated, "Fucked up our lives. I'll probably miss a semester of classes because I can't get to the campus."

"Who knows if I have a job waiting for me?" Jason added. "They were none too pleased when I told them I wouldn't be able to work for a while."

Frank said, "Everyone deserves a decent burial, even enemies killed in combat. Do what you need to do, and don't worry about my feelings. Besides, he's not really enemy."

Brad struggled to speak; Jason put his arm on his shoulder, and said, "Don't strain yourself, Hon; I think I know what you're trying to say. He's probably saying something about forgiveness like Jesus did."

Brad nodded his head in agreement and Jason continued, "He's not the only one to commit suicide because he couldn't cope with being gay. Unfortunately, a fair number of fundamentalist Christians have done the same, but they usually do it in private."

Paco said, "In the home, some old guys are still bitter about what happened to them in Vietnam, and they make life miserable for themselves and those around them. The ones who put it behind them can be pleasant to be around. It's a whole lot easier to see that and apply it to someone else. When it's me, damn, it's hard to do."

Joe asked, "What'd you two do today?"

"Went to see a doctor like we were told in the ER," Paco began, "orthopedists near here. They had to work us in because we didn't have appointments, but they examined us thoroughly, or at least they did me, took x-rays, and said the treatment in the ER was good. My foot injuries are not all that serious: bad sprain or maybe hairline fracture that doesn't show up on x-rays. Need to stay off of it at least a week and have them look at it again."

"Same here," Jason said. "Doesn't look like a serious fracture. They put on a different kind of splint and said come back in a week. They couldn't say how long I'd be unable to work, but were cautiously optimistic saying about a week. Somehow I have to go to Fairfax and see the doctor designated as my primary care physician on my insurance about the other injuries. Now I have to figure out how I can get there on the metro and bus."

"When I get back, maybe I can take you there," Omar offered, "if we can work around my teaching schedule."

"Thanks," Jason replied. "I need to do laundry too. Hard to carry laundry on the bus and metro."

"You can do laundry at our place," Omar offered, "but I can still take you to the doctor when I get back."

"I'm doing laundry tomorrow morning," Joe said. "You can do your laundry so I can show you where things are. You'll be coming there anyway, won't you? We noticed you'd been there while we were gone today."

"Thanks," Jason said. "That'd help a lot."

Paco said, "I've got to go to Baltimore to see a doctor too. "I haven't designated a primary care physician yet, but now's time to do it. Can't be running back to DC every time I get the flu. Mostly doctors at the nursing home look after me for something minor, but can't ask them to tend to this."

"I can take you there when I get back," Omar offered.

"Thanks, man." Paco replied. "That's not necessary. I found out there's good train service from here to central Baltimore and not far from there to where I'd likely find a doctor. I can take a cab from the train station."

"I have the week off; I could take you somewhere on Friday," Joe offered. "I could drive Frank's car."

"Let's wait and see," Jason added. "You guys've been more than generous. Don't know what we'd have done without you."

"Yeah," Paco said. "Soon as we get halfway back to normal, we'll make it up to you."

Joe said, "Weather'll be nice soon, and maybe we can have a big outdoor bash and put this behind us."

Omar smiled, "Yeah, must be nice here in spring." He stood to go and suddenly observed, "Hey, these beds have white sheets on them."

Paco said; "You just now noticing? Most hospitals and nursing homes use white sheets."

"Wonder where the hospital gets them," Omar asked. "We need three white sheets to bury the guy in."

Paco replied, "In our homes there's a linen service. They just deliver clean sheets and pillow cases couple of times a week and take the dirty ones away."

"Hmmm," Omar said. "There must be a linen service here; maybe I could get sheets there. They must have old sheets that're worn out and can't be used anymore."

"As big a place as this hospital is, they might have their own laundry," Paco said. "Maybe ask the nurses."

"Maybe that nice guy in intensive care," Joe suggested.

"See if he's on duty on the way out," Joe said. "Yalla, we've got to go before they kick us out. See you tomorrow for laundry. Too bad you don't have your phones."

"Oh, we didn't tell you!" Jason exclaimed. "We got our phones back and coats too."

"Great, so we can contact you," Omar said as put his hand gently on Brad's free arm and recited the sura of healing in Arabic.

They continued with their usual goodbyes.

CHAPTER 35

Tuesday, March 4, 2008
Washington, DC, USA

In mid-morning, a doctor and technicians were examining and treating Brad with curtains closed around his bed. Paco had been required to leave; Jason was away doing laundry.

A man in his sixties strode into the room without knocking and exclaimed, "There you are!"

He stood five feet ten, had closely trimmed silver gray hair, and his steel gray eyes penetrated through brass-frame glasses. A tailor-made heavy dark brown leather jacket open in the front revealed an olive-green and white-striped long sleeved shirt, along with dark olive green pants that covered his rugged physique that would have fit a younger man.

Startled, Frank said, "Dad! What're you doing here?"

His father replied, "A more relevant question is what the hell're you doing here? After the hospital called, I got the first flight I could to see what the hell you're up to that'd get you into this public hospital right at the same time as that gay bar bombing. I bet that other person they've got you sharing a room with is one of those homo perverts."

He didn't even ask how I am, Frank thought, becoming angry. *All he cares about is a gay person in here.*

"Keep your voice down," Frank said. "He can hear you. For your information, he's one of my best friends and a work colleague and was injured the same place I was."

"And where the hell was that?" the older man asked.

"In the gay bar," Frank spat out the words. "Just in case it makes a difference to you, it was in the line of duty."

His father shouted, "What the hell were you doing in a gay bar and how could that be in the line of duty?"

A nurse stepped out and said softly, "Please keep your voices lower; you're disturbing the patient."

Frank said, "It's classified and you don't have a need to know. You of all persons should know that."

Paco walked in on crutches, startled, and Frank said, "This is my father."

"Paco Mendoza," he said holding out his right hand while balancing on crutches.

"Bart Reynolds," the older man said, holding out his hand for a perfunctory handshake. "General Bart Reynolds. What is your status here?"

"I'm looking after Frank," Paco replied. "I can't work, so I keep him company and help."

"Paco's my friend," Frank stated. "I want him here."

"You injured at the same time?" Bart Reynolds asked.

"Yes, he was," Frank replied annoyed.

"I suppose that was in the line of duty also," Bart Reynolds continued, cynically and disdainfully.

Paco said emphatically, "I was exercising my right of free association guaranteed by the U.S. Constitution."

Bart Reynolds said with a smirk. "Mendoza. That's Hispanic. You one of those Cubans who're taking over the whole damned state of Florida?"

Paco answered, "My family are from Mexico."

"Wetbacks," Bart Reynolds blurted out.

"That's enough, Dad," Frank said forcefully. "Paco's a friend I met in Ohio."

"Ohio?" Bart Reynolds continued. "You came all the way to DC to drag him to homo queer pervert places?"

"I said that's enough!" Frank said. "Paco doesn't drag me anywhere. I told you I was there in the line of duty."

A distinguished-looking black man stepped from behind the curtains wearing a white smock over a dress shirt with a tie and dress slacks, indicating he was likely a medical doctor, and said, "I'm going to have to ask you to leave. You're disturbing our patient and interfering with our procedure. We asked you once to be quiet."

"You can't kick me out," Bart Reynolds said angrily, observing he was black. "I'm his father."

"I can and I will," the doctor said. "Being father of a patient does not give you the right to disturb and interfere with treatment of other patients, and it seems you are disturbing this patient as well."

"If I have to go, why doesn't he?" Bart Reynolds continued, defiantly pointing to Paco.

"Dad, I said that's enough!" Frank almost shouted. "I want him here; besides he's a nurse. He helps, not hinders."

"Now I've heard it all," Bart Reynolds continued tauntingly. "A queer homo male illegal immigrant treating military officers. How could you know anything about treating military of this country with proper respect?"

Paco, his anger at the point of explosion said with seething anger, "I am a citizen of the United States of America, and I know a damn sight more about how to treat military personnel than you do. Wait'll you end up in a VA nursing home and you'll see how the nurses treat you."

The doctor said, "Will you leave *now* or I'll call hospital security to have you removed."

Bart Reynolds, stunned, realizing he had no choice, walked to the door and then turned back. "Just wait. We're getting you transferred to the Bethesda Navy Medical Center where you can get decent medical treatment. No son of Bart Reynolds is going to put up with this."

Frank angrily sat up on the bed and nearly shouted, "That's all I am to you, son of Bart Reynolds. Well Frank Reynolds doesn't want to go to Bethesda Navy hospital."

Bart Reynolds stormed noisily down the corridor.

The doctor said, "I need to tend to this patient. A nurse should see you; maybe you can push the call button."

"That's OK, doctor, thank you," Paco said. "I *am* a nurse and we'll call the floor nurse for assistance."

He hobbled to Frank's bedside, called the nurse, felt Frank's wrist and said, "Pulse rate seems to be high. I'll catch the nurse on her way and make sure she brings the blood pressure monitor."

When they returned, the floor nurse said, "Your blood pressure's elevated, but not to the danger point." She patted Frank's free hand and said, "Seems like you are in good hands. Try to relax as much as you can."

CHAPTER 36

Tuesday, March 4, 2008
Washington, DC, USA

Promptly at 2 p.m. a U.S. Army colonel with a name tag that read "GRANGER" below many rows of ribbons knocked and entered Frank and Brad's hospital room.

Paco struggled to stand, but Colonel Granger said, "Please keep your seat; Otis Granger."

"Paco Mendoza," he said, shaking hands.

Colonel Granger shook Jason's left hand, exchanging greetings, and then said to Brad, "You're Bradley Spencer. Please don't strain yourself. We'll want to talk to you, but only when you're well enough."

"Er, do you want us to leave?" Paco asked.

He replied, "I don't like to ask you to leave with your injuries, but if you feel like fresh air it might be best."

Frank said to Paco, "Maybe you two need to go out on your own, to a movie or something."

Jason smiled slightly as he said, "Yeah, there must be a movie theater in this city somewhere."

When Paco and Jason had gone and the television was turned off, Colonel Granger sat next to Frank's bed and said, "I want to touch base with you on a couple of things. We really appreciate your sergeant coming to see me personally yesterday. We could get involved right away and start working with the FBI much sooner than if information had come through normal channels."

"It was just my duty," Frank said.

"Yes, we know," Colonel said. "Still it's commendable, considering you're in the hospital. Our investigators will be at Fort Meade soon, speaking with the three corporals. What we'd like to know now is how you got the information that prompted you to bring it to Sergeant Beasley's attention."

Frank nodded towards Brad. "He met a person in that bar who he thought was acting strangely and also Arab…" and continued to explain the circumstances.

As Frank was speaking, Bart Reynolds barged into the room and stopped, seeing a U.S. Army colonel in uniform.

Frank said awkwardly, "This is my father."

"Otis Granger, DoDIG," he said, offering a handshake.

Bart Reynolds took his hand and said haughtily, "Bart Reynolds; General Bart Reynolds."

Colonel Granger immediately stated, "Bartholomew Lee Jackson Reynolds, Major General U.S. Marine Corps, Retired. You've been in the Marine Corps personnel section involving yourself in Major Reynolds's hospitalization and duty assignment."

"I suppose that's why you're here, then," Bart Reynolds replied. "Investigating why he was in that homo pervert place and this asinine claim it was in the line of duty. Reynoldses have been a distinguished Marine Corps family for three generations, and I'm not about to allow anything to besmirch the family name now. That's why I'm getting him medically retired and hush up the whole mess. Also get him transferred to Bethesda Medical Center, where he can get decent treatment and not be associated with homo perverts."

Colonel Granger said forcefully, "As a matter of fact, no! Major Reynolds was injured in the line of duty on a project for us. There are crucial things he hasn't had an opportunity to tell us, so now that he's able to communicate, I'm here to find out what he discovered. We're equally interested in trying to 'hush this up,' as you say, but for completely different reasons."

Bart Reynolds continued aggressively, "What kind of duty would take him to a gay bar? He's commander of the U.S. Marine Corps guards at the NSA."

Colonel Granger replied, "General, surely you are not that... er... naïve. We do not use our best military talent on positions like commander of a security detail. That's a cover. If anyone'd realize that, you should."

Bart Reynolds, taken aback, continued blustering. "Cover for what? What the hell do you have him doing that would take him into a place like that?"

Not once has he mentioned his son by name, Colonel Granger observed to himself. *It must've been hell for him growing up.* "General," he responded forcefully, "You must truly be naïve if you don't realize this is classified."

"I'm a General Officer," Bart Reynolds blurted out. "I have the highest security clearance."

"You *were* a General Officer," Colonel Granger replied. "Being retired gives you privileges, but not involvement in military investigations. You, of all people, should know access to classified information requires a need to know, and you do not have that."

"What do you mean I don't have a need to know?" Bart Reynolds retorted angrily. "My family's honor is at stake."

Colonel Granger answered, "That does not justify access to highly sensitive intelligence operations of the U.S. Armed Forces. Moreover, your family's honor is not at stake. Major Reynolds has conducted himself in an exemplary manner."

"Well, we'll see about that," Bart Reynolds replied angrily. "You can't talk to me that way and get by with it."

"General," Colonel Granger replied with increasing anger, "you are interfering in highly sensitive operations involving the security of the United States. Such interference could, as a minimum, lead to an investigation about your motives. At the absolute least, it would be viewed as conduct unbecoming an officer. You must be aware that being retired does not grant you immunity from prosecution. You can be recalled to active duty to face charges. I certainly hope we don't get to that point."

Bart Reynolds's face turned red, seized with rage.

Colonel Granger then said, more calmly, "Will you please leave us alone to continue our discussion."

Bart Reynolds, choking his rage, said forcefully, "You can't throw me out of here. This is a public hospital."

Colonel Granger stated, "I'm notifying hospital personnel if you appear here again, the Pentagon is to be notified immediately and Metropolitan Police if necessary. Interfering with the care of hospital patients is a criminal offense, both from civilian and military perspectives."

Bart Reynolds spun around and stalked out of the room and down the corridor noisily as before.

Colonel Granger said, "Major Reynolds, perhaps you should use the call button to have someone look at Mr. Spencer. It might be useful if she examined you too. I regret it's come to this. I'll stay until she gets here, but we won't discuss any more today."

Frank pushed the call button then said, "Thanks for coming to my defense and protection, Sir."

"Major, we're not doing it for you, although you deserve it," Colonel Granger replied. "We're doing it for ourselves. If it benefits you at the same time, we're pleased."

"You heard him say he's trying to get me transferred to Bethesda Medical Center," Frank said. "Can he do that?"

"I doubt it," Colonel Granger answered, "but independent of anything he's doing, we're beginning the process of having you transferred as soon as you are medically able. It's definitely in our interests to have you in a more secure place than a public hospital. I suspect if you think about it, you might realize it's in your interest as well. At a U.S. Armed Forces medical facility, it's much easier to keep certain persons away from you."

"You mean persons like my father?" Frank asked.

"Yes, that, now that this incident occurred," Colonel Granger answered, "but also the media."

"I see," Frank responded. "One reason I don't want to go to Bethesda is I want to be with Brad."

"We anticipated that, too," Colonel Granger replied. "It's very much in our interests that Mr. Spencer be in a more secure location as well. The real issue is being medically stable enough to make the transfer. Also, from a practical perspective, there's the issue of who pays. When a military person is treated in a civilian facility, especially if it's in the line of duty, the U.S. government pays. Naturally, the Defense Department wants to minimize such payments and provide care in its own facilities."

"Oh, OK," Frank said. "Can our friends be with us there? Will security allow that?"

Colonel Granger answered, "I don't know the details of security arrangements. There must obviously be some arrangement where family members and friends can be allowed on a case-by-case basis, but there needs to be care and discretion about the nature of your relationship. I'm most definitely not asking you anything, and I don't want you to tell anything, but I'm sure you know what I mean. Moreover, as I am sure you're aware, the Navy has a more tolerant attitude about such things."

Frank said, "Thank you again, Sir. I understand."

The floor nurse arrived, and Colonel Granger said, "I'm sorry to say that the last visitor upset these two patients. Please let me emphasize from the perspective of the U.S. Armed Forces we do not want that individual here, and I intend to inform hospital administration on my way out."

"Got ya, Sir," the nurse said and immediately took Brad's pulse and blood pressure.

Colonel Granger walked towards the door, saying, "Best wishes for your speedy recovery."

Walking to the elevator, he thought, *Before speaking to hospital administration, I can call the Pentagon and Marine Corps brass. Bart Reynolds has sympathizers. If I act quick enough, we can make an end run around him and his types.*

CHAPTER 37

Tuesday, March 4, 2008
Lafayette, Virginia, USA

"I'll get Fatima," Nassar said to Roula in Arabic when they arrived home from a long tedious drive in silence. "Can you get the boys' room ready for the two men who'll stay here?"

With a blank expression, she mumbled, "*la.*"

Nassar, stunned by his wife's refusal, started to demand she do it, but instead walked to the Roberts's house.

Velma greeted him warmly, saying, "I'll get Fatima. She's real anxious to see you."

"*Baba,*" Fatima shouted in Arabic, hugging him.

He put his arms around Fatima, who asked in Arabic, "How's mama?"

Nassar answered in Arabic, "Mommy's not well."

"What's wrong?" Fatima asked in Arabic.

"Upset over Marwan and Ahmed," he said in Arabic.

"Ahmed too?" she asked in Arabic, tears in her eyes.

"Yes, dear," Nassar continued in Arabic. "We don't know where he is. We can talk about that later. Let's go now. You're going to have to help a lot. People are coming to stay overnight tonight."

Velma, not understanding what was said, touched Fatima saying, "Go get your things. We can help carry them." To Nassar, "Fatima's such a precious girl, a delight to have around. She missed you terribly."

Nassar somberly said, "Roula isn't doing good."

"Oh? What's wrong?" Velma asked.

"She won't talk to me or anyone," he explained. "The loss of both of her boys hit her hard."

"Both of them?" Velma asked.

"We can't locate our older boy, Ahmed," Nassar replied. "I had to report him missing to the police."

"That's sad," Velma said. To Fatima, "It was real good having you. You can come back any time, but your daddy wants to be with you." To Nassar, "I told people at school her brother's funeral's tomorrow and she'll be absent."

"Thanks," Nassar replied.

"Shane and me'll be there if it's OK," Velma said. "Said I'd not be at work; Shane's takin' the day off too."

Nassar said, "Yes, it's OK. Our burials usually have people from the community show up. A short service in the funeral home, then men'll go to the cemetery."

"We don't rightly know how to act at a Muslim funeral," she said, "but figured we could just pay our respects quietly, if ya don't mind havin' Christians there."

Nassar said, "There's no problem with Christians. We'd be pleased to have you and Mr. Shane."

"While I'm at it, I should tell you people're fixin' supper for y'all tonight," she added. "I'm just supposed to call 'em and tell them when to bring the food over."

He asked, stunned, "Bring food to our house tonight?"

"They can bring it to our house and you come over here if Roula's not doin' well," Velma replied. "It's the custom here. Someone has a death in the family, folks take food so they don't have to worry about cookin' with so much other things goin' on. You're local folks and part of our community, so we want to do what's right; we made sure there's no pork and no Jell-O, neither."

Nassar, fumbling for words, said, "I don't know what to say. We never had anything like this done for us before."

She added, "Let me know what time you'll be back from doin' what you gotta do tonight. While I'm on the subject, Jolene, our pastor, said we'd have lunch for you tomorrow at our church after the funeral. That's our custom, but don't know how you feel about goin' inside a church."

Nassar said, "This's too much to think about right now. We've got no problems going inside churches. We should go. They should be at the funeral home soon, and I need to be there. We've got to get the boys' room ready for two men who're coming; one's an imam and'll recite the Holy Scriptures tomorrow. Fatima needs to get the room ready."

Velma said, "I can come help Fatima if you like."

At home, Fatima rushed to give her mother a hug. Roula gave no response, but looked briefly at Fatima.

She sure don't seem well, Velma thought, *She's upset with the loss of her boys, but not to say nothin' to her own daughter?*

Nassar gently put his hand on Fatima's shoulder as she was beginning to cry and said in Arabic, "*Hayat baba*, you'll have to do things around the house to help. *Baba* has to go to be with Marwan right now. You're such a good girl; please get Marwan's and Ahmed's room ready for guests we're having tonight. Ms. Velma said she'd help you."

His cell phone rang and he answered it and spoke a few words in Arabic. Then he said, "That's the imam. They'll be in Blacksburg in about thirty minutes."

"Sure," Velma replied. "If you'd call us before you leave Blacksburg to sort of give an idea, that'd help. Make sure we got the food ready to start eatin'."

Nassar gave his daughter another hug and left.

CHAPTER 38

After supper, with the door to their room open and dull noise coming from the corridor during hospital visiting hours, Brad watched television and Frank read a John Grisham novel. A middle-aged woman, bundled for winter with heavier winter gear than would be required for a Washington winter, knocked and came in. Brad's face changed from surprise to happiness, to tears of joy, and pain.

"Bradley!" she exclaimed as she rushed to hug him as best as she could. "How are you, dear? We're so worried."

He struggled to speak, then winced with pain.

"Oh, my baby boy," she said with tears in her eyes, leaning to touch him. "Don't try to say anything; I see you can't talk. I just want to know you're going to be OK."

He pointed to Frank and nodded.

"Oh, I shouldn't say things in front of him?" she asked.

When Brad moved his head from side to side, Frank said, "He probably wants me to do the talking. We're good friends and were injured at the same time. You must be his mother. I'm Frank Reynolds. The hospital must've called you as next of kin."

"Oh, sorry, I didn't introduce myself," she said. "I'm Marian Spencer. Bradley's our baby, only not a baby now. His father and I decided I should come right now because I can get off work easier on short notice. He'll come on the weekend, if it's OK."

"Very pleased to meet you, Mrs. Spencer," Frank said and turned off the television. "Sorry we can't offer better hospitality; please take off your coat and have a chair."

She sat close to Brad, saying, "Thank you, you're so nice and polite. What can you tell me about Bradley? It's so impolite to talk in front of him, but I just have to know."

"I can't tell you much, Ma'am," Frank began. "They give information only to next of kin. I've heard doctors and nurses say he's going to be OK. Right now they seem mostly concerned with urgent treatment until he's stabilized."

"That's what they do where we're from," she said, "only tell next of kin. We're from Minneapolis."

"Brad's told us a lot about how good it was to grow up there with a nice family, church, and the like."

"Oh, he told you about us and the church," Mrs. Spencer said, as Brad's face lit up.

"Right now, they're trying to introduce solid food," Frank continued, "in his case, through a straw. Main thing is potty training, then they can remove the IV."

"Oh, dear," Mrs. Spencer commented, "but it sounds positive if you can eat something."

"I'm looking forward to sinking my teeth into some solid food," Frank said. "Oops. Sorry, Brad." *Gee, I'm so chatty and upbeat,* he said to himself. *Being around Brad, Paco, and others maybe taught me social skills. Maybe there all along and I needed to have my façade ripped away.*

"Can you tell me what happened to Bradley?" Mrs. Spencer asked. "I mean the nature of his injuries?"

"I don't know details," Frank replied. "It seems no serious internal injuries. Something sharp hit his head and face, or maybe he hit it, and it caused a gash down the side of his head, face, and shoulder. Maybe broken bones. I heard them say there's no need for immediate surgery."

"What about your injuries, if you don't mind me asking, Frank?" Mrs. Spencer said. "I think that's what you said is your name. I get flustered at times like this, but I'm pretty good at names. Have to be, as an elementary school teacher."

"Yes, I'm Frank," he replied. "I've got broken bones, some pretty bad cuts and bruises too, but they'll heal."

"Oh, good," Mrs. Spencer said. "Oh, not good you're injured, but good you'll recover in time. Could you tell me how you were injured? We, my husband and I, watch the news, of course, and heard about an explosion in a bar here in Washington. Is that where you two were? At first the news said it was a terrorist plot. We couldn't imagine you'd be involved in any of that, dear, but with your speaking Arabic, living in Jordan, and working for the government translating Arabic, well, we just thought there might be some connection. Now it seems that it was just one poor young Muslim man upset about being gay and acting alone. And, dear, there's no problem with us if you were at a gay bar. We figured things out when we visited here last summer and spent so much time with that very nice young man who's your friend; Jason, I think his name is. How is he, by the way? Oh, you can't tell me. Of course we wish it weren't this way. We'd love to have a daughter-in-law and grandchildren, but we already have grandchildren and this is just the way God made things and we are fine. Oh, dear, here I am babbling. Sorry."

Brad showed relief and tears came to his eyes again.

There's that problem out of the way, Frank thought, and said, "It's more complex than that, Ma'am. There're sensitive national security issues we really can't talk about now. I can say this: Because Brad's attentive to things relating to Arabs and actually took the initiative to do something, the situation wasn't much worse. I'm sure more details will come out eventually, but maybe that's all I should say for right now."

"It seems you are involved with this too, and not just as a friend who was at the bar," Mrs. Spencer commented.

"In a way, yes," Frank replied. "Brad and I are friends, and we work at the same place."

"Oh, you're an Arabic translator?" Mrs. Spencer asked.

"No, the Marine security guards."

"We saw the nice young security guards when Bradley gave us a tour," Mrs. Spencer said. "You're one of them? You look older."

"I'm their commander," Frank added. "I'm a Marine officer, so maybe you can see this is a sensitive area for me."

Mrs. Spencer replied, "I understand. We heard a lot about 'don't ask; don't tell' when Clinton was first president—Bradley was just a boy then—but there hasn't been much about that for a long time."

"No, Ma'am," Frank confirmed. "You asked about Jason. I'm sure Brad'd want to tell you he was hurt in the same accident, but not badly. He and my friend went out to get some fresh air and maybe to a movie. I suspect they'll be here soon. They were with us at the bar. My friend was injured also, but not confined to bed. He and Jason have been with us almost constantly; they're a big help. My friend's a nurse. They've been staying with us every night."

"Yes, I've heard hospitals these days allow family to stay overnight," Mrs. Spencer almost interrupted. "I came prepared to stay overnight with Bradley if they'll let me. They wouldn't let me bring luggage upstairs; had to have it x-rayed and leave it in a secure area. I guess I can get it later. Bradley's father said in a city as big as Washington I could get a hotel room if necessary. He travels on business and knows more about such things than I do. He said there's nothing big going on in Washington this week that'd fill all the hotels. Oh, speaking of Bradley's father, I should call him and tell him I'm here and how Bradley is. Excuse me, I won't be long."

She walked out of the room, but near enough Frank and Brad could hear, "Hello, Sweetheart. I'm with Bradley in his hospital room."

Gee, after all of this time, he's still her sweetheart, Frank mused.

284

She continued, "Not as bad as we imagined. He's conscious, but has a bad cut on his head, face, and lips, so he can't talk. He's aware of everything."

(pause)

"There's a nice man sharing the room with him who told me most of what happened," she continued. "He was injured in the same place as Bradley and is a good friend."

(pause)

"Yes, it's where we thought it was," she added.

(pause)

"The other man says Bradley's a hero," she continued, "but it's all hush-hush. Sensitive national security stuff. I'll call you later when things settle down. I want to go back with him now. I just wanted to tell you I got here and he's better than we thought."

(pause)

"Love you. Bye," she said and came back into the room, saying, "Your father sends his love."

I thought that affection like that was only in movies and television programs, Frank said to himself.

She took a tissue from a box on the table next to Brad's bed and began dabbing at his tears, saying, "Try to be careful about that, love. The salty water hurts your lips. Oh, there's so much I want to tell you, dear, and ask you, but you don't need me fussing over you right now."

Frank thought, *At least she realizes she's fussing too much. My mother couldn't leave her bottle long enough to care for anyone, much less make a trip to Washington.* He said, "It's good of you to come from Minneapolis on such short notice."

"It's the least I could do," she said. "Bradley's such a dear boy. Did your family visit? Where're you from?"

Frank's answered, "I'm from Florida, Ma'am. My father was here earlier."

At that moment, Jason walked into the room, followed by Paco, a bit slower on crutches.

CHAPTER 39

Sun was setting behind the Appalachian Mountain ridge west of town, with hues of gold and pink surrounding clouds in the sky, when the hearse arrived at the back of McWhorter Funeral Home, a large three-story white wooden house and a long-time landmark in the center of town. Omar and Joe, dressed for the mountain winter, wore hoodies, Joe's in colors for the University of Michigan and Omar's in colors for the University of Minnesota, both of which would blend well in this university town. Wearing old blue jeans and old athletic shoes, they got out of the hearse, stretching after five hours cramped inside. The driver and a co-worker removed Marwan's remains in a simple wooden box.

A man in his fifties with a dark suit, white shirt, and dark blue tie, typical of a funeral director, greeted them. "Ralph McWhorter. One of you must be Mr. Abu Deeb." He led them into a richly appointed office and said, "You're here to preside over the funeral."

"Yes," Omar replied. "I'm an imam, similar to Christian clergy. Mr. Hammoud asked me to help with preparation and recite the Holy Scriptures."

Ralph McWhorter asked Joe, "Are you an imam also?"

He replied, "No, I'm an attorney, but I'm not here in a professional capacity; just supporting the family."

Ralph McWhorter asked, "Could you tell us about the family? Clergy often give useful information that a family experiencing a death finds difficult."

"I don't know them well," Omar said, and then explained his and Joe's interactions with the family. Joe commented that Marwan's wound seemed large.

Ralph McWhorter continued, "As I said on the phone, we've not had a Muslim funeral here. We want to be accommodating because we want to serve this community, and it's becoming more diverse than when my family first started this business some years ago. Diversity's been good for the community, but you have to be patient with us.

"After talking to Mr. Hammoud on the phone, the best would be for you to come early tomorrow morning and prepare the remains instead of tonight, followed by a service here in our chapel, then burial in the cemetery immediately afterwards. Would that be appropriate?"

"Yes, that's good," Omar said. "We know we can't follow traditions fully like in an Islamic country."

"What would they be?" Ralph McWhorter asked.

"In most Muslim traditions," Omar replied, "preparation's at home. Male members of the family, or female if the one being buried were a woman or girl, would lay the body to face Mecca. The body's washed with soap and water, purified three times. We say ritual prayers for the dead and recite Holy Scriptures. We also anoint the body with perfumes for the dead. Surely you know the story of three wise men visiting the baby Jesus bringing gifts of gold, frankincense, and myrrh. Myrrh's a traditional Middle Eastern perfume to anoint the dead."

"Yes, I've heard it many times," Ralph McCoy said. "There's no myrrh in this country that I've heard about."

"I got some at a shop in Washington," Omar said, lifting a small plastic bag. "The body's then wrapped in three white pieces of cloth. I have them too, basic hospital sheets."

A man in his late thirties, dressed typical of a university professor in a tweed jacket with leather patches on the elbow under his winter coat, was shown in. They exchanged greetings with Dr. Imran Ashfaq, and Omar asked him about Muslim burial traditions in Pakistan. He concurred with Omar; then Ralph McWhorter commented, "Dr. Ashfaq went with us to the cemetery. We found a plot that seems good and faces Mecca. Mr. Hammoud agreed on the phone. He could buy a family plot to make sure other family members will eventually be buried like that. Do you have an idea how many will be at the service?"

Omar answered, "It seems there's only the family, including a cousin. I don't know if there'll be others or if any of the local Islamic community will attend. For Arabs, a burial is a low key event. There's a memorial service after forty days that larger numbers attend. It's an Arab cultural tradition, because Arab Christians do the same thing."

Imran Ashfaq said, "I'll be there tomorrow, but I doubt others in the Islamic community would attend. They weren't close to the Hammouds and, as you said, it's a low key event. People have classes and other commitments; many of our members are students."

"Another issue," Ralph McWhorter said, "apparently you don't want him buried in a coffin."

Omar replied, "No. If we follow tradition, four men would carry him wrapped in cloths to the grave site. Usually it's a long procession on foot. At the gravesite, someone recites the Holy Scriptures and says a few words; Mr. Hammoud wants me to do that. Others could say favorable comments about the person if they want. Here that will apparently happen at the separate service. Only men would go to the gravesite. Everyone, Muslims at least, would recite a scripture any Muslim would know. The body's placed in the grave facing Mecca wrapped only in cloths, mourners throw three handfuls of dirt into the grave, and they walk away. After forty steps, the mourners stop and repeat the scripture again. Is that how you'd do it, Dr. Imran?"

He concurred.

Ralph McWhorter said, "We can accommodate all except maybe burying the remains only wrapped in cloths; regulations and cemetery policy might require a casket. I'll check and let you know. There's plenty of space for the hearse to park as far away from the gravesite as needed for you to make a long procession. I presume there're four of you big and sturdy enough to carry him. I don't have a sense of his size and weight."

"From what I saw in the hospital, he's about average, about like Omar and me," Joe commented.

"That's how I remember him from Friday prayers," Imran Ashfaq added. "I can help carry. If there's Nassar and his cousin and one of you two, that should be enough."

Ralph McWhorter continued, "The forecast for tomorrow is a clear, calm, cold day, typical of late winter. Here in the mountains, things can change rapidly. If it's raining or snowing, we can put a tent over the gravesite."

"That'd be good," Omar said. "These things are ultimately up to Mr. Hammoud."

"I understand," Ralph McWhorter said. "I also need to discuss with him when we should pick them up tomorrow morning and, of course, financial arrangements."

"Oh, you pick them up at their house?" Omar asked.

"Yes," Ralph McWhorter replied. "It's more convenient to use our limousine to pick up family members to bring to the funeral home and to the cemetery. It relieves stress when they don't need to provide their own transportation."

Omar replied, "That's good. I'd have thought he'd be here by now. I called him a good forty-five minutes ago."

"We can go to the preparation room to see what it's like for tomorrow morning," Ralph McWhorter said.

"I hope I can be excused from preparation," Imran Ashfaq said. "We have young children to get ready for school and my wife works.

If Nassar needs me, of course I'll be here; one Muslim always helps a fellow Muslim in need. I've rearranged my schedule for the other things. I can go with you now and wait for Nassar. It'd be good to see him tonight before the service tomorrow."

"There'll be Joe and me, along with Nassar and a cousin, to prepare him," Omar said. "Four should be enough."

"Our preparation room isn't big," Ralph McWhorter said. "I doubt we could accommodate more than four."

Inside the preparation room, two persons, one the driver, were wearing only pants and t-shirts covered by plastic aprons. Marwan lay covered on the preparation table.

"The best we can tell," Ralph McWhorter said, "the preparation table's in an east-west direction and we laid him facing east. You indicated Mecca's east of here."

"Yes, east and a little south," Imran Ashfaq said. "I'm sure this's good enough."

"What will you need?" Ralph McWhorter asked.

Omar replied, "Just soap, water, and sponges."

"You said his injuries are rather substantial and maybe best not viewed by persons not used to such," Ralph McWhorter added. "We could make them less visible."

Omar replied, "That sounds like a good idea."

Ralph McWhorter continued, "We can't transport him to the cemetery covered only in cloths. The remains must be in a container while in transit like when we brought him here."

"We understand," Omar said. "Apparently Mr. Hammoud accepted that fact. Can you use the same box?"

"Yes, we could," Ralph McWhorter answered. "That's all I can think of right now, unless you have something."

Omar said, "Muslims must purify themselves by washing after contact with the dead. Nassar and his cousin will return home and surely shower there. I don't know how many bathrooms they have;

it could really help if you have shower facilities here for Joe and me and a place to change."

"We have a small shower for our staff to clean after messy situations," Ralph McWhorter said. "You could use that and an empty room to change. Also there's the hotel down on the corner that owes us favors because we've referred business there. If there's an empty room, maybe you could shower and change there. Anything else?"

"No, not right now," Omar replied. "We appreciate your sensitivity. Can you think of anything, Dr. Imran?"

Imran Ashfaq thought, and then answered, "Not right now."

Hearing soft melodic doorbell tones, Ralph McWhorter said, "That must be Mr. Hammoud. "Excuse me a moment."

"I'll go with you, if I may," Omar said. "Perhaps it'd be best if I spoke with him in Arabic to review things we've talked about. He speaks good English, but it's better in emotional situations to speak one's native language."

CHAPTER 40

Tuesday, March 4, 2008
Washington, DC, USA

In Frank and Brad's hospital room, Mrs. Spencer gave Jason a big hug, saying, "Jason, so nice to see you!"

He hugged her in return with his free arm, saying, "Good to see you too. What brings you here?"

She replied, "When the hospital called, one of us, Bradley's father or me, had to come. I could get off work easiest. His father will come for the weekend. Our name was in Bradley's wallet as next of kin. It's so good to see you, and we're happy you're taking good care of him. I just told Bradley we figured out your relationship last summer and we know where you were when you were hurt. We're sorry as we can be that you're hurt, but not upset over anything else."

Jason smiled, speechless, giving her another hug.

"Oh, I don't mean to ignore you," Mrs. Spencer said to Paco, now beside Frank's bed. "I'm Marian Spencer, Bradley's mother. You must be Frank's friend."

He replied, "Nice to meet you. I'm Paco Mendoza. Yes, Frank's pretty special. Brad too, but not the same way."

"You're hurt too," she said. "I hope it's not serious. Someone big like you must not get around well on crutches."

Paco replied, "Nothing broken. I'll be able to walk normally pretty soon." *She sure is the doting type*, he thought.

Frank asked, "What'd you two do? Find a movie?"

"Yes," Paco answered. "Went to *The Sure Thing*, a sissy romantic thing. We ate, too. That's why we're late."

Mrs. Spencer said, "If I could get to a kitchen, I'd just love to make some real home cooked food for you boys. I could fix some real American roast beef and potatoes, or maybe some Swedish meatballs and mashed potatoes. We're not Swedish, but there're enough of them in Minnesota we know how to make good meatballs. Oh, we should stop talking about food with Brad not able to eat, and Frank too."

Frank said, "My kitchen's not used much except when Brad comes to cook Middle Eastern food. I'd love to be there now and you cooking as much as you like."

"Oh, yes, Bradley's a good cook," Mrs. Spencer said. "He wanted to learn from me and I was glad to teach him, but he learned pretty quickly on his own. He cooked nice meals for us when we were here last summer, didn't he Jason?"

Jason smiled and said, "Speaking of eating, what about you? Have you eaten? How long've you been here?"

"I just got here, maybe half an hour ago," Mrs. Spencer replied. "No, I haven't eaten; I've been so concerned about Bradley I couldn't think about eating. Now that he's in good hands and not as bad as we imagined, I could eat something."

"I don't know if the hospital cafeteria's still open," Jason said, "but there's likely a snack bar. Say, where're you staying? We might get you something to eat in town depending on where you stay."

"I thought I'd stay here with Bradley if they'd let me," Mrs. Spencer replied. "My bags are downstairs in security. It seems you two have been staying here. I can just stay here and maybe you go home and get a good night's rest, not that we wouldn't like to have you around."

"Oh, thanks," Jason said. "I live way out in Virginia and no way to get home since I can't drive."

"Oh, I insist," Mrs. Spencer said. "Go get a hotel room. I was willing to pay for one, so I'll just pay for you."

"Thanks a lot, Mrs. Spencer," Jason said. "Honestly, the best thing you could do for me would be to stay here during the day tomorrow. I have to go where I work and fill them in on what I'm working on. If you could be here and help Paco, that'd be great. Besides, you've been traveling all day and I've mostly been resting."

"Well, OK," Mrs. Spencer said. "We thought I might have to stay at a hotel anyway."

"You're welcome to stay at my place," Frank offered, "if you have a way to get there. If not tonight, the next nights. I have a guest room and it'd be my pleasure."

Brad stirred using his free hand to point to himself.

"Oh, what is it, dear?" Mrs. Spencer asked. "Do you want something? Can I get you something?"

Brad shook his head side to side and laid his head to the side shutting his eyes to indicate sleep.

"I think he means you sleep at his place," Jason said.

"Oh, yes, dear, of course I could do that," Mrs. Spencer replied. "Thank you for the offer, too, Frank. I'd take you up on that, but can't sleep both places. Can I take a taxi?"

Frank replied, "That's the problem. I live close to Brad. There's no public transportation and a taxi, if you could get one, would cost a fortune; probably as much as a hotel. Maybe tomorrow you could drive my car there with Jason to show you the way. It's parked here in DC. I'd like to get it off the streets and parked where I live."

"Joe and Omar still have the keys," Paco said, "but maybe they left the keys at their place."

Brad sat up in the bed holding out his fist moving up and down and then attempting to point to himself.

"Oh, dear," Mrs. Spencer said to Brad. "You're trying to say something again."

Jason interrupted, "I think he's trying to say you can drive his car. This is like charades we played when I was a kid. I was pretty good."

"Yes, dear, I could do that," Mrs. Spencer said. "I don't know what people'd say about an old lady like me driving such a spiffy red car; maybe it'd be fun."

"Speaking of friends," Jason interjected, "do you suppose she could stay at Omar and Joe's place? At least tonight. They're going to be gone for a couple of nights."

"Yeah, why not," Paco added. "They keep their apartment pretty well and there's plenty of room."

"Oh, who are they?" Mrs. Spencer asked. "I don't want to impose on anyone."

"They're a couple of guys who've become good friends," Frank said. "They like to be helpful and hospitable; part of their culture."

"Their culture?" Mrs. Spencer asked.

Jason explained their backgrounds and Mrs. Spencer replied, "Bradley's always had an attraction for Middle Eastern people ever since he studied Arabic and went to Jordan. How'd they feel if a woman comes to their place? I sure don't want to do anything against their culture."

"They've had women in their apartment as guests," Frank said. "Brad and I were there with women present."

Jason added, "They're not a couple. They're two young professional guys who share an apartment close to where they work because rent's so high in Washington."

"Oh, sounds impressive," Mrs. Spencer added. "How do you know them?"

"Brad and I took a class Omar taught," Frank answered and explained more details.

"They're cool hanging out with us, too," Paco added.

"Omar's from Minneapolis," Jason added, "or rather spent the last six years there. That's another reason he and Brad hit it off, and they both speak Arabic. You need to eat something. We'll get your bags and go to their place and see. There're plenty of places to eat around there and, if you don't feel comfortable staying, a couple of hotels're right there."

"Oh, OK," Mrs. Spencer said, somewhat reluctantly. "It wouldn't hurt to go look. You say they're away?"

"They went to a funeral out of town," Jason answered. "They might be back tomorrow night, but unlikely."

"Oh, a funeral?" Mrs. Spencer continued asking. "Was it something to do with the explosion you were all in? I guess not, because the news said no one was killed except that one young Muslim man who committed suicide."

"That's whose funeral it is," Jason replied. "Omar's also an Islamic imam, like a priest or a pastor. He performed the last rites here in the hospital, and his father asked if he'd do whatever they do at his burial. They live down in Southwest Virginia, about 250 miles from here. I hope it doesn't bother you staying at two Muslim guys' place, especially if they're participating in the funeral of the guy who did this to us."

"Mrs. Spencer said, "No, I don't think their being Muslim would bother me, especially after you say they don't have problems with women being there. It's just going into strangers' house, but I can probably get over that. Some people from our church made a big tour of the Holy Land, spending time with both the Jews and the Arabs, staying in their homes, trying to understand the conflict and contribute to peace. They came back saying that the Arabs were so nice and hospitable, and they were mostly Muslim. And the church had a series of Sunday School lessons on Islam. Oh, that was almost ten years ago and I don't remember all the details, but there was something about Arab hospitality. That may have been where Bradley first got some of his interest in learning Arabic; he was active in the youth group at church then, and they were learning about Islam."

Brad shook his head up and down then raised his hand and pointed his finger toward the door and began thrusting.

"Oh," Mrs. Spencer said flustered. "I think he's saying we should go now."

She walked to Brad's bed to give him a kiss, saying, "See you tomorrow, dear. I see you're in good hands. I'll call your father and tell him more. Our prayers have been answered, and we'll keep on praying."

Jason touched Brad's hand and said, "See you in a bit." He put on his coat, turned to the others in the room, and said, "Yalla, bye, as Joe says, whatever that means."

He took Mrs. Spencer's elbow with his free arm and guided her to the elevator.

CHAPTER 41

Tuesday, March 4, 2008
Blacksburg, Virginia, USA

In Ralph McWhorter's office with Omar, Nassar said, "Sorry I'm late. I went to the station and called the sheriff's office because I know the deputies. They said they'd keep an eye on things. One of them knows a retired man who might be willing to come to the station for a few hours. Best not to leave it unattended, especially after those men bombed our house. Someone might stop to buy gas, see a sign on the door that it's closed, and things might happen. I don't care about losing business, but I don't want my station and garage damaged."

"That sounds like a good idea," Ralph McWhorter said.

Bombed his house? Omar thought. *Sounds serious.*

"People here've been so nice," Nassar continued. "They're even having supper for us when we get back home; people from our neighbors' church."

"That's the way folks do things here when there's a death, Mr. Hammoud," Ralph McWhorter added.

Their neighbors' church? Omar thought again. *I have a lot to learn about local customs.*

Ralph McWhorter said, "I should leave you alone a few minutes. Please knock when you're ready."

For the next few minutes, Omar recounted in Arabic what he had discussed with Ralph McWhorter, emphasizing their willingness to conform to Islamic tradition the best they could, that he had taken risks preparing the grave, and saying he needed to discuss financial arrangements.

Nassar replied in Arabic, "He seems to be a good man. I know I need to pay him, but I didn't have a chance to go to the bank. Can he trust me until tomorrow?"

Omar replied in Arabic, "I suspect he wants to finalize arrangements and have you sign a contract. I'm sure he doesn't want money right now. Put it in the hands of Allah and it'll work out."

In the preparation room, Nassar looked sad seeing Marwan covered by a sheet, but otherwise had no expression.

Imran Ashfaq immediately took Nassar's hands in both of his saying, "Nassar, I'm so sorry about your son." He then began reciting the first part of the *shahada*, "There is no god but God...", using Arabic like almost all Muslims, even if it is not a language they speak. He then recited in Arabic passages from Sura 36 of the Koran, the sura of death, including, "...give life to the dead and record that which they have forwarded and that which they have left behind, ... And the trumpet will be blown and men will slide forth out of their tombs to the Lord."

Faint moisture came to Nassar's eyes as he continued to hold Imran Ashfaq's hands and merely said, "Thanks."

Joe greeted Nassar solemnly, after which Ralph McWhorter said, "Perhaps I should speak with Mr. Hammoud. It shouldn't take long." To Omar and Joe, "You can sit in our waiting area if you like. You could also take a short walk downtown and get some fresh air. There's always something of interest to young people in a town like this."

Nassar said to Omar and Joe, "Sorry you have to wait. You heard me say people're preparing supper for us. That must include you, because you're staying at our house."

This's the first time Nassar said we're staying at his house, Omar thought. *He knows we're Middle Eastern and would assume it. The local Islamic community didn't provide food, but a Christian church did. Maybe this'd be a good research topic.*

"It's OK, Abou Ahmed," Omar said in English. "Maybe Dr. Imran can tell us where we might go."

Imran Ashfaq replied, "You can walk with me if you like. I'm going back to my office." To Ralph McWhorter and Nassar, "I'll see you tomorrow morning at 10:30, *insha Allah*."

Joe, Omar, and Imran Ashfaq walked down Draper Road, passing student-oriented shops where Joe commented, "This is downtown? It looks like the group of shops around the University of Michigan campus."

Imran Ashfaq laughed and replied, "Blacksburg never really had a downtown. Until the 1960s, students lived on the campus and there were only a few shops for them. Town was in Christiansburg. Enrollment skyrocketed and the population of the town exploded, but commercial development was at the edge of town. Now, even with 30,000 students, downtown's about like it always was: a couple of banks, town hall, and a post office. Here's where I turn. Would you like to walk with me and see the campus?"

"Not this time," Omar replied. "It seems like a nice, quaint place, even if it is a major university. A big difference from the University of Minnesota, right in the middle of the city of Minneapolis."

They said goodbyes, then Omar and Joe walked quietly one block up College Avenue and down Main Street, looking in shop windows, when Joe nudged Omar, saying, "Look at that. Their mascot's a turkey! Maroon and orange turkeys on t-shirts and some say 'Fighting Gobblers.' They also seem to call themselves Hokies."

"Yeah," Omar said. "That beats the Minnesota gopher. This seems like such a nice place. It's hard to imagine there was that massacre here a year ago."

Back at the funeral home, they said goodbyes to Ralph McWhorter and went with Nassar to his house.

CHAPTER 42

Tuesday, March 4, 2008
Lafayette, Virginia, USA

At their house, holding a hot pan with big, fluffy, golden brown biscuits, Velma greeted Roula, Nassar, Abou Nidal, Omar, and Joe. "C'mon in. I'm gettin' things out of th' oven. Take your coats off and make y'rselves at home."

After introductions, Omar and Joe, food aromas whetting their appetites well after their normal dinnertime, said, "Pleased to meet you; thanks for your hospitality."

She thought, *They're young and good lookin'. Wouldn't of thought an imam'd be like that; dressed sorta sloppy, too.* She said, "Nothin' formal. Help y'rselves." To Nassar, "Thought you, Roula, and Abou Needle could sit in the livin' room with Shane if y' like; maybe Roula'd feel best in there." To Omar and Joe, "You can sit in the family room with us or wherever y' like. Cobbler's bakin' too. Had peaches in the freezer we put up last summer."

A tall woman in her forties walked up wearing a simple pantsuit and said, "Please let me introduce myself. I'm Jolene Robbins, pastor of the Robertses' church. You're Mr. and Mrs. Hammoud. I'm so sorry about the loss of your son. Maybe we can speak briefly later."

Nassar replied, "I'm Nassar Hammoud; this is my wife, Roula. We appreciate your church's hospitality."

Jolene Robbins thought: *The older man must be the imam, but he's sure dressed casually. The young men must be friends of the sons.* She said to Abou Nidal, "You're the imam who'll lead the service tomorrow."

Abou Nidal replied, "No; cousin of Abou Ahmed."

Omar said, "I'm the imam, Omar Abu Deeb."

Jolene Robbins said, "You're younger than I expected. I'm pleased to meet you. I was hoping we might have a few words together after you eat."

Omar replied, "A pleasure," explained briefly his background and their sloppy clothes, and introduced Joe.

The bar was set with simple food that could be cooked elsewhere and carried here: stewed chicken, hamburger and macaroni casserole, green bean casserole, coleslaw, fruit salad, and a chocolate cake. Margarine and a pitcher of ice water sat next to plastic cups and paper napkins.

In the living room, Shane said, "Welcome. Wish it could be better circumstances. Mrs. Hammoud, sorry 'bout your son. He was a good boy."

Nassar helped Roula, saying, "Thank you, Mr. Shane. It's good of you to have us here. I need to help Roula."

Shane thought: *Poor lady; lots of tragedies at once.* He said, "Velma 'n' me's plannin' to be at th' funeral, if that's OK with you."

Nassar replied, "We'd be honored and pleased to have you and Ms. Velma there."

Shane said, "I'm goin' to look for dessert and put on coffee. Just make y'rselves at home."

Meanwhile, in the family room, Jolene Robbins said, "Omar, is it OK if I call you Omar? You said you just finished school? What education does an imam need?"

He replied, "That's one issue of Islam in this country. There's no formal organization, no formal education, or other requirements. A man can say he's an imam and if enough people accept that, he is. In Islamic societies, that's not a problem because Islam's integrated into society and leaders naturally emerge. Apparently, some fundamentalist Christian sects in this country are similar."

Jolene Robbins replied, "Yes, that's true, especially in Virginia and the South. You're educated, though."

He replied, "I have a PhD in Islamic theology. In a city like Washington with well-educated professionals, an imam would have to be well versed in Islam to be accepted; not necessarily a PhD, but I wanted to be an Islamic scholar. I surrendered to Allah and I believe that's where I'm being called. I'm only a part time assistant imam, and I was selected in a recruiting and interview process. I'm also a research fellow at George Washington University."

"Very impressive," Jolene Robbins said, deferentially. "How long have you been there?"

"About six months," Omar replied, and explained his background in Yemen and Minnesota.

Jolene Robbins said, "May I ask how you came to be here with the Hammoud family?"

"It's the work of Allah," Omar said and explained.

"So good of you," Jolene Robbins said. "The Christian clergy in the area know there's an Islamic community in Blacksburg, but we've not known of an imam."

"I've just met the leader of the community," Omar replied. "He doesn't view himself as an imam. He's a professor at Virginia Tech. He'll be at the burial tomorrow."

Velma said, "Cobbler's cooling." To Shane who had walked in, "Honey, go get some ice cream from the freezer, should be some vanilla, and tell the girls to come get dessert and bring dirty dishes."

Jolene Robbins turned to Joe. "I don't mean to ignore you. You're a lawyer, you say?"

"Yes, ma'am," Joe answered. "I'm with the Attorney General's office. I've been there a couple of years."

"Your accent sounds Midwestern," she commented.

"I'm from Michigan," Joe replied. "My parents are Lebanese, but I was born and grew up in Dearborn, just outside of Detroit." He then explained his background.

Upon seeing Fatima along with Amelia, Omar went to her and said in Arabic, "You must be Miss Fatima. Your father's talked about you."

She replied shyly in Arabic, "Yes, I'm Fatima."

"I'm Omar," he said in Arabic. "Nice to meet you."

Fatima blushed, then Velma said, "You two rinse y'r plates and put 'em in the dishwasher like y' always does. Y'r folks is in the livin' room if y' want to say somethin' before you get cobbler and ice cream; there's cake too."

Meanwhile, Jolene Robbins rinsed her plate and put it in the dishwasher and took cobbler and ice cream thinking, *These two young men have started their careers at the top; very prestigious jobs in Washington. I wonder if Velma and Shane realize what extraordinary guests they have. Maybe I'll mention it sometime; not now, or they'd be intimidated, Velma especially. They seem nice down-to-earth persons. There's Joe rinsing his plate; bet he did that back home. They're very attractive too.*

Velma said to Joe, "You're guests; I'll take the plates."

We're guests and the lady pastor isn't, Omar said to himself. After taking dessert and sitting, he asked, "What about you, ma'am, if I may ask? I've met Christian clergy, but never knew much about their backgrounds and how they came to be pastors."

Jolene Robbins replied, "Like you, I felt a calling. I was well into my thirties, working in a dead-end job as a librarian in a small town in eastern Virginia. My marriage wasn't going well, and I didn't have children. I followed God's calling and enrolled in a seminary. I'm Methodist, so maybe you know bishops assign us to congregations."

Velma sat to eat and Omar said, "We appreciate your having us in your home for dinner. This is a custom I've not been exposed to yet. Is this what you do when someone is buried? Is this a Christian custom?"

"When there's a death," Velma replied, "folks usually takes food to their house, at least 'round here. Figure they've got lots on their mind and not up to cookin' or shoppin', so neighbors, family, and friends just does it. Bein' that Roula isn't doing good, I said we'd have the food over here. They're s'posed to take leftovers home with 'em."

"It's not specifically Christian," Jolene Robbins added. "I don't know anything in scripture that says that, but there're references throughout about sharing food. Muslims don't do things like this?"

Omar replied, "Hospitality is very much part of Arab culture; not only Muslims, because Arab Christians do it too. We'd help a family in need, but providing food before a burial is not something I've been exposed to. It's nice, though. I heard something about lunch at the church tomorrow. Is that a Christian custom?"

"That's what we do 'round here," Velma replied. "The funeral's usually 'bout lunchtime and people got t' eat, so women of the church serve lunch. Mostly funerals are in the church, so when they go to the cemetery, some ladies just stays behind to get lunch ready."

"This might be a more local custom," Jolene Robbins added. "I've heard of funerals up North where the family of the deceased caters a meal at a local restaurant because family and friends are traveling from out of town and it's their responsibility to feed them, especially if there's a matriarch."

"There's some of that in Michigan where I'm from," Joe commented, "but not among Muslims."

Jolene Robbins asked, "There're some people at our church who know the young man and wondering if they could go to the funeral. I know Shane and Velma are going, but I didn't know if it'd be appropriate for others to attend."

"There was an announcement in the *News Messenger* tonight along with the other death and funeral listings," Velma said. "Guess th' funeral home announced it. The Hammoud boys was pretty well thought of at school, even if they wasn't in the social whirl. Don't know if others would show up. Maybe not, bein' it's in Blacksburg."

Oh, no, Joe thought. *In the newspaper. Will troublemakers find out and come picket?*

Omar said, "In Muslim countries, there'd only be a cemetery burial, but in the U.S., like tomorrow, there's sometimes a service at the funeral home with scriptures and comments from the public, followed by only the men going to the cemetery for the burial itself."

Velma interjected, "Me 'n' Shane was just goin' to be quiet and pay our respects."

"That'd be fine," Omar replied. "People like you two neighbors could also say a few words about him too."

"Who've you arranged to say things?" Velma asked.

Omar replied, "No one. We don't ask; they just do it."

"Around here, people'd wait to be asked," Jolene Robbins said. "It's part of the funeral arrangements I'd make when I am presiding over a funeral."

"Shane and me could say a few words," Velma said.

"I'm sure that'd be appreciated," Omar said.

"If you want other people to say something, I'm sure the two who asked me about the funeral would say something too," Jolene Robbins suggested. "One's the vice-principal of the middle school and was the young man's soccer coach. He was sad to hear he had died like this when I announced it at church Sunday morning. He can leave school easily enough."

She announced it at the church service on Sunday morning? Omar thought.

"The other's a young man his age, the son of the vice principal," Jolene Robbins continued. "They were on the same soccer team and friends through school, then went to New River Community College together. He can arrange his work schedule."

"That sounds good," Omar replied. "I didn't know Marwan at all. If others can say things, it'll be good for the family to hear."

"I'll call them," Jolene Robbins said. "Based on what you said, I could go to the service, but not to the cemetery. I must admit curiosity because I've never been to an Islamic service. Also I genuinely want to pay my respects."

Omar replied, "You'd be very welcome."

The rest of the evening was spent with coffee and general conversation.

CHAPTER 43

Wednesday, March 5, 2008
Blacksburg, Virginia, USA

"Good we saw this place walking by last night," Joe said as he dug into buckwheat pancakes at Gillie's Restaurant on a chilly, clear morning. "It's vegetarian, so no bacon or ham."

"Yeah," Omar said, barely nibbling on his breakfast burrito with scrambled eggs. "I'm too stressed; no appetite."

Joe put his hand on Omar's forearm, saying, "You handled things well, especially when he was uncovered."

"Thanks," Omar said. "You were good washing him. I was reciting scriptures, so didn't do too much touching."

Joe, who wore a regular dark business suit, said, "It sure was nice of that hotel to let us shower and change. Wonder if we could stay there tonight."

Omar, who wore a dark herringbone tweed sports jacket and black pants with a white shirt and navy blue tie, replied, "That'd be more comfortable, for sure. Have to see what Nassar has in mind. I couldn't run out at a time like this. Say, I'd better get back down there."

The funeral chapel, a room with an altar devoid of overtly Christian symbols, had rich, dark wood panels, fine draperies and curtains, a plush carpet, and pews padded with rich cloth upholstery, seating perhaps forty persons. Marwan's remains were in a wooden box on a funeral bier at front, turned off center to face Mecca.

An assistant brought two flower arrangements, saying, "These came this morning."

Omar and Joe noticed one was from Shane and Velma Roberts and the other from Jolene Robbins.

He brought another small flower arrangement and asked Omar, "Is it OK to set this one on the casket?"

Omar replied, "We don't have flowers at burials, but there's no problem with the flowers sitting there."

Omar and Joe saw a card that read, "Your soccer buddies."

Ralph McWhorter greeted them and said, "We can bury him in the cloths. We'll have to charge to dispose of the box; not for us, but for the crematorium because it has to be disposed of properly for health reasons."

"I can't imagine there'd be any problem," Omar said.

Velma and Shane arrived dressed like for church. Jolene Robbins arrived soon after, wearing a navy blue woman's dress suit. Two men came in, the older slightly stocky with closely trimmed salt-and-pepper dark brown hair, black wire-rimmed glasses, and wearing a medium-gray suit. He looked the school teacher-administrator he was. The younger, whose family resemblance showed he was his son, was in his early twenties, slightly taller with an athletic build. He wore a gray blazer and black slacks.

Introductions were made to Gordon and Jordan Hicks, who said, "Marwan was a nice guy and a good friend."

Gordon Hicks said, "Jolene told us men go to the cemetery. Jordan and I'd like to go along, if we can. Shane says he would, too."

"You'd be welcome," Omar replied. "I'm sure Marwan's father'd appreciate that."

With sudden inspiration, Joe looked at Omar, whose eyes showed he understood, and said to Jordan, "Maybe you'd like to help carry Marwan. Traditionally it's four persons. Marwan only has a father and older cousin, so we need two more. Joe's one."

Jordan Hicks said, "I'd be honored."

Omar greeted Imran Ashfaq and introduced him.

"Perhaps we could speak briefly later, Dr. Ashfaq," Jolene Robbins said. "It'd be good to know someone in the Islamic community. Maybe during lunch at the church, if you'll be there."

"I hadn't thought about it," Imran Ashfaq replied. "I could be there for a short while."

Omar asked Imran Ashfaq to join him on the left-side front pew, saying, "At the cemetery, you can be with me and not have to carry him. It'd be good if you could recite something in English."

Ralph McWhorter led Nassar, Roula, Fatima, and Abou Nidal to the first row on the right-hand side; all were dressed informally. Roula was expressionless; she wore a dark blue headscarf covering her hair. Omar and Imran Ashfaq immediately greeted them.

At the lectern Omar recited the words of the *shahada* in Arabic then in English, "'There is no god but God, and Mohammad is the messenger of God.' Those words were spoken into Marwan's ears as he was near his transition into death. He was a good Muslim man. In his belongings in the hospital he had his moushaf and rosary that all who follow the way of the Prophet would have. When he enters the grave and his soul is reunited with him, his punishment will surely be brief for whatever sins he may have committed. When the angels Munkar and Nakir tell him to sit up and ask him 'Who is your Lord?' Marwan will be able to respond, just as we heard, 'There is no god but God, and Mohammad is his messenger.'

"On the day of judgment, Marwan will surely be judged worthy. He will be resurrected from his grave right here in Blacksburg, Virginia, in the United States of America, to join the Prophet Mohammad, peace be upon Him, as he walks across the bridge to the entrance to heaven.

"I did not have the privilege of knowing Marwan until moments before his passing. I'm sure I would have known a fine young man. Many of you here can speak to that, and I turn now to you."

310

Nassar stood and said in English, "Marwan was a good boy. I spoke words in Arabic into his ears in the hospital when he was born:

God is great
I witness that there is no god but God
I witness that Mohammad is the messenger of God
Rise up for prayer
Rise up for salvation
God is great
There is no god but God

He heard the *Fatiha* spoken to him when he came home. He went to prayers every Friday; he wanted to go." In Arabic, "Allah will forgive him for whatever he has done, and he will be with us in heaven."

Abou Nidal stood and faced Nassar, Roula, and Fatima, saying in Arabic, "You lost a good boy and brother. He was a fine Muslim man. We went to prayers together every Friday; he talked to me, asking questions. At the resurrection he'll be in heaven with all of us, and we'll enjoy having him around, just like we did in our house."

Shane stood and said, "Marwan was a big little boy when Velma and me moved next door, 'bout six. Him and his big brother played lots. Boys'll be boys, but they never done nothin' to disturb us and th' other neighbors. When his little sister come along and our girl Amelia too, they didn't mind playin' with little girls some. He played well with other kids, no matter who they was."

"When he got big enough to do chores, he was always good takin' care of the yard, mowin' the grass, and stuff. Never complained that we could tell; cheerful and glad to do it. Couple a times when we's away on vacation, I hired him to take care of my yard. Always did a good job."

"I kinda hated to see him go when he 'n' his brother moved up to Northern Virginia, but folks gotta go where work is. We feel sorry for th' Hammouds. They's good people and good neighbors. The

Good Lord works in mysterious ways, but we know they believe in the same God. We all liked your boy and're sorry he's gone."

Velma stood and said, "Shane's told you what good neighbors the Hammouds is, even though we've not been all that close. Their kids, 'specially Marwan and Fatima, was the best kids around. As Shane said, he didn't mind being around the girls when they was growin' up, even though he was a few years older. He was good about lookin' after his little sister and Amelia too, when she got old enough to do things with 'em. 'Course he did boy things too; played on the soccer teams and stuff like that. He was good about helpin' his mom in the flower beds and things. Seemed to take special pride in gettin' some pretty flowers growin' and takin' care of 'em."

"We missed seein' him and his big brother around when they moved off to Northern Virginia, but kids grow up and gotta leave the nest sometime. Be nice if we c'd keep on protectin' them, but just not meant to be. Like Shane says, Marwan believed in the same God, and now we can be comforted God'll lead him where he belongs next."

Most were dabbing their eyes when Gordon Hicks stood and began, "I knew Marwan first when he was a big little boy playing on the soccer team I coached. He was the same age as my boy Jordan here. I was their coach for, oh, I don't know how many years; three or four, maybe. Marwan and Jordan hit it off from the beginning. Marwan was always good with other boys too. We had mostly winning seasons because all of the boys got along well with each other.

"Later on, when I was no longer their coach, Marwan and Jordan were still friends, and Marwan was at our house quite a few times; we were always happy to have him around. When he got a little bigger, on Fridays he'd say he had to go to prayers. That's when we got to know more about his being Muslim. He didn't say a whole lot, but we knew then that it was something he did because he wanted to. We knew he was a child of the same God as ours, even if he did go to his prayers on Friday and we went on Sunday.

"I also knew Marwan at the middle school where I'm the assistant principal. I never had direct dealings with him, which is good because discipline cases come to me. Still, because he was one of my boys from the soccer team, I kept my eye on him. He was a good student. Always well behaved in the class. That's when he discovered computers.

"After he and Jordan got into high school, he wasn't around our house much anymore, but we'd see him, and he and Jordan hung out, especially with computer-related things. I know a couple of times when they were going to New River Community College, they'd ride together. I'll let Jordan say more, because I know he wants to.

"Your boy Marwan was a good boy and a fine young man. I share your loss too. It's comforting to hear the words, even if they're not the exact same words we'd say; he'll be with God in heaven where he deserves to be."

When his father sat down, Jordan Hicks stood and said, "As my father just told you, I've known Marwan since we were kids on the soccer team. Marwan was one of the fun guys to be around. He was kinda shy, but with a group he could open up with he'd be fun. He calmed us down when we wanted to do something wild. The main thing that stuck out about Marwan was he always treated everyone nice, no matter who they were and would go out of his way to help.

"He and I were both really into computers in high school and then at New River Community College. Most of the time he'd ride over there with his brother, but the last year it was just him and me would go together sometimes.

"When we were in high school, we kind of drifted apart socially, but that was when I started asking him what he believed. I asked him if there was anything like a Sunday school like we have, and he said 'no,' that his father always taught them the prayers. After a while, he said it's what he feels inside when he goes to the prayers on Friday that makes him believe. He said he'd like to know more about his religion, but there wasn't much chance to learn.

"Hearing these things from you reminds me of the things Marwan said when I kept pressing him, that he really was a man of God who believed from the inside out, so to speak. When he said he doesn't know what he believes, but just feels it inside, it made me wonder how many of our Christian kids could say that. How many of us feel what we believe inside? We always knew it was the same God, even if he was a different religion, and now I can feel inside like he must have, that he'll be with God in heaven too."

All were even more overcome with emotion and sat quietly while Omar recited the prayer for the dead in Arabic.

Imran Ashfaq stood and said, "There's one prayer Muslims recite on many occasions, including passing of the body and soul into the grave. It represents all that's in our Holy Q'ran, condensed into seven verses. I'll recite in English, because it's the common language for most Muslims worldwide."

As he recited, Shane, Velma, Gordon Hicks, and Jordan Hicks all realized that was the same prayer that Pastor Jolene had read to them in church on Sunday.

Imran Ashfaq then began reciting the *Fatiha* in Arabic, and all the Muslims except Roula immediately began reciting themselves.

Omar looked to Ralph McWhorter to signal this part of the service was over.

Gordon Hicks went to Fatima, who he knew slightly from school, expressing condolences.

Jordan Hicks said to Abou Nidal, "You run the gas station. Nice to see you again; sorry it has to be like this."

Abou Nidal gave a warm handshake, saying, "Jamal al Khatib. *Ahlan.*" He thought in Arabic, *He's one of the nice boys who stop by; always friendly and nice, sometimes buys something to eat or drink, and says hello and goodbye.*

Gordon Hicks, also recognizing Abou Nidal from the gas station, shook hands, expressing sympathies. Both Jordan and Gordon Hicks shook hands with Nassar, whom they knew slightly from the station and parents night at school, expressing condolences and saying they'd be at the cemetery.

CHAPTER 44

Wednesday, March 5, 2008
Tehran, Iran

Just past dawn on a cold overcast morning, a VIP transport plane of the Fuerza Aérea Venezolana landed at a highly sensitive, restricted military airport outside the city of Tehran after an overnight flight. While the VIP attendant gently awakened the Deputy Oil Minister and his personal assistant in private cabins, the crew chief shook Ahmed, saying roughly in Spanish, "Get up! Come!" He pushed Ahmed down a stairway, gesturing away from a black Mercedes-Benz, shouting in Spanish and pointing, "Over there!"

Ahmed, not understanding but sensing he had to move, walked about ten feet and stood thinking, *It's cold. Where the hell are we? It's damned cold for Venezuela or Colombia, but didn't we learn in school Bogotá's cold?*

The crew chief walked to the VIP attendant, who exchanged a few words with him, saying in Spanish, "Send him to that building so he can't see us when we leave. You've taken his documents, haven't you? We need his passport and driver's license; the iPod's for me!"

"Yes sir!" The crew chief answered in Spanish. "We got those on the way from Tripoli after we made sure he'd be sound asleep. I'll get his coat."

"Let him freeze," the attendant said in Spanish. Then he said, "Oh, go ahead. We can't use a heavy coat like that."

The crew chief gave Ahmed his winter jacket and said roughly in Spanish, "Go!" pointing to a building.

Ahmed thought, *The signs are in Arabic. I wish I'd learned the characters better when Dad tried to teach us. Maybe it's all a dream; I'm so sleepy.*

Groggy, he stumbled inside, thankful to be warm. He was in a large open room, empty this hour of the morning, thinking, *There's a couch. I'll sit until they come get me again.*

Several minutes later he was awakened by a man in a military uniform speaking a language he did not understand.

Time to go back to the plane, Ahmed thought, starting to walk towards the door, but he was roughly grabbed by the shoulder by the man who continued to shout.

Damn, Ahmed thought. *I wish I'd taken Spanish in school, but that doesn't sound like the same language others spoke. Isn't Arabic either. There are signs in Arabic letters; maybe he speaks Arabic.* "I need to catch the airplane," he said in simple Arabic.

The official continued his angry shouting.

With increasing frustration, Ahmed almost shouted, *"Arabi, inglisi,* Arabic, English."

The official grabbed him by the arm and roughly led him to an office where a senior official was sitting and said in Persian, "He doesn't seem to understand me. He says something that sounds like 'Arabic, English.'"

The senior official gave what sounded like an expletive, thought a moment, then said in Persian, "The men in the control tower speak English. Get one of them."

An air traffic controller ordered, "Identify yourself."

"Ahmed Hammoud," he answered.

"Documents," the controller demanded.

Ahmed reached into his pants pocket. Finding nothing, he began searching the pockets of his jacket and then said in near panic, "Must be in the airplane."

"What airplane?" the controller asked roughly.

"The plane from Venezuela that was taking me where I'm supposed to go," Ahmed answered.

After a brief discussion with the senior official, the air controller said sternly to Ahmed, "You don't sound like someone from Venezuela; you sound American."

Ahmed blurted out, "No, Palestinian! Where am I?"

"The Islamic Republic of Iran," the controller said.

Iran! Then with sudden realization he had been dumped, fear turned to terror as Ahmed choked away tears. The air traffic controller and the senior official again had a brief conversation, and the flight controller turned abruptly and left.

After calling the oil ministry, the senior official said in Persian, "They'll call me back. He might be a spy the Venezuelans are infiltrating into this country, maybe to stir up trouble with our Arab minority. Take him to the other room and watch him closely."

After several more minutes, the senior official said in Persian, "The Venezuelan officials deny knowing anything about him and even began to get angry when pushed for details. When we pointed out that he must have come on their plane, they said that he must've stowed away, maybe slipping onboard in Libya when they stopped to refuel. That's something the asshole Gadafi would do, infiltrate someone into this country to spy or sabotage. I'll contact security. They know how to get information out of him."

CHAPTER 45

Wednesday, March 5, 2008
Blacksburg, Virginia, USA

After the service at the funeral home, with temperatures warming in the sunshine, the hearse was followed by the funeral car, Imran Ashfaq's car, and Gordon Hicks's car as it progressed slowly along North Main Street with headlights on, led by a patrol car of the Blacksburg town police. Traffic on both sides stopped. An occasional older man would remove his hat and bow his head in accordance with an almost forgotten tradition.

In the cemetery, the hearse and cars stopped about fifty yards from the grave. With the assistance of the drivers, the box carrying Marwan's remains was pulled out of the hearse and the lid removed. Nassar and Abou Nidal lifted Marwan's head and shoulders; Joe motioned to Jordan Hicks to help lift his legs and feet. Once in position, they walked towards the gravesite carrying Marwan on their shoulders. Omar and Imran Ashfaq led the procession, reciting scriptures in Arabic. Shane and Gordon Hicks walked somberly behind.

When Marwan's body was placed on the burial lowering device, Omar and Imran Ashfaq, standing at the head, repeated scriptures in Arabic and English, with the Muslims reciting them as well. Omar walked to the pile of dirt, pulled back the artificial green grass cover, and reached for a handful of dirt. When the body was lowered into the grave, Omar threw one handful of dirt and returned for a second. The Muslim men each took a handful of dirt in turn, throwing it into the grave. Omar and Joe used eye contact to indicate to Shane, Gordon Hicks, and Jordan Hicks that they were welcome to join the activity, which they did.

After each man had thrown three handfuls of dirt, Omar led a procession which Imran Ashfaq, Nassar, and Abou Nidal followed. Joe hesitated just long enough to signal Shane, Gordon Hicks, and Jordan Hicks that they would be welcome to follow. Omar led the procession in roughly a circular pattern, counting the steps. At the fortieth step, Omar began reciting the *Fatiha* in Arabic with the Muslims joining. When the *Fatiha* was finished, Omar walked to Nassar to take his two hands in his and say a few words of sympathy in Arabic, to which Nassar merely said, "*Shouqran.*"

Out the corner of his eye, Joe noticed a man in a trench coat standing behind the vehicles, close enough to observe and hear.

I wonder who that is, he thought. *He was at the service. He's young and well dressed. Maybe another one of Marwan's friends, but why is he shy and not joining us? He's coming towards me.*

Now I remember where I saw him before, the young man thought. *He was on the legal team from the Attorney General's office in Washington, down to arrange a plea bargain for those two young Arab guys they caught smuggling. They tried to make me believe he was on an orientation tour.* He held out his hand and said, "Marcus Porter of the *Roanoke Times.* I recognize you from when you were on an orientation tour of the federal court in Roanoke and I covered a trial of two young men caught smuggling."

Joe, startled, thought, *What the fuck! Wait. The judge did say there was a reporter in the courtroom. Shit. He knows who I am and who I work for. I can't just blow him off; can't get the media pissed off.*

"I'm here in a personal capacity," Joe replied. "This is a private gathering. There's nothing I can say to the media."

He turned to walk away when Marcus Porter said, "Wait, please," handing Joe his press card. "I intend to cover this funeral in a decent respectful way, not like the tabloids. I want to get this to print before it becomes sensationalized; you surely know what I mean. He seems to have been a respectable, well-liked person."

"How'd you find out about this burial?" Joe asked.

"I called funeral homes in the area once we had a name," Marcus Porter answered. "The *Post* called us yesterday afternoon when they broke the story of his identity and asked us if we could find out where the funeral'd be. My editor said he would, but only if we cover the story. I've got a lot to write about already. I hoped you could give me more, show more what he was like, not what tabloids would make him into."

"Sorry, I've got to run," Joe said. "The church is serving lunch, and that's where I have to go now quickly." He turned to go, thinking, *Oh, shit, maybe I shouldn't have said that. Now he might try to find us.*

"What church?" Marcus Porter asked. "I'm from around here. They're from Lafayette, and I can go to every church in the area until I find you, if that's what it would take. Please just tell me, and it'll be easier. I've already told you I want to give respectful coverage."

"A church in Shawsville," Joe answered. "Methodist, I think. Now I must go." He walked away hastily, thinking, *The words just came out of me. Maybe Allah wants this to happen.*

Omar asked Joe, "Who were you talking to?"

"That's what I need to tell you, urgently," Joe said. "He's from the media. Could we ride to the church with someone else so I can tell you without the family around?"

Omar replied, "Maybe we can ride with Dr. Imran."

CHAPTER 46

Wednesday, March 5, 2008
Shawsville, Virginia, USA

On the drive to the church, Joe told Omar and Imran Ashfaq about the newspaper reporter, explaining to Imran Ashfaq that Marwan was the gay bar bomber.

"Allah have mercy," he said. "Does Nassar know?"

"Nassar and a cousin in Arlington know," Omar said, explaining briefly. "I don't know if they've told others."

"The gay bar bombing was news nationally," Imran Ashfaq said, "but nothing locally about the bomber."

"I suspect he was so distraught at being gay he took the only way out he knew, acting like a martyr," Omar stated. "We need to do something for Muslims who think they're gay, but that's not today's discussion."

Inside the church, Velma said, "Come help yourself. That sure was a nice way you conducted the service."

"Thanks," Omar said.

Food aromas came from fried chicken with cream gravy, mashed potatoes, hamburger and macaroni casserole, broccoli and cheese casserole, green peas and mushrooms, coleslaw, three-bean salad, carrot cake, coconut cream pie, a big plate of chocolate chip cookies, sweetened and unsweetened ice tea, lemonade, and a large pot of creamy, light-brown-colored soup.

Omar asked, "What kind of soup is this?"

"Probably peanut soup," Imran Ashfaq replied. "It's a Virginia specialty."

"That's what Jason talked about," Joe commented.

Jolene Robbins walked up and said, "You're trying my peanut soup. That's a specialty I make for these occasions."

"I'll try some too," Joe said.

"Dr. Ashfaq, I was wondering if you and I could have a word. Maybe we could sit over there," Jolene Robbins said.

"Yes, of course," Imran Ashfaq replied.

Sitting across from him, she said, "Thank you for talking with me. It'd be good to know more about Islamic activities in the area. Some fellow clergy and I want to know more and have some communication."

"We're always open for that type of interaction," Imran Ashfaq replied. "What do you have in mind?"

"Please let me get to that later," she said. "There's an immediate concern right now. It's Mrs. Hammoud. She doesn't seem well, more than just grieving loss of her son."

"I've noticed that she's non-responsive," he said, "but I don't know her; I've not met her before."

"Some years ago when I was a seminary student," she continued, "I did an internship as a chaplain in a mental health institution. There were people like that there. They had a trauma and couldn't cope, so they just shut down. I'm certainly not qualified to make a diagnosis. Their neighbors, the Robertses, know her better and say she wasn't this way. I think she needs to see a doctor. Of course recommending someone see a doctor for a possible mental condition is something to be considered very carefully. I'd have great difficulty recommending a member of my congregation take that step, and certainly not someone I barely know. I thought I'd at least mention my concerns to you because you're in a pastoral role, even though it's not your main activity."

"I see your point," he replied. "Having her see a doctor might be beneficial. There's one doctor in our community who might be good. I don't know Nassar well enough to make that kind of suggestion. Mental health issues are on everyone's mind, and nowhere more so than around Virginia Tech. Some people in our community might accept some form of early intervention on a mental health issue, but Nassar and his boys were barely part of our community."

"It raised the awareness of the clergy I know," she added, "especially after news media reported the mother had sought exorcism for him from the minister of their church."

"Dr. Omar seems to have a rapport with them," he said. "Maybe he can suggest a way to approach Nassar."

"Good idea, once he's free," she replied.

Meanwhile, Jordan Hicks had stood behind the chair next to Joe and asked, "Is it OK if I join you two guys?"

Joe replied, "Yes, sure, our pleasure."

"*Ahlan*," Omar said. "That's 'welcome' in Arabic."

Jordan Hicks said, "Most of your prayers were in Arabic. You're not from the U.S., are you?"

"I'm from Yemen," Omar replied. He explained his background briefly and that Muslims usually recite prayers in Arabic, the language of the Prophet, even though they are not Arabic speaking.

"Cool," Jordan Hicks said, and then asked Joe, "You speak Arabic too. What country are you from?"

Joe answered, "Sorry to disappoint you; I'm from Michigan. My parents're from Lebanon. We spoke Arabic at home, but people my age speak English."

"Really? Cool," Jordan Hicks said. "What brings you two down here? That was cool the way you led the service. Don't want to be disrespectful calling a funeral 'cool.'"

"It's OK," Omar replied. "You were very respectful in your remarks. I'm sure the family appreciated them."

Jordan Hicks said, "Thanks. It's the first time I did anything like this and was nervous, but I always like to talk, too much, my girlfriend tells me. Marwan was a nice guy. Are you a Muslim pastor or something like Pastor Jolene?"

"In a way, yes," Omar answered. "I'm an assistant imam in Washington." He explained briefly the circumstances that led to Nassar's asking him to be here.

"That's awesome," Jordan Hicks exclaimed. "Come all the way down here to help the family." Then to Joe, "Are you an imam too?"

Joe explained briefly that they were friends and roommates and that he came to support Omar.

"Cool," Jordan Hicks said. "What work do you do?"

Joe answered, "I'm a lawyer with the U.S. Attorney General's office."

"Awesome, really awesome," Jordan Hicks exclaimed. "So you're really high up. You seem so young."

Joe smiled, "Well I'm twenty-six, almost twenty-seven. I'm pretty low down in the organization but, yeah, it's a good position."

"You just moved there?" Jordan Hicks asked Omar. "What'd you do before?"

Omar explained his background and current positions.

"Here you seemed like two regular guys, not much older than me," Jordan Hicks continued. "Instead you're big guys from Washington who came down here for an ordinary guy like Marwan."

"No one's an ordinary guy in Islam," Omar said. "Christianity believes the same. We're all special in the eyes of Allah, God."

"We *are* just two regular guys," Joe interjected. "What makes you think we're not?"

Jordan Hicks replied, "You're both big in Washington. You're way up high in the government and he's at a big university there."

Joe replied, "We're ordinary guys who believed in ourselves and took opportunity when we found it. My father's an office worker immigrant from Lebanon. I grew up in a working class suburb of

Detroit. Lebanese strive to achieve, so when I had the opportunity to go to the University of Michigan and Michigan Law School, I took it. It's only thirty-five miles away, which helped."

Omar smiled and said, "I'd never qualify as a regular guy," and explained his background.

"Wow, awesome!" Jordan Hicks exclaimed.

Joe interjected, "It was a struggle too, and I'm still paying off student loans."

Jordan Hicks responded, "You guys're giving me inspiration. I've been thinking I should go to Virginia Tech and study marketing, get a real degree. I was always good at computers and thought I wanted to work in computers; but didn't think I was good enough for a big university like Tech, so I went to New River where Marwan went. I still like computers, but now that I'm selling computer stuff, I think I'm more outgoing, not enough of a geek. I like selling things, so I might be good at marketing, but it's a big step."

"Great," Joe said enthusiastically. "It is a big step. It was a big step for me to go to Michigan, but I had a feeling inside, maybe like you have, that's where I should go."

Jordan Hicks continued, "Growing up and going to high school 'round here, Virginia Tech's that place up in Blacksburg, really close, but where all the big important kids from Northern Virginia and Richmond go to school, not little insignificant guys like us here. Local people'd think we're strange, wanting to go to a big time university like Tech. My dad wanted to be a teacher, so he went to Radford; that's a small university in Radford, the next town over from Christiansburg. That was OK."

"We have sort of the same situation where I'm from," Joe said. "Eastern Michigan is the smaller state university in Ypsilanti, the town next to Ann Arbor. It used to be a teachers' college. Some people feel more comfortable there than the big U of M. Go where you feel drawn to go."

Omar said, "Surrendering to Allah's not unique to Islam. Christianity's the same. If you feel you should go to Virginia Tech, maybe that's God's way of saying it's right for you."

"You know Christian beliefs, too," Jordan Hicks said.

"Yes," Omar replied. "That's what coming here to study Islamic theology was all about, study in the context of other religions. I also taught courses in comparative religion at UMD, the University of Minnesota-Duluth, one of those smaller state universities."

"Oh, really?" Jordan Hicks said. "Guys from Tech I work with at the store are regular guys. I can fit in with them, even if I am from Podunk Shawsville. This's been great, talking to you two. How long you here for?"

"Unless Nassar really needs us for something, we'll likely go back tomorrow," Omar replied. "He wants us to drive a car up there for him, and I need to be at the center for Friday prayers if possible."

"Say, I've really got to go now," Jordan Hicks said as he stood to take his dishes to the kitchen. "I'd sure like to talk to you guys some more. Is there any chance you'd want to stop by the store where I work? It's close to the mall between Blacksburg and Christiansburg."

"I don't know if we'd have time or transportation," Joe replied, "but I sure would like to if we can."

"You said it's a computer store," Omar said. "Would we be able to check email there?"

"We don't have public internet access like in some places," Jordan Hicks answered. "We just sell computer stuff, but we could arrange a connection to the internet. I'll definitely be working tonight because I took the morning off. I'm on day shift tomorrow, so I'll be there after 10 until about 6 when some of the part-time guys come in."

Omar reached across the table to shake hands and said, "It's really good to meet you, Jordan, and know Marwan had such good friends. We'll do what we can to get by, *insha Allah*. That means 'God willing.' Some really pious people say it to reinforce belief that everything in life is according to God's will. Most people, Muslims and others, just say it to mean 'hopefully.'"

Jordan Hicks smiled and said, "in-shall-uh," took his dishes to the kitchen, and quickly left.

Omar and Joe sat engaging in small talk, wanting to relax after a stressful morning.

CHAPTER 47

Frank and Brad lay in a private room in a secure wing of Bethesda Naval Hospital, stressed and exhausted after a move from DC General Hospital. Neither felt like watching television and lay listlessly napping. Marian Spencer, who had been allowed in the secure area as next of kin, sat reading a novel. All were jolted when the telephone rang.

Frank answered and after a pause said, "I know you can't visit. It's a secure wing."

(pause)

"It doesn't make a shit who you are," Frank said, agitated. "The DIA told you you're not welcome!"

(pause)

Brad, beginning to stir, agitated, began flailing around with one arm to reach something.

"What do you want, dear?" Marian Spencer asked.

He pointed to the nurse call button.

"I wouldn't give word for you to come to this room even if I could," Frank continued.

(pause)

"Oh, you want to call the nurse?" Marian Spencer said then pushed the button.

Frank shouted into the phone, "Since you obviously haven't figured it out, we're both badly injured. We're here to recover, not entertain the likes of you and feed your ego."

(pause)

"F– forget my poor mother," he continued, red in the face and visibly shaking. "You know as well as I do she cares only for her bottle and couldn't care less about me."

(pause)

"Go the hell back to Florida!" Frank shouted. "If you try to call again, I will do everything I can to stop the call from coming through! Don't contact me again! Ever!"

Frank slammed down the phone even more upset, arteries at his temples throbbing. Marian Spencer, stunned, rushed to his bedside, taking his hand into hers.

"Oh, dear," she said. "This is obviously upsetting you. It must've been your father."

"Yes," Frank said. "Sorry you had to be exposed to it."

"No need to be sorry," Marian Spencer said as she patted his hand. "If you were one of my students, I'd just put my arms around you and give you a big hug."

"Thanks," Frank mumbled. "I appreciate that."

"Breaking off contact with a member of your family is upsetting and stressful," Marian Spencer continued. "You don't have any brothers and sisters, it seems."

"No," Frank said quietly.

"We don't need to go into that now," Marian Spencer said as she patted his hand. "We can be your family now. We just need you to get well and out of here."

"Thanks," Frank said, mustering up a smile.

"Bradley wanted me to call the nurse," she said, taking her hand away. "You two likely need sedatives. A nice warm cup of herbal tea would be nice too; wonder if they have any. Maybe I should go get some tonight. I'll go back to Bradley now. I'm sooo sorry."

When a nurse came in, Marian Spencer nodded towards Frank and said, "He had an upsetting phone call; actually, I think it's upsetting both of them."

The nurse measured Frank's blood pressure, felt his pulse, and said, "That's not good. We should give you a mild sedative. You've been stressed enough today with your move, and now this."

She took Brad's blood pressure and pulse and said, "Oh, not good, either. Not at the danger level, but definitely not good. We'll get you a sedative too."

Marian Spencer took Brad's hand and said, "You've always been a good sensitive boy, thinking of others first."

Within moments the nurse returned and said, "I'll give this glass to Major Reynolds, then I'll give some to you IV. This's mild; something you get over the counter. You'll feel better and relax; maybe sleep."

"Thanks," Frank said as he drank.

"You just relax now," she said. "We're not allowed to disconnect telephones; patients' right to have contact, but I can turn the ringer down."

I don't suppose you have some herbal tea?" Marian Spencer asked. "That's what I always do when I'm a little stressed: Sit down, put my feet up, and have a cup of Tension Tamer tea."

"Oh, that sounds good," the nurse replied. "Maybe I need to try that myself. We just have regular tea here. I can bring you a cup."

"Oh, no, thanks," Marian Spencer replied, "but maybe I can bring my own tomorrow. Would that be OK?"

"Sure thing, honey," she answered as she left.

Marian Spencer said, "Maybe I'll go down to the snack bar and see if I can get a cup of herbal tea. I know you boys'll want to rest, so I'll just let you be for a while."

She blew a kiss towards Brad, took her purse, and left. Brad and Frank gradually drifted into a light slumber.

CHAPTER 48

Wednesday, March 5, 2008
Shawsville, Virginia, USA

Imran Ashfaq said, "Dr. Omar, Ms. Jolene and I wonder if we could speak with you."

"Yes, of course," Omar replied.

Jordan Hicks rushed back in, saying to Joe, "There's a guy who wants to see you outside. Now I really gotta go."

Must be that newspaper reporter, Joe said to himself and rushed outside with only his suit coat on.

Marcus Porter held out his hand, saying, "Marcus Porter, in case you don't remember. I don't recall yours."

Joe indifferently shook hands, saying, "Joe Shaito. You know who I am, so you know I'm with the Attorney General's office. I realize more than most people here it's important to keep good relations with the media, the responsible ones. I'm here in strictly a private capacity. There's not much I can say, even off the record. I'm not trying to blow you off."

"I *am* responsible," Marcus Porter stated. "I intend to get the Pulitzer Prize, and I won't get it for muckraking and sensationalism. I want to write this story in a responsible way before tabloids get it. What private capacity brings you here?"

"I'm helping my friend," Joe said. "It's cold; we should go inside. I suppose it's OK to invite you into the church."

"Most churches are open to people who want to go in for good reasons," Marcus Porter said.

Joe thought, *I'm not a good lawyer for nothing. I've got to control the questioning myself.*

Meanwhile, Imran Ashfaq said to Omar, "Ms. Jolene thinks Mrs. Roula might need a doctor. I'm concerned too."

Jolene Robbins explained the reasons for her concern, and Omar concurred. "I don't know if this's temporary or not; after all, she lost her son, her other son is missing, and I've recently learned someone bombed their house." She quickly added, "There were people like her at the hospital where I worked; it wasn't temporary. Does Mr. Hammoud recognize how serious this is?"

"He must think it's temporary," Omar said. "He told Fatima she should stay home from school to take care of her mother and help."

Jolene Robbins stated, "He can't do that in Virginia; children can't be kept out of school to work at home."

"I didn't know that," Imran Ashfaq said.

"I didn't know either," Omar commented, "but it makes sense. Someone needs to tell Nassar."

"We thought you might, because you seem to have a rapport with him," Imran Ashfaq said. "There's a doctor in our community I could call who might be willing to see Mrs. Roula on short notice. I don't know Nassar well enough to suggest he take his wife to a doctor."

"Does Nassar know him?" Omar asked.

"I doubt it," Imran Ashfaq answered. "Nassar doesn't interact with people the community."

"I can talk to him," Omar said, "maybe in Arabic; he might be more comfortable. I'll ask him to come over."

"Do you want me here?" Jolene Robbins asked. "He might not want a woman interfering in his family things."

Omar said, "That one's difficult. He might feel better that one woman is showing concern for his wife, but he might be offended too. I think I'd err on the side of having you here. If something comes up in our Arabic conversation indicating he's uncomfortable, I can make eye contact and you can excuse yourself."

Meanwhile, Joe said to Marcus Porter, "Why's the *Post* interested in the burial of an insignificant guy like Marwan Hammoud? Why're you so eager?"

Marcus Porter said incredulously, "Surely you know the circumstances how he died."

"I want to hear from you," Joe responded.

He's aggressive, Marcus Porter thought. *I'd tell him to fuck off, but he might be able to cause problems.* "Surely you heard of the gay bar bomber," he said.

"What about it?" Joe said aggressively. "Police closed the case, so why're you here?"

Irritated, Marcus Porter answered, "Police released the name and address late yesterday. It was too late for the *Post*'s last edition, so they broke the story this morning and wanted to cover the funeral. They contacted my editor."

"That still doesn't explain why it's newsworthy," Joe continued. "So what if he's the gay bar bomber? Police said he acted alone."

Marcus Porter said, "Guys are distraught about being gay, even to the point of suicide, but they don't blow up places terrorist style."

"Now you're digging up a terrorist connection." Joe retorted. "What makes you think you'll find it down here?"

"No, damn it!" Marcus Porter exclaimed. "I'm not trying to dig up a terrorist connection, but you know what? The tabloids just might. After all, he has an Arab name and it wouldn't take much to find out it was an Islamic funeral."

"So now you're ethnic profiling," Joe continued. "Would you be so interested if he were, say, Korean?"

Damn, Marcus Porter thought. *He goes right for the jugular. Picks Korean, knowing the Virginia Tech shooter was Korean.* "Damn it!" he said. "I've been cooperative and all you're doing is attacking me, and you said you understand cooperating with the media. I could start asking people directly, but I thought you might be cooperative. Tabloids get a hold of this, you're really going to have ethnic profiling, and it won't be pretty. If I get something in print portraying him as a decent American kid, even if he is Arab-American who happened to be gay, public might not be so stirred up when the tabloids pick up on it. You said you're here in a private capacity and can't talk. I accept that. Maybe you can tell me who to talk to, so this doesn't get sensationalized."

Joe replied, "I get your point. I was a bit aggressive. Surely you can see this's a sensitive situation. It's important to know just how much you know before I cooperate, but you must understand that absolutely nothing ties this to the Attorney General's office and my position there."

"I understand," Marcus Porter replied. "The tabloids might not. Who here knows he's the gay bar bomber?"

Joe answered, "His father; I doubt he's told anyone. I suspect others don't know. I haven't heard anything, and I suspect I would if it were in the news."

"We got it too late for our New River Valley edition," Marcus Porter said. "It made the Roanoke Valley edition this morning. It'll be on the radio and television news today."

"We worried demonstrators would be here," Joe said. "I thought you were here to cover demonstrations."

"Don't kid yourself," Marcus Porter stated, "if there were demonstrators, I'd do everything I could to rush it into print. That'd be a real scoop, but there's not always satisfaction in getting scoops like that. You haven't said why this church is providing lunch for a Muslim family."

"I can't answer that," Joe replied. "Not avoiding the question; I just don't know. The neighbors had something to do with it."

"Are they here? Can I meet them?" Marcus Porter asked. "Sounds like they're in that room. Smells like food."

Joe replied, "I don't know how they'd react to your coming into a private affair with a grieving family."

"Maybe ask the pastor; is he here?" Marcus Porter said.

"She," Joe answered. "And, yes, she's inside, or was."

Meanwhile, Omar asked Nassar to join them and expressed their concern over Roula.

Nassar replied in Arabic, "She's not well. You heard me tell Fatima to stay home and help her until she's better."

Omar replied in Arabic, "Ms. Jolene thinks it's more serious than that. She also said it's illegal for you to keep Fatima from school; you could get into trouble for that."

He repeated in English what he said to Nassar, and Jolene Robbins described her hospital experience.

Nassar said in anguish, "My wife's only been to a hospital to give birth. She couldn't go to a hospital again."

Jolene Robbins said, "She may not need to go to a hospital, but at least she should see a doctor. Don't worry about help at home. The people at the church can help."

Imran Ashfaq said, "There's a doctor in our community; I don't know if you know him: Dr. Roohani; he's from Iran. He's Muslim and sensitive about seeing the wife of another Muslim man. I'm sure he'd let you be there while he examines her. I can call him and make an appointment for you."

Nassar, bewildered, mumbled, "I don't know."

Imran Ashfaq persisted and said, "I'll call him as soon as I get back to my office and find his number."

Jolene Robbins said, "Use my office; come with me."

Omar said to Nassar in Arabic, "You've been teaching your family that Islam means surrender to Allah. If it's the will of Allah, you'll be able to take her to the doctor soon."

Nassar said in Arabic, "You said I'll get in trouble if Fatima stays at home from school."

Omar replied in Arabic, "I'm sure it'll be OK for a day or two. We can talk to Mr. Gordon, the vice-principal."

Imran Ashfaq returned with Jolene Robbins and said, "He'll call me back; his receptionist knows it's urgent. I really need to go now. Thanks again. I look forward to finding ways we can cooperate."

In the meantime, Joe and Marcus Porter entered the fellowship hall; Marcus Porter said, "There're the two men who led the service. One of them must be your friend. Is the lady with them the pastor?"

"Yes," Joe replied.

Marcus Porter asked, "Who's the guy with him?"

"Leader of the Islamic community in Blacksburg," Joe answered.

"Why'd your friend come all the way here to lead the burial?" Marcus Porter asked. "Couldn't this guy do it?"

"Actually, it's not necessary to have an imam for a burial," Joe replied, "but Mr. Hammoud specifically asked my friend to lead the service."

"Why's that?" Marcus Porter asked.

"You'll have to ask them," Joe said. "I'm not trying to blow you off. He's one of my very best friends, and I don't want to disrespect the friendship by speaking for him."

"Oh, OK," Marcus Porter said. "It looks like they're deep in discussion; not a good idea to go disturb them now. Say, what work does Mr. Hammoud do?"

Joe explained, and Marcus Porter said, "Oh, I've heard of him. I've heard people in Roanoke talk about a good place in Montgomery County to get service on older European cars. That'd make a good story too."

"Always looking for a good story," Joe said.

Marcus Porter retorted, "Yes, of course. That looks like the lady who spoke at the burial."

"Yes," Joe confirmed. "She seems to be in charge of organizing food, both last night and today."

"Oh, last night too?" Marcus Porter asked.

"Yes," Joe answered. "She said it's a local custom to take food when there's a death in the family. They thought it more convenient at their house, not the Hammouds'."

"Yes, that's the custom here," Marcus Porter said. "Look, they're heading this way." He greeted Imran Ashfaq, introducing himself with his press card, and said, "Could I have a word with you?"

Imran Ashfaq shook hands and said, "I'm sorry, I have to rush now. I have an appointment in my office very soon."

Marcus Porter handed a notepad. "Maybe I can call for an appointment? What's your phone number?"

Imran Ashfaq hastily wrote down a phone number and exchanged goodbyes.

Marcus Porter then said, "There's the neighbor lady again; do you suppose I might talk to her?"

Joe said, "I'll ask and see what she says."

"Do you suppose I might get something to eat?" Marcus Porter asked. "I'm starved; no time for breakfast."

"I can ask," Joe said.

CHAPTER 49

Wednesday, March 5, 2008
Shawsville, Virginia, USA

Joe approached Velma. "A reporter from the *Roanoke Times* would like to talk to you."

"Why'd the *Ro'noke Times* wanta talk to me?" she asked. "'Bout bombin' the Hammouds' house, I bet."

"No," Joe replied. "He's covering Marwan Hammoud's funeral and wants to talk to people who knew him. He heard you at the funeral home. He seems OK, but I'm not telling you whether you should talk to him. That's your decision."

"Don't hurt to talk, but why'd the paper be interested?" Velma asked.

"Maybe let him tell you," Joe said. "He asked if he might get something to eat. Says he's hungry; must not've had breakfast. I didn't know if it's appropriate to ask."

Velma replied, "The Good Lord said we should feed the hungry, and He and the disciples fed plenty of people, so guess we could let him eat. Plenty of food."

Marcus Porter introduced himself to Velma, showed his press card, and said, "Thanks for letting me eat. May I ask you some things?"

"Help y'rself," Velma replied. "What kinda things?"

"Thanks, this looks really good," Marcus Porter said. "One question is why a Methodist church is having lunch for a Muslim family."

"They's good neighbors," she replied. "Methodist churches, at least this one, makes food for families that have a loss, after a funeral."

"Yes, I know," Marcus Porter said. "I grew up in a Methodist church in Bluefield. My mom prepared food for families in the church who had a loss, and they did it for us when my Granddad died, but he was a leader in the church. Do y' s'pose you could sit down and talk a little bit?"

"The Good Lord said we should show charity to everone, not just Methodists," Velma said. "The Hammouds is nice people and seems they don't have no one to do things for them during this tragedy, so we just pitched in and did it even if they's not Christians. Why're you so interested in the Hammouds? They're nice people, but not so special to make the newspapers come to a funeral."

Marcus Porter said, "I want to write a story about what Marwan Hammoud's really like, his family and friends, not what some tabloids would publish. I want to get the real story out before tabloids go to work on him."

"What's a tabloid? Why'd a tabloid want to publish something bad about Marwan?" Velma asked.

She's pretty sharp, Marcus Porter thought. *She speaks with a pretty heavy local accent and uses bad grammar, but seems right on top of things and cautious. Lots of people in West Virginia like her. Have to be careful about misjudging 'em.* He said, "A tabloid's a sort of newspaper that publishes on small size paper, not large sheets like the *Roanoke Times* and *News-Messenger*. They try to publish things to get people's attention, usually bad things about people. You can see them in supermarkets."

"Oh, y' mean like the *National Enquirer*," Velma said. "Don't see why any decent self-respectin' person'd read that, but why'd Marwan Hammoud be of interest to them?"

Marcus Porter answered, "Yes, like the *Enquirer*. You'd be surprised who reads and believes it. There's some things about the

340

circumstances in which Marwan Hammoud died that tabloids would love to sensationalize."

"Oh, you mean that explosion in the gay bar up there," Velma said. "Guess Shane, that's my husband, was right when he thought Marwan's involved in that. Oh, this poor family if them tabloids as you calls 'em tells 'bout this. Don't know how much more they can take; no family deserves this. Sometimes makes one wonder just why the Good Lord lets things happen. Some'd say it's God's punishment because they's Muslim. Shane and me don't believe that, and Jolene don't either; she's the pastor."

"If I can write a true story about the family," Marcus Porter said, "it can't help but make things easier on them. Is there anything about him that'd have suggested he's gay?"

Velma replied, "Well, don't guess I'd know what to look for. Maybe he played with his little sister and my daughter? He played with his brother and other boys, too. Can't tell you much more; besides, I got to finish puttin' up food for them to take home and help clean the kitchen."

"Thanks," Marcus Porter replied. "Could I get in touch with you and your husband later?"

"Guess I don't mind if you get in touch," Velma said. "Can't speak for my husband, but don't think he'd mind. You seem nice, and we wanta do what's right by the Hammouds."

"May I call you later and come over?" he asked.

"Guess you c'n call," Velma said. "It's up to my husband if he wants to talk to you, but I do gotta go now."

He asked, "May I have your phone number, please?"

She answered, "Look it up in the phone directory. Shane Roberts. Not bein' rude. Easier'n me goin' to find somethin' to write on. Take your time finishin'. Bring your plate to the kitchen if you don't mind."

"OK," he said. "Thanks again for letting me eat."

Meanwhile, Joe went to Omar and Jolene Robbins, asking, "Mind if I join you?"

"Please," Jolene Robbins said. "Who's the young man sitting over there? Friend of yours?"

"That's one thing I was coming to tell you, Reverend Robbins," Joe began. "He's a reporter for the *Roanoke Times* and wants to talk to you. He approached me at the cemetery, wanting more information about Marwan Hammoud. He knew who I am because he'd seen me in court that time I was in Roanoke before. I can't tell you that you should talk to him; that's strictly your choice. My lawyer instincts make me think he's professional and respectful."

"Call me Jolene," she said, "but why'd a reporter be interested in talking to me and come to his funeral?"

"You'll find out soon enough," Joe began. "Marwan Hammoud was the gay bar bomber. You've surely heard about that. He said it was reported in the *Washington Post* today and in the Roanoke editions of the *Roanoke Times*. It was too late for your local edition this morning."

Jolene Robbins replied, "The Robertses guessed that might be the case, but we didn't tell anyone. The last I heard, police concluded it was a single person acting alone who was distraught over being gay. Hard to imagine it's someone next door. Sometimes I preach about love and acceptance of homosexuals; some don't like it, but they're coming around. I suppose you knew this before you came here."

"Yes," Omar answered. *They knew he was the gay bar bomber and still did all this. Never underestimate people,* he said to himself.

Jolene Robbins asked, "Does his family know?"

"Nassar knows," Omar said, and explained about being with Nassar identifying his son.

"That was good of you," Jolene Robbins said. "That's what being a good pastor, or imam, is about. But why's the *Roanoke Times* interested?"

Joe explained Marcus Porter's interest in writing a story before it goes to the tabloids.

"Oh, good," Jolene Robbins agreed, "but why does he want to talk to me?"

Joe replied, "He wants to write about a Methodist church providing lunch in the church for the family."

"I could talk to him along those lines," Jolene Robbins said. "First we need to wind things up here and get the Hammouds home. Mrs. Hammoud is not well."

"Yes, I noticed," Joe said. "But, say, what's this about someone bombing the Hammouds' house? I've heard a few brief comments. Maybe I'm too much of a lawyer, but that could be a hate crime."

"All I know is what the Robertses told me," Jolene Robbins replied. "Talk to them; they saw it firsthand."

Marcus Porter approached, held out his press card, and said, "You're Reverend Robbins, I believe; Marcus Porter of the *Roanoke Times*. May I have a word with you?"

She held out her hand, and said, "Jolene Robbins. Please have a seat. I really can't talk now because we have to arrange transportation for everyone, but perhaps later."

"Thank you," Marcus Porter said, held his hand to Omar saying, "You must be Mr. Shaito's friend; you led the service." To Jolene Robbins, "Thanks for letting me come in and eat. It's really good of you to do this for this family at a difficult time. I'd like to ask some questions and write about it, but I want to express my appreciation first."

Jolene Robbins replied, "Your appreciation is gracious. As Jesus said, if you've done it for the least of these my brethren, you have done it for me. I'm sure Dr. Abu Deeb here can give you similar words from the Prophet."

He said, "Please call me Omar. Hospitality to those in need is fundamental to Islam and the entire Arab culture."

343

Marcus Porter said, "I grew up in a Methodist church. We didn't do anything like this; maybe we didn't have an opportunity. We did do good things for people in need."

"I'm sure you did," Jolene Robbins replied. "We Methodists are good at that. I really must go now and tend to the transportation. Mr. Porter, Marcus, I'd be pleased to talk to you, although I'm not sure what I could add. Maybe you can contact me later." To Joe and Omar, "We need to get you back to the Hammouds'. Velma and Shane'll take the Hammouds home, but that's all who'll fit in their small car. I hope Gordon won't mind taking you and the other gentleman home. Or maybe I could take the two of you, but I need to see how soon they're ready to go."

Marcus Porter said, "I can take you two. That way we can visit more."

"Thanks," Jolene Robbins said. "It'd help me today."

"I need to thank the people in the kitchen," Omar said, picking up the cue. "I'll be right back."

"Me too," Joe said.

As soon as they were in the kitchen, Joe said to Omar, "Sorry I made a decision for you. You don't have to talk to this reporter if you don't want to, but I think he can be an ally in lots of ways."

Omar smiled and put his hand on Joe's shoulder saying, "It's OK, habibi. I'm stressed and exhausted; I don't mind you making a decision or two. You always know what's best."

CHAPTER 50

Joe, sensing Omar's fatigue, climbed into the backseat of Marcus Porter's late model two-door Honda Civic so Omar could have the front, and said, "Good of you to take us. I'm sure Reverend Jolene appreciates it."

"Yes, thanks," Omar said. "She's had a busy, stressful day; lots on her mind. She's a good pastor."

"You're a good pastor, too," Marcus Porter added.

"You know your way around," Joe commented as Marcus drove without hesitating and asking for directions.

"I live not far from here, closer towards Roanoke in Salem," Marcus Porter replied. "I went to Virginia Tech and spent lot of time around there. Not much around here I don't know. To tell the truth, I found their address and stopped by on the way over. Say, what're you guys doing this evening? I'd like to get together and talk more. Yes, I want a story, but you two seem like nice guys, about my age, and really interesting. I like to meet new people. I could show you places in Roanoke. You're tired, but maybe we'd get something to eat. Just have to get in touch with my girlfriend; we don't have specific plans."

"Oh, I don't know," Omar said wearily. "We're staying with the Hammouds and need to see what they are doing."

Joe hastily added, "We're not blowing you off. I'd like to spend time with you too. I've met members of the media in Washington, but none I could get to know on a personal level as well as professional. It's just we're not sure what we're expected to do tonight with the Hammouds."

"Yes," Omar added. "I'd like to get to know you too. I've never known anyone from the media. I'm just tired."

"I understand," Marcus Porter said. "Maybe tomorrow? If you'd like, you could come to Roanoke tomorrow and I can show you around the paper and we could have lunch; an early lunch, if you need to go on to Washington."

"That might work," Omar said.

Joe added, "Tonight's not out of the question; but it'd have to be around here. We halfway promised Jordan Hicks we'd visit him in the computer shop where he works. Blacksburg's a neat town. It'd be nice to see more of it."

Marcus Porter said, "That'd work for me. I used to live in Blacksburg and know my way around, and I'd like to meet Jordan and ask him more about Marwan Hammoud."

Joe said, "To be honest, I'm hoping the Hammouds want to be alone, but we have to be sensitive to what they want. We're all Arabs, and hospitality's big in the culture."

"You're Arabs," Marcus Porter said. "It kind of slipped my mind. I see you as regular guys from this country."

"Well we are," Joe replied. "I'm Arab, but also very much American. I'm from Michigan."

"I'm from Yemen," Omar said, "but I've been here six years, going to school, and hopefully will stay here."

Marcus Porter continued, "Say, I hope to see the Robertses tonight. I told Mrs. Roberts I'd call her and arrange to come over. If they'll see me, I can find you and we can go to Blacksburg and wherever that guy's store is. We need to exchange phone numbers if that's OK."

Joe said, "Marcus, I'm pleased to be with you, but we know you want stories. Being a lawyer, I can say we have to draw definite lines up front. This's the first time I've been in this situation, so we have to establish very clearly, going overboard if necessary, just what's on the record and what's off. If we err, it has to be on the side of being too cautious. I'm not willing to talk socially if there's even the remotest chance it'll end up in print. You seem professional and respectful, but I'd rather take the risk of offending you now than being sorry later. Hope you understand."

Marcus Porter, taken somewhat aback, answered, "Yes, sure, you're right. Trust me; I have a reputation to maintain. The absolute last thing a budding judicial reporter wants is to have the Office of Attorney General of the United States pissed off and be on its shit list. Just tell me clearly if I don't seem to be getting it, where to draw the line."

"OK," Joe said. "Lawyers have more practice. We have to keep our professional and social lives separate."

Omar said, "I'm in a similar situation. I don't know how much I can tell you. I'd like to get to know you, but there're limits to what I can say."

"Yes, I know, clergy confidentiality," Marcus Porter replied. "I admit I haven't had many dealings with clergy and confidentiality, but I know it must be respected. If I pry too much, just tell me. I don't want lightning to strike me. We're here; this is the turn into Lafayette."

CHAPTER 51

Thursday, March 6, 2008
Troutville, Virginia, USA

On an average cloudy, cool, winter day, Joe was driving a classic 1980s model Mercedes Benz north on I-81 leaving the Roanoke area. Omar commented, "It was good of Marcus to show us the newspaper plant."

Joe said, "Now that I know him better, he's a nice guy, on the ball, and knows what he needs to do to get his story and be professional about it. He'll go far."

"His story in the *Roanoke Times* today was good, short, and to the point," Omar said.

"Yes, thoughtful without sensationalizing things," Joe concurred. "The part about the Methodist church was good."

"Omar added, "It was a good time with him in Blacksburg last night, even if I was tired."

"Yeah, Joe agreed. "I like that restaurant he took us to. Quirky, like you'd find around a university. Seems things went OK with you and Marcus when I went to buy t-shirts for my Michigan friends."

Omar answered, "A bit awkward making sure what's on the record and what's off. He seemed genuinely interested in Islam and respectful too. Seemed to go OK with Jordan Hicks when Marcus talked to him while we were checking emails. Jordan can handle himself, but I'm curious what he told Marcus. Maybe we'll find out if *Post* picks up the story. How'd it go with you and him at the Robertses'?"

"Good," Joe answered. "Turns out I didn't really need to be there; Marcus was professional as ever. I was concerned they might be overwhelmed by a newspaper reporter, but I was wrong. As he reminded me, they may have strong accents and use bad grammar, but they're no dummies. His accent's almost as strong."

"Aren't too many 'country' people like them in Minnesota, despite the Lake Woebegone stories," Omar said.

"Lots of blacks like that in DC," Joe continued. "Some come from poor backgrounds and their speech and mannerisms show it, but many are pretty bright."

"I haven't been in DC long enough to observe," Omar replied, "but I'm sure you're right. Say, did you find out more about that bombing at the Hammouds'?"

"Yeah," Joe answered. He described events as told by Shane and Velma Roberts, including reporting to the sheriff.

"That sucks," Omar said. "What'd the sheriff do?"

"They don't know," Joe answered. "Tomorrow I'm going to see Roger. This could be a federal hate crime."

"Did Marcus hear it?" Omar asked.

"Yes, he heard it all," Joe replied. "He was interested; wouldn't be surprised if that ends up in a story too."

"Hope we can read about it in the *Post*," Omar said.

"We can likely look up the *Roanoke Times* online," Joe said, "but, yes, it'd be good to get a story about hate crime against Arabs in the *Post*."

After a few moments, Omar said, "You were going to tell me more about what Jason said on the phone."

"Oh, yeah," Joe began and explained Frank and Brad were moved to a secure wing at Bethesda Naval hospital and that Paco and Jason haven't gotten a security clearance to visit yet.

Omar said, "It's going to be more difficult to visit them up in Maryland. Will we get in through security?"

"We have to be on an approved list," Joe replied. "According to Jason, it's actually easier to get there from our apartment: Get on the red line by DuPont Circle, and the Metro goes straight to the hospital. Brad's mother's there. She came just after we left; his father'll come this weekend. Brad's mom wants to go to his place and stay there. They'll take Frank's car, but they couldn't find the keys."

"Oh, shit," Omar said. "They must be at home someplace. I don't remember who drove his car last."

"I think it was me," Joe replied, "when I drove to Baltimore and Laurel."

"It's good we were able to get an early start," Omar commented. "Fortunately, Nassar was able to take Roula to a doctor this morning. I don't need to tell you how people in our culture feel about mental illness."

After a few more moments, Joe said, "Oh, here's Lexington. That's where Washington and Lee Law School is located. One of the best."

They engaged in small talk off and on until they got to the DC metropolitan area.

CHAPTER 52

Thursday, March 6, 2008
Shawsville, Virginia, USA

In early afternoon, Maggie Burns, counselor at Shawsville Middle School, came to Gordon Hicks's office saying, "You should hear about this, Gordon, it's about Fatima Hammoud."

Surprised, he asked, "What about her? She seems like a nice girl; a little shy. Please sit down."

The counselor said, "There was an incident in the lunch room; a girl taunted her, saying, 'fatty with the faggy brother, an A-rab bitch with a c-word needing the d-word'. There was more, but surely you get the idea."

Gordon Hicks replied, "What brought on that?"

"Bullying," the counselor replied. "Fatima'd done nothing to provoke her; and even if she had, there's no justification for anything like this."

"For sure," he concurred.

"Have you seen the paper today?" the counselor asked. "Her brother was identified as the gay bar bomber."

Gordon Hicks, surprised, said, "I knew he was killed in an accident in Washington, but that's something I wouldn't imagine. I'm sure you're right, but it's unbelievable."

"I agree. He was a student here before I started, so I didn't know him, but from the newspaper description he was a nice, well-liked young man. It cited comments at his funeral by a school official and soccer coach. That must've been you."

"Yes," he replied, "Jordan said something about a newspaper reporter talking to him, but we didn't have time to talk about it. Did it say he's gay?"

"In the article he said he wouldn't be gay any more, just before he set off the bomb," she added.

Gordon Hicks commented, "Homosexuality's a fact of life. We have it here in this school, as you're aware. No need to discuss that now. Who said these things?"

"A girl named Karlee Bates," she began. "Her family lives beyond Ironto in the hollows. She's been a troublemaker along with others of her extended family."

"Yes, I know who you're describing," Gordon Hicks said. "Runs in the family. I've had others in here, mostly boys. At lunch you say?"

"Yes," she continued. "Fatima was with friends. She was sad and depressed because of her brother's funeral."

"I'm sure," he said. "Her mother isn't well. She was supposedly staying home to take care of her."

Maggie Burns continued. "She said her father took her mother to the doctor today and said it'd be best if she came on to school. She didn't want to miss school, either, because she's doing well and likes school. When she got to her next class, she was sobbing. One of her friends told the teacher. It was Jared Lindsey, who teaches math. Because he's young and male, he didn't want to get too close to her, so he asked one of her friends to take her to my office. Fatima didn't want to tell me much, but I got this much out of her and the girls with her at the table. I asked the secretary to take her to the nurse's room, where she can be quiet."

"Good for you," Gordon Hicks said. "I should speak to her, but first I need to talk to the Bates girl and hear what she says. You should be with me while I talk to her."

Soon the counselor arrived with a girl about thirteen, well into puberty, with straight, light brown unkempt hair, dressed sloppily in jeans and a long-sleeved boy's shirt.

Gordon Hicks began gently, saying, "Ms. Burns tells me you had an altercation in the lunch room, Karlee."

Karlee Bates replied, "What's that? Ain't been in no fights, if that's what y' mean."

He continued, "We have reports you verbally attacked another student and said things that were not very nice."

Karlee Bates said, "Oh, you mean that A-rab cunt bitch everone calls Fatty. I didn't attack her; just told her things."

Gordon Hicks winced at the obscenity and said, "What motivated you to do that? Had she said anything to you?"

Karlee Bates replied, "We don't need A-rab terr'ists like her 'n' her family. Her fuckin' fag brother bombed that bar where other fags hang out. Told her she needs a real man to put his dick in her cunt to show her what it's like, but no guy 'round here'd want t' fuck her A-rab hole."

Gordon Hicks, showing revulsion, said emphatically, "We do not use that kind of language here! Do not let me hear you talk that way again. You didn't answer my question. Had Fatima said or done anything to you?"

Karlee Bates replied, "No, she didn't say nothin' to me; didn't have to. Everone's talkin' about her brother. Her other brother's a sissy too. Her family even had my brother and cousins locked up, claimin' they bombed their house. They's the terr'ists. Don't need their type here."

Gordon Hicks said, "That is not acceptable behavior, and we won't tolerate it."

"Oh, yeah?" Karlee Bates retorted, "What y' goin' t' do 'bout it?"

Gordon Hicks said, "We can suspend you from school or expel you; private schooling so you can't hurt others."

"Yeah, right." Karlee Bates said. "Y' ain't scarin' me none. This fucked-up school ain't for shit, anyway."

Gordon Hicks said, "That's enough! Ms. Burns will take you to the detention room."

Karlee remained seated; Gordon Hicks said forcefully, "You'll go with Ms. Burns to the detention room."

"Oh, fuck you," Karlee Bates said, got up and walked to the door where the counselor took her by the arm.

Gordon Hicks thought, while regaining composure, *I've got to tell Henry for sure, but we need to do something with Fatima Hammoud first. Don't think she should go home on the school bus. I'd take her home myself, but wouldn't be right taking home a young Muslim girl just into puberty. Velma might have some ideas.* He explained the situation on the phone to her.

(pause)

He said, "I haven't seen her yet. Maggie Burns, the counselor, said she's crying, but trying to be brave."

(pause)

"Oh, you can?" Gordon Hicks said relieved. "That'd be great. She can stay in the nurse's room until you get here."

(longer pause)

"Didn't think of that," he replied. "I'll call and see. You know if we release her from school early in someone else's custody, we have to have permission from a parent. Do you have her father's phone number?"

(pause)

"Thanks, Velma," Gordon Hicks concluded.

He made another call, saying, "Jolene, Gordon Hicks."

(pause)

"Velma suggested I call you," he said, and explained, concluding, "Velma'll take her home with her when she gets off work. She also suggested you might be able to keep her at the church if you're not too busy."

(pause)

"That might work," Gordon Hicks said. "Let her stay in the church parlor or Sunday school room. She could do school work or bring a library book. I'll call you back. Thanks a lot."

He asked the secretary to call Nassar Hammoud. He and the counselor told Fatima about plans if her father agreed.

Soon after, the secretary said, "Mr. Hammoud was at a hospital with his wife and couldn't talk. When I told him it was from the school and about his daughter, he said it was OK for her to stay with Rev. Robbins and go home with Velma. I told him to call you later."

Gordon Hicks thanked the secretary, told the counselor and Fatima what arrangements were made, then went to the office of Henry Bower, the school principal, knocked, and walked in saying, "Henry, something's just happened you need to know about."

Henry Bower, in his sixties, hair completely gray, had a robust build showing he had been an athlete. He wore a dress shirt and tie with notable lack of style.

Looking over his glasses, he asked, "What's that?"

Gordon Hicks, noting Henry Bower did not ask him to sit down, sat anyway and described the situation.

Henry Bower responded, "Oh, yes, I read about the Hammoud boy's funeral and some other things about him and his family in the paper this morning. Who was it doing the attacking, as you say?"

"Karlee Bates," Gordon Hicks answered. "There've been several Bates children here."

"Yes, I'm aware," Henry Bowers responded with a sigh. "What did Fatima Hammoud do to provoke this?"

"Nothing!" Gordon Hicks said annoyed. "What makes you think Fatima would provoke her?"

"Well something must've made the Bates girl do that," Henry Bower replied.

Gordon Hicks stated, "By Karlee's own admission, Fatima did absolutely nothing. Karlee took it on herself to say she was an Arab c-word, that her brother was a fag terrorist. She says Arabs don't belong and used a whole lot more vile obscene words. Henry, even if Fatima had said something, no one deserves that kind of attack."

"Well, her brother did bomb that gay bar like a terrorist," Henry Bower began.

"Henry," Gordon Hicks exclaimed interrupting. "Fatima is not responsible for what her brother did."

"But they're Arabs, and everyone's suspicious of Arabs these days," Henry Bower replied.

"Henry!" Gordon Hicks exclaimed. "It seems like you're trying to justify what Karlee did. Fatima and her brothers are Americans, as American as you and me and our children and the other kids in this school. It's wrong to attack someone just because of ethnicity. I want to give her a week's disciplinary suspension."

"Oh, I don't know about that, Gordon," Henry Bowers said. "I'm not justifying what she did, but just don't want to get people riled up by making a bigger deal out of it than it is. Suspend her and lots of people get upset. People're upset enough with a terrorist bomber growing up here. Just let it ride. Give her a warning."

"How can you say that, Henry?" Gordon Hicks exclaimed. "Would you be so tolerant of this kind of abuse if Fatima were attacked because she were black?"

Henry Bower, taken aback, replied, "Of course not! We'd have every civil rights group on our backs."

Gordon Hicks, seething with anger, responded, "So it's OK if there's no civil rights group to get upset because she's Arab, but not OK if she is black. Henry, I cannot accept that double standard. I'm going to suspend her for a week. If you don't like it, you can overrule me in writing."

Gordon Hicks walked to the door, paused, and turned to say, "You might notify the superintendent and others in the county school administration office so they can have a heads up if the media and school board find out about this."

Henry Bowers, visibly angry, almost shouted, "Are you threatening me, Gordon?"

Gordon Hicks, his anger turning to exasperation, said, "No, Henry, I'm not threatening you. I'm trying to save your rear end in case the superintendent finds out some other way. I will say that I'll not be in the slightest bit upset if they do find out, but they're not going to find out from me."

Gordon Hicks stalked out, thinking, *Damn it, when're they going to make him retire! He's old enough. Don't want to push it too hard because they might think I'm angling for his job.*

He stopped to sec the counselor, who said Jolene Robbins had come to get Fatima. Gordon Hicks told her about giving Karlee Bates a one-week disciplinary suspension but omitted the tense discussion with Henry Bowers. The counselor agreed wholeheartedly, saying she would process the paperwork for his signature. He returned to his office to stare at the wall for a moment's relief.

CHAPTER 53

Thursday, March 6, 2008
Washington, DC, USA

Inside their apartment after Abou Tarek dropped them off in the car they had driven for Nassar, Joe said to Omar, "Looks like Paco and Jason have been here. A woman's been here, too; must be Brad's mother."

Omar said, "I can get the answering machine."

"Go ahead," Joe said. "I need to find Frank's car keys."

"FBI wants us to call," Omar said, "and you've got a message to call home. Nothing else important."

Soon Joe said, "I found them in your room. Sorry, you're on the phone."

Omar nodded while speaking. "I was there in a strictly private capacity. In case you don't realize it, I'm not a paid undercover informant for the FBI."

(long pause)

"OK, maybe I overreacted," Omar said. "I've shown you, Joe has too, if we find something that might possibly damage the interests of the U.S., I'll report it. I don't go looking for things when I'm in a strictly private capacity, especially in my role as an imam. But, no, nothing remotely related to the things you're investigating."

(pause)

"He's right here," Omar said. "I can't speak for him."

Joe immediately shook his head side to side.

"He doesn't have anything to say either," Omar added, said goodbye and hung up, and commented, "Gee, that guy's persistent."

"Persistence makes for a good lawyer, and journalist, too, the FBI too," Joe replied.

While Omar was rummaging through mail, Joe called and said in Arabic, "Mama, its Joe. Sorry I wasn't here when you called; you know I went away with Omar."

(pause)

"Good, considering the circumstances," Joe replied in Arabic. "Sad. He'll meet the Prophet on resurrection day. Omar assured everyone in his prayers."

(pause)

That was abrupt, he thought. *Usually she's more talkative.* "*Marhaba, Baba,*" he said in Arabic to his father.

(pause)

"We just got back from the mountains of Virginia," Joe continued in Arabic. "I helped Omar with an Islamic burial."

(pause)

"What?" Joe said in Arabic. "Not again. I told you I'm not ready to get married."

(pause)

"You want me to get married and then divorced?" Joe exclaimed with disbelief in Arabic.

(pause)

"After what baby's born?" He asked in Arabic.

(pause)

"What!?" Joe asked in Arabic. "You want me to marry her, get her pregnant, and then get divorced?"

(pause)

"That's disgusting," Joe said angrily in Arabic. "That's contrary to anything the Prophet says about family."

(pause)

"How can the imam say that?" Joe asked in Arabic. "I had plenty of classes in Islam growing up. You should know. You made me go to them."

(pause)

"Just because he says he's an imam doesn't make it right," Joe stated forcefully in Arabic. "He's not my imam. I have an imam who's an expert on Islam right here."

(pause)

"What?" Joe shouted in Arabic. "Money's on its way?"

(pause)

"This has gone too far," Joe exclaimed angrily in Arabic. "The family of a woman pays money the imam will give to you so I marry their daughter, get her pregnant, and then get divorced! That's not only immoral, but illegal. Don't expect me to be a part of that!"

(pause)

"No, and that's final!" Joe shouted in Arabic. "I'm not going against everything in Islam I believe in, and I'm not doing anything illegal to jeopardize my job and career!"

Joe listened in disbelief then held the receiver, the call disconnected. He slammed down the receiver and stood shaking, seething in anger, on the verge of tears.

Omar, seeing Joe more upset than he had ever seen him, placed his hand on Joe's shoulder, faced him, and asked, "Habibi, what is it?"

Joe, sobbing, said, "He disowned me."

Omar moved closer, put his arm further around Joe's shoulder, and said, "You don't deserve that."

Joe moved closer, almost instinctively had arms around Omar in a close embrace, and blurted out, "He wanted me to be a… a… gigolo."

"Habibi, I heard most of it," Omar said; "I couldn't help it. Everything you said is right. It is against Islam, but now's not the time for a theological discussion."

After a few moments, Joe pulled back and through sniffles said, "Thanks, habibi."

They sat on the couch, Omar's arm around Joe's shoulder; Joe said, "I don't know if I'm hurt, angry, or both. I can't believe he'd treat me that way. In Lebanese culture, the children's role is to make parents look good but, damn it, not this way! I need time to think. I can't let that so-called imam get away with this, even if my family's involved. Being an imam doesn't put him above the law."

"For sure," Omar replied, "like Mohammad in Lackawanna. But we don't need a discussion of the role of imams. You're right, and a good Muslim."

"Thanks, habibi," Joe said again. "I'm going to see Roger tomorrow anyway about the hate crime against the Hammouds. I can tell him about this too."

They sat a few moments; then Omar said, "I suppose we should call the guys in the hospital before it's too late. We also need to eat. That early lunch is wearing off."

"I'm in no mood to eat," Joe said.

"Yes, I know," Omar said, "but you've got to eat. You need nourishment now more than ever."

"If you say so," Joe said indifferently. "I don't suppose there's anything in the kitchen. I don't feel like going out."

Omar said. "Let's call the guys, then see."

"Would you please call, habibi?" Joe asked.

"Jason, Omar," he spoke into the phone.

(pause)

"Good," Omar answered, "considering what the trip was for. Stressful too. We can tell you more about it when we see you again. How're Frank and Brad?"

(pause)

"Good to hear," he said. "We'll visit soon as we can."

(pause)

"Oh, you think we'll be approved by tomorrow," Omar replied. "We'll probably be out tomorrow night."

(pause)

"We noticed you and Paco both'd been staying here," Omar said. "There're some women's things in Joe's room too; must be Brad's mother."

(pause)

"No problem at all," Omar replied. "We're glad we're able to accommodate her."

(pause)

"Joe found the keys," Omar continued, "but there's no need for her to stay in a hotel tonight, especially if she's taking Frank's car to Maryland tomorrow."

(pause)

Omar said, "You and Paco can have my bed like before. Joe and I will sleep on the couch and cushions."

Joe winced.

"Oh, Paco's not coming tonight?" Omar said. "Come ahead; we'll make some kind of sleeping arrangements. What time'll you be here? We'll be here after possibly going out for something to eat."

(pause)

"OK, she'll come ahead, then you'll come when they make you leave," Omar repeated. "See you then. Give our best to Paco, Frank, and Brad."

After goodbyes, Omar said, "You likely heard that. Jason and Mrs. Spencer are coming over tonight. They're letting Paco stay in the hospital, but not Jason; his 'I am a nurse' thing again."

"Yeah," Joe said, "and we're sleeping on the couch."

"No," Omar replied. "You and I sleep in my bed and let Jason sleep on the couch."

"Oh, good," Joe said. "I don't know how much sleep I'll get. I hope I don't keep you awake."

"Little risk of that," Omar said. "I'll probably be unconscious. Let's eat. I'm really hungry now. I looked; there's still some soup. Looks like they ate most of the bread and sandwich stuff. Not much else but macaroni and cheese mix and some pasta and pasta sauce."

"Whatever," Joe said. "I don't feel like eating. Yes, I know I need to. If you don't feel like making something in the kitchen, let's go somewhere so long as it's not Lebanese. Maybe something simple like that Greek place."

Omar said, "OK. It'll be a good hour at least before Mrs. Spencer gets here."

CHAPTER 54

Nassar knocked while Velma was preparing supper and said, "I've come for Fatima."

"She's downstairs playing with Amelia," Velma replied. "Come on in out of the cold. How's Roula?"

"Not good," he said. "I had to take her to a hospital."

"That's too bad," Velma said, "but if it gets her the help she needs...."

"I should take Fatima now," Nassar said.

"Oh, please let her stay and play with Amelia," Velma said. "She's already done her homework. Gordon Hicks wants you to call if y' haven't done it yet. Maybe do it in private while she's here."

Nassar said, "I need to find his phone number."

"I c'n give y' his number if y' like. Say, why don't you all just come have supper with us," Velma offered, "and that nice man who lives with you. It's nothin' fancy, but I'm fixin' it right now and there's plenty."

Nassar said, "You've done so much already. We have all that food from yesterday."

"Oh, that'll keep," Velma said. "You must've had a bad day, Fatima too, and don't need to worry 'bout food."

Nassar, with little capacity for resistance, said, "OK."

"Be ready in half hour or so," Velma said. "You come when y're ready. Here, I'll get Gordon's number for you."

Nassar and Abou Nidal returned later; Shane said to Nassar, "So sorry t' hear 'bout Roula in the hospital."

"Taking her for observation for two weeks," Nassar said. "The doctor was very concerned, immediately referred me to a psychiatrist, and used his influence to get me in. The psychiatrist gave her a preliminary screening and said she needs to go to a hospital immediately and made arrangements for me to take her to St. Albans Hospital in Fairlawn, next to Radford. Don't know if they can help her much if they can't talk the same language. It's in Allah's hands now."

"Must be rough on y' at home too, havin' t' do things by yourself and take care of Fatima, too." Shane commented. "It would be for me."

Nassar agreed. "Fatima's old enough to do housework and on days she goes to school she can just stay at home after school until we get there. Don't know what I'm going to do tomorrow. School says she should stay home until Monday."

Velma overheard and said, "We might have a solution for y'. I's goin' t' tell y' later. An older lady at the church, Lucy Simpson, Fatima knows her, says she's willin' to come help y' all out for two weeks for nothin'; just give her gas money or I s'pose give her gas. After that, if y' want t' keep her on, y' c'n work it out t' pay her."

Nassar sat up stunned, "Oh, I don't know...."

"Jolene said it might be a problem 'cause Muslims don't allow women to be alone with men they's not related too," Velma said. "She's an older lady, about old enough to be your mother. Maybe that'd make it OK?"

"It's not that," Nassar replied. "It's just that it doesn't feel right to keep accepting things."

"That's what neighbors are for," Velma said.

"Mr. Gordon told me what happened at school today," Nassar said. With Roula's problems, it's a lot to deal with."

"I c'n imagine," Velma said. "That's why Jolene thought y' might want some help and arranged it with Lucy. You c'n think about it some and ask Fatima; she knows Lucy. I'll go get the girls, and we c'n start eatin'." She called them, turned back, and said, "And don't you give any more thought to them people saying bad things 'cause you're Arabs. I learned from Gordon today it's the same family who bombed y'r house. Just some rednecks; local people here don't like'm neither. There's bad people everwhere, but 'round here lots more good folks than bad."

Fatima hugged her father, asking in Arabic, "How's Mama?"

"Mama's very sick, *hayat baba*," he answered in Arabic. "She's in the hospital."

"Oh," Fatima replied, and began sobbing.

"It's in the hands of Allah, now," he continued in Arabic. Switching to English, he said, "Mrs. Velma says you know a nice lady who'll come help us with housework and stay with you."

Fatima said, "Oh, who?"

"Lucy," Velma said. "The lady in the church nursery."

"Oh, yes," Fatima answered. "She's nice. She's coming to our house?"

"If y'r father wants her to," Velma replied.

"It might be good," Nassar said. "I'll give her more than just gas, but we can work that out later. Could she come tomorrow? Fatima's supposed to stay home from school."

"Yes," Velma answered. "That's why we worked it out so quick. Let's all eat, and we c'n talk about it afterwards."

"We usually says grace, that's a prayer, before we eats our dinner," Shane said. "Does it bother you if we pray?"

"No," Nassar answered. "The Prophet says Christians are people recognized by our holy Q'ran, so we can pray with Christians. You prayed with us yesterday."

"Let's bow our heads," Shane said. "Dear Lord, we thanks You for th' food. Bless it and may it provide nourishment for our bodies to live th' way You wants us to live. Bless your daughter Roula; heal her that she may be back with her family soon. Bless and guide her family during her stay in the hospital. Your blessings on all of us that we may follow Your will. In Jesus' name, Amen."

Velma and Amelia said "Amen" and raised their heads.

When all had finished, Velma said, "You girls help y'r selves t'dessert. Rest of us'll have coffee with ours. You c'n go back downstairs, if that's OK with you, Nassar."

She brought a lemon pie and went to clean the kitchen. Shane brought coffee and led them to the family room.

Shane asked Nassar, "Y' have any idea how long Roula'll be in the hospital?"

Nassar said, "Not sure. They'll let her stay a week without insurance or deposit of money. The state'll provide one week's hospitalization because of the focus on mental health after what happened at Virginia Tech. Don't know what'll happen if she's not well by then."

"Oh," Shane said. "You don't have no insurance?"

"No," Nassar replied. "It's hard to get and very expensive for self-employed persons, so we just decided we'd pay if we needed something. We're all healthy and never imagined anything like this."

"They wants you to pay cash up front?" Shane said.

"Yes," Nassar answered, "and I don't have much cash after paying for Marwan's burial. I've got inventory at the station and cars to be sold, but not much cash right now."

"Can't y' borrow money from th' bank 'gainst that?" Shane asked. "I know at Velma's bank folks is borrowin' money 'gainst things they own if they's in a tight spot."

"I stopped by the bank today on my way from the hospital," Nassar said. "They told me lending's tight and I shouldn't expect to be able to borrow much if anything. They gave me forms to fill out, but didn't sound favorable."

"Oh, what bank is that?" Shane asked. "Don't sound like th' way they does things at Velma's bank."

"Wachovia in Christiansburg," Nassar replied.

"Why don't y' talk to Velma when she comes back in here," Shane suggested. "She's not involved in them types decisions, but knows somethin' 'bout how th' bank works. In your culture, y' don't like to talk about business things with women, I suppose."

"Nassar replied, "I'm getting used to it. The person I talked to at my bank is a woman. After bad things people're saying against Arabs, I wonder if that's the problem."

Abou Nidal asked to be excused. After goodbyes, Shane said to Velma, "When y're at a good stoppin' place, Nassar has somethin' 'bout the bank t' ask y'."

When Velma came into the family room, Nassar recounted the visit to his bank.

"I told 'm that y'r bank lends money t' people in a tight spot if they got property to lend against," Shane interjected.

"What bank do you use?" Velma asked Nassar.

"Wachovia in Christiansburg," Nassar answered.

Velma said, "There's rumors th' whole company might be in a bad place and little branches like Christiansburg're told to tighten up."

"I've been doing business with this bank for over 20 years," Nassar said. "When the government was helping me get settled and start a business, they were cooperative and glad to help. Only then it was the local bank, Bank of Christiansburg. Now it's been bought by other banks. Seems they don't care about good customers anymore."

"Yes, that's what happens when banks get bought out," Velma said. "We're lucky we haven't been bought by anyone, but 're buyin' other small ones right here in this area and we're still First National of Christiansburg. I'm not supposed t' say much, but looks like we'll merge with some other banks over 'n eastern part of Virginia. Might change our name, but operations'll be run from right here in Christiansburg. Anyway, what more specific y' tryin' t' do?"

He explained the same things as earlier to Shane. Velma replied, "What about a home equity loan? How much equity y' have in your house?"

"Equity? What's that?" Nassar asked.

"That's what the value of th' house is t' you after y' pays off what y' owe on it," Velma answered. "How much y' still owe on y'r house, if I may ask a pers'nal question."

Nassar looked confused and asked, "How much do we owe to who? We paid all our taxes."

"Owin' on a mortgage," Velma clarified.

"Nassar replied, "We paid that off over five years ago."

"Then y' have a fair 'mount of equity in th' house," Velma said. "Banks 're still makin' home equity loans, or at least First National is. Things're getting' tighter with some bad mortgages 'round the country, but so far it's not affectin' sound home equity loans."

"I don't know much about that," Nassar said.

"It's a loan where you can use the equity in y'r home for collateral," Velma began explaining. "The bank lends y' the money and y' don't have to pay it back 'til the house is sold. Y' have t' pay the interest, though. Y' can even establish a line of credit, which means you don't actually borrow money 'til y' needs it."

"I haven't heard of a loan like that," Nassar said. "I don't have to pay it back?"

"Well, y' can pay it back if y' wants to," Velma answered. "It means when y' sell the house some day, the bank gets its money first and y' only get what's left."

"Sounds like it might be good," Nassar replied. "Do you think I could borrow money like this from your bank?"

"I don't make decisions like that," Velma said, "but what I can do is have y' come in and talk to the manager. I'd say that chances are good if you're willin' to transfer all of y'r business t' our bank. With y'r station, you sh'd have plenty of bankin' business with credit cards 'n' all that. He might want y' to go get some health and life insurance too."

"I don't think I'd have any problem transferring my business to your bank," Nassar said. "Those people at my bank haven't been very nice to deal with recently."

"When I go in tomorrow mornin', I'll tell Rob you'll be in and give 'im a brief rundown of th' history," Velma said. "Anyways, don't want t' get y'r hopes up, but I think chances're good enough y' sh'd at least come see. Sh'd I go call Lucy and tell'er to come over t'morrow mornin', say 'bout 9 o'clock?"

"Yes, please call her," Nassar said. "I have so much on my mind it's hard to think about everything."

"We understand," Velma said. "Glad we c'n help."

While Velma made a phone call, Shane added, "We feel like you'd do it for us, too, if things were reversed."

CHAPTER 55

Thursday, March 6, 2008
Washington, DC, USA

After eating, Omar and Joe listlessly watched television, Joe mostly rehearsing what to tell Roger. Soon, a mature woman wearing a heavy winter coat with crumpled stylish winter clothes knocked and came in.

They immediately leaped to their feet, Omar saying, "You must be Mrs. Spencer. Please come in and sit down."

"Yes, I'm Marian Spencer," she replied. "You must be the two nice young gentlemen who allowed me to stay in your apartment. I wanted to go to the hotel just down at the corner, but Jason and Paco kept saying you'd insist I stay here. It's so wonderful of you to do all the things for my dear Bradley and Frank too. I just wish I could give you both a big hug, but people say that Muslims don't do that."

Omar said: I'm Omar, Omar Abu Deeb."

"I'm Joe," he said. "Yusef Shaito but called Joe. Can we get you something to eat or drink? Tea?"

Mrs. Spencer replied, "Oh thank you so much. A cup of that Tension Tamer tea would be so nice. You might've noticed I bought some herbal tea at that little grocery store close to here. When I've had a stressful day—I'm an elementary school teacher in case you don't know—the very best thing is to sit down, raise my legs, and relax with a cup of Tension Tamer. I hope you don't mind my buying things to put in your cabinets. I wanted to buy some food, but didn't know what to buy. I just ate a little breakfast here and had my other meals at the hospital. I think Jason and Paco might've eaten something here. Tomorrow I'll move to Bradley's place, now that there's a car for me to drive, so I can buy lots of things for you guys and replenish your supplies. Sometime soon, I'll make us all a nice meal out at Bradley's place."

Joe said, "That's very kind of you. I'll make the tea for you and have some myself. Do you want some, habibi?"

Omar said, "Yes, I'll have a cup. I'll come with you; you can't carry three cups easily." To Mrs. Spencer, "Would you like something in your tea?"

"Oh, nothing, thanks," she replied as Joe hurried to the kitchen. "Tension Tamer's good just the way it is. Besides, I don't need sugar and really don't drink much milk except for some cereal in the morning. That reminds me, you're low on milk here. I'll see about getting you some more."

"Oh, that's OK," Omar said. "One of us can go out if we really need some for tomorrow morning."

Joe found mugs and tea bags, saying, "Maybe I'll have Tension Tamer myself. What do you want?"

Omar put his hand on Joe's shoulder with a slight smile, then selected peppermint.

Returning, Omar asked, "How're Brad and Frank?"

"Oh, they're both stable," she answered. "They're trying to let them stabilize after the big move to that Navy hospital and the big scene Frank had with his father. Nurses and doctors talk to me some about Bradley, but're pretty closemouthed about Frank because they're supposed to talk only to next of kin. Paco manages to get some information out of the nurses because he's a nurse, and he even manipulated things somehow to let him stay overnight tonight. That's good for him and Frank too, of course. The poor guy, cast on his foot and can't walk very well, even with the crutches. A big guy like him must find it hard to get around. It's a long walk from the hospital to the metro station and in this cold weather, although it's not as cold as in Minneapolis.

"I'm glad I'll be able to drive the boys around tomorrow so they can take showers and change clothes. Paco's going to keep his things at Frank's house, but try to spend as much time as he can at the hospital. I'll be at Bradley's place, which is only about a half mile away from Frank's, they say, so I can take Paco back and forth. Hope they'll let me drive through the security gate and drop him off at the hospital door so he doesn't have to walk so far. Jason was going to move to Bradley's place and sleep on the couch, being as they wouldn't let him stay overnight at the hospital, but Frank said he could sleep in his spare bedroom, so he'll do that.

"Maybe next week they'll start some kind of treatment for both Bradley and Frank. They want Bradley to start eating, even if it's only soup through a straw. Frank could eat now if somehow he could manage to use a bedpan or get to the bathroom. My husband will be here tomorrow night, so we can take turns sitting with Bradley and running errands. I hear you have the keys to Frank's car, so I can drive it tomorrow and park it at Frank's place. I'll be driving Bradley's little car most of the time, but maybe Norman, that's my husband, can drive Frank's car over the weekend."

Omar and especially Joe were having difficulty focusing as he thought, *She said Frank had a big scene with his father. Don't want to follow through with her now, but he and I might have something in common. I should at least pretend to be listening to what she says.*

When Mrs. Spencer paused for a breath, Omar interrupted, "I can help you over the weekend, show you around. Tomorrow I'll be busy. Friday is the Islamic holy day, if you didn't know already. Maybe they told you I'm a part-time assistant imam at the Islamic Center here."

"Yes, they told me something like that," she replied. "They said you're also a professor at a big university here, George Washington,

I think they said. Frank and Bradley had a class with you, and that's how you met them. I know Bradley wants to go back to school and get a master's degree someday. I guess that's what he was doing with you in this class, starting his master's degree. He's always been fascinated by the Middle East and the Arab culture. You must be Arab; both of you look a little bit like Arabs. We're mostly blond and blue eyes in Minnesota, but in Minneapolis, there're people from all over. You even talk with a little bit of an accent. Where do you come from? You," she looked at Joe, "don't have any accent at all. You talk like a regular American."

Omar interjected, "I'm not a professor, just a visiting scholar. I do teach classes and research. Brad and Frank were in one of my extension classes at a community college. They were very good students."

"Bradley's the most wonderful student," Mrs. Spencer said. "Always top of his class in school. We were so worried when he wanted to go to Jordan to study and so relieved that he got a job working right here where we thought he'd be safe. We'd've never dreamed he'd be hurt in a bomb blast here because of his job."

Joe interrupted, "He wasn't targeted because of his job. He was just in the wrong place at the wrong time."

Mrs. Spencer asked, "What is it you do here? They said a lawyer for a big agency. You're so young to be in such an important position. You must've been a good student also. I'm sure your parents miss you too, like we miss our Bradley, but parents have to let go sometime. We're fortunate we can get away to come be with him when he needs us."

If only she knew, Joe thought, *but now's not the time*. He replied, "Yes, I was a good student. The Attorney General's office recruited me from Michigan Law School. I had better offers, but decided to take this one."

Omar jumped in. "I'm from Yemen. I've been in this country six years now. Allah willing, I'll get a green card and stay here. I studied

Islamic theology at the University of Minnesota. Brad and I were actually at the university at the same time, but didn't have a chance to meet. I'm glad we met here. He's a very nice person and good friend."

Mrs. Spencer said, "You said a minute ago that it was just a coincidence that Bradley was where that bomb went off. I know it was a gay bar and we're OK with that, but wasn't it a young Arab man setting off a terrorist bomb? I couldn't talk to Bradley about it, and it just didn't feel right asking the others, being they're hurt too."

Oh shit, Joe and Omar each thought. *She's a nice lady and she'll eventually find out; now's not the time for details.* Joe said, "He was American like me, even if his parents are Arab. He was distraught over being gay, and this was the best way he could deal with it. He even tried to make people go away from him so they wouldn't be killed."

"You'll find out soon enough," Omar interjected. "We just got back from his burial. I was asked to recite scriptures from the Holy Q'ran we use for Islamic burials. Joe helped. There's no hint of terrorism; just a decent immigrant family whose son couldn't handle his feelings."

Mrs. Spencer said, "Oh, that's so sad he was distraught over being gay. We realized last summer that Bradley's gay and Jason's his boyfriend. We had suspicions before, but didn't want to acknowledge them. We wish it weren't this way, because being gay can be so difficult; but he's still our baby, and we love him just as much as ever. From what we've learned, that's the way God made him; he didn't choose to be gay, so who're we to object? Of course, it would've been nice if he were to get married and have some children, but Jason is so nice maybe he can be our second son-in-law. Of course, we haven't had a chance to talk to them to see if they think about settling down together someday. And we do have grandchildren. Our daughter has three children who we adore, and we'll be content with them."

"We didn't know Brad had a sister," Joe interjected.

Mrs. Spencer began again. "Ellen's seven years older than Bradley. It's like we had two different families. That might've been best, because we could appreciate each of them individually in their own right, without too much competition for attention. They were not very close. Oh, they got along fine and still do and care for each other, and Bradley adores his nieces and nephew, but they didn't live in the same house all that many years. Ellen went away to university and then got married and they moved away and settled down in New Mexico. Her husband's a rocket scientist, truthfully. They live in Alamogordo, where the rocket research work goes on. We don't know too much about it because it's all hush-hush.

"We go down there to visit them. It's a whole lot easier for us to go down there than for them to pack up three kids and come to Minnesota. It's a nice, interesting place, too, once you get used to the desert. That's where the White Sands are, those fascinating huge sand dunes of pure white sand. There're some pretty places up in the mountains too. They have a really lovely house built in Southwestern design out of adobe. Looks just like in the picture books. It's up a little ways on the mountainside overlooking the town by the space museum. Really beautiful at sunset. Bradley really liked it there too when he visited before he moved to Maryland. He said it reminded him of Jordan. Here, I have some pictures. Do either of you have siblings?"

Whew, both Joe and Omar thought.

I'd better jump in, Joe thought. *This's painful for Omar.* "I have an older sister. She's only four years older, but likewise we're not close. She married young, before I went to university. They have their own family and are close to my parents, but I haven't been around them much."

Joe paused. Then Omar explained briefly his family's being killed and continued, "It was really hard on me, but I've managed to get through it. It gave me the freedom to come to this country, start a new life, and follow my dream to study Islamic theology and become an imam."

"Oh, you poor thing," Marian Spencer began. "I wish we'd known you in Minneapolis so we could've made you one of our family. You're such a nice young man, about the same age as Bradley, and he seems to like you a lot, although he can't say so directly now with his injuries."

"Thank you for your concern, ma'am," Omar said interrupting. "I appreciate that." *I'm probably thankful,* Omar thought. *They seem like a wonderful family and I do like Brad a lot, but not sure if I'd've liked this smothering attention. Guess I got to be too independent and self-sufficient.*

Before Mrs. Spencer could begin again, they were startled by the entry door buzzer.

CHAPTER 56

When Jason entered, Omar and Joe each gave him three kisses and motioned him to sit between them on the couch.

Mrs. Spencer thought, *They're kissing him on the cheek, but don't let women hug them. Surely they're not all involved. They went to great lengths to explain that Omar and Joe aren't gay, just roommates.*

Joe said, "We're having tea. Can we get you some? We're ready for refills."

Mrs. Spencer immediately stood and said, "Let me get it for you. You've been so kind to me, the least I can do is make you tea. What would each of you like?"

Jason replied, "Thanks ma'am. I was never a tea drinker until I met Brad. What kind of tea do you have?"

"Oh, I just finished having some Tension Tamer," Mrs. Spencer answered. "I don't know what the other two had. I know I bought some mint and chamomile too. I think I'll have chamomile now; it's good for bedtime; makes me sleep better. I think I am going to be ready to go to bed soon, if that's OK with the rest of you."

"Tension Tamer; what's that?" Jason asked.

"Oh, just a mixture of herbs that helps take the edge off, like how I was when I got here," Mrs. Spencer replied. "When I've had a stressful day at school, I just come home and put my feet up with a good cup of Tension Tamer. You should try it."

"OK, I'll take that," Jason said.

Joe thought, *She said camel meal, or whatever helps her sleep. Maybe I'll have that. Maybe Omar'll take the cue and help her in the kitchen. Damn, I hate to feel this way, but I'm not in the mood to be sociable and especially smothered with attention. Allah, forgive me.* He said, "Maybe I'll have some of that camel meal."

Omar said, "I'll help you. You can't carry four cups. I'll get mine and Joe's."

When they were alone, Jason said, "Man, you don't look chipper; don't sound chipper either. You OK?"

Joe, in a low voice, replied, "I just had a very upsetting phone call with my father. I can tell you more later in private. I don't want to go into it now, especially with her here. She's a nice lady, but I don't know how long I could control myself if she smothers me with attention."

"I know what you're talking about," Jason said putting his hand on Joe's shoulder, "It's great for Brad, but she's so nervous, she's... well, you know."

Omar came in with his and Joe's mugs; Mrs. Spencer with hers and Jason's, saying, "Here you go, dear. How was Bradley when you left? And Frank too?"

"They were both asleep," Jason answered.

"Oh, good," Mrs. Spencer answered. "Things at that hospital seem good. They seem to do a good job of taking care of them. Really professional. Of course that other hospital was good too. Too bad about the lack of security there. So far no military person has been back to see them; they must want them to be stabilized first."

Omar said to Jason, "It seems we're ready for bed. Joe and I'll sleep in my bed, but that leaves you with the couch for tonight, if that's OK."

He said, "Sure; I'm just glad to have a place to crash."

"Oh, what time'll you boys want to get up in the morning?" Mrs. Spencer asked. "I'd love to make breakfast for you if there's something in the kitchen, but I don't want to be too early."

379

"I need to go to my office in the morning," Joe said, "but I don't have to be there at a specific time. I might just sleep 'til I wake up, but I don't normally sleep late."

"I probably need to get up fairly early, maybe 7:30 at the latest," Omar said. "Fridays are a busy day at the center, but not much in the morning."

"They don't really want us to come to the hospital until about 10," Mrs. Spencer said. "Maybe I need to get up early so I can get ready, get my things packed, get breakfast for you boys, and then go get Frank's car, wherever it is, and be on my way. I suppose you'll be going with me, Jason."

"Yes, ma'am," Jason answered. "I need to take both mine and Paco's things."

Omar said, "You don't need to fix breakfast for us. We can just each figure out what we have and eat it. Don't misunderstand; we do appreciate your offer, but this time let's just play it by ear."

Joe said, "I'll show you where Frank's car is parked. You should be able to find your way out there easily. Just straight down Connecticut and then cutting over to Wisconsin. I can show Jason on a map and he can guide you. If you need help in the afternoon, I'll gladly go with you to Maryland and help you get settled. It won't take me long tomorrow morning in my office."

"Oh, don't you go worrying about me," Mrs. Spencer said. "I can find my way around, I'm sure. After all, I get around Minneapolis and St. Paul just fine. Washington's laid out a bit more complicated, but I can manage. You just go on about your business. You've been so wonderful to Bradley and these boys. We just don't want to impose on you any more. I'm sure we'll be seeing you. You'll be coming to the hospital to visit, I'm sure. Let's see what happens next week. Now if it's OK, I'm ready for bed."

"OK," Omar said. "You can use the bathroom first."

When Mrs. Spencer was in the bathroom, Omar asked, "How are you, habibi? We haven't had a chance to ask."

"Better," Jason replied. "I don't have as many aches and pains. I won't know about my arm until I go back to a doctor; I have to see a doctor my insurance'll pay for. Maybe once I'm settled in Frank's place, it'll be easier to get around, not that we don't appreciate your hospitality. If I can convince Mrs. Spencer to leave Brad's bedside, maybe she can take me next week. I don't know how long Brad's father will be here, but he probably has to go back on Monday."

"I might be able to take you," Omar offered, "depending on how things are at the university."

"I can ask for another day off," Joe said. "Maybe I could take you, if Omar doesn't need to use his car."

"You two've done more than enough," Jason said. "Let's just see. I'm too exhausted to think right now."

"Me too," Omar said. "I'll get some blankets for you."

During the next several minutes, Mrs. Spencer finished in the bathroom; the three men took turns in the bathroom, undressing to their underwear and then going to bed.

When the light was off, Joe put his hand on Omar's shoulder, saying, "Thanks for being supportive. I can't imagine what it'd be like without you here."

He began sobbing again while Omar put his arms around him. They moved into a close embrace.

After some moments, Omar felt himself stirring, startled, as he thought, *Why'm I getting hard? I'd better move quick, so Joe doesn't notice it.*

At the same time, Joe realized he was becoming erect and in near panic thought, *What the hell! I'm hard. I can't let Omar feel this!*

Almost simultaneously, both flipped over to avoid contact, moved apart, and went to sleep.

CHAPTER 57

Friday, March 7, 2008
Arlington, Virginia, USA

While dressing in the morning for her job at a convenience store, Hanan Salameh was startled by a phone call.

After a short terse greeting in Arabic, followed by a brief pause as she listened, she said in Arabic, "What do you mean, I have to make him stay quiet? He's grown, almost 21, and doesn't take orders from me."

(pause)

"This's typical of you," she said in Arabic. "You're so absorbed in yourself, you don't understand he did it for you."

(pause)

"Yes, for you!" she said in Arabic, "so you'd notice him, pay attention to him, be proud of him. Not ignore him like you have since he was born."

(pause)

"Don't think I wasn't aware of what you were up to," she said in Arabic. "You never cared for me. A marriage that would allow you to stay in this country. As soon as you knew it was a boy so you could be called 'Abou Wissam,' you moved out and left me to take care of him."

(pause)

"You took care how?" she asked in Arabic. "You sent money, but what about other problems? Like when he got in trouble in high school because they were teasing him."

(pause)

She continued in Arabic, "That caused the problem. Instead of dealing with him, you got rid of him by getting him into that Saudi Arabian high school. No one wants to hire someone who went to that school. That's where he met other boys who got him involved with that imam."

(pause)

She screamed in Arabic, "All you care about is that he doesn't lead someone to you. He could go to prison for life or be executed, and you wouldn't care."

(pause)

"Why'd you send your lawyer to him to tell him to plead guilty and not say anything?" she asked in Arabic.

(pause)

"It sounds like you're threatening him, based on what the lawyer told him," she continued in Arabic. "What can you threaten him with? He expects the maximum sentence."

(pause)

"What?" she screamed in disbelief in Arabic. "Something will happen to me, if he doesn't cooperate?"

(pause)

"Yes, I know you're paying for this house," she replied in Arabic. "But that doesn't mean you can kick me out. I'm your wife, remember. Wives have rights in this country."

(pause)

"Divorce me," she said emphatically in Arabic. "That's what I've wanted to do for years, but you refuse."

(pause)

"You harm me in any way, and I'm going straight to the authorities!" she said.

She jumped, startled, hearing the phone crash down on the other end as she thought angrily in Arabic, *He hasn't done that since before Wissam was born, thanks be to Allah. He said it in English too. He thinks I'll take his threats seriously. He has another think coming. Women in this country have rights, even Arab women.*

CHAPTER 58

Roger Chen said to Joe, "Please come in. Surprised to see you dressed up today."

"I thought I'd blend in," Joe replied, shaking hands.

"Please sit," Roger Chen said. "How was your trip?"

Joe answered, "Good, considering. A burial isn't pleasant, but Omar did a great job."

"Good," Roger Chen said.

"It's not all good," Joe continued. "That's one thing I came to talk about. The same night their son was killed, there was a bomb attack on their home that has all the indicators of a hate crime." He explained details concluding, "I know I'm not objective, but I can't just sit and let this go unreported when Arabs are targeted."

Roger Chen said. "It sure seems like a hate crime, and I'd sure not sit quietly if it were against Chinese-Americans. You're not objective and not in a position to follow through. I can make a phone call. You said other things."

Joe replied, "I've told you about pressure on me to marry someone. It's come to a head, and now there's money involved." He related the conversation with his father.

"Oh," Roger Chen said. "That's heavy stuff."

"What bothers me the most," Joe responded, "is the moral issues of wanting me to get married, have a baby, and get divorced.

That goes against Islam. I'm also incensed at the legal issues of money paid."

"There can be legal issues about a preplanned divorce and the ability of the person to stay in the country," Roger Chen began. "A child complicates the issue too. So far this is hypothetical because nothing has happened, but you're right to bring it to our attention. This could fall under the law on human trafficking as well as others."

"That imam is the one that I want to do something about," Joe added, "perverting Islam like that and in addition breaking the law. Maybe I'm out for revenge for what it did to my relationship with my father. I suppose my father might be guilty too, if he actually takes money, but I won't give evidence against my father."

"That's understandable," Roger Chen said. "I'll make some calls. Can you give me the name of the imam?"

"Wael al Askari," Joe answered.

Roger Chen handed him a pad and a pen saying, "Please write it down so we can have the spelling right".

"That's a problem," Joe said as he wrote. "When names are transliterated from Arabic into English, the spelling can vary, and I'm not sure how his name is spelled in English; I'll give my best guess."

"Same with Chinese names, too," Roger Chen said. "We need to keep you out of this. I'll not report back to you to keep you legally ignorant, so to speak."

"I understand," Joe said. "Thanks again. Sorry to be presenting you with all of these issues."

"No problem," Roger Chen answered. "That's what we're here for."

Joe stood, shook hands, and said, "See you Monday."

When Joe left, Roger Chen asked his administrative assistant to call Roosevelt "Rosie" Jordan. After exchanging pleasantries, Roger Chen said, "I've got a couple of things for you. I could probably find someone across the street at your headquarters, but I've always worked with you."

(pause)

"It's Joe, again," Roger Chen began. "I called you with something he reported a couple of weeks ago." He recounted what Joe had told him.

(pause)

Roger Chen added, "I told Joe we'd keep him out of the one in Michigan and not report back. For that matter, you don't need to report back to me."

(pause)

"Always good to talk to you Rosie," Roger Chen concluded. "Wish it were on more pleasant topics."

As Joe walked out of the building, he wondered, *What should I do now? There's laundry to do, but I'm in no mood to do housework and laundry now. Maybe go to the hospital and see if they need my help. Scout the place out and take Omar with me later, or tell him how to get there.*

Strange, Omar seemed distant this morning. Maybe he did feel me getting hard. No telling what he thinks about me.

There're Friday prayers today. I usually go with Omar after work. I can just go early today. Can't call Omar because he might be busy doing something at the center. I can send a text. First, I should call the guys at the hospital.

Late in the afternoon, as Omar rode the Metro, he thought, *Seems weird coming home by myself after prayers. Since November, it's been Joe and me together and then getting something to eat. Joe seemed distant at home this morning, and he sent texts he was going to prayers early and then to the hospital. Maybe he did feel me get hard last night. Now what does he think about me?*

CHAPTER 59

Saturday, March 8, 2008
Tehran, Iran

The afternoon of the first day back to work after the Islamic weekend, the junior official in the operations section of the highly sensitive military airport brought cups of coffee for his boss and himself, an afternoon ritual, and said in Persian, "You remember that young guy we found here a few days ago? I heard what happened to him. They tried to break him down, but he wouldn't say any more than he said here, so it must've been the Venezuelan bastards dumped him."

"Typical," the senior official said in Persian.

"They decided to put him in with one of the groups of Iraqis we're training to attack the new Iraqi army and the Americans," the junior official continued in Persian. "At least he can speak their language."

"Suicide squads," the senior officer said in Persian.

"Yes, them," the junior officer confirmed in Persian. "Except, of course, they don't know they're suicide squads."

The senior officer continued in Persian, "Make them think we're supporting al Sadr when in fact we're setting them up for defeat so we can move in and take over with our own loyalists among the Shia in Iraq. Al Sadr's a loose cannon; he'd never buckle under our control. In the meantime, we harass the so-called Iraqi army and the Americans to keep the place unstable for us to move in."

"Exactly," the junior officer agreed in Persian. "Gets this guy out of our hair too. Let him get killed or captured by American or Iraqi forces."

"He must be pretty damned naïve to let the Venezuelans trick him into being brought here," the senior official concurred in Persian. "It's pretty sure he's American. Aren't they worried he'll sabotage things to help the Americans?"

"Seems not," the junior official replied in Persian. "He's adamant he's Palestinian; says he hates Americans."

Smirking, the senior official said in Persian, "This group we're training must really like that he's Palestinian, one of the Sunni scum."

"I hear he's not fitting in very well," the junior official added in Persian. "They might even push him out in front and hasten his demise."

The senior official chuckled. Having finished the coffee, both returned to the pretense of working.

BOOK 3

RETRIBUTIONS

CHAPTER 1

Tuesday, March 11, 2008
Fort Meade, Maryland, USA

Colonel Granger was driving with U.S. Air Force Colonel Lane Harrison, Deputy Chief of U.S. Air Force Personnel, to the National Security Agency, saying, "Damn, why'd he force our hand by going to Marine Corps personnel now?"

"We weren't prepared to take action today," Colonel Harrison concurred, "and I've got too much other work."

"Same here," Colonel Granger added. "Had to come yesterday to inform the director, set up this meeting, and contact the FBI. Hope they managed a lawyer."

Colonel Harrison said, "It's our gut reaction he's not involved with terrorists; just an arrogant ass who likes to throw his weight around; but in situations like this, we can't rely on gut reactions."

"For sure," Colonel Granger replied.

In the office of the NSA director, Admiral Lance Ricketts, U.S. Navy Retired, Sidney Balucci of NSA's legal staff, and Amy Grafton of the Baltimore field office of the FBI were introduced; Colonel Ross was called in.

Admiral Ricketts, standing, pointedly did not invite Colonel Ross to sit in the vacant chair in front of his desk, saying, "You know Colonel Granger, and perhaps you know Colonel Harrison of Air Force personnel. You also know Sid Balucci. You'll be introduced to the lady shortly."

Colonel Ross said, "Er, yes."

Colonel Granger began, "You precipitated this meeting by contacting Marine Corps personnel to demand Major Frank Reynolds be discharged from the service or at least relieved from duties here at the NSA."

Colonel Ross replied, "He was injured in the gay bar bombing and unfit for duty. I didn't want him here in the first place, you remember. What concern is it to the DIA?"

Colonel Granger answered, "First, you exceeded your authority and Marine Corps personnel reported it to us because we're involved in Major Reynolds's assignment here. Exceeding your authority is not of concern to the DIA. What is of concern is that Major Reynolds was injured in the line of duty; your attempt to influence his assignment interferes with an investigation involving national security being conducted by our agency."

Colonel Ross blurted out, "Line of duty? What duty?"

"You should know what duty," Colonel Granger said. "You were present when it was assigned."

Colonel Ross replied testily, "Oh, that? You know as well as I do that was just a cover to tell Major Reynolds he wasn't going to be discharged for being homosexual because you didn't have the courage to discharge him; afraid it would expose a big security blunder on your part."

Colonel Granger stated forcefully, "You're making assumptions and throwing out accusations. Major Reynolds was indeed injured in the line of duty, and you are interfering with a sensitive national security investigation!"

"Ha!" Colonel Ross spat out. "What line of duty and sensitive national security investigation could there be in the gay bar bombing?"

Colonel Granger said forcefully, "You do not have a need to know, nor do the others in this room! Now, let's get to the point why we're having this meeting."

Admiral Ricketts stated, "Exceeding your authority is very much of interest to me and the NSA, because you did not inform me, much less consult with me. Larger issues are at stake, and I am not going to pursue that insult now." He handed a sheet of paper to Colonel Ross, saying, "Did you write and sign this? This is a copy; the DIA has the original."

"Uh, where'd you get this?" Colonel Ross asked stammering. "And why's it at the DIA?"

Colonel Granger stated, "It came to us by legitimate means, and you were informed it would be. The question is whether you acknowledge you wrote and signed this letter. We can, of course, perform handwriting and ink analyses and use other means to establish that you wrote it."

Colonel Ross said, "Yes, I wrote it. Those security guards were harassing honest people coming to work, making them wait out in the cold, just to get in and do their job. They were complaining to me, and rightfully so."

Admiral Rickets stated forcefully, "Again, you exceeded your authority. Fortunately, Major Reynolds, against whom you seem to have a vendetta, was astute enough to ignore your inappropriate order, continue the increased security that was clearly justified, and prevented the attempted terrorist attack on this facility that you are very well aware of because you were called in and informed on Saturday, just like I was."

"OK," Colonel Ross said defiantly. "So what? Maybe I was a little, shall we say, overeager in wanting to take care of the people who stood out in the cold. It all worked out OK. What's the big deal; you're raking me over the coals for something trivial like this?"

Admiral Ricketts, now angry, forcefully stated, "Sid Balucci is here to give you legal counsel if you want it, until you can obtain your own attorney. You will surely want to have your own attorney, and we are not going to say much until you've obtained your own counsel. Treason is among the most, if not the most serious crime that can be committed in this country, far from some trivial incident. Because of the seriousness of the potential charge, we're giving you the opportunity to consult with Sid before you say anything."

Colonel Ross, in disbelief, replied, "You've got to be kidding. Is this some kind of a joke, Lance? Treason is nothing to joke about."

Admiral Ricketts stated forcefully, "It is far from a joke that you issued an inappropriate order that, if followed, could have allowed enemies of this country to enter this facility to set off explosives. The order was issued only two days before the attempted act. It should not come as a surprise to you that an investigation is underway to discover the extent of your complicity with the group behind this potentially heinous terrorist act."

Colonel Ross suddenly became pale, shaken, and faint, stumbling to reach for the empty chair, saying, "Can I sit down? I can't believe you'd do this to me."

"Yes, sit down," Admiral Ricketts said. "Effective immediately you are relieved from duties here at the NSA. Agent Grafton from the FBI will accompany you to your office and observe you while you remove any personal items, which will be scrutinized thoroughly. We require you to leave your cell phone and personal laptop computer, if you brought the computer to the office."

Colonel Granger said, "We can, of course, obtain court orders to require you to surrender the cell phone, laptop, and other personal items and require you to remain in custody until we obtain the orders. The same is true for any items related to the NSA that you have at home. Agent Grafton will accompany you to your home to take possession of such items for this investigation. Mr. Balucci can advise you of your legal rights and potential consequences if you do not cooperate voluntarily and require us to get court orders. If you want to have your own attorney present, you can remain in our custody until he or she arrives."

Colonel Ross stammered, "What the hell?" Turning to Sid Balucci, he asked, "What's going on?"

"Do as they say," Sidney Balucci answered, "but don't say another word until you can talk to your own attorney. I cannot represent you beyond giving immediate advice. When in doubt, always remain quiet until you have your own legal counsel. Complying with reasonable requests is in your best interests. Forcing them to get court orders is not."

Colonel Granger began again, "We don't feel it's necessary to arrest you and keep you in custody for the time being. We are asking you to voluntarily surrender your passport to Agent Grafton."

Sidney Balucci nodded.

Colonel Harrison said, "You will be placed on administrative leave beginning immediately. For the time being, you will receive full pay and benefits. It should be apparent your career's over. Even if you're cleared of criminal charges, your actions are sufficient to justify your immediate termination from active military service."

Colonel Ross said, "I'm close to retirement."

Colonel Harrison stated, "You should consult your own lawyer on this issue. For actions as egregious as yours, even if there is no criminal activity, retirement is often not an option. I'm not prepared to discuss the issue further."

Admiral Ricketts stood to terminate the meeting, first turning to Colonel Granger and Colonel Harrison and asking, "Do either of you have anything else?"

When they said no, Admiral Ricketts spoke to Colonel Ross. "You can stay here to consult with Sid Balucci a few moments. Agent Grafton and I will step outside. Then agent Grafton will accompany you to your office to prepare for your immediate departure."

Once outside the office with the door closed, Colonels Granger and Harrison shook hands with Agent Grafton and Admiral Ricketts and returned to the Pentagon.

CHAPTER 2

Wednesday, March 12, 2008
Washington, DC, USA

Colonel Granger opened a 2 p.m. meeting in a secure conference room in the operations center of the DIA located at Bolling Air Force Base, saying, "Welcome. We're meeting in our facility here because it's less visible than FBI headquarters downtown and not as far to drive for our colleague from Baltimore. Let's begin with introductions. We all know Rosie Jordan, Chief of Operations of the FBI Operations Technology Center at Quantico."

Roosevelt "Rosie" Jordan was a tall, large-framed African-American man in his mid-fifties. His bright, friendly brown eyes belied his no-nonsense approach. He wore the FBI "uniform," a gray pin-stripe suit, the jacket of which hung over his chair back.

"Next is Reid Sandoval of the Baltimore FBI Field Office." Colonel Granger indicated a man in his mid-forties with thinning medium brown hair, light brown eyes with frameless glasses, and medium frame and height. He too wore the FBI "uniform," a solid gray suit.

"Cranford Brooks is with the Washington FBI field office," Colonel Granger continued. "Some of you know Rhonda Philips, political and foreign policy specialist of the DIA, who I asked to be here to assess sensitive issues."

Rhonda Philips, a petite woman in her mid-fifties, had short, professionally styled brown hair falling just below her ears and showing increasing amounts of gray. Faux tortoise-shell plastic-rimmed half-glasses hung on a strap around her neck and would cover her blue-gray eyes when she took notes and read. She wore a long-sleeved red suit jacket with matching skirt and a white blouse. Block-heel white shoes gave her height and matched her ample white leather bag. Her ruby jewelry was tasteful and expensive.

Colonel Granger then said, "Rosie, this's an FBI operation supported by us. Please take over, if you like."

"While you're standing, please give an overview," Rosie Jordan said.

Colonel Granger began with Frank's visit to him on February 29 and explained details including the very recent confrontation with Colonel Ross. He mentioned briefly his, Rhonda Philips's, and Rosie Jordan's previous involvement with Frank, offering to explain details if they became relevant.

Rosie Jordan turned to Reid Sandoval, who explained his office's private discussions with Brad and official meetings with Frank and Sergeant Beasley and continued, "We were involved again when Wissam Salameh was arrested and charged. We've attempted to interrogate him, but he refuses to say anything. We've allowed visits from his mother. His father has not visited but sent an attorney who's obviously Arab or Arab-American. We kept Wissam Salameh as long as we could without arraignment while we and the Washington office investigated.

"The attorney sent by the father was present at the arraignment as defense attorney, as was a U.S. attorney prosecutor. When the suspect pleaded guilty, the judge became suspicious and asked him if his attorney had explained the severity of the crime, that he could receive the death penalty or life imprisonment if found guilty. The attorney looked at the suspect sternly and almost imperceptibly nodded his head to signal he should say yes. The suspect was frightened, that's putting it mildly. The judge stated, 'He hasn't explained that to you, has he?' The suspect stammered 'No.' The judge gave the attorney a stern lecture and entered a plea of 'not guilty' on the suspect's behalf.

"The attorney left angrily, apparently saying something in Arabic. We suspect he threatened something. It must involve someone else, because there's little he can threaten the suspect with. He's from Arlington, and the Washington field office is investigating.

"Our last involvement was yesterday, when Colonel Ross was arrested and our agent accompanied him while he took personal things from his office and turned over his cell phone and laptop computer. She also took his passport. We're searching his office, getting warrants to search his house and examine his bank accounts. The agent who accompanied him to his house said he was scared, er, scared to death; that he's either an extremely good actor or, as Colonel Granger said, not guilty of treason but an arrogant ass."

Rosie Jordan replied, "Thanks, Reid. As we discussed, it's best to turn everything over to the Washington field office and coordinate from our operations center. Now let's have Cranford report."

Cranford Brooks described all the issues he and the Washington field office had been involved with and continued, "Reid mentioned Wissam Salameh. He grew up in Arlington, raised by his mother. It's suspicious someone would commute from Arlington to Fort Meade for a low paying job as a cleaner. It's unlikely his mother could pay for his transportation, because she's a clerk in a convenience store. That leaves his father, who may have paid, but let's save that for a moment.

"His mother is a Palestinian immigrant who's had a green card since childhood. She's estranged, but not divorced from her husband, Saeed Salameh, apparently a long time. She was cautious talking to us, as though she were afraid of something. We sensed it might help if she were interrogated by a female agent, ideally an Arab-American woman. You're working on that, Rosie.

"The father, Saeed Salameh, heads a charity to support Palestinians in Gaza. The bureau suspects the charity's a front to funnel money to Hamas, but we haven't been able to prove that. We haven't aggressively pursued the issue because we have higher priority activities. There're many legitimate charitable needs in Gaza, and it would cause public relations problems if we're viewed as harassing them. There're cases in Texas and Florida right now in which so-called charities support Hamas more overtly than we can detect at Saeed Salameh's organization. An attempt by his son to set off a bomb in the NSA isn't consistent with fund raising for Hamas under the guise of charity. We're wondering whether the father is involved.

"Wissam attended public schools in Arlington most of his life. Sometime in high school, he transferred to a private high school in Fairfax financed by Saudi Arabia. We've been suspicious of this high school, but so far we've not discovered anything amiss with the school itself, even though we've charged specific students with terrorism shortly after graduation. The majority of the parents are indignant at the thought the school would support terrorism and insist they themselves are strongly opposed to terrorist activities and would protest if they suspected it. Again, we have a sensitive foreign relations issue.

"Another angle we're investigating is an imam in Arlington who meets with young Muslim men in the area and with whom Marwan Hammoud and his brother were involved. I'm getting ahead of myself. Marwan Hammoud has an older brother, Ahmed, who has completely disappeared, along with a car owned by the father, Nassar Hammoud. At Mr. Abu Deeb's urging, the father reported his son's disappearance and missing car to the Arlington police and notified us.

"In yet another twist that seems not to have a direct bearing on the case, Mr. Shaito and Mr. Abu Deeb were in the hospital with their friends right after the gay bar bombing and gave last rites for Marwan Hammoud." He described Omar's rapport with the Hammoud family and their recent trip to Southwest Virginia for Marwan's burial.

"So far as the public know, the gay bar bombing's a single event, and we want it to remain that way. Even in law enforcement circles, not many know there's irrefutable indication the two bombings, one actual and one attempted, are related and the common thread is an imam in Arlington.

"The mosque in Arlington seems to be a Saudi-supported mosque. Saudi Arabia directly or indirectly supports several mosques in this country. We could conceivably get someone undercover to find out more about this imam like we did recently in New Jersey, you may have read, but that has to go through you, Rosie, and it's apparently hard as hell to find willing and reliable young undercover agents who can pose as good Muslims. More practically, with the death of Marwan Hammoud, the disappearance of his brother, and the arrest of Wissam Salameh, any imam involved would be lying very low or have fled, so an undercover agent couldn't discover much.

"That's all I can report now. I'll answer any questions."

"Thanks, Cranford," Rosie said. "You've done a commendable job. Any questions or comments? Rhonda, you've been taking notes furiously."

She began, "Let's get homosexuality out of the way so it doesn't distract us. Society's attitude towards homosexuality has changed considerably, despite loud rhetoric from a few. No matter who wins the presidential election, there'll be a change in policy towards gays in the armed forces. The response to the gay bar bombing was horror and compassion, not anti-gay, despite that so-called church in Kansas. We could discuss this more, but politically homosexuality will not be a significant issue.

"There's something worrisome about Wissam Salameh's father. If he's involved with Hamas, then something's seriously inconsistent or really frightening. Hamas are viewed as terrorists by our government, but so far terrorist activities have been aimed towards Israel. Terrorist activities within the U.S., and especially an attack against a U.S. government target, would set back any cause that Hamas might aspire to and is unthinkable. A Hamas attack on a gay bar makes no sense whatever. Hamas, like most Islamists, do not accept homosexuality, but they're pragmatists with one goal in mind, not religious zealots.

"If the son is estranged from his father like his mother is, the son may have acted independently or on behalf of some other group. If so, that could explain why his father's attorney pushed him to plead guilty to deflect attention away from his father's support of Hamas. You've likely figured out it's a threat against his mother they're trying to hold over him. That's not my remit, but more a woman's instinct.

"There's an inconsistency with his son going to the Saudi Arabian school and being involved with an imam at the Saudi Arabian–supported mosque. The Saudi Arabian government does not support Hamas. The Saudi Arabian government does support this high school, much like the U.S. government supports American schools in many cities in the world, directly or indirectly. It exists primarily for children of Saudi Arabian and other Arab diplomats who're in the Washington area. The FBI can speak more to this. If the son is also involved with Hamas, which I doubt, then it's not consistent for him to be involved with an imam at a Saudi Arabian mosque.

"We're raising more questions than we're answering, but we need to ask the right questions before we can make progress. It might help to have the CIA in on this."

"Thanks, Rhonda," Rosie Jordan said. "We haven't consulted the CIA yet. I can contact them to see if they want to be involved or at least give input. We're aware of that Saudi Arabian school. We don't see it as a threat, but can't be sure.

"Like Rhonda said, we've raised more questions than answered, but we seem to be on the right track. We should meet again, say, a week from today."

CHAPTER 3

Friday, March 14, 2008
Bethesda, Maryland, USA

Frank and Brad lay listlessly when the phone rang; Frank almost screamed, "Patrick! How'd you find me here?"

(pause)

"In the hospital about two weeks," he answered, "not all at Bethesda. Glad you were persistent and found me."

(pause)

"Sure! It'd be great to see you," he exclaimed. "We're in a secure wing. Don't know if we can get you a clearance for today, but they're making me sit and go places in a wheelchair. I'll get them to wheel me out to where we can visit."

(pause)

"They don't want certain persons to contact me," Frank said. "I'll tell you more when you're here."

(pause)

"That's what I thought," Frank said, "with Felicia and Pete. How are they by the way? Tell me when you get here."

(pause)

Frank said goodbye, smiled, then said to Brad, "Guess what? Patrick's here. Don't try to talk. Thought I'd lose contact with him after his wedding."

After lunch and naps, an orderly pushed Frank in a wheelchair to a public area where Patrick used both hands to grasp one of Frank's and said, "Hey, Bud, great to see you. I can take the wheelchair now."

Frank replied, "You don't know how much it means to me for you to visit. You're the first visitor, other than Paco and some official ones."

Patrick smiled and replied, "You're the one who said in the military great friends become great memories; I'm determined not to let that happen. I'm here on business, but for sure I was going to see you and Felicia, and family, of course. I'll make a quick trip to Alabama on Monday and let my mother spoil me for St. Patrick's Day. How are you? I see you're pretty bunged up."

Frank chuckled, said, "I'll live," and described briefly his injuries and expectations of full recovery.

"Good to hear," Patrick replied. "How much longer you in the hospital for?"

"They'd like me to go to a nursing facility soon," Frank answered. "As soon as I can get around on crutches, they want me out of a hospital bed. They'd consider sending me home, if I had someone home to take care of me."

"That doesn't sound so bad, considering," Patrick said.

"Yeah," Frank agreed. "Paco's injured too, but not as bad. He gets around on crutches and can do light duty. He missed classes and is frantically trying to catch up. He'd like to stay at home and take care of me, but at the same time he has his job and school. He's not going to quit school; I wouldn't let him, anyway. I'll just let the Navy figure out what to do with me next. There're security issues too."

"You mentioned security issues and you're on a secure wing," Patrick said. "You said it's classified."

"I can tell some things," Frank replied, "but enough about me for now. What's going on with you?"

His eyes lit up as he exclaimed, "We're expecting!"

Frank said, "Great! You seem really happy. None of my friends has had a baby before. When?"

"Patrick answered, "End of summer and really happy! Always wanted a family. Elsie's happy too.""

"Will the little Patrick or Elsie be born in Brussels?"

"That's the plan," Patrick answered. "Elsie's mom wants her to return to Columbus, of course. It's like I'm irrelevant, just like Elsie's dad was irrelevant when she was born. So far, she hasn't suggested she'll come be with us when the baby's born, but I suspect that's coming. My mom's dropped hints about how it was good her mother was there when Anna Marie and I were born. Doctors and hospitals in Brussels are just fine and—who knows?—he or she might want to be a Belgian citizen someday."

"And let Uncle Sam pay too," Frank added, smiling.

"Yes, that's true," Patrick said. "You're bringing up things we've had to start thinking about seriously. We have to make some career decisions. With a child to support, it's tempting to make a career of the Army and let the Army pay the medical bills, but somehow it doesn't feel right to be a 'lifer' and move at the Army's beck and call. Elsie doesn't want to be an Army wife either. For now, she can keep her job and take maternity leave. She doesn't want to be a total stay-at-home mom, but any career she'd want isn't compatible with my being in the Army.

"We don't know where we want to settle down, and that affects what kind of job each of us might get. After Elsie's travelled all over the world, literally, and I've been a fair number of places, we sure don't want to settle down in stereotypical Middle America where life revolves around the PTA and kids' soccer. Nothing wrong with that, and we'll do plenty of it, but not as the mainstay of our life."

"Settle down; what's that mean?" Frank asked sarcastically. "I've never done anything that resembles settling down. My parents've been trying to settle down since they retired and moved to Florida; it's not been happy for them, but they wouldn't be happy anywhere doing anything."

"Oh, Bud, sorry to hear," Patrick said. "You've talked about your parents some, but not as bitter-sounding as this."

"My father's one reason I'm in a secure wing," Frank stated. He then described his father's visits and a phone call.

"That's terrible," Patrick exclaimed.

Frank replied, "Actually, it's a relief. Now I'm out from under him and can break all the subconscious control I allowed him to have over me. As soon as I can get to a Marine Corps personnel office, I'm changing my next of kin and home of record. Don't know who I'll pick. They'd take a dim view of Paco as next of kin. I'm pretty sure I'm going to need a lawyer anyway, so maybe I'll ask him or her."

"Need a lawyer?" Patrick asked, "You suing the bar?"

"No, nothing like that," Frank answered. "The bar didn't do anything wrong. There may be a move to force me out of the service, maybe forced medical retirement."

"You said in the line of duty," Patrick replied.

"Exactly," Frank confirmed. "I can tell you most of it," and explained the ostensible second assignment he had with the DIA. He concluded, "Sounds like a dorky stupid assignment, which it is, but I didn't have much choice. They're right, though. Terrorists could be using gay bars for drops and meetings, thinking they'd not be suspected there."

Patrick asked, "If they assigned you to this, why'd they want you out of the service?"

"It was the DIA who wanted me to do this," Frank explained. "Not all in the Marine Corps were in agreement."

"I see," Patrick said. "You mentioned Paco's going to school. How're things with him?"

Frank smiled, "He's doing well, considering. He's been with me almost constantly in the hospital and brought his books. This week, he moved back to Baltimore. He can go back to work on light duty, but he really wanted to get back to classes. I encouraged him.

After a while we were getting on each other's nerves, running out of things to talk about, no real privacy. Getting his BS in nursing is a big deal for him."

Patrick chuckled, "You're sounding like an old married couple: getting on each other's nerves. Elsie and I do that at times. You still thinking about studying foreign affairs?"

"Yeah," Frank replied. "Did I tell you about the course I took in Middle Eastern affairs?" He explained how he'd taken the course with Brad, met Omar, and become good friends with him and Joe. He concluded, "They're really great, helping all of us get through this, especially Paco and Jason, who can't drive. Who'd've thought we'd become such good friends with two young Muslim guys?"

"Yeah. In this country at least," Patrick commented, "seems the Muslims pretty much stick to themselves. In Lebanon, people of all religions can be friends, at least among the younger ones. How'd they know you were injured? Were they in the bar with you?"

That's a clever way of asking if they're gay, Frank thought, then replied, "No, they're good Muslims and wouldn't go to a bar to drink." He explained events, concluding, "I sure hope you get to meet them sometime. Enough about me. How're your folks and sister?"

"Great, thanks for asking," Patrick replied. "Anna Marie's getting married in June. We'll be back for her wedding, or at least I will. Hope Elsie's OK to travel."

Frank then asked, "How's Felicia and family?"

"They're doing great," Patrick answered. "Felicia's really blossoming as a high-ranking Navy wife. She might get a job, though. Kids are well settled and she's bored. God sure smiled on Felicia when He had her meet Pete. They're coming to visit you, if you want them to that is."

Frank, surprised, said, "Sure, I'd love to see them. They're not upset, knowing it was in the gay bar bombing?"

"I don't think that'd bother them," Patrick said.

Frank asked, "Would you like to say hello to Brad? He's kind of lonely after his parents went back home."

"Sure," Patrick replied. "Always nice to talk to him."

"That's one of the problems," Frank said. "He can't talk because his lip's badly injured. It's frustrating for him not to talk, because he's so sociable."

An orderly pushed Brad's wheelchair to the visiting area. Patrick stood, smiled, and touched his hand and shoulder, saying, "Hey, Bud. Good to see you. Not like this, but good you're going to be OK."

Brad tried to smile, but stopped in pain.

Patrick said, "Hey, Bud, no need to try to speak. I'll look at your eyes and you can move your hand and fingers."

They then had a somewhat contorted conversation, with Brad trying to respond non-verbally and Patrick being especially understanding and attentive. After a while, Brad motioned for someone to return him to his room. Patrick stood ready to leave. Brad shook his head vigorously from side to side, pointing back and forth to Patrick and Frank.

Patrick said to Brad, "Oh, it's you who needs to go; Frank and I can stay here longer." He grasped one of Brad's hands and said, "Good seeing you, Bud. Sorry, I can't say goodbye Lebanese style, but you know I mean it."

Patrick and Frank continued in small talk for several minutes when an orderly said, "Dinnertime, Major."

Frank chuckled and said, "They feed us early; I'd better go, or I'll be sent to bed without supper."

CHAPTER 4

Monday, March 17, 2008
Washington, DC, USA

Roger Chen said, "Hello, Randy" on the phone to Randolph Walker, U.S. Attorney for the Western District of Virginia.

(pause)

"I'm familiar with the case," Roger Chen interrupted. "I referred it to the FBI. You must have it now."

(pause)

Roger Chen explained Joe's involvement.

(pause)

"That sounds like a good idea for him to go there," Roger Chen agreed. "Why don't we have a teleconference with you, me, and Joe? You can tell him directly."

(pause)

Roger Chen concluded with arrangements for the teleconference and thought, *Joe's been preoccupied since he came back. He's under a lot of stress with family problems and his good friends in the hospital. At least it's not affecting his work yet. Maybe going down there might get him away from stress here.*

Later in the afternoon, Roger and Joe were in front of a large flat screen monitor with Randy Walker, who was wearing a green tie for St. Patrick's Day.

After greetings, Roger Chen said, "I told Joe what you told me, Randy. Why don't you go over it again briefly?"

"You know the case," Randy Walker began. "The FBI turned it over to us this morning. I started looking through details and thought I'd call you. We might need assistance, especially from Joe, because it's a hate crime against Arabs."

"I'm sure we can spare him," Roger Chen said. "One of our jobs is support to the field."

Joe asked, "What do you want me to do? I know the family and am familiar with the case." Joe explained briefly his trip and events that led to hearing about the bombing.

"We heard the gay bar bomber was a local person," Randy Walker confirmed. "I didn't make the connection until now, and local newspapers played it down."

"We met a reporter from the *Roanoke Times*," Joe continued and explained his involvement. He concluded, "I suspect he'll be covering the run-up to the trial and the trial itself. That could be to our advantage, unless it prejudices a potential jury and there's a change of venue."

"That must've been Marcus Porter," Randy Walker said. "He's a young judicial reporter for the *Roanoke Times* and does a pretty good job. So far, there isn't any sensationalism. I doubt we'd have a request for change of venue."

Roger Chen interjected, "What's the case look like to you, Randy? Good chance for conviction?"

"It looks pretty straightforward," Randy Walker answered. "We can go to a grand jury next week, and then it depends on when the case can be scheduled before a judge."

"Do you think you'll have any problems with jury selection?" Roger Chen continued, asking, "A jury that's not prejudiced against Arabs after nine-eleven?"

"No," Randy Walker continued. "People here're fair and open minded and don't put up with hurting people just to be mean because they're a different ethnic group. Marcus must've been the one writing favorable stories about Arab immigrants' making

411

positive contributions to the community. One was about a man who services and repairs foreign cars, especially old classics; that must be Nassar Hammoud, whose house was the target. He's well thought of here. Lots of people like me have just heard about him and don't know his name or many details."

"Could the defense claim prejudice from all the favorable publicity?" Joe asked.

"It's possible," Randy Walker replied. "It'll likely be the public defender; they can't afford an attorney, I'm sure."

"Virginians are pretty well known for prejudice against blacks, or were," Joe continued. "Would that apply to Arabs? The trial will be in Roanoke, which is an industrial city, from what I could tell. I'm not questioning your judgment, but thinking of things that might be relevant."

Randy Walker smiled, "You must be thinking back to the fifties and the school segregation cases."

"Yes," Joe confirmed, "We heard about them in civil rights law and also in history classes."

"Virginia's a diverse state," Randy Walker replied. "That was in the eastern part and along the Southside. Local governments here in the west and up in northern Virginia fought that one tooth and toenail. It forced them to segregate schools that were never segregated before and cost taxpayers a bundle. There aren't that many blacks around here and those that were have always been integrated into the community. Roanoke had a black mayor in the seventies, with blacks about 25 percent of the population. Don't forget, Virginia had a black governor in the eighties too."

Joe said, "Yes. We learned that too."

Roger Chen added, "I live in Virginia and I don't know much about it. I'm a typical northern Virginian who moved from somewhere else and see myself as a citizen of the nation; Virginia's just where I get my driver's license and register my car. Like Joe, I know what I learned in school."

Randy Walker chuckled and said, "Yes, I know, 'inside the beltway' thinking, just like that judge said last time you were down here. Are you recording this? I could say some things off the record."

Roger Chen replied, "No; what's on your mind?"

He began, "Biggest prejudice here's towards country people, ones who live out in the hollows on the fringe of society. They barely get by distilling moonshine and these days growing marijuana. There's no legal protection for them because they're white, 'poor white trash,' lots of people call them. The defendants fall into this category. I don't think a jury'll have much sympathy for them."

"It's pretty straightforward, then," Roger Chen said.

"Yes," Randy Walker agreed, "but we in the field know not to take too much for granted. If we get Judge Bishop, you met her before, she's a stickler for doing things right. You'd better have your ducks in a row, dot your i's, cross your t's."

"Sometimes judges like that are the best," Joe said.

"Oh, yes; I hope we get her," Randy Walker replied. "She can make things rough for us at times, but she'll keep the defense in line."

"Are the defendants in custody yet?" Roger asked.

"No, no need," Randy Walker answered. "They've been convicted on state charges of malicious mischief and're doing community service, cleaning out pens at the animal shelter. Montgomery County officials have them on a short leash. We can serve and arraign them any time we like."

"Malicious mischief!" Joe exclaimed. "Is that all? Virginia has hate crime statutes, doesn't it? I was wondering why the state of Virginia didn't try them for a hate crime."

"Probably didn't cross their mind," Randy Walker suggested. "Hate crimes are pretty rare around here, maybe nonexistent. A local Commonwealth's Attorney likely has more things on his mind. Another thing about Virginia is lawyers don't like to litigate if at all possible. Something about our tradition; attorneys will go out of their way to avoid getting into court for much of anything.

I can look up the details of the state case, and I'm sure we'll have to before we go to trial. I'd guess the Commonwealth's Attorney in Montgomery County worked out a deal with whomever was the defense counsel to keep it simple."

"Oh, that bad," Joe commented.

"Overall it's not that bad," Randy Walker replied. "At least the courts are not clogged with trivial open-and-shut cases, like in some states, but that's another conversation."

Joe then asked, "What is it you'd like me there for?"

Randy Walker replied, "I said we need to get our ducks in a row, dot our i's and cross our t's. You were good at that last time, so I thought you might do it again. We have good trial lawyers, especially James Edward Goodwin, who represented us on that case before. Still it's good to get insight from someone at the top."

Joe said, "Thanks, OK. I can do that."

Randy Walker added, "As I told Roger, it'd be good to have your input on Arab culture, since this is a hate crime against Arabs. Now that I know you already know the family, it may be even better to have you involved. You might prepare them better than we could for what might happen on the witness stand. You might examine them."

"I don't know about examining them," Joe replied, "but I could talk to them and prepare them and the neighbors too. I talked with them when I was there and encouraged them to allow this to be pursued as a hate crime."

"When do you want him?" Roger Chen asked.

Randy Walker answered, "Before the grand jury meets; it might be good if you come just to look over the case and discuss it. Maybe not talk to the family yet, but if you're already friends with them, no problem."

"They're closer to my roommate," Joe replied. "Maybe I shouldn't meet them this time. They'd insist I stay at their house, and as an Arab I couldn't refuse. Nassar Hammoud's wife is in the hospital and I wouldn't want to stay there."

Friday this week could be good, even if it is Good Friday," Randy Walker said. "It's not a federal holiday, so we'll be working. If you have plans for Easter weekend, it might not work for you."

"I'm Muslim," Joe said with a chuckle. "Good Friday and Easter don't affect me one way or another."

They concluded. Joe and Roger Chen discussed briefly what Joe was doing and when he might get away.

Maybe Omar and I could spend the weekend down there, Joe thought. *Maybe that's what we need to release tension, and Blacksburg's a nice place. We're both trying to pretend nothing happened, but it's just not the same. I'll tell him tonight and see what he says.*

CHAPTER 5

Rosie Jordan opened a meeting at the FBI Operations Technology Center at the Quantico Marine Corps Base on the Potomac River south of Washington. Attending were Colonel Otis Granger, Cranford Brooks, Rhonda Philips, and for the first time Lawrence Briscoe, a thirty-something Middle Eastern terror groups specialist from the CIA. He was tall and lanky, wore small-diameter circular-lens glasses in brown plastic frames that covered intense blue-gray eyes, had curly light red-brown disheveled hair, and wore a tweed jacket with leather sleeve patches, pale yellow shirt and green tie, and dark brown pants.

Rosie Jordan introduced him, saying, "Larry, we've briefed you. Do you want anything clarified now?"

"No, not now," he answered in a distinct accent reflecting upbringing in a small central Texas town.

"Cranford has a lot to tell us," Rosie Jordan said.

Cranford Brooks began, "A female agent found Hanan Salameh very forthcoming. She came to the U.S. with her refugee parents some forty years ago as a young girl and got a green card. Through an arranged marriage, her husband came to the U.S., got a green card, and later became a citizen; he didn't allow her to apply for citizenship. It's clear the marriage was arranged for the purpose of allowing him to stay in the U.S. with no intention of any semblance of marriage. He insisted on impregnating her by what some would consider rape, in order to have an additional claim to U.S. residence. She claims it was also so he could be called Abou Wissam, which is important in Arab cultures."

"It's traditional to call an Arab man Abou and the name of his oldest son," Larry Briscoe confirmed, and explained the Arab custom. "If he's married and didn't want it known it's a sham marriage, he'd have to have a child. As head of charity collecting money from other Arabs, it'd be important to be Abou something."

Cranford Brooks continued, "In addition to those benefits, he was able to get a U.S. passport."

"We're increasingly aware U.S. passports are just a commodity for the benefit of the holder, especially among Middle Easterners," Rosie Jordan commented. "They have no sense of citizenship and often go home, once they have a passport to travel freely most places in the world."

Cranford Brooks continued, "Ms. Salameh is despondent over losing her son through imprisonment or death. He's all she has. Her parents were killed in an automobile accident many years ago; we're beginning to wonder if it was an accident. She has no relatives in this country, no close friends. Taking care of him was her sole purpose in life. With him gone, she has no will to live except to get revenge on her husband, get a divorce, keep him from selling their house, and get a financial settlement out of him, not for herself but to make him suffer. She may have faint hope she can have a home for Wissam if he gets out of prison.

"We arranged social services counseling and put her in touch with Islamic support networks. Her well-being is important, so we've stretched the definition of witness protection to provide security for her. As Rhonda suggested, it's likely her husband, through his attorney, who's threatening harm to her to keep Wissam silent and plead guilty. We arranged for her to visit him so she could say she's secure and nothing can harm her. Of course, we can't listen so we don't know if she actually did. We just learned he refused to see the lawyer his father sent.

"We'd like her to go back more often to reassure him, but it's tedious to go from Arlington to the detention facility by public transport. She has a car, but doesn't know how to drive. When Wissam went to the Saudi Arabian high school in Fairfax, she scraped together money to buy an old car for him to go back and forth. Security at Fort Meade noticed the car'd been parked a long time, seemingly abandoned, and told her she must move it. We arranged for it to be delivered to her. Social services recommends she takes driving lessons. Her husband had convinced her Muslim women don't drive.

"She told us Wissam was shy, sensitive, and clingy. When he was a boy, he participated in normal boy things, playing soccer, etc. Things were OK until he went to middle school. He had friends, mostly boys in the neighborhood, and was a good but not outstanding student. In middle school, when boys begin noticing girls and vice versa, he noticed girls, but girls weren't interested in him. He was short, skinny, and had an acne problem. Boys and a few girls teased him, calling him 'Wissy the sissy' and 'salami ...' you can guess what. This continued when he went to a public high school, where he was more withdrawn and his schoolwork suffered.

"In a sudden flurry of activity, anger, and resentment, Saeed Salameh enrolled Wissam in the Saudi Arabian school in Fairfax. Wissam and his mother were not consulted. Wissam was indifferent, but his grades improved.

"After high school, he couldn't get a job, although she doesn't think he tried very hard. She doesn't know what he did during the day when she worked, but there was no indication he was involved in undesirable activity. He got involved with an imam at a mosque in Arlington. Ms. Salameh was pleased he had friends, although she never met them. He was often gone at night in his car, but never stayed out late and didn't show signs of drinking, drugs, or other things teenagers get involved with. She also noticed bitterness came over him that he didn't show before; he was detached, edgy, and angry. He didn't confide in her.

"One day last month, he announced he had a job as a cleaner in Maryland that the imam had arranged. She asked him whether it was worth driving so far for a low-paying job and wondered if he couldn't get a cleaning job closer. He brushed her off, saying it was the will of Allah. That's all she knew about his job until she got a phone call the day after he was arrested. She was worried sick because he didn't come home the night before.

"We investigated at the schools in Arlington, but didn't get anything useful; just confirmed what Ms. Salameh told us. We didn't go to the Saudi Arabian high school for many reasons, including sensitive international relations issues.

"Everything points to an imam in Arlington. We've gotten it from three different places now: Joe Shaito, who was talking to Marwan Hammoud; Omar Abu Deeb, who heard a cousin of Nassar Hammoud say he suspected the imam; and now Ms. Salameh. It's highly likely Marwan, Ahmed, and Wissam were acquainted.

"We've identified the mosque, but so far we haven't found out what's going on there. We can't just go in asking. The imam is likely underground or has fled the country.

"As mentioned last time, Saeed Salameh heads a charity we've long suspected collects money to support Hamas. We have no indication Hamas is involved in terrorist activity in the U.S. It's completely out of character that Hamas, working through Saeed Salameh and his son, would try to set off a bomb in the NSA. Everything indicates there was almost no connection between father and son. It seems just a coincidence. That's all I have."

"Thanks, Cranford," Rosie Jordan said.

Larry Briscoe began, "It's difficult to imagine, almost unthinkable, there'd be any connection between Hamas and a Saudi Arabian group, or al Qaeda for that matter, and certainly not inside this country. Hamas gets support mostly from Iran and is loosely allied with Hizbollah in Lebanon, which is supported by Iran. I'd agree it's a coincidence.

"Is the imam acting alone, or is someone behind this? If some Middle Eastern group's behind him, something's strange. Al Qaeda's a continuing threat and would likely do anything to get into this country and create havoc, but bombing a gay bar and a section of the NSA just doesn't fit their modus operandi. They go for big, visible targets like the Madrid train station, the London transport system, and bombs on trans-Atlantic flights. Al Qaeda's loosely connected, so maybe a splinter group's gone off another direction. It's possible he's a loose cannon with delusions of grandeur, operating on his own. With an idea of connections in the Middle East, I might come up with more."

Rhonda Philips began, "There'd be a lot of adverse political fallout if it were known a foreign terrorist group were able to get a potential bomber with explosives into the NSA. There'd be less fallout if it were a random act from, shall we say, a misguided individual acting alone. There's no indication Hamas is involved, although the media'd have a field day if they discover his father's connected to Hamas. If there's a public trial, this'll surely come out.

"From a purely political fallout point of view, it'd be best if he pleaded guilty and were sentenced quietly, with a minimum of media coverage. We can't base our decisions strictly on what's politically expedient. We need to get in there and find out who's behind him.

"The gay bar bombing's a distraction. We can't ignore it, because the two situations are related, but it just gets in the way. There'd be little if any fallout if the public found out terrorists were targeting gay bars, other than alarm that terrorists were able to operate in the U.S. with impunity as suicide bombers. In a perverse way, if it came out terrorists were behind the bombing, that extremist self-identified church in Kansas would be seen as supporting terrorists, which could hopefully silence them.

"On international issues, I agree with Larry. With respect to the Saudi Arabian high school, this is essentially the opposite side of American schools or international schools in many foreign countries. I don't know if there's one in Riyadh, but if there weren't, I'd be surprised. Even though they're not part of the U.S. government, they operate with its approval and encouragement, and the government'd be upset if there were something done to shut them down or restrict their operations. This is not my area of expertise, so I can speak only in general terms."

Cranford Brooks added, "When Wissam Salameh refused to see his father's attorney, we told him he's free to have an attorney of his choice. He can take his time to select an attorney, and if he doesn't, the court will appoint an attorney to represent him. He confirmed he understands and says he wants to talk to his mother again. We're trying to arrange it as soon as possible."

Rosie Jordan said, "Otis, we haven't heard from you."

Colonel Granger replied, "This situation caused us to thoroughly inspect all aspects of security at the NSA and other places in the Washington area where the U.S. Marine Corps provides security; we're in the process of doing it all over the U.S. and abroad. The NSA security detail operated in an exemplary manner. We'll recommend Major Reynolds, Sergeant Beasley, and the three guards for commendation medals. We need to decide if we want to make it public.

"We did learn we need to pay more attention to places where homosexuals congregate, even if the assignment for Major Reynolds was not intended to be serious. This is to the chagrin of those who believe homosexuality is incompatible with anything to do with the U.S. Armed Forces.

"For Colonel Edward Ross, so far we're finding nothing, unless you at the FBI have anything to report. We've begun the process of removing him from the service. That's all I have, but I'll take questions and comments."

Somewhat abruptly, as was his style, Rosie Jordan gave a brief recap and ended the meeting.

CHAPTER 6

Tuesday, March 18, 2008
Washington, DC, USA

While sitting as his desk at George Washington University, Omar thought, *I should go home, catch up with Joe, and have dinner. I used to be eager to get home. Now it's hard to get motivated. I bet he wants to move somewhere else.*

His cell phone jarred him out of his thoughts; he answered in Arabic, "Hello, Abou Ahmed. How are things with you? Fine?"

(pause)

"That's good; how's Ms. Roula?" he asked in Arabic.

(pause)

"Sorry to hear," he continued in Arabic. "I might ask someone here if there's an Arabic speaking psychologist."

(pause)

"Oh, at BWI airport?" he said in Arabic. "Abou Tarek now has it and you want me to drive it down to you?"

(pause)

"What? That's too generous!" he exclaimed in Arabic and thought: *He wants to give me a car! Arabs can't turn down a sincere offer, but this is too much!* "Let me see if I understand. You want me to drive the car found at the airport down there, drive another car back, then go back for the 40th day prayers for Marwan in another car you'll find for me, and then you'll give me one for my own."

(pause)

"Yes, I understand," he answered in Arabic. "Abou Tarek can't keep it longer, and he and his sons can't get away to take it to you. I work too. In fact, I have two jobs."

(pause)

Damn, I don't want to get sucked up into his car business, he thought. *He does sound desperate; Islam says we should help people in need and he's going to give me a car.* "I can't tell you right now," he replied in Arabic. "I'll get back to you. You want me to come for the 40th day prayers. I don't know if I could get away two times. That'd be in the middle of the week, which is difficult."

(pause)

He continued in Arabic, "Do things like you would back in Palestine or Lebanon for the 40th day prayers, but don't be afraid to bring others into your traditions, Muslim and non-Muslim. Dr. Imran was very nice and helpful, and you have nice Christian friends and neighbors."

(pause)

He asked about Fatima and Abou Nidal, exchanged pleasantries, and said goodbye, thinking, *Allah works in mysterious ways. Last night Joe said he has to go to Roanoke on business and asked if I wanted to go with him. I kind of blew him off, saying I was busy. I am busy, but I feel bad I was short. Maybe he's trying to be nice and maybe he wants to go back to being friends like before. The strain this past week was just too much, and I get short tempered. Yeah, it'd be nice to go back where we were and pretend it didn't happen. But what can I say? I'm sorry I got hard in bed with you? That'd raise more questions than it'd solve.*

Maybe offer the car he wants to give me to Joe; that might relieve the strain. I should call the FBI about finding the car at BWI before I go home. Ahmed must've dumped the car and flown somewhere.

Later at home, Joe came out of the kitchen upon hearing Omar unlock the door and said, "Oh, there you are. I wasn't sure when you'd be home, so I started making a sandwich. I can stop if you want to go out."

Omar replied, "Yes, OK, I have some interesting things to tell you. What about that Greek place? It's quick and good and not expensive."

At the restaurant, Omar recounted the conversation with Nassar about someone to drive the car down. "The thought came to me you might want to drive the car to Roanoke," Omar continued. "You could do a favor for Abou Ahmed and give yourself a way to get around. He said he'd have another car for you to drive back. He seemed pretty desperate."

"I suppose I could," Joe replied. "I can ask Roger tomorrow and call Randy too. You want to go with me?"

"No," Omar said. "I'm sorry I was so short with you yesterday, but I've got too much work. You need to be there on a weekday, probably Friday, and we'd need to spend part of Thursday going down. I just can't take that much time on short notice. I've got lectures, papers to grade, and all of that, not to mention the work at the center. I could justify missing work at the center last time because I was leading the burial, but not this time. Besides, and I haven't had a chance to tell you, he wants me back down there for 40th day prayers for Marwan. That's April 9, a Wednesday. I just can't take time off right now."

Joe said, "Maybe Jason would like to go with me. He said he should visit his family, but can't drive yet."

"Good idea," Omar said. "He's mentioned it a couple of times. He must be bored and antsy; can't work, can't paint. I know I'd be."

Joe said, "I'll ask him tonight. Say, are we going to the hospital tonight? I'd just as soon stay home and see what I need to organize if I go. Maybe do laundry. You could go without me if you like." He thought, *Maybe he'll go by himself and I can be alone.*

Omar thought, *I don't think I'm in the mood to go all that way, alone or not. He said he's doing laundry, so that may keep him out of the apartment a while.* "No," he replied. "I'll just stay home. I need to catch up on some reading. We've been there almost every day. I know it's good to be supportive, but they're settled in.

"I haven't told you the most important thing. Abou Ahmed wants to give me a car when they have 40th day prayers. I already have a car, so you can have it. It's a classic; an old sporty BMW he says. It'd be ideal for a lawyer."

Joe, stunned, thought, *What! He wants to give me a car? Maybe he's not upset with me after all, but I can't accept that. It's too much.* He blurted out, "What? You want to give me a car? Thanks, habibi, but that's too much! You're the one who deserves it, after what you did for them."

Omar was dejected. *I thought he'd be pleased and maybe we could go back to being friends. At least he called me "habibi."*

Oh, I shouldn't have been so abrupt with him, Joe thought. *Seems like he's trying to get past what happened, and here I was short. We're both Arabs, and Arabs don't refuse gifts like that; but damn it, I'm American too.* He smiled and said, "Sorry, habibi, if I was so abrupt. You took me by surprise. That's very generous of you. If you want to sell me your car, I'd be grateful and pleased, but I'm too much of an American to accept this kind of generosity. He's offering the car to you, so you should take it."

Omar thought a moment. *At least he's not refusing me. Maybe he's right; it's too generous of a gift.* He said, "I wouldn't sell you my car; I'd give it to you. We don't need to decide right now; it's a couple of weeks 'til I go to the 40th day prayers, if I go."

"Oh, you may not go?" Joe asked.

"I'll probably go," Omar answered. "I have enough time to arrange things. I don't feel like letting them down, but I can't promise I can get away from the university. The center would probably let me go. Say, you might be down there anyway. Could you get off part of a day for the prayers?"

"I'm sure I could," Joe answered. "I am supposed to be working with the family, getting ready for the trial."

Joe called Jason, who was pleased to accept the offer, and then told Omar, who said, "Sounds good, habibi. I'll call Nassar back and say you'll do it."

They spent the rest of the night uneventfully, feeling a little less tension and strain, but still cautious.

CHAPTER 7

On a clear, sunshiny day, with no weather-related distractions now that they were outside the metropolitan area, Joe and Jason traveled on I-66 west in a big BMW Joe recognized as the car Marwan had when they met at Rory's.

Joe, perplexed at Jason's being so quiet, said, "You're awfully quiet, like you're worried."

"Not sure how much longer I'll have a job," Jason replied. "They don't seem eager for me to come back."

"Oh," Joe replied. "How easy is it to get another job?"

"Don't know; haven't paid attention to the job market," Jason answered. "My skills are getting rusty. Could mean going back to school."

Joe replied, "I'd be pretty hard pressed to go back to school again. Where'd you go?"

"Don't know," Jason answered. "Not motivated. Been working to make a living while I paint. Starving artist. Hah!"

Joe said, "Tough looking for job you don't like."

"I don't dislike it," Jason said. "It's just painting's what I live for, and being with Brad."

"If you move in with him, you might work in Maryland," Joe said. "You've both said you'd like to."

"Yeah, we say that, but we haven't talked seriously," Jason replied. "You've seen my apartment; plenty of clutter. You've also seen what a neat freak he is. I've been living there since Marian went back home. It's a mess. I have an excuse that my arm's in a sling, but it's supposed to come off next week and I have to clean it up.

"We'd have to move to at least a two bedroom place so I could have my own space to clutter. Don't know if he could put up with my messiness or I with his neatness. We manage on weekends, but don't know over the long run. Sure, we love each other, or did; but love goes only so far when a slob and a neat freak try to live together."

"Hey, you aren't that much of a slob," Joe said. "What do you mean *did* love?"

Jason choking back emotion, exclaimed, "I don't know what the hell'll happen between us after all this! Haven't been able to talk to him in three fuckin' weeks! Well I can talk *to* him, but he can't fuckin' answer. And I don't talk too much to him because that makes him try, and it hurts him. The wonderful thing in our relationship was we could talk about anything and all things; we felt we belonged together. Also not being able to 'do' anything. It's not that our relationship's all sex. If the sex hadn't been so great, we likely wouldn't've connected so well otherwise."

"I see," Joe said awkwardly.

Jason asked, "Are you uncomfortable talking about gay sex? We've become good friends, so I didn't think about it."

"It's OK," Joe said. "I had gay friends in Michigan, but not close enough to talk about their sex life."

Jason said, "You should've known me before I met Brad; maybe a good Muslim boy wouldn't appreciate that."

Joe replied, "I'm human, even if I am a good Muslim. I wouldn't want to hear graphic descriptions, gay or straight, but I can't imagine you'd tell those. I've come across things in legal cases you probably wouldn't imagine. I'm always interested in what friends have to say, and I can be a good listener, so go ahead."

428

Jason began, "I don't know if you can imagine what it's like, a redneck from Southside Virginia, definitely breaking the mold to go away to college, going off to the big city, Richmond, to study art. Talk about a fish out of water."

"I sort of get an idea," Joe answered. "There were factory workers' kids I grew up with who went to Eastern or Michigan. Can't identify personally, even if my family was pretty ordinary. I was expected to go to university and bring status to the family. That has its own set of problems, but that's another topic. I want to ask you more about rednecks, as you call them, for this case, but later."

"Yeah, sure. I'll tell you what I can, and you're coming to my place and can see rednecks there. Realizing I'm gay only added to my insecurities, sent me looking for other guys to make me feel better. And there were plenty available, probably just like me, looking for the same thing. When I moved up here, I was really out of my element. Richmond's still a Southern city. Up here's a different world. I looked for ways to cover up my insecurities the best way I knew how, only here the guys weren't exactly throwing themselves at me. But I did all right. Then I met Brad."

"I can identify with that," Joe replied. "Washington's a stuck-up city. Say, how'd you and Brad meet?"

"He and I kept ending up at the same bars and clubs, both coming into the city because we couldn't find anything where we lived," Jason said. "One dance club in particular. When I saw him from a distance and saw he was so damned cute, I got hard on the spot."

Got a hard-on looking at someone? Joe said to himself. *I never got hard without trying, except that night.*

"I danced with him a few times," Jason continued, "but if you ever watched gay guys dance, it's kind of hard to know who's dancing with whom. After a few times, we kind of got closer and talked some. Got mixed signals from him. It was like he wanted to be closer, but was holding back. We actually went off and talked a few times, just idle chatter.

429

"One night we seemed to be hitting it off, and I suggested we go to Rory's, which you know has a dark room. He wasn't having any part of a dark room. That embarrassed and upset me; really fed my insecurities. I was ready to go home, but then he suggested we go to his place. I wasn't keen to go all the way to Maryland, but my other head was doing my thinking. We ended up spending the weekend together, and then another, and another. Great sex brought us together, but being able to talk kept the relationship going. It was Easter weekend two years ago we decided we're boyfriends. We went to church together and realized we connected at so many levels.

"Now who knows what'll happen? It's tearing me up to see him like that, not knowing what he feels, what he thinks, what'll happen. I can't just walk out on him now, not that I'd want to; but I'm sure having trouble coping. I'm grateful to get away for the weekend, see my family. I can't tell them about this, but at least I can get my mind off it for a while."

Joe said, "I can't identify with what you're going through, but I'm trying to understand the best I can."

"Thanks," Jason said. "I've not been able to talk to anyone about this. Say, you ever had a girlfriend?"

"No," Joe answered. "At Michigan I was too busy. Yeah, I had friends who were girls and friends who were guys, but no one special. Since I've been in Washington, it's hard to break into a social scene. It's complicated, because I don't think it's right to date non-Muslim girls. I don't have religious hang-ups. I've got plenty non-Muslim friends of both sexes; but if we were to get serious, it gets too complicated. Marrying a non-Muslim would create more problems than I want to imagine."

"I sort of understand that," Jason replied, "although Brad and I are pretty compatible about religion. Another thing, he wants to go back to school. Wants to take advantage of being in DC to get a master's degree in international affairs, specializing in Middle Eastern things."

"Joe replied, "Frank too. Both talked to Omar about it.""

"Hey," Jason said laughing, "Maybe I can find a place to study in DC too. Then we can all move together into one of those big old houses. Plenty of room for all of us. Frank'd have to be alone in a room so Paco could come down to visit. Brad and I would be together and we could set up space in the basement for my shit, my studio. You and Omar could be together, not as a couple."

"Oh, I don't know about that," Joe replied.

"What!" Jason exclaimed. "You're a couple now?"

Joe fumbled, "No, nothing like that; just the opposite. I don't know how long Omar wants to live with me."

"Oh?" Jason exclaimed. "Why not?"

Joe said, "Something happened. He tries to be nice, but I suspect he's just waiting 'til the lease's up to move out."

Jason asked, "What happened? If you want to talk about it, I'm a pretty good listener too."

Joe thought, *If I say I don't want to talk about it, that'd really be an insult. But, damn it, how can I tell him what really happened?* He began, "I can tell *you* but you must not tell anyone else. It's pointless to ask you not to tell Brad when you can talk again, but I can't stand the thought of anyone else knowing. Please."

Jason thought, *It must be pretty bad for Mr. Cool Joe Shaito to be so uptight.* He replied, "Yes, sure."

"It was that last night you and Mrs. Marian were staying at our apartment," Joe began. "Things'd been pretty emotional before she arrived. I'd just gotten off the phone with my father."

"Yes," Jason said. "I remember."

Joe continued, "Omar'd been hugging me. It started with his hand on my shoulder and ended up in a tight embrace. I needed that. No one's hugged me that way since I was a kid, when my mother would at times."

"Hug therapy," Jason said with a smile. "Works every time, and yeah, nothing like that happened in my family."

Hesitating, Joe continued, "Omar and I were sleeping in the same bed. He hugged me because I was upset again. Then, how can I say this, I got a hard-on. I immediately flipped over so he wouldn't feel it and get the wrong idea. He must've felt it, because he flipped over too."

"Is that it?" Jason asked.

"Yes," Joe answered. "Things haven't been the same. It's kind of hard to put in words, but there's tension. It's like we don't feel as comfortable in each other's company like we did before. What else could it be other than he felt me hard?"

"It might be lots of things," Jason answered.

"Like what?" Joe blurted out.

"Well, maybe he didn't feel a thing, but was picking up on your discomfort," Jason offered.

"Then why'd he flip over so suddenly?" Joe remarked.

"Well, you said you flipped over," Jason replied. "Maybe he was surprised and hurt because he'd been comforting you."

"What else could I do?" Joe asked in anguish. "I couldn't let him feel me hard."

"Just how bad is it between you now?" Jason asked. "Did he actually say anything about wanting to move out?"

"No, nothing like that," Joe answered. "We're both trying to act like nothing happened, but tension's there. The lease isn't up until November, and he actually offered to give me a car Nassar Hammoud is going to give him, maybe as penance for moving out. Of course I turned it down."

"What?" Jason asked incredulously. "What's this about a car he's giving you?"

Joe explained, and Jason agreed. "Accepting a gift like that wouldn't make me feel comfortable either. It doesn't seem like it's penance for something he's going to do, but a peace offering, a signal he wants to get back to normal."

"Hadn't thought about that," Joe said. "And he actually called me 'habibi' again."

"Listen," Jason said. "There must be more to this. You need to talk to him. Tell him honestly what happened. It probably won't be bad as you imagined."

"Why'd I get a hard-on like that?" Joe asked. "What can I say when he asks me why?"

"Look," Jason blurted out. "Getting hard's a response to intense feelings, and the situation was pretty intense. It doesn't have to be what you seem to be thinking."

"You think so?" Joe asked.

"Yeah," Jason reiterated. "Man, you need to talk to him. Otherwise, it'll tear both of you up inside."

At this point traffic was heavy as I-66 and I-81 merged; Joe said, "Better pay attention to the traffic."

Once on I-81 southbound, Joe told Jason brief details of the case, how it involved rednecks, and asked about them. After a while, Jason drifted off to sleep.

CHAPTER 8

Joe came home about 8:30 p.m. and Omar said, "Oh, there you are! I was wondering if I should check on you. I figured you had bad traffic on Easter Sunday, but not this late."

He was concerned about me? Joe thought. *Maybe he cares about our friendship after all. It never occurred to me to call him.* "Oh, you were concerned," he replied. "I drove Jason to Laurel after we stopped at his apartment. Then I had to fight traffic to take the car to Abou Tarek, who brought me here; I couldn't face the Metro."

"How was it with Jason's family?" Omar asked. "Oh, you seem frazzled. Would you like a cup of tea?"

Joe said, "Thanks. What I actually need is something to eat. I'll fix something if we have food, after I take my bags to my room. A cup of tea'd be great to go with it."

Omar, said, "I'll heat the water; what kind of tea?"

Joe answered, "Make two of whatever you're having." He took his bags to the bedroom thinking, *He's being really attentive. Maybe there's more to it, like Jason says. How can I bring this subject up? I just can't.*

When he came back, Omar had set sandwich makings on the table and was bringing two cups of tea.

Joe made a sandwich and said, "I stayed overnight at his sister's place. I'd've rather stayed in a motel, but can't refuse hospitality even if it's not Middle Eastern. Nassar wanted me to stay too, but I told him I already had a commitment, thankfully. There's a lot to tell, but let me eat first. I saw your new car. Nice! The car he had me drive back's cool too, an old Peugeot roadster owned by an American who works at the French Embassy.

"Jason wanted to go to Easter Sunday church services with his family. They asked me to go, not really expecting me to, but I thought why not? Nothing in Islam says I can't go to a Christian church service."

"How was it?" Omar asked.

"Compared to our prayers and Friday sermon, it was quite a change," Joe replied. "They were exuberant, shall we say. Jason said this's an evangelical church; not all are this way, and not the one he and Brad attend in Laurel. After church, we had a big family Easter lunch at Jason's parents' house, Easter ham with all the trimmings. They cooked a chicken just for me, but others ate it too. Say, why don't you tell me what's been going on here, while I finish eating."

Omar said, "I went to the hospital yesterday and today. Brad's lonely with Jason gone and Frank getting attention from visitors, friends from Annapolis. He couldn't talk, but appreciated me being there."

"That's good," Joe said. "I need to go see them soon."

Omar replied, "I'm sure Brad'll be pleased to have Jason back. Did he say when he'd go back to work?"

"Probably this week," Joe answered.

"I bet he's eager for that," Omar commented, "but Brad'll be all alone; we should spend more time with him."

"I don't know how eager he is to get back to work," Joe replied. "He's afraid he'll lose his job. He's worried about his and Brad's relationship, too."

"Oh, why?" Omar asked.

"Anxiety over how injuries'll affect things. Say, why don't you ask him yourself? I don't mind telling you, and I'm sure he wouldn't mind my telling, but I get the idea he'd like it if you ask him directly. I sense he's a bit jealous, maybe envious is a better word, of attention Brad and Frank get when he's injured too. He's a genuinely nice person and good to talk to. He gave me useful information for our case too."

Omar asked, "How's the case going?"

Joe replied, "There's more than one kind of redneck. The ones Jason identifies with are parochial, not very sophisticated, and not always well educated, but they do function in society and have social essentials. For the most part they're law abiding, but can get disorderly at times. The ones who bombed the Hammoud's house are reclusive; live back up in the sticks, and don't interact with outsiders except when they have to go to school or buy something. They distill moonshine alcohol and now grow marijuana. Respect for law's not part of their culture.

"I met Marcus Friday night. He confirmed what Randy said about a prospective jury's being fair. He's eager for lots of media publicity because he could feed the news to the *Post* and wherever else he can manage."

"He'd be good to have on your side," Omar concurred.

"Let's be careful about counting him on our side," Joe said. "I'm sure he'd cozy up to the defense if he could get a good story. We wouldn't tell him our legal strategy, but he wouldn't do anything to hurt us."

Omar asked, "How's that going?"

"Good," Joe replied. "We have ideas. Right now about all I could say would be in legal jargon. You want to hear more about Nassar, and it's getting late."

"OK," Omar replied.

"There was another incident," Joe said, and described the incident with Fatima at the middle school.

"Oh," Omar said. "That's terrible. What's going to happen about that, if anything?"

"I'll call Randy on Monday morning," Joe replied. "We'll have to decide whether we want to bring this out as further evidence of deliberate hate crime. Nassar didn't tell me much; it was Velma, when I went to see her and Shane about testifying at the trial.

"I spent all day Saturday with Nassar. It's difficult for him with Ms. Roula gone and Fatima alone. He has a lady from the Robertses' church who he pays to do housework and look after Fatima. Ms. Roula is not doing well." He described Nassar's concerns, then continued, "Every state has some type of public mental health care. Virginia must have something.

"Another thing is Marwan's 40th day prayers. I'll tell you about that; then, I'm sorry, I have to go to bed. Nassar seems overwhelmed. He's determined to follow tradition, which I encouraged, but seems muddled and confused. I told him to contact Dr. Imran, but he's reluctant. I don't know if it's shyness or being overwhelmed. He said he's Pakistani and this is an Arab thing. I strongly advised he contact Jordan Hicks. Remember he said he could've had more of Marwan's friends for the burial if there'd been more time. Also said to contact his neighbors; I reminded him that in Lebanon, this is an Arab cultural thing and Christians have 40th day prayers too that both Christians and Muslims go to."

Omar replied, "Good. Did Nassar contact Jordan?"

"Not while I was there," Joe replied. "I thought maybe I'd contact him or, better yet, both you and I. We promised to keep in touch with him; this'd be a good reason to make a friendly phone call. We also talked about the tradition of posting notices with Marwan's picture. I encouraged him; just because he's not in an Arab country, there's no reason he can't follow tradition. He could even have the notice in both Arabic and English. So what if no one comes as a result; he'd feel good he's followed tradition. I said he could go to Kinko's; I even offered to go with him if I'm down working on the case.

"Also said he should contact Marcus. I called Marcus when I passed through Roanoke again; needed to talk to him anyway. He'll see about having a notice posted in the New River section of the *Roanoke Times*. There's a local newspaper that'd likely post a notice too. I can probably arrange to be there on the 9th. Are you going?"

"Don't know yet," Omar replied. "I feel obligated to keep supporting Nassar, but I do have two jobs. If it's Allah's will, I'll gladly go. It'll be good to have you there too."

"Yes, insha Allah," Joe said. He stifled another yawn, saying, "Sorry, time to call it a night."

"OK," Omar said. "Good to have you back, habibi."

Joe, exhausted, merely said, "Thanks."

CHAPTER 9

Rosie Jordan opened a task force meeting with the same group as before. "Thanks for coming out here again. We don't have any breakthroughs, but it's useful to share what we have and get feedback. Otis, maybe you can start."

Colonel Granger began, "Major Frank Reynolds will leave the hospital soon and stay in a relatively secure location until he recovers enough to return to work. Our biggest concern has been interference of his father." He recounted events with General Reynolds. "He's nothing but persistent. He continued quietly behind the scenes with some of his friends at Marine Headquarters to arrange a quiet medical retirement. As soon as I found out, we immediately began the process to recall General Reynolds to active duty and charge him with interfering with this inquiry. He was formally notified and advised to get an attorney. He promised to stop if we would drop the action. We agreed to suspend, not drop.

"Major Reynolds has detractors at Marine Corps Headquarters, and some would like to remove him from the service with medical retirement. He will certainly fight that, and we support him. We're eager to have him back on duty as soon as possible, even if he is on crutches or in a wheelchair. His sergeant will retire soon, and we don't want two new persons in charge of that guard detail.

"Briefly, on two other things we're working on jointly with the FBI. First, Colonel Edward Ross: We're not finding anything except arrogance of power. We're in no hurry to bring this to a close, so he's still on the hook, so to speak. A few in the Pentagon are trying to hush it up and let him retire, but others consider how many lives could've been lost had his orders been followed and want punishment. He'll likely receive the most severe administrative punishment he can receive and be discharged. We could possibly court martial him, but that would involve a public trial.

"The last involves Bradley Spencer. We've kept him in Bethesda Naval Hospital, mostly for his safety; we couldn't be sure he wasn't targeted because he works in the Arabic language section. That possibility seems to have faded, so we're considering whether we should let his health insurance take over and transfer him to a civilian hospital. The FBI has more to say. Any questions or comments?"

Rhonda Philips, who today wore a royal blue pants suit with light blue blouse, spoke up. "As you and I've been discussing, Otis, it'd not necessarily be a bad thing if events at the NSA become public. It might even be beneficial because it shows that the threat is still real in this country, but we're on top of things and prevented a disaster. It might helpful if Major Reynolds and the others received commendation medals publicly and maybe put a stop to some of his detractors.

"We might not want it to come out publicly, or just not yet, that the gay bar bombing and the attempted bombing at the NSA are related until we can find out who's behind them. Let's avoid a knee-jerk reaction that publicity on the NSA case should be avoided, including details about the young man who's in custody in Baltimore."

Rosie Jordan turned to Cranford Brooks, who began, "First, with respect to Edward Ross, we haven't closed the case, but we're not actively investigating. We can't find any evidence of treason. We're pleased to allow the DoD pursue the case as it sees fit and keep him stewing for a while, if that serves a purpose. Of course, there's the right of *habeas corpus*, constitutional rights to speedy trials, etc.

"With respect to Bradley Spencer, we still have concerns. Until we find out more about who's behind these two events, we can't be sure he's not being targeted. It's an interesting coincidence, maybe too much, that he was in the bar when it was bombed, even if it was apparently suicide. He could be a key witness, and we want to keep him safe.

"The primary question is where to send him next. He needs medical monitoring while he heals from injuries and also needs reconstructive surgery so he can talk again. His care and protection is primarily our responsibility because he has no direct connection with the Defense Department. The DoD does have good hospitals that treat combat injuries, including reconstructive surgery. Ideally we'd like him out of the Washington area. We'll keep working with you, Otis.

"About whether to keep things quiet, for now we wouldn't like too much more publicity that might connect these two cases in the public's eye until we find out more about who's behind them. The suspect in custody in Baltimore isn't saying anything and doesn't want to talk to an attorney, not even the public defender who's representing him. He's busy with other cases and is content to let this one ride for a while, which serves our purposes just fine.

"His mother continues to visit regularly; one of our female agents brings her. She talks openly to the agent, but hasn't told us anything significant. We hope with positive contact from his mother he might open up. The biggest thing is her husband kept calling and harassing her, threatening to go to the house to force her to leave if she or the boy says anything. She obtained unlisted telephone numbers and installed an alarm system. She has a divorce lawyer too. We haven't found out more about that mosque in Arlington. I'll gladly take any questions."

Larry Briscoe slowly and deliberately sat up and said, "After our last meeting, we contacted resources in Gaza about this purported charity. They gave a preliminary report. There is some charitable activity, but also some suspicious activity. They'll get back to us.

"We've had our people looking into the possibility of Hamas's involvement in the bombings. Their reaction is same as mine: this is not the type of thing that Hamas would do. This must be some other group, and it's a coincidence that it involves the son of someone involved with Hamas."

Rosie Jordan briefly summarized the day's proceedings and said, "Let's wait until we have more significant developments before we have another meeting. Thanks to all of you for coming."

CHAPTER 10

Thursday, March 27, 2008
Cabin John, Maryland, USA

On a cool, overcast day, with no weather distractions, and normal traffic for early afternoon, Omar was driving Jason and his belongings to his apartment and said, "You must be eager to go back to work."

"I guess," Jason said. "Sick leave is running out. Don't know how much longer I'll be working there, though."

"Oh?" Omar said pretending surprise.

Jason said, "They wouldn't fire me on the spot, but I could get all the shit work until they find some reason to let me go or I decide to quit." After commenting he didn't dislike the job, but wasn't fond of it either, he added, "Sorry I'm down and depressed. It's a stressful time."

"I imagine," Omar said. "You know I'll do what I can."

"Yeah," Jason replied. "I don't know what we'd've done without you, but we can't keep on using you, either."

"That's a basic premise of Islam," Omar said, "but this may not be the time for a religious discussion."

"A religious discussion's OK," Jason said. "I'm getting into it more, now that I'm with Brad and we're going to church regularly, or I was getting into it. Any heavy discussion is best with Brad when, if, he can talk again."

He's really down, Omar thought, *saying if Brad can talk again.* He said, "We might not be running into you as much, now that you're going home, but that doesn't mean losing contact with you. Hope we'll continue to get together in a more relaxed way than in the hospital."

"Oh, thanks, yeah," Jason replied.

"You're always welcome," Omar added. "I'm not much of a cook, but there're nice restaurants in our area."

"I'm not much of a cook either," Jason said.

"But that doesn't mean you have to always come into DC," Omar continued. "I'd be pleased to go to Virginia. Haven't been there much. Joe'll have a car of his own, I guess you know, so we don't always have to be together."

Hmm, Jason thought. *Does this mean he's upset with Joe? Wonder if they've talked. Should I say something? Nah, but if the subject comes up.* He replied, "Yeah, Joe told me he'll take this car and you'll get a classic BMW. Either or both of you are welcome. It was really good being with Joe on the trip home. You're good to be with too. You two also are good to be with together. It's like you kind of go together."

"Thanks," Omar said. "I heard Brad's being moved, but wasn't able to get the full story."

He changed the topic quickly, Jason thought, then said, "I haven't heard much either; they don't tell me much. They're sending him some place in Texas where there're good facilities to treat bomb injuries."

"All the way to Texas," Omar commented. "You going there to visit him?"

"Doubt it," Jason answered dejectedly. "Can't take off work; and if I lose my job, can't afford it. What'd I go for? Can't talk to him."

"You seem negative," Omar said. "You're so devoted."

"After all of this, I just don't know," Jason said choking away tears. "I don't know if he's the same person I was devoted to. Don't know if I'm the same person."

"Oh," Omar said. "Hadn't thought of it that way."

Sobbing, Jason blurted out, "We haven't fuckin' talked in a fuckin' month! How can I know who he is anymore?"

Omar concentrated on driving as they crossed the Potomac River, thinking, *He's really upset. Allah, help me know what to say and do next.* He put his hand on Jason's knee and said, "I can't identify with your situation, but I can imagine it's difficult in a relationship when you can't communicate through no cause of your own."

"Sorry," Jason said through the sobs and tears.

"No need to be sorry," Omar replied. "We all have times that cause us to cry. You can open up with me."

Jason said, "I know, but sorry for the strong language."

Omar chuckled and said, "Why should you be sorry about that? You think because I'm an imam I'm bothered by such language? I'm certainly not the most clean-mouthed person. You haven't been around me yet when I'm upset."

Jason forced a slight smile saying, "OK. I don't know if Joe told you, but it's the way we could talk to each other that made us so devoted, as you put it. Brad and I could talk about anything, whether laughing and joking, intellectual, our lives and ambitions, times we were upset with each other and otherwise, even silly stuff like what's on TV. Now we just look in each other's eyes and get frustrated, angry, maybe angry at each other. It's gotten to where I hate to be with him at times, but I can't stay away either."

That sounds a little like what's going on between Joe and me, Omar thought. *If only he knew I had to fuck it up by getting a hard on. There, I even used the "f" word.* "No one can completely understand another," he said, "but I understand more than you might think. You do seem so close to each other in many ways."

Jason replied, "We were very intimate too, if that's what you mean, but you may not want to hear about that."

"Why not?" Omar asked. "Because I am an imam? I'm human. While Islam doesn't condone sex outside of marriage, doesn't mean we shut our brains off. We have normal instincts and feelings, and our bodies function normally, even if I don't have active sexual relations. What about your pastor? Can't imagine she shuts her brain off either."

What? "Bodies function normally," Jason thought. *Wonder if he means Joe getting a hard on. Why'd he bring it up now? Maybe this is the opening.* "No, she doesn't shut her brain off," he replied. "She doesn't talk about her sex life, but she has a girlfriend and doesn't hide they enjoy being sexual."

Omar said, "If she can have normal sexual thoughts, why shouldn't an imam like me?"

"Haven't thought about," Jason said. "When we've been together, the subject of, er, intimacy didn't come up."

"Go ahead and say it," Omar said. "It's sex. The word can sound crude at times, but there's no need to always find euphemisms. It's apparent that you and Brad were intimate, as you say. Frank and Paco too."

Jason said, "That's another part of the frustration. We haven't been able to have sex for a month and, as you say, we have normal instincts and our bodies function normally. I'm not about to go find someone else, so long as things're the way they are. The tension's building up though. Just standing holding Brad's hand is enough to get me hard. It's not that I have strong sexual desires for him right that moment, but the combination of pent-up desire, emotional stress, and tension are enough to make it happen. Some things in the body just can't be controlled."

What? Omar thought. *Did Joe tell him I got hard? He said it just happens; can't be controlled. Maybe that's what it was about. Do I dare ask him? Dare tell him?* "What? You say it just happens spontaneously, stress and tension are enough?" he asked.

"Er, yes," Jason replied, "or at least for me, especially here lately. I don't know about Brad. I don't dare try to find out; that'd just add to the frustration."

Omar, tense and nervous said, "I always thought it needed some stimulation to get hard. Maybe what you just said explains what happened to me recently. It's kind of hard to talk about. It's that night Mrs. Spencer was at our apartment. The day Joe had the disturbing call from his father. You were there too."

"Yes, I remember," Jason said.

"When Joe and I went to bed together," Omar continued, "Joe got upset again and started crying. I held him to console him; kind of close. Then I started getting hard. I couldn't have Joe notice this, so I turned over. He must've felt me, because he flipped over. It seems like he's been avoiding me since, although I'm trying to make up for it and trying to let him know it didn't mean anything. I feel he's being nice until the lease is up and he can move out."

Jason thought: *What? He got hard? Joe said he got hard. Wait. They both got hard. Oh....*

Omar continued driving, perplexed at Jason's silence, and wondered, *Did I make a mistake in telling him?*

"You and Joe should talk, and soon!" Jason said emphatically. "Seems like there's a big misunderstanding."

Omar asked, "Did Joe say anything to you about this?"

Jason pondered. *How can I answer and not lie?* "No, Joe didn't say anything about you getting hard," he answered.

"Omar said. "I was beginning to wonder, because you were slow to answer. Thought you might be upset."

"Upset?" Jason asked surprised. "Why? It's something that happens spontaneously to all of us. Nothing to be upset about. I was thinking how good friends you two are and how bad it'd be if something happened."

"Yeah, Joe's special," Omar said. "One of the very best friends I've had. Sort of like you and Brad, someone to talk to and share."

"Then you should share this," Jason emphasized.

"Yes, I know now," Omar replied. "Tension's pretty bad, but it's damned difficult to bring up topics like this, even with someone like Joe."

Traffic became heavy, so Omar focused on driving with little conversation.

CHAPTER 11

Sunday, March 30, 2008
Annapolis, Maryland, USA

The Ramos family were spending a lazy Sunday afternoon, first nice day of early spring, Felicia preparing a cook out, Pete in the family room reading, children away playing.

Frank, also in the family room, leaned against a padded stool on the one buttock not covered by a cast, using a computer. It was his second full day here. He wore a red plaid robe two sizes larger than normal to cover the cast over his thighs and hips. He could walk on crutches and otherwise take care of himself, albeit awkwardly. With Felicia's Filipino upbringing and Pete's "tough love" Navy family upbringing, they communicated he was expected to take care of himself, but they would be there if something were needed.

He rummaged through a long list of unread emails, thinking, *Here's one from D… my father. I'm in no mood to look at this no matter what. Let's see the date. Yep, after I told him I want no contact. Delete it. Here's one from Ali, last week. Hasn't heard from me in a while. I'll send him a short note and fill him in later.*

He read one from Colonel Granger and then said, "Pete, could I bother you for a moment? Is there a printer?"

"It's below the computer table, out of sight," Pete replied. "You need to turn on the button on the back. Here, I'll get it. Forgot for a moment you can't bend down."

"Thanks," Frank said, while Pete turned on the printer. "I was wanting to talk to you about this anyway when we were alone. Maybe you'd have time now?"

"Sure," Pete answered, handing Frank the printouts.

"These forms are to change my next of kin in my official records," Frank explained. "Colonel Granger suggested you might be a good choice, and of course I'd be delighted. Some things happened recently between me and my father. I'll not go into details, but I need to sever all contact, and Colonel Granger agreed."

Pete replied, "Frank, I feel honored and privileged you'd ask me and of course I'll do it. You're a fine man and a fine officer, and we're pleased to know you.

"We're both third generation military and know how things work, especially 'need to know.' When they checked us out as a suitable place for you, they told me a few things about your father and why they want to keep him away from ongoing investigations. I don't know details, and don't want to know. From the little I do know, it's understandable you'd want to sever relations. Put me down as next of kin. I can arrange for the forms to be witnessed and sent."

"Thanks," Frank replied. "You don't know how much it means to me to be here staying with you. It's so much better than a nursing home, and more secure, too."

"We're sorry it has to be in the former maid's quarters, but that's the only place we could put up a bed on the first floor, and you have a private bath," Pete said then chuckled. "Who, knows, maybe it was one of my ancestors who stayed there. If you need anything else, let me know."

Frank continued rummaging through emails. *Here's one from Jason. Brad sent to Brooke Army Medical Center in San Antonio. That's one of the military's best hospitals; the burn center's there. They'd have good plastic surgeons. That's all. Now I can start deleting.*

After several minutes, he saw a small pick-up truck drive up and heard Pete say, "The girls are here."

When they came inside, Frank recognized Christina, who gave Pete a hug and kiss saying, "Hello, Daddy."

He then said, "Hello, Becky, welcome," to the other woman, giving her a hug and kiss on the cheek.

Christina wore men's blue jeans, a plaid man's shirt, casual white athletic shoes, and simple diamond stud earrings. She had a hint of lipstick and other makeup. Becky stood about five six with a slightly robust buxom figure, very closely cropped medium brown hair, and no makeup; she also dressed in men's clothing.

Pete said, "Frank, you remember Christina. This is her friend Becky Bishop. Ladies, this is Major Frank Reynolds."

Frank smiled, saying, "Very pleased to meet you. Sorry I can't greet you more appropriately."

Cristina touched his hand that was holding a crutch saying, "We understand. Daddy and Felicia told us you're here. Nice to see you again. It's been a year or so, hasn't it?"

Frank replied, "Something like that, when Patrick and Elsie announced their wedding here in this room. No, wait, you were at their wedding in Munich?"

"You're right," Christina answered, "but it was such a big event it's hard to remember who was there."

"It's very good of your father and stepmother to have me while I recover," Frank added.

"Oh, don't call her my stepmother," Christina said teasingly. "I look on Felicia as my big sister. I'm so glad Daddy married her. Speaking of her, I'll go to the kitchen to see what help she needs."

Frank awkwardly sat again while Pete asked Becky, "How was your trip to Roanoke last weekend?"

"Good," Becky answered, smiling. "Mom presided over everything, just like she does in the courtroom."

Pete explained, "Becky's mother's a federal judge."

Becky added, "Yeah, and attorneys call her 'hell on wheels' because she's so strict and a stickler for details. My mom's a pistol, and they respect her for it."

"Sounds like an interesting lady," Frank said.

"I'm glad I'm here, now that I'm grown and working," Becky said. "Roanoke's a good place to grow up. Good for Mom, too; doubt she'd have gone as far in a bigger place."

"Oh, how's that, if I may ask?" Frank asked.

"In bigger cities there's more competition and influential congressmen have their favorites," Becky began. "Mom was appointed by Clinton. There was an opening that'd been vacant for a while, just before the '98 elections. It looked like the Republicans might take Congress, so Clinton wanted the vacancy filled pretty quick. The Western District of Virginia's pretty big, but not a lot of population and tended Republican. Mom was one of the few Democrats who was qualified. She and Dad had been prominent in Democratic politics for years, although Mom kept a low profile working for the Commonwealth's Attorney."

"Commonwealth's Attorney?" Frank asked.

"In Virginia, that's what they call the attorney who represents the state in legal actions," Becky explained. "They're called district attorneys in some other places.

"Mom worked for the Commonwealth's Attorney almost all her career, especially when we kids were growing up. She graduated from law school and while she was single worked for a law firm as a gofer junior attorney. Dad was a salesman for a legal supply house and met Mom; he owns the company now. They got married and soon had children. Mom wasn't going to give up her career; but she wanted basically a nine-to-five job while we were growing up. Because they were active in Democratic Party politics, she was visible when an opening in the Commonwealth Attorney's office came up. The Attorney General was a Democrat and a woman, Mary Sue Terry, if that name registers with you, Pete, so she was a natural for the appointment. Not that she was unqualified and got the job because she's a woman; Mom's as well qualified as any man, if not more so; but it helped her break into the 'good ol' boy' network, and she progressed right along up to the top when this federal judgeship came along."

"Good for her," Pete said. "You seem proud of her."

"Yeah," Becky answered, "but there was a time, when I was in high school and college, having a mom who prosecuted young people for, shall we say, 'antisocial' behavior wasn't cool. She would've liked me to follow her footsteps, but didn't put the faintest pressure on me. She did her own thing, so I was free to do my own thing too. When my very best friend decided to go to law school, that took off what little pressure there was."

"Sounds great," Frank commented. "I didn't have any choice. Reynolds were always Marine Corps officers. What did you study, and what do you do now?"

"After a master's in computer engineering from Virginia Tech, I moved to Northern Virginia. I worked for a big IT company, the one where Christina works now. That's where we met. After a little while, I moved on to a smaller company at a higher position."

Christina returned. "Daddy, you're supposed to start the grill and put the meat on. Felicia asked me to pour wine. You want red as usual, Becks? What about you, Frank?"

Frank answered, "No one said anything about no alcohol, and I'm not taking medication. I'll take red."

"What do you do, Frank?" Becky asked while Christina poured. "I know you're in the Marines."

Frank answered. "I'm commander of the Marine Guard security detail at the NSA at Fort Meade."

"Oh, sounds impressive," Becky said.

"Truth be told, it's not," Frank replied. "It's mostly a figurehead position; the guards and the sergeant do the work. He checks with me from time to time as a courtesy."

As Christina set Frank's glass down, she said softly, "You were injured in the bombing at Rory's, weren't you? We went there a couple of times, but it's not our type of place. We usually go to The Phase or Nellie's."

Frank thought, hearing the names of Washington's best known lesbian bars, *They're a couple. Pete and Felicia obviously accept them. Must've figured out Paco and me.*

The children came home and all sat to eat. The rest of the day was spent in pleasant conversation, Frank feeling more relaxed than in a long time.

CHAPTER 12

Tuesday, April 1, 2008
Washington, DC, USA

Cranford Brooks greeted Omar in FBI headquarters for a 2 p.m. meeting, exchanged pleasantries, and said, "There're a couple of situations we could use some help with.

"The first involves Joe Shaito and a racket by an imam to arrange marriages," Cranford Brooks said. "Such things are commonplace, unfortunately; we have trouble getting information to arrest them and put a stop to it. Do you by chance know someone we could send in undercover? You're not available, but maybe you know of someone. Surely you understand we can't contact Joe directly."

"I understand about Joe," Omar replied, "but I don't think I can help you. The imam in Michigan is Shia and I'm Sunni. Joe's one of the few Shiites I know well at all. Sending a Sunni there would not only do you no good, but would immediately cause suspicion. Surely you've heard about the difference between Shia and Sunni."

Cranford Brooks replied, "I've heard about it, but didn't think it'd affect things here. I thought you got along."

"We get along," Omar replied, "or at least we're not antagonistic. It's not that I wouldn't want to help you. I don't approve of this type of activity in any way. It's against the words of the Prophet and destroys the image of Islam."

"OK," Cranford Brooks said. "The next issue's the attempted bombing at the NSA. As you know, we're almost certain the would-be bomber and Marwan Hammoud were involved with an imam at a mosque on Glebe Road in Arlington. Anything you can tell us?"

"I checked around," Omar replied. "Had to be careful because people'd get suspicious if I ask too many questions. No one had any useful information. You might contact Marwan Hammoud's cousins in Arlington; one is named Tarek. They don't like the imam at that mosque, or so their father said. I don't know them. It's likely they're unsophisticated working class people. They might get suspicious and upset if authorities come asking questions. Palestinians don't trust any kind of authority figure, even though they may've been born and educated in this country."

"That might be a possibility," Cranford Brooks said as he made notes.

"None of this must ever come back on me," Omar continued. "If somehow they find out I referred you to them, I'll... let's just say I'll be extremely angry and unhappy."

"Gotcha," Cranford Brooks replied. "It'd be good if we could get into that mosque. Do you have any ideas how?"

"You know I'm willing to help," Omar said, "but if either the Islamic Center or the university knew I'd be helping you, I'd lose both jobs, and I need the jobs to get a green card. You're helping me get a green card, but I have to work for a living too and can't jeopardize that."

"OK," Cranford Brooks said. "Let me try you with one more item. What do you know about a charity called Gaza Children's Education Fund?"

Omar, perplexed, asked, "What should I know?"

"It's a Palestinian charity in northern Virginia," Cranford Brooks said. "One of the key persons in our investigations runs it. We're not convinced it's legitimate."

"I've not heard of that one," Omar replied. "We come across Islamic charities all the time, some rather dubious. They try to involve our center, but we have our own charitable activities. If I find out something, I'd have no problem telling you. What's the connection, if I may ask?"

"Let's just say a person with this charity is related to one of the bombers or would-be bombers, and it doesn't fit. Palestinians in Gaza haven't shown any inclination to terrorize the U.S. so far."

"You're right," Omar confirmed. "This's an issue I don't deal with much, but people in the program at George Washington do. If I hear anything, I'll let you know."

"Thanks," Cranford Broods said. "Thanks for coming. We didn't agree on what we'd pay you for your time. Do you have an amount in mind?"

Omar, surprised, said, "I wasn't expecting to be paid, and I haven't told you anything worth paying for, not that I'm holding out anything. I just don't have any information. Now, if you want me to do a study or consult with you on some specific topic, like the difference between Sunni and Shia in the U.S., we can talk. I want to help. This is my country now, and I want to do my part to be of service. You know I hate terrorists, and'll do anything to get rid of them, Allah willing, but there are things I just cannot do."

"I understand," Cranford Brooks said as he stood. "We really do appreciate what you've done. I'll get you an escort to the front door. You probably know some of the things I mentioned are confidential. We know you'll talk to Joe, which is OK. He works for the Attorney General just across the street, and there's no problem their knowing."

"I understand," Omar replied and thought, *Joe works right across the street. Wonder if he'd be free.*

After being escorted to the exit, he sent a text, "Are you free right now? I'm close. Coffee?"

He continued to think: *We've hardly talked for a week, but I was busy getting a paper ready. Maybe he's pissed off at me and doesn't want to meet me. Can't say I'd blame him.*

His phone rang, and he answered, "Hello, habibi."

(pause)

"Yes, right across the street," Omar said eagerly.

(pause)

Omar replied, smiling. "I'll be right over."

In the Justice Department building, Joe gave Omar a warm handshake. In the snack bar, Omar recounted the conversation with Cranford Brooks.

"Sounds like they want to take it serious," Joe said. "My father's involved, but damn it, it's that imam too. Sorry, habibi, this's a challenge for me."

Omar said, "I wanted to let you know as soon as I could. Sorry I haven't been available much. You know I'm working these days to get a manuscript sent for publication."

"Yeah, I know," Joe said dejectedly. *Like I thought, he doesn't want to talk to me much. Jason said I need to talk to him, but if he avoids me, how can I? But I've been avoiding bringing up the subject myself.*

Omar said, "We haven't been to Mama Ayesha's in a long time. Let's have some comfort food tonight. Weather's OK. We can talk about going to Marwan's 40th day prayers."

Joe perked up, replying, "Yeah. I don't know yet when I'd be going to Roanoke, but they want me there soon."

"I need to get back to the university this afternoon," Omar said. "Why don't we meet at Mama Ayesha's. Maybe early before it gets crowded."

"Six or six-thirty is good," Joe answered.

"Good for me," Omar said. "See you about 6:30."

CHAPTER 13

"Sorry I'm late," Omar said as he took a seat at a table in Mama Ayesha's where Joe was waiting.

"No problem," Joe said. "I just got here. There're some specials: bamiel bil lahmeh; not sure if you've had it but very Lebanese, lamb stewed with okra and tomatoes. That with fattoush would make a nice meal."

"Don't know if I'm much into okra," Omar said, "but I haven't had much and not Lebanese style."

"Well there's chicken kabbsseh, a rice dish with almonds on top," Joe continued.

"That sounds good," Omar said, "and a big fattoush."

The bus boy brought glasses of water and the traditional Lebanese meze with eggplant dip called moutabal, chick pea paste called hummus, two different kinds of olives, turnips pickled in beet juice and turned shocking pink called kubbis lift, a parsley-based salad called tabbouleh, finger-sized spinach pastries and cheese pastries, lettuce, carrots, radishes, and cucumber. Also flat Lebanese bread baked fresh that day.

Recognizing Omar and Joe from their previous visit, he smiled and said, "*Ahlan,*" then continued in Arabic, "Welcome back. Good to see you again."

They both smiled and said, "*Marhaba, shouqran.*"

Damn, what's his name? Joe thought. *I remember he wants to be a lawyer.*

"Good to see you again, too," Omar said in Arabic. "I hoped we'd see you at the Islamic Center."

The bus boy replied in Arabic, "I've been so busy here; Fridays are some of our busiest days. I just rush to the mosque near me in Alexandria and pray quickly; often don't stay for the sermon." Then in a lower voice, "Christians run this place and are not always understanding."

Joe asked in Arabic, "Anything on law school?"

He replied in Arabic, "No. I started looking, but they're too expensive and I don't have much free time. I'm trying to get my girlfriend over here. She was in law school too. The only way she can get a visa is if we're married, and even then we have to prove it's a real marriage. I can't go back to Lebanon, and she can't come here. The waiter's coming. Maybe we can talk more when I clean your table."

The waiter asked in English, "Are you ready to order? Would you like me to explain anything on the menu?"

Joe, annoyed, gave his order in Arabic. Before the waiter could respond, Omar gave his order in Arabic and Joe added the fattoush should be large to be shared.

The waiter, taken aback that two young seemingly American men spoke Arabic, one with a Levantine accent, said in Arabic, "To drink? We have some very fine Lebanese wines; Chateau Ksara, you probably know it."

Joe said tersely in Arabic, "We're Muslim and do not drink alcohol. Water's fine."

Omar asked, "Are you thinking the same thing I am?"

"About what?" Joe replied perplexed.

"What the man I met today said about finding someone to go into a certain location you're very familiar with," Omar answered. "The bus boy."

"Oh," Joe replied. "So long as it's not associated with me. He could fit in well. He's Shia, has the right accent, and the right age. Maybe an arrangement could be made to get him and his girlfriend into a law school."

Omar said, "I could tell the guy I talked to today and also state it's completely up to them to screen, make contact, and work out details. I don't want anything to do with it, and surely you don't either."

"No!" Joe affirmed. "It could be good for this guy. Get him out of here; seems he doesn't like it much."

"Can't remember his name," Omar said.

"I'm trying to remember too," Joe added. "Pretty sure it was Timo, but can't remember his family name."

Omar said, "I can maybe ask for a phone number because of some research project."

Joe said, "Say this food's great like last time. Too bad the attitude of the waiter doesn't match." After a few moments, "I checked about going to Roanoke next week. We're planning on my arriving on Tuesday night, going to Blacksburg for the 40th day prayers, and then back to the office. I need to see Nassar and others to solidify their testimony. They're fine with my going to the prayers."

"Oh, good," Omar replied.

Joe said, "Aren't you going to pick up the car Nassar's giving you? Maybe we can both fly down on Tuesday night and you can drive your new car back."

Omar said, "Maybe you can fly, because your costs are being paid. I can't afford air fare. Why can't we drive down in my car, soon to be your car, then you drive it back?"

Joe thought, *He's still pissed off, but he's right. I wasn't very thoughtful about his financial situation.*

"Sorry, I'm distracted by things back h... back in Michigan," Joe replied. "Sure, we can go down in your car, and I'll drive it back. Might be better; I wouldn't want to take an official U.S. Government car to the prayers."

The waiter asked in English, "Dessert? Coffee?"

Omar replied in Arabic, "*La*," omitting *shouqran* in "No, thank you." In Arabic he said, "Bring us the check."

Soon, the bus boy came to clear away the dishes, and Omar said in Arabic, "We forgot to get your name and phone number last time. We might be interested in talking to you about a research project at the university."

"The university?" the bus boy asked in Arabic.

Omar continued in Arabic as he got a pen and one of his university business cards and explained his position at George Washington University. He added, "I can't promise anyone'll call you, but some of my colleagues might like to get data from persons like you. Write it in Arabic if you like; if someone picks it up by mistake, they likely wouldn't recognize your private information."

The bus boy hastily wrote his name and phone number and said, "I need to hurry; the waiter's coming with your check. I'll come back for the rest in a few minutes."

Omar looked at the card, saying, "Haitham Haider. You're right about his first name; Timo's the nickname."

They paid the bill, leaving a smaller tip than normal but giving Timo a tip too.

CHAPTER 14

Tuesday, April 8, 2008
Haymarket, Virginia, USA

Having left urban traffic driving along I-66 west, with weather warming, Omar said while driving, "It's great Brad can email and chat at the hospital in Texas."

"Yeah," Joe answered. "For someone outgoing and sociable as he is, being unable to communicate must've been torture. I haven't written to him as much as I'd like. Jason's relieved too. Any idea how long he'll be there?"

"We've exchanged a few emails," Omar said, "even some in Arabic. He doesn't know how long; they'll do surgery on his lips soon. His mother was there during her spring break and his father too, for a weekend."

Joe added, "He's lucky in the parents Allah gave him. It's good to see Jason in a better mood too. Say, we should do more things with him if we can. We just passed by his place. Maybe we can see him on the way back."

Omar replied, "I'll try to stop for lunch or coffee. Did you hear Frank might go back to work soon?"

"I got a short email," Joe answered. "I'm sorry I haven't been to see him, but it's too much of a hassle to go to Annapolis without a car. Maybe next week if he's still there. Brad's kept us all together socially. With him in Texas, who knows? We might drift apart."

"You may be right," Omar concurred. "I enjoyed their company and hope we can keep it going."

He says "we," but he and I are so distant these days, Joe thought. *Talk about mixed signals!* "I enjoy it too," he said. "Good to get outside my limited circle of legal people. Say, has anyone heard from Paco?"

"No," Omar answered, "at least I haven't. Maybe call Frank and find out more. I presume he can use his cell phone."

Joe said, "I could call him too, but I have lots on my mind with the shit back in Michigan and this trial coming up. Say where're we going to eat? I'm a little hungry. Jason showed me a place in Harrisonburg where lots of people stop. I'll be good and hungry by then."

After lunch, they drove mostly in silence and exchanging small talk while they admired the beautiful colors of the flowering trees typical of the Shenandoah Valley this time of year.

Roanoke, Virginia, USA

"There it is," Joe said, as they drove on I-581, the spur into the city. "That English Tudor building. Take the next exit."

Hotel Roanoke, Roanoke, Virginia

"Stop in front," Joe said. "I'll get the bags and meet you inside after you park." *Oh, shit,* he said to himself. *I didn't remember to contact the hotel to say that Omar's with me. When I've been here before, there've been two beds in the room, and the rate's the same for two as for one.*

463

At reception, an attractive young man in his early twenties whose name badge read 'Kent' smiled and said, "Hello, Mr. Shaito, nice to see you again."

He remembers me, Joe thought. *Everyone here's friendly, but he's exceptionally so.*

"Hello… Kent," Joe said. "You remember my name."

"I try to remember names of special visitors," he said.

I'm a special visitor? Joe thought.

After a moment Kent said, "One person, three nights."

"It's two persons," Joe said. "I forgot to notify you a friend's with me tonight and tomorrow night. Your rates are the same, single or double, so I didn't think it would matter."

"Oh," the desk clerk said, smiling, "You have a nice king size bedroom. Do you need an extra key?"

Joe thought: *Oh, no, that won't do.* "No, or rather yes," he stammered, "but I thought all of your rooms have two beds. Can you change that to two beds?"

Kent said. "I can look, but we're fully booked. …No, sorry, that's all we have."

Joe gulped. "OK, and yes, two keys."

The bellman opened the door to a luxurious room with a king sized bed, gave the keys to Joe, and began to turn on lights and describe the features of the room. Joe hastily gave him five dollars and said no need to continue.

He turned to Omar and blurted out while he hastily opened his luggage and took out a toilet kit, "I fucked up and forgot to tell them you'd join me. I thought all rooms have two beds. This is all they have available. Sorry."

Before Omar could respond, Joe rushed into the bathroom. When he returned, Omar, in his underwear, went into the bathroom. When he returned, Joe was in bed with the light off on his side, clinging to the outer edge of the bed as far as he could. Omar climbed into bed, turned out the remaining light, and also clung to the outer side.

After some ten restless minutes, Joe thought, *Damn it! This is stupid. I made a bad situation worse, being so blunt. We've been avoiding this talk long enough. Can't be worse than lying here like this.* "Habibi, are you awake?" he asked.

"Yes," Omar answered.

"It's time to tell you something," Joe said. "You remember the last time we were in bed you were holding me because I was really upset. While you were holding me, I got a hard on. I didn't mean to. It just happened. I turned over but it must've been too late because you felt it and suddenly turned over. Really, I didn't mean anything. Jason says it just happens when someone's emotionally stressed. Will you forgive me?" *Whew, I didn't think I could do it.*

Omar thought, *What? He got hard and turned over?*

Joe thought, *He's silent. He's really pissed off.*

Omar stammered, "Did you say you got a hard on, and that's why you turned over so quickly?"

"Er, yes," Joe answered. "But I didn't mean to."

"I don't know quite how to tell you this," Omar said hesitatingly. "I got hard too. That's why I turned over so quickly so you wouldn't feel it, and I was sure you did feel it, and that's the reason you turned over so quick. I didn't mean it, either. I talked to Jason too, and he said it just happens."

"What?" Joe said. "You got hard and didn't feel me?"

"No," Omar answered. "I mean, yes, I got hard, but, no, I didn't feel you."

Joe, with notable relief said, "I didn't feel you. I just thought you felt me and were upset and had the wrong idea."

"Same here," Omar replied.

"You're not upset with me?" Joe asked.

"No!" Omar answered emphatically. "You're my very best friend. It's been painful to think you're pissed off at me and going to move when the lease is up."

"How could I think a thing like that?" Joe asked. "Not only are you the best friend I have but the best roommate I've ever had too. I wouldn't want to move anywhere unless you move with me."

Hesitating, Joe gradually moved towards the middle of the bed, not wanting to go too far.

"Now I know why Jason was so strong saying I need to talk to you," Omar said as he also moved towards the center. "He'd already talked to you, but wasn't going to tell me."

"Yes," Joe said, as he inched closer to the middle. "More and more I am seeing what a great guy he is."

"Yeah," Omar said, as he too inched to the middle.

They moved to the point of being able to put arms and hands on each other's shoulders, but were hesitant to go further.

After a few minutes of relaxed silence, touching each other, Omar said, "Habibi. You don't know how happy I am we talked like this. I'll be much more relaxed tomorrow when I have to meet so many people and lead the prayers, but suddenly I'm exhausted. I suppose relief from all of the built-up stress and tension."

"Me too," Joe replied. "I'll sleep much better now."

CHAPTER 15

Wednesday, April 9, 2008
Roanoke, Virginia, USA

Near the end of a long tiring day, Joe and Omar were eating a late supper at the Texas Tavern, a big hamburger for each, sharing a big basket of french fries, and drinking Pepsi-Colas, avoiding the famous hotdogs because they certainly had pork. The Texas Tavern has been a Roanoke institution for some forty years. Located right in the city center and open twenty-four/seven, its customers were top city officials, professionals from downtown offices, homeless, and everyone in between.

Texas Tavern, Downtown Roanoke, Virginia

"Munching, Omar asked, "How'd you find this place?"
"Guys at the office come here pretty often," Joe answered. "Marcus told me too."

"I've seen places like this in old movies," Omar said; "didn't know they existed any more."

"Me neither until I came here," Joe said. "Couldn't eat here often with all the grease, but hits the spot tonight."

"For sure," Omar concurred. "The lunch Nassar had at the Middle Eastern restaurant in Blacksburg was good, but that was a few hours ago."

"You were great again," Joe said. "You should really be proud of yourself; I'm sure Allah is too."

"Thanks," Omar said. "It was tricky, arranging things with different people and no one to help much except you."

"I'm sure that little mosque isn't used to having many Christians in it," Joe commented. "Dr. Imran tried to be gracious and hospitable, but seemed overwhelmed."

Al-Ihsan Masjid Mosque, Blacksburg, Virginia

"So was I," Omar said, "but I had to be calm."

Joe added, "Good to see Jordan Hicks again. He just received his acceptance for Virginia Tech. Did he tell you?"

"That's great," Omar replied. "I barely talked to him; too busy with Nassar and the family. It was great some of Marwan's soccer buddies and other friends came."

"The soccer trophy in memory of Marwan that he presented was nice," Joe said. "Little boys can handle and display it without worrying about damaging it. Say, did you play soccer when you were growing up?"

"Oh, yes," Omar answered. "Every Yemini boy would kick a football around at some point. Nothing organized like here; just out on a playground or some vacant space when hopefully some guy had a football. What about you?"

"Oh, yes, when I was young," Joe answered. "Later I got involved in school and not really into sports. Lebanese are football, soccer, nuts, especially back in Lebanon. Even here, especially among the older men, everything almost came to a stop during the last world cup.... How's Ms. Roula? You were going to see her."

"Not good," Omar answered, "or not any better. She's not opening up. Not having someone to speak Arabic isn't helping. We said some prayers. They have to do something soon. This hospital's not willing to keep her without payment, understandably. Virginia has state hospitals set up regionally. There could be a psychologist who speaks Arabic on call in Northern Virginia, but they try to keep patients close to home. It looks like they might transfer her to a state hospital near Roanoke and send an Arabic speaking psychologist down here, at least to see if there's progress."

Walking back to the hotel, Joe asked, "What time're you leaving tomorrow? You going to see Jason?"

"Not too early," Omar answered. "Let's say I leave about 10:00; that'll put me where Jason works about 2:00. Maybe he could take a coffee break."

"Why don't you come to the office with me tomorrow morning," Joe said. "It'd be good for you to meet the people I'm working with. We might talk about your testifying."

"Testify about what?" Omar asked.

"You're their imam, they're a good family, upstanding, asset to the community, etc." Joe replied. "In lots of similar trials, Christian clergy testify about what good Christians the persons are, and you could do the same for Muslims."

When they entered the hotel, Kent looked up and said, "Oh, hello, Mr. Shaito. Is this your friend?"

"Yes," Joe said. "This is Dr. Abu Deeb."

"Hello," Omar said.

"Are you enjoying Roanoke?" Kent asked.

"We've been in Blacksburg most of the day," Omar replied. "I haven't seen much of Roanoke yet."

"Oh, to Virginia Tech?" Kent continued.

Joe intervened, "No. We were at 40th day prayers for a person who died recently. Dr. Abu Deeb is an Islamic imam. He knows the family and led the prayers."

Kent, "Oh, you're an imam. But you're so...."

Omar smiled, "I know. I'm young. You expect an old man with bushy hair and a long beard. Sorry to disappoint. Good night."

Kent responded, "Good night, and enjoy your stay, Mr. Shaito and Mr., er, Dr. Abu Deeb."

CHAPTER 16

After lunch at the Academy Officer's Club with Pete Ramos, Frank and Colonel Granger went to a private room where Colonel Granger said, "We had you released on a Friday so you can have the weekend to adjust to regular life."

"Thanks," Frank replied, wearing a perfectly pressed uniform for the first time in over a month.

"We're eager for you to be back to work," Colonel Granger continued. "Sergeant Beasley retires soon; there's controversy over his replacement. Some want an old-line, drill-sergeant type, seeing you as weakened and needing a strong sergeant to keep you in line. We see you as a strong leader and want you there to take charge and stay in charge."

Frank replied, "Thank you, Sir."

"You're welcome," Colonel Granger replied. "Thanks aren't necessary, though. You have a good record, especially when faced with adverse circumstances not of your making. We can't condone that caper to drop would-be terrorists in Mexico, but no need to go into that now. It's people like you we want to have in responsible positions."

"Just doing my job, Sir," Frank replied.

Colonel Granger continued, "We've recommended you, Sergeant Beasley, and the three guys on duty that day for commendation medals. When they're approved, we'll have a ceremony. We're not sure, yet, if we want to notify the media. There's strong sentiment to make it public and publicize the fact that your vigilance averted a serious terror attack. The ceremony will be at the NSA, with the commander doing the honors. You might be interested to know Colonel Ross has been relieved of duties."

Frank beamed saying merely, "Thanks."

"Can you think of anything?" Colonel Granger asked.

"I'm eager to go to work and actually do something for a change," Frank replied. "I was hoping, now that I can get around normally, I'd go to Texas to visit Brad; he's lonely. Maybe I could go on a weekend."

Colonel Granger replied, "Let me see about that. We might be able to send you there to do something for us. We're still interested in him, even though he's not in the DoD. If he's able to communicate, which apparently he is, maybe you'll get information from him. Maybe you only want a social visit."

"With all due respect, Sir," Frank replied. "A social visit was what I had in mind. It might depend on what you want, and if he knows what you want and why. Let me think about it once I know what you might want."

"OK, fair enough," Colonel Granger answered.

"The way we communicate is by computer messenger," Frank added. "He still can't talk, but he's able to type and, I presume, write. I was going just to be with him in person, even if he can't talk."

"I see," Colonel Granger said. "Do you need a ride?"

Frank answered, "A friend's bringing my car from home later today. You could drop me at Pete's quarters."

Later in the day, Paco arrived in Frank's SUV. All enjoyed a sumptuous meal of Filipino food that Felicia prepared as Frank's farewell dinner. They exchanged warm goodbyes when Frank and Paco left.

CHAPTER 17

Tuesday, April 29, 2008
Roanoke, Virginia, USA

After greetings, Ashley Sue Hunter, Esq., federal public defender for the Western District of Virginia, handed a file to Richard Harris, saying, "Here's a case I'd like you to take."

He had a small private criminal defense practice and worked freelance as a criminal defense lawyer for public defenders, federal, state, and local. He was wearing a lawyer's "uniform" of a grey pinstripe suit from a good men's store, white shirt, solid dark burgundy red tie, black wing-tip shoes, and faux tortoise shell eyeglasses, all designed to reflect a twenty-six-year-old lawyer on his way up. Ashley Sue Hunter, an attractive woman in her early thirties, wore a beige professional woman's suit with a light blue blouse; her budget-professional clothes, shoes, and eyeglasses were carefully selected to reflect a professional appearance but not intimidate clients with upscale clothes.

He asked, "Why me? Not that I don't appreciate it."

"You're making good progress in your career," she replied. "This case'd give you a boost."

"Thanks for the flattery," he said smiling. "Cut the bullshit, Ashley Sue. You're a nice and fair person, but not totally altruistic; must be something else to it."

"You go right to the quick," she said, chuckling. "You're a good criminal defense attorney. There'd be no doubt you'll give them the best defense possible and no chance of appeal on grounds of inadequate defense from a public defender."

"You're suggesting they'll be found guilty?" he asked.

"Of course not!" she replied with mock indignation. "The public defender's office must consider all eventualities."

He thought, *It'd take a miracle to win this case, but could still be good for the reputation.* "Flattery again," he said. "Why not take this one yourself?"

"I wasn't flattering you," she replied. "You're among the best. You aren't shy, but not a publicity hound either. There's another big reason why I'm not taking the case; otherwise, I might consider it. If this case goes to trial and is heard before Judge Bishop, and I hope it will, she'd have to recuse herself. Not only would that not be good for publicity, but could be a crap shoot of whom we'd get for a judge."

"Oh, I see," Richard Harris replied. "I heard you and Judge Bishop are close."

"Her daughter Becky and I were very best friends growing up; I spent as much time at her house as my own," she explained. "When I wanted to study law, she was my mentor. We're not so close now, because it wouldn't be good for either of us to socialize a lot, but when Becks comes home, you better believe I'm over there."

"I see," he replied. "The couple of times I've been in front of her, she's been rough on attorneys."

"And fair too," she retorted. "The best chance we have to get these guys off is with her as judge, and you sure aren't shy in front of her. She respects you for that." She pulled her chair closer and said in a lower voice, "You've likely figured out it'd take a miracle to get these guys off. These aren't the type to receive miracles."

"That describes most of your clients," he said. "What's different about these?"

She replied, "It'll get media attention; that's what's different. We need to be seen by the media as giving a strong defense, protecting the legal rights of all accused. Some'll think it's a waste of taxpayer money to defend, in their view, worthless rednecks, but in judicial circles and the media it'll be seen positively. Besides, you're photogenic."

"OK, I get it," he said. "I need to think a day or maybe two, but I'll probably take the case. You know me well enough by now that I'm not going to leave you hanging. I noticed a prosecution witness speaks Arabic and the court needs to provide an interpreter; implies they may have an Arabic speaking lawyer."

"I suspect it might be the young Arab-American guy who was here on that first case you handled for us."

He replied, "The guy on the phony orientation tour. Don't we need an Arabic speaker too?" he asked.

"I'm looking into that," she replied as he stood to leave.

CHAPTER 18

Tuesday, April 29, 2008
Quantico, Virginia, USA

Rosie Jordan opened a task force meeting at the usual time with the same persons as before. "Welcome. Cranford has new information for us; then we'll go to others."

Cranford Brooks began, "Our focal point is who's behind the attempted NSA bombing, although there're lots of peripheral issues. The suspect still refuses to say anything; not even to his mother. The public defender suspects he's becoming depressed, even suicidal, and may be mentally incompetent to participate in his defense. There'll be a motion for a court-ordered psychological evaluation. That could delay the trial, maybe indefinitely, which is fine with us. The longer we have to investigate who's behind this, the better. He's been put on a suicide watch. His father's attorney kept showing up, purporting to represent him, but the suspect refused to talk to him. Officials threatened to report him to legal authorities for malpractice, and he hasn't come back.

"Interesting things happened with the suspect's mother and father. One day while she was working at the convenience store, a man speaking Arabic said he represented her husband and she'd better stop the divorce and stop making trouble. She immediately hit the button to call police. She engaged him in conversation in Arabic until the police arrived and she told them he'd threatened her. The police arrested him. He claimed he was working for her husband, not a robber. To cut the story short, he has a Jordanian passport with a tourist visa and is not allowed to work. Arlington police are holding him, but will turn him over to immigration authorities. We had to notify the Jordanian embassy. So far, the embassy hasn't done anything other than visit him in jail once; there's no indication the Jordanian government is protesting. This also works to our benefit, because we were able to get a court order to go into the so-called charity to look for hiring aliens illegally. In the process, we can maybe find out more."

Rhonda Philips, who in recognition of the season wore a cherry-blossom-pink dress and complementary pale cream jacket, interrupted. "It's to be expected the Jordanian government hasn't done more. It doesn't care much about its Palestinian citizens, although things changed with a Palestinian queen. The Jordanian government wouldn't condone working in the U.S. illegally and'll probably let him face our justice. They'd have to take him back if we deport him; I wouldn't be surprised if they found reasons to prosecute him too. Larry, what do you think?"

Larry Briscoe said, "You're right on, Rhonda."

Cranford Brooks continued. "Mrs. Salameh thought someone tried to get into the house. She received letters from her husband saying he'd come take everything because it was his property and would evict her. She even thought she heard noises one night, so we arranged an off-duty Arlington policewoman to stay overnight with her.

"One night Mrs. Salameh and the policewoman heard someone trying to get in and called police. Saeed Salameh and an assistant were caught trying to break into the house and were arrested. Saeed Salameh protested loudly it was his house, but was booked and put in jail. The next day his attorney got him and the assistant out on bail granted by a lenient judge who was easily convinced Saeed Salameh was misguided and just trying to exercise what he thought was his right to enter what he believed to be his own property. The charges still stand because there's a restraining order on his entering the property until the divorce is settled, but there'll likely be a plea bargain. One good thing is he was required to surrender his U.S. passport and Palestinian travel documents.

"This doesn't get us closer to finding out who's behind the attempted bombing at the NSA. We know it can be traced to a mosque in Arlington. Until we can get inside or someone starts talking, we've hit a dead end."

Rhonda Philips interrupted. "The media might work to our advantage if we go public. Maybe a good investigative reporter can get information. I'm not close enough to the situation to offer specifics, but the thought occurred to me."

"Thanks again, Rhonda," Cranford Brooks replied. "That's worth considering."

Rosie Jordan interjected, "Maybe we need someone from the Attorney General's office to join us. I'll look into that. Larry, we haven't heard from you."

Larry Briscoe began, "Reports from Gaza confirm your suspicions. It'd be difficult to use evidence from our sources in a U.S. courtroom, but I'm not a lawyer. I agree we should have someone from the AG here.

"Our sources in Palestine confirm bombing inside the U.S. is definitely not a Hamas modus operandi; this so-called charity and the father of the suspect are very likely not involved. It doesn't sound like al Qaeda either, although there're those in al Qaeda who'd like to put the NSA out of business, especially the Arabic language section. Al Qaeda's doing increasingly desperate things, but still our analysts don't see this as one of their operations. As I mentioned, maybe it's one of the splinter groups. There're plenty.

"I'll get back to you when I know more. If you learn more about that imam, let me know. The tentative name you gave is a Palestinian name. A Palestinian imam in a Saudi mosque is interesting. So far all we've done is run the name through our databases here. We can try to get more from our sources in the region. There are Palestinians in many countries, so it takes a bit of effort. Any questions?"

Rosie Jordan turned to Colonel Granger, saying, "Otis?"

He began, "Not much over and above what's been said. We have commendation medals approved for Major Reynolds, Sergeant Beasley, and the three guards on duty. The only other thing I can add is former Air Force Colonel Edward Ross's officer's commission was removed and he was given the rank of Senior Airman, the lowest enlisted rank that can be assigned when an officer's commission is revoked. There was sentiment for having him face a court martial and receive a dishonorable discharge. Colonel, er, Airman Ross would likely have fought it legally with publicity. Some would've liked the publicity, but we deferred to your judgment that it's best to avoid it until we've resolved issues. Instead it appears he'll be given a general discharge and not allowed to retire. Any questions?"

Rosie Jordan then said, "Thanks to all of you for coming. We'll be in touch about any further meetings."

CHAPTER 19

Sunday, May 4, 2008
Sulaymaniyah, Iraq

D r. Ali Salman listlessly sipped tea at his desk when a medical assistant entered, saying in Kurdish-accented Arabic, "Dr. Ali, you should see a prisoner with bad facial injuries."

Dr. Ali, as he was called, was associate director of the plastic surgery clinic of the Burn & Plastic Surgery Hospital. A sign with his name and title in English, Kurdish, and Arabic read he was associate medical director of the Viktor Ilarionov Memorial Clinic, a name created and recognized only by him as a tribute to his beloved Viktor. A wall plaque in Kurdish, Arabic, and English read that funding was provided by the U.S. Agency for International Development.

Burn & Plastic Surgery Emergency Hospital,
Sulaymaniyah, Kurdistan, Iraq

His nondescript black pants, light blue shirt, and black shoes had come from the nearby bazaar; a clean white smock was on top. His longish, dark red-brown hair with a small moustache and goatee completed his appearance.

Because most war causalities had facial injuries, it was natural that Dr. Ali, a cosmetic surgeon, would be associate director of the plastic surgery clinic, with a local doctor nominally in charge. It was also a convenient place to keep him under the watchful eyes of the Kurdish government, which ruled the autonomous region of northern Iraq, and the CIA, which provided resources. Treating civilians not only provided favorable public relations, but also provided cover for other activities not known to the general public, such as treating combatants from both sides to glean intelligence information. The location in the second city and cultural capital of Kurdish Iraq provided security and a calm atmosphere.

After preparing the examination room, Dr. Ali returned to sip tea and read the *New England Journal of Medicine*.

Having few friends, he reflected on yet another boring weekend. Being from the minority Alawite religious sect of the ruling family of Syria, and with the name 'Ali' used mostly by Alawites and the dominant Shia of southern Iraq, he was viewed suspiciously by predominantly Sunni Kurds. He spoke only a smattering of Kurdish.

He also reflected on his contradictory feelings about working for the CIA. He was grateful to the intelligence services of the U.S. for being alive. Cooperation with the DIA allowed him to be released from prison in Baghdad. The DIA transferred his case to the CIA and arranged an eventual transfer to the clinic in Sulaymaniyah. He was grateful to be able to practice medicine, even if under the CIA.

The assistant escorted a disheveled young man in shabby hospital pajamas, his face and head covered with bandages; Dr. Ali, offering his hand to shake, said in Arabic, "*Marhaba*, I'm Dr. Ali."

The patient gave a halfhearted feeble handshake and mumbled something unintelligible.

Inside the examining room, Dr. Ali said in Arabic, "I didn't catch your name; can you please tell me again?"

The patient blurted out, "Marwan."

"I'll remove your bandages so I can examine you," Dr. Ali continued in Arabic. "This might hurt; I'll be gentle."

Gee, he's treating me nice, the patient thought in English. *He seems to be Arab.* "Ouch!" he screamed.

"Sorry." Dr. Ali then spoke in Arabic, "These bandages weren't applied carefully. I'll get something to soften the scabs."

Dr. Ali looked in a cabinet, thinking in English: *He used an English word, "ouch." Something strange about him.*

The patient thought in English, *He's being nice, and he used the English word "sorry." Is he setting me up? Who gives a shit? They're going to kill me.*

Dr. Ali applied light oil through the gauze, saying in Arabic, "Let's leave them while I examine you. Open your mouth, please." He went through the routine of an examination, thinking in English, *I can get a urine sample, penile swab, and blood test later if I do surgery.* "Your overall health seems OK, good enough for surgery. Let's look at those wounds, if we can get the bandages off."

Surgery! The patient thought in English. *They're going to kill me and harvest my organs.*

After removing bandages, Dr. Ali examined the patient's wounds and then said in Arabic, "Marwan, your face can be restored, but it'll need a few surgeries, with time to heal in between. We can fix the wounds on your shoulders and arms so scars won't be too obvious; for most people, areas normally covered by clothes aren't as important as the face."

What the hell! the patient thought in English. *Restore my face? If they're going to kill me, why do that?*

"I'm not busy today," Dr. Ali continued in Arabic. "We can begin preparations today and start surgery when I can get qualified assistants. How does that sound to you?"

He sounds legitimate, the patient thought in English. He replied in Arabic, "Why do you want to do surgery on my face? They're going to kill me, if not here, then later."

"Why do they want to kill you?" Dr. Ali asked in Arabic, thinking in English: *He speaks with an accent like mine.*

"Don't you know?" the patient blurted out in Arabic. "I'm not one of them. They don't trust me. They would've killed me earlier, except Iranians wouldn't let them. Are you playing some kind of game?"

Dr. Ali, not really surprised, considering all he had heard and seen in this clinic, said in Arabic, "Your accent isn't Iraqi nor the accent the Kurds have when they speak Arabic. Who are you really, and where are you from?"

The patient sat in stoic silence until Dr. Ali spoke again in Arabic, "We're in a doctor-patient relationship. I'm ethically bound not to repeat anything you tell me in confidence. I see you don't trust me, and I can understand that. You don't have to tell me anything except what I need to know to be able to treat you properly. Your accent sounds Levantine. Is that where you're from?"

The patient answered in Arabic, "You mean Lebanese? No, I'm Palestinian, but from the camps in Lebanon."

"Oh, that explains it," Dr. Ali replied in Arabic. He thought in English, *There's something fishy here. If he were genuinely Levantine, he'd know the meaning of the word. He speaks simple Arabic like Brahim and Boudi, who learned it at home with no education in Arabic.*

The patient asked in Arabic, "Where are you from?"

Dr. Ali answered in Arabic, "From Syria."

"So why're you here?" the patient continued in Arabic.

Dr. Ali replied in Arabic, "Things are not good for cosmetic surgeons in Syria. I found this clinic that genuinely helps people to give them back their nice faces. Do you need to bring anything from the other place? We'll keep you here, so I can tend to you as you heal."

He wanted to add that the patient wouldn't have to worry about someone killing him, but thought the better of it.

The patient stammered in Arabic, "No."

"OK," Dr. Ali said in Arabic. "I'll put fresh bandages on, more carefully this time. I'll fix it so you can take a bath, if not a full shower. Maybe get you regular clothes at the bazaar; it's right out the door. In the meantime, you might be able to wear some of mine. They might not fit well, but at least you can get out of those pajamas."

CHAPTER 20

Sunday, May 4, 2008
Laurel, Maryland, USA

On a warm, sunny, spring afternoon, Omar parked in front of Frank's townhouse, where Joe said to Frank, who was standing at the doorway, "Come see Omar's new car; Paco too."

Frank exclaimed, "Wow, this's in perfect condition."

"Yeah," Omar replied. "He restores and resells classic European cars, and he's good at it."

"Bet it's fun to drive too," Paco said.

"For sure," Omar agreed enthusiastically. "I'll gladly give you a ride and let you drive."

Frank asked, "He gave it to you for saying prayers?"

"No!" Omar answered. "We don't receive gifts for things in our role as imams. I've been doing lots of other things for him and his family. He's in the automobile business and offered me a car. That's what Arabs do: offer something in their line of work. I thought it overly generous, but to refuse would be an unimaginable insult."

Jason drove up in Brad's candy-apple red Mini Cooper and got out, carrying two bags of food for the meal they were preparing for Joe and Omar in appreciation. He wore his signature faded plaid Bermuda shorts, a well-washed VCU t-shirt, and white athletic shoes. As soon as the food was put in the kitchen, hugs and three Arab kisses were exchanged.

Frank and Paco brought drinks and asked, "How hungry are you two? Paco's going to start the fire and grill the meat when we're ready to eat."

Joe and Omar looked at each other and Joe said, "I had kind of a late breakfast. Whenever you want's fine with me."

"Same here," Omar added.

Joe asked Frank, "How is it to be back at work?"

Frank answered smiling, "They think I'm a hero; troops showing lots of respect. The sergeant's even more deferential. If they've figured out I was injured in the gay bar bombing, they're not letting on or don't care. They're awarding commendation medals to me, the sergeant, and the three guards on duty."

"Probably don't care," Joe said. "It's pretty clear to us at the AG that being gay's not a big deal anymore. Congratulations on the medals."

"Congratulations!" Omar said.

"Things going well in Roanoke?" Jason asked.

Joe answered, "Good. We have a strong case, but have to be on our toes. The public defender has good lawyers."

"Please fill me in, if you can, what this's about," Frank asked. "I only heard indirectly about some defamation case."

"Not exactly defamation," Joe began. "It's a hate crime and involves the same family that gave Omar the car."

He explained the situation and Paco said, "That's a crime big enough to get the federal government involved?"

"Yes, a hate crime because it's denying civil rights solely because of their ethnic background," Joe stated.

"Gee, people shouted bad things at us because we're Mexicans all the time, and no one treated it as a crime," Paco stated. "But, then, no one tried to bomb our house."

"Likely because no one was upset enough or didn't know enough to report it to the FBI," Joe replied. "Also denying civil rights involves more than just calling names. Even so, the Hammouds likely wouldn't have reported this as a federal hate crime on their own."

"Who reported it?" Paco asked.

Joe answered, "I did," and explained further.

"Good for you," Paco exclaimed. "Nothing like that happened to us Mexicans."

"Nothing like that happened to us Arabs in Dearborn, either," Joe replied. "Now that I know the law and can report it, something might happen. This might be the first case of violence towards Arabs going to trial in the U.S. and get media attention."

"You'll be a TV star, like those lawyers in the O.J. Simpson trial, way back when I was a kid," Jason said.

"Yeah, sure," Joe said, chuckling. "I'm not the lead attorney and not likely to get much media attention, but if it happens, for sure I'm not going to be playing to the cameras like the lawyers on that case. I was a kid too, but we heard enough about it in law school."

"You're getting ahead of me," Frank said. "You said local guys bombed their house because they're Arabs. How did they know they're Arab in the first place?"

Joe explained details of the defendants' past interaction with Nassar and his garage.

When Paco and Frank heard Joe say "gas station on the interstate," they looked at each other and Frank said, "Where? What kind of station?"

Joe replied, "It's on I-81 in a rural area, no towns around, but if it means anything to you, it's the Ironto exit, the first exit past Christiansburg on the way to Roanoke. It used to be Texaco, but now Shell."

Frank said, "We may have stopped there when we were driving back from Alabama. If this's the place, we saw guys driving away without paying. I remember it because the young kid working there was upset because his father'd be really angry. I can identify with an angry father, so I gave the kid money so he wouldn't get in trouble. Paco got on my case, saying I shouldn't have been so quick to help."

Paco added, "I was talking with the kid when the guys drove off; Frank was in the restroom. If it's who we think it is, they said 'A-rabs' didn't belong; that's how they pronounced 'Arab.' I'm pretty sure they'd bullied him, maybe sexually abused him."

Joe asked, "Do you have any proof you were there?"

"I used my credit card to pay for the gas," Frank replied. "I should be able to find receipts."

He went upstairs, and Joe asked Paco, "How can you be sure the kid was bullied or sexually abused? This might be the Hammouds' older son who's missing."

"Let's just say that I've been there," Paco answered, "before I grew to my current size, that is. Not too many messed with me after I became a teenager and had a big growth spurt. I remember hearing them saying 'fuckin' A-rabs' and something about reaming his ass again."

"This could help our case if we can prove you were there," Joe replied. "You two'd have to testify, and the defense would certainly try to discredit you in every way possible, but I'm getting ahead of myself."

Frank returned with a piece of paper saying, "Here. Hammoud Motors, Elliston, Virginia, November 27, 2006."

"Sounds like the place," Joe said. "Paco says you heard the defendants making comments about fuckin' A-rabs."

"Yes, thinking back and remembering," Frank replied.

"This could really add to our case," Joe said. "I just told Paco you'd have to go testify, and be prepared for the defense to try to destroy you."

"Plenty of people have tried to destroy me before," Frank stated with a smirk. "I can handle this one."

"I'm not shy, either," Paco said.

"When'll this trial be?" Frank asked.

"The arraignment's tomorrow," Joe said. "I don't need to be there for that. Then the judge'll schedule jury selection dates and proceed right into the trial. Don't know how long that'll take, but I suspect we'll begin in a couple of weeks."

"Hope it's after school's out," Paco answered. "Today's my last day of fun. Then hitting the books for finals. I should start the charcoal now."

Omar turned to Frank. "You went to Texas last weekend; how's Brad?"

"Yes, I took him his laptop," Frank began. "I got a military flight; lots of flights to San Antonio with all the bases there. I was eager to see him before I got involved in work again. He couldn't talk, but with body language and written notes; I also got some information the DIA wanted. I got a rental car and took Brad to see some of the sights. San Antonio's a nice place. You should all go sometime."

"Oh, he's able to get up and go out?" Omar asked.

"Everything but his lip's OK now," Frank continued. "He's scheduled to have surgery this week."

Paco came in, said the charcoal was ready, and asked how they liked their steaks cooked.

CHAPTER 21

Monday, May 12, 2008
Sulaymaniyah, Iraq

Dr. Ali sat at his desk, more bored than usual. After finishing one medical journal, he decided to go to his living quarters to find another one, passing through the sitting room where the patient was watching television from a shabby easy chair, thoroughly engrossed in an English-language automobile show on BBC World. Dr. Ali watched quietly for a moment and then shuffled his feet and coughed to announce his presence.

The patient jumped up, startled, as Dr. Ali said in English, "Sorry to disturb you. I see you know English."

After a longish moment, the patient replied in Arabic, "Oh, I just like cars, so I found this channel to watch."

"What program is this?" Dr. Ali continued in English. "It sounds British. What is it about cars you're into?"

The patient stammered in simple Arabic, "I used to work on cars, repairing them."

"Cut the bullshit, Marwan, or whatever your name is," Dr. Ali said in English. "It's obvious you know English. In addition, you speak Arabic like someone who learned it at home. Who are you?"

The patient stammered in English, "Er, Ahmed. Marwan's my brother. Yes, I learned Arabic at home. We *are* Palestinian, and I do work on cars."

Dr. Ali said, "From now on we're speaking English. I learned cosmetic surgery in English, and it's much more effective to treat you if we speak English, which is obviously your native language."

"OK," Ahmed replied and asked, "Where'd you learn English, if you're from Syria? You talk like an American."

"I went to elementary school and part of middle school in the U.S.," he explained, "then I continued at the International School in Damascus, which was mostly American. And you? Your accent is definitely American."

"I watched a lot of television," Ahmed answered.

"All American kids watch television a lot," Dr. Ali replied. "You don't have to tell me. This doesn't affect my ability to treat you. Just don't bullshit me."

Ahmed was silent a moment then said, "OK. I grew up in Virginia, but I don't want to tell you more."

"That's fine," Dr. Ali replied, "just so long as you're truthful when I need to know medical things."

He walked into his living quarters, got the journal he was looking for, and returned to it without further comment.

CHAPTER 22

Joe, James Edward Goodwin, and Randy Walker were discussing the trial that would begin in less than an hour; James Edward commented, "It looks like we got a good jury. We eliminated the woman with the Jewish-sounding name with a peremptory challenge and could've used more."

James Edward Goodwin, the lead trial attorney, was in his mid-twenties, graduated about two years ago from Washington and Lee Law School in nearby Lexington, was average height and build with brown hair and eyes, all reflecting ancestry from the original colonists who settled Virginia.

Joe said, "It'd be useful to know the background of the Arabic-speaking attorney the defense has. I'll ask Roger."

"His name is Yuhana Khalil," Randy Walker said.

"An Arab Christian name," Joe commented. "He might be a refugee from Iraq. Lots of Christians have been forced to leave Arab countries, and some resettled here."

"How come it's Christian?" James Edward asked.

"Yuhana can be translated as 'John' or 'Jonathan,'" Joe replied. "It's from the Christian bible. Muslims wouldn't use that name. Khalil is generally a Christian family name."

"Like John the Baptist, the apostle John, and Jonathan, the best friend of David," James Edward suggested.

"I suppose," Joe said. "We need to be careful not to underestimate him just because he's an immigrant."

"Don't underestimate Rich Harris, either," James Edward added.

"You two are as good as they come," Randy Walker said. "I'm not worried, but we all know strong cases were lost by complacent prosecutors, not won by outstanding defense."

"Will the public defender be there?" Joe asked. "Her name isn't on the list of defense attorneys."

"I wouldn't expect her to be there except as a spectator," Randy Walker answered. "She likely wants to avoid a conflict of interest or, more likely, not put Martha in a position where she has to recuse herself."

Joe asked, "Why'd there be a conflict of interest?"

Randy Walker explained, "Roanoke's a small city, and we in legal circles know about each other." He then explained the connection between Judge Bishop and Ashley Sue Hunter. "If Martha were to preside over a case that Ashley Sue were defending, almost any prosecutor, definitely me, would file an appeal if we lost, claiming conflict of interest and judicial misconduct. Martha knows that and wouldn't allow herself to be in that position. Martha's the most ethical judge around."

"Gee, these are things that we up in the headquarters don't think about too much," Joe said.

"Martha's a pistol for sure," Randy Walker replied. "That's why we often want her to preside over cases when we're strongest on the case being tried on its merits."

"Doesn't this interfere with the public defender's ability to do her job if she has to avoid appearing in front of one of the judges in this district?" Joe asked.

"Not really," Randy Walker said. "Ashley Sue's not much of a trial lawyer. She's a damned good attorney, don't get me wrong. But she'd likely be the first to tell you courtroom trial is not her strength. Public defense down here in the 'backwaters' works best with someone who has a good legal mind and ability to manage. She can hire good trial lawyers on a contract basis, like Rich Harris.

"Let's review our strategy one last time. I'll be sitting at the prosecuting table with you, although you two'll take the lead. The jury expects the lead prosecutor to be there and make the opening and final remarks."

They reviewed legal strategy one last time, packed briefcases, put on suit coats, and walked the short distance to the Poff Federal Building where courtrooms are located.

CHAPTER 23

Wednesday, May 21, 2008
Roanoke, Virginia, USA

At 10:00 a.m. sharp, court was called to order in a Federal Courtroom of the Poff Federal Building for the case of *U.S. vs. Bates, Bates, and Barns*. Judge Martha Bishop, in her fifties, entered wearing a black robe covering her slightly robust figure. Randy Walker, James Edward, and Joe sat confidently at the prosecutors table. Kyle Bates, Kody Bates, and Keith Barnes sat at the defense table, Rich Harris and Yuhana Khalil separating them. They had freshly trimmed hair and were clean shaven. They also had new, clean clothes with long-sleeved shirts covering their many tattoos.

Nassar, Abou Nidal, and other witnesses sat near the front of the courtroom, which had more spectators than usual. In a far corner, Ashley Sue Hunter was observing. Marcus Porter, dressed in a jacket and tie, sat near the front with a tape recorder and note pad. Others from the media had notepads, pads of artist paper, and colored chalk.

Randy Walker gave opening remarks for the prosecution, saying that Congress passed hate crime legislation so persons of all ethnic and national backgrounds in the U.S. could have the right to live without fear of losing their life and property. He explained the defendants were being tried for hate crimes of denying the Hammouds' civil rights by setting off a bomb because they were

Arab. He depicted them as refugees successfully living a productive life, contributing to the community for over twenty-five years.

Rich Harris gave opening remarks for the defense with good oratorical skills, telling the jury the defendants were on trial for denying civil rights, not bombing a house. He emphasized it was the duty of the prosecution to prove intent to commit a crime, not just a prank. He also subtly mentioned provisions against double jeopardy, in which persons cannot be tried twice for the same crime, emphasizing the prosecution must prove a separate crime.

James Edward began by calling Darrell Williams, dressed in a summer uniform, who was established as a deputy sheriff in Montgomery County. He led the deputy through events of the night of February 29 and then had him identify the person he apprehended at the Hammoud's house. James Edward continued, "Have you seen the three defendants before?"

"Unfortunately, many times," Deputy Williams said.

Rich Harris stood and stated, "Object, Your Honor. The defendants are not on trial for many times, but this one time."

James Edward immediately responded, "Counselor knows it's permissible to use past similar criminal activity in a trial, but I'll withdraw the question and ask another. "Deputy Williams, when did you see the other two defendants next, after you left the Hammouds' residence with the person you just identified as the one you apprehended?"

"Almost immediately," Deputy Williams answered. "Another deputy responded to my radio bulletin to look for their car and stopped them right after they turned onto old Highway 460 from Lafayette. I was there within minutes. We took all three to the jail and booked them."

James Edward then asked how well he knew Nassar. He replied that Nassar Hammoud's gasoline station was a frequent stop for coffee and restroom breaks, that Nassar was sometimes there, and they sometimes exchanged a few words.

Rich Harris, on cross examination, first tried to establish the deputy was friendly with Nassar and not objective. Deputy Williams stated Nassar was only occasionally in the station because he worked in the garage most of the time, so no strong acquaintance developed.

Rich Harris then asked, "Do you know what kind of a crime these three men are charged with?"

Deputy Williams replied, "Both you and the prosecutor said it's a federal hate crime, denying civil rights."

"Do you know the difference between a so-called hate crime and arson?" Rich Harris continued quickly.

"I'm no lawyer," Deputy Williams said, "but yes."

"Nothing in your testimony indicates intent to deny civil rights." Rich Harris continued, "It indicates just a prank."

"I wouldn't say bombing a house is a prank," Deputy Williams answered. "Damaging their house and settin' it on fire sure seems like denying some kind of important right."

"Did you hear the defendants say any words or give any other sign or signal they were denying rights of the victims because of who they are?" Rich Harris asked.

Deputy Williams replied, "I don't recall anything."

"So you didn't observe a federal crime that these men are being tried for," Rich Harris stated assertively.

"Object, Your Honor," James Edward said as he stood up. "The witness is being asked to give a conclusion that he admits he is not qualified to make."

"Sustained," Judge Bishop said matter-of-factly.

"Let's review your testimony about seeing two of the defendants within moments after leaving the Hammoud's house," Rich Harris continued. "How can you be sure it's the same two persons who were at the Hammoud's residence? Did you actually see them there?"

"No, I didn't see them there, but I saw their car," Deputy Williams answered.

"Just answer the question without offering other information," Rich Harris stated. "If you didn't see them, how can you be sure?"

"As I just said," Deputy Williams answered, "I saw their car stopped just a few moments later. They were in the custody of the other deputy when I got there."

"How do you know it was the same car?" he asked.

"I saw it drive away from the house just as I arrived," Deputy Williams answered.

"Did you have positive identification?" Rich Harris continued asking. "It was dark. Did you see license plates?"

"No, but they were the same license plates Mr. Roberts saw and gave me the number," Deputy Williams answered.

"You did not actually see the license plates yourself, is that right?" Rich Harris continued.

"No." Deputy Williams answered. "I did not see them myself until I saw the car the other deputy had stopped."

"You can't be sure it's the same two persons who were in the car at the Hammoud's house," Rich Harris stated.

"No, that's not right," Deputy Williams answered forcefully. "Unless they're some kind of magicians, there's no way they could've changed cars and some others got in."

"You cannot place these two defendants in that car at that moment in front of the Hammoud house, is that right?" Rich Harris stated.

James Edward stood and said, "Objection, Your Honor. Counselor is harassing and badgering the witness by asking the same questions repeatedly in different forms."

"Your Honor," Richard Harris responded, "the witness has contradicted himself. I'm merely asking him to clarify."

Judge Bishop said, "I will allow the question this time. I am warning you, counselor, you are extremely close to the edge of what's allowable."

Rich Harris repeated the question, and Deputy Williams answered "No."

"No further questions," Rich Harris said smugly.

James Edward called Nassar Hammoud. After being sworn in using a Koran from the public library, Nassar was asked to describe his background, emphasizing fleeing Lebanon as a Palestinian refugee, being resettled, building a good life for himself and his family, and emphasizing how he thought they had fit into the community. Then he led Nassar through events of the night of February 29.

In cross examination, Rich Harris said, "You knew the defendants before the night of February 29, didn't you?"

When Nassar answered "Yes," Rich Harris continued, "Under what circumstances did you know them?" Nassar, guided by Rich Harris, described towing the car and its being driven away when Ahmed was there.

"Their anger was justified," Rich Harris asserted.

Nassar replied, "I don't see they were justified. I towed the car because the state police told me to, and I'm entitled to be paid. I'm also entitled to be paid for my repair work."

"You can understand why they might be angry with you, can't you?" he asked aggressively.

James Edward immediately leaped to his feet and said, "Objection, Your Honor. This calls for a conclusion of the witness. The witness is not qualified to know how they felt."

"Sustained," Judge Bishop said.

"What did you hear any of the defendants say the night of February 29?" Richard asked.

Nassar answered, "I didn't hear them say anything."

"No further questions," Rich Harris said smugly.

"Your Honor," James Edward said, "Our next witness would like to be questioned in Arabic. We notified you and the court replied the Arabic interpreter will be available this afternoon. If you would like, we can call another witness."

Judge Bishop said, "The court will recess for lunch and reconvene at promptly one o'clock."

Soon the prosecution team gathered in their conference room, eating sandwiches quietly, when Joe finally spoke. "You're awfully quiet, James Edward."

James Edward replied, "Just going over how Rich got the upper hand and scored points. Thinking about what we need to do now."

"Don't be so pessimistic," Randy Walker said. "We have an idea of his strategy: just a prank, no intent, already been punished. He knows he can't use double jeopardy, but he can plant ideas in the jury's mind."

Randy Walker handed a sheet of paper to Joe, saying, "Here's the background on the Arabic interpreter."

Joe commented, "Originally from Maine. Studied undergrad in Vermont. Just before the first Gulf War he was studying and doing research at Mosul University in Iraq. Later continued his research in Kuwait. Got a doctorate in Arabic language, literature, and culture from the University of North Carolina–Chapel Hill in 1998. A professor at Washington and Lee University. Sounds qualified."

They finished eating quickly and returned to court.

CHAPTER 24

Thursday, May 22, 2008
Roanoke, Virginia, USA

When court was called to order again, Judge Bishop introduced Dr. Ames Hanford as the Arabic interpreter and told the prosecution to resume its case.

Joe called Jamal al Khatib who was sworn in with the Koran and said in Arabic, "You're usually called by another name. What is it?"

After the question was repeated in English, he answered in Arabic, "People call me Abou Nidal."

After interpretation, Joe asked in Arabic, "Why are you called that?"

After interpretation, he answered in Arabic, "Nidal is my son. In our culture, a man takes his oldest son's name."

Before Ames Hanford could interpret, Yuhana Khalil stood saying in English, "Object Your Honor. Arab customs of names are interesting, but not relevant here."

Judge Bishop, startled, thought, *He obviously knows I haven't heard the answer in English. Bet he's trying to show the jury he really does understand Arabic.* She looked at him and said, "Counselor, you have not shown the courtesy of allowing the court to hear the English interpretation. If you resume your seat, you may give your objection after we know what the defendant has answered."

Yuhana Khalil, with mock contrition, sat while Ames Hanford interpreted. Then he stood again and repeated his objection.

Joe said, "Your Honor, this is an important line of enquiry to establish the witness's character."

Judge Bishop said, "Overruled. You can continue now, but you must get on with the case, not go off on tangents."

Joe then asked in Arabic, "Where is your son now?"

After interpretations, Abou Nidal replied in Arabic, "Nidal stayed in Lebanon to be with his mother, my dear wife, who had to stay with her mother, who was sick."

Yuhana Khalil waited impatiently for interpretations and then stood to say in English, "Object, Your Honor. The witness's family situation years ago, no matter how sad, is not relevant for this case. The defense stipulates the witness had emotionally difficult family experiences, that his character is adequate, and does not need to be established."

"Your Honor," Joe responded, "it's important to establish the witness's background in order to be able to understand the context in which his testimony is given."

Judge Bishop said, "Objection sustained. Counselor, get on with your case."

Damn! Joe thought. *Now I can't build sympathy with the jury. This guy's sharp.*

Hey, this guy seems good, Ashley Sue Hunter thought, *We just thought he'd do the Arabic work.*

This guy seems good, Randy Walker thought. *If anyone can match him, Joe can.*

This guy seems good, Rich Harris thought. *We figured he'd just do Arabic things. Maybe I'll get him to do more.*

Shit! James Edward thought. *We might've underestimated this guy. Joe warned us. I just thought he had a mail-order degree and speaks Arabic.*

Joe asked in Arabic, "Abou Nidal, where do you live?"

After interpretation, he replied in Arabic, "You mean in the house with Nassar, Mrs. Roula, and Miss Fatima?"

After interpretation, Joe said, "Yes that's what I meant." He then led Abou Nidal, slowly because of interpretation, through events of the night of February 29, concluding with Abou Nidal's saying he heard shouting of "fuckin' A-rabs, you bomb us, we bomb you," the final words in clear English.

Joe paused for dramatic effect, then said in English, "No further questions, Your Honor," which was interpreted.

Yuhana Khalil began in Arabic. "Mr. al Khatib, we're using an Arabic language interpreter because of you. That means you don't speak English, does it not?"

When the question was interpreted, Abou Nidal replied in Arabic, "I understand English and speak a little. Here in court, I want to be sure I understand and can answer good."

After interpreting the response, Yuhana Khalil forcefully said in Arabic, "How can you say what you heard the defendants say if you don't understand English?"

Abou Nidal waited for interpretation and answered firmly in Arabic, "I didn't say I don't understand English, especially the 'dirty' words. I've been in this country twenty-five years, working in a gasoline station and garage. I understood clearly what they said."

After interpretation, Yuhana Khalil said Arabic, "You said you helped the family out of the house. Is that right?"

After interpretation, Abou Nidal merely answered "Yes" in Arabic, which was interpreted.

Then Yuhana Khalil asked in Arabic, "How can you be sure what you heard? You were distracted helping others?"

After interpretation, Abou Nidal answered in Arabic, "My hearing is good; the ones I helped didn't make noise."

Then after interpretation, Yuhana Khalil asked in Arabic, "Have you seen the defendants before?"

After interpretation, Abou Nidal answered in Arabic, "They come to the station sometimes to buy gas; they have to pay before they can pump. Sometimes they steal candy."

When that was interpreted, Yuhana Khalil asked in Arabic, "Do you talk to them?"

Abou Nidal answered in Arabic, "All they say to me is how much gas, but to each other, loud enough for me to hear, 'Fuckin' A-rabs.'"

After interpretation, Yuhana Khalil said in Arabic, "You must call the police when they steal. They'd be upset and have a reason for calling you names, wouldn't they?"

Joe was halfway out of his chair to object following the interpretation, but before he could say anything, Abou Nidal replied in Arabic, "No, I don't call the police. It isn't worth it for just a candy bar."

Then, after interpretation, Yuhana Khalil asked, "What is your immigration status?"

After interpretation, Abou Nidal answered in Arabic, "Immigration status? What do you mean?"

When interpreted, Yuhana Khalil said forcefully in Arabic, "You don't know your immigration status? You must be here illegally."

Joe stood waiting during the interpretation and then said in English, "Object, Your Honor. Counselor is harassing the witness and making unwarranted accusations."

Yuhana Khalil replied, "I'm establishing the credibility of the witness. If he can't remember his immigration status, how can he remember what he heard?"

Judge Bishop looked at Yuhana Khalil sternly and said, "Objection sustained! Counselor, you must know better than to make a comment like that in this courtroom. If it happens again, I'll hold you in contempt of court!"

Ashley Sue Hunter thought, *I need to brief him about Martha, but that was good. Sows doubt with the jury.*

Yuhana Khalil, with mock contrition, meekly said, "No further questions, Your Honor."

Randy Walker hastily passed a note to James Edward, reading: 'Calling DC to get going on immigration status' and hastily walked out the door.

504

Judge Bishop looked at Joe and said, "Your witness."

Joe thought, *Let him rest. We can recall him later.* He said, "Your Honor, we reserve the right to call this witness later. We have no further questions at this time."

Judge Bishop thought, *He's a good lawyer. The witness is agitated and tired. It's been a long tiresome afternoon.* She glanced at the clock and said, "The court will convene tomorrow morning at 9 o'clock."

When the prosecution team gathered in the conference room, Randy Walker said, "I just talked to Roger. He'll get documentation of Mr. al Khatib's immigration status and send it to us, probably tomorrow. We can recall him then."

"Ok, good," Joe replied. "I'm sure we could get something from Abou Nidal himself, too. He was just too nervous. I suspect Nassar takes care of things for him."

James Edward said, "That guy Yuhana 'something' is good. We sure underestimated him with an online degree from the sticks of West Virginia."

"I didn't underestimate him," Joe retorted. "Immigrants are often very bright and work below their ability because opportunities are closed. I grew up in an immigrant community; I know. I admit I let my guard down and he struck some good points, but I didn't underestimate him."

James Edward added, "Between him and Rich, we're going to struggle to win this case."

"Don't be so pessimistic," Randy Walker interjected. "He's on the verge of losing the jury. Joe's developing sympathy even though he got cut off. That was a brilliant move to let him go and recall later. But, yes, he's sharp. He knows when to move quickly and go right for the jugular. He's going to end up getting Martha and the jury pissed off if he keeps up those antics. It's been a long, tiring day. We can meet at 8:30 in the morning and go over tomorrow's plans."

CHAPTER 25

Friday, May 23, 2008
Sulaymaniyah, Iraq

When *Top Gear*, a popular automotive show on BBC World, ended, Ahmed sat lethargically as a news anchor said, "We now go to the United States, where judicial history was made. For the first time, persons are being tried for hate crimes against Arabs in U.S. federal courts. Also, for the first time, the Arabic language was used by prosecution and defense to both question a witness and receive testimony. We go to Jennifer Jackson in Roanoke, Virginia."

He became alert as the screen showed a photograph of a young woman on the left side and a map with an outline of Virginia and a star at the location of Roanoke on the right.

"Judicial history was made in the United States today here in Roanoke, a small city in the Appalachian Mountain region of Virginia," an American-accented voice said. "Three men are being tried for a hate crime, denying civil rights of long-time Palestinian immigrants by bombing their house. This is the first time hate crimes against Arabs have been tried in a U.S. federal court...."

He leaped to his feet to see drawings of three men; she continued, "... Nassar Hammoud has lived in the United States over twenty years. He, his wife, young daughter, and an older cousin escaped after a bomb was set off. Fortunately, there was no serious damage. The defendants allegedly shouted they bombed the house because they were Arabs...."

He felt cold sweat as his knees became weak, holding onto the chair, while she continued, "... Judicial history was made a second way when both prosecution and defense interrogated the cousin using the Arabic language and the witness responded in Arabic. This is the first time lawyers on both sides asked questions in Arabic while an interpreter interpreted for the judge and jury. Jennifer Jackson for BBC World News in Roanoke, Virginia."

Ahmed rushed into Dr. Ali's office shouting, "Dr. Ali, Dr. Ali, you've got to help me!"

Dr. Ali, startled, said, "Calm down; what's going on?"

"My parents' house was bombed," Ahmed blurted out. "I just saw it on TV. Three guys being tried. I know them. I've got to go tell them, help my family."

"On television?" Dr. Ali asked. "Why would this be on television here in Iraq?"

Ahmed continued, "On BBC. Something about judicial history in the U.S. Couldn't focus when I saw it's my family."

Dr. Ali asked, "What do you think I can do for you?"

He looked Dr. Ali in the eye and said, "I'm not very smart; pretty stupid at times, but not so dumb I can't figure out this isn't an ordinary clinic. You're involved with the U.S. You've got to help me. You're the only one I can turn to."

Dr. Ali said, "News items are repeated. Let's look so I can see for myself. Let's see CNN. It's from the U.S."

After a sailing show, a woman with an Australian accent said, "Welcome to *CNN World Report*. We first go to the United States for breaking news in which the U.S. government announced at the close of business yesterday, Eastern U.S. time, that on the first of March a person was arrested entering the National Security Agency carrying explosives. We go to Lateesha Wilcox in Baltimore."

She appeared on the half of the screen while a photograph of Wissam Salameh, seemingly from a high-school yearbook, appeared on the other half. "CNN has learned more about the terror suspect who was apprehended in March attempting to enter the National Security Agency at nearby Fort Meade, Maryland, with explosives. He was identified as Wissam Salameh, a native-born U.S. citizen of Palestinian descent residing in Arlington, Virginia...."

Ahmed turned pale, reached for a chair as his knees buckled, saying, "Shit! They got Wissam."

"... He has been held since March 1st, pending investigations and medical examinations," she continued, while Dr. Ali asked, "What? This doesn't sound like anything about your parents. You're involved in this?"

"... The defendant's attorney, the public defender, issued a statement he concurred with keeping events secret until now so he could prepare his case and the accused could have medical and psychological evaluations," she said.

Ahmed whimpered, "Something different."

"... It seems authorities picked the end of the work day just before the long Memorial Day holiday weekend to minimize public attention, ..." she continued as Dr. Ali said, "You said you need my help to get you to the U.S. to help your parents because their house was bombed and there's some kind of trial. Now you're involved with terrorists. What game are you playing?"

"... In a related event," she continued, "the U.S. Department of Defense yesterday awarded commendation medals to the U.S. Marine Corps guards who apprehended the accused terrorist...."

Ahmed broke into tears, saying, "Not playing games. This doesn't involve my parents; I still need to help them."

"... Corporals Tyler Adams, Michael Kleinberg, and Daniel Morales, along with their superiors First Sergeant Walter Beasley and Major Frank Reynolds, were awarded medals in a public ceremony at the National Security Agency for their diligence in having increased security and being alert to apprehend the accused...," the commentary continued, showing them in full dress uniforms.

Dr. Ali thought, *That's Frank!*

"… CNN will bring you more on this breaking news as it's known. Lateesha Wilcox, CNN, Baltimore."

"We now go to Baghdad, where suicide bombers…," the news anchor continued while Dr. Ali said, "If you're not playing games, what're you doing? You say your parents' house was bombed and you need to help them. Then you panic when a terrorist is arrested."

"But I did see it on television," Ahmed stammered through sobs. "This is something else. You have to help me, Dr. Ali. My life's ruined for sure, but at least I can help my parents. I know this guy who was arrested. In a way I helped him, but we're not terrorists."

"What are you?" Dr. Ali asked, "but don't tell me. I'm not ethically bound to confidentially about terrorism."

"I'll tell anything," Ahmed continued anguished, "so long as it gets me to my parents. My life's fucked, but at least I can help them."

"In Northwest Pakistan…," the news continued while Ahmed, choking away sobs, said, "The guys who bombed my parents' house; I know them. They messed me up bad."

During an advertisement for a bank in Nigeria, Ahmed continued, "This guy Wissam I know too. Me and my brother were in a group with him at the mosque."

"Wait a minute," Dr. Ali interrupted. "I can't make any sense of what you're telling me, but I'm not sure I want to."

The news anchor returned and began, "We return to the United States for another of our top stories. Judicial history was made in the United States today in two ways: For the first time a hate crime against Arabs in the United States is being tried in a federal courtroom. Second, in that trial, the Arabic language is being used both by a witness giving testimony and also by lawyers for both sides. We go now to Cynthia Albritton in Roanoke, Virginia."

509

A young reporter on the steps of the Poff Federal Building said, "History was made today here in the mountain and valley city of Roanoke as a hate crime is being prosecuted for acts against Arabs in the United States...."

The screen switched to an artist's sketch of the three defendants. Ahmed showed hatred, pain, and anguish.

"Three men are charged with denying the civil rights of an Arab family who have lived over twenty years in the small community of Lafayette in neighboring Montgomery County, by setting off a bomb at their house...," she continued.

The screen switched to a picture of the Hammoud family house, causing Ahmed to scream, "That's my house!"

"... The defendants were heard shouting they bombed the house of Arabs because Arabs bombed the United States," she continued. "The case is tried as a federal hate crime because it is directed against persons of a specific ethnic background...."

The screen showed a gasoline station as she continued more details about the nature of the crime and the family.

Ahmed began crying again as she continued, "History was made a second way when the Arabic language was used in the courtroom by attorneys both for the prosecution and defense to question a witness who answered in Arabic...."

The screen showed artists' drawings of Joe and Yuhana Khalil while the commentator explained their backgrounds.

The screen then switched to a drawing of Abou Nidal, causing Ahmed to shout through tears, "That's Abou Nidal!"

"Who's Abou Nidal?" Dr. Ali asked.

"My uncle," he said. "Not really, but we call him that."

Meanwhile, the commentator mentioned Abou Nidal's relationship to the family and showed an artist's drawing of Ames Hanford, explaining his role.

Dr. Ali thought, *What do I do now? I can't push him away, but there's no way I want to be involved in terrorism.*

"… CNN will bring you news as the trial progresses. Cynthia Albritton, CNN news, Roanoke, Virginia." The news anchor continued, "In France, President Sarkozy.…"

Dr. Ali said, "I see you're not playing games about your parents. Still, I don't see the connection with that terrorist, and I don't want to know. Why do you want to go back now so urgently, if you could get in trouble? What can you do for your parents in this trial that's so important?"

Ahmed, sobbing as the television was heard in the background, mumbled, "[inaudible] me anyway."

Dr. Ali reduced the volume, asking, "What'd you say?"

Ahmed stood and almost screamed, "I don't give a shit. They're going to get me anyway. Might as well go this way. After what those guys did to me, I don't have anything to live for, but I have to go to my parents and help them."

"They did something bad to you too?" Dr. Ali asked.

Ahmed blurted out, "They ruined me as a man."

"What!?" Dr. Ali exclaimed. "How'd they do that?"

Ahmed replied hesitatingly, "They, er, forced me."

Dr. Ali asked, "How does that ruin you as a man?" then shuddered, realizing what had happened and his own rape.

"They did things the Q'ran says men shouldn't do with other men," Ahmed said. "They might've made me gay."

"Why would that make you gay?" Dr. Ali asked.

"They must be gay to do that and, er, it went inside of me," Ahmed continued.

Dr. Ali said, "That doesn't make you gay! Doesn't mean they're gay. This is an act of violence, not a sex act, and getting it in you, as you say, doesn't make a person gay."

Ahmed, barely lucid, asked, "Are you sure?"

Dr. Ali, replied, "Yes! It doesn't happen that way!" *Should I tell him?* Then he said, "I was raped too; got it in me. No details, but I know what I'm talking about."

Ahmed looked at Dr. Ali, asking, "You're not gay?"

"That didn't make me gay!" Dr. Ali replied.

"The Holy Q'ran that says if one man does things with another he can't go to heaven," Ahmed continued.

"I'm not Muslim; I'm Alawite, if that means anything to you," Dr. Ali replied. "Besides, I'm not religious, so I don't know what the Q'ran says. I can't imagine that any God would condemn a person for something that he did not do deliberately, something that someone else did by force.

"Oh, OK, maybe," Ahmed mumbled.

Dr. Ali asked, "How do you want to help?"

"Tell what they did to me," Ahmed replied.

Doubt that'd help, Dr. Ali thought. *His word against theirs, but he seems desperate.*

"Let them know I'm alive," Ahmed continued. "Tell them I'm sorry I ran away."

Dr. Ali put his hand on Ahmed's shoulder and said, "I'm not sure what, if anything, I can do for you, but I'm still your doctor. You've had a big emotional shock. Let's give you a physical exam just to make sure everything's OK."

Dr. Ali examined Ahmed's upper torso and checked his reflexes through his jeans, and then said, "Everything's fine. Your heart rate and blood pressure are elevated, understandably. It's lunchtime."

A guard escorted Ahmed to the dining hall while Dr. Ali went by himself, pointedly avoiding being with Ahmed.

CHAPTER 26

When the prosecution team gathered before court convened, James Edward exclaimed, "Hey, we made national news!"

Randy Walker smiled and said, "It wasn't just national. I had calls from BBC and al Jazeera too."

"Really?" Joe asked. "I was at the Hammouds' last night, talking to Abou Nidal. Of course I had to stay for dinner. We didn't watch TV. What about?"

"First time a hate crime against Arabs has been tried in a federal court," James Edward replied. "Also first time Arabic was used to both interrogate and answer and by both the prosecution and defense. There were artist drawings of you and Yuhana Khalil. Your friend Marcus must've orchestrated this."

"I wouldn't say he's my friend," Joe said. "We got to know each other after Marwan Hammoud's burial and 40th day prayers and a couple of times after that. He's being friendly to get good stories, but I'm using him too, to get background for this case. He's been professional in every respect, as well as a nice guy. We agreed without actually speaking we'd not get together while the trial's going on."

"Next thing you know, he'll get in front of the camera," James Edward said, laughing.

"Have to lose his West Virginia accent," Joe chuckled.

Randy Walker interrupted, "The interpreter can't be here today; he'd made plans for the long holiday weekend. We have to wait until Tuesday to recall Mr. al Khatib. The other Montgomery County Sheriff's deputy we want to call isn't available today, either. He'd made holiday plans too. We could've subpoenaed him, but no need to irritate local law enforcement people. Let's review who else we have to testify today." He went through the list, then said, "That shouldn't take all day. Maybe Martha'll want to dismiss early because of the holiday." After discussion of the witnesses and strategy for the day, he said, "Time to go."

When court was called to order, James Edward called Shane Roberts, who wore a suit and tie he would wear to church and was sworn with a bible. Velma left the courtroom.

James Edward guided his testimony through establishing their relationship with the Hammoud family and events of the night of February 29, concluding, "Can you tell us which defendant you caught at the Hammouds' house."

Shane answered, "Th' one at the end on my left."

James Edward then led him through the next events that night, and Shane concluded, "... that's when I heard the guys in the car shouting."

"What did you hear?" James Edward asked.

Shane replied forcefully, "I want all y' t' know I don't like t' use language like this in public, but it's important so I'll say it." He paused and stated, "One of 'em in the car said, 'Serves you right, you fuckin' A-rab assholes. You bomb us, we bomb you back.'" He gulped, paused, then continued, "Th' other one said: 'Yeah, you mother-fuckin' A-rabs, there's more of this if you don't get outta here. We don't want no fuckin' A-rabs 'round here.'"

James Edward continued, leading him through the rest of the events, and sat as Rich Harris stood to begin. "Mr. Roberts, you identified one of the defendants as the one you captured. How can you be sure? You testified it was dark."

"Weren't that dark," he answered. "There was lights from th' windows and a street light. Besides, I saw him bein' put in th' sheriff's car, and the car light was on."

"How can you be so sure?" Rich Harris asked. "Any light there was dim."

James Edward leaped to his feet saying, "Object, Your Honor. Counselor is harassing the witness. The witness has already testified he saw the accused close enough to identify him. Counselor is accusing the witness of perjury."

"Your Honor, this is a crucial point because the witness identified one of the accused in the light of the courtroom based on what he saw in the dark," Rich Harris stated.

"Objection sustained," Judge Bishop stated, silently wondering, *How much more can I let him get by with? He's doing what he can for a strong defense; can't fault him for that.*

Rich Harris then asked, "You testified you heard words shouted from the car saying 'the other one.' Is that correct?"

Shane answered, "Suppose so. Don't remember the exact words I said."

"We can ask the court recorder to read back your testimony," Rich Harris stated.

"I ain't arguin' with ya," Shane said. "Just don't remember the exact words, but was somethin' close to that."

James Edward stood and said, "Object Your Honor. Counselor is harassing the witness. The prosecution has no objection to the court reporter reading back the testimony."

"Sustained," Judge Bishop said. Looking at Rich Harris she said, "One more time and I'll hold you in contempt of court. The court recorder will read the testimony."

The court reporter, a middle-aged woman who gave the appearance of being "prim and proper," repeated very matter-of-factly and neutrally what had been said.

Rich Harris then asked, "When you say 'the other one,' that implies there were only two persons in the car. How can you be sure there were only two persons in the car?"

"Don't imply no such thing," Shane answered tersely. "Means I only heard two. There was only two sittin' in the car when I went to get the license plate number."

"So there could have been more persons in the car?" Rich Harris continued aggressively.

"S'pose so, if some'n's hidin' in the back seat," he replied and quickly added, "or in the trunk."

"The court reporter read very specific words you claim you heard," Rich Harris stated. "How can you be sure those were the exact words spoken by the persons in the car?"

"I wrote 'em down soon as I could," Shane answered.

"How long until you wrote it?" Rich Harris asked.

"'Bout ten or fifteen minutes," Shane answered.

"So you can't be sure, can you?" Rich Harris stated.

James Edward stood but before he could object, Rich Harris said, "I withdraw the question. No further questions."

Joe's face lit up with a sudden inspiration and quickly passed a note reading, "Let me question him."

James Edward, perplexed, looked to Randy Walker, to whom the note was quickly passed, and who nodded.

Joe stood and said, "Your Honor, the prosecution would like to ask more questions of this witness." *He seems pretty bright and to catch on quickly*, Joe thought. *I hope he'll understand where I'm leading him.* He said, "Mr. Roberts, you testified to what you heard the defendants say from their car, and the court reporter read it back. It's very important to know exactly how certain words were pronounced. Could you please repeat for the court how words were pronounced indicating the ethnic group, the type of people, to whom the persons shouting were referring?"

Shane sat a moment, confused, then suddenly said, "Oh, y' mean that they's Arabs."

"Yes," Joe confirmed. "Is that how the persons shouting pronounced the word?"

"Nope," Shane answered. "They said 'A-rabs'."

"If I may, I would like you to confirm that," Joe continued. "That's a long 'a' like in 'say' or 'bay,' then 'rabs.' Is that correct? Can you please repeat it to be sure?"

Rich Harris jumped to his feet saying, "Objection, Your Honor. Counselor is leading the witness, telling him what to say. The witness has already answered the question."

Joe responded, "Your Honor, I'm merely asking him to confirm what he and the court reporter have said. This will be an important point as we develop our case."

Develop our case? James Edward thought. *We haven't talked about this.*

"Objection overruled," Judge Bishop said.

"That's right," Shane Roberts confirmed. "A-rabs."

"That will be all, thank you," Joe said.

Shane stepped down as Joe whispered to James Edward, "Tell you later; may be onto something."

When Shane sat down, James Edward said, "The prosecution calls Mrs. Velma Roberts. She's waiting outside the courtroom, if you'd like someone to get her."

Judge Bishop looked at the clock and said, "It's time for a short recess. Court will resume in twenty minutes. You can ask Ms. Roberts to be in the courtroom then."

Joe spoke softly to his colleagues. "We need to subpoena Ames Hanford to testify when he's here. Calling an Arab 'A-rab' is a big insult. It's about like calling a black person the 'n' word. Ames Hanford will surely verify that. It's a risk, but not much downside."

"A few local people call them 'A-rabs'," Randy Walker said. "The defense reminded the jury we need to prove intent. This might not be intent, but just the normal way of speaking."

James Edward added, "Calling a black person 'nigger' would never be acceptable even if it were the normal way of speaking. Maybe we can get that across. Let's go for it."

Randy Walker replied, "OK. As you said, there's little downside risk. Let's stretch our legs and tell her to come in."

CHAPTER 27

After she was sworn in, James Edward said, "Mrs. Roberts, please tell us if you are related to anyone in the courtroom."

She replied, "That's my husband, Shane, over there."

"You were waiting outside the courtroom before we called you," he continued. "Is that right?"

"Yes, that's right," she answered.

"Why was that?" he asked.

"'Cause you said it'd be best if I didn't hear what Shane had to say," Velma answered.

"What else were you told?" he asked.

"I have th' right to stay in th' courtroom if I want," she replied. "Proceedin's of the court're open to the public, and no one can keep me from bein' inside here if I want."

"You testify under oath you remained outside the courtroom voluntarily, not because you were required to do so," James Edward stated. "Is that correct?"

"Yes, that's correct," Velma affirmed.

James Edward led her through events of the night of February 29. She testified Shane told her to write down what she heard and James Edward asked her to read what she wrote.

Velma unfolded a sheet of paper and said, looking at the jury, "I want all of ya t' know that I don't never use this kind of language.

Wrote it down and am readin' it to you 'cause I know I got to and it's important, but makes me sick to my stomach." She then stated the same set of words as Shane's.

"Thank you, Mrs. Roberts; that must be difficult for you," James Edward continued. "If you will, it's important to know exactly how they pronounced the word used to describe the ethnic group to which they were referring. Can you please repeat exactly how they pronounced the word?"

Velma paused, not completely understanding, then said, "You mean them bein' Arabs."

"James Edward said, "Yes. How was it pronounced?"

She replied, "They said 'A-rabs.'"

James Edward led her through other events that night and then said he had no further questions.

Rich Harris began, "Mrs. Roberts, you identified under oath that a defendant was led handcuffed to the sheriff's car. How can you be sure which one? It was dark and you were some distance away."

"Weren't that dark," she said. "My eyesight's plenty good. Besides, I'm good at rememberin' people; gotta be, working in a bank."

"Mrs. Roberts," he continued, "you were in the courtroom yesterday with your husband. Didn't your husband tell you which one was being led to the patrol car? Remember you're under oath."

Velma stiffened angrily as James Edward leaped to his feet saying, "Object, Your Honor. Counselor's harassing the witness and accusing her of perjury."

Judge Bishop said forcefully, "Sustained."

Rich Harris said, "Let me rephrase that. Did you discuss the identity of the defendants with anyone?"

Velma, still tense, answered forcefully, "No I did not. Shane and me has more important things to discuss."

He then said, "You testified you heard words shouted from a car. How can you be sure they were spoken by the defendants here?"

"I can't be," she answered. "I never testified they was the ones who spoke those words, just that I heard 'em."

Rich Harris, taken aback at Velma's directness, said, "You testified the way a certain word was pronounced. Wouldn't you say that's the normal way lots of people in this area pronounce that word?"

She answered tersely, "No, I wouldn't say it's normal. Prob'bly some would, but that don't make it right."

"Why do you say it's not right if plenty of people pronounce things that way?" he said.

Velma, bristling, answered, "Just 'cause lots of people calls us rednecks don't make it right. It's rude to call someone somethin' th' ain't, even if it's bad pronouncin'. Arabs is fine people, 't least ones we know. Wouldn't be respectful to call them that other word."

He continued, "Mrs. Roberts, do you usually do what your husband tells you to do?"

"Pretty much," Velma answered quickly then hastily added, "But..."

Rich Harris interrupted forcefully, "Just answer the question, which you have. You testified your husband told you what to write down so you did what he told you to do."

James Edward jumped to his feet but before he could say anything, Velma bristling with anger replied, "I most certainly did not testify to that!"

James Edward forcefully stated, "Object, Your Honor. Counselor is harassing the witness and implying perjury. We can request the recorder read back her testimony."

Judge Bishop said forcefully, "Sustained."

Damn, Judge Bishop thought, *He's goading me into declaring him in contempt of court and maybe get sympathy from one or two jurors. Well I'm not going to give him the satisfaction.*

Joe hastily wrote a note: "Let me question her."

"No further questions," Rich Harris said and sat down.

Joe stood and said, "The prosecution has additional questions for this witness. Mrs. Roberts, would you please clarify for the record what your husband told you the night of February 29 about writing down words you heard."

Velma answered, "Shane asked me if I heard what they shouted from the car. I said, 'Yes, ever word.' He then told me to go write down the words I heard; might be important."

Joe then said, "Your Honor, we'd like the court recorder to read back the testimony Mrs. Roberts gave on this point."

Judge Bishop asked the court recorder to read back the testimony, which she did in a monotone voice.

"Mrs. Roberts," Joe said, "just to clarify and be sure the court understands, did your husband, or anyone, at that point in time, or any time, tell you what words to write down?"

"No, never!" Velma answered emphatically.

Joe then asked, "Defense counsel asked if you do what your husband tells you to do. You answered that you pretty much do. Is that correct? We can have the court recorder read the testimony, but I'd like to hear it from you, if that's OK."

Velma replied, "Yes, that's correct."

"Then you were going to add something else," Joe continued. "What was that?"

"I was goin' to say that Shane pretty much does what I say, too," she answered.

He then asked, "Would you please explain a bit more. You say you do what he tells you to and then you say he does what you say. How can it be both ways?"

Velma, annoyed, answered, "Shane and me has a good relation. We trusts each other. If he sees or knows somethin' I don't, he tells me what to do and I do it 'cause I trusts him. Likewise, if I sees or knows somethin' he don't, then I tells him and he does it."

"Thank you, Mrs. Roberts," Joe said. "That's all."

Rich Harris half stood and said, "No further questions."

When Velma had stepped down, Joe said, "The prosecution would like to recall Mr. Shane Roberts." When he was in the witness stand, Joe asked, "Mr. Roberts, you're still under oath. Did you hear your wife's testimony a moment ago describing your relationship?"

"Yes I did," Shane answered.

"Would you please describe in your own words the relationship between you and your wife," Joe requested.

Hope he understands what I'm doing, Joe thought. *Velma seemed a little pissed off.*

"Velma and me gets along fine," Shane answered.

"Would you say, then, you don't have disagreements?" Joe continued to ask.

"Velma 'n' me has our disagreements," Shane answered. "S'pose all married couples do, but w' always talks 'em out."

Joe asked, "Your wife testified she does what you say and you do what she says. Do you agree?"

He said, "Yes, 'cept it's us'ly me doin' what she says."

Joe continued, "What exactly did you tell your wife to do about writing down the words shouted from the car?"

"I told her to go write down what she heard while she could remember it; might be important," Shane said.

"Did you at that time, or at any time, discuss with her words she should write down or did write down?" Joe asked.

"No, definitely not," Shane answered emphatically. "I don't never use language like that with Velma and wouldn't on this occasion neither."

"Thank you, no further questions," Joe said.

Rich Harris half stood and said, "No further questions."

James Edward stood and said, "Your Honor, our next witness says he can be available with fifteen to twenty minutes' notice. He would also be willing to come Tuesday. Two other witnesses requested they be postponed until Tuesday because of the holiday. As you know, we have one witness scheduled for Tuesday when the Arabic interpreter will be here."

Judge Bishop thought a moment and said, "Court's adjourned until Tuesday at 9 a.m."

Later, Randy Walker, James Edward, and Joe were in the Hotel Roanoke, treating themselves to a leisurely nice lunch. After placing orders, James Edward said to Joe, "That was a brilliant move to jump in and start interrogating Velma and then her husband."

Joe smiled and said, "Thanks. It was just a hunch. I've been with them in their home and have an idea how they get along. I also figured they're pretty bright people, even if they don't have much education and speak with poor grammar. Plenty of people in Dearborn misjudge Lebanese immigrants for the same reason. I thought I'd take a risk." Sensing James Edward's jealousy, he added, "You were great setting it up. You were brilliant in getting the court reporter to read back those words; let the jury hear them repeated a few times to stick in their mind. I wouldn't have thought of that."

"I'm surprised Rich let himself get in a trap like that," James Edward added, a bit mollified. "He's sharp and usually doesn't fall for things like that."

Randy Walker smiled and said, "You were both great. Don't underestimate Rich Harris. He might sound a little desperate, but remember all he has to do is get one juror on his side. I don't think he's falling into any trap. What're you guys doing this weekend? You going back to DC, Joe? You going to your folks, James Edward?"

"No, everyone I know there is either going away or busy," Joe replied. "A friend from up there's coming to meet me for dinner tonight; he's on his way to Martinsville to do the family thing for the holidays. Since we're through early, I'll try to find a mosque that has Friday prayers early. Other than that, I'll just hang out here. There's a lot of this part of Virginia I haven't seen. Maybe I'll go to Blacksburg and see more of Virginia Tech."

I'm staying here with my girlfriend," James Edward answered. "Hope we can go to Smith Mountain Lake. We'd planned to go with Rich like we often do on weekends; his folks have a place there. Since we ended up on opposite sides of this trial, we decided we'd better forget going to the lake together. My girlfriend thinks she's found a place; she has some relatives with a place there." To Joe, "Hey, why don't you come up tomorrow or Sunday, if we can work out something? I'll have to call you to confirm, but it'd be great to have you. My girlfriend can maybe find a girl for you if we go out dancing or something."

Joe, recalling days in Ann Arbor when he was included in social things, smiled and said, "Sure. Sounds great."

They continued to exchange small talk over their leisurely lunch and then parted company.

CHAPTER 28

Friday, May 23, 2008
Roanoke, Virginia, USA

Joe lay watching the evening news; a reporter was discussing the softening housing market, thinking, *Guess we're old news now.* The reporter concluded, "… Aaron Golightly, *ABC News*, Las Vegas." Another reporter began, "Now for a story we're following about the trial for an alleged hate crime against Arabs, we go to Roanoke, Virginia."

"Action in the courtroom today focused on testimony of next door neighbors of the alleged victims," she began, as a split screen showed artist drawings of Shane and Velma Roberts. "Both husband and wife testified they heard the defendants shout: 'Expletive A-rabs, you bomb us, we bomb you,' followed by another phrase using the term 'A-rab' that can't be repeated on television. Prosecution attorneys asked questions focusing on the pronunciation of 'A-rab' versus 'Arab,' suggesting a strategy of linking mispronunciation of 'Arab' to the hate crime. Testimony ended early because of the holiday and will continue on Tuesday. Ginger Hicks, *ABC News*, Roanoke, Virginia."

When the news changed to other topics, Joe flipped through a newspaper, heard a knock, and leaped off the bed.

He had a big smile as Jason entered wearing his trademark plaid shorts and polo shirt and gave him a big bear hug, saying, "Hey, Mr. TV celebrity!"

Joe, expecting a discreet Arab hug with three kisses, squeezed him in return and said, "You've seen the news."

"Yeah," Jason said. "Those artist's drawings don't do you justice. I should paint one of you. Tell me more over dinner; I'm hungry. Nice room! I've heard about the Hotel Roanoke, but never saw it from the inside. Too rich for my blood, and I'd have no reason to stay overnight in Roanoke."

Joe replied, "Not a place I'd normally stay either. The government gets a special rate to put all its people here."

"Maybe I'll bring Brad down here for a weekend if things continue to work out between us," Jason added.

"You still sound uncertain," Joe commented. "How is he? Still in the hospital?"

"No," Jason answered. "He left the hospital after the surgery. Bandages should be removed next week. He's in New Mexico now."

"New Mexico?" Joe said. "Thought he was in Texas."

Jason replied. "Let's go and I'll tell you while we eat."

"Where do you want to go?" Joe asked. "I know this great greasy spoon chili and hamburger place."

"Oh, you mean the Texas Tavern," Jason said. "That's a Roanoke institution for ages, and everyone from anywhere around here knows about it. It's good, but I was thinking more about Macado's. That's pretty much of an institution too, more upscale, quiet and relaxing, and gay friendly too."

"I've been there a couple of times with guys from the office," Joe replied. "One in Blacksburg, too. Didn't know it's a gay place. Guys at the office aren't gay."

"It's not a gay place," Jason stated, "only that gay people can go there and feel comfortable and not be harassed. Most people wouldn't know the difference and don't care."

During the short walk across the railroad tracks to the Market Square area in shirtsleeves because of the pleasant night, Joe described events in the courtroom, asking Jason about the local pronunciation of "Arab."

"Older people or some really country rednecks might say 'A-rab,'" Jason replied. "These days most'd say 'Arab.'"

"Would persons pronouncing it 'A-rab' mean it to be offensive?" Joe continued to ask. "More important, would other local people, not Arabs, view it as offensive?"

Jason said, "I'd say the person pronouncing it would have to know the correct way and then do it wrong in order for it to be offensive. Some rednecks wouldn't know the right way or care. As for others, they'd think the person was crude and ignorant, but probably not deliberately offensive."

Joe said, "I hope the defense doesn't get a hold of you. Oh well, it was a longshot."

In Macado's while waiting to give their orders, Jason said, "Those two guys over there are probably gay."

"I wouldn't've noticed," Joe said.

"That's my point," Jason said. "Most wouldn't."

After their orders were taken, Joe asked, "What's this about Brad going to New Mexico?"

Jason began, "After hopefully the last surgery, they wanted to free the bed space; he didn't need to be hospitalized, just go somewhere to get the dressings changed and attention if something happened. They looked for a nursing home, but of course Marian, Mrs. Spencer, wanted him home in Minneapolis. They said it's too far from a military hospital where he could go in an emergency."

Joe said. "Sounds like her."

"To cut the story short, they arranged for him to stay with his sister in New Mexico," Jason explained. "There's a big Air Force base with a hospital there. There's a really big Army hospital in El Paso, little over an hour's drive."

"She talked about her daughter in New Mexico," Joe said. "Sounds like it worked out well for Brad."

"Er, no," Jason replied. "It was a real disruption, having Brad there with the children. They were used to him before he was injured and freaked out seeing him all bandaged, having to eat through a straw, and not being able to talk. Brad and his sister get along well and could've coped, but the children were getting on Brad's nerves. The thought of going to a nursing home with sick old people wasn't appealing either. In the end he went to a condo in a resort town up in the mountains, about an hour away. They didn't tell the military people; Brad just drives down to the Air Force hospital. He uses one of their cars, which's awkward for his sister and brother in law."

"Sounds like it's working out, then," Joe said.

"Pretty much," Jason said. "He has to go out in town to buy things with his bandages and can't talk, so it's awkward. He's weak after being in a hospital bed for so long and not being able to eat properly, but he's getting there."

"Thought you might've gone there this long weekend," Joe said, "but guess you have family obligations."

"Family obligations aren't that big for Memorial Day," Jason stated. "Can hardly wait to see him, but only when we can talk and he's fit enough. Soon as those bandages are off, I'm out there."

Joe was about to hesitate about dessert when Jason asked for a menu again, saying, "I haven't had a decent dessert in months. Since Brad's not cooking, I'm losing weight and can't afford to do that."

Joe said, "I thought you look skinnier. I might be gaining, eating out all the time, but can't let you eat alone."

Both ate dessert. Then Jason said, "Say, you're not doing anything tonight, are you? Let's go dancing."

"Dancing?" Joe said surprised.

"Yeah, dancing," Jason replied enthusiastically. "You've been dancing before. You're not a total nerd."

"Yeah, in Ann Arbor," Joe said. "Where'd we go?"

"There's a gay bar downtown here called The Park," Jason answered. "Friends told me it's pretty good."

"Oh, a gay bar," Joe said hesitatingly. "I don't know about that. What if someone sees me there?"

"If someone recognizes you, they're probably just as concerned about being seen as you are," Jason continued. "Besides, you're not that well known yet. I'll stay overnight and go home in the morning."

Joe thought, *He's knows there's only one bed in my room. With all we've gone through with different people sharing beds, I guess he thinks it's OK. Yeah, it'd be good to get out and let off some pressure; I haven't been out dancing or partying since I moved to DC, but to a gay bar?*

Jason said, "Come on. It'll do us both good. I haven't been dancing, or doing anything physical for that matter, since February. You're stressed too. I can see it in your face. That place may be close, and we can walk. I'll go ask."

Before Joe could say anything, Jason asked the greeter, thinking, *I'd better get us there soon before he changes his mind. I don't want to go alone; I'd probably be hit on all night. I just want to dance and move!* He returned and said, "It's just a couple of blocks from here on Salem Avenue, right on the way to the hotel. Let's go."

They were seated drinking beer for Jason and cranberry juice for Joe with a few young men and women at other tables; Jason commented, "See, this isn't just for gays."

Soon a young man in his early twenties dressed in clean blue jeans, a clean polo shirt with an alligator on the breast, and basic white athletic shoes, approached and said with a big smile, "Hello, Mr. Shaito, or should I say Yusef?"

"It's Joe; everyone calls me that," he replied instinctively. Suddenly recognizing him, he said, "Er, Kent."

"You really are getting good publicity with your trial," Kent said, "you along with the other lawyers. Don't worry, I know how to be discreet about who I see in here, especially hotel guests. You have a new friend with you."

Jason stood, put his left hand on Kent's shoulder, shook hands with his right hand, and said, grinning, "Jason. We gay boys have straight friends too, don't we? Joe's just keeping me company while I pass through town. My boyfriend's in New Mexico, and I need to get out and move. He gives me permission to go out with Joe, knowing I'll be safe." He pulled Joe out of the chair, saying, "Let's go dance." To Kent, winking, "Find us and dance with us."

The Park, Roanoke, Virginia

Over the next couple of hours, Joe and Jason danced, mostly with each other, but also with Kent and some of Kent's friends. After a while, Kent made a point of saying goodbye to Jason and Joe, exchanging a warm but not overly close hug with Jason. He then hugged Joe, who responded awkwardly as Kent said with a smile, "See you in the hotel, straight boy."

Back in the hotel room, Jason quickly stripped to his boxers and went into the bathroom. Joe stood uncomfortably in only his briefs and rushed into the bathroom when Jason came out. When Joe came out, Jason was in the bed on the far side. Joe climbed into bed and turned out the light.

Jason, moved closer to the middle, laid his hand on Joe's back and said, "Thanks for going with me and letting me stay overnight. I was about to explode with all the pent up energy."

Joe said, "You're welcome. Thanks for dragging me along, even if I was reluctant."

Both went quickly to sleep.

Saturday, May 24, 2008

When each realized the other was awake, they looked at each other and said, "Good morning."

Jason said, "You go shower first; I'm the interloper."

Joe replied, "Nah, you go ahead. I can shower after you leave. I suppose you need to get on your way pretty quick."

"Yeah," Jason answered, "but not that quick. We can go get breakfast. I'll treat because you let me stay over."

He went into the bathroom while Joe dressed. Soon he came out of the bathroom with wet stringy long hair, naked, looking to find clean clothes.

Gee, again, Joe thought. *I guess I'll never get used to this lack of modesty. Are all gay guys that way?*

As they rode the elevator down to the lobby, Jason asked, "Where do you want to have breakfast?"

"Haven't really thought about it," Joe answered. "I usually grab a coffee and roll on the way to the office. There's always the hotel coffee shop."

"Nah, likely super expensive," Jason replied. "Must be someplace on the way out of town."

They passed in sight of reception, where Kent caught their eye, smiled slightly, and gave a slight discreet wave.

"I'll go ask," Jason said. In a fairly loud voice, he asked, "Are there good places to have breakfast on the way out of town to Martinsville?"

Kent thought and said, "There's IHOP on Franklin Road just before you get to Tanglewood Mall." Lowering his voice, "It's cheaper than this place and better too."

Jason replied fairly loudly, "Thanks." Then lowering his voice said, "Your guest's virtue is still intact, and my boyfriend doesn't have anything to worry about. Nice to be a guest in your hotel."

They went in separate cars to IHOP for a leisurely breakfast, parting company in the parking lot, with another big bear hug, which Joe returned readily.

CHAPTER 29

Tuesday, May 27, 2008
Roanoke, Virginia, USA

About 7:30 a.m., Joe rushed into the conference room where Randy Walker was waiting and said, "Thanks again for coming in yesterday on a holiday to help."

"You're welcome," Joe answered.

Randy Walker said, "Here's the brief. Please look at it one last time. We need to be at her office when it opens."

While Joe looked at the brief, his mind drifted: *Randy's call to come to the office yesterday and send James Edward to DC saved me from a tricky situation. It seemed I might be expected to spend the night with the girl they fixed me up with. She was nice and fun to be with, but I wasn't ready for sex.*

Randy Walker interrupted, "I forgot to mention James Edward's calling soon. Like I told him, wish it could've been you who went to DC to meet the guy who wants to testify, especially since you know his family, but we're committed to use the Arabic interpreter today and need you for that. You also want to question Dr. Hanford too."

"I understand," Joe said. "I didn't have any reason to go back to DC. James Edward's folks are close, so he got to spend part of Memorial Day with them."

Soon Randy Walker said, "James Edward's on the line." After greetings, "What can you tell us? We're trying to set up an early meeting with Martha and Rich."

"I've had one meeting with Ahmed Hammoud," James Edward began. "Didn't learn much. His attorney, a public defender, was present. As you know he's incarcerated and under investigation for fighting with militants in Iraq. Also seems he's implicated in the attempted NSA bombing."

Joe, surprised, asked, "How's that?"

"Don't know much yet," James Edward replied. "He insists on seeing the guy who's charged and is willing to tell what he knows."

"Is he trying to plea bargain?" Randy Walker asked.

"So far, no," James Edward said. "Says his life is over so he wants to help his parents and get back at the guys we're prosecuting and maybe do something to help the guy charged with the NSA bombing. He seems depressed; his attorney was cautious. He's eager, almost desperate, to testify against the defendants, like he has a score to settle. On his attorney's advice, he didn't go into detail."

"Do we want him to testify?" Randy Walker asked.

"Not sure yet," James Edward replied. "We need to keep our options open. Rich might take advantage of his depressed state, involvement in the other crime, and need for revenge to tear him to shreds. He also has bandages on his face, and I haven't had a chance to find out what for. That might have some impact. I need more time."

"I'll ask Martha to delay at least a day," Randy Walker said. "Joe helped a lot preparing a brief showing precedents to delay a trial due to unexpected witnesses; I'll give it to her this morning. Can you have more later today?"

"I'll do my best," James Edward replied. "I'm supposed to see him again this morning."

"Can you get a sense of how soon he could get here?" Randy Walker asked. "Martha'll want to know."

"He'd need release on bail to allow him to travel, I suspect," James Edward answered. "I can't imagine someone'd agree to his being taken to Roanoke by U.S. Marshalls and held in custody in

Roanoke just so he can testify in our trial. That'd also feed into Rich's attempt to destroy his credibility."

Randy Walker asked, "Has the topic of bail come up?"

"So far, no," James Edward replied. "I was only with them about an hour. I doubt his lawyer has even thought of release on bail."

"If a judge there knows we're interested in him as a witness in another federal trial," Randy Walker said, "he or she might be more inclined to grant bail, but someone would have to come up with money or pledge property. Likely have to be his family."

"I doubt Nassar Hammoud even knows what bail is," Joe added. "Someone needs to discuss it with him; I don't think it should be me. Wonder if Omar'd do it. He knows them better than I do."

"Would he have money?" Randy Walker asked.

"I wouldn't know," Joe replied. "His business seems to be good, but he's had some heavy expenses lately."

"He'd need a lawyer here," Randy Walker said. "The public defender here couldn't represent him and the defendants both. Do the Hammouds have a lawyer?"

Joe answered, "I doubt it. I suppose I could find out, but maybe we should wait and see if he's coming down here."

"Yes," Randy Walker agreed. "There's always Montgomery County or maybe Roanoke Legal Aid, but let's not get ahead of ourselves. Let's see what happens with your meeting this morning, James Edward."

Wait," Joe said suddenly. "Ask him if he remembers a time about two years ago when two guys in a SUV with Florida plates stopped at the gas station just as the defendants were driving away shouting something about Arabs. One guy gave him some money."

"Huh?" James Edward said. "What's this all about?"

"Maybe a longshot," Joe answered. "A couple of my friends said they stopped at Nassar's gas station…" and explained briefly what had happened. "I can tell you more later. My friends are willing to come down here to testify."

"We'd better go now," Randy Walker said. "We'll look to hear from you, maybe at lunch or when court dismisses."

Randy Walker and Joe were in Judge Bishop's chambers; Rich Harris rushed in, saying, "Sorry to be late, Your Honor."

"That's all right, counselor," Judge Bishop said. "It's very short notice." Turning to Randy Walker, she asked, "Counselor, you asked for this meeting. What do you have?"

Randy Walker began, "A witness came forward over the weekend who we may want to call. We'd like the option to delay until we can file a formal request."

"The old surprise witness trick," Rich Harris stated.

Randy Walker responded, "Your Honor, our office has had a long-standing relationship with this court and we have never used tricks of any sort."

Judge Bishop replied, "That's right, counselor."

"The situation is a surprise to us as well," Randy Walker added. "The possible witness, as we informed you, is the son of the victims. We did not look for him; he contacted U.S. authorities stating that he wants to come here to testify. We've only had one short contact with him; Mr. Goodwin is in Washington right now speaking with him and his attorney. Because he's insistent, we feel we have a professional obligation to pursue his request and see if it's appropriate to subpoena him. Your Honor, here's a brief we prepared to show case precedents of similar cases in which the judge granted delays or failed to grant delays and was overturned."

He handed the legal brief to Judge Bishop and Rich Harris, who said, "Most of those cases are for the defense, not the prosecution. They wouldn't apply here."

"It has been well established that the procedure applies both to prosecution and defense," Randy Walker said.

"Thank you, counselor," Judge Bishop stated. "I'll take this under advisement and let you know as soon as possible."

"While we are on the subject, Your Honor," Randy Walker continued, "Mr. Shaito has also been notified by two other potential witnesses of their willingness to testify. We will include their names on the subpoena as well."

"Duly noted, counselor," Judge Bishop stated. "Court will convene in five minutes."

CHAPTER 30

Tuesday, May 27, 2008
Roanoke, Virginia, USA

Court came to order with Joe calling Abou Nidal, handing him a sheet of paper, and asking in Arabic, "Abou Nidal, this document is in English. Do you recognize it?"

Dr. Hanford interpreted while Abou Nidal replied in Arabic, "It says I can be in this country."

After interpretation into English, Joe said, "Your Honor, the prosecution would like to place this document into the record. If the witness would like, we can ask Dr. Hanford to read the document and interpret it into Arabic."

Judge Bishop took the document, examined it briefly, gave it to Rich Harris to examine, and said, "The document is to be entered as prosecution exhibit A." To Abou Nidal, "Would you like to have this document translated?"

Dr. Hanford interpreted the question, and Abou Nidal said in Arabic, "It's not necessary," which was interpreted.

Joe asked in Arabic, "Abou Nidal, do you have any other documents that show your right to be in this country?"

After interpretation, Abou Nidal removed a card from his wallet; Joe said in English, "The prosecution would like to have a copy made of this card and place it into evidence. In addition, we request that it be stipulated that this is a so-called green card issued by the U.S. Government to legal residents who are not U.S. citizens. We could call a government official to testify as to the authenticity of the card."

Judge Bishop asked Rich Harris, "Do you stipulate?"

After a brief conversation with Yuhana Khalil while examining the card, he stated, "We so stipulate."

Joe continued in Arabic, "In your previous testimony you said you had contact with the defendants when they bought gasoline and stole candy. We can read back your testimony if you like. The question now is whether there were other occasions you saw the defendants at the station, but did not have contact with them."

After interpretation into English, Abou Nidal answered in Arabic, "Yes that's what I said in my previous testimony. One time they drove away without paying for a repair bill."

Dr. Hanford interpreted; then Joe said in Arabic, "Please describe this incident and who else was present."

After interpretation, Yuhana Khalil said in English, "Object, Your Honor. The defendants are not being tried for alleged crimes that may have occurred at a gasoline station. This line of testimony is inappropriate and irrelevant."

Rich Harris thought, *He's good. I wouldn't have objected. She'll overrule; Joe Shaito knows his law. At least he's trying to cast doubt in the mind of the jury.*

"Your Honor," Joe stated, "it has been well established, especially in cases of denying civil rights due to ethnicity or national origin, that evidence of previous actions of the defendants along the same line is admissible."

Judge Bishop said tersely, "Objection overruled. You may answer the question."

Dr. Hanford explained the situation in Arabic to Abou Nidal, not interpreting word-for-word, looking cautiously at Joe and Yuhana Khalil to see whether there was an objection.

"Ahmed, that's Nassar's oldest son, met them when they came to pick up a car that had been repaired," Abou Nidal began answering in Arabic. "They drove off shouting something. They must have had their own key, because we still had the key by the cash register."

When interpreted, Joe asked in Arabic, "Was anyone else present to see what was happening?"

After interpretation, Abou Nidal answered in Arabic, "Two customers in an SUV were buying gas. They must've used a credit card, because they didn't come in the store to pay. One of them talked to Ahmed, and the other gave Ahmed some money. When Ahmed came into the store, I asked him about the money. He said the guy felt sorry for him because Nassar would be angry for letting the guys drive away and gave him money to pay their bill. I told him *I* was angry with him for taking money he didn't earn. Islam says you can't keep money you don't earn. I said I wouldn't tell Nassar if he gave the money to the mosque the next Friday. I also told him I'd explain to Nassar it wasn't his fault."

Again after interpretation, Joe said in Arabic, "Thank you. That is all for now from the prosecution."

While Dr. Hanford interpreted, Joe sat and Yuhana Khalil began in Arabic. "Abou Nidal, you testified you heard the defendants in conversation and shouting. You also testified you saw them through the window. How can you hear someone if you're inside looking through a window?"

After interpretation, Abou Nidal, answered in Arabic, "I did not testify that I heard them. I testified I saw them. I think it's possible to read back the testimony. I knew they were talking by seeing their lips move and watching their bodies."

While Dr. Hanford interpreted, Yuhana Khalil thought in Arabic, *He's alert and testy today.* He said in Arabic, "You don't know what the defendants actually said. For all you know, they could have said, 'Have a good day.'"

After interpretation, Abou Nidal replied in Arabic, "Ahmed told me they said, 'Fuckin' A-rabs.'"

Yuhana Khalil stated in English, "Your Honor, we request this statement be removed from the record. This is secondhand hearsay testimony that is not allowable."

Joe immediately responded in English, "Your Honor, the witness testified to what he heard, not what the defendants said. This is not hearsay, but a statement of fact."

Judge Bishop said, "The testimony stays in the record. The jury is instructed to be aware that the testimony is what the witness says he heard, not what the defendants said."

Dr. Hanford interpreted what had transpired, and Yuhana Khalil said he had no further questions.

Judge Bishop called a twenty-minute recess.

CHAPTER 31

Tuesday, May 27, 2008
Roanoke, Virginia, USA

When court was called to order again, Joe called Dr. Ames Hanford; when he was sworn in, Joe asked, "Dr. Hanford, you are called to testify as an expert in the Arabic language and culture, and you are being paid a fee to testify as an expert. Is that what you understand?"

"Yes it is," he replied.

"Has anyone discussed with you what testimony you should give in exchange for this fee?" Joe continued.

Dr. Hanford answered, "No, not at all."

"In testimony earlier today," Joe said, "you heard the ethnic group to which the victims belong pronounced in a certain way. Do you know to which pronunciation I refer?"

"You must be referring to 'Arab,'" he replied.

"Yes; did you hear another pronunciation?" Joe asked.

"I heard Mr. al Khatib use another pronunciation that he said he heard," Dr. Hanford replied. "He used it and he is Arab, but I don't like to say it in public."

"Why don't you like to say it in public?" Joe asked.

"I don't like to say it in private either," Dr. Hanford added. "Most Arabs, if not all, consider it to be offensive."

"Thank you, no further questions," Joe said and sat.

Rich Harris asked aggressively, "Dr. Hanford, you're engaged as an expert in the Arabic language. Yet, the supposedly expert testimony you're giving is pronunciation of words in English. Therefore, your testimony is outside your area of expertise, is it not?"

Dr. Hanford replied, "I believe the other counselor stated my expertise is in the area of the Arabic language and culture. I believe the court reporter can go back and read exactly what was said. To be more precise, my expertise, in addition to the Arabic language, is in cultural linguistics. If you wish to examine my CV, you can see I've published research on the interaction of culture and language, including pronunciation, especially when native speakers of a language live in a location that has another dominant language. Because I work with the Arabic language, one of my studies is on Arabic-speaking persons in the U.S."

Rich Harris continued, "You live in Southwest Virginia; Lexington, I believe. Therefore, you must be aware that pronunciation of 'A-rab' is a normal way of speaking for many local residents of this area."

Dr. Hanford stated, "Yes, I believe I've heard that pronunciation by some local residents. The fact that it's the normal pronunciation of some persons does not make it less offensive. If they've seen television at all, they would've heard the proper term for Arabs. In many parts of the U.S., some persons normally used the terms 'dago,' 'wop,' 'mick,' 'kraut,' 'spic,' 'greaser,' 'chink,' and I could go on and on to refer to ethnic minorities; but that does not make the terms any less offensive."

"But these persons didn't intend to offend, would you say?" Richard Harris continued.

Dr. Hanford replied, "We have just discussed my expertise. It does not include psychology. Therefore, I cannot testify to what anyone intended or intends. What I would say, though, is that it's irrelevant. If we go back a few years, many persons, especially here in the South, normally used the 'n-word' to refer to African-Americans. We know now that this word is so extremely offensive that it is seldom if ever used by anyone publicly or privately."

Rich Harris said, "Are you now saying that calling someone an A-rab is equivalent to using the n-word?"

Dr. Hanford replied, "In order to answer that question I would have to do research comparing the reactions of a broad sample of each group in multiple contexts, controlling for age, education, length of time in the country, and several other variables. My hypothesis would be that the two expressions are essentially equivalent."

Rich Harris, frustrated, snapped his question. "Just give a simple 'yes' or 'no' answer and spare us a lecture."

Dr. Hanford replied, "I just told you I am unable to give a 'yes' or 'no' answer until there is more research done on the subject. I did say that my hypothesis, that is my prior expectation, is that the two expressions are equivalent and equally offensive in certain contexts."

Rich Harris, annoyed, said, "No further questions."

Joe also said, "No further questions."

Judge Bishop asked, "Counselors, do you have any further need for Dr. Hanford's service as an interpreter?"

When they answered "no," Judge Bishop thanked him and a court clerk led him outside to process his pay.

Joe said, "The prosecution calls the Reverend Jolene Robbins." When she was sworn in, he established her position as a pastor in Shawsville and then asked, "Are you acquainted with the victims in this case, the Hammoud family?" He established they were neighbors of the Robertses and their church did things for the Hammoud family.

Joe then asked, "Are you aware of the crime for which the defendants are being tried?"

"It has been well publicized," she replied; "denying the Hammoud family civil rights because they're Arabs."

"When did you first become aware of events that led to the defendants' being charged with this crime?" Joe asked.

"The next day," Jolene Robbins answered. "The first of March." Then she continued to describe events.

Whew, she didn't say anything about Marwan's death, Joe thought. Then he asked, "To clarify for the record, you understand religion is not involved in the crime the defendants are charged with, do you not? The charge is denying civil rights due to their ethnicity, not religion."

"Yes, I understand that," Jolene Robbins replied.

Continuing, he said, "Please remember what you heard Mrs. Roberts say to you. Did you hear that the bomb was because they were Arabs or because they were Muslims? Also, to be sure you and the court understand, you are being asked to testify what you heard, not what Mrs. Roberts said."

"I definitely heard her say 'because they're Arabs,'" she answered. "She verified it later when she told me she had written down what she heard."

"What did you hear her say that she had written down?" Joe asked. "Please note again I'm asking what you heard, not what Mrs. Roberts said."

"Actually, I read most of it myself," she answered. "She couldn't bring herself to speak the obscenities."

"Can you please tell us what you read," Joe asked.

Jolene Robbins paused and said, "From the best of my memory it was, 'Serves you right, you f-word A-rab a-holes. You bomb us, we bomb you back.' Then, 'Yeah, you m-f A-rabs. There's more of this if you don't get out of here. We don't want no f-word A-rabs here.' If necessary, I can say the actual words, but I'd prefer not."

"That's not necessary, thank you," Joe said. "Now let's please turn to your earlier testimony that you told your congregation on Sunday morning there was a bombing at the Hammouds' house because they're Arabs. Can you please tell us what individual reactions were?

Please note I'm not asking you to violate clergy confidentiality, only what you heard in public or semi-public conversations."

"Some of them were concerned and upset that something like this could happen in our community," Jolene Robbins replied. "One person even said they could not imagine that so much hate against Arabs still existed so long after nine-eleven. 'Hate' was the person's actual word; we hadn't heard the term 'hate crime' used."

"Did you hear anything, from your congregation or elsewhere, that someone thought attacks against Arabs were justified because of Arab bombings of Americans?" Joe asked. "Again, we're asking you what you heard, not what someone said; and again, we're not asking you to violate clergy confidentiality."

"None whatever," she answered emphatically.

"Thank you. That'll be all," Joe said and sat down.

Rich Harris began, "Reverend Robbins, as a member of the clergy, wouldn't you say your experience is distorted? Distorted in a good way, but still distorted. With your congregation, you deal with what is right, good, and moral, and therefore not ordinary behavior of non-religious, non-churchgoing persons."

Jolene Robbins replied, "In my experience, it's just the opposite. While members of my congregation are indeed as you describe, aspiring to be good and moral persons, clergy have to deal with all sorts. Some people walk into the church 'off the street,' so to speak, asking for help, help as they view help. Also members of my congregation are exposed to less-than-good behavior and come to me for guidance and counseling. To answer your question directly, my experience is distorted, but opposite from what you suggest."

"In your testimony, you said a member of your congregation used the word 'hate,' even though not aware of the term 'hate crime,'" Rich Harris continued. "How can you be sure the person wasn't familiar with so-called 'hate crimes' from some other source?"

"I obviously can't be sure," Jolene Robbins stated. "What I said, or meant to say, is none of us were aware of the term 'hate crime' as it was later used to describe this case, because no charges had been made at that point."

Rich Harris asked, "You testified what you heard and read some two months ago, first of March, you said; how can you be sure after such a long time? Have you seen or heard the words that were allegedly written down since then?"

She stated, "No, I have not seen them since then. In my testimony, I said 'to the best of my memory,' and that is a true statement. One skill a pastor acquires, if he or she does not have it already, is good memory."

When Rich Harris and Joe said they had no further questions, Judge Bishop said, "Court is recessed until 1:30."

Randy Walker checked his telephone and said, "There's a message from James Edward. Let's hurry and have lunch sent in." Outside he said, "That was a good job interrogating those witnesses, especially the pastor."

"Thanks," Joe replied. "I was a little nervous because I wasn't well prepared, since James Edward was supposed to question her. Mostly, I was concerned about questioning a Christian clergyperson because I'm not Christian and don't know much about them. Also my Michigan accent might have some subtle effect on the jury because I'm an obvious outsider questioning one of their own. He wouldn't have that problem. I haven't talked to him about religion, but I assume he's Christian and Protestant like most people around here."

"Oh, you did just fine," Randy Walker said. "Yes, Goodwins are a prominent family in Virginia and have been since colonial days. They're well-known Episcopalians going back to the Church of England days, but I don't know about James Edward. Younger generations often stray from the paths of their forebears. I'm surprised you didn't raise the topic of pronunciation of Arab with the pastor."

"I thought about it, but decided not to," Joe replied. "I wasn't sure how she'd answer, and besides, sometimes it's best to leave an issue a little open ended and linger in the mind of the jury. I was concerned Dr. Hanford overwhelmed the jury with all the academic talk."

"I don't think that's a problem," Randy Walker said. "Actually, it may've helped. You may not have noticed the black woman was paying especially close attention when the 'n' word was mentioned. Rich was noticeably flustered too, and the jury might've picked up on it."

"Oh, good," Joe commented. "It sure made it easier that he brought up the 'n' word himself. I wasn't sure how to move the testimony that way. James Edward was going to do it."

At their office, they went straight to the conference room where lunch was waiting.

CHAPTER 32

Tuesday, May 27, 2008
Roanoke, Virginia, USA

After lunch, James Edward reported on the speakerphone, "Ahmed Hammoud can possibly help us, and it might be a humanitarian thing to get him down there to be with his family. We have to be cautious. He seems emotionally fragile and maybe mentally fragile."

"Why's that?" Randy Walker asked.

"He's lucid most of the time, but gets close to crying when he talks about what the defendants did to him. Rich might push him over the edge. We should arrange a psychological exam before we put him on the stand."

"What did they do to him?" Randy Walker asked.

"Beat him up," James Edward answered, "but something's not right. Getting beat up usually doesn't cause someone to be as emotionally upset as he seems to be. He keeps referring back to how he's ruined, unclean, can never be raised on the day of judgment, and not appear before Allah. I don't know much about Islam, but getting beaten up surely wouldn't make him unclean."

Joe interrupted, "It could've been sexual." *Paco did say something about rape.*

"Sexual?" James Edward exclaimed.

"Yes," Joe continued. "Islam prohibits sex acts between men, and some Muslims take an even more extreme view. If the defendants forced themselves on him, he might view himself permanently ruined and not worthy of being raised to meet Allah on the day of judgment."

"If that's what happened," James Edward countered, "it isn't his fault. Why would that ruin him before Allah?"

"It wouldn't," Joe answered, "but in some Middle Eastern cultures, if a woman's raped it's her fault, and she's often punished or killed. It's cultural, not religious. It could apply to men too. I can talk to Omar. He might also talk to the guy. He was a federal prison chaplain. Of course he's bound by clergy confidentiality and wouldn't do anything specifically to help us."

"Wouldn't hurt," Randy Walker said. "There're a psychiatrist and psychologist we work with here; we can have them examine him. We use them when the defense uses an insanity defense or claims defendants are mentally unfit to stand trial. Their experience is to assess mental fitness. Do you know if he's had contact with his family?"

"Some," James Edward answered. "He's really upset over his brother's death and concerned about his mother."

"Did you find out about the charges against him and getting him released on bail?" Randy asked.

"Not much," James Edward replied. "That's still being investigated. On the attempted NSA bombing, he's agreeing to tell what he knows if he's allowed to testify in our case. They're taking him to Baltimore this afternoon."

"What about two guys seeing the defendants drive off and giving Ahmed some money?" Joe asked.

"Oh, yes," James Edward replied. "I almost forgot. "He remembers the situation well. His father got really pissed off because he allowed them to drive off, even though his uncle tried to defend him. Also, his uncle made him give the money to the mosque."

"This could be the strongest testimony he can give," Joe stated. "My friends can testify too."

"We need to hurry," Randy Walker said, interrupting. "What are you doing this afternoon?"

"Nose around here in the AG office to find out what I can about the other two cases he's involved with," James Edward replied. "I'll send you a message like before."

"Make yourself comfortable at my desk," Joe said with a chuckle. "Really wish you were here. Bye."

"Time to dash," Randy Walker said. "Bye for now."

CHAPTER 33

Tuesday, May 27, 2008
Roanoke, Virginia, USA

Back in court, Joe called Deputy Sheriff Clayton Evans of the Montgomery County Sheriff's department to the stand. He was dressed like his colleague in a summer uniform. Joe asked, "Would you please tell the court if you are acquainted with any of the defendants in a professional capacity."

"I know all three of them," he answered.

"How frequently have you encountered them in your official duties, and for what reasons?" Joe asked.

"I, like the other patrolmen in the Eastern part of the county, have met them quite a few times," he answered. "Until this last time, it was minor traffic offenses, fightin', disturbin' the peace, and the like."

"Would you please tell us what happened this last time and when that was," Joe asked.

He consulted notes and said, "The night of February 29th, I was on routine patrol westbound on old highway 460 comin' from the Roanoke County line towards Shawsville. At the turnout from Lafayette, a car sped out at a high rate of speed, turned right spinnin' its wheels, and was fishtailin'. I immediately turned on the flashin' lights to pull it over. At first it didn't seem it'd stop, but eventually did. I recognized it because I had stopped it a few times before. Just as I was about to give the license plate number to the dispatcher, I heard a bulletin to look out for a car with those license plates. I radioed the dispatcher that I had just stopped the car. She said I was to apprehend the driver and any passengers and wait for Deputy Williams, who'd be coming soon.

"I apprehended the driver, Kody Bates, and handcuffed him. It looked like th' other one was goin' to run away. I pulled out my pistol and told him to stop, apprehended him, and handcuffed him. It was Keith Barnes. I put both of 'em in the back of the cruiser, notified the dispatcher, and waited for instructions. Deputy Williams arrived soon with the other defendant. We took them to the jail in Christiansburg and booked them, including reckless driving for Kody Bates."

Joe said he had no further questions; Rich Harris began, "Deputy Evans, you've testified two of the defendants drove away from the scene of the crime. How can you be sure?"

Deputy Evans replied, "That's not what I testified. I said they were in the same car that Deputy Williams reported he saw driving away from the crime scene."

Rich Harris then asked, "Deputy Evans, you've been referring to your notes. You obviously did not write them down while you were driving; when did you make them?"

"The next day when I came on duty," he answered.

Rich Harris said, "How can you be sure it was just a few minutes; Isn't it easy to forget something that precise?"

"Yes, it's easy to forget," Deputy Evans answered. "That's why the dispatcher keeps precise times and there are monitoring devices on the car. I consult these to be sure."

Rich Harris said he had no further questions.

Joe, with sudden inspiration, stood and said, "We'd like to ask additional questions of this witness. Deputy Evans, would you please consult your notes and tell us the times the specific events happened to which you have testified."

He replied, "It was 9:18 p.m. when I saw the car turning onto the highway and I turned on the lights to signal them to pull over. It was 9:21 p.m. when I heard the bulletin to watch for the car. At 9:22 p.m. I radioed the license plate and received instructions to apprehend and hold the driver and occupants. By 9:27 I had the suspects in custody in the back of the patrol car and I told the dispatcher. At 9:30 Deputy Williams arrived with the other defendant. At 10:05 we booked them and took them to the jail."

"Based on your knowledge of law enforcement and driving times," Joe continued, "would it've been possible for the car to change drivers, pick up, or let out passengers?"

"I can say with confidence it'd be impossible," Deputy Evans answered, "unless it had been planned and rehearsed; and then it still may have been impossible."

Joe and Rich Harris had no further questions. Then Joe said, "The prosecution calls Daniel Cohen."

A distinguished middle-aged man dressed in a business suit took the stand. Preliminary questions established him as an urban architect involved in property development.

"Mr. Cohen, are you acquainted with Nassar Hammoud?" Joe asked. "If so, in what capacity?"

"I've known him for twenty years at least," he answered. "I heard he works on old classic European cars, so I took my Mercedes to him. It's still running in great shape, thanks to him. I bought another one from him a few years later, and it's running just fine too."

"How long have you known he's Arab?" Joe asked.

"From the outset," he replied. "When I first saw him, I wasn't going to let just anyone touch my car, so I asked him about his experience. He said he'd come from Lebanon, where he worked on this type of cars. I assumed he's Lebanese; those of us who are old Mercedes buffs know it's *the* car of choice in Lebanon. They're Arabs."

"When did you learn he's Palestinian?" Joe continued.

"Oh, pretty early on," Daniel Cohen replied, his mountain-and-valley Southwest Virginia accent becoming apparent. "Maybe it was when I asked him how he happened to settle in a remote part of Montgomery County. I joked that I hoped he wouldn't take it out on my car that I'm Jewish. He joked in return and went to work on it."

"Has there been any other discussion about his being Arab?" Joe asked.

Daniel Cohen thought then answered, "After nine-eleven, he made a comment about how bad it was that Arabs attacked the U.S. I agreed, and the subject was dropped."

"Would you say your dealings with Nassar Hammoud have been satisfactory in all respects?" Joe asked.

"Yes," Daniel Cohen stated. "In all respects."

Joe then asked, "How long have you and your family lived in this area, Mr. Cohen?"

"I was born here," he replied. "My parents were too, in this area, not in Roanoke itself. One of my grandfathers came to the coal fields about the turn of last century as an itinerant peddler. He married a Jewish girl, a daughter of another peddler, settled down, and the rest is history, as the saying goes. The stereotype is Jewish people gravitate to urban areas, so they ended up in Roanoke."

"It would seem you're well acquainted with attitudes and viewpoints of people in this region," Joe commented.

"Yes," he replied. "Coming from a family of merchants, we pick that up readily."

"In your opinion, then, is it normal for local people to set off a bomb in someone's house as a prank?" Joe asked.

"Definitely not!" Daniel Cohen answered.

"No further questions," Joe stated.

Rich Harris said he had no questions.

Joe said, "The prosecution calls Charles Dalton."

A man in his forties in a business suit came forward. Preliminary questions established that he was an attorney.

Randy Walker thought, *An attorney who knows Nassar Hammoud and might do him a favor.*

"Mr. Dalton," Joe continued, "what do you understand about the nature of the charges against the defendants?"

"Only what I read in newspapers and hear on the news," he replied. "My specialty's property law, especially commercial development, law of contracts, water rights, and the like. I haven't been exposed to criminal law since law school, and hate-crime legislation hadn't been passed then. Because of my legal education, I might have a little bit better perspective than the general public."

Oh, no exposure to criminal law, Randy Walker thought. *I've seen him at bar association meetings, but never really talked to him. Maybe someone else in his firm....*

"Are you acquainted with the victim, Nassar Hammoud; and if so, in what respect?" Joe continued.

"Yes," he began. "He works on an old Peugeot I inherited a few years back when Peugeot was selling a few cars in the U.S. I managed to keep it going a while with local mechanics, but over time it was showing lots of wear. Peugeot had withdrawn from the U.S. market, and I was on the verge of abandoning it. I'd really become attached to it; it's kind of nice to be unique and drive an old classic lots of people don't recognize. Then I heard about Nassar. I go to Montgomery County pretty often because of all the development in the New River Valley, so I just stopped by one day. He's taken care of my car ever since. It's been ten or more years now."

Joe continued, "Have you been satisfied with his work and business dealings with you?"

"Yes, very satisfied in every respect," he answered. "Nassar's in a monopoly position because he knows I'd have to go to Washington or Norfolk to get service otherwise, and maybe not even there, but he's always been fair in how much he charges me and in delivering when he says he'll finish. If he's delayed getting parts, he always calls me. He even came to Roanoke to get my car with his car carrier one time and didn't charge much extra."

"How long have you known he's Arab?" Joe asked.

"From the beginning," he answered.

"Did you have any discussions with Nassar or others about his Arab ethnicity?" Joe continued.

"No, not that I can think of," Charles Dalton replied. "There might've been a comment around nine-eleven."

Joe asked, "How long have you, and your family before you, lived in this area?"

He answered, "I was born here. Daltons have lived in Southwest Virginia since before Revolutionary War days."

"Would you say you have a good sense of attitudes and viewpoints of the local people?" Joe Shaito asked.

"Yes, in addition to family background—and some Daltons have been politically prominent—being a property lawyer involved in development requires knowledge of local culture," he replied.

"In your view, would it be normal for local people to set off a bomb in someone's house as a prank?" Joe asked.

"No, not at all," he replied. "Southwest Virginians are people like people anywhere with their human frailties, but in my observation, this's not a prank someone would play."

"No further questions," Joe said and sat down.

"No questions from the defense," Rich Harris stated.

Randy Walker stood, saying, "Your Honor, that's all the we have for now. As you know, we want to call others."

Judge Bishop stated, "Court is recessed until further notice. The jury is instructed not to discuss the case."

While walking towards their office, Randy Walker said, "Let's go to that coffee shop close to the office. No need to be in a hurry. There's nothing from James Edward."

"I could use something," Joe said, "at least coffee."

"You did all the work today," Randy Walker said. "I'll treat. It's always possible I'll have to give closing arguments tomorrow if Martha doesn't approve our delay. I don't think Rich's going to call any defense witnesses; probably just try to attack our case."

"Yes, that's the sense I get," Joe concurred. "He didn't examine our last two witnesses. It seems he made a couple of blunders when he was questioning our other witnesses and their responses supported our case, not his."

"Yes, maybe," Randy Walker replied, "but don't underestimate Rich. He can be sly and clever like a fox. All he has to do is put doubt in the mind of one person." He received a text on his cell phone and said, "Listen to this: some members of the jury are requesting they be taken to the scene of the crime and observe for themselves the distances. One of us has to go along, of course. You've been there; James Edward may or may not be back. They couldn't get things arranged by tomorrow, so it'll be Thursday at the earliest. I should go; it'd help me develop closing arguments. Also means I'm off the hook for a day at least."

As they walked back to their office, he said, "Take the day off tomorrow."

CHAPTER 34

Rosie Jordan opened a task force meeting and introduced Roger Chen. Then he said, "We've had very significant breakthroughs, so why don't we get started with Cranford."

Cranford Brooks began, "Ahmed Hammoud, older son of the family whose house was bombed, contacted U.S. authorities. Larry should explain more before I continue."

Lawrence Briscoe began, "Many CIA operations and activities are secret, even from a group like this, so there's a limit to what I can tell you." He explained events in Iraq that led to Ahmed's contact with US authorities. "Because he claimed he's a citizen, we brought him to the U.S. and turned him over to the FBI. Any questions?"

Rhonda Philips, wearing a very stylish fresh, pale green dress, asked, "Is Dr. Ali Salman involved, by chance?"

Larry Briscoe answered, "Yes, he is. How'd you know?"

"In a previous task force Rosie and Otis know about, I met Dr. Ali under circumstances that're best kept secret," she said. "It has nothing to do with this case; just curiosity."

Cranford Brooks continued. "We've verified Ahmed Hammoud is who he claims to be and a U.S. citizen. He claims his passport and other ID were stolen in Venezuela, of all places. He's in custody charged with treason, among other things. The CIA is investigating Iraq and Venezuela. He has a story that is so bizarre it seems to be true. Charges against him would probably be difficult to prove in court, but it's too soon to comment. He'll be released on bail to testify against the defendants in Roanoke, which is his burning desire. Roger can speak to that."

"Charges against him haven't been brought to us, yet," Roger Chen stated. "I, too, suspect it'd be hard to prove in court if the alleged crimes occurred in Iraq. He could help our case in Roanoke, but it's not all that clear cut. We're also concerned about his emotional and mental stability."

"We're aware he's emotionally fragile, shall we say," Cranford Brooks continued, "so we've been cautious. He's given very valuable information. He gave us names of others in the group at the mosque in Arlington and names of imams. It seems there are two imams who are potentially involved; we'll get to that shortly.

"We contacted other group members one by one; they were nervous, wondering what'd happen to them now that it's public Wissam Salameh's been charged. We were very cautious to respect their legal rights, notified them they are not under investigation at the moment, and informed them things could be easier in the future if they cooperated now and told us about activities of others. We were very careful to indicate they are not expected to implicate themselves and we're not offering plea bargains."

Rhonda Philips interrupted, "Is there a plea bargain with the defendant in Baltimore? Some in Congress are very interested and the way it was kept quiet for so long. They would be most upset if there's any notion of a plea bargain."

"No plea bargain's been offered," Roger Chen stated.

Cranford Brooks continued, "All were fairly consistent. The primary imam is from Saudi Arabia, and we've known that Saudi Arabia supports this mosque. There's a Palestinian imam from Lebanon who actually led the group of young men born in the U.S. who had Palestinian parents. This imam convinced them the U.S. government disrespects Islam and was targeting Arab Muslims, especially Palestinians, in the U.S., spying on them, monitoring conversations at the NSA, etc.

"It's not clear who came up with the idea to set off a bomb at the NSA, but it seems likely the imam manipulated them into thinking it was their idea. He also manipulated them into thinking they needed to set off a diversionary bomb. That's when Ahmed Hammoud insisted they bomb a gay bar in DC because he claimed being gay is against Islam and gays cause so many problems in the world.

"The group selected the two who were the weakest and most easily influenced to do the bombings. They even called Wissam 'Wissy the sissy' behind his back, just like when he was in high school. Ahmed also had his brother go to the gay bar a few times to see what it was like, where he apparently met Joe Shaito. Ahmed claims he had no idea his brother was gay.

"The imam arranged the explosives, being very careful not to disclose sources. Intermediaries were used to make actual deliveries. A couple of them said they heard the imam went back to Lebanon. Others said he just disappeared. They have pretty much avoided contact with each other since. Questions or comments so far?"

Larry Briscoe spoke up, "When you gave us the name of the suspected Palestinian imam, we started investigating further. For the other Saudi Arabian imam, we've known that some Saudi Arabians have supported some of the al Qaeda splinter groups, especially in Lebanon, even though the Saudi Arabian government is strongly opposed. His family name, al Qhatani, is a prominent family name there. There's a person with this name in Guantanamo, but we have to be careful about drawing implications based only on family name; it's more like a tribe. It'd be interesting to know how long the two imams have been in this country. Maybe it was before we started monitoring names on flight manifests.

"The Palestinian imam might be with one of the al Qaeda wannabe groups like Intifada in Palestine and Fatah al Islam in

Lebanon, which is mostly a Palestinian operation but with some Saudi Arabians involved. You may remember, it tried to take over a Palestinian refugee camp in Lebanon, but was routed in bloody battles by the Lebanese army. If this group is now trying to infiltrate the U.S., this is indeed very serious. Domestic terrorism is the FBI's responsibility, but we're very eager to cooperate."

Cranford Brooks said, "Some of them thought the Palestinian imam hadn't been here long. If so, he would need assistance from someone who's been here longer and has connections to get the explosives. That points even more to the Saudi Arabian imam's being involved. Thanks Larry. The Palestinian imam is likely beyond our reach now, but maybe not the Saudi Arabian.

"Ahmed Hammoud insisted he see Wissam Salameh. Yesterday, he went to Baltimore and they talked. Of course, we don't know what was said, but it broke his silence. He's willing to see his mother and also asked to see his lawyer. Roger can tell us more."

Roger Chen began, "His attorney, the public defender, contacted the U.S. Attorney prosecuting the case and said the defendant's ready to plead guilty and accept whatever sentence the court gives him, apparently including the death penalty. He doesn't want his mother to suffer more by having a trial and wants to get it over. So, Rhonda, no suggestion of a plea bargain, and we don't expect one. I don't think we want to push for a death penalty either."

"Certain members of congress will be pleased to hear that," Rhonda Philips stated. "A quick and quiet verdict would suit almost everyone. The public ceremony to award the commendation medals went over well too. From my remit of political and international relations, we're coming out well on this otherwise nasty situation."

"That trial in Roanoke is getting good press in the Middle East too," Larry Briscoe added.

"For sure," Rhonda Philips agreed. "The only major network covering the trial on a regular basis now is al Jazeera, but it's playing well. If it ends in a conviction, it'll go some ways towards countering the images of anti-Islam they have of this country."

Roger Chen interjected, "Let's be careful not to confuse issues. The trial in Roanoke is not about the Islamic religion. The defendants are being tried for hate crimes against Arabs because of their ethnicity, not their religion."

Cranford Brooks said, "That's all I have. I'd gladly take questions or comments."

Rosie Jordan said, "Otis, you haven't said anything."

Colonel Granger said, "There's one major incident that's more sad than disturbing. The public presentation of commendation medals was not totally public and by invitation only because it was inside the NSA, which is a secure area. Because the entire Marine Security Detail was present, watching their colleagues receiving awards, security was handled temporarily by MPs from Fort Meade. To cut the story short, General Reynolds showed up without an invitation, demanding to be admitted so he could take some of the glory for his son's being awarded the medal with the media present. He was bordering on belligerence. The MPs contacted me, and I suggested he be arrested. Of course, he tried to contact his buddies at Marine headquarters, but some of them were becoming annoyed and others remembered his arrogance when on active duty. In brief, he's in custody. He'll no doubt be released, but there'll be some kind of sanctions. Major Reynolds knows nothing of this yet."

"Thanks for coming," Rosie Jordan said abruptly. "We've made significant breakthroughs. I'm sure we'll meet again soon."

He recapped the discussion; they said goodbye and left.

CHAPTER 35

Saturday, May 31, 2008
Harrisonburg, Virginia, USA

Omar was driving southbound on I-81 thinking, while Ahmed dozed, *Here I am getting involved again. Never thought an imam's life would be easy, but not with a family a long way outside Washington. Allah works in strange ways. It helps Joe too. I'm hungry. Here's Harrisonburg; Shoney's is right off the interstate.*

Ahmed woke up and mumbled, "Uh, where are we?"

"We're stopping to eat," Omar said. "I'm hungry; you must be too."

"Not really," Ahmed said. "I'll wait here."

Omar, irritated, said, "No, come on. You need to eat and I'll pay. Your father'd be really pissed off if I brought you home without having eaten, and you know that!"

Omar ordered grilled chicken, reasonably sure it wouldn't be cooked with a pork product. Ahmed ordered a hamburger. Both sat in silence until food was delivered.

Finally, Omar commented, "Your father gave me this car. It was really nice and generous of him. I appreciate it."

"I thought I recognized it," Ahmed answered. "That's the one I was hoping he'd give me."

Omar replied, "Oh, you can have it then. I didn't know you were expecting it. I can get another car."

Ahmed, nibbling, said, "No, he gave it to you. My life's over. All I have left to do is testify against those guys."

Omar replied gently, "Maybe we should talk about this, but in the car when it's private."

Ahmed grunted, "OK."

The rest of lunch was small talk, and Ahmed engaged reluctantly.

Driving again, Omar said, "You said your life's over. Why don't you tell me about it. Remember, I'm an imam, and anything you say to me is confidential. That's why they released you to me, because I'm a federal prison chaplain."

Ahmed in anguish said, "They took away my manhood. Now I can never join the Prophet in heaven; not get married. My life is ruined and all because of them."

Oh, it is *serious*, Omar thought. "Why do you think that?" he asked very gently.

Choking back tears, Ahmed said, "They did things to me the Prophet said men must never do with other men."

Omar said, "They did them to you, not you to them."

Ahmed replied fumbling words, "But they left me unclean, if you know what I mean."

Omar said softly, "I think I know what you mean, but it doesn't make a difference. Allah would never condemn you and keep you from going to heaven. Allah accepts all who are clean in spirit and mind. Physical things don't matter."

Ahmed said stammering, "Really? Are you sure?"

He said, "I have a PhD in Islamic theology and know some things. I can't speak for Allah, but I'm pretty sure."

Oh, a PhD like those stuck up bastards at Virginia Tech, Ahmed thought dejectedly. *Here I thought he was a regular guy, even if he's an imam, someone I might talk to. Guess not.*

"Oh," he muttered and turned away.

Omar, taken aback, thought, *That was abrupt. Here I thought I was getting him to open up.* He drove in silence and then suddenly realized, *Maybe because I said I have a PhD. They're intimidated because others at their mosque have PhDs and MDs. Jordan Hicks was intimidated, and he went to the same school.* He asked, "Do you know Jordan Hicks?"

Ahmed, startled, said, "Er, what's that?"

"I asked if you remember Jordan Hicks," he repeated.

"Yes, sort of," Ahmed answered. "He was a friend of my brother. What about him?"

"He's starting Virginia Tech in the fall," Omar replied. "He was intimidated by PhDs there. Then after talking to me and my friend and working with some Virginia Tech guys, he realized there's no reason to be intimidated."

"How do you know him?" Ahmed stammered.

At Marwan's burial he said very good things about Marwan, like at a Muslim burial," Omar replied. "Then at the 40th day prayers, he said other good things and presented a Marwan Hammoud memorial trophy for kids' soccer."

"Oh, you knew Marwan, and they had 40th day prayers?" Ahmed asked, becoming more alert.

"Your family didn't tell you about his burial and 40th day prayers?" Omar asked.

"They only said Marwan's dead," Ahmed said. "It was my little sister who told me, but my father confirmed it."

Omar then explained briefly his interaction with Marwan and the family. He continued, "At first everyone was surprised I'm an imam, being so young; they were expecting some old fart in a robe and long beard. A few were intimidated when they learned I have a PhD and my friend who was with me—you'll meet him this afternoon—is a lawyer with the U.S. Attorney General. We told them that we're just ordinary guys who worked our asses off. Say, don't you know Dr. Imran Ashfaq at your mosque in Blacksburg?"

"You know him too?" Ahmed asked.

"He was very helpful at Marwan's burial and the 40th day prayers. He's a nice guy and has a PhD."

"I knew who he was," Ahmed said. "The Virginia Tech people at the mosque were so stuck up we had nothing to do with them. We just went to Friday prayers and left."

"That's what Jordan Hicks thought until he realized once you get to know them, Virginia Tech people and the PhDs are just ordinary guys," Omar continued. "Just because they have a PhD doesn't make them any better than anyone else, just more specialized."

"OK, I guess," Ahmed muttered. After hesitating, he asked, "Do you know how my brother died?"

"Yes," Omar answered.

"You know it was at that bar," Ahmed asked, "and the guys at the 40th day prayers knew where too?"

"You mean the gay bar? Yes," Omar answered.

"Oh," Ahmed said. "Islam says being gay's wrong."

Omar replied, "It's open to question what the Prophet actually said and what He meant. The Prophet did say certain physical acts shouldn't be done, but that's not the same thing as saying being gay is condemned. Let's not go into that now; it's not really important. What *is* important is all who truly repent will join the Prophet in heaven. I'm sure Marwan will be there with the Prophet when you get there."

"Oh, OK," Ahmed muttered.

Omar added, "I don't want to keep on you about your beliefs, but it seems you're driven to testify against these guys to get revenge for what they did to you."

"Yeah," Ahmed replied. "They hurt me pretty bad."

"The sacred words of Islam tell us that we must not seek revenge against those who hurt us," Omar stated.

"The imam in Arlington said the Prophet tells us we must fight back and defend ourselves," Ahmed said.

"It's not clear he really was a true imam, but let's not go there," Omar said. "The Prophet does say we can defend ourselves under attack, but this is years later and you're not under attack. Let's stop and think about why the Q'ran says we shouldn't seek revenge. It's not to be easy on persons who hurt us; it's for our benefit. Carrying hatred and wanting revenge inside can eat us up inside and hurt us bad."

"How can it hurt me more than I've been hurt already?" Ahmed argued.

Not wanting to answer directly, Omar said, "Islam has a strong sense of justice. Justice isn't the same as revenge. It's what motivates you inside that's important. Only you can know that."

"OK," Ahmed mumbled.

Omar added, "An imam's a spiritual guide and prayer leader, not someone who tells you what to think or do or not do. Islam's about surrender to the will of Allah, which is a very personal thing."

They rode in silence several minutes when Omar said, "We're going to stop in Roanoke to pick up one of the lawyers. He's also my best friend and roommate. He wants to meet you and talk to you while we go on to Lafayette. We should stop so I can text him and say when we'll be there. There must be a rest area coming up. Wouldn't hurt for me to stop at a rest area anyway."

"There's a rest area past Lexington, between there and Roanoke," Ahmed replied.

In Roanoke, Omar introduced Ahmed and Joe, saying, "You're driving, if that's OK. That way you two can talk easier."

Once out of urban traffic, Joe said, "On Monday morning early, we've arranged for you to see doctors. You've been through some heavy stuff. The defense attorney will push you to or beyond your limits. We need to be sure you can handle it. Hope this is OK with you."

"Er, I guess," Ahmed replied, bewildered.

"We found a lawyer to represent you *pro bono*," Joe continued. "He's a colleague of a customer of your father who agreed to represent you at no charge while you testify. Sorry to hit you with all these things, but some things we need to know if you testify. Do you remember, just after Thanksgiving 2006, the defendants driving off without paying?"

Ahmed replied, "Yes; my father was really pissed off."

Joe led him through the events that day and asked, "Could you identify those two? We can get them down here to testify, but we have to make sure you can identify them. The defense attorney'll challenge you, so we have to be positively sure your identification is solid."

Ahmed mumbled, "Can you give me a hint?"

"No, that's the point," Joe explained. "You have to be able to look around the courtroom and pick them out. If we were to show you photographs or something ahead of time, not only would it be unethical and damage our case if found out, but it could put you in a position of breaking down under the intense questioning. Think about it. You don't have to answer right now."

When they arrived in Lafayette, Fatima rushed to hug Ahmed and began crying. Nassar hugged his son; Abou Nidal followed.

Joe and Omar stood aside until Nassar noticed them and quickly shook Omar's hand, saying effusively in Arabic, "Thank you so much for bringing my boy home, Dr. Omar. You too, Mr. Joe. Now we have to go inside for coffee. Then we'll have a nice dinner to welcome home our missing son."

Omar said firmly in Arabic, "No, not this time, Abou Ahmed. You deserve to have Ahmed all to yourself. Besides, I'm really tired. We'll be in touch tomorrow."

CHAPTER 36

Tuesday, June 3, 2008
Roanoke, Virginia, USA

"What do the doctors' reports say?" James Edward asked as they reviewed strategy for the day over morning coffee.

Randy Walker said, "He can testify; might be worse if he were denied the opportunity. His lawyer'll be there."

James Edward said, "Here's the background on Yuhana Khalil. Forgot to give it to you before."

Joe commented as he read, "Just as I suspected, Iraqi Christian resettled here. A lawyer in Iraq, so it's natural he'd be one here. Must be bright and ambitious; a Christian lawyer in Iraq would have to be. Distance learning courses here and a couple of courses at West Virginia University law school. Passed the bar exam the first try.

"Practices in a small town in southwestern West Virginia. Not too successful, not for lack of competence, but people're more comfortable with locals. Married a woman from the local Catholic church; picked up some business that way, mostly routine real estate transfers and the like. Does *pro bono* work for persons who can't pay much and who other attorneys don't want. Has a modest record of trial success. Also federal and state public defender jobs.

"It remains to be seen whether he'll have a subtle, maybe unconscious prejudice against Palestinians. They've have been disliked by other Arabs for thousands of years."

Court was called to order. James Edward called Ahmed Hammoud, who was dressed in nice school clothes, freshly laundered and pressed by Lucy Simpson. He was sworn in with the Koran and established as being born in Blacksburg, growing up in Lafayette, and going to school in Elliston.

James Edward asked, "Do you know the defendants?"

When he answered 'yes', James Edward said, "Please tell the court when and how you got to know them."

Ahmed said he knew them around the high school. Then he continued, "They followed me home from school, forced me to go with them, and sexually assaulted me," and briefly described when.

"Sexual assault can mean many things from unwanted touching or exposure to full penetration and other things," James Edward said. "Can you tell us in brief general terms what they did to you?"

Rich Harris stood and said, "Object, Your Honor. The defendants are not charged with sexual assault. Counselor's asking for sensational details not relevant to the case."

"Your Honor," James Edward responded, "counselor knows full well the defendants are charged with denying victims' civil rights because they're Arabs. It's permissible to bring evidence of other similar activities. Sexual assault is certainly denial of civil rights, and we will establish very soon it's because of the witness's ethnicity."

"The question will stand for now," Judge Bishop said. "Counselor, you're stretching and need to keep to the point."

Ahmed, sobbing, said, "I was penetrated."

James Edward then asked, "What reason did the defendants give, if any, for assaulting you?"

Ahmed replied, "Said they didn't want A-rabs messing with their girls; called me an A-rab sissy boy."

James Edward continued, "Did they use protection?"

Ahmed blurted out, "No."

"Object, Your Honor," Rich Harris said forcefully. "This testimony is not only irrelevant but prejudicial."

Judge Bishop sternly looked at James Edward, saying, "The question has already been answered, but I would have sustained the objection. You must not pursue this line of questioning. The jury is instructed to disregard the answer."

James Edward then asked, "Mr. Hammoud, have you had other encounters with these defendants?"

Ahmed said, "You mean at the gas station when they drove off without paying? They called me an A-rab asshole and said they'd ream it again, then said they weren't going to pay the bill; they didn't want to have fuckin' A-rabs here and would bomb us like A-rabs bombed them."

While Ahmed was testifying, Joe sent a text message.

"Who else heard them?" James Edward asked.

"Two guys buying gas," Ahmed replied.

Paco and Frank entered the courtroom quietly and took seats far apart, with other spectators around them. Omar entered through another door.

James Edward asked, "Would you please look around the courtroom and see if you recognize those two persons."

After looking around the courtroom several moments, Ahmed pointed to Paco and said, "I think one of 'em's there; it'd help if he stood up." Paco stood and Ahmed said, "Yes, that's him. He talked to that guy over there," he pointed to Kody Bates, "who said he wasn't going to pay and drove away screaming about bombing our house."

James Edward then said, "You said there were two persons who heard. Is the other person present?"

After another search for a few moments, Ahmed pointed to Frank. "Might be that guy there."

"Please tell us what transpired between you and this person you've just identified," James Edward requested.

Ahmed replied, "He said the car drove away without paying. I answered my father'd be really angry; he gave me $100 so my father wouldn't have to know."

"What'd you do with it?" James Edward asked.

"My uncle must've seen because he made me give it to the mosque, saying Muslims can't keep money they don't earn from their own work," Ahmed replied.

James Edward said he had no more questions; Rich Harris began, "How many times have you seen the two men you identified?"

Ahmed looked at his attorney, who gave a signal to be cautious, then answered, "Just told you, at the station."

"What about photographs or physical descriptions?" Rich Harris asked."

Looking at his attorney, Ahmed answered, "No."

Rich Harris then said, "You can't be sure they're the persons you saw, can you? You had to ask one to stand up."

James Edward jumped up saying, "Object, Your Honor. Counselor is harassing the witness."

Judge Bishop said, "Sustained."

"I'll rephrase that," Rich Harris said. "How can you be sure this was the same person you saw almost two years ago?"

Ahmed looked at his attorney and answered, "After he stood up, it was easy. He's big and tall."

"Did he say anything else to you?" Rich Harris asked.

Ahmed's attorney gave a signal and he answered, "He said these guys'd done something bad to me, hadn't they, er, and that some gay guys might defend me."

Rich Harris then said, "You testified your uncle heard you and the person you just identified discussing why he gave you money. Were you shouting? How could he hear?"

Ahmed's attorney shook his head to indicate 'no' and made the sign of a trap; James Edward said, "Object, Your Honor. Counselor's statement is false. We request the witness's testimony on this issue be read by the recorder."

Rich Harris then said, "I'll give the question in another way. How was it possible your uncle observed this person whom you just identified gave you money?"

James Edward said, "Object, Your Honor, we did not request the question be rephrased; we requested the court recorder read the witness's original testimony on this issue."

Judge Bishop asked the recorder to repeat the question, during which Ahmed realized the trap and said, "That's not what I said. You just heard I said 'my uncle must've *seen*.'"

"Now let's go to that fantastic story that you were abducted and sexually assaulted," Richard Harris said. "How can you expect us to believe you if no one heard them say you were being allegedly abducted because you're Arab?"

"Object, Your Honor," James Edward said. "Counselor's leading and harassing the witness and asking for an unwarranted conclusion."

"Sustained!" Judge Bishop stated forcefully.

"I'll rephrase," Richard Harris said. "Who, else, *if anyone*, heard you were assaulted because you're Arab?"

Ahmed replied, "My brother and sister might've."

"They can't testify to confirm, can they?" Richard Harris asked.

Seeing his attorney's sign, Ahmed answered, "No."

"Your brother's dead, isn't he?" Rich Harris asked. "What were the circumstances of his death?"

Just as Ahmed was beginning to sob, James Edward stated, "Object, Your Honor. The death of the witness's brother is an established fact that can be readily verified. The circumstances of his death have no bearing whatever."

Judge Bishop forcefully stated, "Sustained."

Rich Harris then continued, "Was anyone else present when this alleged sexual abuse occurred?"

Ahmed answered, "No."

Rich Harris stated, "You have no proof that sexual assault occurred. For all we know, it was just a little scuffle high school boys get into all the time."

Joe hastily passed a note to James Edward while Ahmed, with increasing anguish and looking at his attorney, blurted out, "No, it wasn't like that. They raped me."

Joe thought, *I hope Ahmed catches on to what we're doing; we didn't prepare him for this.*

"No further questions," Rich Harris stated.

James Edward stated, "Your Honor, we have additional questions for this witness. "Could you please tell us if it's possible for you to identify the attackers' private parts and tattoos in the area if you were required to do so. Please note we are not asking you to identify them now in this courtroom, but whether you could."

Ahmed struggled to say, "Yes."

When James Edward said no further questions, Yuhana Khalil stood and said, "Your Honor, we have additional questions." To Ahmed, gently, "*Marhaba*, Ahmed. We know it's difficult because of the passing of your brother, but we need to know whether you'd say you're a good Muslim?"

James Edward rose, "Object, Your Honor. The witness's religion is not an issue here. It has been established by previous testimony that this trial is for hate crimes committed because of the victims' Arab ethnicity, not their religion. Counselor very well knows that not all Arabs are Muslim and introducing the Islamic religion is irrelevant."

Yuhana Khalil, smarting at the obvious reference to his Christianity, responded, "Your Honor, this question raises a vital point about the witness's credibility. There is a huge amount of precedent in courts in this country in which witnesses have been called upon to identify themselves as good Christians. The same precedent must necessarily apply to Muslims. The witness testified he attends a mosque and is obviously Muslim. Therefore, there can be no objection to asking the witness to identify himself as a good Muslim."

Judge Bishop said, "Objection overruled. You can answer the question."

Ahmed said, "Yes, I s'pose."

"Then isn't it true that good Muslims would not look at another man's midsection?" Yuhana Khalil said.

"Er, yes," Ahmed answered.

"Then how can you claim you could identify private parts?" Yuhana Khali asked.

Ahmed blurted out, "They forced me to look."

"How can someone force you to look?" Yuhana Khalil asked quickly. "You can always close your eyes."

Ahmed replied, "They pulled my hair hard and forced me to look directly at them."

Yuhana Khalil then asked, "Wouldn't you say one man's private parts are just about like any other's?"

"But not tattoos," Ahmed blurted out on the verge of collapse before James Edward leaped to his feet saying, "Object, Your Honor. Counselor is asking the witness for a conclusion he is obviously incapable of making. Furthermore, he's going into lurid details to which the defense itself objected. If this line of questioning is pursued, the prosecution will request a court-ordered medical examination of the defendants to be compared with the witness's descriptions."

Judge Bishop, obviously displeased, stated, "The objection is sustained, but this court will not order any examination nor tolerate any questioning along these lines."

Yuhana Khalil said, "No more questions, Your Honor."

Judge Bishop, noting Ahmed's condition, said, "You may step down. The court will recess for twenty minutes."

During the recess, James Edward said to Joe, "That sure was brilliant about private parts and tattoos."

It just popped into my mind," Joe replied. "I noticed the defendants have tattoos visible on the parts of their body not covered with their shirts. Why'd they wear long sleeves in this hot weather if it were not to cover up tattoos?"

CHAPTER 37

Tuesday, June 3, 2008
Roanoke, Virginia, USA

When court resumed, James Edward stated, "The prosecution calls Francisco Mendoza," and established he lived in Baltimore and was a nurse at the Veterans' Administration nursing home.

Ahmed sat next to his father, becoming increasingly agitated and causing his father to tell him quietly to be still.

James Edward led Paco through testimony that he had voluntarily remained outside the courtroom at prosecution request, that he was aware it was his right to be inside, and that he had heard the previous witness's testimony only since he had been in the courtroom. James Edward led him through testimony in which he identified Ahmed and described their interaction at the gasoline station and then asked if Paco could identify any of the defendants.

Paco replied, "The one in the middle. He left without paying and shouted threats about reaming his rear end and bombing their house."

"Please repeat and confirm for the court how the defendant pronounced the word that describes Mr. Hammoud's ethnicity," James Edward requested.

Paco replied, "You mean Arab that he called 'A-rab.'"

"Have you had any contact with Mr. Ahmed Hammoud since that date?" James Edward asked.

"No, not at all," Paco answered firmly.

Omar observed Ahmed losing composure, beginning to cry, and led him out of the courtroom.

James Edward said he had no more questions. Then Rich Harris began, "Paco, where are you from?"

Oh, Rich must've studied Spanish and knows Paco's a nickname for "Francisco," James Edward thought. *No one has used that nickname for him here in court.*

"I said earlier I'm from Baltimore," Paco answered, "and Paco's a name that only friends, family, and my patients call me. I am Francisco or Mr. Mendoza."

"I asked you where you are from, Fran-cis-co," Rich Harris stated combatively, "not where you live."

He replied, "Where I grew up? Hamilton, Ohio."

"No!" Rich Harris stated emphatically. "Where are you from? Where were you born?"

"Oh," Paco answered, annoyed. "Why didn't you say so? I was born in Mexico, but I have...."

"Just answer the question," Rich Harris interrupted. "What is your status?"

"What status do you mean?" Paco asked.

"Your immigration status, of course," Richard Harris stated condescendingly. "Are you illegal?"

James Edward stood to object, but before he could, Paco stated, "I am a citizen of the United States!"

"What proof do you have of that?" Rich Harris asked.

James Edward, still standing, stated, "Object, Your Honor. Counselor is harassing the witness and accusing him of perjury. Counselor knows full well there is no requirement in the United States for citizens of our country to carry and produce proof of citizenship. As we have done with a previous witness, we can obtain and produce documentation, should the court require such proof."

Rich Harris, with mock indignation said, "Your Honor, I am merely determining the credibility of the witness."

Judge Bishop, scowling, said, "Objection sustained."

"Francisco, you testified that it was getting dark," Rich Harris stated. "How can you be sure of your identifications?"

Paco replied, "I most definitely did not testify to that. It was broad open daylight; I could see very well."

"Even so," Richard Harris continued, "it's been a long time; how can you be so sure who you saw?"

Paco replied, "Growing up as a Mexican kid in Hamilton, Ohio, one learns quickly to recognize bullies."

"You're accusing this defendant of being a bully with no good reason, aren't you?" Rich Harris asked combatively.

"Threatening to ream his ass again and bomb his house sure sounds like bullying to me," Paco answered.

"As big and husky as you are, it's difficult to imagine anyone would bully you," Richard Harris continued combatively. "You were the bully, weren't you? How many times did you beat someone up?"

James Edward immediately said, "Object, Your Honor. This is a totally unwarranted attack on his character."

"Sustained!" Judge Bishop stated forcefully.

"Isn't it true you had a cell phone ready to call authorities and intimidated the defendant by threatening him, causing him to flee for his own safety?" Rich Harris asked.

"I had a cell phone, and I would have used it to call 911 if there'd been violence," Paco stated. "Working as a nurse in a veterans' home, I deal with effects of violence all the time and will do what I can to prevent it. As for threatening, I don't view asking what's going on as a threat."

Rich Harris stated haughtily he had no further questions, after which James Edward called Frank and established his residence, occupation, and that he had been present on the day in question.

He also established that Frank remained outside the courtroom voluntarily.

Joe received a text message from Omar reading, "Ahmed with me at hotel. Call when you can."

"Previous witnesses have testified you were at the Hammoud gas station on November 27, 2006," James Edward continued. "Can you confirm that?"

Frank showed the sales receipt for gasoline on that day, which James Edward requested be placed into evidence.

"The witness testified you gave him money. Did you in fact give him money, and how much?" James Edward asked.

"Yes I did," Frank answered, "one hundred dollars."

"What was your motive?" James Edward asked.

"He said his father would be really angry because the car drove away without paying," Frank stated. "I've had lots of experience with an angry father and felt sorry for him."

James Edward then asked, "Was there any further dialogue between you and Mr. Ahmed Hammoud?"

"He said thanks, or something similar," Frank replied.

James Edward indicated no further questions, and Rich Harris began by asking, "Major Reynolds, you normally buy your way out of trouble by paying money, don't you?"

James Edward objected, which Judge Bishop sustained.

"Previous testimony indicates you were away when most of the confrontation between Francisco and the defendant occurred. Where were you?" Rich Harris asked.

Frank answered, "In the restroom."

"As you came from the restroom, you saw Paco Mendoza intimidating the defendant, didn't you?" Rich Harris asked.

"I saw nothing of the sort!" Frank stated.

"What is your relationship to Paco?" Rich Harris asked. "Intimate friends, so that he moved to Maryland to be with you and traveled together with you. Right?"

Joe immediately jumped up and said, "Object, Your Honor. Counselor is harassing the witness and jumping to conclusions. It has no bearing on this case whether they are casual acquaintances or professional colleagues and friends."

"Counselors will approach the bench, and that includes you, Mr. Shaito," Judge Bishop ordered.

In front and with the noise neutralizing device on, she looked at Rich Harris and stated forcefully, "I have tolerated your misconduct enough. If you cross the line one more time, I will hold you in contempt of court, but not until the case is over. Action will be filed with the Bar Association as well." Then, turning to James Edward and Joe, she said, "Your theatrical stunts having witnesses waiting outside the courtroom as though this were stage drama are pushing the envelope. Get on with your cases." Then after the noise neutralizing device was turned off, she said, "Objection sustained!"

Joe thought, *One of them has to testify about their relationship. Hope James Edward and Randy trust me.*

When Rich Harris said no further questions, Joe stood to say, "The prosecution recalls Francisco Mendoza." He thought, *Paco's bright. Better to ask him than Frank.*

"Mr. Mendoza," Joe began, "you testified you're a nurse with the Veteran's Administration. In this capacity you would naturally be involved with former military personnel. Do you also have contact with active duty personnel?"

Paco, confused, answered, "Yes, sometimes."

"Major Reynolds is an active duty military officer," Joe continued. "Have you had contact with him in a professional work-related capacity?"

Paco replied, "Yes, he comes to the nursing home sometimes to visit Marine Corps veterans."

"Would you say, then, that your friendship and professional contacts are related?" Joe asked.

"Yes, definitely," Paco answered.

"Would you please tell us why you two were traveling together through this area on that day?" he asked.

"We were returning from the wedding of a friend in Alabama, a military friend," Paco answered.

Joe said there were no further questions. When Rich Harris stated he had no further questions, Randy Walker stood and said the prosecution rests its case.

Rich Harris said, "The defense moves the case be dismissed for failure to prove a credible case. We've heard only unsupported allegations and lurid details that have no relevance."

Judge Bishop, anticipating the request, stated, "Motion denied. The defense will proceed with its case."

"The defense rests," Rich Harris stated.

"Court will convene tomorrow morning to hear closing arguments," Judge Bishop ordered and promptly left.

While prosecution attorneys walked to their office, James Edward said to Joe, "That was brilliant how you jumped onto that gay accusation and deflected it, setting things straight."

"Be careful how you use the word 'straight,'" Joe chuckled. "I didn't tell you guys Paco and Frank *are* a gay couple. There's more to it, but I need to call Omar urgently. He has Ahmed with him in the hotel."

While Joe called Omar, James Edward told Randy Walker what Judge Bishop had said at the bench.

"Like I thought," Randy Walker commented, "Rich Harris knew exactly what he was doing all the time and was probably trying to get Martha to hold him in contempt publicly just to get sympathy from one juror."

Joe finished his call and interrupted, "Ahmed had a breakdown and is in our hotel room. He needs a doctor. Omar didn't want to do anything until we could contact you, Randy, and maybe get the doctors who saw him yesterday."

"OK, I'll get on it right away," Randy Walker said.

"I was saying," Joe continued, "Paco and Frank are a couple," and explained briefly how the friendship developed.

James Edward replied, "This is the twenty-first century. I suppose we all have gay friends and acquaintances."

"There's more to how much I was involved with Marwan Hammoud's death as the gay bar bomber, too," Joe said. "not keeping secrets, but no need to go into tragic details if it isn't relevant. Maybe I should tell you now."

"We need to do something about Ahmed first," Randy Walker said. "Get him an HIV test too. I need to spend the afternoon finishing closing arguments. Unless there's something urgent that affects our final arguments, let's save that until later."

CHAPTER 38

Tuesday, June 3, 2008
Roanoke, Virginia, USA

Joe, Frank, and Paco were sitting in Macado's ordering dinner; Joe had explained that Omar would hopefully join them later because he was busy with Ahmed at a hospital. Joe had spent most of the afternoon with Frank and Paco because Ahmed was distraught, crying uncontrollably, mostly in a fetal position. To give Omar and Ahmed privacy, Joe gave Frank and Paco a leisurely tour of Roanoke.

"This restaurant is a nice place," Frank commented.

"It's gay friendly, or so Jason says," Joe commented, and described briefly Jason's recent visit and going to a nearby gay bar to dance. They all said how much they enjoyed Jason's company.

"Maybe we can stop to see him on the way home," Paco said. "He should be back from New Mexico now."

"When're you going home?" Joe asked. "After closing arguments tomorrow morning, I'm free until the jury gives its verdict; I just have to stay close. Maybe we can do something in the afternoon and evening if you two can stay over."

Frank replied, "Hadn't thought much about it. I don't have anything to get back for."

Paco said, "School's out and summer school doesn't start for a few days. I can probably trade work with someone who has a weekend." After orders were taken, he said, "You almost lost me when you asked how we knew each other."

"You caught on quick," Joe replied. "I remembered you said you'd used that story to deflect attention. It's true, so you weren't perjuring yourself. The defense attorney must've picked up on Ahmed's testimony about gays. The judge sure picked up on it. She's been letting him push the limit all during this trial, but not this time."

"Her daughter's lesbian," Frank stated.

"What!" Joe exclaimed. "How would you know?"

"I met her daughter and her partner," Frank replied, and explained. He concluded, "I was going to mention it before, but we were all preoccupied. Interesting coincidence it was actually her mother who's the judge in this trial."

"No shit," Joe said. "The defense attorney's one sharp guy; he's been pushing her to the limit all trial long. This attempt to make them think you're gay pushed her button. Now I see why. She's hell on wheels."

"That's what Becky, her daughter, says," Frank chuckled. "But how can that defense attorney be one sharp guy if he made so many mistakes and got overruled?"

"Oh, he didn't make mistakes," Joe answered. "It was part of his strategy to get the judge pissed off at him, maybe hold him in contempt of court, and get sympathy from one of the jurors. He only needs one to be doubtful to get a hung jury and maybe get them off."

They were engaging in small talk when Omar arrived, showing extreme exhaustion on his face and body.

Joe went to him, saying, "Habibi, you OK?"

Paco immediately stopped eating, looked directly at Omar, and said, "Hey, man, you don't look good at all. Maybe I need to examine you and get you to a doctor too."

Omar slid into the booth, saying, "It's been one hell of a day. Maybe I just need something to eat; didn't have lunch."

Without looking at the menu, he ordered a chicken sandwich and soft drink. He sat slumped with obvious letdown while others continued eating in silence.

Joe asked, "How's Ahmed?"

"Not good," Omar replied. "Nothing life threatening unless he becomes suicidal, but don't think there's much danger of that. He's still Muslim and wouldn't take his own life and he doesn't have misguided notions about virgins on the path to heaven. He's in a psychiatric unit, and they likely have him under routine suicide watch."

"Oh," the others muttered glumly as Paco said, "Hey, man, that's heavy. Know sorta what you're talking about. A few of the old guys in our home get that way occasionally when the pain, psychological or physical, gets too much for them to deal with. I'm not a psychiatric nurse, but if I can do anything to help, help you that is, let me know."

"Thanks," Omar muttered. "The biggest part of the problem is insurance requirements of hospitals in this country. The psychiatrist Randy arranged thankfully intervened and got him admitted as an indigent. Nassar thought he was going to have to be responsible; just wanted to take Ahmed home to rest, thinking he'd be OK after a while. After his experience with Roula in the private psychiatric hospital and now the state mental hospital, he was saying as much as he loves his remaining son, he just doesn't have the money. The psychiatrist finally convinced him Ahmed's legally an adult and there's no obligation for parents to pay. Nassar felt a moral obligation—not his words—and was beside himself."

Joe added, "Seems it's taken care of, at least for now."

"Something'll have to be worked out soon, but they're focusing on stabilizing him right now," Omar said.

"Was he violent?" Paco asked.

"No, not at all," Omar replied. "Just the opposite. He did not respond to anything, just saying, 'I killed my brother.' I tried to reason with him, but it was clear he wasn't going to respond. He wouldn't move when his father tried to get him up to take him home. Even when the EMTs came to take him to the hospital, he wouldn't move. He didn't resist when they fastened him to one of those cots to take him away."

"God," Paco stated, "I do need me to look you over."

"Should we call a taxi to go to the hotel?" Joe asked.

"Nah," Omar replied. "By the time a taxi'd get here, we'd be halfway there. I can still walk, but for sure I'm at the point of collapse. I need to get in bed."

"You go ahead," Frank stated. "I'll pay and catch up later. You can all pay me later. Oh, what the hell, I'll treat."

Paco wrote a name on a scrap of paper, gave it to Frank, and said, "See if you can find a pharmacy open and get this; it's a non-prescription sedative and tranquilizer. Surely a town as big as Roanoke would have a pharmacy open or on call."

A short while later, Paco examined Omar as best he could, saying, "Your pulse is high, but I don't find anything else of immediate concern. Your other vital signs seem OK. You're basically in good health; you take care of yourself."

"Yeah," Omar muttered.

"Most we could do is take you to an emergency room, and about all they'd do is put you in a hospital bed until someone could examine you tomorrow. Might as well stay here in the hotel bed."

Omar awkwardly undressed to his underwear and got in bed, but didn't go to sleep until Frank arrived several minutes later.

Frank and Paco went to their room. Joe went to bed and promptly went to sleep as well.

CHAPTER 39

Joe left a note asking Omar to send him a text message when he woke up, sent text messages to Frank and Paco saying the same, and then went to the office. Later, he and James Edward were in the courtroom while Randy Walker gave closing arguments, which tied together testimony and evidence presented at different times. He emphasized the definition of hate crimes and legal precedents of proof for such crimes. He showed how the testimony and evidence presented fit that proof. He also made an appeal to emotions, describing the Hammoud family as decent and hard-working, contributing to the community, and not deserving to have their property damaged and be threatened because of their ethnicity.

Rich Harris used emotion to attack the prosecution's case, saying testimony was unreliable; it had lurid irrelevant details because it could not build a credible case. He reemphasized the definition of hate crimes, stating how serious they are, and stated that the prosecution's case would be frivolous if it were not so serious. He asserted that the defendants at most played a prank, a state crime not a federal one, and have paid the price.

After Rich Harris's remarks, Judge Bishop declared a lunch recess. Joe saw text messages saying Omar was on the way to the hospital and wanted Joe to call when he could. Paco said he was going to the hospital to be with Omar. Joe phoned Omar, who said he was with Ahmed and Paco. Joe then called Frank, who said he was hanging out and stayed in the hotel to deal with issues about his mother. Joe said to meet him at the courthouse and listen to the Judge's instructions to the jury and they'd meet afterwards.

Judge Bishop gave instructions to the jury, which were articulate and well organized. She reiterated the defendants were being tried for a federal crime of denying civil rights because of ethnicity, and it was the duty of the prosecution to prove a federal crime or crimes. She described the type of evidence needed to prove the crimes and the varying degrees of credibility to attach to each type of evidence. She concluded, emphasizing the three were being tried individually, even though they were being tried at the same time. She stated that the jury must return three verdicts.

When she finished, Marcus Porter rushed to talk to Randy Walker, using eye contact to hint to Joe he would see him later. Meanwhile, some from the media rushed to Frank, pushing a microphone in front of him, one asking, "Where's your boyfriend?"

Frank said he had nothing to say.

"That means he is your boyfriend, then; don't ask, don't tell," another stated.

Marcus Porter rushed up in front of Frank, saying loudly, "Major Reynolds, wouldn't you say that your testimony was the frosting on the cake of the prosecution's case?" He then walked forward, forcing Frank to move backward and said barely audibly, "Go to that side door, protesting loudly so you can get out of their way."

Frank suddenly caught on and almost screamed, "How many times do I need to tell you, I have nothing to say," and walked rapidly to the door, with Marcus Porter following.

As they approached the door, Marcus said loudly, "Oh you're avoiding the question." In a lower voice, "Go wait by the security guard at the door; I'll tell Joe."

Marcus Porter returned to where Randy Walker was speaking. "We have no comments for the moment. The local media know the U.S. Attorney's office in Roanoke cooperates with the media in order to preserve the right to fair and open public prosecution in accordance with the U.S. Constitution. We will call a press conference when we have comments to make. For those of you not with the local media, please contact our office and leave your contact details so you can be notified. That will be all for today."

Marcus Porter passed close to Joe heading to the defense table and said softly, "Frank's waiting by security."

Meanwhile, Rich Harris was commenting about the prosecution's failure to present an adequate case. Some were questioning Yuhana Khalil about his background; he took the opportunity to subtly promote himself in a professionally appropriate way while answering.

Meanwhile, Joe went to the security area, stood next to Frank sidewise, pretending to be looking for someone, and said, "Wait here and we'll be back to get you."

When the prosecuting team was heading towards their office, Frank walked ahead of them. Joe brushed against him and said, "We'll follow you and shield you. Turn right and keep on."

Soon Joe and Frank sat in a coffee shop commiserating over Frank's encounter with the media, and Joe asked, "Other than that, how's your day been? You said something about your mother."

Frank replied. "I haven't told Paco because I didn't want him to worry while he had finals. Maybe you can give some legal insights or just listen."

"Sure," Joe replied.

"I told you my father was arrested trying to crash the award ceremony. He's under house arrest in the DC area. He tried to contact me a few times, but I refused."

"House arrest?" Joe replied surprised.

Frank continued, "He pulled enough strings to get out of confinement, but some guys he's bullied through the years want to make him pay a price. Also the DIA's really pissed at him and wants to keep him under wraps. They're deciding whether to recall him to active duty for a court martial or charge him as a civilian. Plenty are dragging their heels, wanting him to stew as long as possible."

Joe responded, "I can't give much insight there. Military law's a special area I don't know anything about."

"That's not all of it," Frank added. "I told them I'd severed all ties with him and not to get me involved. Now it's my mother. You know she's alcoholic. She had a bad car wreck under the influence, lots of persons injured including her, was hospitalized, and now faces legal problems."

"What kind of problems?" Joe asked.

"If one person dies, which now seems unlikely, vehicular homicide," Frank continued. "I'm sure you can imagine all sorts of other criminal acts, not to mention insurance, and all sorts of civil liability issues. She's hospitalized in critical condition."

"Oh my god," Joe replied. "You must be concerned."

"Not that concerned," Frank said. "She's a human being, but beyond that, I've completely washed my hands of anything to do with my biological parents. There's a move to make her serve jail time and go to rehab once she gets out of the hospital. She's been in scrapes before; and my father, I should say her husband, pulled strings for her to go to a few days' rehab and get off with a fine. I told the person who contacted me that so far as I'm concerned she can be in rehab the rest of her life. She's obviously a danger to others, not to mention to herself."

"I had to deal with some of this in legal aid clinics in law school," Joe said. "I can brush up and let you know."

Frank said, "Thanks. They can do with her legally what they like. Another issue came up this morning. A lawyer finally found me. Their house has been vacant a long time and is not being maintained, an eyesore to the neighborhood, to say the least. Neighbors are up in arms, not only about an eyesore, but the danger of someone breaking into the house, maybe even squatting, and creating a risk for them. The lawyer wanted me to go to Florida and tend to the house. My, er, sperm donor says I should take care of it. I told the lawyer in no uncertain terms that I would not go to Florida. I have no interest whatever in that house. Still, the neighbors are decent people and don't deserve to be put at risk. I told the lawyer to hire house-sitters or whatever; my parents have plenty of money. My question is what obligation do I have legally, and what could come back on me?"

"That's easy to answer," Joe said. "You have no legal obligation unless you have some legal interest in the house."

"Their wills apparently leave their property to me," Frank said. "I don't intend to claim that inheritance. If I'm required to take it, I'll give every last penny to charity."

"That wouldn't normally give you enough legal interest that you could be held responsible," Joe replied. "One question is whether you've prepared a will to specify that anything you inherit will go to whatever charity you want."

"No, I hadn't thought of that. I do have a will; we're pretty much obligated to have a will if combat's a possibility. I definitely need to change it, now that Paco's in my life. I don't want to go to a base legal office to rewrite my will because of questions about being with Paco."

Joe agreed. "For sure you need to do something. You don't have to use a military lawyer. You can use any lawyer in Maryland, or wherever your legal residence is. I'm not expert enough in this type of law and not licensed to practice in Maryland. I could help find you one, though."

"Gee thanks," Frank said. "Pete would surely have a lawyer too; I can ask him or, if not, get you to find one."

"OK," Joe replied. "Who's Pete, if I may ask?"

Frank explained briefly about knowing Pete Ramos, and Joe said, "Oh, I remember. What are your thoughts for the rest of the day? I'm free until a verdict is announced. I just need to stay close enough to go to the court on short notice. I need to get in touch with Omar and see what's going on with him at the hospital. Paco's with him, I hear."

"Yeah, Paco kind of pushed himself on Omar and insisted he go along," Frank said. "He's worried about Omar and thought since he's a nurse he could help with the guy. Maybe we go to the hospital and see what's going on."

"I doubt we could do much good at the hospital, and they might not want us around," Joe said. "I suspect Ahmed's father is there, so two more'd be a crowd. For sure I need to call. I need to change clothes and call from the hotel, if that's OK with you."

"Sure, I'm just hanging out," he said.

"As soon as I get changed and we know what's going on with Omar and Paco, we can come back into town," Joe suggested. "There's a pretty decent small art museum here and some other museums. Say, I heard of a good place up on the parkway we could go to dinner."

They paid their bill and walked to the hotel.

CHAPTER 40

Wednesday, June 4, 2008
Peaks of Otter, Virginia, USA

Frank drove up winding roads to the Blue Ridge Parkway on a clear early summer evening when days were long and the air clear before the mid-summer haze set in. They arrived at Peaks of Otter Lodge by a small lake on the slopes of Virginia's Blue Ridge Mountains below two towering mountain peaks for which the lodge was named.

While eating from a sumptuous buffet, Paco commented, "Nice and cool here in the mountains; getting warm in the city. I could use a beer. Do any of you mind?"

"Why should we mind?" Joe asked. "You've drunk beer around us before."

"Just didn't want to be the only one drinking," Paco replied. "I suspect lover boy won't drink, especially driving these winding roads in the dark."

"Nothing for me," Frank replied. "It's bad enough to manage those roads sober."

"I'll drive so you can have something," Joe offered, "if you trust me on those roads."

"You sure?" Frank asked. "I sure could use a glass of wine, and for sure I'd trust you. Say, this is really a nice place; somewhere to come for a romantic getaway."

Paco nudged him gently chuckling, "Gee, aren't you getting mellow; romantic getaway, no less."

They ordered drinks, engaged in small talk, then Joe asked, "Are you two going home soon, now that the trial's over except for the verdict? It sure was good you stayed over an extra day. It'd be great to have you here longer."

"Sometime tomorrow," Frank replied. "I don't think we're in a huge hurry to get back, at least I'm not. Maybe after lunch and get to Jason's in time for dinner. We haven't talked about it, so I don't want to speak for lover boy."

"Fine with me," Paco answered, "although I'm in no hurry. Nice to have a break after finals." To Omar, "You want help getting him to the state hospital tomorrow?"

"I can handle it," Omar said. "Maybe Joe can help if something's needed." After a short pause he hastily added, "I do appreciate it. I didn't express appreciation very well earlier. I'm not used to having people do things for me and taking care of me. I was kind of annoyed when you insisted the nurse and doctor at the hospital examine me too. Now I realize it was a good thing and you were concerned and caring. Thanks."

"Yeah, man, I noticed," Paco said. "I'm used to that. Lots of old guys in our home aren't used to having people take care of them."

Omar replied, "Thanks to you and especially the doctors, Nassar was convinced Ahmed needs to be in the state hospital, at least for a while, same place his mother is. I hope we can get him transferred early. I need to get back tomorrow too. Friday's a big day at the center."

"Whoa, man!" Paco said emphatically. "You're not in any condition to drive anywhere tomorrow and certainly not go to work so soon. Maybe I do need to go with you and get that doctor to knock some sense into your head."

Joe said forcefully, "Habibi, he's right! You've been working at the center a good ten months without a single day off except when you were down here at a burial and 40th day prayers, and even then you were working. Surely they understand imams can get sick and need time off."

Omar became indignant but then realized they had a point and said, "OK, let me think about it."

After finishing dessert, while they relaxed Joe suddenly remembered and said to Omar, "Doesn't Nassar realize Ahmed's under arrest and out on bail, mostly because you're a federal prison chaplain who's responsible for him?"

"Good point, Habibi," Omar said. "Sorry. I've been under so much stress I didn't think about that. Here I am a prison chaplain. I should know these things."

"Hey, lighten up," Paco interjected. "You may be a prison chaplain, an imam, and all that, but you're still human. You need to pay attention to your own health right now."

"What's this about things he did in Iraq?" Frank asked. "Maybe it's none of my business."

"It's a long, bizarre, convoluted story, and I don't know all the details myself," Joe replied. He then gave a brief summary of Ahmed's activities.

Frank and Paco exchanged surprised looks, causing Joe to ask, "Did I say something wrong?"

"No," Frank answered. "We think we might know the doctor, the cosmetic surgeon. Where in Iraq?"

"Don't know," Joe replied. "We didn't ask. It's in an area that doesn't have too many Arabs or they didn't speak Arabic much and the doctor spoke perfect English."

"Sounds like Kurdistan," Omar offered.

"That fits," Frank said. "Sounds like the guy we know." He described briefly how they knew Ali, concluding, "There's more to the story, but that's probably best not told in a public place."

"OK," Joe said. "If something more comes of this, we can ask you. Say, you think we should go? I've had a busy day, and it seems Omar needs to get to bed soon."

"Yeah," Omar muttered. "It's not that I don't enjoy your company, but I'm still exhausted. Maybe I will call the center and tell them I'm not feeling well."

"According to the map, there's a short road that goes from here to the interstate," Joe said. "Maybe we can find it and have an easier drive back."

Later, when Joe was driving them down the very steep and winding Virginia Highway 43, he commented, "Oh my God, this's even worse than the roads we drove to get here. At least we can get to the interstate soon." As they approached Roanoke, he said, "Hey, we don't have to get up early in the morning. Maybe we can go have a late leisurely breakfast. Jason found an IHOP when he was here and he and I went."

Paco said, "Yeah, IHOP's great."

CHAPTER 41

Friday, June 6, 2008
Roanoke, Virginia, USA

Over lunch, Joe said to Omar, "Damn, how much longer will they deliberate? Maybe he did convince one juror and they're hung. They asked the judge for clarifications yesterday, which she gave this morning. How was your day? You find an Islamic chaplain for the hospital?"

"No," he replied. "The guy at the Islamic educational place said he'd do what he can, but I'm the official chaplain for now. Say, when should we to go to prayers?"

Later inside the mosque, Joe felt his phone vibrating. Leaving before prayers ended, they soon were in the courtroom where large numbers of the media had gathered; camera crews were outside. Nassar rushed in dressed in work clothes and sat next to Omar.

Court was called to order, and then the jury foreman stated Kyle Bates had been found guilty of a first degree crime and the other two of lesser crimes of aiding, abetting, and conspiracy. Judge Bishop remanded the defendants into custody awaiting sentencing.

Persons from the media rushed to the defense and prosecution tables and swarmed around Nassar, shouting questions about whether he felt vindicated.

Nassar stammered, "Please not all at once."

A reporter for Arabic-language *al Jazeera* pushed forward, asking in Arabic, "Abou Ahmed, how do you feel about your great victory for Arabs in the U.S.?"

Omar spoke to him tersely in Arabic. "Can't you see he's overwhelmed? Show respect and maybe he can answer."

"Who are you?" the *al Jazeera* reporter replied combatively in Arabic. "You're not his son."

Omar answered in Arabic, "I'm an imam who has offered guidance. You're obviously Arab. Now please show respect of our Arab culture and maybe he can say something once these other rude reporters stop." He said forcefully in English, "Show some respect. Can't you see he's in a difficult position with you harassing him all at once? Mr. Hammoud will give a statement when it's appropriate."

"And who are you?" one of the reporters asked testily.

"I'm an imam," Omar answered. "In case you don't know, it's like a Christian pastor or priest."

Marcus Porter rushed up, saying softly, "Mr. Hammoud, follow me and I'll run interference. I'll find you later for a statement if I may."

Pretending to fire questions, he led Omar and Nassar through a cluster of aggressive reporters and cameramen. Outside, he directed them to a nearby coffee shop.

Meanwhile, the reporter from Arabic al Jazeera subtly accused Yuhana Khalil in Arabic of betraying his heritage by defending persons who bombed Arabs' house.

Yuhana Khalil replied calmly in Arabic, "In the United States, all persons accused of a crime are entitled to an open trial and rigorous defense; the government pays if necessary. All are presumed innocent until proven guilty by a jury of ordinary people. Arab countries can't make such claims. I'm pleased to have had an opportunity to participate in such a system of justice. Questions about the trial must be directed to the public defender's office."

He then packed his material while Rich Harris stated that all questions must be directed to the public defender's office.

Meanwhile, reporters were shouting questions to Randy Walker, James Edward, and Joe about a victory. Randy Walker said their office would call a press conference. He stated he did not view this as victory because justice was not a game or a war with victors and losers.

Marcus Porter led Joe to the coffee shop where Omar and Nassar waited; he asked Nassar if he felt vindicated.

"I just want to live with my family in peace and get on with my life." Nassar replied. "We're not full of hate like some Arabs, even though bad things happened to us. I don't want bad things to happen to those guys, but they do need to be punished. Now I need to go; Fatima'll be home alone."

Omar gave Nassar three kisses and said he would be in touch before he went back to Washington. Joe likewise gave three kisses, while Marcus Porter shook his hand.

"How do you feel about feel your victory for Arab rights in this country?" Marcus Porter asked Joe. "Although Randy said it wasn't a victory. You can go on or off the record."

"You can take it on the record," Joe replied. "I agree completely with Randy. This is not a victory; this is justice, and it's not just for Arabs. It's basic human rights for all ethnic groups in this country. Just because they brought me down from Washington to interrogate witnesses in Arabic doesn't mean this is an Arab issue. Like your wanting the Pulitzer Prize, I want to achieve great things, but not as an Arab rights specialist."

"I really pushed your button," Marcus Porter said teasingly, then to Omar, "What's it feel like to be the spiritual guide for this trial?"

Omar replied, "Spiritual guide?"

"You're the imam, spiritual guide you said," Marcus Porter replied. "You had lots of contact with the victims."

"That's all strictly private," Omar said. "Nothing I can say about that on the record or off."

"Christian pastors and priests speak up on justice," Marcus Porter said. "You don't want to say something?"

"My guidance to them didn't have anything to do with this trial; what I did was strictly private," Omar continued. "Off the record, Islam has a strong sense of justice, but we don't say much in public."

"OK," Marcus Porter said and abruptly got up to go. "Sorry, wanta try to find some of the jury to see if they have comments. I'll find you later. When're you two leaving?"

"Haven't thought about it," Joe answered. "I'm sure I need to be in the office here on Monday."

"Haven't thought about it, either," Omar said. "No reason to rush, but no reason to stick around. Gotta get back and start the research again. Got some great ideas here."

"Let's get together before you go, like last time," Marcus Porter said as he rushed away.

Joe and Omar sat silently. Then Omar asked, "What do you want to do now?

"Not sure," Joe answered. "Get out of this suit, but don't want to hang around the hotel; media'd be all over me. What do you have in mind? Going to the hospital today?"

"No, not today," Omar answered. "Ahmed needs time to settle in without me around every day. Maybe tomorrow. For sure, at least once before I go."

"Say, if you are not in a huge hurry to go home, maybe we could do something, go somewhere," Joe suggested. "It sure would be good to do something without the stress."

"Yeah," Omar replied. "You heard me say I got lots of good ideas down here, but haven't had time to follow thorough, especially with Robertses and Ms. Jolene. Maybe we could visit them."

"Say, they've been so nice and served us dinner and lunch," Joe said. "Maybe we should take them out to eat, like maybe Sunday after church."

"Yeah, combine business with pleasure. Who do we call to arrange it? Ms. Velma?" Omar asked. "I'd call, but you seem to know her better."

"OK," Joe agreed. "Let's wait until back at the hotel."

After changing to casual clothes, Joe called Velma, exchanged pleasantries, asked if she had heard the verdict, which she had, and invited them to lunch on Sunday.

After pauses and monosyllabic responses, Joe said, "Just a moment, I'll ask Omar. She says no good restaurants there; we'd have to go to Christiansburg or Salem to find something good, and that might be a problem. She said if we want, we could bring food there like a picnic. What do you think?"

"Haven't thought of it that way," Omar said. "Guess we could. Make sure it's not too much work for her. It was she who did the cleanup both times before."

"He said OK," Joe said, "but we don't want you to be left with the cleanup."

(pause)

"We haven't talked about it," Joe continued. "You, Mr. Shane, and Amelia for sure. Nassar, Fatima, and Abou Nidal, if he isn't working; Ms. Jolene for sure."

(pause)

"Oh, OK." Joe said. "We're going out but we'll have our phones with us." To Omar, "She's going to call Ms. Jolene and get back to us. Maybe we can have a picnic at the church; they have a nice place outdoors if it isn't raining. Say, where do you want to go now?"

"Maybe a movie?" Omar answered. "Media wouldn't be looking for you there."

"They're going to call back; Randy might call, Marcus too," Joe said. "Let's go to a museum; not likely media there, and no problem if the phone rings."

As they neared Center in the Square in central Roanoke where museums were located, Joe's phone rang; after a few pleasantries he said, "Here, I'll give the phone to him." To Omar, "It's Ms. Jolene."

Omar exchanged pleasantries and said, "I've never done anything like that before. I suppose I could, but I don't want to be the center of attention."

(pause)

"He's attended church services before," Omar continued. "I can ask him." To Joe, "She wants us to go to the church service, me to say a prayer and maybe say a few words, and both of us to church coffee afterwards."

Omar gave him the phone and Joe expressed his willingness to attend a service and meet people, but expressed reservations over taking credit for the trial.

(pause)

"Under those circumstances, it'd be a pleasure to be there and provide a meal for you afterwards," he replied. "What time?" To Omar, "It seems set. This is a new experience for sure."

"For me too," Omar concurred. "We managed to pull it together for the Eid party; I guess we can do it now."

Omar said, "Say, who else should we invite? Now that it's at the church and we're bringing food, maybe invite some more who'd be comfortable in a church."

"There're Jordan Hicks and his father, who'd likely be there anyway; his mother too, if she's there."

"Yeah," Joe agreed, "and maybe Marcus too."

They continued with their plans as they wandered around museums.

BOOK 4

RAMIFICATIONS

CHAPTER 1

In the evening before bedtime, Joe and Omar nibbled leftover food in their hotel room, Joe commenting, "That went well, if I do say so myself. People seemed to enjoy themselves, and the food was good. Good you suggested going straight to Blacksburg after the hospital in Catawba. The drive up back roads was interesting."

"Yeah," Omar agreed, "like coming into a completely different world going up that steep hill into Blacksburg. It's so backward out of Catawba; Blacksburg's modern."

Joe asked, "How are Ms. Roula and Ahmed doing? Hard for me to tell, not being around them much."

Omar replied, "I'm cautiously optimistic, but maybe it's wishful thinking. Ahmed seemed a little more responsive; at least he moves around. Ms. Roula has a little more facial expression, now that her son is around."

Joe added, "Jordan's really excited about going to Virginia Tech."

"I didn't talk to him much, but heard his father has a new job," Omar said. "He told Fatima he'd see her at the high school; he'll be assistant principal."

"His wife was talking to Mrs. Velma," Joe said. "The principal at the middle school got in trouble over that situation with the redneck girl and was forced to retire. They offered the job to Mr. Gordon; he refused and got the job at the high school instead."

"Same ol' political shit," Omar said. "I'm learning there's lots of that at the university too."

"Marcus really worked the crowd," Joe added. "He was paying attention to those people talking to you after church."

"They commented about my prayer and the few words I spoke," Omar replied. "He was interested in how people in a place like Shawsville felt about Muslims in their midst."

"You were great as usual," Joe said. "You always are."

"Thanks again," Omar said. "Next thing we know, tabloids'll say 'Imam crashes church to say prayer.'"

"Did you hear Marcus say the reason the jury deliberated so long was they couldn't decide whether to find them all guilty of the same crimes or two of lesser crimes?" Joe added. "Too bad Imran Ashfaq couldn't make it."

"He's met with Ms. Jolene some," Omar said. "What're we going to do with the leftover food? I'm going tomorrow and could possibly take a little with me, but most would go bad before I get home. You going to eat more?"

"Not tonight," Joe answered. "We might see how much we can cram into the mini bar, and maybe I can eat it tomorrow, but don't think I can eat that much and likely don't want to. Say, when're you going tomorrow?"

"Haven't thought about it a lot," Omar replied. "I'm having dinner with Jason, so I don't want to leave too early; maybe after lunch here."

Joe said, "I haven't told you yet. I got a text message from Randy. He's called a press conference for tomorrow morning. You might as well come to that. Maybe we'll all go to lunch. No doubt Marcus will be there, but don't know if he'd go to lunch with us."

"Don't know if I'd want them swarming all over me like they did in the courtroom," Omar said.

"I haven't been to Randy's press conferences," Joe said. "Knowing him, I'm sure he'd keep it under control. It's up to you. Just a thought."

"Let me see how I feel tomorrow," Omar said. "If you don't want any more food, we should do something with it."

"What about offering it to Kent in reception," Joe suggested. "He's always been especially nice."

After giving food to Kent and taking a walk, they went to bed.

CHAPTER 2

Tuesday, June 10, 2008
Washington, DC, USA

Joe arrived home in the evening, having had coffee with Jason. Omar greeted him with a hug and three kisses. They talked about their trips and visits with Jason while Joe took his bags to his bedroom.

Omar said, "You've gotten lots of calls from your mother."

"She must've seen me on the news and wants to congratulate me and break the ice," Joe said as he called and said in Arabic, "Mama, it's Joe."

(pause)

"Calm down," Joe said in Arabic. "Who's arrested?"

(pause)

Joe replied in Arabic, "You expect me to get him off?"

(pause)

"Mama, things don't work that way in this country. I can't get him off and keep him from being deported," he continued in Arabic.

(pause)

"Oh, that's why you paid for me to go to law school, to help you out when he breaks the law," Joe said and thought bitterly, *What about the student loans I'm paying?* He added in Arabic, "He disowned me, remember?"

(pause)

"How can you say that, Mama?" he said in Arabic. "What he wanted me to do is not only illegal but also immoral. It's against Islam, the words of the Prophet."

(pause)

"I don't give a... care what the imam says," Joe said angrily in Arabic. "Just because he says that doesn't make it true. I went to Islamic school all those years, remember? You made me go, and you did pay for that."

(pause)

"Oh, the so-called imam's arrested too?" Joe continued in Arabic, "and you expect me to get him off too? No way, even if I could. He deserves to be charged for what he did."

(pause)

"Stop crying, Mama," Joe continued in Arabic. "What other young guy ran away too?"

(pause)

"Look, Mama, I can't do it!" Joe stated in Arabic. "I just helped Arabs to get their rights in this country. It was a big case. I'm sure you saw it on TV. You haven't said one word about how you feel about that."

(pause)

"So that's how you know I can do it and I'm just being stubborn, forgetting my heritage, what you did for me?" Joe said angrily in Arabic. "Well that's not the way it works! I don't think we have anything else to say. Bye."

He immediately began sobbing, crying full tears, when Omar gave him a tight embrace, saying, "I heard everything. You don't deserve that."

Joe stopped crying enough to say, "She didn't even say she was proud of me for what I did in the trial; she doesn't care. All she cares about is my father! And, oh, Timo apparently did go there. Some young guy from Lebanon who lived with them agreed to marry the girl then disappeared."

The phone rang. Omar answered, then said to Joe, "For you. Some woman. Do you want to take it?"

Joe took the phone and said angrily after a pause, "How dare I talk to her what way, Najat?"

(pause)

"What about the stigma of having both a father and a brother in prison?" Joe said angrily. "You grew up in this country. You know I can't do things like that, and I wouldn't if I could. What they wanted me to do is illegal, immoral, and against Islam."

(pause)

"Fuck that so-called imam, and sorry if I offend you," Joe continued. "In case you don't recall, I went to Islamic school; I'm a pretty good student and I happened to learn something about Islam. That so-called imam doesn't know shit. In case you don't remember, my best friend is an imam, has a PhD in Islamic theology, and knows a thing or two."

(pause)

"Why does she have to come live with me?" he asked.

(pause)

"You think only about yourself, Najat," Joe continued angrily. "Stigma of having a father in jail. Too disrupting for your family if she lives with you. Think about her for a change. She'd be miserable here. She doesn't know a soul. The only other Arabs are mostly high-level officials. Very few Arab Shia here. She doesn't speak English that well. Why does she have to move anywhere?"

(pause)

"Listen, Najat, we don't even know what'll happen to them yet, and here you are worrying about not having to take care of her," Joe said. "She's my mother and I'll help take care of her, but that doesn't mean I'll bring her to live with me, where she'd be miserable. Don't expect me to do anything for that person who used to consider he was my father and disowned me. I couldn't even if I wanted to."

(pause)

"Najat, I just finished a successful case to uphold Arab rights in this country," Joe continued. "I was on television; I know you saw it. Not once have you or she said anything. All you care about is your own selfish issues. You can call me if something serious needs to be discussed about our mother. Otherwise I have nothing else to say."

He hung up the phone seething with anger and said, "I can't believe this. My own family. It's not that Najat and I were ever close and she can be a bitch, but all of them?"

Omar asked, "What can I do for you now?"

"I don't know," Joe said. "Just be here. I'm so angry I can't think straight."

"I'll be right here for whatever you want and need," Omar said. "What can I get you? Tea? Coffee?"

"Do we have any of that Tension Tamer Mrs. Spencer left?" Joe asked. "I sure could use my tensions tamed."

"I'll go look," Omar said. "What about eating? I was sort of waiting until you got here. You eat with Jason?"

"No, just coffee," Joe answered. "I'm so upset now I couldn't possibly eat anything."

"I understand," Omar said, "but you have to eat."

"Yeah, I know," Joe said. "What've we got here?"

"Not much," Omar answered. "I just got back and was waiting for you to go shopping."

"I guess I could walk somewhere with you," Joe said.

As they walked, Omar said, "I forgot to mention, Jason's coming next weekend. Spending the night."

"Yeah, he told me," Joe replied.

"We can work out who sleeps where when he gets here," Omar said, "Maybe he can have one of our beds. After all, you and I shared the bed all that time in Roanoke, even if it was a king-sized."

"Yeah," Joe said. "I don't know quite how to ask this, habibi, but can I sleep with you tonight? I don't feel like being alone. It felt weird alone last night in Roanoke too."

Wednesday, June 10, 2008

Joe knocked and entered Roger Chen's office, doing his best to be composed and professional, but obviously upset.

Roger Chen stood, smiled, shook his hand, and congratulated him on the great job in Roanoke. Then, noticing Joe's expression, he said, "You don't look so good."

Joe recounted his phone calls and concluded with, "I don't think I should be looking to see what my father and the imam are charged with, but I'd really like to know. You're the first one I thought of to find out for me."

Later in the afternoon, Joe returned to his boss's office, where Roger Chen said, "The imam was caught with a large amount of U.S. currency in his possession at the Detroit airport returning to the U.S., more than the legal limit that he did not declare. He was immediately arrested and charged with currency violations and is being investigated for other crimes relating to the marriage racket. Your father's being investigated for conspiracy, aiding, and abetting. Beyond that, I couldn't find out much because the cases have not been turned over to us yet."

"God," Joe said. "I know I reported them, but when the reality hits, it's another thing. I told you I don't want to testify against my father, but I sure would like that fake imam to be investigated and prosecuted to the limit. I know I'm not objective with all sorts of conflicts of interest, but I do want to know the progress and my mother and sister sure aren't going to tell me."

"I know," Roger Chen said. "We'll do everything on our end to keep you out of it. Would you want us to inform you if your father is formally charged and prosecuted?"

"Why do I have to make these decisions?" Joe asked rhetorically. "I know I should stay legally and professionally ignorant, but damn it, it's my family and I just have to know. Would they really deport him if he's guilty?"

"I'm no expert in immigration law," Roger Chen said; "from what I know, I'd say yes. He's not a citizen, is he?"

"No," Joe answered. "I could do research myself, on my own time that is."

Roger Chen said, "You don't need to tell me that. I know you well enough now that you're not going to take advantage of us, timewise or otherwise."

Joe struggled through the rest of the day, looking forward to being with Omar again.

CHAPTER 3

Wednesday, June 11, 2008
Quantico, Virginia, USA

Rosie Jordan opened a task-force meeting. "We have things mostly wrapped up now. Cranford, let's begin with you."

He began, "For the attempted bombing of the NSA that got us together in the first place, things are essentially concluded. It opened other issues that we'll get to. Wissam Salameh pleaded guilty and has been sentenced. Maybe you can fill us in on that in a minute, Roger. He didn't act alone, and attention went to a so-called imam and the group he led. Actually it looks like two imams. The Saudi Arabian imam has been in the position for a few years and is seemingly legitimate. That doesn't mean he can't be involved. Larry can fill us in."

Larry Briscoe began, "We traced the Palestinian so-called imam, Abdulmalik Abu Salim, to Lebanon where he fled. Lebanese authorities found him trying to stir up trouble in a Palestinian refugee camp and captured him. As we suspected, he's with one of the al Qaeda wannabe groups, Fatah al-Islam which split off from Fatah al-Intifada a couple of years ago. It stirred up trouble in a Palestinian refugee camp in Tripoli, Lebanon, and had to be subdued in bloody battles by the Lebanese army. We can't get him back here to prosecute, but he'll face some kind of justice there.

"The Saudi imam has dubious connections in Saudi Arabia. We let the Saudi Arabian authorities know our suspicions. If they prove to be justified, the Saudi authorities have ways to deal with him. We can't say what that'll be, but likely pretty harsh. Rhonda, you have anything to add?"

She replied, "Many in congress are pleased the defendant pleaded guilty and was sentenced and seemed especially pleased over the public award ceremony for the guards who apprehended him.

"About the imams, Lebanese are not barbaric. They may not be the most humane, but we don't have to worry about international relations and political fallout. With respect to the Saudi Arabian imam, it could cause problems if we tried to deal with him in this country. I concur it would be better to let the Saudi Arabian government deal with him."

Cranford Brooks continued, "Thanks, Larry and Rhonda. We likely won't charge the other young men in his group. About the most we could charge them with is conspiracy, which would be hard to prove and open ourselves up to publicity that might not be good. They're pretty scared and not likely to get involved in anything anytime soon. It's pointless to file charges against Ahmed Hammoud for things he might have done in Iraq."

Roger Chen said, "For Ahmed Hammoud, charges haven't formally been dropped, but it seems likely they will. The trial for Wissam Salameh in Baltimore was short. He gave a guilty plea and he stated he completely understood the consequences. The judge sentenced him to 50 years but held out the possibility that the sentence could be reviewed after a psychiatric medical exam. He was sentenced to a medium security prison in Wisconsin, close to a prison-system psychiatric medical center nearby in Minnesota."

Rhonda Phillips interrupted. "A few in Congress would be upset if he's getting off light for mental health reasons."

Cranford Brooks replied, "There's no indication he'd get off lighter, but could get needed treatment. We're relocating his mother near the hospital in Minnesota under the witness protection program when her divorce is complete, house sold, etc. That area has Arab Muslims and is known for being tolerant and accepting. We want to keep her safe so maybe she can testify against her husband. Larry."

Larry Briscoe responded, "Our sources in Gaza confirmed his so-called charity indeed does support Hamas and not just its charitable activities. We've given you the information we have and will continue to dig."

While Larry Briscoe was speaking, an administrative assistant spoke to Roger Chen, who excused himself.

Cranford Brooks added, "You might've been following two similar cases in Florida and Texas that are having prolonged legal battles. We can get him for hiring illegal immigrants, if nothing else, but we want to hold out for something more serious. We don't expect much from his soon-to-be ex-wife, but every little bit helps. It keeps her close to Wissam, which can help."

Rhonda Philips spoke up, "Good for you. The poor woman needs a break for a change. Glad to hear things are moving in a good direction for her."

Roger Chen returned, saying, "The judge in Roanoke just passed sentence. The one convicted of a first degree crime is sentenced to 15 years in a medium security facility in far upstate New York. The other two got the maximum sentence of ten years and were sent to a medium security facility in rural Minnesota, not the one where Wissam Salameh is going, and the other to a medium security prison in a remote part of western Oregon. All three have an option of having a sentence reduced and parole if they participate in job training programs and get jobs. The U.S. Attorney in Roanoke speculated the judge wanted to get them as far away as possible from influence of family and also far away from each other. If you watched news of the trial on TV, you must've gotten some indication of their background."

"Like some of the old sitcoms when I was a child," Rhonda Philips added. "Only it wasn't all that funny for me because there were people like that from the Ozarks of Missouri where I grew up. Maybe I'm an old softie, but it's not going to do the country's interests any harm to have them in those places, and it might do them some good."

Rosie Jordan asked for input from Colonel Granger, who declined, then concluded by saying, "Thanks again for all of you coming. It seems we can put another task force behind us and hope we don't have other soon. We'll be in touch if something comes up."

All exchanged pleasantries and left.

CHAPTER 4

Tuesday, June 24, 2008
Washington, DC, USA

Roger Chen called Joe to his office and told him, "I've heard from Detroit. The so-called imam, being caught 'red-handed,' is trying to plea-bargain by implicating your father and others. The FBI must've gotten a tip to search him when he arrived at the airport. The search is legitimate and the evidence can be used with no problem, so it seems certain he'll be convicted and deported; the plea-bargain is over whether he'll have to serve time here in the U.S."

"Oh," Joe said.

"Your father's been implicated in receiving money on two occasions, one he apparently was required to return when you refused. The other was for some other young man he claimed was his adopted son who would marry a Lebanese woman. The Detroit office is assessing how strong the evidence is; as it stands now, it would be just one person's word against another and might not be credible before a jury. I think they're holding out for a plea bargain, will deport your father, and that would be the end."

"Oh," Joe said glumly.

"There's no indication you'd be involved in any way," Roger continued. "There's not much you could say that's not hearsay. The person I talked to seemed to think this 'adopted son' might be an FBI informant whom they would not pursue, but that was just speculation; and were it some other circumstance, I'd not mention it to you."

Joe replied, "My mother said someone fled."

"That's all I have," Roger Chen added, "and that's likely all I'll have unless I go asking them for more information, and I'm not sure I want to do that."

"I understand," Joe replied. "Do you know what kind of legal defense my father has? Everyone deserves a strong defense, even if it's for a despicable marriage racket. He is my father and I could pay for his defense, but for sure I wouldn't want anyone to know. I still know good lawyers there."

Roger Chen replied, "It's easy to understand why you might want to do this, but don't be so hasty; give yourself time to think. You've seen public defenders at work. Some're damned good. Of course I don't know if your father is represented by the public defender or not, but if he is, he might be as well represented as those guys in Roanoke. Sometimes it's best to let things happen."

"Oh, OK," Joe said and paused just a moment. "Now that I'm here, there's one thing I want to ask you. You remember I've talked about my friend Brad who was badly injured in the gay bar bombing? He's been recuperating in New Mexico and has invited all of us for the Fourth of July to celebrate the end of his treatment and return to normal life. The Fourth is on Friday. In order to get good air fares, we thought we'd go on Wednesday and come back Tuesday. I know I've been away a lot when I was in Roanoke, but I can arrange my work to be away a week."

"Oh, go enjoy," Roger said. "I know you'll take care of your work; you always do. I've never been to New Mexico; it must be interesting, but isn't it hot this time of year?"

"I've never been there either," Joe said. "That's one reason I want to go. Brad said it's up in the mountains, something like 7,000 feet, so it's not so hot. He did say we might go down to where the temperature'd be above 100."

Joe got up to leave when Roger said, "That wasn't the only thing I called you here for. We always need new staff to replace guys who move up and on. We're wondering about the guy you worked with in Roanoke, James Edward Goodwin. What do you think about his coming here to work? He made a favorable impression when he was here. Do you know if he'd even want to move here?"

"Yes," Joe replied enthusiastically. "He was great to work with, and we became pretty friendly. He knows his law for sure and has other good skills. His family is from up this direction, some rural area between Charlottesville and here. I suspect, he'd like to be closer. He has a pretty steady girlfriend who might have something to say, but the one time she implied she might be ready to move on from Roanoke."

"The defense attorney from Iraq was impressive too," Roger Chen said. "He's older than we ideally like to hire in an entry level position, although you know we can't discriminate due to age. There're some agencies here who'd like to have an Arabic speaking Muslim lawyer on their staff. Again, we can't discriminate."

"It might not work," Joe said. "He's not Muslim."

"Oh, what is he then?" Roger Chen asked."

"He's Christian," Joe replied. "It's obvious from his name. It was also in that information I asked you for."

"Oh, you can tell his religion from his name?" Roger Chen said. "I didn't read that information we got for you."

"Yes, usually," Joe answered and briefly explained the significance his name. "A Christian lawyer in Iraq would have something on the ball."

"I'll pass his name on to some other agencies anyway," Roger Chen said. "I'll also ask Randy sometime soon when I talk to him about James Edward Goodwin. I don't like to snatch someone out from under him."

"Maybe Yuhana Khalil could work in Roanoke, taking James Edward's place," Joe offered.

Joe returned to his desk, excited about New Mexico.

CHAPTER 5

Wednesday, July 2, 2008
Ruidoso, New Mexico, USA

In late afternoon on a clear sunshiny warm day, temperature in the 80s, Joe and Omar parked their rental car in front of Brad's condo, and Jason flung open the door. He was wearing olive-green shorts and a New Mexico flag t-shirt. He was clean shaven, and his hair was short and professionally styled. Hugs and three kisses were exchanged. Brad rushed out of the kitchen, wiping his hands on a New Mexico apron and also giving big hugs and three kisses.

Later, they were all sitting on the balcony, Joe and Omar in casual shorts and polo shirts, and Brad with a black Ruidoso t-shirt, khaki shorts, wireless framed glasses, and closely trimmed hair. Omar said, "You two really changed your appearance."

They smiled and Jason said, "When I got here, I saw Brad looking older, more mature. It looked and felt good, so I decided to go for it too. I asked him to take me to get my hair cut. He had seen a barber shop downtown and dropped me there while he went shopping. The barber was a right-winger; had anti-gun control and other right-wing stuff laying around. He complained while I was waiting that tourists take up seats, keeping regular customers away, so I just walked out.

"Brad'd seen another barber shop close to a copy center he used, and took me there. Cool place. Looks like an old fashioned barbershop, but pretty high tech. Can look on their website and see a camera that shows how many are waiting. The barber's a retired high school teacher in computers. He also had a really big-screen TV streaming Texas Honky Tonk music with Willy Nelson. Not my style of music, but cool.

The other customers were all about his age, old enough to be my grandfather. Interesting to hear them talking to each other. At first, I thought they were kind of locals, like the rednecks back in Southside Virginia. Then I found one of them was the immediate past state forester for New Mexico; retired in the area. Has a PhD in forestry. Others educated and successful too. They also looked on me kind of as their pet while watching all my hair get cut off. He did a good job, don't you think? Gave him a big tip."

"We've both been through a lot; I have for sure," Brad added. "Time to grow up, leave the preppy look as part of a great past life. New image for a new job."

"New job?" Joe asked.

"Yeah," Brad replied. "Maybe CIA. Leave details for later when Frank and Paco get here and not repeat. They're flying into El Paso; about a two-and-a-half-hour drive."

"You're really into the New Mexico thing," Omar said.

"There's a cool shop downtown, Noisy Water Winery and apparel shop," Brad replied. "You'll have to go."

"Noisy water?" Joe asked.

"Bad translation of the town's name," Brad explained. "'*Ruidoso*' means noisy in Spanish; named for the Río Ruidoso, *río* means river. Runs through the middle of town, a glorified creek. Lots of rapids, so it can be noisy. 'Noisy river' got badly translated to 'noisy water.' I like it here; I've felt good since I got here. In a way, sorry to go."

"We saw some cool UFO and alien t-shirts at the UFO museum in Roswell," Joe said. "I was tempted to buy some; maybe on the way back to the airport."

"I've been tempted to stop there," Brad said. "I've only been to Roswell to pick up Jason.

"The museum's cool," Joe said. "It's not just about the UFO landing in New Mexico, but in Nevada too, and they associated extraterrestrial phenomena with lots of things."

"I didn't know much about them, but it's interesting," Omar said. "Nice drive up here too."

Jason added, "There's a great art gallery in San Patricio on the way. Two famous American painters married and moved there years ago; Peter Hurd's from Roswell and married Henriette Wyeth. Great stuff there. Wish I could afford to buy some. Almost missed my flight looking."

THREE GENERATIONS OF ARTISTS

Located on the family's ranch in San Patricio, New Mexico, the Hurd La Rinconada Gallery is home to the spectacular works of the Hurd family: Peter, Henriette Wyeth and their son Michael. The gallery also features a selection of works by renowned artists N.C. and Andrew Wyeth.

Hurd La Rinconda Gallery, San Patricio, New Mexico

The doorbell rang; Brad said, "Frank and Paco."

Hugs and three kisses were exchanged, Frank saying, "Sorry we're late. Paco wanted to go across the border, since we were in El Paso. It was so hot we didn't stay long."

Paco handed Brad a bag. "Here're fresh papayas from Mexico for breakfast if you like."

Frank handed a bag. "We stopped near a small town, Tularosa, I think, and got pistachios and New Mexico wine. Didn't know New Mexico produced wine."

"Thanks!" Brad said, hugging them. "Some New Mexico wine's good. Make yourselves at home. Jason has beer."

Later over dinner, Paco said, "This food is great. The chips are blue. Everything's almost as good as my Mami would make, but a different taste. The enchiladas are blue."

"They're blue corn tortillas, a New Mexico specialty," Brad replied. "This's New Mexican food, a cuisine all its own. I taught myself to cook it, with not much else to do. Kind of fun. Uses green chiles, not red.

"Tomorrow, we might stay around close. There's neat stuff nearby. Carrizozo, the little county seat town, has colorful painted burro statues. Then there're the ancient lava flows, ancient petroglyphs, Smoky Bear Museum is in Capitán, and Lincoln's the place Billy the Kid hung out."

Burro statues in Carrizozo, New Mexico

"Carrizozo's an artists' community," Jason said. "Not my type of art, but still fun."

"I've heard about Billy the Kid in old wild west movies," Omar said. "Fun to see where it actually happened."

Billy the Kid Museum, Lincoln, New Mexico

"Sounds good to me," Joe said. "I heard about Smoky Bear when I was a kid."

"Me too," both Frank and Paco added; "Only you can prevent forest fires."

"On the Fourth, my sister's invited us to Alamogordo to the Fourth of July parade and a cookout," Brad continued. "We can also go to the White Sands and the space museum if it's open. That night there's a fireworks show here at the Inn of the Mountain Gods, the fancy upscale hotel and casino on the Native American reservation next to town."

"July Fourth on an Indian reservation?" Frank asked.

"Why not?" Brad said. "They live in this country too. Besides, it appeals to the tourists at their fancy hotel."

They finished a leisurely meal and drinks and went to bed fairly early for a busy time the next day.

CHAPTER 6

Thursday, July 3, 2008
Ruidoso, New Mexico, USA

On a pleasantly cool sunshiny morning sitting on the balcony, all were enjoying a sumptuous breakfast prepared by Brad: scrambled eggs a la Mexicana, refried beans, warm flour tortillas, *frituras de manzana*, and fresh papaya. All commented the papaya was good and all but Paco saying they had never eaten it before.

While they were eating and drinking steaming mugs of coffee, Paco said, "Say, these tortillas are great. Where'd you get them? Is there a *tortillería* here that makes 'em fresh?"

"Yeah, one of the supermarkets has a *tortillería* where you can watch a lady making them," Brad replied.

"These *frituras de manzana*, apple fritters you'd call 'em, are like my cousin makes in his bakery in Ohio," Paco added. "He got the recipe from a bakery in New Mexico."

"Got them at the same supermarket," Brad said. "They make 'em fresh every day in their in-store bakery. Lots of apples, *manzanas* in Spanish, grown close to here, so that's likely why your cousin got the recipe from New Mexico."

All raved over the food, to which Brad replied, "Glad you like it, but I hope you don't mind if I don't make breakfast every morning. There'll be plenty of breakfast food, and we can just help ourselves."

"Sure," Frank said.

"Hey, man, we'll buy it too," Paco offered. "We didn't come here to eat your food; just tell us what to buy."

After a lull, Joe said, "Yesterday you said something about a new job and you'd tell us later."

"Oh, yeah," Brad replied. "There's reluctance to send me back to the Arabic language section; still not sure if I'd attract terrorists. The CIA contacted me and even sent someone here to talk to me. They always need people who know Arabic and the culture. It seemed positive. I'll follow through when I get back home."

Frank asked, "Are you interested?"

"Probably," Brad replied. "I was ready to do something different anyway. You know I want to get a master's. Don't know if CIA'd support it. I'd have to move to Virginia; too far to commute from Laurel."

"Sounds exciting," Omar said.

"What about your job, Jason?" Joe asked.

"Same ol'," Jason replied. "Not trying to get rid of me, but doing nothing to keep me. Had plenty of time to think about what I want to do next and have a good idea. Some friends back home are in the furniture industry. Maybe you know furniture's big in Martinsville and High Point, North Carolina. Been talking to them, and now I'm going to be a furniture designer. They say the furniture industry in this country's stale and needs fresh designs. I'm a good designer, so why not furniture?"

"Will you be moving back home, then?" Joe asked.

"No way!" Jason stated emphatically. "You've been to Martinsville. High Point isn't any better. Don't have to actually live there to design furniture."

"Do you have to go back to school?" Joe asked.

"Probably not. I'll probably go to Helsinki for a while to learn more about furniture technology and design."

"Helsinki?" Omar commented. "Why there?"

"Helsinki, and Finland in general, is one of the best design centers in the world, especially in furniture," Jason replied. "Finns are great with bright color combinations, but tasteful. You know me and color."

"Oh, like IKEA," Frank commented.

"IKEA's from Sweden, not Finland," Jason chuckled. "Same idea, contemporary design but more upscale's what I have in mind. Integrate cloth and leather, leather in bright color, not the dull white and black used now. Solid leather all around's not good for cushioning; won't let it breathe. Needs cloth upholstery on the bottoms and sides; cloth could have complementary colors."

After a pause and coffee refills, Jason said, "Oh, I forgot to tell you guys the bad news about Chad, the bartender at Rory's whose face was so badly hurt. His insurance won't cover cosmetic surgery and he's pretty bummed out about it. Some guys are talking about taking up a collection, but cosmetic surgery is so damned expensive."

"I'm sure thankful mine was paid for," Brad said. "I've been getting paid all along and not having too many extra expenses, so maybe I can donate."

"Any idea how much it'd be?" Joe asked.

Frank and Paco looked at each other and to Joe and Omar. Then Frank said, "Remember we told you we know a cosmetic surgeon in Iraq. It'd sure be something if he could go there, medical tourism. It couldn't cost as much as here."

"I might know who he is," Joe said. "Ahmed Hammoud had cosmetic surgery from him. There was something that he was involved with the CIA. Wonder if the CIA'd send him there to keep this from getting too much publicity if there's a fund raising drive."

"I'm going to have more discussions with the CIA," Brad said. "Maybe I can inquire. They want me pretty bad, so maybe I can push them a little.

"Don't want to rush you too much, guys, but we need to go pretty soon. We don't have to do everything today if we're tired, but'd be less crowded today than the weekend."

Friday, July 4, 2008

All were sitting on the balcony at night, drinking wine and juice, when Frank said, "Great two days, Brad. You really outdid yourself making all these plans."

"The White Sands are amazing," Omar said. "Lot of this area is like Yemen, mountains and desert, but nothing like the White Sands."

White Sands National Monument, New Mexico

"Glad you enjoyed it," Brad said. "From now on, though, I thought we'd just hang out, go do things on your own if you like. Plenty to do around here. Just ask."

"That Fourth of July parade was neat," Jason said. "Seemed funny to see all the Hispanics out front waving the American flag; only the whites'd do it back home. Come to think of it, I haven't seen a Fourth of July parade in ages."

"Most of these Hispanics have been here for generations," Brad added. "Part of the U.S. since 1845 and no connection with Mexico or desire to be Mexican."

"Mexicans are pretty patriotic in general," Paco said.

Frank yawned and said, "I need to turn in. Still on Eastern time and it's been a long day. Good day but tiring."

"Me too," Paco added. "We old guys can't keep up."

Saturday, July 5, 2008

Frank and Paco had gone out exploring on their own. Brad and Omar were sitting on the balcony having a theological discussion about religion and homosexuality, among other topics, Omar mentioning maybe he wanted to reach out to young gay Muslims.

Joe and Jason were driving to the supermarket with a *tortillaría* and in-store bakery.

Joe asked, "Say, how're things going with you and Brad, if I may ask? You can tell me to butt out if you like, but last time we talked seriously you were concerned, and now it seems like you're distant, or not as close as before."

Jason replied, "Actually I'm glad to have someone to talk to. You're one friend I can really talk to. There's a good coffee shop just around the corner on the main road. Easier to talk there; no hurry to go shopping. There it is. Zocca, very popular local coffee shop."

Sipping coffee, Jason began, "You picked up on things; not the same between us, but maybe for the better."

"Oh, you're breaking up?" Joe asked.

"No, nothing like that at all," Jason continued. "You saw we've changed, hair styles, clothes, more mature. Kind of like forced to grow up fast."

"You weren't immature before," Joe said, "but go on."

"We're both different persons than before," Jason continued. "It's like we're falling in love again."

"Sounds positive," Joe commented.

"Yeah, and the sex's great as ever." Jason said. "You and Omar seem to be back as good friends as before."

"Yeah, thanks for asking," Joe replied, and explained what happened that night in Roanoke. "If Brad gets that job with the CIA, you think you might live together now?"

"I doubt it," Jason answered. "You heard me talk about a neat freak and a slob living together. Besides, we've both realized we need to put ourselves first. He wants to get a master's degree, and I want to go to Helsinki. Tough to live together; great to be closer, though."

For sure look out for yourself first," Joe concurred. "I can't identify, having never been in a relationship, but I'm learning more about putting myself first, not hurting others of course. The big trial in Roanoke caused me to think about my future. Need to make sure I'm not typecast as the Arab, Muslim government attorney, but maybe focus on human rights law. That's another conversation for another day."

"We'd better go to the grocery store and get back," Jason said. "It's great talking with you, just us two alone."

You're one of my best friends now," Joe added. "I'm so glad you invited us. It's been great being together, and especially here. New Mexico's nice."

"Enchanted you, hasn't it?" Jason chuckled. "The Land of Enchantment. You could come visit me in Helsinki too," he continued. "Maybe we could have a reunion there, but for sure you and Omar if he wants to."

"Great! I've never been to Europe, except the U.K., if you consider that Europe," Joe said.

Later that night, Frank said, "Hope you guys don't mind if we leave tomorrow morning. We've got an early flight Monday and it's over two hours' drive from here, so we'd be better off staying in El Paso."

"Yeah, and I'd like to go back to Juárez, too, now that we have a better idea what border crossing is like," Paco said. "There're some things I want to buy like we used to get in Mexico when we'd go visit family."

All reflected on great times together and then went to bed.

Monday, July 7, 2008

Joe and Omar drove into town for breakfast, giving Brad and Jason time alone for the last time in a while. Jason would ride back to the Roswell airport with them, since it turned out he was on the same flight to Dallas.

After tearful goodbyes with Brad, they left in time for a stop at the art gallery in San Patricio, leaving the UFO Museum for another visit.

They said goodbyes with warm hugs in the Dallas-Fort Worth airport, promising to be in touch back home. Jason found his flight to Dulles Airport, while Omar and Joe found their flight to Reagan National.

CHAPTER 7

Sunday, October 12, 2008
Annapolis, Maryland, USA

On a beautiful fall afternoon, sunshiny and warm, Felicia greeted Paco and Frank warmly and took the bouquet they offered. Inside, all huddled around Patrick and Elsie and a baby Patrick held in his arms. Pete rushed to greet them, offering drinks; Christina and Becky, along with another woman about the same age, were cooing over the baby.

She looks familiar, Frank and Paco each thought.

Patrick looked up with a big smile on his face, saying, "Hey, Bud. Good to see you. Sorry I can't get up. Come meet Caroline Marie. You too, Paco."

Paco went forward, saying, "She's cute; your hair, but her mother's blue eyes."

"Yeah," Frank said hesitatingly, "nice red hair. Haven't been around babies before, so don't know what to say or do. For sure I'm pleased for you. You must be proud of her."

"Come sit down next to us; you want to hold her?" Patrick said. "She's good natured and likes men. I'll really have to watch her when she's a teenager."

"Oh," Frank said cautiously. "I've never held a baby."

"Come here, little cutie," Paco said as Patrick handed her over to him.

Caroline smiled and cooed at Paco, who was beaming. He handed her to Patrick, who then handed her over to Frank, where she puckered up her face and began whimpering.

Patrick said, "Relax. Hold her for a while, and smile. Babies pick up your feelings. If you're scared, she is too."

After a moment, Caroline calmed down and smiled, causing Frank to smile back.

Elsie reached out and said, "I can take her now. You wouldn't think that Patrick has anything else on his mind but her, would you? I do know he's real eager to see you again."

"Yeah," Patrick replied. "What've you been up to, Bud? You too, Paco."

Frank and Paco explained briefly what had been going on while the ladies started fussing over the baby again.

Pete interrupted and said, "These guys haven't been introduced to our other guest. This's Ashley Sue Hunter, Becky's friend from Roanoke."

Wait, Frank said to himself. *They mentioned her name in the office with the Joe. Must've seen her in the courtroom.*

Frank stood and said, "Very pleased to meet you." To Becky and Christina, "You too. Sorry we got carried away. You, too Elsie. We didn't greet properly either."

"No problem," Elsie smiled. "Happens all the time nowadays."

Paco greeted Elsie, saying to the other women: I'm Paco, Frank's friend."

"Nice to meet you," Ashley Sue said. "I've actually seen you two before, but you likely aren't aware."

"I am," Frank said smiling. "The prosecuting attorneys mentioned you. You sat back in the corner of the courtroom. The rest of you must know the trial we're talking about."

Becky, Christina, and Pete all nodded yes while Patrick said, "I was able to follow most of it on TV news. I must not've seen it where you were involved."

"I got some of it flying back and forth to the U.S.," Elsie commented, "but I didn't recall you two in the trial."

Ashley Sue said, "They gave the testimony that sealed the case for the prosecution," and explained briefly. "By then, lots of the media had stopped their continuous coverage, but a reporter for the *Roanoke Times* fed coverage to the *Post* and appeared in front of cameras for some of the networks, mostly foreign ones, who didn't have their own reporters there."

"We saw him, or I suppose it was him," Becky said. "I remember a West Virginia accent sounding strange on whatever network it was."

"Rumor has it that he'll get a big move out of this," Ashley Sue said. "He's destined for bigger things; someone good like him wouldn't stay in Roanoke."

"Just look at you," Becky commented. "Someone good like you isn't staying in Roanoke, even if you weren't on the news every day."

"I haven't gotten the job yet," Ashley Sue said.

"What job is it?" Elsie asked. "With Caroline, I didn't hear enough of the conversation to get a good idea."

"It's head of the public defender's office for the Alexandria Division of the Eastern District of Virginia," Ashley Sue said. "The same job I have in Roanoke for the Western District, but more population and much smaller area; basically just Northern Virginia."

"You'll represent defendants in court?" Patrick asked. "From what I saw, some guy was the public defender."

"It's an administrative job mostly," Ashley Sue explained. "Rich was a contract attorney I hired. I oversee things and get defenders on contract. Courtroom trial isn't my strong suit."

While Pete started the charcoal, Paco asked, "How'd you feel about moving away from Roanoke? Seemed like a nice place when we were there. I know what it was like when I moved from Ohio, leaving family and friends."

"It'll be tough," Ashley Sue replied. "I lived in Roanoke all my life except when away at university and law school, and both of them were less than fifty miles away."

"I can't identify with that," Christina Ramos said. "Being a Navy brat, I moved around a lot."

"Same here," Frank said. "Marine Corps brat."

"Maybe I can find a man and become more domestic," Ashley Sue chuckled. "I haven't been able to find someone in Roanoke who wants me and my legal baggage, career and all. Not enough men there like Beck's father when he married her mother. Hardly anyone more domestic than she is, and she has a great career."

"We'd get her up closer to us," Becky said. "Ashley Sue and I've been best of buds since Montessori school. Can't imagine life too far away from her."

"Did you move here to be with Frank?" Ashley Sue asked Paco. "They told me you two're together."

"No," Paco answered. Then he explained, concluding, "I can identify with you some. I was in my thirties, never been away from home, and needed to broaden my horizons."

"Speaking of great career," Becky said, "Mom's another one who might move up because of that trial. If Obama wins the election, and it's looking more like he will, she might be appointed to a vacancy if one occurs on the Appeals Court for the Fourth Circuit in Richmond. She's had some discreet feelers tossed to her."

"Oh, really?" Ashley Sue said. "I hadn't heard that rumor yet, but something like that'd be really quiet."

"What happened to that guy you used in Roanoke to defend the defendants?" Frank asked. "Seems like the judge, your mother, was really pi ... er upset with him."

"Not really," Ashley Sue replied. "Yes, he pushed her past her limit and she had to call him on it, but she respects Rich; other judges do too. He does go to the limits and maybe a little beyond at times; that's what a good defense attorney's supposed to do. Rumor has it he has offers from some big city law firms. Again, someone that good's not going to stay in Roanoke unless he wants to."

"Yes, everyone's entitled to a strong defense, paid by the government if necessary; presumed innocent until proven guilty," Paco said. "Learned it in citizenship preparation."

"Oh, you weren't a citizen born here?" Ashley Sue asked. "You said you were from Ohio and emphasized in the courtroom that you're a citizen."

"I am now," Paco said and explained briefly.

Caroline began whimpering and fussing, causing Elsie to say, "Oh, bet it's time to change a diaper. She's probably ready for a nap too. Maybe she'll sleep a while and let us have lunch in peace, not that she's a bad baby. She's great."

Patrick jumped up and picked up Caroline, saying, "I'll go change her and put her down." Then he rushed up the stairs.

"Gee," I hardly get to do anything for her when Patrick's around," Elsie said smiling.

Ashley Sue spoke up. "How're you handling your career, if I may ask? I hear you're with an airline."

Elsie explained her lingering frustration with her flight attendant job and that she was ready for a career change, saying with a smile, "I'm not much of the stay-at-home mom, although it's been great these couple of months. I'm not very domestic either; Patrick and I always shared domestic duties. He'd probably be a stay-at-home dad if he could. I'm on leave of absence for a few months and still get some benefits like low cost flights, which allowed us to come here for her baptism. Gives me plenty of time to think what I do next."

"How long're you here for?" Frank asked. "Felicia did say something about a baptism when she invited us."

"Sorry we didn't tell you directly," Elsie replied. "We've both been too busy for emailing, as you can imagine. Just a couple of weeks. We flew into Philadelphia Friday; still jetlagged, especially Caroline.

We're going to Alabama on Tuesday, right after the holiday, to see Patrick's folks, then they're coming with us to Columbus for the baptism."

"Oh, in Columbus," Frank commented.

Elsie replied, "After going to Alabama to get married, we just had to have her baptism with my parents so all their friends and the few family we have could attend. There's a new priest everyone just loves, and he agreed to do it without meeting us. It's low key, and we didn't send invitations. We want it that way on purpose, but of course we want good friends like you to come. Felicia and Pete are godparents."

Paco replied, "I have to work next weekend, but maybe I can trade. Haven't seen the folks in Hamilton for a while. Maybe pop in for a quick visit. Can't confirm now."

Frank said, "I don't have to worry about getting off for a weekend. Might be a good time to go check on my house that's for sale. It's rented now.

"Speaking of that trial advancing careers, our good friend Joe was one of the prosecuting attorneys. He's already at the top, being at the Attorney General's office in Washington; don't know how much higher he could go."

"He's really good and will go places," Ashley Sue said. "He might become chief deputy in a larger district, not a small one like the western district of Virginia. Another one who seems to have benefited from the trial was the Iraqi guy we hired. Seems the U.S. Attorney wants to hire him for the Abingdon office. They need more people down there with increasing crime along the I-81 corridor and in the coal fields. He'd fit right in, being from West Virginia."

Frank said, "If I may bring up another point about the trial, Becky, it seems that your mother got really upset right after that defense attorney tried to show Paco and me as a gay couple. Do you think it's because you're in a relationship that it upset her?"

Becky replied, "Mom accepts our relationship for sure. It's hard to imagine she'd get really upset over that issue."

"I think it might've been the proverbial last straw," Ashley Sue said. "It's kind of hard to imagine that one thing alone would upset her to that point, but for sure Martha'd be ticked off at what Rich was trying to do over the gay issue."

Felicia announced she was going upstairs to get the children and they could all go to the table. Patrick returned with Timmy; Denise followed. All held hands for the traditional blessing, Frank and Paco feeling even more comfortable. After very pleasant conversation over the meal and afterwards, warm genuine goodbyes were exchanged.

AFTERWORD

AFTERWORD

Welcome to the part of this book where I tell some of my secrets, explain choices, give thanks and apologies, and otherwise express what's on my mind.

This story began eight years ago but was delayed by two major international moves and especially by an accident with broken bones that kept me from writing for about a year. The delays were perhaps providential. Many of the events that were fictional when I wrote them, originating only from inspirations, have come to pass recently. Maybe not in the exact form as in this book, but close. These include a gay bar bombing, the successes and plights of Arab Americans in the U.S., evolving issues of gay and lesbian rights, unfortunate increase in hate crimes and violence against minorities in the U.S., infiltration of the U.S. by Islamic terrorists, and weakness of school administrators, to mention a few.

When I finished *Three Kisses*, a prequel of sorts, and got it ready to be published (only to have to revise it later, but that's another story), I thought my creative writing was spent. Before I could shut down my computer though, some of the leading characters tapped me on the shoulder, saying, "Not so hasty; you aren't through with us yet." Almost immediately the inspiration for a bare-bones sketch of a plot started spinning in my head. I had no idea how the plot and subplots would evolve. All I knew is that I had to start writing, and the story would evolve as I went along. As with *Three Kisses*, inspirations just came to me. Of course they came with the need to do more research on some items, but almost none is deliberate creation.

Even though this is a sequel, I was mindful that the story line had to stand alone and that readers shouldn't have to read *Three Kisses* first. Nonetheless, I did throw in a few tidbits to pique your interest to go read it.

It was apparent from the outset that the focal point of the action had to be in Washington, DC. There still needed to be another primary location, and it had to be within a reasonable distance of Washington, say a three-hundred-mile radius, and in a semi-rural area. There were possibilities, but inspiration kept leading me to the mountains of Southwest Virginia, where some of the action in *Three Kisses* occurred. Not only was there continuity with *Three Kisses*, but also information about the area was readily available. After I had received the inspiration and started writing about events of the area, the sad unfortunate shooting at Virginia Tech in nearby Blacksburg occurred. This event, tragic though it was, fit ideally in the story line.

It was also apparent early on that a small part of the action must take place in Iraq, and the semi-autonomous Kurdish area of northern Iraq fit best. When I wrote that part of the story and created a fictional clinic, a trip to Iraq was the furthest thing from my mind. Then, about a year later when I actually did go to Kurdistan on other business, lo and behold the hospital and clinic were right there and fit the description perfectly and no longer needed to be fiction.

The concluding location in Ruidoso, New Mexico, came as a logical location when Brad needed a place to recuperate. Ruidoso is a well-known year-round mountain resort town with ample information readily available.

All characters are fictional. There are no composites or thin disguises. A few politicians and public office holders are mentioned by name because they fit the story line ideally. The words attributed to them are entirely fictional and come from my inspirations. They do not necessarily represent my views nor those of the publisher. If one looks just a little below the surface, the fictional phrases uttered by public figures are similar in style to what these persons have actually said.

Despite the fact that the characters are fictional in all respects, some bizarre coincidences occurred. Once, when traveling in winter and I was unexpectedly snow bound at a hotel for three days, one of the hotel employees was the spittin' image (to use an old-fashioned Southern U.S. term) of Jason to the last detail, except for the plaid shorts Jason always wore in the summer. Also, the alter ego of Brad came into my life a good six years after Brad was created and is a good friend to this day.

Almost all locations, including businesses, are actual; otherwise the story would be contrived. No promotional consideration was received. Macado's Restaurants are favorite well-established institutions all over Southwest Virginia. Shoney's Restaurants are well established all over the southeast U.S. and are favorite stops, especially along interstates. The Hotel Roanoke is an old railroad hotel that has been known for its luxury for many years. Zocca is a favorite coffee shop in Ruidoso that has received local awards.

There are exceptions: Rory's gay bar in Washington is fictional. There are gay bars in Washington in that neighborhood, but not at that exact location. I have no idea what facilities are available inside these bars, nor if any of them resemble the fictional Rory's. Also, McWhorter's Funeral Home in Blacksburg is fictional, as is Ralph McWhorter. A very similar funeral home with another name did exist in Blacksburg. To avoid direct connection with that funeral home, fictional names were chosen. The clinic and hospital in Sulaymaniyah, Kurdistan, exist, as shown by the photographs. The notion that it is financed by the CIA is entirely fictional.

Geographical locations like Toronto, Maiquetía, Stuttgart, Munich, and Sulaymaniyah follow necessarily from the plot. Russellville comes from a random choice made when writing *Three Kisses*.

Several serendipitous events show that fictional events in this story line are indeed realistic. In addition to the tragic shootings at Virginia Tech that occurred shortly before that part of the story was written, they include the well-known ongoing coverage of the activities of the National Security Agency that has occurred since this story was written. After I had written about the investigation of a suspected Hamas fund raiser, news accounts reported actual trials of similar persons first in Florida and then in Texas.

Many dear friends and several casual acquaintances have contributed greatly to this story. Some of them do not know they contributed nor how they contributed. Many of them would not want to be identified by name, so I will not identify any. You know who you are. Great hugs and kisses where appropriate, and eternal thanks and gratitude.

DISCUSSION QUESTIONS
for *DAY OF JUDGMENT*

Please use these discussion questions for your book reading groups or just for yourself. Reader feedback or additional questions and/or comments is always welcome.

1. Some characters from *Three Kisses* tapped me on the shoulder and said you are not through with us. New characters come into this book, which is the second in a series, but also designed to be read alone. All characters are based on real people I have encountered in places I have lived and in my travels, not always in favorable circumstances. Are they stereotypical? What makes a character stereotypical? Which characters stand out as being well developed? Which are underdeveloped. How do character descriptions of physical features, clothes, mannerisms contribute to the story?

2. A major motivation and inspiration for my writing is to bring life to otherwise obscure communities, some of which can be described charitably as less-than-charming. Which communities in the plot and subplots most effectively bring out the influence of communities on the characters and vice-versa? Which communities could be developed more?

3. Continued romantic developments between some of the characters are presented in subplots. How are these subplots effective in contributing to the main plot?

4. Omar and Joe have developed what is called a "bromance" in current jargon. How does their relationship contribute to the story line? How do you see this relationship evolving as additional books in the series are written?

5. Writing about a rape scene was challenging and required several iterations. What are your impressions of how this scene was written? How effective is the communication of the aftermath on Ahmed's activities, emotions, and mind sets?

6. How effectively is the funeral scene presented blending Muslim traditions with long-standing small-town American traditions like traffic stopping, men removing their hats, lunch afterwards in a church?

7. Currently, the issue of bullying in schools has become a major issue, especially in the U.S., with wide spread criticism of school administrators. How to you feel about bullying as described by the characters and administrators at Shawsville Middle School.

8. Currently, we are receiving news of young men acting alone to set off bombs in public places, conduct mass shootings, drive trucks into crowds. We are often horrified, grateful that does not involve anyone close to us. But what if it does? How would you feel if you lived in a small community like Lafayette, Virginia, and learned that a neighbor you knew for years growing up had been the bomber in Washington, DC?

9. The story has sub-plots of two very different wedding scenes. What is your reaction to these two scenarios? How effectively do they contribute to the main plot and character development?

10. Mental health has become very relevant and with a wide spectrum of opinions on the topic. How relevant are the mental health issues and institutions in this story today even though written a few years ago?

11. The story presents some of the activities of the NSA and people who work there, a "hot" topic right now. How realistic are the descriptions of the NSA in your view based on current news reports?

12. The story describes in detail the various activities of the federal judicial process, especially the activities of public defenders. How effective are these descriptions in presenting actual, realistic descriptions of federal justice?

13. The story also describes the activities of the FBI in unraveling the plot. How effectively have these activities been presented?

14. A subplot describes fictional activity by a Palestinian in the US using a fake charity to raise money to support terrorism by Hamas in Palestine. The story is based on actual criminal fund raising activities being tried in courts in Florida and Texas. In the main plot, the Hammoud family, Palestinian refugees have lived a peaceful life in the U.S. for over 20 years. Other Palestinians have been living in the U.S. for some time? How do the story line, main plot, and subplot, affect your views of Palestinians in the U.S. and in other countries where they have sought refuge?

15. The story is written to entertain as well as to inform and foster tolerance, acceptance, and respect. How effectively have these intentions been accomplished.

16. What other discussion questions come to your mind? Please let me know by email to HeathDanielsAuthor@gmail.com or on my website HeathDanielsBooks.com.

An excerpt from the forthcoming

JUSTICE!

PROLOGUE 1

Monday, November 25, 2013
Mogadishu, Somalia

On a warm yet not hot evening with little humidity, normal in the desert near the horn of East Africa, in declining twilight, Qasim Abdikarim waited off to the side in the refugee camp of those waiting to be airlifted to the U.S. for resettlement. He was in his mid-thirties, tall and distinguished, with neatly trimmed facial hair. He had a triangular-shaped black face and tightly curled black hair kept trimmed by his wife. He wore a tailor-made robe, carefully designed to come only to his ankles, and a Somali headdress.

Soon, a man approached him, looking carefully to see whether someone might see their meeting in the dimming light. He was average height and had the physical features of Arabs from Iraq and Syria. He was dressed in an Arab robe and headdress that covered most of his skin, not revealing he had lighter skin than black Somalis. As soon as he recognized Qasim, he walked to him, gave him an embrace and three Arab kisses, saying "marhaba" in Arabic, a language that most educated Somalis like Qasim understood and spoke. In the process, he deftly slipped a package into a pocket in Qasim's robe.

Continuing in Arabic, he asked, "When are you going?"

"Maybe tomorrow," Qasim answered in Arabic. "A young guy in our group who knows English heard them say something about wanting us there before Thursday, a big holiday in the U.S."

"Where are you going?" the Arab man asked.

"Somewhere in Texas, he heard them say," Qasim replied. "Somewhere I can open up a shop like I had here; also learn English."

"Good. We don't have anyone there to recruit for us yet," the Arab man said. "Contact our people in California and Minnesota. They're sending guys our way to fight for us. They'll tell you how to get guys you recruit to Turkey and into Syria. There's enough money in that package to get started with one or two tickets."

"OK," Qasim muttered.

"Be careful, though," the Arab man added. "Lots of Muslims in America are apostate Wahabis, or don't accept the true DAESH way yet."

"Yeah," Qasim said. "ISIS, they call it,"

"Maybe convert some of the locals like the guys in California do," the Arab man continued, "and convince them to come fight for what is right."

"OK," Qasim muttered again. "You know I found you plenty here, some to go to Nigeria."

"Yes," the Arab man said. "Just watch out for the Wahabis who think they are the true Islam. We are the ones who follow the way of the ancestors and re-established the caliphate. Most authorities over there are looking for al Shabab, so they don't pay much attention to us. Maybe the Americans don't even know the difference between us and al Shabab."

"Indeed," Qasim said. "We are Salafi who believe in the way of the ancestors and will get you good people."

The Arab man took his leave to find other potential operatives who were infiltrated into the group.

PROLOGUE 2

Tuesday, December 25, 2013
Redwood, Texas, USA

On a cool, pleasant and sunny early winter day, typical of south-central Texas, four Somali men, recently resettled refugees, sat around a table in a makeshift tea shop in an abandoned gasoline station and garage. They were sipping tea and grumbling about their misfortune of ending up in a small, poor town. All of their conversation was in Somali, only one person understanding English. Redwood was at the fringe of both the Austin and San Antonio metropolitan areas, a suburb of the smaller city of San Marcos, and almost entirely Hispanic. Very few local people were outside; most were with family or friends celebrating Christmas. Inexpensive, often well-used Christmas decorations adorned local houses.

Yasir Farhan, wizened with wrinkled black skin and looking older than his actual forties from long exposure to the sea, had shaggy, longish, tightly curled black hair. He was huddled in a shabby, long-sleeved robe, faded even more than its original light blue color, with a jacket. He said, "Damn, it's cold. Why couldn't they have settled me in Florida, where it's warm and next to the sea so I could work on a ship? I'm freezing my balls off."

"At least they didn't send you to North Dakota, like they did my cousin; now that's cold, and there's even snow there," Raqe Shire added. Raqe was in his late twenties or early thirties, wearing jeans and a shabby, faded hoodie. He had smooth black skin and tightly curled black hair in need of a trim.

"I wonder if we'll get snow here?" Zaid Rahim asked. "It'd be fun to see it for the first time." He was nineteen or twenty with boyish good looks and smooth black skin. His hair was closely trimmed; he wore neat blue jeans and a long-sleeved shirt covered by a hoodie.

"Not if you had to work in it," Raqe replied. "My cousin had worked in oil fields in Sudan, so they sent him to work outdoors in the oil fields up there."

"At least he got to work in something he knew something about," Yasir added bitterly. "Here they've got me working in construction, pushing a wheel barrow. All I know is the sea."

"Just what'd you do at sea?" Zaid asked.

"Hush, boy," Yasir snapped back. "You're not supposed to know."

"What have they got you doing here?" Raqe asked.

"I'm supposed to start school in January," Zaid answered. "Studying for something they call the GED, some kind of a certificate that'd help me get jobs and maybe into something they call a community college. I finished school at home, so there's a possibility I can do some things here. Right now, I just work in that food store. I speak English, so they might want me to work at the cash register late at night when no one else wants to work."

He speaks English, Qasim Abdikarim thought, having sat quietly listening to all. *That could be useful once we get organized and start finding locals to recruit. He's working in a shop. Maybe he can learn and help us open a shop here selling fruit and vegetables like our friends who settled in California. There's no place in this miserable little town to buy anything good and fresh. Maybe we can expand this tea shop if they send more Somalis here.*

655

"At least we don't have to work today," Yasir said in Somali. "Infidel holiday, Christmas. Everyone excited about being with families while our families are back home being harassed by Ethiopian soldiers. Back to work tomorrow."

At least they didn't serve us a holiday meal with that foul American food like they did for that Thanksgiving dinner, or whatever they called it, when we first got here," Raqe responded.

"I kind of liked it," Zaid commented.

"Christians are people of the book," Qasim said, speaking for the first time. "Their Jesus was the last great prophet before our Mohammed, peace be upon Him. Today is Jesus's birthday. Of course, we shouldn't be celebrating like they are, in pagan ways, but we shouldn't condemn them either." *Besides, these Christians might be useful to us, he thought. The local Muslims certainly aren't.*

"It's good of you to open this tea shop," Raqe said. "Nothing else is open in this miserable little town today."

"This'll be our community center," Qasim replied. "When we get a few other Somalis here, my wife'll start selling our kind of food. There're halal things in Austin we can bring here to sell, and we can sell fruits and vegetables."

"Good," Yasir said. "Other shops here treat us like shit."

"For sure," Raqe agreed. "These Mexicans here don't want to have anything to do with blacks, and the few local blacks here treat us worse because we don't speak their language and aren't Christian. There's not any place to get our hair cut; they don't know how to cut African hair."

"They took me to a place in San Marcos to cut my hair," Zaid commented. "Said I had to have a decent haircut to work in the store. There's a black barber there who knows how to cut our hair, but he doesn't like Africans, even though that's where his ancestors came from."

"They gave us shitty rooms to live in too," Raqe added. "No place to pray either."

I've run into Muslims in San Marcos who treat me like I'm some leper too," Zaid added.

"They aren't Muslims," Qasim said vehemently. "They've become westernized and have forgotten the true ways of the Salaf. The authorities who brought us here think that just because they claimed to be Muslim we would associate with them. How could we possibly pray with apostates like them? When we get enough true Salafi here who can give us money, this'll be our mosque. We'll fix it up inside."

"We need to go show them what the true way is, just like we did back home," Raqe said.

"Let's not be too hasty," Qasim interjected. "When the time is right, we'll know what to do. These Americans need to know what the true path of Islam is. They tolerate those apostate mosques." *We need to get to know each other well enough first and see who else'll be sent here to join us, he thought. Then we can start recruiting locals to send over there to build the caliphate.*

A tall, graceful woman in her mid-twenties walked to where they sat, showing natural beauty in her Somali face. She was wearing an elegant burgundy robe she had made herself that came exactly to her ankles and a gold-colored headscarf completely covering her hair, obscuring her age. Qasim ordered her to bring more tea for everyone. She obediently went back inside where a pot of boiling water sat on an old hotplate.

The rest of the afternoon was spent grumbling over their unhappiness, the unfairness of their situations as resettled refugees, and their anger at being stranded in a land of infidel Christians and apostate Muslims, and in idle chatter.

PROLOGUE 3

On a hot humid afternoon—fall comes late to South-Central Texas—at about 1:30 p.m., Sammy Lee Jones and Wesley Stokes were sipping coffee after lunch in a Cracker Barrel restaurant while their wives shopped out front. They had stopped for lunch after services at the Church of the Prince of Peace, as was their habit. Both men were in their fifties and suntanned from many years working in excavation and building demolition in the rapidly developing I-35 corridor from north of Austin to south of San Antonio.

"Say, what'd ya think of Pastor Bobby Ray's call fer 'nuther Ko-ran burnin' day right here?" Sammy Lee asked.

"Them Muslims're trying to take over the whole damned world," Wesley replied. "Just look what they done in this A-rab spring, killin' off the decent Christians in Egypt. Gotta stop 'em. Burnin' their Ko-ran's th' least we could do to show 'em."

"Yeah," Sammy Lee agreed. "Last time that pastor in Florida got hisself in big trouble when he tried to burn the Ko-ran, but went ahead and did it anyway. Bobby Ray says it might not get so much publicity here, but we gotta show 'em we're Texans and we don't put up with that kind of shit. Pardon my language; we just come from church."

"When's he gonna do it?" Wesley asked.

"Don't know," Sammy Lee answered. "Hope it's not sometime we're working. Wanna be there to participate."

"Maybe on a Friday, but sometime after work," Wesley said. "That's the day they're s'pposed to be prayin' to that Allah character, they call him."

"Yeah," Sammy Lee concurred. "That's what they said on that Austin television station that had that story about that new nigger Muslim mosque in that old gas station in Redwood. Y'see that?"

"Yeah, gotta glimpse of it," Wesley said. "One of them nigger guys from there works on one of the sites I work on; pushes the wheel barrow. Complains about the heat and humidity and he's from Africa where it's s'pposed to be like that all the time. On Friday, he even goes off and bows down and does somethin' like praying. Damn niggers. Got enuff of our own, includin' a nigger Muslim president. Don't need t' be bringing other ones from Africa.

"Y'heard about them high school kids in Buda who got in trouble 'cause they didn't want no nigger bitch teachin''em. Sure don't need no niggers teachin' our kids."

"Maybe go burn a Ko-ran at that mosque they got set up in that old gas station," Sammy Lee added.

"Maybe even blow the damn place up," Wesley suggested.

"Gotta be careful 'bout that," Sammy Lee retorted. "Might kill someone. Not that them nigger Muslims don't deserve to be killed.

"Look what happened to them guys back in East Texas where we're from. Tied that old nigger to a pickup truck and drug him 'til he died. Executed one of 'em in Huntsville fer murder."

"Well, shouldn't go 'round killing 'em for fun, even if he was a worthless ol' nigger," Wesley retorted. "Deserved to be punished, but death penalty just for killing a nigger?"

"Yeah. … Companies almost beggin' people t' go to work here," Wesley added. "Bet that's how them nigger Muslims got jobs so easy."

"Yeah, fastest growin' place in whole country, 'specially San Marcos,"

Sammy Lee said. "You 'n' I got jobs here; none back home in East Texas. But damn we have to put up with all them meskins here too."

At that point, their wives returned and they parted company until they saw each other the following Sunday.

PROLOGUE 4

Wednesday, October 30, 2014
Washington DC, USA

In midafternoon, Yusef 'Joe' Shaito, senior staff attorney for the U.S. Attorney General's Office, rushed to the office of his former supervisor, now a close colleague, Roger Chen, beaming with excitement.

Roger Chen, a Chinese-American in his forties, startled, seeing Joe's excitement, said, "You got the job!" He stood to shake his hand with his left hand on Joe's shoulder and added, "Number two deputy AG for the Western District of Texas; just right for you. One of the largest and most important judicial districts in the U.S. We'll miss you here, of course."

Roger reflected on working with 'Joe', as he called him, for some seven years, watching him mature and rise as high as he could for the time being in the headquarters of the US Attorney General: *We kept him here as long as we could, getting him promotions, not that he didn't deserve them. I knew at some point we'd lose him and here it is. Of course, I gave him the highest recommendations. Hopefully they'll realize how lucky they are to get him. Maybe we can get him back when there's a senior opening here.*

"I'll miss working here, for sure, but you know this is a big step," Joe said, sitting. "I have to be honest; I won't miss living in Washington. San Antonio seems like a much nicer and friendlier city."

He reflected on working with Roger for seven years: *With a boss like Roger, the experience here was great. He got his promotions and brought me along with him, finding ways to promote me as well. Of course, I deserved them. Without Roger, I may have tried to move earlier to another city.*

Living with Omar as a roommate and best friend was a factor too, but he's ready to move too. I'm over thirty now and still single. Wonder how many Muslim women there are there. ...

"We've settled in here," Roger Chen replied, "so this is home now. The kids are into high school activities in a big way. I might have been able to move up in a district office, but things are going so well here. I can see that a guy like you might not be all that happy with the social scene here. Things are bigger and better in Texas, they say. When do you move?"

"I'm not sure yet," Joe replied. "Of course, they want me to start soon, but there's nothing really urgent to get me there next week. They realize I need to wrap things up things here. Maybe sometime between Thanksgiving and Christmas. You may remember the Eid al Adha was a couple of weeks ago, so there are no more significant holidays until Thanksgiving. I might want to stay here for that. Christmas doesn't have much significance for a Muslim, so maybe that's the best time to move and get settled. I'll need to go sometime to find a place to live."

Roger Chen smiled, "Yes I remember that first Eid al Adha dinner you had and invited Lisa and me. Say, maybe you and Omar'd like to come over for Thanksgiving. You know I've got to talk it over with Lisa first. We may invite some other friends and families too. Those Thanksgiving turkeys're big. The kids are teenagers now, so they can join in."

"Sounds good to me," Joe replied. "I can't speak for Omar. Someone at the university might invite him, but there's been lots of tension there he's trying to avoid. International politics are becoming big-time issues with the conflicts in Yemen, and Omar's Yemeni, you know. Also, Sunni and Shia issues are getting really tense and spilling over. I'd better let him tell you about that if the subject comes up.

"One good thing about San Antonio is it doesn't seem to be politicized, or not politicized in that way. You know I've turned down feelers before when they wanted me just because I'm Arab-American Muslim. People in San Antonio seem to want me for my human rights and civil rights expertise and don't care about my religion and ethnicity. But then again, immigration issues are heating up. As you know, the Western District of Texas extends a long ways along the Mexican border. Maybe they want me because I'm neutral, neither Hispanic nor Anglo."

"Sounds good," Roger Chen said. "Let's have a long lunch someday soon and talk more about it. Check your calendar and let me know."

"Sure thing," Joe said and left, exchanging pleasantries. He walked back to his office thinking, *New job, new life. Maybe now I should leave 'Joe' behind and be 'Yusef'. Joe' is what kids in school back in Dearborn called me because they couldn't pronounce Yusef right and it continued through university and law school. That's what everyone here calls me too, but I'm making a break. Omar calls me Joe too, but he'd understand.*

This is going to be bittersweet. Omar and I've been best friends and roommates for six years now. It's hard to imagine living somewhere without him, but it's time to settle down and maybe get married. He's looking for other jobs, too, so all good things come to an end. Most of our good friends have moved away, too. Maybe I can find a nice Muslim girl in Texas. Sure haven't here.

PROLOGUE 5

Later at home, after changing clothes, he heard Omar come in, rushed to greet him, and said, "I got the job!"

Omar Abu Deeb, who was also in his early thirties, stood about five feet eight inches with average build, had slightly wavy black hair and brown eyes. Taking off his coat and sweater, he said, "Great! Good for you. You were so excited about the possibility you'd get it."

"Yeah, I'm excited, but sad leaving here after we've been together so long. It's been six years."

"Yeah, Omar said. "That's what I've been thinking too. Things're looking positive for me at North Carolina, so I might be moving too, but not for a while; not until next summer. As the old saying goes, better not count my chickens before they hatch."

Joe said, "That'd be where Brad and Jason are."

They reflected on their very good friends Bradley Spencer and Jason Henderson, a couple who had moved to North Carolina in late summer for Brad to start a master's degree program.

Omar said, "Yeah, I haven't told Brad yet, but I'm pretty sure I'll go down there to present a paper and interview."

"Maybe we can all go there for a reunion when you get the job," Joe said smiling. "Of course, you could all come to San Antonio."

Sounds good," Omar said. "Frank said San Antonio's really nice. Brad, too, but he didn't get to see much of it when he was in the hospital there. We haven't had a good reunion since we all visited Jason in Helsinki; when was it, four years ago?"

"Yeah," Joe replied. "Say, let's go to Mama Ayesha's for dinner and celebrate. Weather's still nice enough to walk."

While walking and eating at one of Washington's best-known Lebanese restaurants, they reflected on their other good friends Frank Reynolds and Paco Mendoza, a couple who were also good friends of Brad and Jason. Joe said, "Yeah it was really cool to see that part of Europe. Helsinki's a nice city. Those two big cathedrals are nice, even if they are Christian. Turku was even better."

"Yes," Omar commented, "There are Muslims in Helsinki who go back a century and a half from the days Finland was part of the Russian empire. I got some research ideas there. Sort of got me going on my publication career, the peaceful interaction of Muslims and Orthodox Christians; there was no conflict like there is in Russia today.

"I liked Turku, too; good atmosphere. The historic old cathedral there is nice too, and also the old castle. Nice little art museum there too. Too bad the mosque there was way out in the suburbs and there was no way to get to it. At least you and I could have prayers by ourselves Friday night on the ferry. Otherwise the booze cruise atmosphere didn't do much for me."

"Yeah, didn't do much for me either," Joe agreed. "I sure liked that day trip to Tallinn, though. The old walled city is charming and there was that great new art museum that Jason took us too. That was cool too."

"Stockholm was great too," Omar added. "Lots of Muslims there. Maybe I'll go back one day. There must be some good research ideas there too."

"Speaking of mosques," Joe said, "what about leaving your job at the Islamic Center here? You haven't seemed too happy there lately."

"So it's obvious to you," Omar said. "I've been trying not to show it, not even to you. It's getting involved much too much in political things and losing sight of what Islam's all about, especially situations in Somalia and Yemen. They seem to think I should want to get involved because I'm Yemeni."

"Oh, like the university, too," Joe replied.

"Yes," Omar said downcast. "Here I was with a dream of being an imam at the largest mosque in Washington, DC, but now that I'm here, it's becoming a nightmare. That's why I haven't said too much; it's too much of a blow to my ego to admit my dream was too selfish. I felt much better when I was a part-time imam at that small community in Duluth, like I really belonged and made a difference. I wish I could go to some place like that again. Maybe there's a similar mosque in North Carolina."

"Hey, lighten up on yourself, habibi," Joe said. "You did what you thought Allah wanted for you at the time, but circumstances change. We all have dreams that get shattered. You're the theologian, but maybe Allah wants them to be shattered because different things are in store for you now that you have a green card, a tenured position in the university, and citizenship pending.

"Say, we were going to Duluth together, but never got around to it. Now it's getting cold up there and I have to start thinking about moving soon."

They both reflected on two young Yemeni-American guys from New York state whom Joe had helped prosecute and were sent to prison in Duluth. They became involved with the mosque in Duluth for which Omar was a part-time imam when they were on parole and released.

"Interesting that you should mention that," Omar said. "I haven't had a chance to tell you yet. Brahim's getting married to the daughter of a Pakistani professor and wants me to be the imam overseeing the process. There's no imam in Duluth now, so they want me. I might go and you could go with me. The weather's not so bad yet; it can still be Indian summer."

"What about the other guy, Boudi?" Joe asked. "I wasn't close to them like you were. They might not want to be reminded I prosecuted them. I'm still a little curious, though. They were good guys who just got caught up in things by that so-called imam. Still, they broke the law and paid the price. No need to go into that."

"Yeah," Omar said. "Going to prison and then settling in Duluth may have been the best thing that could have happened to them. They never would've gone anywhere if they had stayed in Lackawanna. Brahim now wants to get a PhD in library science. That's one reason why they want to get married soon. He's looking for places to go where she can go with him.

"Boudi's doing great; manager of a gym in a town close by. He and his wife seem to have settled in well, even if they did have to get married when she was pregnant. Their little boy is getting big. His wife's family's finally coming around to accept him now that there's a child, even if they did have a Muslim wedding."

After a leisurely meal, they went home reflecting on their personal successes, Joe as a son of Lebanese immigrants and Omar as an orphan who surrendered to the will of Allah and found himself first in Minnesota and then in Washington, DC.

THANK YOU

FOR READING

DAY OF JUDGMENT

It was my pleasure to write it for your entertainment and enlightenment. Please let me hear from you about your thoughts and feedback.

Please consider writing a review for Amazon, Goodreads, newspapers, and wherever else you go to find thoughtful reviews.

Please sign up to receive my periodic newsletter. Send your name and email address.

Blessings,
—Heath Daniels

HeathDanielsAuthor@gmail.com
HeathDanielsBooks.com
Facebook: Heath Daniels, and Heath Daniels Books

HEATH DANIELS is a semi-retired professor and consultant for international activities. He was born and grew up in the U.S. where he worked for many years, moving often to different locations. He now lives part-time in the U.S. and part-time abroad; mostly in the U.S. His work allows him to travel extensively. In the process, he has developed a large network of colleagues and friends who have contributed directly and indirectly to the knowledge he has brought into this book. When he is not thinking of ways to spoil his grandchildren, he writes, reads, and travels. Throughout his life, he has been a keen observer of current events with special interests in culture and language, history, and spirituality, and reads extensively on the subjects. He has written and published extensively on professional topics.

53191891R00374

Made in the USA
Lexington, KY
25 September 2019